CSC

THE STATIONMASTER'S DAUGHTER

Also by Maggie Craig

The River Flows On
When The Lights Come On Again

THE STATIONMASTER'S DAUGHTER

Maggie Craig

HEADLINE

First published in 2000
by HEADLINE BOOK PUBLISHING

10 9 8 7 6 5 4 3 2 1

All characters in this publication are fictitious and any resemblance to real persons, living or dead, is purely coincidental.

British Library Cataloguing in Publication Data

Craig, Maggie
The stationmaster's daughter
I. Title
823.9'14[F]

ISBN 0 7472 7451 7

Typeset by Avon Dataset Ltd, Bidford-on-Avon, Warks

Printed and bound in Great Britain by
Mackays of Chatham PLC, Chatham, Kent

HEADLINE BOOK PUBLISHING
A division of the Hodder Headline Group
338 Euston Road
London NW1 3BH

www.headline.co.uk
www.hodderheadline.com

To railway children everywhere:
from a Blue Train kid

And to Sandy, Kathleen and Pat –
who were also lucky enough
to have the stationmaster for a father

Acknowledgements

I should like to thank Margaret Stewart for most generously giving of her time to tell me about her childhood in Partick. The memories she shared with me were an invaluable source of information and inspiration.

I am indebted also to Louise Logan for searching through the legal texts in order to be able to furnish me with advice on a point of law.

Thanks are also due to my son. Ably assisted by his sister, he made sure that I kept my nose to the grindstone throughout a long and enjoyable summer. He also made me laugh a lot – which was just as important.

PART I
1935

Chapter 1

Although some perceptive [illegible] Caroline [illegible] When [illegible] had learned [illegible] and the master [illegible] her hair as her [illegible] newly found [illegible].

Easter Pictures was [illegible] had [illegible] the same [illegible] example, the [illegible]

[illegible] every [illegible].

Sitting up straight in [illegible]

[illegible]

[illegible] to take [illegible].

Caro leaned forward to pick up the [illegible] the housemaid [illegible] brought [illegible] into the garden of the [illegible] house. She was happy [illegible] the trouble which went [illegible]

Despite the hand-down [illegible] against the May madder [illegible] could wear [illegible] of the [illegible] three minutes [illegible] More [illegible] miserable state of [illegible] Caro [illegible] for a minute.

He [illegible] back [illegible]

Chapter 1

Although more perceptive people saw all the other shades within the glossy strands, Caroline Burgess was a redhead as far as most folk were concerned. When she was a child, both she and her brown-haired mother had learned to smile dutifully at the jokes about the milkman and the postie. Her father Archie, who invariably referred to her hair as her crowning glory, teasingly told her it was the colour of newly fitted copper pipe.

Esther Burgess was fond of declaring she would die happy if she had hair the same colour as her daughter, and Carrie herself loved it. Looking pretty in pink was out of the question, of course, but she could wear lots of other colours her friends couldn't. Take, for example, the pale green cotton sundress she had on today. The material had been a bargain for precisely that reason. The shade wouldn't suit everybody.

Sitting up straight in the striped deck-chair, she smoothed the cool cotton down over her knees. She didn't think anyone would be able to tell the garment wasn't a bought one. Esther was a good dressmaker, who took great delight in running up a frock or a skirt out of a few shillings' worth of fabric. She and her daughter had found the cloth for the sundress at one of their favourite shops, a fabric warehouse in Montrose Street up in Glasgow.

Carrie leaned forward to pick up the hand mirror lying on top of the book she'd brought out with her into the garden of the station house. She was happy with her hair, but she could have done without the freckles which went with her typically Scottish colouring.

Despite the broad-brimmed straw hat she wore as protection against the May sunshine, she could swear she'd acquired half a dozen more of the annoying little dots since she'd come outside fifteen minutes ago. Not a very desirable state of affairs – especially with Matthew Campbell due any minute.

He was on back shift this week, and her mother had agreed the two of them could spend some time together today before he went along to the booking office to start his duties. With a bit of luck, Carrie thought, she might be able to convince Esther that Matt could call past *every* day this week. She sighed contentedly. Newly left school, with nothing to do for the next few months but wait for her exam results, the summer stretched before her with what seemed like endless promise.

With a furtive glance towards the back door of the solidly built stone cottage in case her mother might be watching, she fished a slice of lemon out of the jug of lemonade she had made earlier that afternoon in preparation for Matt's visit. Replacing the beaded crochet cover protecting the drink from the insects buzzing about the garden, she applied the fruit to her nose and cheeks. She heard a throaty chuckle.

Starting guiltily, she looked across her father's potato drills to the fence which separated the long garden from the equally long platform of the railway station. Several faces were grinning at her over the palings. The squad of railway navvies was obviously coming off day shift.

Her eyes lit on Ewen Livingstone. He was standing a pace or two behind his workmates, apparently fascinated by something lying on the platform. Bare-headed, he carried his navy working jacket slung over his shoulder, his index finger crooked through its hanging loop. His mop of fair hair appeared not to have seen a comb for a week. As usual. He raised his head and Carrie looked quickly away.

'Lemon juice against the freckles? Sure, we could all be doin' with some of that today, Miss Burgess.'

It was the ganger of the Permanent Way men who had spoken – Martin Sharkey, a middle-aged man almost as wide as he was tall. Sweeping off his bunnet in salute, he wiped his broad and shining forehead with the back of his hand.

'It's a devilish warm day, eh?' Consciously or not, his eyes went to the jug of lemonade. Jumping to her feet, Carrie lifted the chunky green glass pitcher and the tumbler she had put out for Matt and walked over to the fence. Weaving a little to avoid her dress catching on the potato shaws, she picked her way daintily round the edge of the vegetable patch on one of the paths her father had constructed to divide his garden into its different areas.

'Would you like a drink?'

With a sweep of the hand which held the tumbler, she indicated that the invitation encompassed the whole group. She was going to be in trouble if they all accepted, even if each man took a gulp from the same glass. What the heck, she could always fetch the second jug she'd made, left in the scullery to keep cool. The P-way men had a tough job, out in the open all day and subject to the vagaries of the climate. In the case of the west of Scotland, those were considerable: freezing fog, ice, slush and snow; scorching heat and torrential downpours; the fine misty rain which could go on for weeks, penetrating coats and jackets and shoes.

Sometimes, as the old joke went, you got them all at the same time – although that wasn't really a joke at all. Everyone had experienced days when Mother Nature flung all four seasons at you at once.

'No, thanks, lassie,' said one of the men, 'but it's kind o' ye, all the same.' He tipped his bunnet politely and headed off down the platform. Three of the other men followed his lead, leaving only their foreman standing by the fence – and Ewen Livingstone. She darted another glance at him. Was she imagining that faint look of reproach on his pale face?

Sharkey surveyed them both thoughtfully. 'I'll be getting on too, Miss Burgess, but Ewen here will take a glass of your lemonade. Won't you, son?'

They stood for a minute or two gazing after the ganger, watching as he caught up with the rest of the squad. Heavy-footed in their working boots, the men clattered over the bridge to the other platform and then were swallowed up by the cavernous exit at the end of it. It framed a steep flight of stairs which led down into the hustle and bustle of Partick.

Carrie pulled back the bolt on the platform gate. Invisible from the railway side, it was an integral part of the picket fence. Like the villain coming up through the stage floor at the pantomime, she had often enjoyed surprising an unsuspecting passenger by suddenly emerging from the riot of rhododendron bushes – interspersed with the occasional silver birch or rowan tree – which tumbled along both sides of the garden.

'Will you come in for a wee minute?'

Carrie hoped she didn't sound as reluctant as she felt. She'd been avoiding him for over a month, since the railway social club *ceilidh* at Partick Burgh Hall. She owed him an apology for that night when, not to put too fine a point upon it, she had used one young man to make another jealous. She repeated the invitation, forcing herself to look Ewen in the face.

Compared to him, she had to admit her own freckles paled into insignificance. His, darker than his tousled locks, marched across his cheeks and nose in the summer months. Yet underneath them, his complexion was as smooth and creamy as her own.

'Do you want me to?' Ewen asked gravely.

'Of course,' she said, turning about and leading the way back to the deck-chairs. If she got the exam results she was hoping for – and her teachers had said they would be astonished if she didn't – she was heading for nearby Jordanhill College after the summer holidays to start her teacher training. Last month she had met a recently qualified member of the profession at a tennis party up on Partickhill.

The young woman had insisted that one of the most important qualities required when facing a classroom full of children – all potential wee horrors if they spotted the merest hint of weakness – was the ability to act the part. Judging by this performance, I'm halfway there, Carrie thought ruefully.

Some of the tension in the atmosphere dissipated when they reached what Esther Burgess referred to as the lawn. This was to differentiate the square of grass near the back door of the station house where the family sat out in the summer months from the drying green on the other side of the pebbled path which bisected the long back garden.

'I'm manky and mucky,' Ewen said, declining Carrie's invitation to sit in the second deck-chair, set opposite her on the other side of a small home-made garden table. He took a long stride to avoid standing on the flowers which bordered the lawn, threw his heavy jacket on to the grass and sat down on the edge of the drying green. The ground there was raised by several inches, bordered and supported by upended railway sleepers.

'This makes a fine seat.' He stretched his legs out and crossed them at the ankles, the white chuckies which formed the path crunching under the pressure of his heavy boots. He looked around him with every appearance of pleasure, and Carrie felt herself relax a little. Was it possible they could slide back into their previously relaxed friendship as though nothing had happened?

'This is almost like being out in the country,' he said. 'Ye certainly wouldnae think we were between a passenger station and a goods yard.'

'It's the trees and the rhododendron bushes.' She gestured towards the latter. It being May, the extravagant pinky-purple blossoms were just coming into their full glory. 'They screen us off from everything. Even the noise and soot sometimes.' The constant danger of the pernicious black flecks puffed out by steam engines settling on clothes drying on the washing line was the bane of her mother's life. Carrie tried a tentative smile. 'If the wind's blowing in the right direction, that is.'

'Aye,' he replied. 'I don't doubt it.' If he had noticed that wee smile, he hadn't responded to it. His eyes drifted once more over the garden: the vegetables, the raspberry canes, the neatly trimmed grass. 'Your daddy works hard,' he observed. 'Making everything grow. The tatties and the vegetables and the wee flowers and everything. It must be rare having all this right outside your own door.'

'You're not near a park or anything?'

His eyes came back to her face. 'There's no' much grass in Keith Street, hen.'

She knew instantly that the reminder of the difference in their circumstances had been entirely deliberate. Before she could think of some suitably neutral comment, Ewen spoke again, his face thoughtful. 'Apart from the Quaker graveyard, of course.'

'What's that?'

The delivery was faultlessly deadpan. 'A graveyard wi' deid Quakers in it.'

'Walked right into that one,' she conceded, expecting him to grin in triumph. He was nothing if not quick-witted, and he had caught her out like this several times. No smile appeared, however. He continued gazing at her with that pensive and extremely disconcerting look on his face.

'I m-mean,' she stuttered, 'why is there a Quaker g-graveyard in Partick?'

He tilted his chin, angling his face towards the sun. 'Och, there was a group o' them here once. In the olden days, like. When Partick was a wee village. Seemingly there were some folk called Purdon among their leadin' lights. That's why we've got a Purdon Street.'

He was full of wee snippets like that, what he himself called 'another piece of useless information'. Carrie had no idea where he got them all from. She supposed he must read a lot.

'Where is Purdon Street again?' The answer didn't matter. Keeping this harmless conversation going as long as possible did.

'Where the steamie is,' he replied, using the colloquial name for the building which housed the public baths and wash-house. The station house had its own little laundry room off the kitchen, equipped with a clothes boiler, two deep sinks for steeping and rinsing clothes and a mangle for squeezing the water out of them. Many of Partick's overcrowded tenement homes, like those throughout Glasgow, had no such luxuries. On washday the housewives who lived in them pushed prams piled high with their families' dirty clothes to the steamie.

Ewen pretended to catch himself on. 'You wouldnae know where that is, of course. The street the Carnegie Library's on the corner of, then. That's more your kind of level.'

Carrie didn't miss the edge to his voice. So much for having a harmless conversation, slipping back seamlessly into their old easy comradeship. Trying to get her courage up to offer that apology, she studied him over the flowers. He sat framed between a clump of marguerites and the group of red hot pokers Archie Burgess had planted in a circle next to them. The flaming hue of the spiky flowers matched the red neckerchief Ewen wore knotted at his throat, traditional garb for Permanent Way men.

'Catches the sweat,' he had once told her cheerfully, 'and it comes in handy for tying tae the end o' a wagon if you need to leave a warning signal for the man coming behind you.'

She couldn't help noticing he had a hole in the sole of each boot. Embarrassed for him, her eyes slid to his navy reefer jacket, lying on the washing green beside him. That was also traditional gear, as were the brown corduroy trousers he wore. Whether the men bought their working clothes themselves or had them issued free of charge by their employers every two or three years was a perennial bone of contention between them and the railway company.

The jacket was pretty threadbare. The elbows were soon going to be through. Couldn't his mother sew some patches on for him?

With a pang, Carrie realised she didn't even know if he had a mother. The two of them had talked a lot since Ewen had come to work on the railway – almost two years ago now – but somehow their conversations had never really touched on the personal. She had picked up the subtle signals that he preferred it that way.

She hadn't even known he lived in Keith Street until he had mentioned it just now, only that his home lay in one of the crowded streets along towards Partick Cross, on what her mother called the wrong side of Dumbarton Road. Ewen Livingstone belonged, quite literally, on the wrong side of the tracks.

His cheerful description of the state of his working clothes had been perfectly accurate. His trousers and blue collarless shirt were pretty manky. He had his sleeves rolled up and she saw that his muscular forearms had caught the sun. The fine hairs on them were golden, like those at his throat where, under the red neckerchief, the first two or three buttons of his shirt were undone.

'So, do I get a glass of lemonade? Or do I have to roll over and die for Scotland first?' The pale eyes were quizzical.

'What? Oh, sorry.' Carrie hastily lifted the pitcher and poured. 'Is that Bobby you're talking about? Does he roll over and die for Scotland?'

Ewen nodded, but there was a gleam in his light eyes – she had never been able to decide whether they were grey or blue – which told her he knew very well that she was grabbing at any possible topic of conversation except for the one that really mattered.

Bobby was a mongrel of indeterminate parentage but impeccable manners, intelligence and training. His owner Donald Nicholson was a man of few words, but his dog was a great favourite in Partick. Being invited to take him through his various party pieces – giving his right paw, giving his left paw and so on – was considered to be a great social coup. It was a sure sign that his rather taciturn master approved of you.

'Aye. I seen him and Donald when I was on the way tae ma work this morning.'

Resisting the temptation to correct his grammar, Carrie handed over a tumbler of lemonade. He gave her a glimpse of his old smile as he took it out of her hands.

Ewen Livingstone wasn't handsome exactly, although his features were pleasant enough. It was the face-splitting smile and the mischievous twinkle in his eye which made him attractive. Up until the *ceilidh* a month ago, both had almost always been in evidence whenever Carrie and he had met: when he jumped nimbly up on to the platform after working down the line somewhere; when he stopped on his way to and from work to exchange a few words with her.

Caroline Burgess would have been an extremely unobservant young lady indeed if she hadn't realised fairly early on in their relationship that Ewen Livingstone had a wee fancy for her. She would have been lying if she'd claimed to have no feelings for him in return. There had been at least two occasions when she had been in imminent danger of being kissed over the fence. She wasn't entirely sure which one of them had been the first to take a step back . . . or whether or not she was grateful for the physical barrier provided by the wooden palings.

Then, shortly before Christmas last year, Matthew Campbell had arrived at Partick, transferred from Hyndland, the next station up the line. Carrie had taken one look at the new clerk and forgotten all about the young P-way man.

Matt was everything Ewen wasn't: tall and handsome, well-spoken and well-dressed, and with a quiet maturity and sophistication which appealed strongly to Carrie. At twenty-four, he was seven years older than she was. That age gap worried Carrie's mother, but Matt's grave courtesy and respectful attitude were beginning to win her round.

The invitation to afternoon tea extended by his mother had also helped. Esther Burgess had been mightily impressed both by the spacious main-door flat at the posh end of Gardner Street and by Matthew's father. According to her, Charles Campbell was the dead spit of Ronald Colman, and charming with it. Her daughter was inclined to agree with her there, but she had found Matt's mother rather cold. Spotting her curl of the lip at the way Esther raised her pinkie when she drank her tea hadn't exactly endeared Shona Campbell to Carrie either.

Mature and courteous Matt might be, but it had taken him long enough to ask her out. A month ago an exasperated Carrie, convinced the attraction between them was mutual, had decided to do something about it. The railway social club do had seemed the ideal opportunity, especially when she found they were seated at the same table.

He asked her up for the first dance, saw her politely back to her seat at the end of it – and proceeded to stay firmly in his own for the next half hour. Sitting on the opposite side of the round table from him, the noise of accordion and fiddles had made conversation impossible. Then Ewen came bounding up, the fair waves of his hair flying, looking for all the world like Bobby the dog when he spotted one of his favourite humans. He had one girl by the hand and was looking for another to make up a threesome for the Dashing White Sergeant. A plan began to form in Carrie's mind.

It crystallised during the procession of the dance round the hall. Meeting young Mr Campbell, persuaded on to the floor by a colleague to make up a set of two men and girl, Carrie was not at all displeased to be greeted by a ferocious glower. To make sure she was on the right track, she stood up with Ewen for the next dance, a Military Two-Step. Getting up with him the third time for a waltz might have been pushing it a bit – but it did achieve the desired result.

As she came back into the hall from the powder room after the brief interval, Matt stepped out from behind one of the pillars which supported the balcony of the ballroom and took a firm hold of her hand.

'You're dancing every other dance tonight with me,' he told her. His voice was low and husky, his beautiful brown eyes intense. She had made a joke about loving masterful men, but secretly she had been thrilled. To her shame, seeing Ewen's face fall as he came eagerly towards her and then registered that she had her hand in Matt Campbell's had given her only the merest twinge of regret at the time.

She was thoroughly ashamed of herself now that the first heady flush of being Matt's girlfriend had subsided and she was beginning to think straight again. Taking a drink of lemonade, she set her glass down on the table, carefully not too close to her book. She looked up and saw Ewen's light eyes go to her head.

'Are you wearing that for a bet, Miss Burgess?'

The cheeky comment didn't bother her. The brim of her straw hat was rather large. The 'Miss Burgess' did. They had long since gone on to first name terms with each other. If this unusual formality was a measure of how much she had hurt his feelings, she was truly sorry for it. Stalling for time, she removed the hat and laid it on the table. It covered most of the surface, so she took the book on to her lap.

'You've ayeways got yer heid stuck in a book, haven't you? Romantic poetry, nae doot. A' hearts and flowers. Nothing whatsoever to do wi' real life.'

Thirty seconds ago she'd been feeling sorry for him, but now Carrie bristled. 'They're not romantic, as a matter of fact,' she said with an unconscious lift of the chin. 'You might even like some of them.'

He shrugged. 'Read me one, then. I'll bet ye cannae find anything that'll mean something to me. That would mean something to any working man.'

She was more than happy to pick up the challenge. She knew exactly which poem to choose. 'Listen to this,' she urged. 'It's by Robert Louis Stevenson. It's called "From a Railway Carriage".

'Faster than fairies, faster than witches,
Bridges and houses, hedges and ditches;
And charging along like troops in a battle
All through the meadows the horses and cattle:
All of the sight of the hill and the plain
Fly as thick as driving rain;
And ever again, in the wink of an eye,
Painted stations whistle by.'

She broke off, unnerved by the fierce and sullen silence with which Ewen was listening to her. 'It's about a train journey, you see –'

'I'd worked that out,' he growled, giving her one of his do-you-think-my-head-buttons-up-the-back looks. Drawing his legs up in front of him, holding his lemonade in one hand, he bent his head forward and stared down at the stones on the path. 'Read the rest of it,' he commanded, his voice muffled slightly by the posture.

'Here is a child who clambers and scrambles,
All by himself and gathering brambles;
Here is a tramp who stands and gazes;
And here is the green for stringing the daisies!
Here is a cart runaway in the road
Limping along with man and load;
And here is a mill, and there is a river:
Each a glimpse and gone forever!

'Well?' she demanded when she had finished.

Ewen straightened up. 'No' bad,' he admitted grudgingly. 'He's got the rhythm of the train in his words. That's clever, that.'

She closed the book and reached for her lemonade. Ewen tossed the last of his own drink back with a gulp and placed the glass on the path, tilting it against the railway sleeper border so that it wouldn't fall on to the stones. Then he raised his head and fixed her with a penetrating gaze.

'Go on then,' he said softly, both elbows now resting on his knees, his hands loosely clasped between his legs, 'spit it out. You'll feel a whole lot better afterwards. You're quite right, Carrie. Ye do owe me an apology.'

She supposed he didn't have to be a mind-reader to work out why she had invited him in this afternoon. And despite his rough speech and lack of education, he was by no means unintelligent.

'About what happened at the *ceilidh*,' she began and then paused. What was the best way to phrase this? 'I-I'm sorry –' What was she sorry about? That she had hurt his feelings? But men didn't like being reminded of their vulnerabilities, did they? 'I'm sorry about what happened.' She faltered under his steady gaze. 'I mean –'

'Go on,' he said in an infuriatingly encouraging tone. 'I might even throw ye a biscuit if ye manage tae get tae the end o' a sentence. Like rewarding Bobby for giving me a paw.' He gave a short bark of laughter. 'Don't glare at me like that. Ye'll get wrinkles to go wi' your freckles.'

'Ewen Livingstone –'

He rose abruptly to his feet and came towards her, thrusting his hands deep into the pockets of his corduroy trousers as he stood on the path in front of her.

'I'll say it for you, will I, Carrie? You're very sorry you used me to make Matthew Campbell jealous. You're very sorry you got up to dance with me three times for that express purpose. No' because you actually wanted to dance with me. Perish the thought, eh?'

His eyes were boring into her across the red hot pokers. Like red hot pokers. He muttered something she didn't catch, except to realise it was an exclamation of some sort. He took a couple of paces away from her, his angry feet making quite an impression on the path. She'd have to get the rake out and smooth the pebbles over after he'd gone. He stomped back to stand on the other side of the flowers.

'And – although I might just be flatterin' myself here – you're very sorry that I'm only a railway navvy and you're the stationmaster's daughter. Is that no' the sum of it, Carrie?'

Dismayed, and upset that he was so upset, she stood up and went to him, the poetry book sliding unheeded into the canvas seat of the deck-chair. The skirt of her green dress swished against the marguerites as she took a long step between the flowers and over the earth of the border.

'Ewen.' She laid her fingers on his bare forearm but he shook her off, pulling his hands out of his pocket and waving them angrily.

'I suppose you thought you were as well to keep me dangling. On standby, like. Till someone better came along. Someone like Matthew Campbell.' The name was spat out. 'A young gentleman more suited to your superior social status.' He enunciated the final three words with careful and precise sarcasm. 'Is that it, Carrie?' he demanded, nostrils flaring. 'Have I got it right?'

He wasn't much taller than her, but he had his head – fair waves more unruly than ever now – tilted back at a haughty angle. The posture enabled him to look down at her. She studied his face and wondered if he did have it right. Had she refused to let herself care for him because of the difference in their social positions? She didn't want to think that about herself.

'Ewen . . .' she said again. She had no idea what she was going to say to him. He didn't give her any help, simply kept staring down at her with cool and unforgiving eyes. There was a noise behind them: footsteps coming round the side of the house.

'Sorry I'm a wee bit late,' called a cheerful voice. 'Oh!'

It was Matthew. Carrie threw him the swiftest of glances over her shoulder. She was in no doubt now about the colour of Ewen's eyes. They had darkened to an icy winter blue.

'In the name o' God,' he whispered. 'I didnae think you'd do it a second time. I really didnae think anyone would stoop that low.' He took his frosty gaze off the rapidly approaching Matthew Campbell and bent it once more on Carrie. 'I've obviously had far too high an opinion of you, Miss Burgess. I'll not make that mistake again.'

Chapter 2

Now she had two angry young men to deal with. Far too late, Carrie realised how it must look to both of them: that she had engineered this meeting. Nothing could have been further from her mind. Martin Sharkey had all but pushed Ewen into the garden, and their ensuing conversation had simply put Matt's imminent arrival out of her head.

Engineered or not, the encounter was fast turning into a confrontation. Matt and Ewen were looking at each other in a way that made Carrie's blood run cold: sizing each other up.

However much your parents tried to protect you, you couldn't grow up in Glasgow without learning to recognise the warning indicators of an outburst of male violence. It had to do with the stance, the locked eyes, the crackle of tension in air suddenly become icy, the very silence which preceded such explosions.

Those weren't scarce these days. There were so many men out of work. Frustrated and dispirited, with too much time on their hands, they stood about for hours at street corners, ready to take offence at the smallest slight, real or imagined. Sometimes one man simply had to glance at another the wrong way. Then the challenge would ring out. 'Are you looking at me, Jimmy?' And you would find yourself having to hastily cross to the other side of the street to get out of their way. Matt's question was worded differently, but the aggression was exactly the same.

'What's he doing here?'

He took a few slow and deliberate paces towards them, halting a couple of feet from the back door. Beside her, Carrie felt Ewen slowly shifting posture. His eyes, she knew, were fixed on Matt.

An image of dogs about to launch themselves into a yelping and biting scrap slid into her mind. She could practically hear the growls, see the bared teeth and cocked-back ears.

If only she hadn't been so stupid and so selfish the night of the *ceilidh*. She had caused this hostility between two young men who might otherwise have scarcely noticed each other. She knew there were girls who would love to have two boys fighting over them, but she wasn't one of them. She hated this sort of thing.

Like her father, she was a natural peacemaker. Archie Burgess belonged to that other group of men, the ones who would wade in, often at considerable risk to themselves, to break up a fight. In her father's case it was usually a dispute between two late-night drunks at the station. She had anxiously watched him do it on more than one occasion. He always did his best to reassure her afterwards.

'Did ye no' see their arms, lass? No bones in them. Flailing about like the India-rubber man. Drunks are harmless that way. That pair hadnae a hope in hell – excuse my French, hen – of landing a decent punch.'

Despite his protestations, she noticed he always swore her to secrecy about his role in breaking up these fights as far as her mother was concerned.

Her mother! Carrie shot an anxious glance towards the back door of the station house. For some reason she'd never been able to fathom, Esther Burgess had a down on Ewen. This certainly wasn't going to endear him to her. Moving swiftly, Carrie side-stepped neatly over the chuckies – gosh, Ewen had churned them up – bent down and scooped up his shabby navy jacket from the edge of the drying green.

She called once more on her acting skills, consciously making her tone of voice as even and pleasant as possible. 'I invited Ewen in for a glass of lemonade, Matt.'

'You what?'

He hadn't shouted, had barely even raised his voice, but the tight set of his mouth gave him away. He had been charm itself to her since they had started walking out together, but she had known, somehow, that he might have a bit of a temper . . .

Ignoring his question – under the circumstances that seemed the wisest course of action – she held the jacket out to Ewen.

'He was just going when you came in.'

For the second time that afternoon, she laid her hand on Ewen's arm. The springy golden hairs felt slightly damp, the skin underneath them clammy. He didn't shake her off this time, but she had to exert considerable pressure before he took the death-ray glare off Matthew Campbell.

'What?'

She extended her arm, offering him his jacket again. 'I said, you were just going. Weren't you?'

She had the impression he had to re-focus in order to understand what she was saying. His whole concentration had been on Matt. All her fault, Carrie thought miserably. She had made the two of them hate each other.

Feeling more guilty than she ever had in her life, she saw that hate wasn't too strong a word. Judging by the look on Matt's face, Ewen's feelings were more than reciprocated. Surely she wasn't worth all this?

She wasn't certain if Ewen sensed her anxiety, but she felt the bunched muscles under her fingers relax a fraction and he took the jacket from her. 'I'll relieve youse both o' my presence then.'

Matt's lip curled at that 'youse'. That wasn't fair. Ewen hadn't been given the opportunities the two of them had. She wasn't going to part from him on bad terms either. They'd been friends for too long. As though he were a bomb which might go off if she wasn't standing right next to him, she darted forward to the deck-chair, grabbed the book of poetry and whizzed back to the path in about three seconds flat, thrusting the book out to him.

'Why don't you borrow this, Ewen? Give it back to me in a couple of weeks.'

His eyes flickered briefly down to the book, then returned to her face.

'No, thank you, Miss Burgess. I wouldnae want to deprive you o' it.'

'Go on, Ewen,' she urged. 'You'd enjoy it. There are some great poems in here.' He might be childish enough to keep up this 'Miss Burgess' malarkey, but she wasn't going to retaliate.

'Thanks for the lemonade,' he said firmly, and headed off in the direction of the platform gate. Avoiding Matt, still standing close to the back door, he cut across the lawn, apparently intending to leave without so much as a backward glance.

'Oh!' Carrie nearly stamped her foot. 'Don't be so bloody stubborn!'

He stopped and turned, feathery eyebrows raised in disapproval. 'A lady like you shouldnae swear.'

'Well, take the blooming book then.' She held it out again.

Matthew laughed, and sauntered forward to join them both on the grass.

'Not much point in lending him a book, Miss Burgess,' he said. *Miss Burgess?* Good grief, they were both at it now. Honestly, men could be really pompous sometimes.

'Don't you know your wee friend can't actually read?'

Like a train seeing an unexpected red signal up ahead, the conversation ground and screeched to a halt – and a deep and ugly flush stained Ewen's creamy skin.

In the silence which followed, Carrie heard the chug-chug of a locomotive shunting wagons over in the goods yard. Nearer at hand, a blackbird was singing. Somewhere within the mass of rhododendron bushes, she thought. Their singing was at its sweetest at this time of year, when they were building their nest and raising their young.

'He can't write either. It's in the staff records. He can barely manage to set his own name down. You should see his signature in the ledger.' Matt's voice was full of disdain. 'Or what passes for his signature. A child of five could do better. He might as well have made his mark.'

Carrie stared at him, scarcely able to believe her ears. Was this the same man who had been so attentive to her over the past month, who only last week had presented her with a single white rose?

'That's how I see you,' he'd said softly, 'as pure and beautiful as this perfect flower.' It had been an early blossom, a bud on the point of unfurling. She was a rosebud too: a girl poised on the brink of womanhood, ready to open up to the right man, the man who would love her for the rest of her life. The words had thrilled her. So had the long, deep kisses which followed them.

She couldn't understand how the man who was capable of such romantic words and gestures could be standing here now saying these cruel things. She didn't doubt they were true. One look at Ewen's stricken face, deathly pale now that the painful blush had faded, was enough to verify that – as was the way he was refusing to meet her eyes.

Why hadn't it occurred to her that he might not be able to read? She knew, because of his rough accent and bad grammar – and because he'd told her so himself – that he hadn't had much education. He'd left school at fourteen and alternated between casual labouring jobs and long periods on the dole until her father had taken him on as a surfaceman the day after his seventeenth birthday.

'Thanks for the lemonade, Miss Burgess,' he repeated, and strode off once more in the direction of the platform gate.

'Leave it, Carrie.'

Matthew's assumption she was going to do as he said was enough to propel her towards the corner of the house.

'Ewen! Wait!'

He was already on the platform. She was sure he would have pretended not to hear her if he hadn't realised that the gate wasn't properly closed. Hearing the squeak as it swung open behind him, he turned and pushed it to. His hand was coming over the spars to push the bolt home when she reached him.

'Ewen,' she said, placing her fingers over his. 'I'm sorry . . .'

'Take your hand away.'

'Ewen . . .' she repeated helplessly.

'Please take your hand away.'

Lost for words, and not knowing what else to do, she did as he asked. He fastened the bolt in place. Then he met her eyes at last. His own looked completely washed-out, bleak and desolate.

'Goodbye,' he said. 'Goodbye . . . Carrie.'

* * *

'This lemonade's a bit warm. Is there any more in the scullery? And did you speak to your father about the rostering for the weekend?'

Matt was standing by the deck-chairs, apparently quite at ease. More angry with him than she would have believed possible, Carrie chose her words carefully, trying to keep a hold on her temper.

'You didn't need to show him up like that. You made him feel small. You hurt his feelings.'

He shrugged. 'So what? He's a railway navvy. The lowest of the low.' He lowered his long frame into one of the chairs.

'Whatever happened to the brotherhood of the workers, Matthew?' she asked lightly. 'And have you forgotten that my father started off as a shunter?'

Matt was strong in the union, and the all-encompassing National Union of Railwaymen at that, which welcomed members working in all the railway trades: from salaried clerical staff right through to manual labourers. It had been a conscious political decision, he had told her, in line with his socialist ideals.

Unusually for a stationmaster, Carrie's father was also an NUR man, staying loyal to the union which had welcomed him when he had first become a railway servant. That had been back in the days of the old North British Railway Company, for the past twelve years and more part of the mighty LNER – the London and North Eastern Railway.

'Your father worked his way up,' insisted Matt. 'And you're a stationmaster's daughter and I don't think you should forget that.'

Carrie stared at him in disbelief. 'Just because I'm a stationmaster's daughter doesn't mean I consider myself a cut above everybody else!'

'Well, you should.' He paused and studied her, then smiled and held out his hand. 'Come here.' He reached for her, but she stepped back, evading his grasp. It was more than anger. She was disappointed in him.

'Carrie, people like Ewen Livingstone are never going to work their way up. They're not capable of it. He's not on your level and he never will be. Now,' said Matt, looking up from the deck-chair with a winning smile, 'since you *are* the stationmaster's daughter and I'm your young man, am I working this Saturday or am I not?'

As well as *ceilidhs* and dances, the railway social club organised frequent excursions. On Saturday there was one to Oban, the west coast terminus of the West Highland line. Not everyone could go, of course. The stations still had to be manned. Matt had drawn the short straw as far as the booking office was concerned.

Carrie's voice was clipped. 'I did ask Father, but he feels he can't change it. He'd be accused of playing favourites with his daughter's boyfriend.'

Organising the shifts for all the men who worked underneath him was one of Archie Burgess' biggest headaches. When he drew up the rosters for each month he had to make sure everyone had their fair share of day shift, back shift, night shift and rest days. Some men had preferences for one shift over another. They had a considerable amount of respect for their stationmaster, but that didn't stop them making their feelings crystal clear when they didn't get the shift or rest day they had put in for. As Matt had.

'So you're not going to try to persuade him?'

Tight-lipped, Carrie shook her head.

'You could if you really wanted to. You can wind your father round your little finger.'

She'd never heard his voice so cold, nor seen such a scornful look on his handsome face. Was he expecting her to back down over this? She wasn't going to. It was a pity Matt couldn't come to Oban, but she wasn't prepared to put any more pressure on her father. He had enough stresses and strains in his job already.

During the previous winter he had started to experience crippling chest pains. Despite his demands that they stop making such a fuss about nothing, his womenfolk had insisted on calling in the doctor. He had given Archie a thorough examination and told him he needed to watch his diet and relax more. Try to forget about the job when he was off duty. Easier said than done when you more or less lived above the shop.

Matt stood up. 'So you won't speak to him about it?'

'Please try to understand,' Carrie said. 'It could cause my father a lot of trouble. He's got enough on his plate as it is.'

'Right. Fine.' Matt folded his arms across his chest. 'Are you going up the hill to play tennis tomorrow tonight?'

'Yes, I am.'

They'd had this argument yesterday. He had quizzed her about who else would be there, particularly which boys. That was quite flattering in one way . . . but a bit irritating in another.

'Even though I don't want you to go without me?'

Carrie tossed her coppery head. 'You can hardly expect me to give up all my friends for you. To sit at home twiddling my thumbs whenever you're working.'

'I thought people in love only needed each other.'

She let out a sigh of exasperation. 'Matt, that's rubbish and you know it.'

'So, basically, what you're saying is that Ewen Livingstone's feelings matter and mine don't.'

'Matt,' she pleaded, 'that's not at all what I'm saying.'

'That's what it sounds like to me.'

He stood in front of her: tall, elegant – and completely unbending. He *was* waiting for her to back down. Well, he was going to have a very long wait. The faint look of incredulity which flashed across his handsome features when she said nothing almost made her laugh – almost.

'I'd better get to work then,' he said eventually. 'We wouldn't want the stationmaster to think I was trying to get away with anything just because I'm his daughter's boyfriend. Would we now?'

That was two men who had walked out on her today. She was doing well. And she and Matt had parted without making any arrangement to meet again. She heard the back door open, and turned towards the sound.

'Caroline, pet, you're not forgetting that there's more lemonade in here?' Esther Burgess looked curiously at her daughter standing alone by the deck-chairs. 'Carrie? I thought Matthew was paying you a visit today.'

'He's been and gone, Ma,' she said brightly. 'Didn't want to be late for his work. Why don't you come out and have a glass with me?'

Definitely a touch of the actress. At this rate, she thought with grim humour, I'd have been better applying to the Royal Scottish Academy of Music and Drama in Buchanan Street than teacher training college.

Chapter 3

'Caroline Burgess! You never walked through the streets of Partick dressed like that!'

Carrie laid her tennis racquet on the gate-leg table, folded now against the wall of the big square living room of the station house. Glancing down at her divided skirt, she smoothed a hand over its white piqué folds. It was certainly short, stopping a good four inches above the knee, but it wasn't exactly indecent.

Her legs were beginning to acquire a healthy glow. She went to great pains to protect her face from the sun, but light brown legs and arms were fashionable, even if she did sometimes think it wasn't so much a tan as all the freckles joining up with each other. When she looked up again at her mother, her face was glowing with mischief.

She'd had a good time this evening, indulging in a little innocent flirtation with the boy she'd partnered for a game of mixed doubles. It had all been light-hearted fun and taken seriously by neither of them.

Her tennis partner had cheerfully offered to see her home, but she'd told him just as cheerfully not to bother. She was perfectly capable of walking home on her own, especially at this time of year when there was daylight until late at night. Also, although she didn't say this to the young man, she didn't want anyone reporting to Matt that she'd been seen with another lad. Partick was a busy place, only a few miles from the teeming centre of Glasgow, but it was still the village it had once been as far as gossip was concerned.

'I did,' she said now in response to her mother's question. 'I got a couple of wolf whistles, too.'

'With legs like that I'm not surprised,' said her father, emerging from behind the broadsheet pages of the *Evening Citizen*. Ensconced in one of the upholstered dark-red armchairs which flanked the neat tiled fireplace, he lowered the newspaper on to his lap and stretched out his legs on the hearth rug. The grate held its customary seasonal vase of dried flowers, placed there by Esther Burgess every spring and ceremoniously removed in September or October when the first fire of the autumn was lit.

'You get your shapely pins from your mother, you know. Only I'm the only person who ever sees hers. It's a damn' shame.' Relaxing before he went back up to the station to do his nightly rounds, his jacket off and his dark waistcoat unfastened, Archie's eyes twinkled as he surveyed first his daughter and then his wife. The latter stood in the narrow passageway which led from the living room to the back kitchen and wash-house, a tea towel in her hands.

It did Carrie's heart good to hear her father joking like this. In overall command of the railway station, one of the busiest on the Glasgow suburban network, dealing with the rostering of shifts was only one small part of his workload. He had to oversee every aspect of both the passenger and freight traffic sides of the business – and deal with the extensive staff which carried it out.

There were all the different grades of clerks, both on the passenger and the goods side. The porters had their own hierarchy, from the leading porter down through to the lad porters. One of their main duties in the winter was to tend the various coal fires throughout the rambling station buildings: in the waiting rooms on either platform, in the ladies' waiting room on the up platform, in the booking office, the stationmaster's office and their own little room. That was situated on the opposite side of the booking hall from the office where the passenger clerks like Matt worked.

Then there were the signalmen who worked in the box a hundred yards or so beyond the end of the long platform. The goods yard, over on the other side of the station house, had another set of offices full of busy parcels clerks and sidings which echoed all day to the puffing of engines and the calls of drivers and shunters, not to mention the surfacemen. The Permanent Way squads had a brick-built bothy in the goods yard, also heated by a coal fire.

Archie Burgess loved his job, but as he himself drily put it, his staff didn't always work together in perfect peace and harmony. All of their disputes – major or minor – eventually ended up on the big solid desk in his office.

He looked relaxed enough now. With mock solemnity, he tapped the side of his nose with his index finger and threw another wicked look at Esther, his eyes deliberately sliding down to her legs. 'Definitely shapely,' he said. 'Like the rest of her. I'm the only man who can testify to that, as well.'

'Archie Burgess!' Blushing, his wife advanced into the room and flicked the tea towel at him.

'Careful, Mother, you'll have his eye out.'

Father and daughter grinned at each other. It was one of Esther's favourite admonitions. It went along with *Don't eat an apple last thing at night, it'll lie on your breast till morning* and *Always wear clean underwear every day in case you get run over by a tram.*

Carrie had once asked why you would be worrying about the state of your pants and brassiere if you were lying in the middle of

Crow Road with a broken leg. Without a trace of irony, Esther Burgess had drawn herself up to her full – and deeply unimpressive – height and stated that she personally would be black affronted if any member of her family turned up in Casualty at the Western Infirmary wearing grubby underwear. What kind of housewife would the doctors and nurses think she was?

'Aye, dangerous things tea towels, eh, Carrie?' said her father now, the impish look still on his face. 'You'd think folk would handle them with more care, wouldn't you?'

'Och, you!' The cloth was flicked once more in Archie's direction. He lunged forward, grabbed it and pulled. Despite a valiant effort to maintain her stern expression, his wife ended up on his lap, laughing into his face. Carrie laughed too. She loved it when her parents horsed around like this. They were like a couple of weans sometimes.

'You both think you're so smart, don't you?' demanded Esther.

'Nope,' said Archie cheerfully, squeezing her waist. 'We know we are. It runs in the family, you might say. For all those who had the good fortune to be born a Burgess.' He winked outrageously at Carrie.

Opening her mouth to retaliate, Esther was pre-empted by the noise of a train thundering past on the railway line outside, yards from where the family sat. The house, and everything in it, trembled in sympathy.

As a child, Carrie had provoked some hilarity when, a puzzled frown wrinkling her small forehead, she had asked friends of her parents why their house *didn't* shake at regular intervals. Having lived with it all her life, she found the vibration entirely normal and oddly comforting – like listening to the trains at night while she was lying in her bed.

As the noise disappeared into the distance Archie glanced across at the clock which stood, still gently trembling, on the mantelpiece.

'The first Home James,' he murmured.

It was his name for the empty carriages which went through at this time every night, three sets in all, so as to be in the right place for the start of passenger traffic the following morning. With no passengers to consider, they could rattle along at quite a lick, hence the nickname: 'Home, James, and don't spare the horses.'

Carrie moved towards the door. Her father timed his final visit of the day to his domain after he heard the third set of empty carriages pass. That would be in exactly – she checked the clock herself – twenty-nine minutes' time. She'd better get a move on if she wanted a private chat with Matt. She saw her mother's eyes go once more to her bare legs.

'The other girls walked home in their tennis skirts too, Ma,' she said innocently. 'Even the ones that live up on Partickhill.'

The girls who lived up on Partickhill hadn't very far to walk, the tennis courts being close to their homes. From the expression on his face, she could see that had occurred to her father, but what mattered to her mother was that she took the behaviour of those who lived up the hill as a yardstick for her own daughter's behaviour. If they had walked home in their tennis skirts, then it must be all right.

Carrie lifted her racquet from the table and put her other hand on the doorknob. 'All right if I pop along to see Matthew for ten minutes?'

'Aye, on you go, hen,' said her father, the twinkle still in his eye and his wife still on his knee, his arms loosely about her trim waist. They'd be kissing as soon as she went out of the door, thought Carrie fondly. 'I'm sure he'll be glad to see you. And since he's on back shift, there won't be many other people about.'

'You're not going to the station in your tennis skirt?'

'No, Ma, of course not.'

She was tempted, mind, simply to see the look on Matt's face. No, better not. Mr Matthew Campbell, clerk grade three, could be surprisingly strait-laced at times. About some things, at any rate.

The second Home James was approaching as Carrie went out on to the platform, and she stayed where she was for a moment, turning only to secure the bolt of the gate. The instruction to stand well clear had been drummed into her from an early age. As the van glided past, the guard spotted her and raised a hand in greeting.

She stood and watched as the train swung on towards Hyndland, the two paraffin lamps on the back glowing in the May twilight. Checking those were visible was an old railwayman's habit, one she had acquired from her father. If there were two red lights to be seen at the rear of a train all was well. Not only would a following train be able to see it stopped at a signal or a station, it also meant no carriages had become uncoupled, as had been known to happen. Archie Burgess had a fund of railway horror stories, many of them revolving around runaway trains somehow cut loose from their engine and driver.

Despite the whooshing noise made by the heavy door as it slid open over the hard floor of the booking office, Matthew didn't hear her come in. He was concentrating too hard on whatever it was he was doing, perched on a tall stool to one side of the arched ticket window checking tickets off in a huge ledger. Several piles of them, held together by elastic bands, lay on the counter in front of him.

Studying him as he worked, Carrie's fingers itched to brush back the stray lock of hair which was falling forward on to his brow. Like Ewen, he had wavy hair which could sometimes be a little unruly, but there the resemblance stopped. While Ewen was all light eyes and pale skin, Matt was much darker, with soulful brown eyes. He was taller too, and elegantly slim, although with a strength in his arms which made Carrie dizzy.

He heard her at last, and looked up. Sliding off the high stool, he came on to his feet. Even the way he stood was elegant, one foot extended a little to the side, hands casually in his pockets. He was always smartly dressed, a knife-edge crease in his trousers and a neat collar and tie around his neck even when he was off duty. He was a fastidious kind of man.

He stood looking at her gravely, not a trace of a smile on his face. It was obviously up to her to break the ice.

'If I say that I'm sorry, will you say that you're sorry?' she asked.

'Maybe,' he said cautiously.

Walking towards him, her heels tapping on the linoleum, she slowed her steps, swaying a little and swinging her arms as she approached him, trying to get him to drop the serious expression. She was sure she could see a tiny lifting at the corners of his mouth. She stood up on tiptoe to kiss him. She had closed her eyes, but felt his lips curve into a reluctant smile.

'Hussy,' he murmured, but he pulled his hands out of his pockets and fastened them about her waist instead.

'Kiss me back,' she mumbled against his mouth. Her knees turned to jelly when he obliged. Sometimes, though she blushed to admit it, it was she who wanted to go further, not him. Like last week at the pictures. He had given her the choice of the Tivoli or the Rosevale – nothing but the best for the stationmaster's daughter, he'd said. She'd chosen the Tiv – and the special seats at the back designed for courting couples, with no central armrest to get in the way.

He had called her a hussy then too, but once they were ensconced in one of the special seats he had been quite enthusiastic about the idea . . . They hadn't paid much attention to the film.

'*Are* you sorry then?' she demanded as soon as she had got her breath back.

'You promised you'd say it first.'

She pulled back, enough for them to focus clearly on each other's faces. 'I'm sorry if I upset you yesterday.'

He raised his dark eyebrows into two beautiful curves. 'Don't you mean you're sorry you invited *him* into the garden?'

'If that's what upset you, then yes I'm sorry about it. Are you sorry for upsetting me?'

'Och, Carrie,' he blurted out, 'of course I'm sorry! Of course I am. I love you, Caroline Burgess!'

That impassioned outburst required the reward of another kiss. And then another. He was smiling at last, but she fixed him with a stern look.

'Are you sorry for being so nasty to poor Ewen, as well?'

'Of course. But it is true what I said, Carrie. Honest Injun. He can't read or write. I think he only managed his signature because someone else had written it out for him to copy – your father, I think. It looks like his handwriting.'

Continuing to hold her loosely, he swung round and indicated a shelf on the opposite wall which held document boxes and ledgers. 'It's in there somewhere. I could show it to you if you like. There's Livingstone's name written out neatly and then what's obviously his own attempt at it. It's all over the place. Takes up nearly half a foolscap page. Do you want to see it?'

'No,' she said swiftly. 'There's no need.' The mental image of that crudely formed signature was enough – as was the thought of the struggle Ewen must have had to make it. 'I didn't disbelieve you,' she told Matt, 'but you hurt his feelings, and embarrassed him in front of me.'

'I know,' said Matt humbly, 'I don't know what came over me.' He regarded her solemnly for a moment. Then, unexpectedly, he pulled a face: self-mocking and apologetic. It made him look very boyish.

'Well . . . I do know what came over me. I was jealous when I saw you with him, and I lashed out. Reached for whatever weapon came to hand. Please forgive me.' He lifted her hands, bent his head and kissed both sets of fingertips in turn. 'It's only because I love you so much,' he said, looking up at her with liquid eyes.

'It's not my forgiveness you should be asking for,' she replied, refusing to allow that look to melt away her resistance.

Matt dropped her hands and straightened up. His voice was clipped, his words terse. 'You can't honestly expect me to apologise to him personally?'

'That's exactly what I expect.'

The dark eyebrows weren't curved now. They were down over his eyes in two straight lines. Then they lifted again.

'You're a hard taskmaster, Miss Burgess.' He heaved a theatrical sigh. 'But if that's what it takes for you to forgive me . . .'

She jumped in before he could change his mind. 'Tomorrow morning? If he's going on the Oban trip?'

'Wouldn't that be even more embarrassing?' Matt's frown was questioning now, not bad-tempered. 'For him as well as for me? Surely it would be better to wait for a suitable occasion. When I can have a quiet word with him with no other ears flapping.'

'I suppose that's reasonable. How do I know you'll do it, though?'

'You'll just have to trust me.' His hands tightened on her waist. 'Don't you trust me, Carrie?'

'With my life.' They kissed again, but she wasn't letting him off the hook too easily. 'You were awful nasty to him.'

'I was jealous,' he repeated. 'He fancies you.'

That was a statement of fact she couldn't argue with, but she did her best to reassure him. 'He's not even nineteen yet, Matt.'

'And you're not even eighteen. He's much more your age than mine. Do you fancy *him*?'

'I'm very fond of him. As a friend,' she added hastily, seeing Matt's brows draw together once more.

'I don't like you having friends like him.'

'Matt, I told you. You can't expect me to give up my friends for you.'

He bit his lip. 'I know that. I know I'm being unreasonable. It's just that . . . well, I love you so much . . . I want to have you all to myself.'

She lifted her hands from where they had been resting on his chest and put her arms around his neck. 'You've no need to be jealous of Ewen Livingstone,' she assured him. 'Or anyone else for that matter.'

'You do love me, then?'

'Of course I do,' she said, touched by his uncertainty.

'Then prove it,' he said. 'Marry me.'

Chapter 4

'Marry you?' Carrie dropped her hands and took a step back, out of his arms.

'Is it such an unexpected question?'

'Yes . . . no . . . I mean . . . I don't know . . .'

'Don't tell me clever little Miss Burgess is lost for words.' He reached out and tapped her nose with one teasing finger. He seemed to have completely regained his good humour. 'I thought you loved me too, Carrie. What's so odd about me asking you to marry me? You know we've already discussed it.'

Discussed wasn't exactly the word she would have used. The subject had been raised. They'd only known each other properly for a week when he had first mentioned it and she had laughed, assuming he couldn't possibly be serious. She told him now what she had told him then.

'Matt . . . I'm too young to get married.'

His smiled faded. 'So you don't love me, then?'

'Of course I do!' This was becoming exasperating. It was supposed to be women who constantly needed reassurance about these things. She saw his face cloud over. Oh, dear. Now they were back to square one. Taking a mental deep breath, she began trying to explain.

'Matt, you know I'm going to Jordanhill after the holidays. That's going to take me three years for a start –'

He interrupted her. 'Why are you going to the college, Carrie?'

She looked blankly at him. 'To train as a primary teacher, of course. You know that.'

'No, that's not what I mean. Why are you bothering to go to college?'

'Why am I bothering?' she repeated. Truth to tell, both questions had taken her aback, as had the first answer which had popped into her head. *Because my parents want me to.* That didn't seem an entirely satisfactory answer. Nor was it one which Matthew would readily accept. She thought about it. Why *was* she going to Jordanhill?

'Because,' she said slowly, 'it's an interesting and worthwhile thing to do.' She looked up into his face, formulating her answer as she went along. 'Because it'll give me a training. Because it'll allow me to have a career.'

'Which you'll have to give up when you get married.'

'Ye-es,' she agreed reluctantly. She could see exactly where he was headed.

He pressed the point. 'You know that teachers aren't allowed to stay on if they get married.'

'The female ones.'

'Well, of course the female ones, Carrie,' he said irritably. 'Why would men have to give up because they get married?'

She decided to let that one go. The argument which would undoubtedly ensue would only lead them up a blind alley.

'What's your point, Matt?'

'You know very well what my point is, Carrie. If we're going to get married eventually, then you going to Jordanhill really isn't worth it. It unnecessarily delays something which is going to happen anyway.'

He paused, waiting for her to agree with him. When she didn't, he posed a question. 'Tell me something. Are you going to come out as a primary teacher and marry me straightaway?'

She drew her breath in sharply. 'I think you're assuming a bit too much here, Matt. I haven't agreed to marry you at all yet.'

'We love each other, don't we?'

She nodded. Yes, she loved him, but this badgering was beginning to get her a wee bit irritated . . .

'And people who love each other get married?'

She nodded again.

'So,' he went on, 'are you going to marry me – let's see now . . .' he screwed up his face in concentration '. . . in the summer of 1938?'

'I think I would have to work as a primary teacher for a few years, Matt,' she said levelly. 'Otherwise it would be a waste of all that training, wouldn't it?'

'How many years?'

'Matt, how would I know? That would depend.'

He persisted. 'Three years? Five?'

'More like five years,' she allowed.

'So that would be until 1943? Eight years from now? Is that right, Carrie? You ought to be good at arithmetic if you're going to teach it to wee ones. Have I got my sums right?'

'Perfectly correct,' she said tightly.

'I'll be thirty-two in 1943, Carrie. And you expect me to wait for you until then?'

'I don't expect anything,' she burst out. 'I haven't worked any of this out!'

She moved closer to him, hands raised to touch him – or in a plea for him to see things from her point of view – but he took a step back, retreating from her.

'Oh, Matt, try to understand!'

'Maybe *you* should try to understand, Carrie.' His voice was low and throbbing with passion. 'Do you think I'm made of stone? Do you think I can stand to kiss and hold you, to be as close as this to you, and not be able to go any further? For eight long years?'

So that was it. The same old story. She lowered her arms. This was why she had broken up with her last boyfriend. His hands had wandered a bit too far and when she had slapped them away, he had issued the ultimatum. If she wasn't prepared to allow him to take certain liberties then that was it. Carrie frowned. It hadn't seemed to her to be like that with Matthew. Haltingly, she tried to put it into words.

'But, Matt . . . sometimes I feel . . . Well, it always seems to be me who wants to go a wee bit further . . . not you.' She blushed, but struggled on. 'Sometimes I've thought that you don't . . . that you don't really want me . . . in that way.'

'Not want you in that way?' He looked genuinely incredulous. 'Och, Carrie, of course I do! I want you in every way.' He moved closer. The look in his eyes was sending chills racing up and down her spine. 'But I want us to be together properly. Honourably. I've got far too much respect for you for it to be otherwise. And love,' he added, his voice like velvet. 'Lots and lots of that, Carrie. If you'll only let me give it to you.'

She couldn't doubt his sincerity. She raised her hands once more towards him. This time he grabbed them and held them against his chest.

'I'm twenty-four. I thought I was never going to find a girl I wanted to spend the rest of my life with. Then I met you.'

'Oh, Matt,' she breathed.

He curled his long slim fingers around her own. 'I want you to be my wife, Carrie. A wife to set up home with, to have children with, to be happy with for the rest of my life. Don't you want any of those things yourself?'

'Of course I do – but not yet. I'm –'

'Too young,' he supplied flatly. 'Too young for me, you mean. That's what your mother thinks, isn't it?'

He was always so quick to take offence, far too sensitive for his own good. All the same, she was touched that he had allowed her to see that side of him. Most boys, she felt sure, hid their deepest feelings, even from the girls they cared about – maybe particularly from the girls they cared about.

He loved her. If she'd had any doubts before, this intense conversation had swept them all away. So she would coax and cajole and get him into a better mood. It took her ten minutes, but she got her reward in the end: a series of passionate kisses which left her breathless and trembling.

'Maybe I'll not let you have any more until you agree to marry me,' he said when, with one eye on the clock and conscious of Archie's imminent visit to the booking office, they reluctantly separated.

'And they say women are moody,' she teased, delighted to see him in a lighter mood.

'So you'll let me try and persuade you to marry me?'

'I don't suppose I can stop you,' she said happily.

He crooked a finger under her chin. 'Such a lovely face you've got, Caroline Burgess. Like a beautiful wee fairy creature a very lucky man might find at the bottom of his garden.'

'Oh,' she murmured. 'That's so sweet. Do we have time for one more kiss?'

He walked her back along to the platform gate, his arm warm and possessive about her shoulders as they skirted the flower beds which punctuated the platform at regular intervals. They were interspersed with half whisky barrels, doing sterling service now as flower tubs, filled with geraniums and fuchsias and tumbling nasturtiums. Cast-offs from one of the whisky bonds down at Dumbarton, they'd been transported up to Partick in the guard's van. Laughing at something Matt said, Carrie stumbled and almost fell into one of them.

'Mind your papa's flowers.' Slipping his arm around her waist, he drew her closer into him. 'You'd think Mr Burgess had enough to do in his own garden without all this,' he observed as they continued along the platform.

'Are you kidding? He wants to win the Best Station Garden competition again.'

'It's a lot of work,' mused Matt.

'Well,' she said, punching him playfully on the arm, glad they had left behind the intensity of the last half hour, 'his staff could give him some more help. How about you, Mr Campbell?' Although everyone took great pride in gaining a prize in the competition, it was really only Archie, the leading porter and one of the signalmen who were prepared to put their backs into the work required to win one.

'Is that a hint, Miss Burgess?' His laugh was a pleasant sound in the twilight. 'I'm far too impatient for gardening.'

'Impatient? You?' They had reached the gate and she slipped out from under his arm and turned to face him. 'When you can wait so long for certain other things?'

'Not by my own choice,' he said smoothly. He raised his hand to her cheek and gently drew his knuckles down it. 'I'd take you anytime.'

He meant every word of it. She could see that in his dark and dreamy eyes. And she was excited by the direct way he'd put it . . .

'In fact,' he murmured, bending forward and placing his mouth very close to her ear, 'I'd like to make love to you right now. This very minute.' He placed his hands on her shoulders and pushed her against the fence, where the rhododendrons leaned over and formed a halo above her head. 'I'd lay you down under these bushes,' he whispered, 'and I'd pull a handful of petals off and sprinkle them in your hair . . . your very beautiful hair.' He cupped her face in his hands, threading his fingers through the red-gold strands.

'Oh, Matt,' she breathed, 'that's so roman—'

He stopped the words with another kiss. Carrie didn't understand the feelings he was arousing in her. Lost in the pleasures of his mouth, his hands buried deep in her hair, she knew only that they felt good.

Back on her own side of the fence a few moments later, she paused, listening to his footsteps ringing smartly back up the platform. The smell of the Virginia stock which her father had planted in his beloved garden floated to her on the velvet darkness of the night. She was a lucky girl. She lived in a nice house, with a beautiful garden. She had parents who loved her – and each other – and she had Matthew. He wanted her so much. Yet he was prepared to wait for her. She was sure she could win him round about her going to Jordanhill. He would be proud of her.

The third Home James rattled past. Carrie heard the front door open and the sound of her father's footsteps. Regular as clockwork. She slid the bolt on the platform gate, ready to usher him through. His head was bowed as he came round the corner of the house and for a few seconds he was unaware that she was observing him. She almost cried out. His mouth was set in a tight line, one hand lay in a fist on his chest and she didn't like the pallor of his skin. It had a bluish tinge. Then he looked up and spotted her, and his face relaxed.

'Been keeping young Mr Campbell off his work then, have we?'

'I'm afraid so,' she said, moving forward to greet him. 'Are you all right, Daddy?'

'I'm fine, hen.'

'You've got the pains again?'

'Only a wee twinge or two.' He took a breath which struck her as being somewhat cautious, an impression confirmed when he gave a relieved smile. 'That's it past. Don't make a fuss now, there's a good lass. There's no need to say anything to your mother.'

Carrie put her hands on her hips. 'I'll not tell Ma if you'll agree to go and see the doctor if it happens again.'

Archie's lips twitched. 'That's blackmail.'

'It's for your own good, Daddy,' she told him sternly, reaching once more for the gate.

'You're a fine lass,' he said. He patted her arm and went through on to the platform. He paused briefly. 'I couldnae have let Matthew Campbell off the morn. You appreciate that, don't you, pet?'

'Of course, Daddy,' she assured him. 'He knows that too. Ma's going to come with me instead. It'll be a nice outing for her.'

'Aye. And we'll keep what happened just now between you and me and the gatepost?'

'For the moment,' she said steadily. 'You know the conditions of our agreement.'

He laughed and went off to start his rounds.

Matthew gave his stationmaster a report on the evening's activities and went off duty, running lightly down the covered stairs to Dumbarton Road with a spring in his step. Carrie was all his, and she had forgiven him.

He strode along the pavement in the direction of Gardner Street but crossed the main road and went down a side street well before he got there. With a furtive glance behind him to check there was nobody about, he plunged into the dingy close he'd come to know well over the past couple of years. He'd had the foresight to tell his parents he might be required to do a little overtime tonight. He took the stairs two at a time.

There wasn't much conversation in the top flat he visited, but there was uninhibited company – and at a very reasonable price. A man needed an outlet, didn't he? What he had told Carrie was perfectly true. He wasn't made of stone.

Tackling the climb towards his home at the top of Gardner Street some time later, he felt mellow and relaxed. He had handled things well tonight. That was one advantage of being that bit older than Carrie. He'd been as excited as she had been, but he'd managed to hold himself in check. That hadn't been easy. She was so lovely . . . and there was something terribly innocent about the way she responded to him. That was as it should be, he thought solemnly. Carrie was a nice girl, in a different league from the tart with whom he'd spent the last half hour.

That didn't mean he wasn't longing to do with one girl what he had just done with the other – but only once they were married. He wasn't planning to wait eight long years for that particular pleasure either. He lifted his chin to the night air and smiled. Persuading her to change her mind about Jordanhill was a challenge. Despite his recent encounter, the thought of the type of persuasion he might bring to bear to influence that decision was evoking some very pleasurable stirrings. It was good to be young and virile.

He glanced over to the left, where Partickhill Road began. It was one of the discreet streets where the big houses and handsome villas of the neighbourhood stood, including his own former family home.

He'd spent his early years there and visited his grandfather regularly until the great disaster had struck six years ago.

The move to North Gardner Street, which had taken place well before the stock market crash, had been meant to be temporary. From what he had managed to glean, his father would have been more than happy to continue living in his own father's house, but his wife and the old man hadn't got along. Naturally, in the fullness of time, when his grandfather died, Matt and his parents would have moved back to the ancestral home. Some other family occupied it now – dreadfully *nouveau riche*, his mother said disparagingly.

Walking towards his own front door, Matthew reflected, as he often did, on how very different his life might have been if the family fortunes hadn't taken a tumble.

He wouldn't have been working on the railways for a start. He'd probably have fallen into some cushy number in the newspaper business owned by his mother's family. That was all gone now – or as near as dammit. He'd been eighteen in 1929 and although Shona Campbell had been distinctly unimpressed by his choice, going out and getting a job had seemed the heroic thing to do. He wasn't so sure about that now. It was all a bit of a struggle, and he worked damned hard. To make his life even more difficult there was also a log jam of older men in front of him, blocking his path to promotion.

Matt extracted his key from his pocket and walked up the short path. If the Crash hadn't happened he probably wouldn't have had to pay for his pleasures either. In an indiscreet moment last Christmas, when they'd both had far too much to drink, his father had told him of the life he'd known as a young man living in a big house which employed plenty of pretty young parlour maids. To be sure they made a fuss sometimes, but that was all part of the game.

Full of malt whisky and *bonhomie*, Charles Campbell had bestowed some paternal advice.

'But we don't marry that sort, my son.' His arm around Matthew's shoulders, his speech was only slightly slurred. He held his liquor well. Only the frankness of the subject matter indicated how much he'd had of it. 'We marry good girls – pure girls. The sort who have to steel themselves to put up with it. The kind who lie back and think of England. Or in our case Scotland.'

In bed in the darkness of his room, Matt smiled. He couldn't imagine Carrie was going to lie back and think of Scotland. He was going to have the best of both worlds: a good girl and a passionate one.

[illegible] with a hundred or [illegible] travelling companion for the day [illegible] glasses and a [illegible] [illegible]

[illegible]

Chapter 5

Esther Burgess woke up the following morning with a humdinger of a sore throat, putting paid to her plans to replace Matt as Carrie's travelling companion for the day. Swollen glands and a croaky voice didn't stop her issuing her daughter with the usual set of dire warnings, though.

No going off on her own when they got to Oban. It would be better if she chummed up with a couple of nice girls. Even then, they weren't to wander too far away from everyone else. Be careful crossing the street. People drove so fast these days. She wasn't to take any shortcuts or go up any deserted lanes. Terrible things could happen to young girls out on their own . . .

'They're going to Oban, Esther, no' Chicago. I doubt Al Capone'll not be there. Nor the white slave traders either,' said Archie in exasperation, silencing his wife by the simple expedient of sticking a teaspoon of cough medicine in her mouth. 'And the lassie'll miss the train if you go on at her any longer and we cannae have that now, can we?'

Both his wife and daughter had a tendency to leave catching trains until the very last minute. They would stand at the window, cup of tea in hand, watching for the train to come into view before they even left the house. As soon as they spotted it they hastily set down the cup, sped to the door and flew out through the platform gate. It drove him mad. The stationmaster's wife and daughter should set an example to other passengers, not use their special privileges to catch the train by the skin of their teeth.

This morning, however, Carrie eschewed the platform gate for the more sedate and official route to the station: through the front garden and along the public footpath which led up from Crow Road. Matt was coming out into the booking hall as she got there. He smiled when he saw her. It was a sunny, 'good morning' kind of a smile.

Wanting to keep the mood going, she skipped up to him like a little girl. A shaft of sunlight slanted down from the long windows between the booking hall and the platform outside. It caught all the dust motes and Carrie's shining hair, curling smoothly under at the ends. She hadn't slept very well last night, waking early and lying there worrying about her father's health. Realising at half-past five that she was unlikely to get any more sleep, she'd got up and washed her hair. It had dried just in time.

'You look lovely.' Matt's admiring glance took it all in. A neat little red hat with green trimming and a sporty pheasant's feather set off Carrie's forest green lightweight wool costume. The white of her blouse made an ideal contrast, the red and green embroidery on its front placket complementing her ensemble perfectly.

'Give us a kiss, handsome.'

'In front of everyone?'

'Be a devil.'

'If you insist, Miss Burgess,' he murmured, suiting the action to the words. Neither of them noticed a shadow falling across the column of sunlight as, outside on the platform, Ewen Livingstone moved away from the windows which looked into the booking hall.

The special excursion train was already at the platform, itself thronged with people. Leaving Matt to get on with the task of seeing them all off, and spotting her father coming down the platform to do the same, Carrie moved over to a group of girls she knew. Like herself, they were all the daughters of railwaymen. Working on the railways was like being part of a big family. Everyone knew everyone else, even across the different companies.

There weren't nearly so many of those as there once had been. The Grouping of 1923 had absorbed the many smaller companies operating throughout the British Isles into four large ones: the London and North Eastern Railway, the London Midland and Scottish, the Great Western Railway and the Southern Railway. That didn't go far enough for many people, who looked forward to a nationalisation of the whole of Britain's railways. This, they thought, would improve both safety and the working conditions of the employees.

Scotland was divided up between two of the Big Four: the LMS and the LNER. Many thought of the latter as an Edinburgh company. Its headquarters were certainly in the capital, at Waverley Station. However, it was active in other parts of Scotland too, including Glasgow and the west of Scotland. It had inherited Archie Burgess' domain from the old North British Railway Company.

The girls accepted Carrie readily into the circle in which they stood, adjusting their relative positions so she could fit in, and commiserating with her over her mother's sudden illness.

'D'you mind if I come with you?' she asked.

'Nae bother,' said Mary, daughter of a senior parcels clerk. 'We'll see if we can all get a compartment together, shall we?'

'Is Douglas not with you?' asked Carrie, referring to Mary's steady boyfriend, a junior signalman at Partick.

'Aye, but we decided we'd travel with our own friends and meet up when we get to Oban.'

'Douglas doesn't expect you to spend all of your time with him, then?'

'Och, no! We both like to spend time with our friends as well.'

That sounded like a sensible idea, although Matt wouldn't have approved of it. He seemed to think that when you became boyfriend and girlfriend every other friendship had to go out of the window. Another of the girls echoed Carrie's thoughts.

'I thought Matthew Campbell and you would have been going together today.'

'Unfortunately he's got to work.' Carrie pointed him out further up the platform, trying to get the chattering and excited day trippers to stop talking long enough to get themselves on board the train.

'I thought the stationmaster's daughter would have been able to pull some strings about that.'

The words had come from outside the happy circle. The girl who had uttered them stood behind Mary.

'Janice,' said Carrie politely. 'I didn't see you there.'

The shrug of the shoulders was very offhand. 'That doesnae surprise me.'

'Miaow, miaow,' mouthed Mary silently to Carrie. Since childhood there had been an awkwardness between Carrie and Janice Muirhead. Her father was a railway signalman too. Decent and God-fearing though he seemed to some people, Mary wasn't the only person to tell Carrie he was also a bit too free with his hands when his children stepped out of line.

Carrie and Janice had been in the same class at primary school. They had played happily together until Janice had invited Carrie to come home with her after school one day. Esther, who knew all about Davie Muirhead, had forbidden her to go. She hadn't told her daughter the real reason why until much later. The younger Carrie had attributed the refusal of permission to her mother's disapproval of the Muirhead home being on the wrong side of Dumbarton Road, and had blurted out an embarrassing and stumbling apology to Janice, inadvertently communicating that view to the girl. Ever since, Janice had looked on her as a complete snob.

'Don't mind her,' said Mary, steering Carrie towards a carriage door and throwing a smile at an exasperated Matt, who was doing his best to persuade people in a holiday mood and hell-bent on enjoying themselves that it might actually be a good idea if they got on to the train. Departure time was less than two minutes away. He relaxed a little when he reached the girls.

'Shoo, ladies,' he said. 'Your carriage awaits.'

With a sly look at Carrie, Janice turned and bestowed a dazzling smile upon him.

'Anything in trousers,' muttered Mary as they clambered into the train. Janice had taken herself off elsewhere. 'She'll get herself a reputation if she's not careful.'

'She already has,' said one girl darkly. 'Why d'you think she had to take a fortnight off work before Christmas last year?' She looked round the compartment. 'According to what I heard she was recovering from an operation. One that wisnae carried out at the Western Infirmary either,' she added meaningly. 'More likely on old mother MacLeod's kitchen table.' She was referring to a woman in White Street who had a bit of a reputation herself – one for helping girls who got themselves into trouble.

'No!' someone breathed, eyes sparkling with malicious interest. 'You're not serious.'

'I am,' insisted the girl who had spoken first. 'The thrashing her daddy gave her when he found out didnae help much either. Took his belt to her, apparently.'

Mary and Carrie exchanged a look and Carrie hastily changed the subject. She hated this kind of gossip. She also felt sick at the thought of what poor Janice had endured. To have that happen to you, and then for your father to beat you at the end of it . . . She couldn't begin to imagine what it must have been like growing up in a house like that, especially when she thought of her own loving and gentle father. Davie Muirhead was a brute. No love at home, so Janice went looking for it elsewhere – and found the wrong sort. The sort that got a girl into trouble.

Doors slammed. A whistle blew. They were off. Excited chatter ran through every compartment and carriage. The sun was shining, it was a day off and everyone was in high spirits and determined to have a good time.

The train trundled through Hyndland, slowly passing the extensive grounds and grey chimneys of Gartnavel Hospital. Then Carrie caught a glimpse of the twin spires of Jordanhill College, her destination after the summer. As long as my exam results are all right, she reminded herself. It didn't do to tempt fate by being too cocky.

Once they left the cranes of Clydebank and Dumbarton's shipyards behind them the train picked up speed. For a few miles the track stuck close by the river in its lower reaches, the water broadening out as it approached the Tail of the Bank. There were more shipyards on the other shore, at Port Glasgow and Greenock. After they passed the pier at Craigendoran, from where ferries took passengers all over the Firth of Clyde, the north side of the river became much more rural, with green fields, farms and cottages heralding the start of the Highlands.

As Carrie had half expected, it wasn't long before her companions' conversation worked its way round to Mr Matthew Campbell.

'He's quite a catch, Carrie.'

'Aye, he's dead good-looking,' chipped in another admiring voice.

'Absolutely gorgeous,' agreed Mary.

Carrie laughed and glanced out of the window. The train had slowed again. They were chugging through Helensburgh Upper, crossing the Highland Boundary Fault Line, she thought, geography lessons still fresh in her mind. The scenery was growing wilder and more dramatic by the yard, but when Carrie turned from her contemplation of it she couldn't help smiling. The expectant faces turned her way demonstrated that her friends were more interested in quizzing her about Matt than in admiring the beauties of their homeland.

'Is Matthew romantic, Carrie?' Mary asked. 'He looks as if he would be, does he no'?' She looked around at her companions for confirmation. That gave Carrie a couple of seconds to collect her thoughts.

She certainly wasn't going to tell them what he had said about strewing the rhododendron petals in her hair. That would remain beautifully and deliciously private between him and her. However, she told them about his gift of a single rose, and gave them a slightly censored version of the words he'd used when he had presented it to her. That sent them all off into paroxysms of delight.

'Oh, that's dead romantic! See my Douglas? Buying me an extra pickled onion with my bag of chips is his idea of the height of romance.' Mary exaggerated the pronunciation of the word, making it *ro-mance.* Striking a dramatic pose, she twisted round and leaned back over Carrie's lap, making goo-goo eyes at her all the while. 'Obviously when it comes to ro-mance, none o' us has even lived compared to Miss Caroline Burgess!'

Carrie laughed again, revelling in the good-natured banter.

Archie Burgess wore an impressive official hat to indicate his status as stationmaster and esteemed servant of the LNER. It bore the company badge and rather a lot of gold braid. He was inclined to refer to the latter, somewhat irreverently, as scrambled egg. Looking longingly out over Oban Bay, on the opposite side of the street from the shops she was currently being dragged round, Carrie was beginning to think that her brain might be in danger of turning into that very substance.

Understandably enough, Mary had gone off with Douglas when they had disembarked from the train at the busy fishing and ferry port. Poor Douglas had looked quite confused when all the girls in turn had sternly instructed him to make sure Mary got as many pickled onions as she wanted if he was buying her a bag of chips for her lunch.

Appetites sharpened by the journey and the sea air, Carrie and another of the girls whose company she'd enjoyed on the way up had decided to eat first and then go for a walk along the prom together. However, as they came out of the restaurant after their meal, the other girl was approached by a young shunter who shyly asked her to accompany him on a walk. The invitation was politely extended to Carrie too, but she had gracefully declined. She had no wish to play gooseberry and knew very well that this particular young man's eye had been on her friend for quite some time.

Watching them go, she was almost knocked into the road by a raucous group of girls. Was she on her own? They couldn't have that. Despite a protest that she really didn't mind, Carrie found herself being swept along with them.

Her current companions, one of them Janice Muirhead, seemed to consider shopping the main purpose of life – when they weren't giggling furiously or fluttering their collective eyelashes at any of the groups of young men from the day trip who were also wandering around together. Oban being a relatively small place, that was happening all too often.

Coming out of yet another souvenir shop, Carrie began to mentally invent excuses for taking her leave of them. She really would like to walk along the front, get some good sea air into her lungs. Or maybe she could climb up to the coliseum-type structure which dominated the town. She had broached the prospect tentatively ten minutes ago, but it had been brushed aside. Climb up to that big monument? Whatever for?

There was a sudden outburst of giggles and greetings. They sounded like a group of chattering monkeys Carrie remembered from a visit to the zoo last summer. Then she heard a well-known male voice responding to the high and excited female ones.

'Good afternoon, lassies!'

It was Ewen, one hand politely tugging his bunnet in greeting.

'What are you up to, Ewen?' yelled one of the girls. His normally sunny disposition made him a great favourite with everyone.

'I'm away off for a walk,' he said. 'Any o' youse yins want to come wi' me? We could go right along to the Ganavan sands.'

'How far's that?'

'Och, I don't know exactly. Probably about a mile and a half.'

The suggestion was greeted with shrieks of horror.

'Walk all that distance? Not on your nelly! Sorry, Ewen. Anyone fancy afternoon tea instead?' That provoked an enthusiastic response.

Carrie cleared her throat. 'I'll come for a walk with you.'

'Miss Burgess,' he said formally, 'I didnae notice you there.'

The noisy chatter around them ceased abruptly. Carrie was all too aware that Janice Muirhead had narrowed her eyes and that all the girls were regarding both Ewen and her with open curiosity. Everybody knew she and Matthew Campbell were walking out together.

'If y-you'll have me,' she stuttered, and wished the words unsaid when she heard Janice snigger. 'I'd like a decent walk.'

Let them think what they want, she thought defiantly. Why shouldn't I go with him? He is a friend of mine, after all. For one awful moment she thought he was going to turn her down. He looked very serious, almost forbidding. Then he gave her an odd little bow.

'I'd be honoured, Miss Burgess.'

She chanced a quick glance at him as they passed the Columba Hotel. He looked uncomfortable, half-throttled by an unaccustomed stiff collar and tie. His jacket had been pressed and brushed, but it was even shabbier than his working one. It was also a bit neat for size. His shoulders had filled out a lot in the past year.

'Where's the boyfriend today, then?'

'Rostered to work. Somebody has to.'

'Oh, dear, what a pity. I'm so sorry he's missing this very pleasant outing.' Carrie gave him a dirty look. He must have known that Matt was working today. He'd been very much in evidence on the platform before the excursion train had left. They strolled on, past the small jetties from where boat trips left.

'Take the young lady to see the islands and the seals,' offered one man, smiling broadly at Carrie, but addressing his next comment to Ewen. 'Is your lassie not bonnie enough to deserve a wee treat?'

Carrie shook her head apologetically. She'd caught sight of the price chalked up on a blackboard tied to the rail of the esplanade. It wasn't unreasonable, but she doubted very much Ewen would be able to afford it.

'No, thanks,' she said brightly. 'We're needing to stretch our legs.'

They moved on, but before they had gone very far Ewen slowed his pace, looking back over his shoulder. 'Would you have wanted to go?'

'Nope. I'd much rather walk.'

'Let's walk then,' he said tersely.

'Look at that church on the other side of the road!' she said a few moments later. 'The architecture's really modern, isn't it?'

'It must be the new Catholic cathedral,' he growled. 'St Columba's. Seemingly they only built it a few years ago.'

Another piece o' useless information. If he had been in a better mood, she would have teased him about that. It didn't seem advisable at the moment.

They had left the bustle of the town behind them. To their left, the bay was opening out and on their right the road was lined with large and imposing villas. Many had been converted into small hotels, but several were clearly still family homes.

'Lovely houses. Like the mansions up on Partickhill.'

He made an odd noise. It sounded to her like a snort of derision. She thought she knew what that meant: disapproval of the moneyed classes.

'Are you a socialist?'

'I'm no' anything,' he said shortly. 'What's politics ever going to do for the likes o' me?'

She opened her mouth, ready to come out with one of Matt's pronouncements about the need for working-class solidarity. Perhaps not. In any case, considering Matt's upper-middle-class background, she did sometimes think his comments were a bit rich. Even in her own relatively privileged position, Carrie knew a lot more about the realities of working-class life than he did.

She looked out at the sea. It was a beautiful rich blue, sparkling in the sunlight. The big island which sheltered Oban itself had come to an end, but the view in front of her was studded with islets and rocks. Was that Mull in the distance? With his capacity for picking up information, Ewen probably knew, but it didn't look as if she was going to get a civil word out of him today.

A wave of tiredness swept over Carrie. Her sleepless night was starting to tell on her. It was more than simple fatigue. Despite the beauty of her surroundings, she was beginning to feel quite depressed. Earlier in the day she had resolved to put her worries to one side, but now she felt them all crowding in on her again. The surly silence of the young man walking beside her wasn't helping one little bit.

'Are words on ration today, Ewen?' she demanded. She heard the belligerence in her tone. She didn't give a damn if he heard it too. 'Why did you ask me to come for a walk with you if you're not prepared to hold a civilised conversation?'

'I issued a general invitation,' he said stiffly, 'before I saw you were wi' the lassies.'

She stopped dead in the middle of the pavement. 'So you'd rather I left you alone?'

'I didnae say that.' He had stopped too, and they turned to face one other.

'You've hardly said anything!'

'Maybe that's because I don't want tae say too much!'

'What's that supposed to mean?'

He started to speak, then stopped himself. She bunched her hands into fists. 'Ewen Livingstone,' she demanded through gritted teeth, 'if you've got something to say, then say it and let's get it over with!'

'You want to hear what I've got to say, Miss Burgess? You want to bloody hear?'

'Don't swear. It's not necessary if one has an adequate vocabulary.'

'I beg your pardon, I'm sure,' he flung at her. 'I'm no used tae spending time wi' ladies like yourself!'

'Oh! Just tell me what you've got to say. Right now!'

'All right then, I will!' he yelled, then looked around him in embarrassment and lowered his voice. They were standing close to an ice-cream kiosk where several people were waiting to be served.

'Why are you bothering to walk with me?' he asked in a quieter voice. 'Are you still using me to make Matthew Campbell jealous? Hoping the other girls will report back tae him that you went off wi' me? Or do you really fancy a wee bit of rough?'

She drew her breath in on a hiss. 'That's an awful thing to say!'

He folded his arms, lifted his chin and gave her a magnificently disdainful look. 'Aye, well, sometimes the truth is awful, Miss Burgess.'

'Oh, for Pete's sake,' she wailed. 'Stop calling me Miss Burgess. And stop being so horrible. I thought we were friends.' She straightened out her fingers and lifted her hands in a gesture of helplessness. Then she brought them down hard, slicing through the air. 'Oh, just stop it!'

He raised his fair eyebrows. 'People are looking, Miss Burgess.'

'Let them bloody look!'

'Don't swear. It's no' necessary if one has an adequate vocabulary.'

'You'd drive a saint to swear!'

In the middle of Oban esplanade, and to her utter horror, Caroline Burgess burst into tears. She never did that sort of thing. If she had confused herself, she had completely unmanned Ewen. The supercilious look vanished from his face and he took an urgent step towards her.

'Och, lassie, there's no need for that. Don't greet, hen. I didnae mean to upset you. I'm awful, awful sorry. Don't cry, Carrie. Please!'

Peter rowed [illegible]

[illegible] nodded, and [illegible] a hard blow with an [illegible] down and Peter [illegible] had [illegible] [illegible]

[illegible]

[illegible]

The pale light [illegible]

[illegible]

[illegible] one side of [illegible]

[illegible]

[illegible]

Chapter 6

'Better now?'

Carrie nodded, and managed a watery smile before giving her nose a final blow with an extremely sodden handkerchief. He had pulled her to an empty bench further along the esplanade, sat her down and listened to all of it. She had apologised profusely for her bad behaviour at the *ceilidh*, begged him to believe she hadn't intended the confrontation with Matt in the garden to take place, and told him how worried she was about her father and his health.

'A lot better,' she said. 'And thank you for rescuing me back there, too.'

'Rescuing you?'

She nodded her head. 'Yes. If I'd had to look at another mustard pot with *A Present From Oban* painted on it or a whisky glass decorated in lurid colours with a picture of a bagpiper I'd have had the screaming abdabs in the middle of Oban High Street.'

'The screaming abdabs, eh?' he murmured. 'I'd love to have seen those. Personally I love all those calendars wi' cute wee Scottie dogs on them. You know? One black, one white, and with *Frae Bonnie Scotland* written underneath them.'

She gave him a curious look.

'I can pick out some words. I've tried to teach myself to read, but I cannae say I've made much of a job of it.'

'How come you didn't learn at school?'

He rubbed the side of his nose and looked embarrassed. 'Well, I didnae go to school very much, to tell you the truth.'

'I'll bet you regret that now,' she said pertly, beginning to recover.

'You'll never know how much,' he said. His voice was quiet but unmistakably sincere, and she wished she hadn't made the smart comment.

He relaxed his posture. While she'd been recounting her tale of woe, he'd been sitting with one ankle up on the opposite knee, occasionally leaning forward and giving her hand an awkward pat.

'Look,' he said, 'how would it be if I volunteered to help your daddy with the gardening? At the station or at your hoose. I don't know anything about the technical stuff, but I could do some o' the hard labour for him. I suppose it's past the time for digging, but maybe I could do the weeding for him, that kind o' thing.'

'Would you really?'

It was a generous offer, especially when she considered the long hours he already worked.

'Aye. Of course I would. Your daddy's been good tae me. He gave me a job when other people wouldnae.'

She smiled gently at him. 'D'you know something, Ewen Livingstone? You're a very nice person.'

'I like your daddy. I like his daughter too.' He reached out and took a strand of her hair between his thumb and index finger. 'When it comes to you, maybe it's a bit more than liking.' His rough voice had dropped to a whisper, as soft as the sound of the waves slapping against the sea wall beneath their feet.

He began to stroke the smooth tress he held, his touch as light as a feather. 'You've the bonniest hair,' he murmured.

'Ewen . . .' Please don't say any more, she thought. There was too much between them: background, education, status. Not to mention a certain Mr Matthew Campbell. Whether he saw it in her face or got the silent message, Ewen took his hand from her hair and turned his head away to look out over the sea for a moment. Then he got to his feet.

'Still want to walk along to Ganavan?'

She smiled up at him, relieved at how well he had taken her rejection. 'I can't think of anything I'd like better.'

'Can you walk and eat at the same time?'

'I'm willing to give it a try.'

'Then I'll go back to that kiosk and get us both an ice-cream.'

'Is that Mull over there?'

'Aye. Mull of the Mountains,' Ewen said easily, stretching out his legs and crossing them at the ankles. They were sitting on a bench overlooking the Ganavan sands. 'One of the Inner Hebrides.'

Caught by the poetry of the name, Carrie repeated it. '*Mull of the Mountains*. Is that where your family's from?'

Partick was full of folk from the Highlands and Islands. The flow south in search of work had been going on for generations. There were the girls who came to the city's great teaching hospitals to train as nurses and the tall, strapping men who peppered the ranks of the Glasgow police force. Islanders with the sea in their blood manned the merchant ships and passenger liners which sailed all over the globe. They crewed the ferries and the Clyde puffers too: the tough little boats which transported coal and everything else between the Lowlands and the islands and settlements of the rugged West Coast.

The shipyards on both sides of the river provided work for many.

There was a high concentration of Highlanders both in Govan on the south side of the Clyde and in Partick, which sat opposite it on the north bank.

Carrie was pondering something. 'I didn't think Livingstone was a Highland name.'

He assured her that it was. 'Although there's a Gaelic version of it too. We don't come from Mull, though. We belong to Appin, and a wee island called Lismore. They're both up there somewhere. Someone pointed them out to me on a map once.' He had his hands thrust in his pockets, but he lifted his chin to indicate the general direction, and told her that the famous Dr David Livingstone's family had also come from the same area.

'Do you go back to visit?' Carrie knew lots of people did. The flood of people took place in reverse, at least on a temporary basis, during the summer months.

'No. I wouldnae be exactly welcome there, you see.' The bench creaked as he shifted his position on it. 'Don't ask,' he said in response to her look of surprise. 'You don't want tae know.' There was the oddest mix of expressions on his face. 'You don't know what to say now, do you?'

That was too much of a challenge to resist. 'You're a man of mystery, are you?'

His face lit up. 'Aye, I like that. A man of mystery.' He was studying her, surveying the smart little felt hat, his eyes travelling up the pheasant's feather and back down again.

'Very up-to-the-minute,' he pronounced. 'Now, do you call that style Tyrolean or Robin Hood?'

'Either really.'

She was intrigued by the way he was forcibly changing the subject, but also greatly amused by this unexpected interest in fashion. When he ventured the opinion that she was wearing the hat at exactly the right angle, Carrie laughed.

'Is that another of your pieces of useless information? How you should wear a Tyrolean hat? I can't think you're going to find much use for the knowledge yourself.'

He smiled. 'A woman I know likes to buy the fashion magazines when she can afford them. She reads the articles out to me.' His smile grew broader. 'Whether I want to hear them or not.'

'Is she a friend of your mother's?' Now she was unashamedly fishing for information.

'She was.'

'She *was* a friend of your mother? What happened, did they fall out?'

His expression grew sombre. 'My mother died three years ago, Carrie. Not long after my sixteenth birthday.'

She laid an impulsive hand on his shoulder. 'Oh, Ewen, I'm so sorry.'

'Don't be. She loved me and I loved her.'

That answer had bounced straight back at her, and it had sounded a touch defensive. Regretful that she had unwittingly put her foot in it, she asked him what she thought was a practical and unemotional question. 'So do you live with your father?'

He hesitated. Then, with the air of a man who had just made a decision, he said quietly, 'I never knew my father, Carrie. My parents weren't married. I'm illegitimate.' He gave her a crooked smile. 'I'll not soil your ladylike ears with the technical term.'

'Oh,' she breathed. So that's what the big mystery was, and no doubt also the reason for her mother's disapproval of him. Being born out of wedlock was a terrible thing, a subject for gossip by adults and name-calling from your fellow children. It brought a stigma with it, one you would carry to the end of your days. Ewen's tight lips and paled skin seemed to indicate that he had experienced his full share of jibes and taunts.

Her heart filled with sympathy for him. People could be so cruel. Was he wondering now how she was going to react? She hoped he knew her better than that. It was hardly his fault that his parents hadn't been married. That had always been her belief. Why should the sins of the fathers be visited upon the children?

'Would you like to talk about it, Ewen?' she asked briskly. 'I mean, I'll listen if you want to tell me, but don't feel that you have to.'

The grim expression on his face relaxed. 'You're real sweet, Carrie Burgess,' he said softly, 'but no, I don't really want to talk about it. Is that all right?' he asked, his brow furrowing.

'Of course it is.' Anxious to put him at his ease, she went back to practicalities. 'So who do you live with then?'

'I live by myself.'

'By yourself?' She had never heard of anyone of their age living alone. There were plenty of young married couples, of course, but not single people in their teens. 'Who looks after you?'

'I do,' he said proudly. 'I can cook. And clean.'

But not sew, she thought. That explained the lost buttons and the lack of elbow patches on his working jacket.

'Does your mother's friend help you out sometimes?'

'Aye. Her and her mother-in-law. They've lived together since Jimmy died.'

'Jimmy?'

'Son tae one, husband tae the other,' he said briefly. 'He was killed in a shipyard accident. They'd only been married a few years when it happened.'

'How sad. But I suppose his wife and his mother must comfort one another in their loss.'

Ewen burst out laughing.

'What's so funny?'

He had to wipe his eyes before he could speak. 'They never stop fighting, that pair.'

'What do they fight about?'

'Everything and nothing. Both o' them could start an argument in an empty hoose. Sometimes it's over me. I go round there every Sunday for ma dinner and they fight over whose turn it is to cook it, whose turn it is to serve it, which one o' them is the best cook. You should hear the things they call each other. I think "black-hearted bitch" is one o' my personal favourites,' he mused.

Carrie was gazing at him in amazement. 'So why do they stay together?' she asked.

He looked shrewd. 'Because they're actually very fond of each other and they both really loved Jimmy – although his grieving widow miscalls him too, with the old lady shouting at her about no' speaking ill of the dead. You were quite right. They do comfort one other, but they'd die rather than admit that.'

Carrie shook her head. 'Folk are odd, aren't they?'

'They certainly are.'

They sat in comfortable and companionable silence for a while. Then she posed another question. 'Is that how you know all the things you do? Because your mother's friend reads her magazines out to you?'

'Well, I always listen when she does that. Or anybody else, for that matter. There's one or two o' the surfacemen who buy a paper every day. Sometimes we get a real good discussion going about something in the news. And I've got my own wireless set. I've learned a lot from the programmes on that. I saved up for it,' he told her with quiet pride. 'Took me ages. By the time I'd got enough money together I'd grown out o' ma good jacket.'

'So you had a hard choice to make?'

'Aye. The wireless or holey elbows. No choice at all, really,' he said with a grin. 'I talk to people a lot as well. It's amazing what you can learn from other folk.' He took his hands out of his pockets and sat up straight on the bench, his face alive with enthusiasm. 'Before I met you and the lassies today, someone was telling me all about McCaig's Tower. You know, the big monument up on the hill?' They couldn't see it from where they were sitting, but he waved an arm back in the direction of the town.

'I thought it was called McCaig's Folly?'

'Ah, well, but my informant' – he looked sheepish – 'that is, the wee wifie who sold me the gammon roll I had for my dinner, well, she says that a whole heap o' people don't agree with it being called a folly. This Mr McCaig apparently had it built to provide work for unemployed stonemasons. So it wasnae a foolish thing to do at all.'

'No,' Carrie said reflectively. 'It was a good thing.' Like him, she could more than see the point of anything which provided work. 'I'd love to walk to it. There must be a great view from up there.'

'There is. That's where I was this morning. It's a steep climb, mind.'

'So you wouldn't fancy going up again?'

'I don't think we would have the time, hen.'

Dead on cue, a church bell somewhere in the distance began to sound the hour. Warm and relaxed and enjoying his company, Carrie lazily counted the chimes, her eyes closed and her face turned up towards the sun. Five o'clock. Then, with a start, she straightened up abruptly. Five o'clock! Their train home was due to leave in twenty-eight minutes' time!

She was a stationmaster's daughter. She knew the trains had to run on time. Come hell or high water. So why was she standing in front of the buffers of a curiously empty and echoing Oban station gazing in dismay at empty tracks? The special excursion train – Carrie consulted her smart little wrist watch – had left for Glasgow precisely eleven minutes ago.

'My mother's going to kill me.'

Especially, she thought with a silent glance at Ewen, if she finds out how much time I've spent with you today. He might not be Al Capone or a white slave trader, but he was equally as undesirable in Esther Burgess' eyes.

'I doubt it.' The object of her mother's disapproval seemed to be in an infuriatingly cheerful frame of mind. 'Anyway, why don't we check the timetable for the next train and then you can phone home? Your da's probably still on duty, and if he's not someone can pop round to the station house with a message for your parents. Then they won't be worried when you're not on the special.'

It was a sensible suggestion. Carrie should have thought of it herself.

'Will you check the timetable, then?' she asked, waving towards the wall to the right of the booking office where large white posters displayed the details of arrivals and departures. 'I'll see if somebody here will let me phone Partick.' Her eyes lit on the booking-office window. The shutter was down. That was a bad sign. 'Unless they've all gone home for their tea, that is.'

'Eh . . .' said Ewen, sending her an odd little smile. 'I think *you'd* better check the train times.'

'What?' Then she realised. 'Sorry,' she mumbled, blushing at her *faux-pas*.

'Och, you're the very soul o' tact, Miss Burgess,' he said in mock-outrage. They strolled over to the wall. They were in no rush now.

'How long till the next train?'

She showed him, pointing it out.

'Look. Here it is. Glasgow Buchanan Street. You said you can pick some things out. See the capital G for Glasgow? Here it is again for Garelochhead.' She ran her index finger back up the poster, underlined the words and said them slowly, breaking them up into their component syllables.

'Glas-gow Bu-chan-an Street. Now you.'

'Me?'

Ewen looked startled, and a little nervous, but he did as she had done, using his finger to trace along beneath the words, sounding out the names.

'Very good. And you said you know your numbers.'

He peered at the figures. 'I know some o' the numbers.' He sounded anxious.

'Go on,' Carrie encouraged.

He pronounced them carefully. 'Seven . . . two . . . No, it's twenty-two. Seven twenty-two?' He turned to her for confirmation, a little frown between his brows.

'That's right. Seven twenty-two.'

He swung back to the wall. 'But what's this after the seven twenty-two?' She waited, willing him on. His face cleared. 'Och, I know. *PM*. That's right, isn't it?'

She beamed at him. 'Well done!'

'If you tell me I'm a clever boy I might well no' be responsible for my actions, Caroline Burgess. You'll be a dab hand with the infants when you start teaching. Do I get a jelly baby or a dolly mixture for getting it right?'

'I think we're going to need more sustenance than a bag of sweeties if we're not going to be back home till some time around midnight.'

They left the station and went into the street to look for a blue and white *You May Telephone From Here* sign. She had tried knocking on the door of the booking office and the stationmaster's office, but to no avail. There was nobody about.

'Terminus stations,' suggested Ewen. 'They probably do all go home for their tea here. Why should they hang around if nothing's going to happen for another couple of hours?'

A seagull the size of a pampered cat hopped across in front of them, scavenging for scraps of fish left on the jetty which abutted the railway station. The tang of the sea and its bounty was strong. Carrie was preoccupied, worrying about how late it was going to be before they got home.

'My mother *is* going to kill me,' she said mournfully.

Ewen looked amused. 'You're your parents' darling,' he said. 'I imagine you'll survive unscathed.'

He was always doing that, coming up with words she wouldn't have expected him to know. Uneducated he might be. Unintelligent he certainly wasn't.

They headed towards the shops on the seafront; but there didn't seem to be any signs indicating a public telephone. However, there was a chip shop open.

'Can I offer you a fish supper, madam?'

The aroma was certainly enticing, but Carrie chewed her lip. 'Maybe we should keep looking for a phone.' The words were scarcely out of her mouth before she was struck by an unwelcome thought. Matt was still on duty. More than likely she would get him when she called. He wasn't going to be exactly overjoyed when he found out she was stranded in Oban with Ewen Livingstone.

He was saying something, pointing out that nobody was going to be worrying about them yet. Why not enjoy their tea first and then continue the search for a telephone? They'd still be getting the message through a good two hours before the excursion train pulled into Partick without them. It was another sensible suggestion. And, a little voice whispered, it postponed having to make any explanations to Matt.

'Let's eat,' said Ewen decisively. 'In God's fresh air and in God's own country. We can sit on a bench and enjoy the view.'

'Shall we go Dutch on the fish suppers?'

'I offered to treat you.' His wide mouth was set in an uncharacteristically tight line.

'I'm sorry,' she said hurriedly. 'That would be lovely. Thank you.'

'We poor people are proud, you know,' he went on, still frowning at her.

Trying to work out how to smooth the feathers she had unwittingly ruffled, she cast around for the right words. To her relief, she saw his face break into its more customary smile. He'd been teasing her.

Ewen waited out on the street while Carrie went into a hotel to phone. Her heart sank when Matt's voice answered. He should have been off duty for half an hour by now. He wasn't pleased to hear that she'd missed the train. He was even less pleased to find out how late she was going to be home.

'Don't worry,' Carrie said brightly. 'I'm not on my own. There's a couple of us here.' Well, she thought, a couple can be taken to mean a few people, not just two. She crossed her fingers, but the charm didn't work. There was frost in his voice, crackling up to her over the hills and mountains and lochs which separated them.

'Who *exactly* is there with you, Carrie?'

She told him – and heard the sharp intake of breath all the way along the hundred miles of phone line.

'And where are you now?'

'In a hotel.' Now that a cat was out of the bag, she was beginning to feel a bit calmer. She hadn't intended for this to happen, after all.

'Is it a respectable sort of place?'

It was on the tip of her tongue to tell him that the hotel foyer was full of painted *houris* and men who looked as if they might be white slavers or dope fiends. She thought better of it.

'Of course it's respectable, Matt. It's perfectly respectable.' The folding door of the telephone booth was slightly ajar. She pushed it completely shut and looked out through the two glass panels which adorned its upper half.

'There's a receptionist who looks as if she's about a hundred and fifty years old, and the only other person in the place is an old lady with a wee dog on her lap and a fox fur around her shoulders. It's completely hideous, but she looks the very soul of respectability.'

'Don't be flippant, Carrie,' he said irritably. 'Now, listen to me.'

After she came off the phone, she held it in her hand for a second or two and addressed it as though it were the young man to whom she had just been speaking. Correction. The young man who had just been speaking to her. Or perhaps *at her* would be a better choice of words.

'Want me to salute you as well, Matt?' she enquired wryly of the heavy black receiver.

'Everything all right?' Ewen asked as she emerged from the front porch. He was stroking a fluffy ginger cat which was balancing precariously on its dainty paws on the narrow-topped wall which surrounded the hotel's front terrace. 'Did you get through to yer faither?'

'He'd gone for his tea. I got Matthew Campbell.'

'Oh. Him.'

'He speaks highly of you too,' she snapped back, still smarting from the interrogation to which Matt had subjected her, not to mention the set of instructions he had barked out. How could he be so lovely sometimes and so horrible at others?

She was to sit in the hotel until the train left. By herself. Then she was to travel home. In a different compartment from Ewen Livingstone. Preferably a Ladies' Only compartment.

With a wave of the hand, she indicated the hotel behind them and told him that Matt wanted her to wait there until it was time for the train. Ewen scowled.

'I sincerely hope you told him to go and fu—'

Carrie's eyes opened wide and he hastily amended it to 'go and raffle himself'.

'I told him no such thing,' she said sharply, annoyed that he had so very nearly used such an awful word in front of her. 'Matthew Campbell *has* asked me to marry him, you know.'

'He's what?'

'You heard,' she said tightly.

The ginger tom had been revelling in Ewen's stroking. When it abruptly ceased, the cat looked momentarily disgusted. Then he jumped down off the wall, ran along beside it and slunk stealthily around a corner and out of sight. Ewen, his expression grown thunderous, didn't appear to notice.

'I presume you told him you're far too young to get married?'

Now she had another man trying to run her life for her. This was too much.

'What I told him is none of your business, Ewen Livingstone.'

The shutters came down over his cool eyes. 'Right. Fine. Well, away back into that hotel and sip tea. They probably wouldnae let the likes o' me in, anyway. I only hope ye don't die o' boredom. I'll see you at the train.'

He was struck momentarily dumb when she announced her intention of travelling home, alone, in the Ladies' Only compartment. She saw it in his face, though: disbelief, insult, upset. He managed a parting shot before he stomped off.

'If you let him boss you around like this now, what's it going to be like after you're married? Have ye thought of that, Carrie?'

Chapter 7

This was ridiculous. She was the only person in the Ladies' Only compartment. There weren't many people on the entire train, which made it all the sillier that Ewen was sitting a few compartments along from her, probably also on his own.

Elbow propped on the wee table which jutted out from below the window, Carrie contemplated the scenery. It was as spectacular and dramatic on the way down as it had been on the way up. The trouble was, its very grandeur inspired her to think, thoughts racing off in a hundred different directions.

As they emerged from the narrow defile of the Pass of Brander she was confronted by the impressive expanse of Loch Awe. The water was sparkling still in the long summer's evening. She gazed gloomily out at it.

The train sped on. She glimpsed an impressive-looking castle through the trees as they turned round the head of Loch Awe before making brief stops at Dalmally and then Tyndrum Lower. Opposite the station there, a small boy sat on the lower slopes of a gentle hill. He waved at the train. She returned the greeting, moving her arm in a wide and prolonged arc so he would be sure to see her.

Crianlarich was the next stop, then Ardlui at the top of Loch Lomond. After that, it wouldn't take very long to leave the hills behind, re-crossing the Highland Line back into the Lowlands – at which point she herself would have to face the music.

Her mother would be up on the ceiling, but that would wear off once her daughter was safely back in the bosom of her family. Besides, Carrie knew that Esther trusted her really. Her father would pretend to be angry to support his wife, but there would be a twinkle in his eye. What she'd never hear the end of was the stationmaster's daughter managing to miss her train. Her father would tell that story forever and a day. Matt, however, would be hard pressed to see the funny side of any of today's events.

It was a short hop from Tyndrum to Crianlarich, where there was always a longer stop for the engine to take on water, time enough for the passengers to stretch their legs for ten minutes. Carrie stepped out on to the platform at exactly the same moment as Ewen did. They looked along the carriage at each other. He'd taken his jacket off, and had also removed his stiff collar and tie.

'Is there a tea room here?' she asked quietly.

'Famed both far and wide,' he replied. 'Great home-baking, so I'm told.'

'Would you let me treat you this time?'

'A gentleman never lets a lady pay for herself,' he responded loftily. They discovered, however, that they were too late. The renowned tea room was closed for the night, so they had to content themselves with sauntering up and down the platform in the deepening twilight of the Highland night.

That was the plan anyway. The midges had a different idea. The blood-sucking insects, attracted by the smell of warm human skin and the feast which lay beneath it, swarmed around them in seconds. Attacking every piece of exposed skin, their irritation value bore no relationship to their tiny size. They stood it for a couple of minutes, then retreated, Carrie delaying only long enough to fetch her things from the Ladies' Only compartment.

'We couldnae get a cup of tea,' said Ewen with a laugh, still slapping at the beasties which had followed them back into the train, 'but the midgies are getting a drink from us.'

'Wee horrors, aren't they?' she agreed, engaged in the same ritual dance as himself. 'The curse of the West Highlands. My father says that if you kill one of them, ten thousand of his pals come to the funeral.'

'Do you not know how to get rid o' them?' Ewen asked. 'You mix up a paste of sugar and water . . .'

Carrie sat down. 'White or brown?'

'Brown. Demerara's the best.'

'Right.' She was listening carefully. Ewen worked out of doors. He was bound to have learned from the older men a foolproof method of keeping the dreaded midgies at bay. Sitting across from her, perched on the edge of the long upholstered seat, he was miming the mixing-up of the sugar and water, warming to his theme. His hands rose to pat his cheeks.

'Then you spread the paste on your face and arms – and any other exposed parts of the body.'

'And does that keep them away?' she asked eagerly.

'No – but it rots the wee buggers' teeth!'

Laughing at his own joke, he flung himself back into the seat then looked momentarily dismayed. 'Oh, excuse me, I didnae mean to swear in front of you.'

'It's not the swearing I mind,' Carrie said swiftly. 'It's the terrible joke.' This was the way she liked him, friendly and relaxed and talkative. He didn't mean anything by his swearing. It was normal in the company he usually kept. She knew he didn't do it to shock.

'A real luxury this,' he murmured, 'to be sitting on the cushions.'

'Surfacemen usually travel in the guard's van?'

'Aye. We have some good laughs, but the view's no' very good.' He gestured with his thumb towards the window. 'Certainly no' as good as from here. Did you see that dead interesting-looking castle at the head o' Loch Awe and the wean sitting on the hill back at Tyndrum?'

'Yes to both. Did you wave to the wee boy?'

'Aye, of course I did.' He twisted round, angling his body so he could stretch his legs out in the well between the two bench seats. A contemplative smile touched his mouth. 'D'ye think he was clambering and scrambling – all by himself and gathering brambles?'

Carrie sat back in her own seat. 'You liked the poem, then?'

Ewen was checking the disposition of his feet, eyes downcast. Were his eyelashes a little fairer than his hair? She thought she could see some gold in there among the feathery strands. His jaw line was beginning to shadow with the faintest suggestion of stubble, but the skin on his cheeks, as she'd observed before, was as smooth as a baby's. He looked up, and straight at her.

'I loved the poem.'

The train juddered, and pulled slowly away from the platform. Surely it was that jolt which was making her suddenly breathless?

He threw her an odd little glance, then heaved a sigh of deep contentment. 'I could take a lot of this.'

She thought, perhaps, that it might be as well not to enquire exactly what he could take a lot of.

'Do you like the pictures?'

His eyes lifted again, to the space above and behind her head. Underneath the luggage rack made of steel struts and string mesh where Carrie had carefully laid her jacket and hat and where the back of the seat was bolted on to the wall, there were three frames. The one in the middle surrounded a mirror. It was flanked on either side by small posters showing the beauties of Britain, underlined by the message, *It's Quicker By Rail*. On Ewen's side of the compartment there were pictures of Bamburgh and Edinburgh Castles. Carrie's held views of Loch Long and Loch Lomond.

'Aye, they're dead artistic. I love the way they do them.' He lifted a hand in frustration. 'Och, I don't know the word to say what I mean.'

'The style of them?' she suggested.

'That's it. The style. They paint them in a particular style, don't they?'

Ewen examined all of the pictures in turn. There was real appreciation in his eyes. 'I love paintings,' he confided. 'I often go along to the Art Galleries on a Sunday afternoon to look at them.'

'Not looking for talent?' she teased. Glasgow's municipal art gallery, housed in a magnificent red sandstone building over the River Kelvin, on the fringes of Partick, was well-frequented on Sunday afternoons by young members of both sexes. It was a well-known meeting place.

'Why would a man go looking for talent when he's already found perfection?'

He gazed at her, the expression in his eyes exactly the same as it had been when he had been studying the pictures. This time the jolt Carrie experienced had absolutely nothing to do with the motion of the train. He might have been stumped for a word a minute ago, but at other times he could be all too eloquent.

'Ewen . . .' she said, her face troubled. 'Please don't.'

He continued to study her for a moment or two. Then, palms upward in a gesture of hopelessness, he lifted his hands.

'I know, I know. I shouldnae have said it. Like I shouldnae have said what I did this afternoon. Don't bother giving me the wee speech about wanting us to stay friends. I think I know it off by heart by now.'

He looked away from her and leaned his head against the window. 'I don't want you to be in any doubt about how I feel about you.' His voice was quiet but firm. 'I want you to know you have a choice. That I'm here if you need me.'

She thought that was one of the saddest things she had ever heard. He would never be her choice. Judging by the way he was choosing not to meet her eyes, he knew full well she was going to reject him again, yet he was laying his feelings bare to her. His painful honesty and vulnerability brought a lump to her throat.

He was staring out of the window now – or at his own large hand which he had pressed flat against the glass. It was a strong hand, used to hard work, his splayed fingers blunt and powerful. Matt's fingers were strong too, but tapering and slender with it.

The train, labouring up one of the steep gradients which characterised the West Highland line, had slowed. Without shifting his position or looking at her Ewen posed a question. 'D'ye want tae change back to the Ladies' Only compartment at Garelochhead?'

'Not if you promise to behave yourself.' She sounded as brisk as her old gym mistress.

She could see one side of his face, and half of the quick smile her words had provoked. It was a lot more than rueful. After a moment or two he sighed and lifted his head. 'I promise. Cross my heart and hope to die.' He raised his eyebrows at her. 'Right then. What would ye like to talk about now?'

Carrie had politely asked the driver before they left Oban if he would do a request stop at Partick for them. Archie Burgess took care to thank the man personally but didn't delay the train any longer than was strictly necessary. They had a timetable to adhere to.

With a wave to the guard and that automatic glance at the rear lights as the train swayed out of the station to complete the final brief stretch of its journey to the city, he walked smartly down the platform towards his erring daughter and her friend. One of them at least betrayed a little anxiety as the stationmaster approached. Ewen was shifting from one foot to the other, waiting for the dressing down.

Standing four-square outside the booking office, Archie did his best to oblige. Carrie wasn't going to undermine his authority in front of his staff, so she acted the meek and penitent daughter and tried not to respond to the answering gleam in her father's eye. She had been relieved to see him waiting for them, especially as Matt was there too, looking far angrier than Archie Burgess did.

He must have been scanning the carriages as they came in. He had his fingers wrapped round the handle of the open door of the Ladies' Only compartment, and stared when he saw Carrie and Ewen emerge from one further up the platform. As though he couldn't believe his eyes, he peered into the empty compartment. That made Ewen chuckle. Not a wise move. Especially as Carrie couldn't entirely contain some amusement either.

After a few questions which Ewen answered nervously but apparently to his stationmaster's satisfaction, Archie gave him a formal rebuke and dispatched him off home. He took his leave of Mr Burgess respectfully, gave Carrie a cheerful wave and completely ignored Matthew, who turned to watch him go with cold eyes.

'Right then, young lady,' barked Archie in a very creditable imitation of a stern patriarch. 'We'll be for home. Your mother wants a word with you too.'

Matthew coughed. Carrie knew what he wanted. She supposed there wasn't any point in putting it off. 'Could Matthew and I have five minutes alone together, Father? Please?'

Grumbling in a token sort of way, Archie told his daughter he'd be waiting for her by the platform gate in exactly five minutes. 'Not a second longer, my girl!'

She turned to Matt. He was so handsome, especially when he looked as he did at the moment, all smouldering eyes and unruly dark hair. Walking over to him, she lifted her face and offered him a kiss, but he jerked his head back.

'Matt? What's the matter?'

His voice was low and impassioned. 'You've spent all day with *him*. That's what's the matter!' He gestured towards the station steps which Ewen had descended a few minutes ago. He'd be walking along a quiet and deserted Dumbarton Road now, heading home to an empty house in Keith Street.

'Matthew,' she said carefully, taking a step back. 'I did not spend all day with him –'

'That's not what I heard.'

She stiffened. 'Not what you heard? From whom, might I ask?'

'It doesn't matter who told me, Carrie.' Matt was holding himself as rigidly as she was. 'What does matter is that you apparently sneaked off with Ewen Livingstone straight after lunch.'

'Sneaked off with him?' She repeated each word with angry precision, both her voice and her temper rising.

'Yes. I understand the two of you weren't seen for the rest of the afternoon.'

Her chin went up. 'What are you implying, Matt?'

'I'm not implying anything.'

The coldness in his voice suggested the exact opposite. 'Don't you think I'm entitled to an explanation of your behaviour?' he demanded. If it hadn't been directed at her, she might have found his haughtiness and air of wounded pride quite magnificent – if a touch theatrical. Her father hadn't subjected her to this kind of an interrogation. She saw no reason why she should take it from Matthew Campbell.

Suddenly she realised who'd supplied him with his information: someone who'd been there when she'd accepted Ewen's invitation to go for a walk, someone who might well have made it her business to notice that the two of them had failed to make the train for the return journey.

'Janice Muirhead told you, didn't she?'

His face betrayed the answer.

'I'll bet she enjoyed that,' said Carrie lightly.

He gave her one of his disdainful looks. 'You're wrong, as a matter of fact. I practically had to force it out of her.'

'Oh, I'm sure you did! Tell me,' she asked with careful sarcasm, 'would this be the same Janice Muirhead we're talking about? The one you recently described to me as a complete trollop? I believe those *were* the words you used.'

'My opinion of her moral character doesn't matter, Carrie. Judging from what you yourself said to me over the telephone, her information was accurate.'

'Don't be so pompous, Matt. You sound like a policeman giving evidence at the Sheriff Court.' Carrie paused, and made a conscious effort to calm herself down. This was escalating into the mother and father of all arguments, rather more than a lovers' tiff. 'I did not *sneak off* with Ewen straight after lunch,' she said, striving to excise the anger and irritation from her voice. 'We bumped into each other in the early afternoon and I was so fed up trailing round the shops with Janice and her friends . . .'

'You didn't get fed up with Ewen Livingstone's company,' he interrupted. 'You were enjoying yourself with him so much that you missed the train home. How could you do that, Carrie? You've got a watch, haven't you?'

Keeping her temper was beginning to require a great deal of effort. That patronising question hadn't helped. 'Ewen and I walked along to the Ganavan sands. It's quite a distance. We got talking and completely forgot the time. But we're both home safe now. Isn't that all that matters?'

She moved towards him, laid a conciliatory hand on his arm. 'It's you I love, Matt,' she said softly.

He looked down at her hand, resting lightly on the sleeve of his dark jacket. 'Is it?'

'You know it is.' Her voice grew gentle. He had sounded very uncertain when he had asked that question, as if he really was unsure of her. That was why he was acting this way, overreacting wildly to her having spent time with Ewen because of that uncertainty.

'I love you, Matthew Campbell. Only you. How many times do I have to tell you?' She willed him to lift his gaze from her hand, and eventually he did.

He gave her a shamefaced smile and a swift kiss on the lips. 'What were you and he talking about?'

'Och, I don't know. Different things. Lots of things.'

He persisted. 'What sort of things?'

'Matt, I can't remember all the things we talked about, but you've got nothing to worry about. Honestly. It was all perfectly innocent.'

She had a sudden mental picture of Ewen leaning his tousled head against the window of the compartment, awkwardly confessing his feelings for her. That was one confidence she certainly wasn't going to betray.

'D'you know what I think, Carrie? I think you don't want to remember, that you don't want to tell me what you and he were talking about.'

'I told you, we talked about a lot of things. We were with each other for quite a while.'

That was the truth, but it had been the wrong thing to say. Matt's eyes flashed with anger. 'You'd have spent a lot less time with him if you'd travelled home in the Ladies' Only compartment,' he snapped. 'Why didn't you do that?'

'Because it was boring sitting on my own.'

'But I had expressly told you not to sit with him, Carrie. Why didn't you?'

'Matt,' she pleaded, 'it shouldn't be about one person telling another one what to do. Isn't it about love?'

He moved his arm, shaking her hand off. 'Aren't you going to promise to obey me when we get married?'

She'd never given that much thought before. It might be what you said when you made your wedding vows, but surely most modern husbands didn't really expect obedience from their wives? Her father didn't. He and his wife discussed family matters, often argued the toss about them. Archie didn't always win those arguments. He wasn't the kind of husband who expected to.

A rogue thought flitted through Carrie's brain. What kind of husband would Ewen Livingstone be? Fun, she thought immediately, always willing to look on the bright side and make jokes and the best of a bad job if the going got rough. She couldn't imagine he would expect his wife to obey him either.

The young man who stood in front of her with such a forbidding expression on his face was also assuming rather a lot.

'I haven't actually agreed to marry you, Matt.' She could hear for herself how haughty she sounded. Well, she was feeling pretty haughty. 'Had you forgotten that?'

'No, I hadn't forgotten. I don't understand why you won't say yes, but I hadn't actually forgotten,' he said bitterly. 'How can I when you keep telling me you're too young for me?' They were glaring at each other now.

'In fact, Carrie, if you're not prepared to make that commitment to me, and if you really can't understand why I'm so upset about you spending all this time with Ewen Livingstone, I'm wondering if we shouldn't perhaps think of calling it a day.'

She took a deep breath. 'I think maybe you're right.'

He hadn't expected her to say that. She saw him rock back on to his heels. 'Is that what you want?' he asked stiffly.

'I think it's for the best, yes.'

They held each other's gaze for a few long seconds.

'Goodbye, Matthew,' she said. 'Thanks for all the places you've taken me to and all that. I do love you, you know. That's the simple truth.' She stomped off up the platform. Her father was holding the gate open for her. Carrie swept through without a word.

'Everything all right, lass?'

'Oh, Daddy!' she burst out, and went into his arms.

Chapter 8

'Hallo there.'

Carrie sat bolt upright in the deck-chair, although the words had been no more than a murmur. It was Ewen, leaning over the fence and the blossoming white flowers of the potato shaws. She walked over to him. She didn't want to have to shout this conversation in a voice loud enough for half of Partick to hear.

'Where are your workmates?' Peering over the palings, she cast a swift glance up and down the platform.

'Already gone,' he assured her. He seemed to understand her desire for discretion. 'I saw you sitting out when we came up on to the platform, so I pretended I'd left something behind at the bothy and had to go back for it.' He shifted the canvas bag in which he carried his tools from one shoulder to the other. 'Did you get an awful row from your ma on Saturday night?'

Carrie shook her head. She'd washed her hair this morning and dried it in the sun. The shiny strands felt like satin on her smooth cheeks. 'Not too bad.'

'I havenae seen you for a few days, though I've been looking out for you since Monday.'

He hadn't seen her because she'd been staying inside as much as humanly possible. Esther had more or less ordered her out today. Since Sunday morning Carrie had busied herself tackling every conceivable task which needed doing around the house. There wasn't a garment unmended, a sock undarned, a shirt lacking a button or a mirror or piece of brasswork unpolished throughout the Burgess home. She had even got out the canteen holding her mother's EPNS fish knives and forks – a prized wedding gift used only on the most special of occasions – and cleaned and polished every single one of them. As Esther had done the very same job herself not two months before, motherly patience was beginning to wear a little thin.

'It's tiring me out just watching you,' she had said firmly as the family sat down to the midday meal Carrie had insisted on preparing – as she had done every day that week. 'You haven't sat still for days. You're going to sit in the sun with a good book this afternoon. You need some fresh air. And a wee rest.'

'Best do as she says, lass,' Archie had chipped in. 'She's fearsome when roused. Take it from one who knows.'

Carrie had smiled mechanically at her father. After dinner was finished, she took a very good book outside with her, one she'd bought some time ago and hadn't got round to reading yet. She'd been looking forward to it. She was on page fifty before she admitted to herself she wasn't taking in a single word.

'I was worried about you. I thought maybe she'd kept you in or something,' said Ewen, his anxious voice recalling Carrie to the present. His concern almost made her laugh. The thought of her mother as some kind of fierce dragon-lady who'd lock her in her room on a diet of bread and water was the first thing she'd found remotely amusing since Saturday night.

'No,' she said, 'she's been all right about it.'

Her mother had been about to hit the roof when she found out that her daughter had spent several hours alone in a railway compartment with a boy of whom she disapproved. However, when she realised Carrie was unable to tell the story herself because she was crying bitterly over her argument with Matt, she had reacted in the same way as her husband and offered the sobbing girl the comfort of her arms.

'Oh, that's good,' Ewen said, his face clearing. 'I found a reception committee waiting for me when I got back home.'

'The two ladies you told me about on Saturday?'

'Aye. Mr Sharkey's son Pascal – you know him, don't you?' Carrie nodded. Pascal Sharkey, a friendly and likeable lad, had been taken on as a clerk earlier in the year. 'He noticed I'd missed the train and mentioned it to his father who unfortunately told the Terrible Two when he bumped into them later on that night. What a row I got for worrying them half to death!' Ewen grinned. 'Then a beaker of cocoa and about four pieces o' the old lady's shortbread. And her shortbread's worth having, let me tell you. I'd have taken the scolding anyway, and no' just for the sustenance. Saturday was a rare day, wasn't it?'

'It was,' Carrie agreed, studying his open face and thinking about it. It *had* been an enjoyable day. The fact she was no longer walking out with Matthew Campbell didn't alter that.

Last night was the first one she hadn't cried herself to sleep over the break-up, but Matt shouldn't have tried to boss her around like that. No girl with any spirit could stand for that sort of treatment. Practically ordering her to sit in the Ladies' Only compartment, for goodness' sake! It wasn't on. She could understand that he'd been jealous, but surely once he'd calmed down he must have realised himself how high-handed he'd been? Only it was Thursday now and he still hadn't come to apologise, so it didn't much look like it.

'Are you all right, Carrie?'

Ewen was looking very concerned. She'd better make an effort. It wasn't his fault. Not directly, at any rate.

'I'm fine.' She gestured towards the platform gate. 'Are you coming in?'

He fixed her with a level look. 'That depends.'

'On what?'

'On when you might be expecting Matthew Campbell to turn up today.'

She looked him straight in the eye. 'I'm not expecting him today. Or any other day for that matter.' It was time she faced facts. If Matthew hadn't come round to apologise the day after their quarrel, he was hardly going to do so five days on. 'We broke up on Saturday night.'

'Oh, really?' Ewen's eyebrows all but disappeared into his fair hair. 'Well, hen, I'd like to say I'm sorry about it, but I cannae be that two-faced, I'm afraid.' He was regarding her with a speculative air. Realising what it meant restored some of her pertness.

'There's no need to look at me like that, Ewen Livingstone,' she said sharply. 'I'm not looking for another boyfriend. Not at the moment, anyway.'

'Would a friend be acceptable?'

'A friend would be fine.'

'Right then,' he said briskly. 'I've something I want to ask you, but no' here.' He glanced at the raised arm of the signal at the end of the platform. 'There's a train due. Can we go some place where every railwayman in the west of Scotland cannae see us?'

'There's a bench round the other side of the house.'

'That's a bit more than a bench,' he said a minute or two later, looking at the wooden seat which sat against the windowless gable of the house.

'My father made it,' she told him proudly. Archie had built a rustic arch over the seat. Taking cuttings from a wild rose which grew elsewhere in the garden, he had trained the small pink blooms to climb up it.

'A bower,' Ewen said. 'That's what you call this. Is that no' right?' He looked questioningly at her.

'I suppose you would call it a bower. It's one of my favourite spots in the garden,' Carrie confided. And, she thought silently, despite the romance of the bower she had sat here with Matt on only one occasion. On grounds of practicality he had insisted that they move. The little briar roses attracted too many bees. Carrie had never minded the hard-working insects. If you kept still, they didn't bother you, simply got on with their work and flew on to the next flower.

She sat down at one end of the slatted seat and indicated to Ewen that he should join her, but he stood for a minute or two looking down at her.

'I shouldn't really sit here, of course,' she joked, becoming slightly uncomfortable under his prolonged scrutiny. 'Redheads don't suit pink!'

'You suit pink roses very well. A beautiful bower for a beautiful maiden,' he concluded softly.

She ought to have reminded him what had just been said about them being friends and nothing more, but instead she said gently, 'You've the soul of a poet, Ewen Livingstone.'

He snorted. 'I'm no poet, but this fellow was.'

He reached into his canvas bag and fished out a package, loosely tied up in brown paper. Curious, giving him an uncertain little smile, Carrie opened it and took out the book which was inside: *A Child's Garden of Verses* by Robert Louis Stevenson. She looked quickly up at him.

'Och, Ewen, that's awful nice of you, but I've already got a copy of this.' She wondered that he hadn't realised that.

'It's not for you. It's for me.'

'For you?'

He gulped and swallowed hard. 'I thought,' he began. 'I mean, that is . . . I wondered if . . . we could use it. You and me.'

The admiring look had left his face. He was very earnest, and obviously nervous. He swallowed again and came out with it.

'Teach me to read, Carrie,' he said. 'Please teach me how to read.'

Chapter 9

'You're going to what?'

'Teach Ewen Livingstone to read,' she repeated. 'We've already begun, although I'll have to get some proper teaching materials. We started this afternoon with Robert Louis Stevenson's poems for children, but they're too difficult for him at the moment.'

The struggle to cope with even the first line of what he referred to as 'the train poem' had dampened Ewen's spirits somewhat, but Carrie had chivvied him along. He had to learn to walk before he could run. His teacher was a novice too, but she would find out the best way of going about things. Or die in the attempt. That last comment, coupled with her obviously growing interest in the project, had brought the smile back to his face.

Carrie wished her new role as Ewen's teacher could have had the same effect on her mother. Esther Burgess, serving spoon poised over the large willow pattern bowl which held what was left of the potatoes, was unusually stony-faced.

The lines on her forehead grew deeper as she looked across the table at her husband. 'Did you know he was illiterate?' she demanded. Carrie winced at the word. It was such a cruel one.

Archie heaved a deep sigh. 'Aye, I knew. He didn't have much schooling. What with one thing and another.'

A look passed between husband and wife.

'That's what worries me,' said Esther, grimly spooning out potatoes on to her daughter's plate without stopping to ask if she wanted them. 'That boy's got a terrible background. You do know that, don't you?'

About to cut into one of the potatoes – grown by her father in their own garden and, she firmly believed, the most delicious food on earth when birstled in the pan with a knob of butter before being brought to the table – Carrie laid down her knife and fork in exasperation.

'Oh, Mother, that's not his fault, is it? And he's trying to improve himself. That's why he's asked me to help him. He's got ambitions. All he needs is a bit more confidence in himself.' She leaned forward over the table, the better to make her point.

Esther shook her head. 'Carrie, when it comes to his family history you don't know the half of it –'

'I know all of it,' she said coolly. 'He told me when we were at Oban. About being illegitimate, I mean.'

She heard her mother's sharp intake of breath, and saw her parents exchange another look. Ridiculous! Was she supposed to pretend she didn't know what the word meant? She wondered how Esther would have reacted if she'd used what Ewen had called the technical term . . .

'Surely you can't blame any child for being born out of wedlock? It's not the child who makes that choice.'

'She's got a point, Esther. Aye, I'll have another tattie.' Archie handed his plate across the table to his wife. 'And you have to give the laddie credit for wanting to better himself.'

'But why does Carrie have to help him do it?' wailed Esther.

'Because I'm the only person he can ask. He doesn't want anyone else to know he can't read and write. You will keep it a secret, won't you?' She looked pleadingly at both of her parents.

'Of course, hen,' said her father. He laid a hand over hers. 'It's a good thing you're doing. That lad could go far if someone would only give him a hand up. He's got something about him – a kind of spark.' He gave his daughter's hand a squeeze, released it and applied himself to his potatoes. 'That's why I gave him a start.'

Carrie smiled into her father's tired eyes. 'I know, Daddy. He's got great respect for you. He's offered to help you in the garden or with the station flower beds, if you would like.'

'In his own time? Och, that's kind o' the boy. I'll maybe take him up on it, lass.'

Perhaps, Carrie thought silently, Ewen's offer could kill not two but three birds with one stone. He would feel happier if he was making some recompense for the time Carrie was going to spend teaching him. Her father would be relieved of a physical burden and a considerable amount of mental stress and strain, and the resulting benefits to Archie's health would endear Ewen to Esther. Her mother's next words shattered this pleasant little idyll.

'So Ewen Livingstone will be calling at the house every day, and we're not to tell people why. You know it won't be long till the tongues start wagging, don't you? What will Matthew Campbell think?'

Carrie picked up her knife and fork again, doing her best to give a nonchalant shrug of the shoulders. 'Why should I care what he thinks? Mmm, these tatties are really tasty, Daddy. Are they the Maris Piper or the Pentland Dells?'

'So you don't care about Matthew any more,' Esther persisted. 'I suppose there's some other reason why you've been crying yourself to sleep every night since Saturday, then? And doing every wee job possible around the house so you don't have to go outside and run the risk of bumping into him?'

'I'm not saying I don't care about Matthew,' said Carrie, finding it more difficult than she expected to meet her mother's shrewd look. 'But I wasn't prepared to be bossed around by him. I told you that, Ma. He owes me an apology.'

'He was concerned about your reputation, Carrie. That says an awful lot for a young man.'

Funny. Now that Matt was no longer walking out with her daughter, Esther seemed inclined to forget all the objections she'd had to him. Even the age difference which had bothered her so much before seemed not to matter now.

'My reputation was perfectly safe, Mother. I know you'll find this hard to believe, but Ewen behaved like a perfect gentleman – at Oban, and while we were on the train.'

Esther snorted in disbelief. Before an infuriated Carrie could respond, Archie intervened. 'I was going to offer to take the plates through and bring the dessert, but I think I'd better no' leave you pair alone in case I come back and find blood on the walls!'

Carrie's expression of self-reproach was a mirror image of her mother's. She leaped up out of her chair. 'You both stay where you are. I'll see to it.'

When she came back through she set down the Eve's pudding which had been keeping warm in the oven of the Baby Belling, carefully placing the enamel ashet on a cork mat in the centre of the table. Then she fetched the jug of custard she'd made and set it down on another one. Handing out the dessert bowls, her back temporarily to Archie, she received a silent message from her mother. Loud and clear. *Let's leave this for now. We don't want to worry your father.*

Carrie gave her a reassuring and apologetic smile. On that point, the Burgess women were in wholehearted agreement.

Ewen proved to be a quick learner, soaking up everything she could give him – and more. Carrie spent some time each evening preparing for the following day's lesson. It was never enough, and she often had to rack her brains to think of something extra.

That was how they came to institute the words of the week, which he had to learn to recognise in their printed form and also to practise using as much as he could in speech. The unlikely conversations which resulted caused them both a fair amount of hilarity, for example when he reported another surfaceman's reaction to his observation that one of their comrades was looking a wee touch *delicate* today. Had he perhaps spent too much time in the pub the night before *consuming intoxicating beverages*?

Martin Sharkey, himself blessed with the silver-tongued eloquence of the Irish, had been mightily amused by Ewen's announcement, after carrying out a particularly dirty job, that he was off to the tap in the bothy to *perform his ablutions*.

Initially the words of the week were taken from the big English dictionary Archie Burgess had bought when his daughter went to secondary school, but later they came from a smaller version Carrie gave Ewen for his nineteenth birthday.

She'd wanted to surprise him by knowing the date – asking her father to look it up in the staff records – and she did. Esther had agreed – with considerable reluctance – that he might have his tea with them that evening. Three weeks on, she wasn't showing much sign of relaxing her disapproval of him, but Archie had insisted.

'Well, Esther, we'll be having tatties and vegetables out of the garden with our meat, I suppose, and the laddie *has* been helping me grow the stuff!'

For to Carrie's surprise, and vague unease, her father had accepted the offer of help in the garden with some alacrity and without the necessity for her to issue any dire threats. So Ewen, stiff and nervous and having performed some very vigorous ablutions at the scullery sink, came in and sat at the table with them. He was voluble in his thanks for this unexpected birthday treat and a little over-enthusiastic in his praise of Esther's cooking – trying that bit too hard to please his hostess – but it all passed pleasantly enough.

They dispatched a substantial meal of tender rump steak stewed with onions and carrots from the garden, accompanied by floury potatoes, buttered cabbage and peas from the same source. Carrie had shelled the latter that afternoon, sitting in a deck-chair on the lawn watching her father and Ewen toiling to keep down the weeds. Despite the disparity in age and status, the two men seemed to get on well together. Much of the conversation which floated across to her was a spirited discussion on the merits of various football teams.

While Esther cleared the plates away, Carrie disappeared into the front room and came back proudly bearing aloft the cake she'd baked and iced earlier in the week. She placed it in front of Ewen, laughing at the expression of amazement on his face as he followed its descent on to the table. To her further amusement, she saw that he was counting its tiny candles, making sure it really was for him.

Digging into the deep pocket of her green sundress, she extracted her present of a dictionary, carefully wrapped in navy blue paper and decorated with a silver bow. She had thought the combination pleasingly masculine. With a flourish, she put that in front of him too.

'For me?' he asked wonderingly, looking up at her as she stood beside him. 'Both o' them?'

'Well, it is your birthday,' she replied, lips twitching. 'Haven't you ever had a cake or a present before?'

She regretted the words the moment they were out of her mouth. Ewen's good-natured face crumpled.

'No' since my mother died.' Apparently overcome, he bent his head and covered his eyes with his hand. Every member of the Burgess family froze in silent sympathy. Even Esther's face softened.

Archie recovered first. 'It's all right, lad,' he said, giving Ewen an embarrassed pat on the arm. 'We understand. Give yourself a wee minute.'

Carrie bent towards him and slid a swift and sympathetic arm along the hunched shoulders. 'I'm so sorry, Ewen,' she whispered, her lips almost touching his ear. 'I didn't think.'

'It's me who should be sorry,' he said a minute or two later. 'Making an exhibition o' myself.' He sat up and squared his shoulders. 'I cannae apologise enough, Mrs Burgess. Mr Burgess.' He managed to look them both in the face.

'No need for apologies, laddie,' said Archie. Esther, watching as her daughter took her arm from Ewen's shoulders, said nothing. Carrie herself was totally focussed on him, her one aim in life at this precise moment to make him feel happier again. Lifting the small navy and silver package, she handed it to him.

'Open your present,' she instructed cheerfully. 'I want to see if you like it.'

His reaction didn't disappoint her. 'An English dictionary! Och, Carrie, that's great!'

She smiled broadly in relief. He sounded really pleased.

Chapter 10

'You seem to be sitting awful close to me.'

'Well,' responded Ewen, his face carefully blank, 'we are reading off the same book.' He indicated it with his index finger. 'I've got to sit close to you to be able to see the words.'

Carrie pursed her lips and looked suspiciously at him. 'Didn't you have to do an eye test when you joined the company?'

They were in their usual place, on the bench round the corner from the kitchen door. It was a hot and still day, with scarcely a breath of wind to disturb the warm air. There were at least two bees busy in the roses which tangled through the trellis above their heads. She could distinguish the different notes of their humming. Like her, Ewen didn't seem to be bothered by the proximity of the industrious little creatures.

'I don't recall,' he said loftily, using one of the current words of the week.

'Pull the other one, Livingstone, it's got bells on,' she said, resolutely ignoring the smile which greeted this sally.

She'd felt very tender towards him since his birthday, touched by the emotion he'd shown that day. However, she was beginning to wonder if she'd conveyed the wrong impression by bestowing that impulsive hug upon him.

'Everyone's got to pass an eye test before they're even considered for a job on the railway,' she said. 'You know that as well as I do.'

Ewen struck a contemplative pose. 'Well . . . no' cloakroom attendants or kiosk assistants, Carrie.'

'You're neither of those,' she pointed out, poking him in the chest to emphasise her point, an action which served merely to broaden his smile. 'You're in the sort of job where you have to be able to see if a signal's changed colour or if there's a dirty great locomotive bearing down on you.'

'Looks like you've answered your own question, then.' The freckles danced across the bridge of his nose as he wrinkled it in a teasing grimace. 'Miss Smart Alec.'

'So,' she demanded, the shimmering curve of her hair swinging as she stuck her chin out, 'there's another reason why you're sitting so close to me?'

'Aye,' he said cheerfully, not a bit abashed. 'I like sitting close to you.'

She should have told him off there and then, got to her feet and forcibly put some space between them, but instead she stayed where she was and spoke soft words into the few inches of warm air which separated them.

'You're incorrigible, Ewen Livingstone.'

He was studying her face. At rather closer range than Carrie found comfortable. 'If I'm a good boy, will you explain to me what big words like that mean?'

'Come off it, pal, you know plenty of big words.'

'What, like wheelbarrow? See when you teach me to write, can that be my first word?'

Carrie raised her eyebrows. 'Wheelbarrow?'

'Ha-bloody-ha,' he said grimly. 'Oh, sorry. I forgot myself again. No, I meant incorrigible. In-corr-ig-ible.' He rolled the word around his mouth like a sweetie.

'Who says I'm teaching you to write?'

He slid down the bench, hooked one leg over the arm of it and rested his wavy locks on her shoulder, looking backwards up at her. 'You did. If I made good progress, you said. And I have, haven't I?'

She couldn't deny him that. 'Yes, you've worked hard. You're all arms and legs,' she observed, surveying him as he lay sprawled beside her. He was wearing his dark brown corduroy working trousers, an open-necked white shirt and his red neckerchief knotted round his throat. Combined with his current posture, the ensemble gave him a rather rakish air. 'You look like a gypsy.'

'Apart from the hair.' His face turned up towards the heat of the sun, his eyelids fluttered shut.

'Mmm,' she agreed. 'It's getting fairer, have you noticed?'

'Och, it aye does that in the summer.'

Carrie didn't really think about what she did next. She lifted one of the tresses in question. The strands of hair felt as smooth and silky as her own. Without opening his eyes, Ewen stretched a hand back, lifted her arm and placed it around his neck, imprisoning it there.

'You're no' resisting,' he murmured.

'It's too hot to resist.'

She saw his lips curve. A minute passed. Two. His warm fingers were curled around her forearm. She flexed her hand, her fingertips feeling the solid thump of his heartbeat. There was a constant hum of noise from the railway, but it seemed quite far away, the area immediately around them very quiet and still. Even the bees had moved on, off to collect pollen from some other flowers.

'This is nice,' he said.

She muttered something non-committal. He opened his eyes,

swivelled his head round on her shoulder and spoke softly into her face. 'Would I be pushing ma luck if I tried anything else?' The pale blue eyes dropped to her mouth, leaving her in little doubt as to what that anything else might be.

'What do you think?'

She'd intended the words to come out briskly, friendly but dismissive. Instead, her voice sounded husky, and oddly breathless.

'What dae I think?' His voice was as warm and lazy as the summer day which shimmered around them. 'What I think is that you'll have tae sound an awful lot more convincing than that, Miss Burgess. If you really don't want me to try anything else.'

Their faces only inches apart, their concentration on each other intense, neither of them heard the sound of the back door opening.

'For the umpteenth time, Mother, Ewen is not my new boyfriend!'

'Does he know that?' muttered Esther darkly. 'The way yon laddie smiles when he sees you. Are you telling me you don't notice the look in his eyes?'

The two women were squaring up to each other in the living room, Ewen having hurriedly made his excuses and left. Before Ma could physically throw him out, thought Carrie wryly. Never mind the look in his eyes when he saw Carrie, there had been something approaching holy terror in those blue-grey pools when he had glanced up to find Esther standing there glaring down at them – hands on hips and more or less breathing fire.

She was adopting the same posture now, using the few minutes before her husband was due home for his tea to express her pent-up feelings.

'He practically had his head in your lap!' she yelled. 'A month ago you were crying your eyes out over Matthew Campbell. I didn't think you were that sort of a lassie, Carrie!'

In the silence which followed this accusation she heard with relief the sound of the back door being pushed open. Pity her hearing hadn't been so acute ten minutes ago. Esther had heard it too. 'That's your father.' She turned to walk through to the kitchen to greet him, throwing a softly spoken threat back over her shoulder. 'Don't think we're finished with this, miss.'

Waiting for sleep to come that night, Carrie reached out a hand to the small bookcase which stood between her bed and the door. The books on the top shelf were adorned with half a dozen soft toys. Like so much of what made her room cosy and pleasant – the plump quilt under which she lay, the embroidered Duchess mats on her dressing-table – they were all her mother's creations.

Gertie the giraffe had always been Carrie's favourite. Made of dark brown felt, her long legs stiffened so she could stand up if necessary, she was covered with small fawn patches to mimic a real giraffe's coat. Each one of the footery wee pieces had been painstakingly cut out and stitched on by Esther.

Carrie stretched out her arms and held Gertie above her head. 'So tell me,' she asked, 'what am I going to do about all this?'

The giraffe regarded her impassively. Apparently she didn't feel capable of expressing an opinion on the subject.

'I don't blame you,' Carrie said softly. 'I'm finding the whole thing quite difficult myself. It's horrible when you know you're making one of the people you love most in the whole world unhappy. How can I convince her there's nothing to worry about? That I think of Ewen as a friend? Like the brother I've never had?'

Now she could have sworn that Gertie's two glassy eyes held a tell-that-to-the-marines-my-girl expression. She put the light out and tucked the toy in beside her, underneath the covers.

Did your brother rest his head on your shoulder while you coiled your arm about his neck? Did the feel of his heartbeat under your fingers give you an odd, fluttery little feeling in your chest and throat?

Yet her feelings for Matt hadn't gone away either. She remembered those passionate kisses and embraces, and how they had made her feel . . .

She allowed the memories to wash over her for a few minutes, blushing in the darkness as she felt her body begin to stir into response. All at once uncomfortably warm, she pushed the covers down and rolled on to her side, blowing out a long exasperated breath. There was no point in thinking like that if Matt didn't want her any more.

Could she be sure of that, though? She knew he'd had equally as strong feelings for her. She couldn't believe he was the kind of man to slough them off with scarcely a backward glance. She had seen him two or three times since the break-up, but only at the station where there were always other people around. Hardly the ideal place for a private chat.

The railway bush telegraph was working well enough as it was. Esther had been entirely right in her prediction. The tongues were wagging about the stationmaster's daughter and the Permanent Way lad. Outside the Burgess family, only Martin Sharkey knew about the reading and writing lessons. Ewen had confided in the older man. Since he had also sworn him to secrecy, everyone else was busily drawing the obvious conclusion.

There was even a joke going the rounds. *Caroline Burgess is seeing someone beneath her station*. She had prised that out of an embarrassed Mary, who in turn had got it from her fiancé Douglas. Carrie turned once more on to her back, remembering to move Gertie so she wouldn't squash her.

None of this made it easy for Matt to approach her. Perhaps she ought to take matters into her own hands. She thought about it for a minute or two, eyes wide open and staring at the dark ceiling.

'Got it,' she whispered. Thinking about Mary and Douglas had given her an idea. She wrapped her arms around Gertie. Within five minutes she was sound asleep.

Chapter 11

'Hello, Carrie.'

Deep in apparent contemplation of an Egyptian mummy in a glass case, she turned immediately at the sound of his voice.

'Hello, Matt,' she responded. Well, her ploy had worked, and there was nobody else in this section of the Art Galleries, although she could have done without spotting Janice Muirhead a few minutes ago. There were lots of people she knew here today. There always were, particularly in the summer. She had come with Mary and Douglas. The former, in on the plot, had agreed they would fade discreetly into the background if they saw Matthew approaching.

The first floor of the building, reached by a couple of impressively sweeping stone staircases, housed a fine collection of paintings; the ground floor a wide variety of museum exhibits. Universally, however, the whole place was always referred to simply as the Art Galleries or Kelvingrove, the latter being the park in which the ornate and beautiful red sandstone building stood.

Some girls professed to find the mummies spooky, shrieking a horrified refusal if a boy suggested visiting the small side gallery which they occupied. Carrie had always heartily despised that attitude. Why some members of her own sex thought they had to behave like empty-headed little pieces of fluff when there were men about was beyond her.

However, this Sunday afternoon she was glad of it. It meant she and Matt were alone together, however briefly. She wouldn't have put it past Janice to be lurking somewhere not very far away, but since this looked like being her best chance of getting him on his own, Carrie plunged in.

'How are you?' she asked.

'How do you think I am?' His voice was low and impassioned. 'Without you in my life?'

'How am I supposed to know how you feel when you haven't tried to see me to tell me?' she responded, striving to keep her voice light, although her heart had leaped into her throat at his words. He still wanted her. *He still wanted her!*

'How could I? You're always with someone when I see you.'

'I'm not with anyone at the moment,' she pointed out. 'And neither are you.' She gestured towards the glass cases. 'I doubt the mummies will clype on us.'

They were standing in a bay formed by two display cases which jutted out into the middle of the room. The mummies within them lay with their heads to the wall and their feet towards the long windows which framed the main building of Glasgow University up on the other side of the Kelvin.

Matt's face showed no response to her joke. Her timing had always been bad when it came to trying to get him to see the funny side of things. He was, as ever, immaculately dressed, but he looked miserable – pale, and thinner than he had been before. He found himself a spare patch of wall between the two exhibits and leaned one shoulder against it, folding his arms across his chest as he did so.

'Where's your little boyfriend today, then?' he asked bitterly. The jealousy in his voice was unmistakable. It was also undeniably exciting. 'Not much point in him coming here, I suppose. He wouldn't be able to read the captions.' Matt extracted one hand from his folded arms and flicked his elegant fingers towards the printed card giving all the known facts about the mummy. A narrow band of spotless white cuff showed beneath the dark material of his jacket.

The gesture he had made was so dismissive, cold and heartless. Yet Carrie could remember only too well what else those long fingers could do . . . Those had been warm and loving things. Thrilling things.

'I suppose he could go upstairs and look at the pictures. That would be about his level.'

Carrie took a deep breath. 'He's not my boyfriend.'

'No?' Matthew pushed himself off the wall and came towards her, peering down into her face. 'You do know that everyone's gossiping about the two of you, don't you?' he sneered. 'I'm surprised your father's letting you see Livingstone, I really am.'

'Let them gossip.' Carrie tilted her chin. She was wearing the same outfit she'd worn to Oban, and the pheasant's feather on her Tyrolean hat bounced with the angry movement of her head. The thought of her father letting – or not letting – her do anything was a fairly mind-boggling concept. That wasn't how things worked in the Burgess family.

She'd been on the point of explaining the situation, making it clear all she was doing was helping someone learn to read and write, but that implied criticism of her father had put her off her stroke. And however hurt Matt was, she couldn't let him get away with those sarcastic comments about Ewen.

'Do you really want to know how I am, Carrie?'

'Why do you think I came here today?'

That stopped him in his tracks, and she saw a spark of hope in his eyes. When he spoke, his words winged their way to her like a simple plea from his heart. 'Come back to me, Carrie. Please.'

'Och, Matt . . .' She took a step towards him. She was almost in his arms.

'You'll have to dump *him*, of course.'

'Matthew, it's not a question of dumping anybody.' She put as much reassurance as she could into her smile. First they would kiss and then she would tell him the whole story, make it crystal clear that while Ewen was her friend, it was Matthew who was her lover. Lover. What a beautiful word that was.

Her smile became dreamy, but he had taken a step away from her. 'If we get back together again, you'll have to promise never to see him again.'

'I'll do no such thing!'

Her defence of her right to see Ewen had been instinctive. It sent Matt right back on to his high horse. 'I can't believe you prefer him to me. An illiterate navvy!' He was sneering now. 'Do you know anything at all about his background, Carrie?'

'That again,' she said contemptuously. Honestly, she might expect it of her parents' generation, but she was bitterly disappointed that Matt didn't appear to have a more modern attitude.

His eyes narrowed. 'He's told you about his mother?' He sounded disbelieving, almost incredulous.

'Of course he has,' she said. 'I know it all. Goodbye, Matt.'

She could feel his eyes boring into her back as she turned and walked away.

'I'm not asking you to put on the pan loaf!' Carrie exclaimed, completely exasperated with her pupil. Both of them seemed to be on a short fuse this warm Monday afternoon.

'It's the way I speak,' Ewen said belligerently. 'It's the way most people I know speak. What's wrong wi' it? I'm no' gonnae speak with marbles in ma mouth for anybody.'

'I'm only saying you might try to be a wee bit more precise when you're talking to certain people. It'll help you get on.'

'What d'ye mean, help me get on?'

'Well, are you planning to stay a P-way man all your life?'

'Something wrong wi' that?' he growled.

'Nothing,' she said carefully. 'It's an important job.' She was feeling a bit fragile, unsettled after her meeting with Matt the day before. Ewen's unusually bad temper wasn't helping at all. 'I just think you could do better for yourself. Maybe consider applying for a clerkship,' she suggested. 'Once you've had a bit more practice at reading and writing.'

'Away and boil yer heid, Carrie,' he said irritably. 'I'm no' brainy enough for that kind o' a job. Look at this,' he said dismissively, gesturing to the words he had painstakingly copied out in the jotter which lay on the gate-leg table. 'It's hopeless.' He sounded disgusted with himself. 'I'm never gonnae be able to write wee enough to get it between the lines.'

'Of course you will,' she said, her voice gentling. 'You're doing really well.'

'Och, Carrie, let's stop kidding ourselves!' He dropped the pencil and thrust out his hands towards her. 'Look at them! They're fine for wielding a pick-axe or a thirty-two-pound hammer, but they're no good for this sort of thing. Far too big and clumsy.'

She shook her head. 'Big,' she agreed, 'but not clumsy.'

She'd seen him using the heavy hammer. There had been a curious grace about it. Stripped to the waist, the muscles in his back and shoulders rippling like wave patterns on a sandy beach under the outgoing tide, he'd swung it with what had looked to her like effortless ease, bringing it down through the air in a smooth arc.

'You had to learn how to use the hammer, didn't you? The pick-axe too. Then you had to practise with them. It's exactly the same with a pencil and paper. They're tools too, that anybody can learn to use. Practice makes perfect, whatever it is you're doing.'

He looked doubtfully at her. Since he wasn't actually biting her head off, she took her courage in both hands and dared to go on. 'You could easily pass a clerkship exam. I've seen the papers. I know you could do it. If you stick in at your reading and writing.'

Her words had penetrated his black mood. 'D'ye really think so, Carrie?'

'I know so,' she said firmly.

Sometimes, when he let his guard down, she got a searing glimpse of exactly how low an opinion he had of himself and his capabilities. Very few people had encouraged him to think otherwise, she supposed: maybe only ever his mother – until he'd been brave enough to seek Carrie's help.

'Come on,' she wheedled, 'try it a few more times.'

He started off well enough, but ran out of space before he was halfway through his surname. 'Och, damn and bloody blast!'

He rose angrily to his feet, snapped the pencil in two and flung it on to the table. 'It's no use. I'll never be able to do it. We might as well admit that and agree to call it a day. Your ma cannae stand me anyway, can she? Hates having me around the place.'

'What had my poor wee pencil done to you?' Carrie asked mildly, ignoring those last observations.

'I'll give you the money for a dozen bloody pencils!' The words came out jerkily and she guessed he'd had to hold himself back from peppering the statement with a few more expletives. 'I'm away,' he said abruptly. 'I'll see you the morn. Or maybe I'll not.'

He edged out from behind the table, but she got up too and came quickly round the other side of it. She laid a light hand on his arm, checking his headlong flight towards the corner of the house.

'Ewen, what's the matter with you today?' She could feel how tense he was. Under her fingers, the muscles of his forearm were as rigid as a washboard. 'Come and sit down again,' she said gently.

He shook his head. 'No. I cannae.'

'Let's walk up to the end of the garden, then,' she suggested, recognising that he was too restless to sit still.

He struck off across the drying green towards the clump of silver birch trees which stood in the farthest corner of the garden, overlooking the goods yard. That was as good a place as any. At least they'd have some privacy over there.

Gazing up at the cloudless blue sky earlier that morning Esther had decreed it to be a rare drying day and highly suitable for what her husband laughingly designated the ceremonial annual wash of the bedclothes. There were two blankets on each side of the square formed by the four clothes poles which defined the business end of the drying green. Carrie had stretched an additional length of rope diagonally between two of the poles for the covers which she personally had trampled in the bath, her soft cotton summer skirt tucked up into her knickers to keep it dry.

Having, perforce, to stop when he came up against the barrier of the fence, Ewen grasped the tops of two of the palings in both hands. She caught up with him and came to stand beside him. Glancing at his hands, she saw that his knuckles were white. He must be holding on very hard indeed.

'Will you tell me what's the matter?'

He stopped pretending to be fascinated by the activities of the sturdy, if unprepossessing, little engine shunting coal trucks about in the goods yards and turned to look at her, releasing his grip on the fence.

'You went to the Art Galleries yesterday. You met Matthew Campbell there.'

It was an accusation, and a demand for her to explain herself. She wasn't sure he had the right to expect a response to either of those, but she answered him anyway.

'I needed to talk to Matthew privately,' she said quietly. 'That was the only place I could be sure of getting him on his own.'

'And you were just talking to him? That's no' the way I heard it.'

You didn't have to be Sherlock Holmes to work out who his informant had been. Carrie's determination not to lose her temper wavered. This was the second time that young lady had stuck her oar in.

'Oh?' she enquired haughtily, taking a step away from him along the fence. 'Tell me, Ewen. What *exactly* did Janice Muirhead say to you?'

He didn't flinch. 'She said you and him were in a wee side room by yourselves for ages. She said she thought you were kissing.'

'Well, she was wrong,' snapped Carrie. 'We most definitely were not kissing.'

'Do you tell me that, Carrie?'

She glared at him, infuriated by his refusal to believe her emphatic denial. Who the hell did he think he was? The thought that he'd take Janice Muirhead's word over her own made her blood boil. She was reminded suddenly of Matt. Hadn't she had a very similar conversation with him – although perhaps interrogation would be a better word – over her afternoon in Oban with Ewen? Her temper cranked up a few notches. She didn't have red hair for nothing.

'Yes!' she yelled. 'I do bloody tell you that! And you'd better bloody believe me! Because it's the truth!'

He folded his arms across his broad chest. 'I've tellt you before about swearing,' he said sternly. 'It doesnae become a lady like you. Don't do it again.'

'Oh!' She clenched her fists in frustration. 'Stop bossing me about! I won't have it!'

'You'd take it from Matthew Campbell!'

'I would not! That's why I split up with him! Remember?'

'So why did you go to the Art Galleries yesterday?'

'Maybe I wanted to sort out how I felt about him! Maybe I'm confused! Maybe I don't know how I feel about *you*!'

Ewen flushed. 'I didnae know you felt anything about me,' he said quietly. In the goods yard, the little locomotive chuntered. Carrie glanced over at it, then returned her eyes to Ewen's face.

'Why do you think I'm helping you to read and write?'

'I've nae bloody idea,' he flung back. Apparently it was all right for him to swear. 'Just why are you doing the Lady Bountiful act?'

She was struck dumb for a full five seconds. Then she let rip. 'How dare you, Ewen Livingstone? Of all the ungrateful . . .' She shook her coppery head. If she hadn't felt the need to speak up for Ewen yesterday, she and Matt might be back together again now.

'You're the main reason I fell out with Matt in the first place!' she yelled. Too angry to watch her words, she stormed furiously on. 'You're quite right, by the way. My mother does hate having you here. I'm having fights with her almost every day over you. And I never fight with my mother!'

His earlier flush had faded. He was pale now, and tight-lipped. 'So why bother? I wouldnae have thought I was worth it.'

'Has the thought ever penetrated your thick skull that I might be helping you because I quite like you?'

He swayed towards her, chin jutting out, his face inches from her own. 'Quite like me?' he howled. 'QUITE LIKE ME? Is that supposed to make me delirious wi' joy, Miss Burgess?'

Delirious. It was his word of the week. The phrase was one she had used to illustrate the different ways it might be used. Fatally, they both realised that at precisely the same moment. For a frozen moment they continued to glare at each other. Then Carrie's lips twitched.

'Well, I do feel quite *affectionate* towards you. Is that better?'

'There's no need to be *supercilious* about it.'

He'd caught on immediately. He waited patiently for her to trot out another former word of the week, and for his own chance to lob one neatly back to her.

'Do you feel I'm *patronising* you, then?'

'Do you think I'm completely *incorrigible*?'

They both burst out laughing. Carrie bent over, hugging her middle. She straightened up, saw he was still in fits and had to lift a hand to his broad shoulder for support.

'Oh, Ewen . . . I haven't laughed so much in ages!'

'Are you really not going back to Matthew Campbell?' he asked a minute or two later, the amusement fading slowly from his face.

'Mind your own business, Livingstone,' she said cheerfully. She had enjoyed the laughter. She didn't want this conversation to get serious again.

He had other ideas. 'Maybe it is my business.'

'You think so?'

'I think it could be. If you would permit it.' He smiled faintly. *Permit* had been another of his words.

She wasn't sure what to say to him. She didn't want to raise any false hopes. Above their heads, the branches of the silver birches creaked as the summer breeze freshened and became brisker. Behind her, she heard sharp thwacks as the blankets on the washing line shook themselves out, reacting to the wind. Ewen lifted his hand to her face.

Big. Definitely not clumsy. His fingers felt like thistledown against her smooth cheek. Or a dandelion clock, perhaps. That was an odd metaphor to pop into her head at a moment when time seemed to have taken it into its head to stand still. The shy fingers on her face became infinitesimally more confident. He bent his head forward.

'No,' she whispered. Then she added two more words. Perhaps to soften the blow. Perhaps because they were what came to mind. 'Not yet,' she said.

Ewen hesitated. 'Is it because you're still confused about how ye feel about him? Or how ye feel about me?'

'Something like that.'

He dropped his hand and took a step back from her. 'And you want me to keep ma distance,' he said in matter-of-fact tones. 'At least for the time being.'

'That's about it,' she agreed.

He took a deep breath, lifted his shoulders and considered. Then he exhaled a long breath. 'I can do that, Carrie. Nae bother at all. But I can keep coming for my lessons?' His fair eyebrows drew together in anxious enquiry.

'Of course you can!' On impulse, grateful for his understanding, she stepped forward, stretched up and kissed him swiftly on the cheek. When she pulled back she saw that he was pointing to the other side of his face.

'This one too. Otherwise I'll be lopsided. Might fall into Dumbarton Road on the way home and get run over by a tram. You wouldnae want that on your conscience, would you?'

'Chancer,' she muttered, but she gave him what he had asked for.

The next day he brought her an apple. 'Because I was so grumpy yesterday,' he said, giving her the sunniest of smiles. Removing the apple from a somewhat crumpled brown paper bag, he extended it to her with a surprisingly elegant flourish of the hand, like an experienced waiter balancing a tray on his fingertips.

'The reddest and shiniest one in the shop. Selected especially for you. That old cow in the greengrocer's round the corner from me –'

She narrowed her eyes at him, but he carried on, unrepentant. 'She is an old cow, Carrie, always trying to palm folk off wi' tatties with black bits in them and suchlike. She didnae want to give me a bag either – because I was only buying the one piece of fruit – but I insisted,' he added proudly. 'I couldnae have your apple jostling around among my tools all day.'

'I'm pleased to hear you stood up for yourself,' Carrie told him gravely. 'And thank you for the apple. Can I save it and eat it later? I'll have it after my tea.'

'But no' too long after your tea,' he admonished. 'Ye shouldnae eat an apple just before you go to bed. You'll no' digest it properly.'

She grinned. 'My mother always says that.'

He had no comment to make on that. She regarded him thoughtfully, and wondered if he thought her mother was an old cow too.

'Here,' he was saying, 'put it back in the poke if ye're no' going to eat it now.' He handed her the bag and explained further. 'I meant it to be an apple for the teacher, like.'

'I could have worked that one out,' Carrie replied in a passable imitation of the way he had growled at her yesterday. 'Right,' she said briskly. 'I want you to start off by writing your name out properly. Six times.'

He sketched her a salute. 'Yes, miss. No, miss. Three bags full, miss.'

She administered a swipe to the back of his head. His hair was so thick he would hardly feel it. 'Less of your impertinence, boy. Now, sit down and let's get on with it.'

She watched him as he wrote. Bent over the jotter, his whole attention was directed towards the task which had defeated him yesterday. His autographs weren't exactly neat, but his handwriting was smaller and more controlled and so far he hadn't run out of space. His lips were slightly parted and she guessed he was completely unaware that his tongue was sticking out a little to one side in concentration. Like a wee laddie at school, she thought fondly.

Chapter 12

Carrie's brolly was fighting a losing battle with the elements.

'Sure, you'd hardly believe it was August, would you now? I'm thinking we should both be making a dash for it, Miss Burgess. Mind and give my regards to your mother, now.'

'I think you're right, Mrs Sharkey,' said Carrie politely. 'And I hope your husband will be better soon,' she added, for she'd been listening to a blow-by-blow account of the ganger's current attack of bronchitis.

She regarded the bent spokes of her umbrella in disgust. It might be summer according to the calendar, but it was blowing a force-eight gale on Dumbarton Road. The accompanying squally showers had been alternating with brief spells of dazzling sunshine all day. What a country!

Bidding farewell to Martin Sharkey's wife, whom she'd bumped into as she came out of the baker's, she folded her now useless protection against the rain, pulled her mother's message bag in closer to her body in an attempt to keep both it and its contents dry and sped towards the covered stairs which led up to the station. It was an obvious shortcut back to the house, especially on a day like this.

Ewen would be coming off duty soon. It was too wet to have their lesson today, but they could have a quick word with each other, protected from the rain by the canopy which projected out from the roof of the station buildings. Coming down the last few steps of the bridge, where the wooden treads came way to stone steps, she saw that her father was already standing under there. She pushed a strand of sodden hair out of her eyes and smiled at him. She hadn't wanted to get any of her hats wet. So now her hair was soaking. Very logical.

'I'm waiting to catch Ewen and his mates when they come off-duty,' said Archie. 'I need to have a word with them about the general manager's visit.'

That exalted being – high heid yin for the entire Scottish region of the LNER – was scheduled to spend most of the following Wednesday afternoon at Partick. A letter from his office at Waverley Station in Edinburgh had communicated his desire to meet the stationmaster's family and, of course, to see as much as possible of the work of the station. He was particularly keen to talk to younger employees, both salaried staff and those in the waged or conciliation grades.

'Is this about the protective clothing dispute, Daddy?'

Archie nodded. That old favourite had reared its head again recently. It had caused a substantial amount of friction when the surfacemen discovered that several of the clerks had blithely indented for new railway-issue waterproof jackets for themselves – and received them.

The Permanent Way staff, whose stock of oilskins kept in the bothy was now so old as to be more or less useless at keeping the rain out, were up in arms about it. They spent a hell of a lot more time out of doors than some clerk who did most of his work sitting in a warm and dry office.

Archie had tried to get them new waterproofs only to be told by the railway offices in Glasgow that the clothing budget for this year was spent. They would have to wait till next spring. Sharkey and his men, facing the approaching autumn and winter without adequate protection against wind and driving rain, had expressed themselves rather frankly on the subject. Sharkey now being off sick with bronchitis had only added force to their argument.

Heavy footsteps were crunching down the wet platform. Archie stuck his head out from under the protection of the canopy. 'Ah, here they come. Like a platoon of soldiers. How are you today, boys?' he asked in a louder voice.

'Wet,' said one man, coming in under the shelter and throwing an uncompromising look at his boss. Under cover of the discussion which ensued, Ewen edged his way round the backs of his workmates. Like the rest of them, he was extremely wet. The sleeves of his heavy jacket were sticking to his arms and his hair, plastered to his head, was beginning to go into curls.

'You look like a drowned rat.'

'So do you.' He reached out a hand and tugged her hair. 'Yee-uch! You'll need to put yourself through the mangle.' He made great play of wiping his fingers on his jacket, grinning at her all the while.

Everyone else was grinning too, something the two of them unfortunately didn't realise until Archie Burgess spoke Ewen's name for the second time. Embarrassed, Carrie did her best to blend into the background as her father and the other P-way men put a proposal to him. Since the general manager wanted to have a formal meeting with as many of the younger members of staff as could be crammed into the booking office, why didn't Ewen take that opportunity to put their complaints to him on the question of waterproof jackets?

'Oh, I couldnae! I wouldnae know where to start!'

Carrie came forward. 'If I helped you, Ewen?'

He turned eagerly to her. 'Would you, Carrie?'

'We'll leave you to convince him then, Miss Burgess,' said the man who'd earlier given the succinct answer to Archie's enquiry after their health. 'Use your womanly wiles on him.' He gave her an outrageous wink. 'Come on, lads. See you later, Ewen.'

There were a few sly glances as they left, plus a parting shot from another of the surfacemen, an older man. 'I cannae imagine he'll be able to resist ye, pet.'

The three of them stood and watched the men head home, trudging through the rain with their heads down.

'I don't think I like the implications of that last statement,' Carrie muttered, but she was talking to herself. Her father was busy trying to convince a panic-stricken Ewen that he was perfectly capable of carrying out the task his mates had saddled him with.

'You'd be helping all your mates,' Archie was saying. 'And yourself too. It never hurts a young man who wants to get on in the railway to seize an opportunity to shine in front of senior management.'

'I doubt I'll shine very brightly, Mr Burgess. I'll more than likely make a pig's ear out o' it.'

'No, you'll not,' insisted Carrie. 'You'll manage it fine. I think,' she went on, 'that you should write down the points you want to make on a wee index card. That'll make you look really businesslike and well-prepared. I've got some of those.'

'Write them down? And then read them out? Carrie, I cannae!'

'Of course you can,' she said robustly. 'If you like, I'll do the writing bit. I'll print the words out in block capitals, and quite large. We'll practise reading them out loud between now and next week. I'll try to stand near you so I can prompt you if necessary.'

He was looking at her very doubtfully. Behind his head, the rain was driving against the glass panels of the screen which supported the roof canopy at both ends of the station buildings. Archie Burgess laughed and clapped them both on the shoulder, joining them together through him.

'I'd give in now, son. You know she'll persuade you in the end.'

On the following Wednesday they all packed into the booking office. Waiting for everyone to assemble, Carrie spoke out of the corner of her mouth.

'It all seems to be going well.'

'It's like the swan,' murmured one of the senior clerks in reply. 'Gliding smoothly on the surface, paddling like hell underneath. Excuse my French, Miss Burgess.'

Accompanied by Archie, and followed by three or four other railway officials, the general manager swept in. He was a tall and elegant man, wearing a well-cut grey suit. He told a couple of surprisingly funny jokes, made a little speech, assured them he was on their side and asked if they had any comments to make.

'Don't be shy, now,' he said encouragingly. 'If you have any complaints, I want to hear them.'

There was some shuffling of feet. One or two minor points were raised. They were either answered there and then, or a promise was made to look into them. Carrie, who hadn't managed to get anywhere near Ewen, chanced a look at where he stood, over by the arched booking-office ticket window. He was looking a little green about the gills, and he was standing next to Matt. That wasn't going to help his confidence.

'Nobody else then?' asked the general manager, looking around the room. He was very pleasant, but both his official position and his commanding presence made him just a wee bit daunting . . . One of the officials glanced up at the clock on the wall.

Carrie caught Ewen's eye. *Go on*, she mouthed. She heard him clear his throat nervously and saw him bring the small white card she'd prepared out of his pocket. If she hadn't been so concerned with willing him through the next few minutes, Matt's double take as he began to read out from it would have been hilarious.

Ewen stumbled over a word and stopped dead for what seemed like ages, but could only have been a second or two. It was a bit stilted at first, but when he had finished reading and looked up, he became more fluent.

'It's not only a matter of fairness,' he said with considerable dignity. 'It's also one of practicality. No' having the right gear leads to people getting soaked and catching a chill, and then they're off work. That's hardly an efficient way of going about things.'

Despite his previous resistance to putting on the pan loaf, he was speaking a good deal more precisely than he normally did. He could do it when he wanted to, the wee toerag.

'You spoke about respect just now,' he went on, warming to his theme. 'You said we young people ought to have respect for the passengers, the company and our colleagues.' He had used the exact words which the general manager had used in his pep talk. 'Well,' he said, lifting a mutinous-looking chin, 'I think respect has to be earned.'

There was an audible intake of breath from one of the officials. Carrie looked anxiously at his boss. Was he going to bawl Ewen out? Sack him on the spot? To her amazement she saw the general manager nod slowly in agreement.

'I also think respect has to be mutual.' Ewen gave Carrie the ghost of a smile, acknowledging his use of a word of the week. 'Some folk – including some of our own colleagues – seem to think Permanent Way men are the lowest of the low.' He couldn't quite prevent his gaze sliding briefly to his left, where Matt was standing. 'But the trains couldnae run without us. And we're out there in all weathers. If the company really had respect for us and the job we do, they'd issue us with the equipment we need.'

He finished, and for a few seconds you could have heard the proverbial pin drop. Then the general manager spoke. 'What's your name, lad?'

'L-Livingstone, s-sir.' So confident a minute or two before, now he was nervous again. Carrie saw Matt's lip curl.

'First name?'

'Ewen.' He looked surprised to have been asked.

'Ewen Livingstone.' The general manager broke off. 'Forebears from Appin, eh?'

'Th-that's right, s-sir.'

'Well, young man, you've made your case very well, and I'm pleased to see someone who's so concerned for the well-being of his workmates. You and your squad will have new oilskins or waterproof jackets by the middle of next week. If they haven't arrived by Wednesday, ask Mr Burgess to get in touch with me immediately.' He walked across to where Ewen stood and stuck out his hand. 'Good day, Mr Livingstone.'

He and his entourage swept out as swiftly as they had swept in. A few mouths had dropped open, including Ewen's. There was a look of astonished delight on his face. He'd succeeded in solving the problem and the general manager of the Scottish region of the LNER had shaken a humble P-way man by the hand and called him 'Mr Livingstone'.

'Well said, Ewen.' That was Douglas, Mary's fiance, perched up on the counter at the back of the booking office. A glower from one of the senior clerks sent him sliding sheepishly off it on to his feet.

'Aye, congratulations . . . *Mr Livingstone*,' put in another of the young signalmen.

'Gather round, *colleagues*,' chipped in a lad porter.

There was general laughter, the younger members of the conciliation grades obviously feeling Ewen had struck some sort of a blow for them too. Several of the clerks were generous-spirited enough to clap him on the back or shake him by the hand as they piled out of the over-crowded office.

Carrie stood back, as pleased as punch. This must be how the teachers of clever pupils feel at prize-giving, she thought. Laughing at someone's parting shot, Ewen spun round as she came up behind him. 'Did I do all right?'

'You know you did,' she said warmly. 'You were great.'

'Aye. Well done,' came a cool voice. 'I'd never have believed you had it in you. Shouldn't you be running along now, though? The company doesn't pay any of us to stand around doing nothing, you know.' Matt gave a cold little laugh. 'Although P-way men do seem to spend an awful lot of time leaning on their shovels.'

Everyone else had disappeared. There were only the three of them in the booking office. Beside her, Carrie felt Ewen stiffen. She sent out a silent but heartfelt message. *Don't rise to it. Please don't rise to it.*

'As a matter of fact,' she heard him saying, 'I'm on my own time at the moment. I've got a rest day today and tomorrow. So no, I don't need to be running along now.'

He had said that last sentence perfectly, each word carefully and precisely enunciated.

'Well, in that case, get out of my booking office.' Matt's voice sank to a low growl. 'Or do I have to throw you out?'

Carrie put herself physically between them. They could both lose their jobs if anything developed here.

'Matt,' she pleaded, looking up into his dark eyes, 'please don't be so horrible. Can't we all be friends?'

'Friends?' he asked bleakly. 'You expect me to be friends with someone who was born in the gutter and who's never going to climb out of it? He'll drag you down there with him, Carrie. Don't you know that going out with him is already beginning to damage your reputation?'

'Right, that's it. *That is it!*'

'Ewen! No!'

But he wasn't listening to her. It all happened so fast. First Ewen thrust her out of the way, then she was watching, horrified, as he grabbed Matt by the throat and slammed him up against the wall. He drew his hand back and made a fist . . . This can't be happening, she thought. Please God, let this not be happening.

'Told-her-about-your-mother-yet?' panted Matt, clawing at the fingers splayed across his throat. Ewen froze.

Carrie darted forward. She had to get him out of here very soon, before anyone else came back in. He seemed dazed, but he had released his grip on Matthew's throat and he was allowing her to pull him away.

'I told you that day at the Art Galleries, Matt,' she said quietly. 'I know all about him being illegitimate.'

Unexpectedly, Matthew laughed. But it was Ewen his gaze was fixed on, not her. 'Didn't have the guts to tell her, Livingstone? Like me to do it for you?'

'Tell me what?'

Neither of them answered her. Matt was smiling: a horrid, knowing, thin-lipped little smile. Ewen stood slumped against the door. He'd been the aggressor, ready and willing to smash his fist into Matthew's face, but right now he looked like a man who'd taken a blow.

'Tell me what?' she asked again.

Ewen straightened up. 'No' here,' he said. 'Not in front of him.' He turned on his heel and wrenched open the door.

They were in Kelvingrove Park, standing in front of one of the statues.

'That's Lord Kelvin.'

'And what's he famous for?' Carrie asked gently. The three words were the first Ewen had uttered since she'd followed him out of the station. They'd taken the tram along Dumbarton Road in complete silence.

'He was a great scientist and inventor. Starting studying at the Uni when he was only eleven years old. Later on he came up with a different temperature scale. Different from Fahrenheit and Centigrade, I mean. They call it degrees Kelvin, after him.'

And what, she wondered, as they walked slowly through the park towards the Art Galleries, are you about to come up with? The trees which lined the path gave way to grass, allowing Glasgow University to come into view. High up on Gilmorehill, its ornate neo-Gothic tower reached into an azure sky, unmarred by the smallest patch of white.

'I've always wanted to climb up there,' said Ewen suddenly. 'I used to imagine jumping off it. Only I wouldnae plummet to the ground like a stone, I'd turn into a bird and fly away. Leave my life behind, become a different person altogether . . .'

His voice trailed off. Thoroughly alarmed by this queer little speech, Carrie tugged on his sleeve.

'Ewen, why don't we go and have afternoon tea somewhere? There's that nice Italian café in Byres Road. My treat. What d'you say?'

He stopped dead under an old beech tree which stood in solitary splendour by the side of the path and looked at her. 'You mean you don't want to know what the great mystery is?'

'Is it such a mystery?'

'There's times when I think the whole world knows. Apart from you. Somehow it hasnae come to your ears. No' for the lack o' some folk trying,' he added, his voice filled with bitterness. He set his back against the trunk of the tree. 'I suppose I always knew it was too much to hope for that you wouldnae find out.'

'You don't have to tell me,' she said firmly. 'Only if you want to.'

The grim expression on his face relaxed. 'You're so sweet, Caroline Burgess,' he said softly. His eyes flickered briefly shut, then opened again. He regarded her thoughtfully. 'My mother was a streetwalker, hen. That's how she made her living.'

'Oh,' breathed Carrie. Only she thought she had spoken, but nothing seemed to have come out.

Chapter 13

'Did you hear what I said, Carrie? My mother went with men for money. She was a prostitute. What folk hereabouts call a *hure*.'

Ewen was still pronouncing his words carefully. He'd uttered that most dreadful of all the insults which could be flung at a woman with an almost delicate precision. Carrie had always thought the Scottish version sounded a great deal worse than its standard English equivalent.

'That makes me the son of a hure, of course.'

'I heard you,' she whispered, wincing at this apparently calm description of himself.

'She hated it, you know,' he said conversationally. 'It made her feel dirty. She was always washing herself. Down there. Between her legs.'

Carrie's face burst into flame. His head tilted back against the tree, Ewen didn't notice the effect his brutally frank words were having on her. He was too busy remembering.

'She was aye cleaning the house, too. Trying to wash them away. All those respectable men who came to her behind their wives' backs. All those respectable men who go to church every Sunday.'

'She brought them home? Her –'

Carrie broke off. She didn't have the vocabulary for this. What was the correct word? Customers? Clients? Ewen gave her another alternative.

'I made her bring them home. She used to go up to Blythswood Square. That was her pitch. One night she came back from work in a hell of a state. One o' the punters had beaten her up, refused to pay for her services.'

Back from work. Her services. It sounded so matter-of-fact.

'So after that I followed her a couple of times, kept out of sight, but within earshot in case she met wi' that kind o' trouble again.'

He turned his head to look at her, a sad little smile playing about his wide mouth. 'Pathetic, eh? What could I have done, skinny wee runt that I was? I didnae have the muscles then that I do now. I could only have been about twelve.'

He looked away again, towards the spire of the university. Carrie wondered what he was really seeing. In his mind's eye.

'She found me out, of course. One of her pals spotted me. Ma hit the roof. *Christ!* My ears rang for a week wi' the tongue-lashing she gave me that night.'

The momentary spurt of amusement faded from his face. 'Then it happened again. Someone else who didnae want to pay for his pleasure.' His voice hardened. 'Or who found some o' that pleasure in hitting a defenceless woman. You get men like that. There's a woman up my close who's married to one o' them. He lays into her every Saturday night when he comes home from the pub. He's no' the only one. No' by a long chalk.'

Carrie shook her head. She knew nothing of this world. For the first time, with a strange mixture of shame and humility and pity for Ewen, she realised how protected and safe her own life had been. 'And you insisted your mother brought them home after that? Did the neighbours not object?

Somehow the shrewd wryness of his glance summed up the huge gulf between them. They'd been brought up in the same small place, but the distance between the way their lives had been led was as great as the millions of miles which separated the earth from the moon.

'Do you think she was the only working girl in Partick, hen?'

That was another phrase Carrie had learned, then. A working girl. And no, it had never really occurred to her that things like that were going on a few hundred yards from her own front door. Lots of things had never occurred to her.

They had to her mother, she realised now. The revelation came with a jolt, like the feeling Carrie sometimes got as she lay in bed, that sense of missing a step: an odd little flutter of blind and unreasoning panic. Life was precarious. Respectability was even more so. One false step and you would plunge into the abyss, falling down a fissure so deep you'd never be able to claw your way back up to the surface.

'She'd take them into the house,' Ewen said, 'and I'd sit outside on the stairs until they had finished.'

She could see him: a skinny wee runt, hunched miserably on a cold tenement landing, his knees drawn up and his tousled head sunk forward on them. Until his mother and the man she'd brought home with her had finished. A business transaction. Something bought and something sold.

She studied his face, watching the shadows cast on it by the sun-dappled leaves above his head as the branches of the old beech tree bobbed gently to and fro.

'She met this man . . . thought he was going to help her get out of it. He was nice to me. At first.' Ewen gave a mirthless laugh. 'That soon changed. He wanted to live off her, you see. There are men like that, too,' he said drily. 'He thought knocking me about a bit would persuade her to go out more. She'd been doing the bare minimum when she met him, enough to pay the rent and keep us going.' Ewen's tone of voice became reflective. 'I think him having a go at me was the final straw.'

'What happened?' whispered Carrie, her heart aching for him. With an upbringing like that, she supposed it was inevitable that he himself would turn to violence when he was roused. The thought of his fist pounding into Matt's face made her sick to her stomach.

'On the night after my sixteenth birthday she couldnae stand it any more,' the quiet voice continued. 'She cooked me a meal – toad-in-the-hole, my favourite. I couldnae figure out why I was getting a treat two days in row. She'd baked me a cake the night before, you see.'

Carrie did see. It must have brought it all back when she'd done the same for his nineteenth birthday.

'She lifted one of the floorboards and showed me where there was some money hidden. Forty pounds that she'd saved. From her work,' he added carefully. 'She kissed me and told me she loved me, said I was the best thing that had ever happened to her.' The deceptively calm voice grew husky. 'I was never to forget that. Then she said she was going out for a walk. I asked if I would come with her, but she just smiled and told me to enjoy my tea. She needed to clear her head.' He paused. 'I'll never know if she managed that. I hope she did.'

He paused again. Carrie's heart was thumping, dreading whatever was coming next.

'What I do know is that she didnae walk very far,' he said at last. 'Only as far as the Clyde. They fished her body out at the Dalmuir Bend a week later.'

Carrie's eyes flooded with tears. She wanted to say something, attempt to offer him some comfort, but she couldn't speak. She moved closer to him and laid her hands on his arms. 'Och, I've made you sad,' he said softly. 'I didnae mean to do that.'

She could only shake her head, and for a few minutes they stood together in silence under the beech tree. 'How did you manage?' she asked at last. 'You were still only a boy.'

'I grew up quickly,' he said drily. 'My ma's pal helped. The money under the floorboards paid the rent for a good long while. Then your father gave me a job. I'll aye be grateful to him for that.' He was studying her face. 'Come on,' he said abruptly. 'I'll walk you home.'

'I'll get the tram.'

'I'll see you to the tram stop then.'

They walked round the outside of the Art Galleries building, not through it as they could have done. It would be full of high-spirited children, dispatched there by harassed mothers wondering if the school holidays were ever going to be over. Some of the wee Partick scruffs would be sticking their tongues out at the middle-class children from Hyndland and Hillhead and Park Circus trailing around dutifully after their mothers or nursemaids.

Rich or poor, well-dressed or in hand-me-downs, most of those children would have loving mothers. Your mother loved you. That was a given fact. Despite his terrible childhood, it was obvious that Ewen's mother had cared very deeply for him. As he walked beside her towards the main road, silent now that his terrible story was told, Carrie hoped with all her heart that he found consolation in that.

She sat on the side seat of the tram, and made the mistake of looking back. He was walking slowly away from the Kelvin Hall, shoulders hunched and head bowed. Her tram gathered speed, clanked over the Kelvin and swung round, heading for Partick Cross. Ewen was lost to view.

Carrie was in her mother's arms, sobbing her heart out. 'Oh, Ma, I didn't know! I never realised what you were talking about all this time! You should have told me!'

Standing beside his entwined womenfolk, her father patted her on the shoulder. 'There, there, lass. Your mother couldn't tell you. You had to hear it for yourself. I'm glad young Ewen found the courage to tell you.'

Carrie lifted her head from her mother's shoulder and wiped her eyes with her hands. Esther's grip on her daughter's waist slackened. 'Come and sit down, pet.' She guided her into one of the big red armchairs, pulled up a footstool and started rubbing her daughter's hands, as she had when Carrie was a child and had gone to play outside on a winter's day forgetting to put her mittens on.

'She's awful cold, Archie. Maybe we should light the fire.'

Once, when she was about ten years old, the three of them had gone on a railway outing to St Andrew's. The *haar* had been down, the East Coast fog. Carrie felt now as she had that day, that there was something important out there, hidden within the folds of the all-enveloping mist, but she couldn't seem to reach it.

A sound came back to her: the deep note of a lighthouse's foghorn, tolling like a muffled bell somewhere in the distance. Her mother's voice, too, seemed to be coming from a long way off. Carrie fought her way up out of the mist, slid one hand out of Esther's grasp, wiped her eyes again and sniffed.

'Don't be daft, Ma, we don't need the fire lit. It's not even the end of August yet.'

Her father was hovering over both of them. She needed to lift those anxious lines from his forehead. 'Maybe I'll just go to bed early with a piggy. That'll keep me warm.'

Esther jumped to her feet. 'Aye, that's the best thing. I'll bring you some soup on a tray and sit with you for a wee while.'

'You take the lassie through to her bedroom, Esther. I'll boil the kettle for the hot water bottle and put the soup on to heat.'

She turned at the door of the living room. Her father was on his way to the kitchen and her mother was at her elbow.

'I'll be all right,' she said, directing the comment at both of them. 'Don't worry about me.'

'You'll be fine,' agreed Esther. 'A good night's sleep and you'll be right as rain. We know that. Don't we, Archie?'

'Aye, of course we do,' he said stoutly.

Her father was watching her. It was the evening of the following day and Carrie was helping him in the garden.

'What next, Daddy?' she asked cheerfully.

She knew she hadn't fooled him, but he smiled and asked her to fetch him the graip. He needed to level out the areas in the potato patch from which they'd already lifted tatties. There would be some still lying there, fallen back below the surface when Carrie or Esther had shaken the shaw free of earth.

'There's maybe enough to do the next couple o' days,' he said. 'Then we can leave the rest to grow a wee bit more.' He scowled at the summer sky. 'If we get some rain to allow them to swell up, that is.'

She fetched the big fork from the garden shed. While the central part of this remarkable structure had been purchased, it had been added to over the years, acquiring what Carrie irreverently referred to as the west wing and the east wing. To her father's considerable amusement, a few school lessons on architecture had supplied her with another description: the semi-Gothic shed.

He raised his tomato plants in the lean-to greenhouse which adjoined it, carefully explaining to his daughter that, contrary to popular opinion, tomatoes were a fruit, not a vegetable. Like an apple or an orange, they carried their seeds on the inside.

He had taught her a lot about gardening. She knew that potatoes were an excellent plant for cleansing the soil, that you should have your early varieties in no later than St Patrick's Day – 17 March – and that you should practise rotation of crops if at all possible.

Apart from five neat rows of raspberry bushes, which needed sturdy and permanent support and consequently had to stay where they were from year to year, Archie religiously followed his own advice. The ground became tired if you continually planted the same thing in it. It wasn't easy soil to work, being heavy and full of clay.

Both he and Carrie were firmly of the opinion that you could probably make very good pots out of it.

He fed and lightened it regularly with bone meal. Sprinkling a little of it along the drills before the seed potatoes were planted had always been one of Carrie's jobs. She couldn't help him much with the heavier jobs, but the lighter tasks were fine.

'Thanks, hen,' he said, taking the graip from her. She'd remembered to bring the old tin basin too, the one in which they usually gathered the tatties. 'You're a big help.'

Her bottom lip wobbled.

'Och, lassie,' he said gently. 'It'll all come out in the wash, you know.'

She raised the back of her hand to her mouth, forced the tears back. 'I keep thinking about Ewen. Wondering how he's feeling.'

'You're fond of the laddie.' It was a statement, not a question, but she gave him a quick nod of agreement anyway. Archie's eyes narrowed consideringly. 'But you're fond of Matthew Campbell too?'

She nodded again. Impossible to tell her father that while fond might be exactly the right word to describe her emotions towards Ewen, it didn't begin to cover the feelings Matt aroused in her. It was the difference between affection and passion, she supposed. Yet that affection had grown very deep over the past couple of months, had begun to seem something very real and solid . . .

'I'm all mixed-up Daddy,' she confessed. 'I don't know what I feel and I don't know what I think.'

'Dangerous occupation, thinking. Probably why lots o' folk try to avoid it altogether. That's better,' he said, seeing her smile. He put his hand on her shoulder and gave it a quick squeeze. 'Will you take some advice from your ancient father?'

'Any time he cares to offer it.'

'Sleep on it, lass. Things aye look clearer in the morning.'

'You think so?' He released her shoulder and started sifting through the earth for the lost potatoes.

'I know so.'

He was right, of course he was. And she would see Ewen tomorrow when he came back to work, and would assure him that what he had told her about his mother would make absolutely no difference to their friendship. She knew he'd be worrying about that.

'I'll go and help Ma get the supper,' she said. 'Would you be wanting some Welsh rarebit?'

'That'll do me fine.' Archie had unearthed three decent-sized potatoes. He stooped, and tossed them gently into the basin.

'You're not scared the cheese will make you dream of your granny?'

That was another of Esther's admonitions, one she'd given up on some time ago. Archie was very fond of toasted cheese before he went to bed at night. He straightened up, winced, and put a hand to his back. Then he started wielding the graip again.

'I wouldnae mind if I did,' he confided, 'my granny was a nice old soul. On ye go now. I'll be in as soon as I've done this.'

'I wish I'd been a boy,' Carrie said suddenly. 'I could have helped you more in the garden.'

He stopped swinging the fork and regarded her with loving eyes. 'I wouldnae want you any different, lass. I'm gey proud of you, you know.' His voice softened as he surveyed her. 'Beauty and brains and a kind heart too. What more could any father want?'

Her lip started to wobble again. She wanted to tell him she was proud of him too, that she loved him with all her heart, put into words how grateful she was for the way he'd brought her up. He had never laid down the law to her as so many other fathers did to their children. Throughout her life he had always shown her that he valued and respected her opinions and wanted to hear them.

She wanted to tell him all of those things, but they were both Scots, with the national tendency to shy away from public protestations of affection, so she didn't. All the same, standing there on the grass and looking at him smiling back at her from the middle of his vegetable patch, she couldn't resist asking a question.

'Shall I give you a kiss?' She took a step towards him, but he laughed and waved a jokingly dismissive hand in the direction of the back door.

'Don't be daft! Away ye go now. Tell your mother I'll be along in a wee minute.'

'What can your father be doing?' said Esther in exasperation fifteen minutes later. Six pieces of bread lay neatly on the rack of the grill pan, already toasted on their undersides. She'd placed slices of cheese on top of all of them, preparatory to sliding the pan back under the heat. She peered out of the window. 'And it'll be getting dark soon. The nights are fair drawing in, you know. Go and give him a shout, lass.'

Hiding a smile, Carrie went to the open back door. *The nights are fair drawing in*. It was an expression lots of people used at this time of year. It stated the obvious, and she didn't think she could be the only person who found it unintentionally hilarious. Summer in Scotland meant long days and light evenings, winter the opposite. There obviously had to be a transitional period, but each year this fact of life took some folk by surprise. There were those who seemed to regard it as a personal affront when the days began to shorten at the end of August.

She went to the open back door. Funny. She couldn't see him. Could he be tidying some tools away in the semi-Gothic shed, or perhaps working out of sight behind it? Maybe he was at the fence, speaking to someone he knew on the platform.

She stepped out into the garden and made her way along the back of the house. She looked in the shed. He wasn't there. She walked the few steps necessary to bring her round the other side of it and stopped dead. Through the tattie shaws she had caught a glimpse of something which shouldn't be there. Something black.

She went closer, and stumbled. She looked down stupidly at the graip. What on earth was it doing there? Never in a million years would her father have tossed it aside so carelessly. He was careful about things like that.

She lifted her eyes again to that unexplained splash of black. It was cloth, a heavy material. Trousers. Her father's black trousers. Lying flat on the ground.

'Ma!' she shouted, her voice thin and high-pitched. 'Ma!'

Carrie did what came naturally. She ran to the station for help. She found Matt. He hardly needed to listen to what she said. One look at her face was enough to send him striding over to the porters' room. He was back in ten seconds flat, throwing out an instruction to the concerned-looking man who was following him into the booking-office.

'Hold the fort till I get back.'

'Is your father all right, pet?' asked the porter anxiously.

Carrie could only shake her head.

'That's what we're going to find out,' said Matt decisively. He reached for her hand. 'Come on, you, let's run.'

Esther was kneeling beside her husband, clutching his limp hand against her breast. Carrie went round and stood behind her, leaving space on the other side of the big body which lay so still and quiet among the potatoes. Matt would be able to do something. Like a great many railwaymen, he was a regular attender at first-aid classes run by the St Andrew's Ambulance Association.

He felt for a pulse: at the wrist and at the throat. He put his finger under Archie's nose. He bent his dark head and listened. Then he looked up at the two women. Carrie saw the compassion in his eyes, and waited while he tried to find a kind way to say it.

She had known anyway. From the moment she had stumbled on the graip. Archie Burgess was beyond first-aid. Her beloved father was beyond any kind of aid.

Chapter 14

There was a huge turnout for Archie's funeral. It brought Partick to a standstill, men doffing their bunnets as the cortège passed and women on the route it took to the church and the cemetery closing their curtains and lowering their window blinds as a mark of respect. The general manager of the LNER, so recently a visitor to the station, came back through from Edinburgh to witness the interment of a loyal and long-standing servant of the company. He even read the lesson at the funeral service.

That meant a lot to Esther, but Carrie found herself more touched by the sincerity of the expressions of sympathy made to them by many less exalted folk. Martin and Rita Sharkey, uncomfortable and uncertain of their welcome in a Protestant church, but nevertheless determined to pay their respects, were among them. With her mother's blessing, Carrie asked Sharkey to be one of the pall-bearers. He accepted with tears in his eyes.

Matthew was another of those carrying a cord as her father was laid to rest. That had been her mother's idea, but Carrie had concurred whole-heartedly with it. She had seen a different side of him since that dreadful moment in the garden – a considerate and sensitive aspect to his nature.

She stood with her mother and watched Martin Sharkey and Matthew and the others – old friends and colleagues all – lay her father to rest. She did so with a mounting sense of unreality, understanding for the first time what people meant when they said they couldn't accept that someone was dead. She couldn't accept that she was never going to see her father again. Absurdly, as they sat at the funeral tea, she kept expecting him to walk through the door. It was like being at a party where the guest of honour was unaccountably absent.

In the days after the funeral there was a steady stream of callers to the station house. Some came to offer practical advice, others simply to express their condolences. Ewen was one of them, part of a small deputation of Permanent Way men, shunters and signalmen, all led by Sharkey. The ganger sat awkwardly opposite her mother in the living room, perched on the edge of one of the red armchairs. Ewen and the other men who'd come with him stood, even more awkwardly, behind it.

Sharkey fished something out of his pocket. It was a red neckerchief, done up as a bundle. Carrie heard the clink of coins as the Irishman leaned forward and held it out to her mother.

'We had a wee whip-round.' He coughed. 'We would be honoured if you and Miss Burgess would accept this small token of the esteem in which we held your husband.'

She saw her mother's eyebrows go up. Please God, she prayed silently, let her accept it in the spirit in which it's being offered. Esther didn't let her down, putting her hand out for the none-too-clean handkerchief, grubby after its sojourn in the deep pocket of the foreman's working jacket.

'Thank you, Martin,' she said gravely. 'And please thank all the other men most sincerely on behalf of Caroline and myself.'

Carrie saw the little group to the door, deliberately taking them through the front porch and round the side of the house to the platform gate. It had been a formal visit. It seemed to require a formal seeing out. They went out on to the platform one by one, solemnly shaking her hand as they did so. Sharkey and Ewen were the last to leave.

'Did you get your waterproof clothing?' she asked, suddenly remembering.

'Thank you, Miss B, we did indeed. They came the day we buried your poor father, God rest his soul.' He crossed himself – hurriedly, as though he were afraid the action might offend her Protestant sensibilities. 'That was something else he did for us.'

'Well,' she said lightly, hoping her voice wasn't going to break, 'Ewen helped quite a bit, did he not?'

She half-turned. He was standing behind her, deliberately hanging back. She had caught a glimpse of him at the funeral, white-faced and sombre at the back of the crowd gathered round the grave, but they hadn't spoken to each other since that day at Kelvingrove when he had made his great revelation. Only a week ago, she realised. It seemed a lot longer.

'Well, I'll be for home,' announced Sharkey. They barely noticed him go.

'How are you?'

She tucked a strand of hair behind her ear and managed a smile. 'Och, I'm fine. Well, not exactly fine, but we'll manage. Everyone's being so kind.'

Ewen's pale eyes were fixed on her face. 'If there's anything I can do, Carrie . . . For you or your ma . . . Well, you know you only have tae ask.'

'Thank you,' she said gravely. 'I appreciate that.'

'I mean it,' he said. 'Anything at all.' His gaze shifted, focussing on what lay behind her. 'Yer faither loved his garden, didn't he?'

'Yes,' she managed. 'He did.'

'It would be a shame for all his good work to go to waste over the autumn. I'd be glad to keep lending a hand. Whatever needs doin' before the winter comes.'

'Thanks, Ewen, but we're going to be out of here long before the winter arrives.'

That had been one of the official visits she and Esther had received. The man from the railway company's headquarters in Glasgow had been very kind too, but Partick was a busy station. It needed a firm hand at the helm. They already had a most suitable candidate in mind. Mrs and Miss Burgess were of course entitled to the statutory period of notice, but it had been tactfully suggested that if they could manage to move out sooner, it would be better for everyone.

Ewen turned surprised eyes on her. 'But that's terrible! Could they no' give you some more time?'

Carrie shrugged. 'There's no real point in delaying. Mrs Sharkey knows of a flat in White Street that might be suitable for us. We're going to look at it tomorrow.'

'White Street's nice,' he offered.

'Is it?' she asked indifferently. 'That's good. Ma would probably prefer somewhere up Crow Road or Hyndland, but we can't afford that.'

'Are ye no' left very well off?'

'You could put it that way,' she said drily. 'There's a pension, but it's not great.'

That had been last night's nasty surprise. Sifting through the family papers while her mother sat listlessly in front of the empty grate, Carrie had discovered that her father's pension amounted to the princely sum of ten shillings a week. Her parents had some savings, but after she'd done the arithmetic and calculated how many weeks or months that would keep them going for, she had realised how quickly the money could evaporate if they didn't have a regular wage coming in.

'I'm going to have to become a wage slave, Ewen,' she told him, striving for lightness. 'I'll not be doing my teacher training now.' That had been a bitter pill to swallow. Her exam results had dropped on to the doormat this morning. She had passed with flying colours.

He frowned. 'Is there no' a bursary ye could get or something?'

'I've written to Jordanhill to ask, but I'm not very hopeful. And I can't imagine that any bursary would pay enough to support two people, can you?'

Carrie gave him a brittle little smile.

She'd anticipated an argument when she told Esther she wouldn't be going to college. She didn't get one. That worried her, as did the fact that her mother was so calm. Frighteningly calm.

On the night of Archie's death the two Burgess woman had clung to each other, weeping. The next day they'd had to compose themselves to deal with the hundred and one things a sudden death, or indeed any death, throws up: the funeral arrangements, informing officialdom, receiving all the visitors and telling the story of Archie's last moments over and over again, working out the state of their finances and exactly how they were going to adjust to their new circumstances.

Finding a new home was the first priority. The harassed and bad-tempered little man at the factor's office gave Carrie the key to the flat in White Street and told her he needed a decision that day. He had other people interested in taking over the tenancy.

She could believe it. It was a sought-after area, and the two apartment room and kitchen was spick and span, if a little poky. Properties on the ground floor usually were, the entrance close to a building cutting into the available space. However small they were, whichever floor they were on, tenement houses in Glasgow were always referred to as houses, never flats.

'Well, Ma, what d'you think?' Carrie asked as they walked through the tiny lobby from the front room – which didn't really seem large enough to merit that title – into the equally small kitchen. It was like a hundred others she had seen: box bed against one wall, huge old range on the other, sink under the window and built-in cupboards occupying the fourth wall of the room. Carrie surveyed the remaining floor space. They'd be hard pressed to fit their dining table and chairs into it.

'It's a bit dark,' said Esther. She was standing staring at the range. Was she thinking of how much she was going to miss her smart and efficient little Baby Belling? There were lots of things they weren't going to be able to bring with them from the station house. Suppressing a pang, Carrie walked over to the window to look out at the back court.

Her mother was right. The house was dark. Hemmed in by tenements front and back, that was inevitable. Her eyes lit on an earth border running alongside the wall which divided their back court from the neighbouring one. There were a few straggly flowers in it.

'Looks like someone does a bit of gardening,' she said brightly.

'That's nice,' said Esther, but she didn't move from her position in front of the range.

Carrie turned, and indicated the built-in cupboards. 'You know,' she said, 'if we stripped those down and painted them a lighter colour that would make a big difference.'

'I suppose it would.' Esther had turned obediently to look, but her face was expressionless, her eyes empty and vacant.

'So shall we take it?' Carrie asked. They didn't really have much choice. Time was of the essence, and the rent was affordable.

'Do as you think best, pet,' said Esther.

It was a phrase Carrie was to hear more and more over the days and weeks which followed. Her mother pretended to listen to discussions about the future, but at the end of them she always left any decisions to be made to her daughter.

It was an awesome responsibility for a seventeen-year-old girl, but Carrie gritted her teeth and got on with it. There was no alternative – although she knew very well that Matthew Campbell wanted to offer her one. He was once again a frequent caller at the station house. As her mother grew more withdrawn, and the day of their removal to White Street drew ever nearer, Carrie was often glad of his company.

He had changed. He seemed softer, more humble somehow. He was also willing to let her hold him at arm's length – as she was doing at the moment. There was still the matter of how awful he had been to Ewen.

'Jealousy,' he told her, as he helped her sort out her father's clothes, a task she'd been dreading. Mary and Douglas were through in the living room, gently encouraging Esther to select which pieces of furniture and ornaments were to make the journey to their new home.

'Somebody could maybe get the use out of this suit.' He refolded a pair of trousers and slipped them neatly on to a hanger, replacing the waistcoat and jacket over them.

'He hardly wore it. That's what he called his funeral suit.' Her breath caught in her throat. 'Only he went to his own before he could wear it to anybody else's!'

'Och, Carrie. Come here.' Matt held out his arms, but she shook her head.

'I'm all right.' She took a deep breath and squared her shoulders. 'You were explaining to me why you were so nasty to poor Ewen.'

Matt dropped his arms. 'I was jealous,' he repeated. 'Plain and simple. I'm not proud of myself, but the green-eyed monster had me in its grip.' When his comments evoked no response, his face grew more serious. 'I love you, you know,' he said quietly.

She did know. Matthew had always known what he wanted, never left her in any doubt about his feelings, but if she'd been too young to marry him before she was still too young to marry him now. What she needed was a job.

She might have her Higher Leaving Certificate, but she wasn't trained for anything. She enquired about doing a course in shorthand

and typing, but even the short ones seemed to cost quite a lot of money. Nor was there any guarantee she would get a position at the end of it. There were so many people looking for work these days.

She wondered about applying to a shop, perhaps one of the high-class ones which required well-spoken and intelligent assistants to deal with their wealthy clientele. She tried several. They all told her the same thing: she was too young, she had no training or experience, come back when she had done something else for a year or two. It was all very dispiriting.

'Are you sure you'll be all right, Carrie?'

'I'll be fine, Mary.' She gave the Baby Belling one last wipe. 'Is that Douglas come for you now?'

Her friend nodded. She'd been helping with the final cleaning of the house, preparatory to Mr and Mrs Gibson, the new stationmaster and his wife, moving in the next day. 'Let's see now,' she said. 'All the floors are done, aren't they? So that means we can take the galvanised bucket and the mop. I've got the sweeping brushes, the stiff one and the softer one. What does that leave you to carry?'

'Just the shovel, the wee brush and the clouts and things. Matthew's calling past when he finishes his shift. He said he'd walk me along to White Street, so he can help me with those.'

Douglas strolled into the kitchen. 'It's gey sad to see it so empty –' he began, and then broke off, yowling in pain and turning accusing eyes on his beloved. 'What did you kick me for, Mary?'

'Men,' she said, rolling her own eyes heavenwards. 'Not the most tactful o' creatures, are they?'

Carrie smiled. 'It's all right,' she said. 'I'll forgive you, Douglas.'

'We could stay with you till Matthew comes,' said Mary. 'It's no bother.'

Carrie shook her head. 'You've done enough already, Mary. Both of you,' she said, including a still rather perplexed-looking Douglas in her thanks. He'd helped with the removal two days before. 'I'm really grateful. My mother just couldn't face coming back today. You know?'

'Aye. I know,' said Mary, her brown eyes soft with sympathy. 'Well, if you're sure, Carrie . . .'

'I'm sure. I'd kind of like a wee while here on my own, anyway.'

'Aye,' repeated Mary. Then she grew brisk, indicating the heavy bucket in the corner of the kitchen. 'Douglas, if you would be so kind.'

After they had left, Carrie walked slowly through the echoing rooms, quickly giving up any pretence she was checking to see that everything had been done. She was saying her goodbyes.

The grate of the living room fire was empty. The vase of dried flowers had made it along the road, but they had no room for the big red armchairs. The beds were staying too. Carrie had negotiated a price for everything they were leaving with the Gibsons. The extra money would come in handy.

She went in and out of her parents' bedroom quickly. That was altogether too painful. Oh, Daddy, she thought, we're going to miss you so very much!

Fighting back tears, she stood in the middle of her own bedroom. This was where she had grown up, dreamed her girl's dreams. She remembered winter days playing in here, evenings spent studying, Sunday afternoons laughingly trying to stand still while Esther pinned up the hem on a skirt, or fitted a new dress on her.

She could see her father carefully carrying through a shovel full of hot coals from the living room to start off her own fire so that she wouldn't be cold. She'd been so well loved and cared for. Now it was up to her to return that love and care, to hold together what was left of the Burgess family.

About to leave the room, she checked herself. She'd almost forgotten Gertie the giraffe, standing up on her stiffened legs in the middle of the bare mattress of Carrie's bed. Holding the stuffed toy to her as though it were a baby, she went out into the garden.

Matthew found her there twenty minutes later, standing with her back to the semi-Gothic shed and clutching Gertie tightly to her bosom.

'Carrie?'

It came out like a dam bursting. 'I can't bear to leave this house! I was so happy here! We were all so happy here!'

He pulled her to him, giraffe and all. 'Life's never going to be the same again,' she said brokenly, her cheek pressed against his shoulder.

His hand was at the back of her head, gently rubbing her hair. 'No,' he agreed, 'but life will be good again, I promise you.'

She began to sob. 'I've always belonged here. I was the stationmaster's daughter. Now I'm not going to belong anywhere.'

His arms felt solid and warm and heavy. Possessive too, but there was something comforting in that now she was adrift in a cold, hard world.

'You could belong with me. You only have to say the word.'

She turned her face up to him, and he bent his dark head and kissed her brow, the gentlest she had ever known him. 'One day I'll be the stationmaster here, Carrie. I could bring you back home.'

Her tear-filled eyes were wide and sad and trusting. 'Could you, Matt? Could you?'

'Say yes,' he urged. 'Please, Carrie, say yes!'

She laid her head once more against his shoulder. Her voice came out muffled by the fine wool of his jacket. 'Not now, Matt. Not now.

Will you . . . will you ask me again another time? When I'm not so upset?'

His arms tightened around her. 'You can count on it.'

A few days' later Carrie had a brainwave. The railway! Although she'd never actually heard of any female clerks – it was regarded as a man's job – she didn't think there was any formal rule about not employing women. She was sure she could pass the exam and that she would be perfectly capable of doing the job.

The pay for a junior clerk wasn't great, but it wasn't awful either. With her father's pension, and if they were really careful, they might just manage to make ends meet. It was also a job she would enjoy and it would keep their connection with the railway.

She composed a careful letter to the general manager in Edinburgh – nothing like going straight to the top – and waited eagerly for his reply. When it arrived, her heart soared. He had arranged an interview for her at the company's offices in central Glasgow.

She told Esther there was some paperwork to be sorted out about her father's pension, put on her forest green costume and her Tyrolean hat, and set off with a spring in her step. With a bit of luck, she might be coming home with news which would really cheer her mother up.

Her optimism was to be short-lived. The man who saw her was very mannerly. He gave her tea out of a china cup and saucer. He sympathised with her in her great loss and told her what an asset men like Archie Burgess were to the railway company. He also made it absolutely clear he had no job to give to Archie's daughter.

'You see, Miss Burgess,' he explained, brushing some biscuit crumbs off his pin-stripe suit, 'whilst you would very probably make an excellent clerk . . .' he smiled benignly at her '. . . or in your case, *clerkess* – we really can't give a man's job to a woman, particularly not with the state the country's in at the moment. A man has a family to support, after all.'

'But I've got my mother to support,' Carrie said in exasperation. 'We're out of the station house and have rent to pay.'

He placed his own cup and saucer on a silver tray on the beautiful mahogany desk between Carrie and himself and stood up. The interview was over. She found herself being ushered politely to the door, biting her lip in disappointment.

'There, there, my dear,' he said soothingly, 'a pretty girl like you will be married soon, I've no doubt. Then you can give all your problems to your husband to sort out.'

She was still smouldering with rage and frustration when she got back to White Street.

'It's only me,' she called as she took her key out of the lock, but there was no reply. She found Esther in the kitchen, sitting on the edge of the box bed with her head bowed. Carrie knelt down in front of her, expecting to see tears, but her mother's face bore the calm expression she was beginning to find just a wee bit unnerving.

Her mother spoke without preamble. 'I've been to the Western Infirmary this afternoon. While you were up in Glasgow.'

Alarmed, Carrie wrapped her fingers round Esther's wrist. 'What's wrong, Ma? Did you have an accident while I was out?'

She looked her mother over in puzzlement. She seemed fine, blooming with health and curiously peaceful. Esther extended her free hand and touched her daughter's face. 'That hat really suits you. You're such a bonnie girl.'

'Ma, tell me what's happened. Are you all right?'

Esther took her hand from Carrie's face and laid it against her own chest.

'I've got a growth,' she said. She placed her hand underneath the curve of her breast, sliding her fingers round towards the armpit. 'Right about here. There's nothing they can do.'

Carrie rose to her feet and sat down heavily on the bed. 'What do you mean, there's nothing they can do? Doctors can work miracles these days. If they catch things in time.'

'I've had it for nearly a year, lass. Seemingly it's spread right through me. That's what the doctor at the Infirmary said, anyway.' She smiled. 'He was very kind.'

'A year! Oh, Ma, why didn't you go to the doctor when you first noticed it?'

'I was more concerned about your father's health. I thought this wee thing I had couldn't matter very much compared to that.' Esther's smile faltered. 'I thought it might go away.'

'Oh, Ma,' Carrie said again, and her eyes filled with tears. In an instant, comforting arms were placed around her, pulling her into the warmth of her mother's body.

'Don't cry for me, pet,' said the quiet voice above her head. 'It means I'll be going to join your father a wee bit sooner than I had thought, that's all.'

'I can't lose the two of you! God couldn't be so cruel!'

'Hush, now. Sit up a wee minute. There now.' Esther had removed her daughter's jaunty little hat. Turning, she placed it carefully on the narrow shelf which ran between the box bed and the cooking range. Then she patted her lap.

'Lay your head down, lass, and I'll stroke your hair.'

Like a little child, Carrie did as her mother bid, curling her legs up on to the bed. When she had been a wee girl, this had been her special treat, a reward for submitting to having her hair brushed and combed and held back with clasps, tied up in rags at night to make ringlets or scraped back from her forehead during the day to make a neat ponytail.

'How long?' she asked, some time later. It might have been five minutes. It might have been fifteen.

The loving hand which was smoothing her hair didn't falter. 'A matter of months. Maybe six.'

She was lying facing the window. The sky was beginning to darken, the days shortening as the autumn approached. Esther must have felt the slight movement of her head, realised what she was looking at.

'The nights are fair drawing in.'

'Aye, Ma,' Carrie said softly. 'That they are.'

Someone had called her name. Lost in thought, she couldn't at first make out where the words had come from.

'Up here,' came the voice again. She lifted her gaze and saw Ewen, sitting atop a wall, a half-munched apple in his hand. He must be on one of his rest days.

'How's it going?' he asked easily.

'Not very well,' she confessed, looking up at him. He wore no jacket or waistcoat, and his blue shirt was collarless and open at the neck. He needed a shave, she noticed. Probably he didn't always bother on the days he wasn't at work.

'Are you not cold?' she enquired. 'It's a bit nippy today.' It was approaching the end of October and there had been a businesslike frost the night before. She had left the buttons of her brown wool jacket open, but she was glad of its warmth and length, skimming down over her hips.

He contradicted her cheerfully. 'It's a beautiful day. Golden, ye might say.' He took two healthy bites from the apple and lobbed it over his shoulder.

She snorted. 'It might be golden for you, but it's been black and sooty for me. I've spent all morning trying to get the blasted range lit.'

She turned away from him, responding to a greeting called out from the other side of the road. There was a thud and she whirled around, startled. Ewen was standing right in front of her. 'Want me to come round and give it a go?'

'No, thanks, I think it's burning all right now.'

Her rejection of his offer had been too swift. His face clouded. 'And your mammy wouldnae give me houseroom anyway?' The coldness in his voice was the last straw. Tears welled up in her eyes. Sometimes she wondered where they all came from. Surely you had to run out of them eventually.

'Och, Carrie,' he said. 'I'm sorry, hen. I didnae meant to upset ye.'

'I don't want to disgrace myself in the middle of the street,' she told him in an anguished whisper. She remembered Oban and managed a strangled laugh. 'Isn't this where we came in?'

'Maybe, but I know a way out. Up ye come.'

Before she had time to think about it, he had interlaced the fingers of his hands to make a step and helped her shin up the wall on which he'd been sitting. Then he was there beside her.

'It's not as far to go on this side. Jump down.' He suited the action to the words and looked up at her in laughing invitation. The surprise had dried her tears. She blinked and swung her legs over. The wall enclosed a small grassy area, overgrown with grass and a few wild flowers. She reviewed the situation. Ewen had done it easily. Then again, he was used to leaping on and off railway platforms.

'Go on,' he urged. 'I double dare you. And I'll catch you anyway.'

He not only caught her, he also held on to her. Carrie looked him straight in the eye and issued a silent dare of her own: for him to go any further. He dared.

He might have looked rough and ready, but he smelled of fresh air and soapy skin and newly washed shirt. She laid her two hands flat on his chest, but she wasn't pushing him away. His mouth was cool and firm on her own and the feel of the bristles on his jaw and upper lip was a new, but not unpleasant, sensation.

When it was over, he pulled back and said a few simple words. 'I've wanted to do that for such a long time.'

A golden day, he'd said. His hair looked golden, sticking out from his head as usual and lit like a halo by the autumn sunlight. She peered over his shoulder and felt his grasp on her waist slacken slightly.

'What is this place?'

'The Quaker graveyard.'

'I don't see any gravestones. Do Quakers not approve of them?'

'I don't know. Can I kiss you again?'

She dropped the contrived fascination with their surroundings and looked sadly at him. 'I don't think that would be a very good idea.'

'Why not?'

'Because I'm going to marry Matthew Campbell. I decided this morning.'

It had been while she'd been struggling to get the range lit, as a matter of fact, sitting on a cold floor surrounded by crumpled up newspaper and half-charred bits of kindling and trying to choose between bursting into tears or swearing her head off at the antiquated piece of machinery, but Ewen didn't need to know that.

His hands slid off her waist. 'Why are you going to marry Matthew Campbell?' he asked, pale to his very lips.

'Because I love him,' Carrie replied, wondering why that was so hard to say. 'Because my mother wants to see me settled.' She shrugged her shoulders. 'Because I've got to marry someone.'

She realised too late that her attempt at flippancy had given an immediate hostage to fortune.

'You've got to marry someone? What's wrong with me, then?'

'You've never asked me,' she whispered.

'Well, I'm asking you now.' Ewen's breath was coming fast and shallow. 'Don't marry him, Carrie. Marry me instead.'

Chapter 15

The words came tumbling out, falling over each other in his urgency to convince her of his case.

'I know I'm no' on your level, but I could pull myself up. I know I could, Carrie. With you helping me with my reading and writing, I could go after a better job, make you proud of me. And we wouldnae need to have children straightaway if ye didnae want to. I could wear a French letter when we went to bed together.'

'Ewen Livingstone!' Her face was burning.

'Think about it, Carrie,' he urged. 'We could have fun together, you and me.'

'Fun?' She said it as though she had no idea what the word meant.

'With you coaching me maybe I could go in for a clerkship. Perhaps even become a stationmaster one day – take you and your ma back to the station house.'

It was the thought of Ewen and her mother living under the same roof that did it. Fatally, she laughed at him – and saw the eager light in his pale eyes fade.

'Ye think I'm no' capable of it?'

She shook her head in denial of that, but it was only her words which penetrated his brain. 'I'm going to marry Matt.'

'Ye cannae marry him, Carrie, ye cannae!'

All she could see was his angry face. His seized her arms above the elbows and pushed her back against the wall of the little graveyard. He looked wild and despairing and it occurred to her to wonder if anyone would hear her if she screamed.

'So you love Matthew Campbell, do ye?'

Several things went through her head then. Before she could express any of them, Ewen spoke again. 'Are you sure ye don't love the fact that he lives up the hill, that his family's well off, that marrying him's going to save you from having to go out and work for a living like normal people? You and your precious mother, you're a right couple o' snobs!'

Carrie squirmed, trying vainly to release herself, the stone wall hard and rough against her back. 'How dare you say that about me?' She was shouting at him now. 'How dare you be rude about my mother!'

'How dare I? This is how I dare!'

He tightened his hold on her arms and jerked her towards him. His mouth was hard and passionate and demanding . . . and despite her anger, she felt herself respond to it. She was kissing him back.

The punishing fingers relaxed their grip. His lips grew gentle and coaxing She relaxed into his body, her arms snaking up around his neck. He made a funny little noise somewhere way back in his throat and slid his hand inside her jacket.

She started violently, but he lifted his mouth off her own long enough to murmur a quick little reassurance. 'It's all right, lassie, it's all right.'

His fingers travelled up over the cream-coloured lacy jumper she wore, found the curve of her breast, began slowly to stroke it. Carrie wondered how it was possible that such a strong hand could be so gentle . . .

He was wrong. This wasn't all right. She began to struggle in earnest. He let go of her.

'What's wrong?' he asked thickly.

'I want you to stop. Right now.'

Carrie eyed him warily. You weren't supposed to lead a man on. That got them to a point where they weren't willing to stop, where they were no longer able to stop. If a girl did that she only had herself to blame. Ewen was staring at her, breathing heavily. Had he reached that point?

'Gonnae tell me you werenae enjoying that? Still gonnae tell me it's Matthew Campbell you love?'

He looked very menacing, bigger somehow, with his hands bunched into fists at his sides. Carrie panicked. 'If you don't let me out of here, I'm going to scream!'

In her whole life, nobody had ever looked at her in such a contemptuous way. 'What d'ye take me for? You really think I'm that kind o' a man? There's a gate over there.' He raised his arm and pointed. 'You'll find it easier to get out that way. We wouldnae want you doing anything that's beneath your dignity, would we now? Like being seen wi' me, for instance.' He hoisted himself up on to the wall.

'So long, Miss Burgess,' he said, his voice laden with sarcasm. 'I would say that it's been nice knowing ye, but ma mammy didnae bring me up to tell lies. Funny that, eh, a woman like her?' He gave her one last, unforgiving look before he dropped out of sight.

Carrie stood staring stupidly at the wall. Then, very slowly, she turned and headed for the gate out on to the street. It was behind two or three poor-looking trees. A golden day, he'd said. None of it felt very golden to her.

She pushed open the heavy wrought-iron gate and walked out

into Keith Street. Ewen was nowhere to be seen, although presumably one of the closes she was walking past led to his house. Some children were playing in the middle of the road. A few of them were barefoot.

Three men stood round a close mouth on the other side of the narrow street. One of them said something and his two friends looked across at her and laughed. She quickened her step, heading for the main road with the sense of escaping from something. Nonetheless, she couldn't help throwing a swift glance back to the wall surrounding the old graveyard just before she turned the corner.

She'd gone in there like a child, clambering up the old stones and jumping down the other side. She'd left like a grown-up, walking sedately through the gate. She was a woman now, not a girl. That part of her life was over.

Chapter 16

'Show of presents?'

Her mother hadn't noticed the note of disapproval in Shona Campbell's voice. The three women were taking afternoon tea together in Byres Road, discussing arrangements for the wedding. Carrie heard the disdain loud and clear, saw also the little wrinkle of the nose which accompanied it. Her future mother-in-law obviously found the custom too working-class for her taste. Esther, she knew, had been fishing for an invitation, anxious to show off the towels and tablecloths and half tea sets her daughter had received up the hill rather than at White Street.

Carrie had privately determined that wild horses wouldn't drag her and her gifts to the Campbell family home any sooner than was strictly necessary. She wasn't going to have Matthew's mother looking down her elegant nose at good friends like Mary and Douglas and Rita Sharkey and her daughters.

'Yes,' she put in, 'we're having it the weekend before, on the Friday night and the Saturday afternoon. You'd be very welcome to come along, Mrs Campbell.'

She'd be Mrs Campbell herself soon. The knot was to be tied on the first Saturday in December. She supposed it was natural to feel a flutter of nerves. Getting married was a big step.

Matt was doing his best to reassure her she'd made the right decision. He was so happy: promising he'd look after her forever, promising her the earth. She'd told him about Esther's diagnosis and he'd simply wrapped his arms about her and held her close for a long, long time. When she finished crying he started planting little kisses all over her face.

'You've got me now,' he said. 'You don't have to cope with it all by yourself. I'll look after you. I'll look after everything.'

After that, his kisses became more passionate . . . Everything became more passionate. Carrie blushed to think of it, but she knew she would have let him go on, had even mumbled as much to him . . . but he had pushed her away.

'Not till we're married,' he'd said hoarsely. 'Then I'll show you how I really feel about you.'

She didn't doubt it. She had to take another drink of coffee. She could really have done with some iced water.

'Anything else I can do for you, ladies?'

It was the café owner's son, a boy Carrie knew to say hello to. Young as he was, he'd obviously inherited not only his father's dark good looks but also his continental charm. He'd been flirting outrageously with her since they'd come in here, and she'd been flirting right back.

Carrie felt a little spurt of childish pleasure when she sensed Shona Campbell's disapproval of the banter being tossed backwards and forwards between the young man and herself. She was going to be living in the same house as this woman very soon, not a prospect she relished – to put it mildly.

Matt said it was the sensible thing to do. They didn't have enough money put by yet to get a decent place of their own. Living with his parents for a few months would allow them to save towards that. She wondered if he was thinking that a few months' delay might see the house in White Street becoming available. She'd chosen not to put that thought into words.

Esther, insisting that all the usual traditions and customs were observed, was throwing herself into the preparations for the wedding with an enthusiasm which some folk were surprised to see in a recently widowed woman. Carrie, the only person able to see the frantic edge underlying the happy bustle of activity, was finding some things almost unbearably poignant.

Stroking one set of particularly good quality towels, Esther had come out with a pleased, 'These will last you a lifetime,' seemingly unaware of the pathos of the statement.

This morning, Carrie had stood back and watched her in animated discussion with the people at the City Bakeries about the wedding cake, and the little favours which were going to adorn it. Esther was determined to give her daughter as good a wedding as she could afford. At the same time, in a display of down-to-earth practicality which took the breath away, she was calculating how much money needed to be left to pay for another up-coming event: one which wouldn't include little silver slippers and bells and lucky horseshoes.

He deserved a treat. These were his last few days as a bachelor. He'd had his stag night, of course, but although a fair amount of drink had been consumed and a great many off-colour stories recounted and dirty jokes told, that had been a relatively sedate celebration. The presence of his father and various other older male relatives had seen to that.

The slope of the street flattened out. Matthew continued to walk purposefully towards Dumbarton Road. It was much better to look confident, not slink along in the shadow of the buildings like a thief.

It was early yet. Most people would still be finishing their tea. All the same, he was glad of the darkness of the evening, the inadequacy of the street lights and the wisps of November fog. He would hate to bump into Carrie or any of her friends tonight.

He felt the usual stirrings at the thought of his bride-to-be. She was so young and lovely, so fresh and untouched – so unlike the young women he was planning on spending the next hour or so with, tarts and strumpets all.

Mind you, they knew their trade. Over the years women like them had taught him a lot. Once they saw the colour of your money they were all over you. Quite literally. He crossed over the main road, his lips curving in anticipation. Tonight was a special occasion. Could he justify the expense of having two girls at once? The thought quickened his blood and his step.

Carrie would be shocked to the core if she knew his plans for the evening. Not that she would ever find out about any of this. Once they were married he wouldn't need the outlet. He was looking forward to doing some teaching himself . . .

That might give her a few shocks too, but it was only to be expected. She was a nice girl, after all, but at the same time she'd be anxious to please him. He turned into the side street. He was definitely going to have two of the strumpets tonight.

Carrie was wearing a grass skirt. Mary had fashioned it out of green crêpe paper, graciously decreeing that she might be allowed to wear her tennis skirt underneath, thus preserving some degree of maidenly modesty. At the moment, however, one of the other girls was kneeling at her feet, shortening the hems of the divided skirt with safety pins.

'They'll give you more money if they get a good flash o' leg. And you've got nice legs, Carrie. What's wrong wi' showing them off a wee bit?'

'It's November,' she muttered, doing her best to scowl at the image looking back at her from the long mirror on the front of the wardrobe. 'I'll freeze.'

'No, you'll not,' said Mary, coming into the front room carrying assorted bits and pieces over her arm. 'You might be a South Sea maiden, but we are letting you keep your jumper on,' she pointed out, looping three shell necklaces over Carrie's head.

'The alternative being?'

'Something your intended wouldn't care for one little bit,' said Mary, grinning wickedly. 'Here, take this.'

'My intended wouldn't care for any of this, I don't think,' she replied, trying to make sense of the piece of white cotton Mary had handed her. It had two straps and a large broderie anglaise frill. An apron?

'They don't go in for this sort of thing up the hill?'

'What d'you think? Mary, what on earth . . .'

Her friend took the material from her, shook it out and swung it up and on to Carrie's head, tying the straps in a large bow under her chin. It was an outsize baby's bonnet.

'There. What do you think?'

'The phrase "dog's breakfast" springs to mind.'

Esther, sitting on the edge of the bed and watching with great interest, chuckled. Carrie caught her eye in the mirror, and heaved a mournful sigh. 'I suppose I'll have to go along with it, Ma.'

'I think you will, pet,' responded Esther, her eyes twinkling.

The girls led Carrie along Dumbarton Road, making as much noise as possible. One of them had a tambourine, two of the others home-made drums: empty biscuit tins and wooden spoons. Mary was in charge of collecting donations for the happy couple – in a chamber pot, as tradition dictated.

'Chuck your change in the chanty!' she yelled happily.

'And I always thought you were such a nice refined girl,' said one man with a roguish wink as he emerged from one of the many pubs on their route. 'You too, Miss Burgess,' he said, taking in her costume.

Carrie winked back. She was beginning to enjoy herself. The noise had brought other drinkers outside, even some she recognised as men who, given half a chance, could drink for Scotland. They cheered her on, tossing jokes into the air and change into the chamber pot. It was the same all the way along the street.

At one hostelry it was suggested the girls ought to sing for their supper. Nothing daunted, Mary launched into *Sweet Sixteen And Never Been Kissed*, which had been a big hit round the dance halls a year or so before. She couldn't hold a tune, and the title prompted hoots of good-natured derision – which made it all the funnier.

When she had finished, one of the men watching came back with *Button Up Your Overcoat*. Everyone joined in. Considering the time of year, it was a good selection, although Carrie had to admit she wasn't feeling the cold. She'd even pushed up the sleeves of her jumper.

Despite the many voices, some of them rather tuneful, Mary's off-key notes were still managing to make themselves heard. Wondering if she was ever going to recover from the fit of the giggles she was having, Carrie swung round towards the pub, aware of a couple of people standing there. She hoped they were enjoying themselves too.

She found she was able to stop laughing rather more easily than she had anticipated. Hands behind his back, one leg bent up so that the sole of his boot rested flat against the wood panelling of the pub frontage, Ewen Livingstone was standing watching her. He didn't look as if he was enjoying himself.

'Hello,' said Carrie. 'How's it going?' Her heart sank when she realised who was standing next to him: Janice Muirhead, gazing at her out of sullen eyes.

'I'm perfectly fine, Miss Burgess,' he said. 'It's real kind o' you to ask.'

Janice giggled, but Ewen didn't crack a smile. He was giving Carrie the top-to-toe treatment, eyes lingering on her bare legs, visible through the paper strips of the grass skirt. He spoke again, his voice too loud. She was glad the impromptu choir had gone on to perform another number.

'No need to ask how it's going wi' you. You're obviously delir . . . delir . . .' He took a run at it. 'Obviously deliriously happy.'

It still hadn't come out quite right. Carrie took a couple of steps towards him. 'Have you been drinking?' Hit by the smell of alcohol on his breath, she reeled back in disgust, but his hand shot out.

'Is it any o' your business if I want to buy myself a wee drink?'

'A wee drink?' she asked contemptuously. 'More like a great big drink.'

His hand tightened, and she remembered how he had held her in the Quaker graveyard. If she hadn't put a stop to it, how far would he have gone that day? *You really think I'm that kind o' a man?* No, she hadn't thought so, but then he'd never struck her as the kind to take strong drink either. She was disappointed in him.

Even in drink he was still strong. His fingers were digging into the soft skin of her forearm like Chinese bracelets, the tests of stoicism they used to do at school.

'You're hurting my arm.'

The words of his reply were perfectly clear but softly spoken, intended for her ears alone:

'You're hurting my heart.'

For a frozen moment, they lost themselves in each other's eyes. Then Janice came sauntering forward.

'Come on, Ewen, this is boring. I thought you and me were going for a walk.' She laid a hand on his shoulder and smiled insolently at Carrie. 'Somewhere nice and quiet.'

She reached between the two of them, placing her free hand on the back of Ewen's head, pulling him round to face her. 'Give us a kiss, handsome.'

Carrie made an exclamation of disgust, and would have turned away, but he was still holding on to her. Janice, lips parted in readiness, stretched up and kissed him. She took her time about it. Ewen responded in kind, but his eyes kept flickering to Carrie, making sure she was watching. She had very little choice.

When Janice finally came up for air, he ignored her, his attention all on Carrie.

'Let go of me,' she said quietly.

'Oh, look, Carrie,' shrieked a voice from behind her. One of the girls had broken off in mid-song. 'It's your *fee-on-say*!'

Her arm was dropped. Janice pulled Ewen away. Carrie turned and saw Matt.

'What exactly do you think you're doing, Carrie?'

She laughed nervously. 'Hello, Matt. Where did you spring from?'

He brushed the question aside. 'Never mind that. What's all this?'

Somehow she had known he would disapprove. Which was, she supposed, why she had accidentally-on-purpose forgotten to mention to him that she was going out with the girls this evening.

'It's only a bit of fun, Matt.'

'Fun? Getting dressed up and begging for money in the street?'

'It's not begging,' she protested. 'It's a way for people to wish us good luck. Everyone does it.'

'You're not everyone,' he said sternly. 'You're the stationmaster's daughter.'

She laid a conciliatory hand on his dark sleeve. 'Och, Matt, my father would have loved all this.'

'Well, I don't, and in a few days' time I'll be your husband. So I'm taking you home right now so you can get out of that silly rig-out. Look at the state of you! And showing your legs off to every Tom, Dick and Harry too.'

He shook her hand off and stood there, waiting. Over his shoulder she could see Ewen and Janet, watching to see how things were going to develop. Mary, despite being out of earshot, must also have sensed that all was not well. Carrie was aware of her friend's anxious eyes on her.

In a few days' time I'll be your husband. I haven't promised to obey you yet, she thought mutinously. His brows were down, straight and angry lines over stormy eyes. He was so angry with her he hadn't even noticed that Ewen was standing a few yards away.

Mary appeared at her shoulder. 'Hello, Matthew,' she said politely. 'Everything all right, Carrie?' An undercurrent of anxiety ran through the simple question.

'I'm taking Caroline home, Mary.'

'Oh?' Mary's eyebrows flew up. 'Are you wanting to go home now, Carrie?'

No, she wasn't. However, this situation was only going to be resolved if one of them was prepared to back down. It wasn't going to be Matthew. That much was obvious. She really didn't want to have a major falling-out with him a matter of days before their wedding. It would upset her mother, for one thing.

Added to which, if she went meekly with him now, and Janice Muirhead used the brains she undoubtedly had to haul Ewen off somewhere, there would be no need for another, potentially rather more dangerous, confrontation to erupt.

'Let's call it a day, Mary. You were only going to tie me up to a lamp-post anyway, weren't you? I think I can live without that.'

Carrie tried to smile. She felt like bursting into tears.

On the day Caroline Burgess married Matthew Campbell, Ewen Livingstone went out with the express intention of getting himself blind drunk. He did it so quietly, sitting in a corner of the pub with some of the other surfaceman, that it was well on into the evening before Martin Sharkey noticed how far gone he was, and put a fatherly hand on his shoulder.

'Is it not about time you were heading for home, lad? I think you've had enough for one day.'

Talkative at last, Ewen began arguing with his foreman. Ignoring the half-coherent protests that another pint of heavy and maybe a wee whisky wouldn't do him any harm, Martin tipped the wink to another man who, like himself, had only had a couple of drinks. One on either side, they picked the boy up and frog-marched him to the half-glazed double doors of the pub.

Ewen gulped and swallowed hard as a fresh blast of December air hit him. The two men supporting him looked at each other. Before they could debate which of them was going to take him home and put him to bed, a girl who'd been leaning against a lamp-post came forward. She looked cold, as though she'd been waiting there for a while. A few flecks of snow swirled about her dark head.

'I'll make sure he gets home safe, Mr Sharkey.' She put her arm around Ewen's waist and he leaned against her, smiling stupidly.

'Janice! I knew ye wouldnae desert me, hen.'

Martin Sharkey knew the girl by sight – and reputation. It wasn't a good one. He looked at Ewen, one floppy arm draped heavily over Janice's shoulders.

'Promise me ye'll no' talk about Caroline Bloody Burgess's wedding dress,' he was saying, his words slurred with the drink. 'Or where she's goin' for her effin' honeymoon.'

'Not a word.'

'Good girl! That's all – that's all every other – every other lassie in Partick's been talking about a' day.' He scowled ferociously. The concentration involved in trying to get the words out was considerable. 'A wee bit boring, d'ye no' think, Janice?'

'Boring as hell,' the girl agreed, and Ewen beamed at her.

Jesus, Mary and Saint Joseph, thought Martin, why hadn't he spotted earlier on that the lad was set on drinking himself into oblivion today? It should have occurred to him. Over the last few weeks his young workmate had been as unhappy as he'd ever seen him. The boy needed some comforting, right enough. If this young lady was hell-bent on providing that, who was he to stop her?

Hell-bent was probably the right word. Good Catholic that he was, he watched their unsteady progress along the street and consoled himself by concluding that in his present state Ewen probably wasn't going to be capable of very much. A quick fumble up the nearest close would be the most Janice could hope for. Martin held out his hand, checking on how much snow was falling. Hopefully that and the snell breeze which was blowing would send the two of them scurrying indoors as well.

A few minutes later Janice was dragging Ewen through to the back court behind her own home. She pulled him out of the way of the cold air whistling through the close and leaned back against the wall. Taking his hand, she guided it up under her threadbare coat and skirt.

'French knickers,' he mumbled, as his fingers found warm female flesh.

'Easy feelers, Ewen. Help yourself. I don't mind.' She opened her mouth to his kiss, and pulled his other hand to her breasts.

He was very rough, but Janice giggled and undid the buttons of her blouse, allowing him even greater access. She seemed to like it.

He'd been this far before with a lassie. A little further, in fact, although never all the way. Meeting Caroline Burgess had arrested his sexual development. He'd had some half-baked idea of keeping himself pure for her. Pathetic. Stupid. Humiliating. Through the alcoholic haze, it came to him that it was only because of her he knew what the last word meant.

Janice's fingers were at the solid brass buckle of his belt. 'D'ye want to, Ewen?' she whispered. 'I'd let you, you know. I know what all you lads are after, and I'm willing to give it. Not like that stuck-up cow Carrie Burgess.'

The hand between her legs tightened convulsively. Janice yelped in pain. 'Ewen! That hurts.'

'Sorry,' he mumbled. He moved both of his hands and placed them carefully on either side of her head, his sweaty palms flat against the cold and damp stone of the building.

'Go on,' Janice said in a wheedling tone, 'it'll be quite safe. I've got some johnnies with me. Do you know how to put them on?' She giggled again. 'I can help you. I've had a lot of practice.'

He was a child again. About eight years old. He'd found these funny balloon things in the drawer under the box bed, had taken them out and started playing with them His mother, coming back into the house after hanging some washing out in the back court, had smacked him hard.

'I need all of those!' she'd cried.

Then she had burst into tears and hugged him to her, rocking him backwards and forwards in her arms. That's when she had told him what she did for a living.

And right now he was no better than any of those men he had learned to hate so much. He was just another drunk pressing some girl up against a cold hard wall, seeking release without caring at all about the person who was providing it. Squalid. That was another big word that he knew thanks to Caroline Bloody Burgess.

He took his hands from the wall and straightened up. 'Ye shouldnae sell yourself so cheap, Janice. You're worth more than this. Goodnight, hen.'

Perplexed, she stood and watched him go, placing one foot precisely in front of the other in the over-careful walk of the drunk.

He made it to his own street before he was sick, the vomit rising in his throat so fast he barely had time to make it to the gutter. When the spasm had passed, he could think of only one place he wanted to go.

His first attempt at vaulting the wall of the old graveyard got him nowhere. He lay sprawled on the ground, winded. He succeeded at the third attempt, but he scraped his side on the way down the wall, his shirt and jacket riding up and exposing sensitive skin to the rough stone. That was going to hurt like buggery in the morning, but at the moment he was feeling no pain. No physical pain, at any rate.

He sat down cross-legged in a corner, bowed his head and wrapped his arms about himself. Like a cowering child, he was trying to make himself as small as possible. This place had always been his bolt-hole. When the nameless ache inside him became too much to cope with, when the knowledge of where the money came from to feed and clothe him overwhelmed him, he had always come here. The old Quakers didn't judge him, or his mother.

He hated everybody, himself most of all. He hated Janice. He hated Matthew Campbell. He hated Caroline Bloody Burgess. No, he didn't. Everyone else, aye, but not her.

She'd be Mrs Matthew Campbell by now. That swine was probably making love to her right this minute. That wouldn't be a sordid fumble up against a close wall. Ewen knew exactly where she was spending her wedding night. Since Esther had been showing off about it for weeks, overwhelmed by Charles Campbell's generosity in paying for the honeymoon, everybody in Partick did.

He could visualise them in their de-luxe suite in their luxurious hotel on the Ayrshire coast. He'd never been in such an establishment, but he'd seen plenty like it at the pictures. The room would be enormous and there would be vases of flowers everywhere. The bed would be huge too and she'd be lying in it waiting for her new husband, her bonnie hair a startling splash of colour against a snowy white pillow.

Matthew Campbell was climbing in beside her. She was turning to him, lips parted, arms open and welcoming . . . With a sob, Ewen swung round and smashed his fist against the graveyard wall. Shite! That had hurt enough to penetrate the fog in his brain.

Welcoming the pain, he did it again. He punched the wall a third time before some sort of sense began to prevail. If he hurt his hand real bad, he wouldn't be able to work. If he didn't work, he wouldn't get paid. He had to live, although he wasn't quite sure why that mattered any more.

He put his grazed and bloody knuckles to his mouth. Christ, they'd probably hurt for days, maybe even weeks. Good. That would remind him of her every moment of the day, whenever he curled his fingers round the shaft of his hammer, or lifted a shovel.

He wouldn't be able to write for a while, but why should he ever want to write again anyway? He'd been practising his skills before she'd gone back to Matthew Campbell, making several attempts at writing a letter to her. He'd even thought about trying to write a wee poem. She liked poems.

His knuckles were stinging now, but it wasn't the pain which was making the tears roll down his face. It was the thought of what he had lost. She had never been his in the first place, but there had been moments, during the happiest summer of his life, when he had dared to hope.

It was winter now. The wind had died down, but the flecks of snow had became large flakes, floating gently down on to the scrubby grass in front of him. In here, they would probably lie for a while. He turned the collar of his reefer jacket up in automatic response, but he wasn't really paying any attention to the weather.

He slid down the wall and rolled over on to his side, drawing his knees up so that he lay like a baby. Eventually, cradled by the bones and dust of the old Quakers, he slept. The soft snow settled on him like a lacy blanket.

All the cosier because of the snow dashing against the long windows, Carrie snuggled deeper under the covers. Matt, propped up on his elbow beside her, was looking amused.

'Liked it then, did you?'

'You could say that,' she murmured. 'Can we do it again?'

He laughed and tapped her nose with one long finger. 'Not going to wait to be asked, my little hussy?'

* * *

She did a lot more than that, baffling the doctors by holding out several months longer than they had predicted. She spent the last two of those months up the hill, despite Shona Campbell's clear reluctance to have a dying woman in her house. In any other family, there might have been an almighty row about it, but that wasn't the way things were done in North Gardner Street.

In a tone of sweet reason, Matthew's mother had asked if it wouldn't be better all round for Mrs Burgess to go into the Infirmary. Easier for everybody, surely. Charles Campbell, as was usual when anything serious was being discussed, was nowhere to be seen.

'Especially you, Caroline,' Shona said, surveying her heavily pregnant daughter-in-law with cool and critical eyes. 'You really shouldn't be going out and about so much in your condition.'

Tired and emotional and exhausted from toiling up and down to White Street to sit with her mother all day and every day, Carrie looked at Matt, a mute appeal in her eyes. Part of her could see very well how difficult it was for him, caught between his mother and his wife like this, but she desperately needed him to support her. He walked over to her, gently touched her face.

'You're very pale,' he said. 'You need to rest more.' His smile was wry. 'If your mother goes into the Western you'll just struggle along there every day, won't you?' Without waiting for an answer, he turned and spoke to his mother. 'Mrs Burgess can have my old room.' He lowered his voice, said something Carrie wasn't supposed to hear, 'It'll not be for long.'

But it was for longer than they all thought – except Carrie herself. She knew exactly how long her mother would hold out. And so it was that as new life began to make its way into the world in one room, across the hall another was slowly ebbing away. Esther lived long enough to hold the baby, although her frail grip had to be supported by her daughter's loving arms.

A few hours after the birth Matt carried his wife through to her mother, laying her gently on the bed beside her. Then he came back with a shawl-wrapped bundle.

'A wee boy,' he said, leaning over and placing his son in Esther's embrace. She was propped up on a heap of pillows, Carrie's arm about the painfully thin and sharp shoulders.

'Och . . . he's so bonnie . . .' Esther's eyes flickered. Her strength was fading fast.

'Aye, Ma,' whispered Carrie, wondering how much emotion a heart could take before it split in two. Joy for her son, aching grief for her mother. She glanced up at Matt, and he gave her a little nod. They'd discussed this before he'd brought her through. 'We're going to call him Archie,' she said gently.

The bony face lit up. 'That's . . . a . . . grand . . . name . . .' Esther smiled down at her grandson. 'Archie . . .' she repeated.

She said that name one more time before the end. It came later that night. Carrie was by her side, holding the baby. Matt stood sentinel behind her chair, one hand resting lightly on her shoulder. He'd given up his attempts to persuade her to go back to their room and lie down several hours ago. She felt his fingers tighten and her head snapped up. Something was happening.

Esther had been motionless for hours, her face impassive. Suddenly her eyes opened wide and a smile of great sweetness suffused her face. She raised her arms, as though she were greeting someone.

'Archie . . .' she said, her voice clear and strong.

There was a quick little breath. Then the room fell silent.

PART II
1937

Chapter 18

Carrie checked the time by the beautiful old grandfather clock which had spent much of its life in the mansion a few hundred yards away on Partickhill Road which had been her father-in-law's childhood home. *A piece of flotsam salvaged from the wreckage of the family fortunes after the fall of the house of Campbell.*

One mocking eyebrow raised, a self-deprecating smile on his handsome face, that was how Charles Campbell always referred to the family's losses in the stock market crash. He had a way with words. He earned some sort of an income at it, writing the occasional article for newspapers and magazines.

Given the erratic nature of that income, the comfort of her surroundings and the fact that he had paid for her honeymoon, Carrie assumed that the fall of the house of Campbell hadn't been total. Presumably there had been some investments left which enabled Matt's parents to live in reasonable style without either of them appearing to exert themselves very much.

Both Charles and Shona Campbell spent most of their time socialising. She played bridge, attended luncheon parties and had friends round for afternoon tea. He played a lot of golf. In the evenings there were cocktail parties and visits to the theatre. With that example before him, Carrie regarded it as all the more commendable that Matt had chosen to follow a career.

She suspected there had been some quixotic gallantry in his deciding to go out and work for a living, a desire to do something concrete about the economic disaster which had befallen his family. That seemed entirely honourable, and for his sake, it distressed her that his mother didn't see it that way. Shona Campbell was less than impressed with the social status of her son's occupation.

Carrie was quite sure she was even less impressed with her daughter-in-law's social standing. That had come as a bit of a shock. The Burgess family had enjoyed a certain position in their own community, a respect earned through Archie's job and the way he'd carried it out. As far as Shona Campbell and many of her friends up the hill here were concerned, you only seemed to be worthy of their attention if you didn't work for a living. Carrie found that attitude hard to understand and even harder to stomach.

The gilded Roman numerals on the clock face were showing twenty-past four. There was no need to worry about Matt just yet. Shoes kicked off, sitting on the hearthrug with her back against an armchair for support, Carrie stretched her legs out in front of the cosy but well-guarded fire burning in the elegant fireplace. The meeting at Partick Burgh Hall wasn't due to finish until half-past.

She glanced at her son, playing with his building blocks on the rug beside her. At least she could keep him safe. Her eyes lingered fondly on the dark waves of Archie's hair, so like his father's. She wondered if the new baby would have the same colouring or take after herself. Maybe she'd have a girl this time. That would be nice, although another boy would be fine too, especially if he turned out to be as happy a baby as Archie.

He looked so adorable in the wee yellow romper-suit with farmyard animals embroidered on the front and the collar. All her own work. She had very little else to do with her time in this house. She'd be a lot busier when the new baby arrived. That great event was still over four months away, well into the new year.

The new baby's soon-to-be big brother was concentrating ferociously at the moment, his normally smooth forehead furrowed and his small pink tongue sticking out of the corner of his mouth. He was trying to build a tower out of his blocks. He could get it two-high, but the addition of a third brick always made it wobble and fall over. Carrie had tried to demonstrate the proper technique to him, but now she was quite literally sitting on her hands. Observing his frustration each time the tower fell, she was desperate to help him, but knew he was determined to perform the task unaided.

'By myself, Mammy!' he had told her ten minutes ago, firmly pushing her helping hands away with his own chubby little fingers. Stubborn and independent. She couldn't imagine where he got that from.

She lifted her head to the large bay window overlooking the tiny but neat front garden and street. Above the beautiful leaded-glass screens which covered the bottom of the panes she could see that the dreich December day was shaping up into a foul night, the rain beginning to lash against the glass. That was good.

Matt had assured her stewards would prevent what he called troublemakers from actually attending the rally, but Carrie knew Partick. Matt's troublemakers – socialists, communists, trade unionists and other opponents of Sir Oswald Mosley's fascist message – were incensed that his Blackshirt supporters were even being permitted to hold a meeting in the Burgh Hall this Saturday afternoon.

They would be waiting outside for them, probably conducting

their own impromptu meeting at Partick's traditional speakers' corner on Peel Street. Both sides had some great orators. That could get folk awful riled up. Look what had happened in the East End of London last year when Mosley himself had addressed the crowd. There had been a riot and people had got hurt.

A miserable day would hopefully make it more likely that a lot of people would slope off home before anything nasty could develop between the opposing factions. The whole thing, and especially Matthew's involvement with it, dismayed Carrie terribly.

Disillusioned with the Labour Party, his own socialism was a thing of the past, as was his membership of the National Union of Railwaymen. At first she had remonstrated with him. Didn't he know what was going on in Germany and Italy? How could he support such an anti-democratic group as the Blackshirts?

He had retaliated by asking her if she really thought democracy was working. Was it doing anything to end the misery of the Depression? Uncertain of the answer to that, she had held her tongue and hoped that, in the fullness of time, he would see the error of his ways. Hating herself for the disloyal thought, she had reflected that his support for left-wing views had also been short-lived.

His parents voted Conservative in the same way as they got up in the morning, went to church each Sunday and knew exactly which were the correct knives and forks to use. It was an article of faith, and quite preposterous that anyone in their social circle should think of holding different views. Sometimes Carrie wondered if Matt's socialism had simply been a method of rebelling against them. Sometimes she wondered if his choice of her as a wife had been an act of rebellion . . .

Her gaze landed on her mother-in-law, sitting at her writing bureau attending to her correspondence: giving and receiving invitations to the social events which were so important to her. There might be a terrible civil war raging in Spain, fascists, communists and socialists fighting each other in the streets of Britain and the pessimists insisting that a war with Germany was simply a matter of time, but Shona Campbell's chief worry still seemed to be finding the ideal cocktail dress.

Archie was tugging at Carrie's skirt, beaming with pride. He had built his tower at last.

'Clever boy!' she cried. 'Three blocks high! Well done, wee man.' She leaned forward and dropped a kiss on his smooth hair.

Should she call on Shona to witness this great event, the possible first signs of Archie's future as the foremost engineer of his generation? As she was contemplating it, he swiped his hand against the bricks and knocked his achievement down.

'Och, Archie!'

'Build it again,' he announced happily and set to doing exactly that.

It was probably just as well. Shona's interest in her grandson was pretty limited. Fishing for information, Carrie had found out that Matthew had been brought up by a succession of nursemaids. The picture which emerged was of a young boy always taking second place to his parents' social life. She had learned not to attempt to discuss the topic with him. He wouldn't hear a word of criticism against his family.

People called his mother beautiful, but Carrie thought Shona Campbell too often looked as if a piece of fish was slowly decomposing under her nose. Like now, when she twisted round in her chair and looked disapprovingly at her daughter-in-law sitting on the floor. Too bad. As her pregnancy advanced, Carrie found it one of the most comfortable postures to adopt. Shona seemed to find most things to do with the getting or rearing of children distasteful, so Carrie was surprised to hear her posing a direct question about one aspect of it.

'Use baby milk? Oh, no, I'm going to breast-feed again. I've already decided.'

Matt's mother closed her discreetly made-up eyes for a second, looking pained. *Breast* obviously counted as a vulgar word in her vocabulary. 'Bottle-feeding is so much more up-to-date and convenient, Caroline.'

Carrie shook her vibrant head. Past the morning sickness stage, she was beginning to bloom, skin and hair shining again.

'I disagree,' she said pleasantly. 'Breast-feeding is a lot more convenient.' Maybe if she kept using the word, Shona would let the subject go. Some hopes. All three members of the Campbell family were like terriers when they got their teeth into something. A somewhat unfortunate metaphor to use when discussing breast-feeding.

'It's unhygienic.' The invisible decomposing fish was firmly in position.

'It's the most hygienic thing there is.' Despite her best efforts, Carrie's voice had sharpened. She was fed-up having to justify everything she did to this cold woman.

Shona wrinkled her elegant nose in obvious distaste. 'Don't you think that nursing the baby yourself is rather . . . lower-class?'

'No, I don't. I think it's natural. You'd have to admit that Archie thrived on it.'

Sensing his mother's gaze, Archie, still in training for his future as a great engineer, looked up briefly and gave her his characteristic wrinkled-nose smile. It was horribly reminiscent of the gesture his grandmother had just made. I'll not hold that against you, son, thought Carrie with the grim and private humour which had saved her sanity several times over the past two years.

Shona stood up in one graceful movement. 'Don't you think Matthew would prefer you to bottle-feed?'

'No, I don't.'

'Have you discussed it with him?'

Mind your own business was the phrase which came to mind, but there was no point in causing trouble unnecessarily. 'Of course.'

'You're terribly stubborn, Caroline. I can't think why your parents brought you up to be so defiant.' Shona gathered up her letters and swept out of the room.

Carrie put her arms under Archie's shoulders and lifted him on to her lap. 'Well, young man, I think I've just been paid a compliment.'

'Compliment,' he repeated.

'Clever boy,' she said automatically, but didn't try to stop him when he squirmed out of her arms and went back to his blocks. Carrie rose slowly to her feet.

'Where Mammy going?'

She laid a reassuring hand on his head. 'Only over to the window, my wee sugar dumpling. I'm going to watch for your daddy coming home.'

She stood in the wood-panelled bay, one eye on the outside world, one eye checking that Archie stayed where he was. At fifteen months, he was becoming alarmingly mobile. She had to watch him like a hawk. The spacious and roomy flat had too many interesting corners ripe for exploration by an inquisitive small boy who was beginning to find his feet.

Spacious and roomy it might be, but it wasn't big enough for Shona Campbell. Like her husband, she'd been used to better things. When it was just the family, she referred to where Carrie and Archie were at the moment as the morning room. When there were guests for dinner it metamorphosed into the drawing room. Brought up in a simpler home, Carrie often found her tongue tripping over the two designations for the one room, a mistake which always put her on the receiving end of a look of withering scorn from her mother-in-law.

She put her hands behind her and leaned back, gazing out at the increasingly wild night. Her twentieth birthday was still a few months away, but here she was, the mother of a toddler and expecting a second child. She'd have preferred a longer gap between the two, but Matt had been horrified when she had mumbled an embarrassed suggestion in the days following Archie's birth that they should practise some form of birth control once they resumed marital relations.

She hadn't known exactly how to put it, and had blurted out

something about French letters. He'd gone on at some length about her using such a coarse expression, had expressed some surprise, and considerable disapproval, that she should even know what it meant.

Carrie sighed. Then she straightened up. The man in question was coming along the road. As far as she could tell from here he looked unscathed.

'Here comes your daddy,' she said. 'Hopefully he's kept himself out of trouble. Let's get to him first before your grandma manages to cause any either.'

'Daddy trouble,' said Archie. 'Grandma trouble.'

Carrie scooped him up and carried him towards the front door. She'd have to give this up soon. He was getting too heavy.

'You know,' she told him, 'it's all very well you being such a good speaker, but I may have to stop confiding in you if you're going to become such a blabbermouth. And your grandma is a sweet and wonderful woman.'

Well, the other one was, she thought, absolving herself from having told her son a fib.

Archie chortled, and started playing with her hair.

'Mother says you told her you're not going to bottle-feed the next baby, that you want to feed him yourself.'

'Him?' asked Carrie, sitting on their bed taking off her stockings. 'It might be a girl, you know.'

'You do realise she found it quite distasteful the last time,' said Matt, ignoring her attempt to divert the conversation.

'*She* wasn't actually doing it. *I* was.'

'Don't be dim, Carrie, you know what I mean. There was the occasion when you sat and fed Archie while Mother's friends were here.'

She stood up and shrugged into her nightie. 'I was dog-tired, Matt. They were all women. I was sitting by the fire and they were at the wee table in the corner playing cards. I had a twin set on and I pushed the jumper up a bit and the cardigan hid most of the rest. There was practically nothing to be seen.'

'That's not what Mother says. She was deeply embarrassed by the whole thing.'

Struggling to hold on to her temper, Carrie folded back the covers and got into bed. 'I'm not really sure it's any of your mother's business, Matt.'

He began unbuttoning his shirt. 'I should have thought you would have appreciated her taking an interest, what with your own mother no longer being with us.'

Carrie slid down on to her side, turning her back to him. Mention

'I'll be gentle,' he promised, 'and I thought the later on in pregnancy you are, the safer it is anyway.'

'I knew I shouldn't have let you read those books the lady doctor loaned me.'

He chuckled, and smothered her protests with kisses.

Afterwards, he fell asleep quickly but Carrie lay awake for a while. Sometimes, despite the spaciousness and the high-ceilinged rooms, she felt stifled here. In the summer she sat out as much as possible. There was a good-sized back garden, with a lawn and flowers kept neat and tidy by a gardener paid for by all the residents of the building.

It was pretty, but a little too regimented for Carrie's taste. She didn't believe flowers were meant to stand in neat rows, like soldiers on parade. She missed the clumps of lupins and marguerites and red hot pokers which had adorned the garden of the station house like splashes of colour on an artist's palette. She missed her father's vegetable patch. She missed the trains.

She had told Matt once, half joking, but part of her completely serious, that she found it difficult to live in a house which didn't shake from time to time. He had looked at her as if she were mad and read her a lecture on how grateful they should be for living in such a nice house well away from the noise and dirt caused by trains and coal trucks.

She listened to him snoring quietly by her side. That was the trouble, of course, he was too comfortable here. She had become a wife and mother, her life changed immeasurably from how it had been before, but Matt had continued to be the son of the household in which he'd grown up. His life had gone on much as it had been before. He had no real responsibilities to cope with.

She would have to use her powers of persuasion on him. A luxury flat was a pipe-dream, not something she really fancied anyway. She'd rather move down the hill, be among people she knew. There were lots of good houses, nice closes and respectable streets. It was simply a matter of finding the right one. Maybe she could get somewhere near the railway. That would be her ideal, much better than any luxury flat.

Up here on the hill it was only at night, when everything else had fallen silent, that she heard the occasional train in the distance. She could hear one now. The sound was absurdly comforting in spite of the memories it brought with it.

On the day she married Matthew she had made a conscious decision not to think about him, but there were unguarded moments, especially at times like this, when Ewen Livingstone stole back into her head like a thief in the night.

of her parents never failed to bring a tear to her eye. Lately she'd been feeling the pain of their loss acutely, with an added dimension which gave it the sharpest of edges. Her mother could have helped and advised her with Archie, shared the pleasure of all the little milestones as he grew and developed. Nor did it take much effort of imagination to visualise a slightly older version of her son helping his grandfather in the garden of the station house.

'I find it a bit distasteful myself, Carrie,' Matt had come round her side of the bed, was pulling the tail of his shirt out from his trousers. Lost in memories and a longing for what now could never be, she looked up blankly.

'Distasteful?'

'When you were feeding Archie, you didn't want me to touch you. Here, I mean.' He trailed his fingertips across her breasts. 'You fed him for nine months. That's a long time for a man to be deprived.'

'It's the best start in life, Matt. Surely that's what you want for our children?'

He tossed his shirt into a corner. 'You're so stubborn, Carrie.'

'That's what your mother said.'

'And? Shift over a wee bit,' he said, sitting down on the edge of the bed to finish removing his trousers.

'And nothing. Matt,' she continued, 'what happened about us getting a place of our own?'

'How many times do I have to say this, Carrie?' he asked irritably. 'Not till we can afford somewhere really nice.'

'The house in White Street was nice enough.'

'No, it wasn't, and you hated that old range, so take that butter-wouldn't-melt-in-my-mouth look off your face, Mrs Campbell Junior. I was thinking of something more like those new flats they're building along at Anniesland.'

'Kelvin Court? You've got delusions of grandeur, Mr Campbell Junior.'

He grinned. It transformed him back into the man she'd fallen in love with. 'Are you coming in this side?' she asked.

'Only if you're going to make it worth my while.'

He stood up to place his trousers over the back of a chair, divested himself of socks and underwear and sent them in the same direction as his shirt. Then he put out the light and got in beside her.

'That's your answer to everything, isn't it?' she asked, but she had rolled over to face him and her hand was already resting on his bare shoulder.

'I don't normally hear you complaining,' he murmured. His own hand was busily seeking, pushing up her nightdress, roaming warm and intimate over her smooth skin.

'Matt . . . I'm not sure if we should . . . what about the baby?'

'We're married,' she told him happily. 'We're allowed to do it whenever we like.'

'So we are.'

He pushed the covers down, exposing her breasts to his hungry gaze. 'It doesn't embarrass you if I look at you like this?'

She shook her shining head, her smile widening when he leaned over to plant a kiss on each breast. She laid a hand on the thick dark waves of his hair.

'You know what is going to embarrass me? Us going to bed so early tonight. I'm a bit worried about facing our fellow guests at breakfast tomorrow.'

He looked up at her, his eyes darkening. There was no amusement left in his face now, only passion.

'Who says we're going to make breakfast?' he asked, and bent his head once more to his work.

He had left Partick. That much she knew. In the middle of his first week back at work after their honeymoon, Matt had come home with an announcement. 'Your wee friend's slung his hook. Gone off to seek his fortune elsewhere, apparently.'

Thinking it more diplomatic to evince little interest in the information, she hadn't asked for any details. She had also told herself sternly that she didn't need them. Later on, when her curiosity got the better of her, she had spoken discreetly to Mary. Could Douglas maybe find out where Ewen was? She'd like to write to him, make sure he was all right. Mary gave her an old-fashioned look and asked if she thought that was wise. Carrie hadn't pressed the point.

It was too late to do it now. Douglas and Mary had married in the summer – Carrie had been matron of honour – and gone to live near Fort William. Douglas was in charge of the signal box at a small highland station and they'd been allocated a railway house. Mary's letters were a joy to read, full of tales of her new neighbours and the beauty of their surroundings and how she and Douglas were knocking their garden into shape. They were really looking forward to eating their own vegetables next summer. Carrie would have to visit. Wee Archie would love it. Matthew was welcome to come too, of course.

Carrie rolled from her back on to her side, and stretched an arm across her sleeping husband. She'd been disappointed by Ewen's behaviour that night before her wedding, but what stuck in her memory wasn't the sheer awfulness of being forced to watch him kissing Janice Muirhead or seeing him the worse for drink.

What she remembered was a handful of softly spoken words. *You're hurting my heart.* She could hear him saying them, see the bleakness in his wintry eyes. He must have been so unhappy . . .

She hoped he'd got over her. She hoped he was keeping up his reading and writing. She hoped he'd met a nice girl. As long as she wasn't called Janice Muirhead. To the best of her knowledge, however, Janice was still swanning about Partick.

Carrie yawned and snuggled into Matt's warm body. She imagined that some men might be put off by their wives being pregnant, but it didn't seem to bother him at all. Quite the reverse. He was a wonderful lover, more passionate than ever. Some of the things he liked to do and tried to coax her into doing . . . well. She suspected they might make even Janice Muirhead blush.

Chapter 19

'Aye, only the one son. I think she tried it the once and didnae like it! Mind you, he's got a wean already and there's another on the way, so maybe he takes after his faither . . . the old goat!'

Carrie, approaching the kitchen door, unannounced and unheard, turned smartly about – or as smartly as a woman in the sixth month of pregnancy could – and headed back to the morning room. She could make herself a cup of tea later.

What she had overheard the daily say to whoever was in the kitchen with her hadn't come as much of a surprise. She had long since put her father-in-law down as having a roving eye. As for Shona trying it once and not liking it – well, Carrie knew exactly what the woman meant.

She put it out of her mind, having other fish to fry today – more or less literally. Heartily sick of eating cold evening meals, she'd decided there was going to be something really tasty for tea tonight, cooked by her own fair hand. The daily was having the afternoon off, which would give Carrie the kitchen to herself, and she was planning a wee foray out to Byres Road to buy the ingredients. The January day was crisp but sunny. The frost on the pavements would soon melt and Archie would enjoy the expedition as much as she would, wrapped up snugly in his pushchair.

There were also guests coming round this Friday evening: Matthew's Uncle Roddy, a journalist on a Glasgow newspaper, and his colleague – according to Matt also his ladyfriend – Josephine Shaw. Carrie liked them both. They were friendly and open and always great company. She was sure they would appreciate a good hot meal on a chilly winter's night.

Shona Campbell's welcome to her much younger brother would no doubt be as cold as one of her collations. She disapproved of his relationship with his colleague – whatever it actually was – and made her feelings all too clear. Carrie found the frigid politeness her mother-in-law displayed towards the poised young woman quite embarrassing. Picking up on the silent messages flashing between Roderick Cunningham and Josephine Shaw last time they'd visited, she suspected they laughed it off once they were alone together. However, once or twice she felt sure she had seen real hurt in Miss Shaw's clear grey eyes.

Her greatest sin seemed to be not speaking with the right accent. Although she never mentioned her family, it was obvious she came from a humble background. It was equally obvious that Roderick was immensely proud of her and her achievements. He was always telling them about some great article she'd written, or some story she'd uncovered – usually to the accompaniment of Miss Shaw herself telling him to shut up.

Shona remained unimpressed. Her brother was letting the side down. Socially, Josephine Shaw was beneath him. Which is probably why she and I get on so well, thought Carrie ruefully.

Roderick also committed the unforgivable sin of having a career which he took seriously. That didn't stop him joking about it and almost everything else in his life. Carrie hadn't known him for very long before she recognised his flippant manner for what it was: a smokescreen he threw up to hide his true feelings.

After lunch, feeling a bit like Christopher Columbus going off in search of America, she betook herself to the fishmonger's in Byres Road which her mother had always declared to be the best in Glasgow. Its marble slab presented Carrie with a cornucopia of fruits of the sea. She chose some luscious-looking haddock and then headed for the greengrocers to buy vegetables and cooking apples. She took her time about it, enjoying the bustling atmosphere of the busy street and the feeling of being out in the world again.

When they got back to North Gardner Street – she could never really bring herself to call it home – she put Archie down for his nap and set to work. The menu was fish in white sauce followed by apple crumble and custard. She made the dessert first, then prepared as much of the main course as could be done in advance.

Carrie laid the fish in the bottom of a large enamel ashet and poured the freshly prepared white sauce over it. She peeled the potatoes, cut them into slices and parboiled them. She would fry them just before serving up the meal. At this time of year the peas had to come out of a tin, but she scraped and chopped carrots and left them to steep in a pan on top of the stove. Once everything was completed to her satisfaction she went through to check on Archie.

He was still sound asleep. That gave her time to have a quick wash and change her clothes. Taking clean underwear out of a drawer, she came upon the canteen of cutlery which held her mother's fish knives and forks. They would provide the perfect finishing touch.

She was in the kitchen washing them when she heard the front door of the flat open. At precisely the same moment, the child inside her began to move. The sensation always made her laugh with delight. She looked up expectantly. It was unlikely that Matt had been let off early, but you never knew. It was his father who put his head round the kitchen door.

'Something smells good,' he said appreciatively.

Carrie beamed at him. 'The baby's kicking me,' she said, wanting to share the pleasure with somebody.

Charles Campbell was beside her in an instant. Before she had quite realised what he intended, his hands were on her stomach. She tried not to recoil. He was the baby's grandfather after all.

'Why, so he is!'

She smiled nervously, wondering when he was going to take his hands away. He looked closely into her face. 'You're looking forward to the new baby coming?'

'Oh, aye. Of course.'

'You're a good little mother to your boy,' he said. 'I'm sure it's hard work sometimes.'

Carrie shrugged. 'I enjoy being with Archie. It's a pleasure.'

Her father-in-law was standing awfully close to her. 'I hope the getting of him gave you as much pleasure. This one, too,' he added, beginning gently to stroke her abdomen.

She swallowed. She hoped he didn't mean what she thought he meant. She also really wished he would take his hands off her. He lifted one of them, but it only travelled as far as her face.

'I hope my son's being good to you, Caroline.'

'M-Matt's very good to me,' she managed. Maybe he'd leave her alone if she pretended to misunderstand what he was on about.

'I'm very glad to hear it,' he murmured. 'I'd like to think the ability to keep a woman happy runs in the family.'

The door bell rang. She felt dizzy with relief.

'What a pity. Just when you and I were getting to know each other better.' He gave her cheek two soft little slaps. 'Another time, my dear.'

Carrie stood staring after him. Surely she had misunderstood. He was calling something from the hall. 'Our guests have arrived.'

She put a smile on her face and went out to meet them.

'My favourite niece-in-law!' cried Roderick.

'Your only niece-in-law, I think.'

'Not the point, dear girl. Keeping well, I trust?'

He kissed her warmly on the cheek and gave her a hug. She'd been taken aback when he had first greeted her that way, but his exuberance had never made her feel uncomfortable. It was the way he was. Her family and their friends had never gone in much for kisses and hugs, but posh people were different, she knew. Maybe she was over-reacting to what had happened in the kitchen.

'Can I get you a drink?' she asked, turning to include Miss Shaw in the conversation. She was standing back, looking wryly amused.

'Those are the most beautiful words I've heard all day,' said Roderick. 'You're an absolute angel, young Mrs Campbell. I should have brought you some flowers.' He paused for dramatic effect, lifted her hand and bestowed a delicate kiss upon it. 'Only no bloom could hope to match your own glow.'

'Stop hamming it up, Roddy,' said Josephine Shaw. She came forward to say hello to Carrie. 'You've been cooking?'

'Yes.' She frowned. 'I hope you both like fish.'

'We love it. There's a new restaurant specialising in it not far from our office. Mr Cunningham would be there every evening if I didn't occasionally remind him he's now a wage slave and no longer has a limitless private income.'

Roderick adopted an air of immense and wounded dignity. 'I'll have you know that I'm proud to call myself a member of the working classes.'

Josephine Shaw put her hands on her hips. 'Away and boil your head and make soup with it, Roddy. Come the revolution you'll be one of the first up against the wall.'

He grinned at her. Carrie laughed. She loved the way this pair were with each other. She had often privately wondered if they *were* more than just good friends. Despite his theatrical manner, there was nothing unmanly about Roderick's broad shoulders and handsome face. Once, watching him as he glanced at Miss Shaw and thought himself unobserved, Carrie had seen a look in his eyes which was not only all-male, but also full of a kind of wistful longing.

'Anything we can do to help?' he asked. 'Set the table or something?'

'Most of it's done, but you could put the cutlery out for me, if you like.'

'Nae bother,' said Miss Shaw, turning at the sound of a key in the lock.

'Ah,' said Charles, 'it's my son and heir. Now we're only waiting for Shona to complete the party.'

Out of sight of his brother-in-law, Roderick rolled his eyes at Carrie. She wondered, not for the first time, how the same parents could have produced a brother and sister who were so different from each other.

'You cooked this yourself?'

'Isn't she clever, Shona?' asked Roderick. He lifted a crystal goblet to his lips and took a healthy swig of the white wine Charles had poured out for everybody except Carrie and Archie. The baby was sitting between his parents, laughing at the faces his great-uncle was pulling at him from the opposite side of the table. Carrie was aware that Matt was very quiet. He seemed to have something on his mind.

Having checked three times that the piece of fish she'd chosen for Archie had absolutely no bones in it, she placed it in his porringer which was lying beside her own plate. The small dish already contained some chopped up peas and carrots. She cut a couple of slices of potato, added them to the fish and placed the porringer on the tray of the high chair, between Archie's own knife, fork and spoon. He was beginning to manage them quite well.

'What?' She had missed the question. Her mother-in-law repeated it, pronouncing each word as though she were talking to a person of limited intelligence.

'Where did the fish come from?'

'The sea?' suggested Roderick. 'Ow!' He turned and glared at Josephine Shaw. That reminded Carrie of Mary and Douglas. Oh, how she wished she was sitting round a table with them!

'The fishmonger's in Byres Road,' she said in response to Shona's question.

'You went out shopping, when you're so obviously *expecting*?'

'I didn't realise it was something I was supposed to be ashamed of,' Carrie said evenly, although her temper was flaring. 'Matthew and I are married, you know.'

Shona drew her breath in sharply. Her son's head snapped up. Charles Campbell, public face firmly in place, looked pained. Roderick and Josephine gazed sympathetically at Carrie.

'What on earth are these?' Shona had picked up one of Esther's fish knives. She turned it over in her hand, examining it as if it were a laboratory specimen.

'They were m-my m-mother's,' stuttered Carrie, realising too late that she must have committed some social gaffe. 'I thought they'd help make the meal special.'

'Don't you know anything?' The cultured voice was as icy as the January night, held at bay by the heavy curtains drawn across the windows of the dining room. 'No one with any breeding eats fish other than with two forks. They're not even silver. For heaven's sake, take them away.'

She dropped the knife on to the tablecloth and made an elaborate gesture of distaste which reminded Carrie of Matt. Both mother and son had a tendency to overdo the dramatics on occasions like these. She was trying to stay angry. It seemed preferable to bursting into tears. Her mother had been so proud of her fish knives and forks . . .

She wished somebody would say something. Somebody did. It was Roderick, his voice unusually hard-edged.

'Caroline has cooked us what smells and looks like a delicious meal, and I think we should all do her the compliment of tucking in and enjoying it.' He picked up his cutlery. '*Bon appétit*, everyone.'

Everyone followed suit, even Shona. No doubt she didn't want to make a scene.

'Delicious,' pronounced Roderick a few moments later. 'Moist . . . juicy . . .' He turned to Miss Shaw. 'Help me out here, Jo. What's the word?'

'Succulent,' she suggested, throwing a smile across the table to Carrie. 'And beautifully cooked.'

She knew what they were doing. She was grateful, touched too, but she was bitterly disappointed that Matt had uttered not one word in her defence.

'For God's sake,' he said irritably as they were getting ready for bed. 'You're making a big fuss over nothing. Apologise to Mother tomorrow and everything will be smoothed over.'

Carrie stared at him, incredulous. 'You want *me* to apologise to *her*? You don't think it should be the other way around?'

'Whatever,' he said absently. The realisation that he wasn't even listening properly made her desperate. She knew she hadn't picked his father up wrong. Charles Campbell really had made those horribly suggestive remarks to her earlier this evening.

'Matt, we've got to move out. I can't stand this any longer. Please, Matt!'

She'd been doing her best not to cry, but she was six months pregnant and worn out by the stresses of the day. She sank down on to the bed.

'Carrie, you're overtired. Walking to Byres Road and back was obviously too much for you, and now you're getting yourself all het up over nothing.'

'It's not nothing,' she sobbed, pressing her fingers to her hot and sweaty forehead. Last time she'd got upset like this she'd ended up being sick. That wasn't good for the baby. She took a deep breath and looked up at him, forcing herself to speak calmly. 'I want a place of our own.'

'And how are we going to afford that when I've had to take a pay cut?'

'A pay cut?' she repeated. 'For everybody?' It was a bit of a blow, but it didn't surprise her. The country might be slowly beginning to pull itself out of the Depression, but there was a long way to go yet. Workers in more than one industry had been obliged to accept a reduction in wages.

Matthew shook his head. 'Not everyone. Only Pascal Sharkey and me.'

'I don't understand.'

He had the oddest of looks on his face. 'We had a slight difference of opinion. Over politics.'

She still didn't understand. Lots of people argued the toss over politics. They were living in interesting times.

'If you must know,' said Matt reluctantly, 'it got a bit heated. He's a socialist, Carrie!' He spat the word out as if it explained everything. 'I ended up taking a swing at him. He retaliated, of course. What else can you expect from a bloody Paddy?'

That statement, and the sneer which accompanied it, defeated her. It was all right for Matthew to lash out, but not for Pascal to defend himself? Like his father Martin, the young man confounded the stereotype of the fighting Irish. She knew him as the most peaceable of lads.

People could, of course, be provoked beyond endurance. That made her think of another occasion in the station booking office when violence had been narrowly avoided. She had seen Ewen Livingstone as the aggressor then. Now she looked at her husband . . . and wondered. She had a dreadful sinking feeling in the pit of her stomach.

'Oh, Matthew,' she breathed, 'whatever possessed you? You might have lost your job.'

'You think I don't know that?' It came out petulantly. 'I was tired and fed up, and he was being all smart and clever, demolishing my argument, making a fool of me in front of other people.'

'So you hit him?' Her voice rose in mingled outrage and disbelief.

He scowled at her. 'You think this unpleasantness between you and my mother doesn't affect me, Carrie? You could make more of an effort to get on with her, you know.'

That took her breath away. By one of those tortuous swings of logic Matthew seemed to specialise in, it was now she who was in the wrong. She stood up and went to stand in front of him.

'Make more of an effort?' she demanded with an angry toss of the head. 'I do nothing *but* make an effort with your bloody mother. Perhaps it might help if Lady Muck would condescend to do the same!'

He had gone very still. 'What did you call my mother?'

'Lady Muck,' she muttered, already ashamed of the impulse which had led her to use the name.

She saw it coming. It was in the darkening of his eyes. She just didn't believe it, that was all. Not when his hand came up. Not when she saw it swing towards her face. Not until she heard the noise it made and felt her cheek sting as he hit her.

He looked as shocked as she felt, and it was she who spoke first. 'I'm going to sleep in Archie's room.' She sounded dazed. She *was* dazed, unable to believe what he had done. Unwilling to believe it.

'No, you're not.'

She started to shake her head, but he grabbed her by the upper arms and spoke softly into her face. 'Would you like another slap, Carrie?'

They went to bed in silence. She lay on her side, facing away from him, and couldn't believe it when she felt his hand snake round her waist.

'I'm tired,' she said, her voice dull.

His hand slid up to her breasts. She pushed it away, but it returned, more demanding this time. 'I'm not in the mood.'

'Maybe not,' he said into the darkness, 'but I am.' His fingers tightened. 'Turn around, Carrie.'

She thought of Archie, lying sleeping on the other side of the dressing room door. She thought of the baby she was carrying. She turned around.

'Shall we take Archie out for a walk? It seems a nice enough day.'

Matt, off duty for the whole weekend, turned from his inspection of the weather and smiled warmly at his young wife. It was shortly after breakfast on Saturday morning, and everyone had gathered in the morning room.

'It's too cold.'

He strode across the room, swung a chair round from the small table in the corner and pulled it up beside her where she sat by the fire, opposite his mother. He sat back to front on the upright chair, straddling it. Laying his hands along the back of it he turned his mouth down, mock mournful.

'Oh, go on,' he said. 'A bit of fresh air will do him good. And you,' he added, 'you're looking a bit peelie-wally.' She had to steel herself not to jump when he stretched out one long finger and touched her lightly on the cheek.

Charles folded the newspaper he'd been reading and threw a glance at the outside world. 'Brrr! I think Caroline's right. I'm out later on this morning, but I'm planning to sit here and toast my toes for the next hour or so. Perhaps your mother would go with you and the young fellow, Matthew.'

'I'm afraid not,' said Shona, arching her beautifully plucked eyebrows. 'I'm meeting a friend for lunch in town, and I want to do some shopping beforehand.'

Matthew stood up and replaced the chair. 'Well, my boy and I are going, aren't we, son?'

Archie, playing happily on the rug at his mother's feet, gave his father a wrinkled-nose smile. 'Walk?' he asked.

'A walk,' Matt confirmed, lifting the little boy into his arms. He splayed his hand out over the small chest, holding Archie strong and secure.

'Mammy come too?'

'Maybe if we ask her nicely.' Father and son turned as one. 'Please come,' Matt said softly.

She went. It might have been because she didn't relish the prospect of being left alone with her father-in-law, or because she didn't want to disappoint Archie. Or perhaps it was because Matthew had asked her nicely.

She walked beside him like a silent ghost. He was being determinedly cheerful, pointing things out to Archie and not showing any irritation at her own lack of conversation. However, when the little boy nodded off on the journey home, Matthew also grew quiet. The air between them began to fizz with tension.

The house was empty when they got back. Matt, who'd lifted the pushchair up the front steps whilst Carrie held the door open, stood in the echoing hallway and looked down at his sleeping son.

'Should we wake him up for his lunch?' he whispered.

She shook her head and pointed to their bedroom. He lifted Archie out of the pushchair. The shawl wrapped around him tangled on a metal bar. Carrie hastened to free it, Matt waiting patiently while she did so. He stood back to let her go ahead of him into their bedroom and through to the dressing room. She pulled back the cot blankets and he laid the baby down. Together, they laid the covers over him and tiptoed out of the small room.

Laying his palm flat on the finger-plate Matthew pushed the door gently closed and walked a few steps away from it. Carrie was standing by their bed. He folded his arms and indicated the dressing room with an inclination of his head. 'You know, whatever the two of us do with our lives, he'll always be our greatest achievement.' His eyes went to her body. 'The one that's coming as well, of course.'

Carrie made no comment.

'Well,' he said, 'shall I make us some lunch?'

She couldn't help smiling at that. 'You wouldn't know where to start.'

'Maybe I'm trying to make a peace offering,' he said. 'Maybe I'm trying to say sorry.' He raised his eyebrows and uncrossed his arms. 'I've never found it an easy thing to do.'

'You hit me,' she said. 'You –' She broke off, sat down on the bed and put the heel of her hand to her mouth. She couldn't bring herself to say that word.

'Carrie . . .' He came towards her, but she put an arm out, trying to fend him off.

'I felt invaded. Used.' She wasn't crying, but Matt was. He slid to his knees in front of her, seized her hands and pressed them to his brow, his head bent over her lap.

'I'm sorry,' he said brokenly. 'I apologise. I don't know what came over me. It'll never happen again, I promise.'

He raised his head and she caught her breath at the sight of those glittering eyes. 'But I love you so much, and I want you so much. You've been busy with Archie lately and concerned about the new baby too, and I understand that, I really do, but I need your time and attention as well.'

'Oh, Matt,' she said sorrowfully.

'Tell me you forgive me, Carrie. Tell me you still love me.'

She was no match for that plea. 'Of course I still love you,' she said, not understanding how he could doubt her, 'but we need a new start, Matt. Away from here.'

He threw his arms about her waist, placed his heavy head against her stomach. 'Anything,' he said. 'Anything you want, my little wife.'

Chapter 20

Knowing Matt would inevitably find their new home small, Carrie was careful to look for the nicest place they could comfortably afford. For starters, it was in a red sandstone block whose entrance passageway and stairs were decorated with beautiful dark green china tiles. A wally close was always a mark of superiority.

Their own two-apartment house had a lovely bay window in the front room and was also on the first floor. One up was the best position, away from the noise and dirt of the street, but not necessitating a strenuous climb carrying washing, messages or babies to the top of the building. As in most tenements in Glasgow, this was indicated on the outside of the building.

The first-floor windows were surmounted by a projecting piece of decorative stonework which followed the lines of the bay. The second-floor ones also had their crowns, although as usual the adornment was a little simpler than on the floor below. The third floor, which had no bay windows, was completely plain. This was common practice. However, Carrie considered her block vastly superior to many others she had seen because there were some architectural frills and furbelows between the third storey and the top floor. The building was undeniably handsome.

Best of all as far as she was concerned was that it was very central: round the corner from the steamie, along from the library and not too far from the station. If she looked out of the side panel of the bay window she could see the trains on the bridge which carried the railway across Dumbarton Road.

There were one or two flies in the ointment. Although most of her new neighbours were friendly, the woman across the landing was anything but. A bleached blonde in her mid-thirties with a cigarette dangling permanently from her lips, she greeted Carrie's friendly overtures with thinly veiled hostility. Baffled, she mentioned it to Matt, who advised her blithely to forget it.

'She's probably jealous of you. She lives with that old wife, doesn't she? Her mother?'

'Mother-in-law, I think,' said Carrie, ladling him out a plate of Scotch broth. They were close enough to the station now for him to come home for his midday meal. She hadn't pointed out this advantage in so many words, but she was planning on cooking him something really tasty each day. 'They're both Mrs Cooke.'

'Where's Mr Cooke?' he asked idly. 'Away working somewhere? At sea? Gone to his reward?' He lifted his eyebrows and his spoon. 'Maybe she murdered him and buried him in the back court.'

'I dunno.' Carrie filled her own plate, sat down and buttered a slice of bread for him. 'I'm not likely to find out either. She seems to find it hard enough to say good morning to me.' She gave Archie his bowl of soup, which had been cooling down on the table, out of his reach. 'Why would she be jealous?'

'Because she lives on her own with the old bat, whereas you have a handsome husband and son.' He smiled across the table at Archie, who beamed in response. Unfortunately, the little boy's mouth was full of Scotch broth at the time. Carrie tutted and stood up to remedy the situation.

'It's all over your hands, you wee toerag!'

Matt laughed. 'You've got your work cut out with him, haven't you?' He applied himself to his own soup. 'And,' he said, several spoonfuls later, 'you're rather nice-looking yourself, Mrs Campbell.'

'Why, thank you, kind sir.' She gave the tray of Archie's high chair one last wipe and slipped back into her chair. If she didn't get to her own soup soon, it would be lukewarm. She reached for her spoon, but Matthew's hand took hers.

'I bet a lot of men are jealous of me,' he said softly.

'Because your wife's a dab hand at making soup?'

'That,' he agreed, his eyes roaming over her face, 'and the rest. Give us a kiss, gorgeous.'

Her broth was growing colder by the second, but she did as he had asked. He was on his best behaviour at the moment. The least she could do was meet him halfway.

The attitude of her nearest neighbour continued to bother Carrie. She found it all the more inexplicable because 'the old bat', as Matthew so charmingly called her, was friendly, and made a great fuss of Archie.

She refused to let it spoil her pleasure in being mistress of her own home at last. Not even the fact that her kitchen was dominated by an old black range identical to the one at White Street could do that. On her first morning in the house, a frosty February day, Carrie decided it wasn't going to beat her, and got busy getting to know her way around it. Within a week she was beginning to appreciate its good points, not least how quickly it dried clothes on the pulley suspended above it.

Unlike White Street, her new home didn't have its own wash-house in the back court. A visit to the steamie in Purdon Street beckoned. Carrie took Archie by the hand, hoisted a wicker basket of washing on to her hip, and set off.

When she got there she stood awkwardly in the doorway, not quite sure of the procedure. The place seemed huge, and very noisy. There were pipes everywhere and clouds of steam condensing on the white-tiled walls. Women stood at deep sinks in individual stalls separated from each other by low and narrow wooden partitions. Some were bent over washboards, other were laughing and calling to each other as they worked. It was all a bit daunting.

The woman in the first stall, attacking a grimy shirt collar with a big bar of Sunlight soap, looked up. 'Is this your first time, hen?'

Someone laughed raucously. 'Look at the wee lad, Rena, no' to mention her belly. It cannae be her first time.'

Carrie's heart sank when the woman who had made the coarse remark stepped forward. It was her unfriendly neighbour, Mrs Cooke. Hair done up in curlers with a scarf over them, a flowery pinny wrapped round her skinny frame, she jabbed a finger at Archie. 'This is no place for a wean. It's dangerous wi' all this hot water aboot.'

'I've n-nowhere to l-leave him.'

The potential dangers of the steamie had occurred to Carrie, but she'd had no choice other than to bring Archie with her. She could hardly have taken him up the hill to her mother-in-law. Relations were a little strained at the moment, Shona being incapable of understanding Carrie's need to be mistress of her own home. She might have left him with Rita Sharkey but after Matthew's contretemps with her eldest son, Carrie would have been embarrassed to ask such a favour. The woman called Rena spoke.

'Stop going on at the lassie, Isa. We'll find something to amuse the wee laddie and keep him out of harm's way while his ma's doing the washing.' She turned to Carrie. 'Miss Burgess as was, isn't it?'

'Yes,' she said gratefully.

'Come on then. I'll show ye the ropes.'

They knew who she was. She'd been accepted into the fold.

Carrie couldn't believe how lucky she was. She'd had another healthy child, a little girl this time.

'A redhead like her mother,' observed Matt, cupping the tiny head gently in his palm and walking slowly up and down in front of the bay window.

Propped up against two pillows watching him, Carrie was feeling rather pleased with herself. Confounding the predictions of all the women around her, her labour had lasted a few hours longer than with Archie, but the memories were already beginning to fade. Mother Nature's gift to mothers: selective amnesia.

She was wearing a pretty white lacy bed jacket which Josephine Shaw had presented her with yesterday when she and Roderick had called past to see the baby. She'd been touched and a little surprised by the evident emotion with which Josephine had held the wee one.

Matt holding his daughter also made a lovely picture. Whatever difficulties they'd had in the first two and a half years of their marriage, Carrie couldn't fault his love for his children. His dark eyes were soft as he surveyed the baby girl. He'd chosen her name: April, for the month of her birth.

'You're not disappointed because we haven't had another boy?'

'Disappointed? Of course not. We've got a gentleman's family now. A boy and a girl. Mind you,' he murmured, coming over and bending forward to carefully lay the shawl-wrapped bundle in the crook of her arm, 'I'm hoping we'll have some more.'

'Not for a while though, Matt.'

Her response had been too quick, and too anxious. The features of the dark face above her own stiffened.

'You don't need to remind that my tap's stopped for the next few weeks, Carrie.'

More than a few, she hoped. That was the last thing on her mind at the moment. He straightened up and looked down at them both.

'I suppose you're determined to nurse her yourself?'

She laid her forefinger along April's downy cheek. 'Of course I am. You enjoy a feed from your mammy, don't you, wee lassie? And Mammy likes feeding you.'

'Carrie, honestly.' Matt looked faintly disgusted. 'Do you have to be quite so graphic?'

Determined the children shouldn't be deprived of contact with their grandparents on her account, Carrie made the effort to visit North Gardner Street from time to time. She'd spent an hour there this afternoon, a short enough period for Charles Campbell to be able to maintain an interest. He'd made faces at three-month-old April and got Archie thoroughly overexcited by some rumbustious play.

Shona had been her usual cool and aloof self. Taking the long way round to avoid having to push the big pram and attached baby seat down the steep slope of Gardner Street – the thought of what could happen if her hands slipped gave her the heebie-jeebies – Carrie was thinking about that as she made her way home.

Matt adored his mother and looked up to his father, but he'd never received the attention he craved from either of them. She guessed that was why he was often so demanding of her. There were times when she thought she had three children, not two.

He was always looking for something he couldn't seem to find, a niche where he would be appreciated and valued. He was good at his job, but that fight with Pascal Sharkey hadn't helped his chances of promotion. He'd blotted his copybook, and there had to be a period of penance before his superiors would trust him again. Most galling of all, Matt's support for Sir Oswald Mosley's political philosophy – the very thing which had caused the fight in the first place – had waned sharply. If only he could find something which would hold his interest and give him some real satisfaction!

April started to grizzle, needing her mother's breast. They were running a bit late today, but feeding her before they had left North Gardner Street hadn't been an option. Shona would have had a fit of the vapours. April's grandfather, on the other hand, would probably have been only too keen on the idea.

As Carrie approached her own close, a young girl who lived on the top floor of the building came running up and asked shyly if she'd like to come and watch the concert she and her friends were about to put on in the back court.

'Oh, I'm sorry, pet,' she said. 'I'd love to, but April's needing fed.'

The child's face fell, and Carrie hesitated. So far these summer holidays the children hadn't had much chance to put on any of their wee shows. The weather had been extremely wet. She was very fond of the girl, who loved to be allowed to help with Archie and April. Her mother was a really nice person too. When Carrie had been convalescing after the birth, she'd sent her daughter down with a large pot of soup and other bits and pieces to keep them going until she was up and about again.

Old Mrs Cooke was coming through the close. Despite her younger namesake's continuing hostility, she'd been a great help in the months since April's birth. She and Archie had taken a real shine to each other. When she'd first offered to mind him for a wee while so his mother could put her feet up for an hour in the afternoon while the baby slept, Carrie had been grateful, but absolutely convinced that her son wouldn't go anywhere without her. She'd ended up muttering 'traitor' to his small retreating back as he toddled off happily hand in hand with the woman he now knew as Auntie Florence.

'There's people out here want to know when the entertainment's starting, young lady. Hello there, Carrie. Are you coming through to watch the bairns?'

She explained her predicament. Florence looked puzzled. 'Feed her outside. Naebody'll mind.'

The older woman led the way to the back court, where an assortment of chairs had been assembled. Most of them were already occupied, mainly by mothers and grannies. There were one or two men present, either on shift work or unemployed. Florence's daughter-in-law Isa was also there, turning to look at the newcomers with cool eyes.

'Sit doon here,' said Florence to Carrie. 'This seat's fine and low.'

A man came over to help unfasten Archie from the baby seat and lift him off. Before he set him down he raised him up into the air a couple of times, causing the little boy to laugh with delight. Carrie took her daughter out of the pram, sat down on the low chair and began unbuttoning her blouse. Dipping into the bundle of covers at the foot of the pram which had been discarded on such a warm day, Florence fished out a shawl. She draped it over Carrie's shoulders.

'There you are, pet,' she said. 'Discretion guaranteed.'

Carrie found herself enjoying the simple entertainment. The children had rehearsed their show well. There were traditional songs and popular songs and a funny sketch involving Hitler and Mussolini. The boy playing the Italian dictator was particularly good. She transferred April from one side to the other and, with the rest of the audience, joined the young performers in a spirited rendition of *Roaming in the Gloaming.*

There was a harsh screeching sound as a sash window above their heads was thrown up. 'In the name o' God, how's a man on night shift supposed to get any sleep with this bloody racket going on?'

The protest was somewhat diluted by the grin on the man's face as he looked down at all the faces looking back up at him. His wife poked her head out of the window beside him. 'Pay him no mind, children. He was getting up for his tea anyway. And I think your singing's lovely.'

The couple lived directly above Carrie. She tilted her head back and gave them both a cheerful wave. Nuzzled against her breast, April had fallen asleep. She adjusted her arms around the sleeping baby and sat back comfortably in the chair, warm and relaxed. She became aware that someone was standing behind her and turned to see who it was.

'Oh, hello, Matt,' she said. 'You're a wee bit early.'

He waited till they'd had their tea and the children were safely asleep. Sometimes he helped get them ready for bed, but tonight he sat and watched in silence as she washed April and Archie in turn in the small round bath in front of the range. Normally, he disposed of the dirty water and put away its receptacle. He made no move to do so tonight.

She dried the children, got them into their nightclothes and put them to bed. Then she settled them down to sleep with a kiss on each small brow and went back through to the kitchen. She went forward to remove the tin bath.

'Leave it,' he said, his voice cracking like a whip. Then he started. What sort of trollop was she to be exposing herself to half of Partick, men as well as women? How did it make him look, that his wife conducted herself in such a common manner?

At first she tried to defend herself, but within five minutes she had fallen silent, no match for the verbal onslaught. He went on and on, his language growing ever coarser. Some of the words he used made her wince. By the time his fury was eventually spent Carrie was pale and trembling.

She stood at the open door of the flat, uncertain of her next move. It was the afternoon of the following day and she felt the need to get out of the house. She was only planning on going downstairs for a few minutes but wasn't sure about leaving the children. No, that was daft. They were both having their afternoon naps, tucked up securely in cot and pram respectively, and with the door left ajar she'd hardly be out of earshot.

She hesitated, hovering on the doorstep. She wasn't feeling very decisive today. The door of the flat opposite opened and Isa Cooke came out with a duster and a can of brass polish in her hands. Head bowed, she appeared lost in thought. She looked up, saw Carrie, and jumped.

'In the name o' the wee man! Have you nothing better to do than lurk about trying to give folk heart attacks?' Her hand went to her bosom, presumably to quell the frantic beating of the organ in question.

In a more cynical mood, Carrie would have recognised that her neighbour was rather making a meal of it. In her present state of mind, she could only stutter out an apology. Her voice trembled as she said the words. Isa Cooke took two steps forward and peered into Carrie's face.

'What the hell's wrang wi' ye?'

'Nothing.' She turned, blindly, to go back in, not wanting to disgrace herself in front of this woman who seemed to dislike her so much. She heard a sigh, felt her arm being taken, and the next thing she knew she was being pushed into one of the chairs set round the table in her neighbour's kitchen.

'Are the weans asleep?'

Carrie nodded.

'You'll be glad to get a wee rest yourself.'

That had been suspiciously close to a friendly comment. Carrie must really have given her a fright. Isa put her can of polish and duster on one shelf and lifted down a packet of cigarettes, a box of matches and an ashtray from another.

'Jimmy and me never had any children,' she said. She lit up, narrowing her eyes against the smoke. 'Then the stupid bugger went and got himself killed in the yard, so that was the end o' that.'

'I'm sorry.'

Isa shrugged, and took a pull on the cigarette. 'Why should you be sorry? It wisnae your fault. He went to work blootered, that was the long and the short o' it. Missed his footing, and down he went. Leaving me wi' his black-hearted bitch of a mother.'

'Who's not home at the moment, I presume,' said Carrie, beginning to recover. She knew it wouldn't have made much difference if the older woman had been there. The two Mrs Cookes seemed positively to enjoy hurling abuse at each other.

'Never mind that.' Isa laid the ashtray on the table and fixed her guest with a penetrating stare. 'You got yourself into trouble with your man yesterday. Am I right?'

Carrie pressed her eyes tightly shut for a few seconds. That was a mistake. It brought back the memory of Matt ranting and raving at her, looking at her out of cold and unforgiving eyes, calling her horrible names.

'The walls here are no' as thick as you might think, hen.'

Carrie put her elbows on the table and sank her head into her hands. She hadn't the heart to deny it. Matt had knocked the heart out of her last night . . . Through the curtain of her hair, she was aware of the cigarette being stubbed out.

'Here,' came Isa's voice a minute or two later, 'you're a nursing mother. You need to keep your strength up.'

A plate with a piece of gingerbread on it was pushed under her nose. It was followed by a cup of milk. The unexpected kindness undid Carrie completely. Tears slid unchecked down her smooth cheeks. Isa said nothing, but she sat down at the table opposite her and waited.

Carrie wiped her eyes with her hands and sniffed. 'Sorry. It's just that this isn't how I expected my life to turn out.'

'You chose him.' If the rough voice had softened before, it became harder again now. 'You didnae have to. You had another choice.'

You had another choice. Carrie's head snapped up. It was as if Ewen had come into the room. She could see him: hair all over the place, open-necked shirt flapping in the breeze, rakish red kerchief knotted at his throat. He was chuckling at her – for being so stupid, probably.

A mother and daughter-in-law living together but arguing with each other all the time . . . A husband and son who'd died in a shipyard accident . . . Ewen laughing himself silly at the thought of the two women consoling each other in their hour of need. Now she could hear him as well as see him. '*I think black-hearted bitch is ma personal favourite*.'

'You're his mother's friend,' she breathed.

'Throw the girl a peanut,' said Isa sourly. 'She's managed to work it out at last.'

Chapter 21

Tears forgotten, Carrie began asking questions. 'Do you know where he is? How he's getting on?'

Isa pretended to study her fingernails. 'Do you care?'

'Of course I do!' Stung, she blurted out the words. 'Ewen was my friend.'

'Funny way to treat a friend.'

'What do you mean?'

The other woman made her wait, lighting another cigarette before she let Carrie have it. It was a bit like standing in the dock knowing you were about to be mercilessly harangued by the lawyer leading the case for the prosecution. Only instead of a neat legal wig, this attacker had a head of tight peroxide curls.

'You know exactly what I mean. You broke Ewen Livingstone's heart. You picked Matthew Campbell over him because you thought you'd have an easier life that way. Up the hill in your main door flat,' she spat out.

'It wasn't like that . . .'

Her impassioned protest was ignored.

'He told you about his mother – who, by the way, was one o' the nicest women I've ever met in my entire life – and you threw it back in his face.' Isa tossed her head. 'D'you think it was easy for him to tell you that story?' She stopped finally for breath and looked accusingly at Carrie.

'No,' she responded sadly. 'I don't think it was easy for him. I don't think anything was ever easy for him.'

'You are dead right there, hen,' said Isa fiercely. She took a couple of angry puffs and then the second cigarette joined the first, stubbed out in the ashtray barely smoked. 'He's done very well for himself. No thanks to you.'

Carrie waited. She could see there was a battle going on. Pride in Ewen was warring with condemnation of herself. Pride won.

'He's working in Edinburgh. Shameful thing for a Glasgow man, eh? He's a clerk at the Waverley. Went in for the exam a year and a half ago. Passed wi' flying colours.'

'He finally made it? I'm so pleased for him!' Carrie sat up in her chair. 'Do you hear from him regularly?'

She was getting an odd look. 'He writes to us once a month. Without fail.'

'He writes? Och, that's just great!'

Carrie was still on the receiving end of that appraising gaze. Then Isa looked pointedly at the plate and cup she'd placed in front of her.

'Drink your milk,' she said. 'And eat your gingerbread. I didnae put out good food for you to let it go to waste.'

She ought to be getting back, but she'd not been brought up to waste food either. 'Lovely gingerbread,' she said a minute or two later, lifting the last crumbs off the plate with a dampened finger.

'Aye,' said Isa grudgingly, 'the old yin's no bad at the baking.'

Carrie finished the milk. 'Thank you. I'd better be getting back now.' She pushed her chair away and stood up. 'See when you next write to Ewen, would you let him know I was asking for him? And that I congratulate him – most warmly – on making clerk.'

Isa gave her a look but said nothing, simply got to her feet and saw her out. Four days later, however, she knocked on Carrie's front door, about half an hour after Matthew had gone to work.

'This came for you.' She turned on her heel and disappeared into her own house. When Carrie looked at the envelope she saw there was one word written on it: her own name.

It took her some time to summon up the courage to open it. Since her conversation with Isa, she'd been prey to an enormous sense of guilt about Ewen. She'd hurt him so badly, ridden roughshod over his feelings. How could she expect him to forgive her? Yet why would he have bothered to write to her if that was how he felt? Maybe he wanted to give her a piece of his mind, but he had written that simple *Carrie* on the envelope. If the letter contained a lambasting, surely he'd have been more formal.

She got on with her chores, settled Archie at the kitchen table with his toy farm, fed April and put her down for her morning nap. Only then did she take a knife out of the cutlery drawer, slide it under the flap and open the envelope.

Dear Carrie, she read as she put the knife back and walked slowly over to stand in front of the range. *Bet you never expected to get a letter from me!* It was as though he was there with her – smiling and friendly, his usual sunny self. She turned the page over to see how he had signed himself. *Your affectionate friend, Ewen Livingstone*. Her eyes misted over. He'd forgiven her. He still called himself her friend.

'Why Mammy crying?'

Archie, engaged in giving a sheep a bareback ride on a cow, had chosen that very moment to look up. Engrossed in Ewen's letter, Carrie answered him rather absently. 'Because I've just had a letter from an old friend, my wee petal.'

Well, now you know who your neighbours are, as it were! I'm glad of the chance that gives me to say how sorry I was when I heard that your mother had passed away. That must have been very difficult for you coming so soon after Mr Burgess' death.

Isa tells me you have a fine wee boy and a beautiful baby daughter. They must be a great consolation to you. I'm sure they keep you busy!

He went on, briefly, to tell her he was doing well, beginning to move up the grades and enjoying the work. *A lot better than being out in all weathers, like I used to have to do. And I know who I have to thank for it all.*

That brought a lump to her throat. She read the whole thing again, right through to *Your affectionate friend, Ewen Livingstone.*

Affectionate. It had been one of their words of the week. That would be why he had chosen that adjective. They'd had a lot of fun over all that, she remembered, thinking back to those sunlit days in the garden of the station house.

She folded the single sheet of paper and slipped it back into the envelope. Stretching up, she tucked the letter in behind the big willow pattern platter which stood in pride of place on the shelf above the range, fitting in neatly under the gas mantle and flanked by two smaller plates in the same design. They had all belonged to her grandmother, Esther's mother. She often kept Mary's latest missive there for a few days, taking it down from time to time to re-read it.

Then she thought about it. However innocent the contents of the letter she had just received, Matt wasn't going to be very happy when he found out that Ewen had written to her. It might be better to get rid of it straightaway. Her fingers were on the envelope, ready to pull it back out and consign it to the flames of the fire – but that seemed a terrible thing to do.

I know who I have to thank for it all. It was sweet of him to say so, but judging by the neat handwriting and excellent spelling, Ewen had put in an awful lot of hard work himself. Her thoughts drifted back once more to that summer three years ago. She was remembering the occasion when he had brought her an apple for the teacher. She could see him in her mind's eye, delving in his tool bag, then presenting it to her with a flourish.

She smiled. She'd keep his letter for a wee while, read it again in a couple of days. Then she would burn it. She pushed it back in behind the plate so that it was completely out of sight. No point in allowing it to cause trouble between her and Matt.

'How was work?'

'Don't ask,' he said gloomily, but he seemed to be in a good enough mood as he took off his jacket and loosened his collar and tie. He'd had a long day today, working over his midday break to cover for a colleague attending a funeral.

'Never mind,' said Carrie as he went to the sink to wash his hands. 'I've made something special for tea tonight.' She grabbed a cloth to protect her hands and crouched in front of the range to take an enamel ashet out of the oven. Turning, she placed the steep-sided dish carefully on a cork mat lying on top of the checked seersucker tablecloth. Archie, who liked his food, regarded his prospective tea with interest. His father peered at it suspiciously.

'Macaroni *au gratin*,' said Carrie proudly.

'That means with cheese sauce, doesn't it?' Matt looked doubtful. 'There's no meat in it, then?'

'I'm afraid not. But I think you'll find it tasty all the same. Give it a try.'

She spooned him out a small portion. After a few mouthfuls he declared it to be excellent and asked for more. Smiling with satisfaction, his young wife obliged.

'Where did you get the recipe?'

'They were demonstrating it at the Empire Exhibition. When I went with Josephine Shaw last month.'

'She seems to like being with our two, doesn't she? Strange thing for a career woman like her.'

Carrie answered non-commitally, 'She likes children.'

'Can't imagine why. They're all horrible wee monsters.' He leaned over and tickled Archie on the stomach.

'Matthew! Not while he's eating, please.'

'Women,' tutted Matt. 'What would you do with them?'

Evidently in total agreement with his father, Archie gave a shrug of his small shoulders and screwed up his face in a gesture of exasperation. Matthew grinned at him and turned to share the moment with Carrie. She smiled back, and the grin transformed itself into a long, slow smile.

'Dessert,' she said brightly, and leaped up to fetch it.

'Well, young man,' said Matthew, 'what have you been doing today?

'I played with my farm.'

'With your sheep? Or your cows?'

'With my sheep *and* my cows.'

The smile was still on Carrie's face as she listened to them. Archie was a very good speaker, but then he'd always had lots of encouragement. She talked to him all the time as she went through her day, and Matt always took an interest when he came home from work. As he was taking an interest now.

'And what did Mammy do today?'

'She got a letter,' said the clear childish voice. 'From an old friend. It made her cry.'

Carrie set a bowl of blancmange on the table. Matt glanced up at her.

'A letter that made you cry? Who was that from?'

'A friend in Edinburgh,' she said brightly.

'I didn't know you had any friends through there.' Matt looked quizzical. 'Anybody I know?'

'No,' she said quickly, 'I don't think so.'

'So what's she called? It is a *she*, is it?'

She hesitated for the merest second. It was long enough. She saw what she had hoped never to see again. Something was happening behind Matt's eyes.

'Isn't that funny, Archie?' He was still speaking in that pleasant tone of voice, but it was sending shivers up and down Carrie's spine. 'Mammy doesn't seem to know the name of her friend. The one she got a letter from today. Isn't that odd? Maybe Mammy's friend can't write very well. That would explain it, wouldn't it?'

Carrie's blood ran cold in her veins. Archie was looking up at his father, not understanding what was going on.

'Don't bring him into it,' she said. 'Please.'

Matt's dark eyes flickered, but he lifted the little boy off his seat and hunkered down in front of him. 'I want you to go through to the front room, Archie, and make sure your sister's all right.'

'Take April some pudding?'

Matt shook his head. 'No, she's too wee for that. You can take your own though.' He spoke without turning around. 'Put some out for him.' In contrast to the way he was speaking to their son, it was a curt order.

Her hands trembling, Carrie obeyed and passed a bowl and spoon over to him. He took it and handed it to Archie. 'Now then,' he said, 'you've not to come back till Daddy comes for you. Understand?'

'Is it a game?'

'Sort of.'

Closing the heavy door behind the boy, Matt put his back to it and surveyed her in silence. She stood between the table and the range, still holding the serving spoon with which she had dished out Archie's blancmange.

She noticed that the weight of her husband's tall and powerful body was pulling on the coats which hung on the back of the door. If he stayed there for much longer, the hanging loops would snap. Even as the thought flitted across her mind, he pushed himself off and took a few steps towards her.

'Where is it?' he asked. The game had begun.

[illegible]

[illegible] the door, with her back [illegible] the bundle. She had [illegible] about her [illegible] anxiously [illegible] had carried [illegible] a [illegible] managed to [illegible]

[illegible]

[illegible]

[illegible]

Chapter 22

'Archie come back through now?'

The door creaked open. Carrie was lying where Matt had left her, on the floor with her back against the wooden cupboards under the box bed. She had her arms curled protectively about her head, still unconsciously trying to shield herself from the slaps and punches he had rained down on her. She hadn't managed to keep many of them out. He'd split her lip, and her left eye felt gritty and swollen.

Archie came round the door and into the room, his eyes as big as saucers. She tried to scramble to her feet, but one leg gave way. She winced as pain stabbed through her thigh. That must have happened when Matt had hurled her against a chair, demanding to know where Ewen's letter was: the letter whose hiding place the movement of her eyes had betrayed.

'I fell, Archie,' she said. 'Your silly mammy fell. Come here and give me a cuddle and that'll maybe help me get up.'

He trotted obediently to her and coiled his arms about her neck. 'Daddy gone back to work?' he asked, his voice muffled as he pressed his small face against her neck.

She pulled him more tightly to her. 'Yes, Daddy's gone back to work.' He was accepting it all, she thought gratefully. He was used to Matt working shifts, coming home and going back out again, and he was too young to question the oddness of his father having left his mother lying hurt on the floor.

He didn't need to know what had really happened here. Nor, even if he had heard anything, would he have understood any of the vile things Matt had said. He had read the letter out loud before crumpling it up and flinging it on the fire. He had seized on that *your affectionate friend* before he did so, demanding to know why Ewen had used that particular word. Carrie had tried to explain it was a simple word game, one they had played while she'd been teaching him to read and write.

'What other games did you and he play?' Matt demanded. He had her pinned down, his fingers handcuffing her wrists to the arms of the big chair in front of the range. To her horror, he accused her of having let Ewen make love to her. She protested in vain that Matt knew better than anybody that she had been a virgin on their wedding night.

'A virgin who knew what French letters were,' he spat into her face. 'That's the sort of things only whores know about. Or sons of whores.'

He kept using that dreadful word, right up until he finally stopped hitting her, his breathing coming fast and ragged. Arms up, she was waiting for the next onslaught when she heard the front door bang with a force which must have echoed down to the close and up to the top floor of the building.

'Go get Auntie Florence and Auntie Isa?'

Dazed, she wondered when Archie had decided to confer that title not only on the old lady, but also on her sharp-tongued daughter-in-law.

'No!'

She had frightened him. He pulled himself out of her arms, and his wee face crumpled. It was hard to smile with a cut lip. It was hard to smile when your heart was breaking. Somehow Carrie managed it.

'Mammy'll be fine.' She made it to her feet. 'See? I'm all right now. I'm fine,' she repeated. She found her way to the chair, extending an arm to bring him with her. That hurt. She settled herself gingerly into the seat. That hurt too. Her eyes went to a stain on the floor, the sticky trail left by the serving spoon she'd been using for the blancmange. It had flown out of her hand when Matthew had struck the first blow, skidding across the floor and ending up in front of the sink. Somebody knocked at the front door.

'Archie, go and say your mammy's a bit busy at the moment.'

'Can't reach the door.' He was standing in front of her, one finger in his mouth. He looked so worried.

'No,' she said gently. 'Of course you can't.'

It took her ages to get there, Archie hovering at her side, the knocking now continuous. 'I'm coming, I'm coming!'

From the front room she heard April start up. Should she go and see to the baby before she opened the door? She couldn't decide. Her head was swimming. In the end, she decided she had to make the knocking stop.

'In the name o' God, we thought he'd killed you all!'

'Shush,' she muttered, falling back against the open door. 'Archie's here . . .'

'Mammy fell,' he piped up.

'Did she, son?' exclaimed Florence. 'Och, that's a shame. Look,' she said, exchanging a swift glance with her daughter-in-law, 'why don't you come across to our hoose while your Auntie Isa helps your mammy? I'm needin' a hand to make some biscuits.'

'Aye.' Isa nodded her head in approval. 'That's a good idea. You run along, wee man.'

Carrie had her head tilted back against the solid wood of the door, but it was still spinning. 'April needs seeing to.'

Her voice seemed to be coming from a long way off, as did the rough one which answered her. 'Well, I can change her, but you'll have to do the ten minutes each side!' She felt her arm being taken and Isa beginning to lead her through to the kitchen.

'April,' she protested. 'Need to feed April.'

'I'll get her for you in a wee minute, but first I'm going to see you into your chair. I hope you werenae planning on going to the dancing the night. You're no' in a very good state to be attempting the foxtrot.'

Isa settled her in front of the range, took a pillow off the bed and tucked it in behind her, and then fetched the baby. With unabashed practicality, she helped Carrie undo her blouse.

'Now,' she said briskly, 'while you're doing that, let's have a look at you. Will you and me be paying a wee visit to the Western Infirmary this evening, d'ye think? We'll have to lash out on a taxi if we do. You're no' fit to walk there and no' fit to be seen either, so the tram's out o' the question.'

'I'm not going to the hospital.' Carrie's voice was a little stronger.

'I'll be the judge o' that, young lady. Let's get you cleaned up and see what the damage is.'

Ten minutes later, Isa grudgingly allowed that hospital treatment wasn't going to be necessary. 'Mind you,' she said, 'you're gonnae have a right keeker the morn. That eye's swelling up nicely. Walloped you good and proper, didn't he? Made a bloody good job of it.'

Carrie almost laughed. Isa was looking her over like an artist surveying a work in progress. 'A wee cup of tea, hen?'

Carrie raised an exploratory finger to her mouth, drawing her breath in on a hiss when it made contact with the cut. 'Make some for yourself if you like. I don't think I can drink anything with this lip.'

'That's where fags come in handy,' said Isa sagely. 'Even if the bugger's planted a few on your mouth, ye can usually find a wee corner to stick your Woodbine.'

'Your Jimmy hit you?' Normally Carrie wouldn't have dreamed of asking such a question, but this wasn't exactly a normal evening.

'Once or twice,' said Isa drily. 'When he had a drink in him. Which was quite a lot o' the time, in actual fact. Not that the old bitch would ever admit her wee boy was capable o' anything like that.'

She dipped into her apron pocket and brought out her cigarettes. 'I thumped him back, mind,' she said thoughtfully. 'He didnae like that. Happy to dish it out, no' so happy to take it. His sort never are.' She lit up and sat down opposite Carrie. 'You're not the type to hit back though, are you?'

'I'm leaving him,' Carrie said calmly. 'I'm taking the children and I'm going.' Her voice shook.

'Of course you are, pet.' Isa blew out some smoke rings. Carrie had seen her do it before, but it was still a good trick. 'I'm no' very sure what you're going to do for money, mind. Or a place to stay.'

Carrie wasn't too sure about that either. Everyone she knew needed all the space they had. Apart from her parents-in-law, that was. Moving back in with them didn't seem a very realistic option . . .

'The three of you can stay with us tonight,' said Isa, 'but it's going to be a wee touch cramped. You'll have to sort something out with your man pretty damn' quick, especially if you don't want the laddie to twig that there's anything up. But none o' us are wanting a repeat performance of tonight's wee episode, are we now?'

Carrie stared at her, panic rising in her throat. 'You think he might do it again?'

'They usually do, hen.' Isa's voice was as dry as sandpaper.

'I could threaten to go to the police.'

Her neighbour looked at her pityingly. 'Don't make me laugh. The police'll no' help you. That would be intervening between husband and wife.' She said the phrase with considerable derision. 'They'll intervene if he murders you like, but no' before.' She stood up and looked down at her. 'You're on your own, kiddo. Except that you've got some friends.'

'I'm very grateful for them,' Carrie said tremulously. 'You and Florence have really come to my rescue tonight. Thank you.'

'Aye, well.' Isa tossed what was left of her cigarette on to the fire. 'Have you finished feeding the wean? Give her here, and I'll change her nappy.'

Matt came home at ten o'clock. He'd been drinking, but he wasn't drunk. He came into the room warily, like a man uncertain of what he was going to find. His eyes ranged over Carrie. She thought he seemed relieved at what he saw. Isa, who'd risen to her feet as soon as they heard the sound of his key in the lock, stood beside her chair like a personal bodyguard. Carrie was glad she was there. Her heart was thumping violently.

'I'd like to speak to my wife.'

'Would you now?'

Carrie waited for Matt to explode. He didn't. He transferred his gaze from Isa back to her. 'Are you all right?' he asked quietly.

'I'm as you see me,' she said levelly. *As you left me*. She considered a nonchalant shrug, but it would undoubtedly make her shoulders hurt more than they already did. Not knowing why he deserved to be given the slightest reassurance, she added something, forcing herself to use the same light tone of voice. 'There doesn't seem to be anything broken.'

'Thank God.' He ran a hand wildly through his hair. 'Oh, thank

God.' He pulled a chair out and dropped into it like an apple falling off a tree. Putting an elbow on the table he leaned forward and shaded his eyes with his hand. Carrie glanced up at Isa. Her mouth was set in a cynical curve.

'Where are the children?' he asked.

Her heart rate had slowed. It was becoming easier to speak. 'With old Mrs Cooke. They're staying there tonight. So am I.'

Matt lifted his head and looked at her. 'I suppose I deserve that.'

Isa laughed. 'You deserve a lot more than that, pal. And I know a few good men who'd be more than happy to make sure you get it when they find out what you did to this lassie.'

Carrie saw panic flash across his face. *Happy to dish it out, no' so happy to take it.* Oh, Matt, she thought sadly, how have we come to this?

'Are you going to tell these few good men about . . . about what I did?' He was finding it hard to meet Isa's implacable gaze. His eyes were shifting all over the place.

'For some reason, your wife doesnae want me to. But I might still do it, a' the same. Let's just say the possibility is always there.' She let that sink in for a minute. 'Do we understand each other?' When he didn't answer her, she repeated the question.

'Yes,' he said, meeting Isa's eyes at last, 'we understand each other.'

Despite her pain and unhappiness, Carrie felt an odd little spurt of amusement. She was damned glad the redoubtable Mrs Cooke was on her side. What was the phrase – a better friend than an enemy?

Isa helped her up out of the chair, issuing instructions to Matt. He could maybe speak to his wife tomorrow. If Carrie felt up to it.

'Ow! Sorry,' she said apologetically to Isa as she made her slow and tortuous way to the door. 'I think everything's stiffened up.'

'Can I help?' Matt was beside her, holding out his hand. She flinched back, and for a few seconds the three of them froze. Unsurprisingly, Isa was the first to recover her composure.

'Bit of a comedian, your husband,' she observed. 'You can open the doors,' she told him roughly. 'That's all.'

Carrie woke early the next morning, aching all over. She gazed at the outside world, visible through the curtains Florence had drawn back last night after she'd put them all to bed. Archie was on a camp bed under the bay window and April was in her pram at Carrie's feet. The day was overcast, and it was drizzling.

Isa and Florence had doubled up in the kitchen, the former threatening the latter with dire consequences if her snoring kept her awake. A panful of cold water was mentioned. Carrie was, however, beginning to see cracks in the apparent mutual hostility. The two women had made a highly effective team yesterday.

Florence had tucked her in like a child, bringing her warm milk and a straw to drink it through. All that was missing was Gertie the giraffe. She lived in Archie's bed now, through the wall from where the three of them lay. Carrie hoped she hadn't been lonely during the night . . .

She closed her eyes and the events of the previous evening started replaying themselves in her mind's eye. The pictures and sensations were so vivid they had her snapping her eyes wide open again and sitting bolt upright to check the children were safe.

Satisfied that they were sleeping peacefully, she subsided slowly on to the pillows. Now she had other pictures in her head. They were all of a very different Matt to the cold-eyed man who had beaten her last night.

She could see him pushing Archie in a swing, kicking a ball around with him in the park, tenderly cupping April's head in his palm, looking up and smiling directly into her own eyes. She flung herself on to her side and had to stifle a cry as the pain in her hip made itself felt.

Oh, God. Oh, God. Oh, God. What was she going to do?

He was full of contrition, unable to apologise enough. It was six o'clock that evening, and they were in their own front room. Isa and Florence were in the kitchen with the children. As far as Archie was concerned, his two aunties were simply paying a neighbourly visit. In reality, Isa had refused to allow Matt to speak to his wife under any other circumstances.

'We'll not be far away,' she'd said meaningly, ostentatiously making sure Carrie was comfortably ensconced in the low nursing seat. She pointed to the upright chair she had carried through and set in the bay window and gave Matt his orders. 'You're too tall. Sit doon.'

He obeyed her without a whimper, but as soon as she left the room, carefully leaving the door half open, he bent forward, hands on knees.

'Don't get up!'

Carrie hadn't realised till that moment how panicky she was at the thought of being left alone with him. He could move much faster than she could, especially at the moment. He hesitated, and settled back into his chair.

'You're scared of me,' he said bleakly.

'Do you blame me? Look at the state I'm in.' She gestured towards her black eye and bruised face. 'I'm in pain, Matthew. Because of what you did. I don't understand how you could do that to me.'

He bit his lip and turned his head to look out of the narrow pane of glass at the end of the bay window. 'I don't understand it either, Carrie. I got so angry . . . it was like a rage . . . a red rage. I knew I was hurting you, but I couldn't seem to stop myself.'

He didn't need to tell her that. He'd been out of control. That was what had been so frightening about it. 'I suppose I was jealous,' he said. 'Because you'd had that letter from Ewen Livingstone.'

'Matt . . . you have absolutely no reason to be jealous of him. I haven't seen him for years. I got his letter via Isa.'

He stopped looking out of the window. 'So why did you hide it behind the plate? You weren't going to tell me about it, were you?'

'No,' she agreed slowly.

He pressed his advantage. 'Wives shouldn't have secrets from their husbands.'

'It wasn't a case of keeping something secret. You and Ewen always hated each other. I knew you'd be angry if you found out that he'd written to me.'

'How does Isa Cooke know him, anyway?'

'She was a friend of his mother.'

'Oh.' There was a wealth of meaning in that little word. Matt's eyes narrowed. 'Did you know that when we moved in here?' She met the suspicious look head on.

'No, of course not. I only found out a few days ago.'

'Were you planning on writing back to him?'

'He and I were good friends once,' Carrie said carefully.

'I don't want you to write back to him. And I don't like him talking about the children either. The three of you belong to me, not him.'

'Of course we do,' she said, although she didn't much care for the way he had put it.

'You do still want to belong to me?' He sounded so humble.

'Och, Matt . . .'

Before she had time to realise what was happening, he was on his feet and striding across the room. She looked up in alarm, but he knelt in front of her, an impassioned torrent of words pouring out of his mouth.

'Please forgive me, Carrie. I'll never do it again, I promise. It'll never happen again. Please, Carrie. Please.'

He said the words over and over, pleading with her. He began to weep.

'Och, Matt . . .' she said again. This was how it had ended before, with him on his knees in front of her. She didn't have the strength left to resist him. It would have been like refusing comfort to Archie or April when they needed her.

Wincing as she walked, Carrie made her way through to the kitchen.

Florence was sitting with Archie on her lap. One of his picture books lay open in front of them.

'All right, pet?' she asked, glancing up.

'Fine. Isa, can I have a quick word?'

They went across the landing. Isa reached for her cigarettes and matches. 'Don't tell me,' she said, 'let me guess. He's been on his hands and knees to you. Crawled across the floor to beg your forgiveness. Swears he'll never do it again.'

Carrie said nothing. That picture was too accurate by half.

'They're all like that the first time, hen.' She tossed the spent match into the fire. 'They'll promise you the earth if you'll only take them back. But once they discover that hitting you is a hell of a good way of getting you to shut up, they'll not stop at just the once.'

Carrie shook her head. 'No, you're wrong. He's really upset. Isa, he's in there sobbing,' she breathed, incredibly moved by the emotion Matt had shown. 'He hates himself for what he did.'

Isa's face remained set in cynical lines. 'I thought you were an educated woman. Have you never heard o' crocodile tears?'

'No,' Carrie said vehemently. 'It's not like that.'

Isa stared at her for a long moment. Then she sighed. 'Fine. I wish you all the best, hen.'

'Can we still be friends?'

'Aye, sure. Why not?'

'Will you thank Ewen for his letter the next time you write back to him?'

'You're no' going to reply to him yourself?'

'I don't think that would be a very good idea.' She hesitated. 'You'll not tell him anything about all this, I presume.'

'And why would you presume that, Mrs Campbell?'

'Because I'm asking you not to. Please.'

That got her a grunt, presumably of assent. 'Have I to say anything else to Ewen?'

'Tell him I wish him well for the future.'

Isa looked unimpressed. 'That's it?'

'That's it,' Carrie said firmly. 'And I do wish him well, Isa. I wish him all the luck in the world.'

Matt was her husband and the father of her children. He loved them all deeply. He was a passionate man, and a jealous one. She had known that from the outset. Now, however unfounded his suspicions, they had resulted in her getting hurt and him tearing himself to pieces over what he had done to her.

Carrie's way was clear. From now on she would have to make absolutely sure she gave him nothing to be jealous about. Not the slightest thing. It was up to her.

PART III
1942

Chapter 23

'Is Archie still liking the school, Carrie?' called the woman in the next stall. 'Now that the novelty's worn off?'

'He loves it. Can't wait to get there every morning.'

'Does your lassie miss him during the day?'

'A bit,' she said, looking with satisfaction at one of April's dresses from which she'd just managed to remove a stain. 'They've always been good pals, my two.'

'You'll need to be giving her a wee brother or sister to keep her company,' shouted another woman. 'Unless you and your man have forgotten how to go about it!'

'Give me a break,' Carrie said cheerfully. 'April's not four yet, you know.'

'Well,' said Rita Sharkey, 'I've borne my Martin eight children and I wouldn't be without a single one of them.'

'Aye, but you're a Catholic. Carrie's a Proddy.'

'And do Catholics and Proddies do it differently?' asked another interested voice.

Carrie grinned, and reached for a grimy shirt. Despite the hard work involved in doing the weekly wash, she felt able to relax here, be herself in a way which no longer seemed possible at home, at least when Matt was around. The public wash-house was a woman's world, a place to let off steam in more ways than one. Some of the discussions she had listened to over the scrubbing boards and sinks would have made a sailor blush.

'Keep it clean,' she suggested now.

'Oh, my,' came a very creditable attempt at a refined Kelvinside accent, 'is our young Mrs Campbell not awfy polite?'

'Born to be a lady,' said Carrie in a superior tone, 'but never required. Although,' she added, 'Isa's new gentleman friend makes us all feel like royalty. I've never met anyone so well-mannered. Stands up when you come into the room and kisses your hand when he says hello.'

She was bombarded with questions. Isa's romance with a Polish soldier had been the talk of the steamie for the past few weeks.

'Is he good-looking, Carrie? What's his name?'

'Where did she meet him? Do you think he might have any friends going spare?'

'Aye, but none o' them are that desperate!'

Carrie grinned again. 'He's called Leon, he's very handsome and she met him at that club for foreign servicemen at St George's Cross. I expect there's a few lonely lads from Warsaw there.'

Like most British cities, particularly the great ports, Glasgow had become quite a cosmopolitan place since the outbreak of war three years before.

'What does old Mrs Cooke think about it?' asked Rita Sharkey. 'Is she worried Isa'll up sticks and leave her on her own?'

'I suppose she might be.' Carrie rested briefly from her labours and considered the point. 'I don't really know.'

She tucked a strand of her red-gold locks under her headscarf. Knotted at the front, it kept her hair neatly and safely off her face and the back of her neck. With so many women working or contributing to the war effort in some way, fashion was being led by practicality these days.

Shortly before the hostilities started, Carrie and the children had been evacuated to the safety of the countryside, but when the air raids everyone feared so much failed to materialise, many of the mothers and children who'd come with them began to drift back home. Matt had written letter after letter pleading with Carrie to return too. Eventually he simply came and fetched his family. She hadn't argued with him. She'd learned the hard way that wasn't a good idea.

She'd learned a lot of things the hard way over the past few years. Unfortunately, how to spot one of Matt's outbursts coming wasn't one of them. Sometimes she would be convinced the ceiling was about to fall in and he'd be as nice as ninepence, wanting to know what on earth was the matter with her. Couldn't she be a bit more cheerful?

At other times it came completely out of the blue. It was almost a relief when it did. The guilt he experienced afterwards guaranteed a few months' respite to follow. The pattern was always the same. Once the fury of the storm was spent he'd come home and throw himself at her feet, making abject apologies and tearful promises never to hurt her again. She had grown so tired of it all, but his need for her forgiveness was overwhelming. Like a broken tree branch borne away on a flooded stream she found herself being swept along with it.

As far as she could she kept it hidden from Archie and April. She didn't want them thinking badly of their daddy. She kept it from Isa and Florence too, not so much because she was fearful of the former carrying out her threat of getting someone to administer a beating to him, but more out of a stubborn pride. She knew they had their suspicions, but Matt had learned some things too: to keep his voice down and to hit her where it wouldn't show. He was careful now only ever to slap her face, not punch it.

He was desperate to join up, but as a railwayman he was in a reserved occupation, permission to resign his post to be granted only under the most exceptional of circumstances. Somehow Carrie got the blame for that. If he had been a single man with no ties the army would surely have welcomed him with open arms.

Offended by his lack of logic, she had answered him back on that one. Her temerity brought down a torrent of verbal abuse on her head. It left Archie and April, sitting at the tea table with them, wide-eyed and pale as their father stormed out of the house. An hour later he came back with ice-creams all round. The smiles returned to the children's faces, but Carrie recognised the pattern: unforgivable behaviour followed by an apology you had no choice but to accept.

In bed later that night, Matt had joked about how quiet she was and tried to coax her into responding to his questing hands and mouth. When she failed to co-operate, he did what he wanted to anyway. That was something else she had grown very tired of.

And yet he had been wonderful during those terrifying nights when the bombs had finally dropped, making sure everyone in the building took shelter and that the necessary supplies and equipment were at hand. She remembered how strong he had been when both her father and her mother had died. He was good in a crisis, needed something like that in his life – a challenge he could rise to. If only he could get an exemption from his job!

Archie gave his mother and sister a nonchalant wave and ran over to join the queue of children waiting to go in at the infants' entrance. Before Carrie could yell at him to avoid the icy puddle in the middle of the playground he glided smoothly over it, the gas-mask case he wore bandolier-style over his coat swinging out in a graceful arc. Just as well, she supposed. He might have more than a term to go before he completed primary one, but he hated his little friends to see his mother babying him.

'Right then, young lady. Out you come.'

Although her daughter would be four years old in less than a month and liked to walk everywhere, Carrie still used the pushchair when she was in a hurry or didn't want to take too long to get somewhere, like on this cold March morning. However, it was milder than she'd thought today. They could take their time going home.

They might have visited April's grandparents – they weren't too far from North Gardner Street – only Charles and Shona Campbell were no longer there. Within a month of war having been declared in

September 1939, they'd taken themselves off to a hotel on the coast which offered very modest rates for long-term residents.

She brought the pushchair to a halt. April had stopped to pat a dog out for a walk with its elderly master. She was very fond of animals, as was her brother, currently trying to persuade his mother to allow him to have a white mouse as a pet. Carrie had offered him a choice.

'You can have a white mouse, or you can have me.' Fortunately, Archie had made the wise decision.

They said goodbye to the elderly man and made their way home. April was chattering away, seeming not to notice that her mother was unusually absent-minded today. Carrie was steeling herself for a confrontation with Matthew.

Almost everybody she knew was doing something towards the war effort. Florence was knitting comforts for the troops. Isa, a part-time shop assistant before the war and now doing a far more physical job in a local factory, made fun of the socks, gloves and scarves in front of her mother-in-law and told everyone else how beautifully made they were.

There was a new resolve in the air. This war was only going to be won if everyone pulled together. It had started as a matter of principle, a refusal to let an evil dictator rewrite the map of Europe and deprive millions of innocent people of their rights and their freedom. Carrie read the newspapers and listened to the wireless. She knew what was going on in Germany and the occupied countries.

Trouble was, that knowledge could made you feel so helpless. Did the people who were suffering know you were thinking about them and sympathising with their plight? She hoped so. She wanted to do an awful lot more than think about it.

As the mother of young children, she was exempt from any obligation to do war work, but some pretty strong encouragement was being offered. Government-run crèches had been established. There was one locally. Without telling Matthew, she had made a tour of inspection last week. It was bright and airy and full of toys and staffed by pleasant nursery nurses – and they could offer April a place for four hours a day, five days a week.

Carrie was sure her daughter would love it. She did miss her brother when he was at school. That night, however, wondering if she was doing the right thing, she had confided her plans to Florence and Isa. 'What if she doesn't settle at the nursery? What if I have to work more than four hours a day, or do odd shifts?'

'Then I'll take her,' said Florence stoutly. 'You know I'd love to, pet. And I'd easy take Archie to and from the school, and keep him afterwards. Nae bother at all.'

So that was all settled. Now all she had to do was get Matt to agree to it. *All she had to do.* That was a laugh. He was going to hit the roof. She knew that for a fact.

The shortage of manpower in the forces had caused a major rethink about railway work remaining a reserved occupation. While amateurs couldn't do the work of drivers and other technical staff, many exemptions had been granted to men in the clerical grades, their posts taken over by women.

Despite being so keen to get an exemption himself, and infuriated when Pascal Sharkey was allowed to go, Matt had heaped scorn on the idea of extensive female labour being used to keep the railways running. Take signal boxes, for example. What woman would have the strength to pull the long and heavy levers which operated the gantries by the track outside? Carrie, who'd tried her hand at the task whilst visiting Mary and Douglas the previous summer, had found it hard to bite her tongue. She told him she was quite sure she'd be capable of it and what's more, she'd like to try.

Matt told her coldly that he'd never heard such a piece of nonsense in his life. And who was she proposing would look after the children if she wasn't here – that old witch across the landing? When she tentatively mentioned the crèche, he declared that no child of his was going to be looked after by strangers for half the week. Carrie's place was at home, looking after him and the children.

'If we're lucky, you'll maybe have a new baby to look after soon,' he had added, giving her a significant look. He had made it painfully clear on a previous occasion that he suspected her of having done something to prevent that. She hadn't, but she'd been given some advice on how she might have done so, and from someone she would previously have considered an unlikely source of such information.

Leon the Polish soldier was long gone. He had been superseded by another impeccably mannered fellow countryman who in turn had been followed by a Free Frenchman. Carrie didn't think Florence needed to worry about losing the companionship of her daughter-in-law but she did worry that Isa was in danger of getting herself a reputation. When she remonstrated with her friend, she was astounded by the response she got.

'We might all be dead tomorrow. I'm having a bit of fun before I'm too old for it. I'm no' the only one, no' by a long chalk.'

'You're not too old to get yourself into trouble,' Carrie had tossed back. 'What would you do then?'

'I'll not get myself into trouble,' came the calm reply. 'If Pierre doesnae do something beforehand, I do it afterwards – if you catch my drift.' She went on to give Carrie the details.

'And that works, does it?'

'I bloody hope so. I'm a bit past the motherhood stage.'

'Oh, Isa!'

Her friend laid a hand on her shoulder. 'I know you mean well, hen, but folk gossip whatever you do. I might as well give them something to talk about.'

Carrie put her key in the lock and ushered April into the house. She was still quiet, silently rehearsing the arguments she was going to put to Matt as to why she should go out to work. She had to persuade him to listen to her without flying off the handle. Or worse. The very thought gave her the usual symptoms: a churning stomach and clammy hands.

She wanted to do her bit, make her contribution to the struggle the whole country was engaged in, but it had occurred to her that going out to work could be important for another reason too. Maybe when Matt saw that she could cope with a part-time job and running the house and caring for the children he'd see her in a different light. She'd long ago lost the status she'd enjoyed while he'd been courting her. She had been the stationmaster's daughter then, and he had liked that. He didn't seem to have any respect for her now.

Carrie knew one thing. They couldn't go on like this. She was dying slowly inside. Another few years of being browbeaten by him and there would be very little left of the girl who used to be Caroline Burgess. Their marriage would be a hollow sham. For both their sakes she had to do something about it.

She filled the kettle and set it on top of the range. Settling April at the table, she gave her a biscuit and a cup of milk. Then she took a sketch pad and pencils from a drawer and laid them beside her.

'After you've finished your piece,' she said.

The little girl beamed at her with a mouth full of biscuit. She was such a cute wee thing, and so loveable. 'Going to draw Bobby,' she announced. Donald Nicholson's faithful canine companion was one of her special friends.

Carrie watched the masterpiece take shape as she sipped her tea. *Obviously going to be a vet when she grows up. Maybe an artist, of course. That would be fine too.*

A doting mama, that was her all right. She could laugh at herself, but she knew that whatever her children's dreams and ambitions might be, it was her job to support them in their endeavours. She would rejoice with them when they succeeded and offer comfort when they met with reverses and disappointments. They needed her strong and happy. She needed herself strong and happy. So did Matt.

For all our sakes then, she thought, for all our sakes.

* * *

He was due home in a few minutes. Everything was ready: house and children spotless, a nice meal – or as nice as rationing would allow – prepared. She would tell him before she served the pudding, reminding him that the children were present. She would also casually drop into the conversation that Isa was coming across later, the excuse being that she wanted help with trying out a new hairstyle.

Isa and Matt lived in a state of armed neutrality, speaking to each other only when absolutely necessary, but Carrie knew he had a healthy respect for their sharp-tongued neighbour. She'd cooked up the plot with her this afternoon. Isa had strict instructions as to exactly what time she was to chap at the door.

'Don't you worry, hen,' she'd said grimly. 'I'll no' go away without seeing you and making sure you're all right.'

Carrie had been forced to tell her the truth about Matt's sporadic but continuing violence over the past couple of years. Isa had reacted angrily, demanding to know why Carrie had kept it to herself for so long, and extracted a solemn promise that she would let her know when it happened again.

'But, Isa,' she protested, 'I'm hoping there won't be a next time. Things are going to be different from now on. As long as I can get him to agree to this.'

'There's one born every minute, Carrie, and you're it,' retorted Isa in exasperation. She gave her a pitying look. 'Does your mammy know you're oot? The leopard doesnae change his spots, you know.'

Carrie shook her head. Hair freshly washed, she intended to leave it loose for the rest of the day. 'No,' she insisted. 'People can change. I know they can.'

She wasn't sure if she was quite so confident about that when she heard Matt come in that evening. She did her best to look natural, head tilted expectantly towards the door. Some hopes. She didn't have butterflies in her stomach, it was more like Hurricanes and Spitfires screaming around in there.

She knew as soon as he entered the room that something had happened. His face was glowing. She walked over to greet him, unable to resist his obvious excitement. He seized her hands.

'They've granted the exemption! I can join up!'

Chapter 24

They talked solidly for the next hour, all through their meal. To be more accurate, Matthew talked and Carrie listened. He was full of it: which service he might be directed towards – army, navy or air force; whether or not he would get a choice about that; how he himself would prefer the army. The Argyll and Sutherland Highlanders would be his first choice of regiment, the most appropriate for a Campbell, didn't she think? They'd been in the Mediterranean since before the outbreak of war. He'd probably end up in North Africa.

His father had served with the Argylls during the Great War. That reminded him, he'd better write to his parents tonight, share the good news with them. He could be whisked away to start basic training within the next two weeks, you know. They'd have to get themselves organised for his departure.

When he stopped to draw breath, Carrie took a deep breath of her own and plunged in. This was the best chance she would ever have to persuade him that she ought to be doing her bit too.

Matt looked faintly startled, but then he shrugged. 'Why not?' He grinned. 'They might even give you my job.'

'I'll only be working part-time,' she pointed out, and started to explain the arrangements which would ensure the children were cared for every minute of the day. Matthew brushed that aside, and went back to talking about his own plans.

Carrie sat back in her chair, wondering whether she ought to be laughing or crying – hysterically, in both cases. She'd been building up to this for weeks, had spent most of today bracing herself for a battle royal. Now the solid wall of his opposition was crumbling away before her eyes. It was a funny old world. She felt giddy with shock and relief.

When Isa came round as arranged shortly after tea, Matthew couldn't resist telling her his news. She listened without comment.

'Could you not have shown a wee bit more enthusiasm?' muttered Carrie as she took her friend by the elbow and steered her through to the front room. 'For my sake, if not for his?' Isa waited until the door was safely shut behind them.

'So he's the blue-eyed boy now, is he? Have you forgotten why you asked me to knock on your door tonight? What you were scared he might do to you?'

'I know, Isa, but I really think him joining up is going to make a big difference. He could come home a changed man. He's always been searching for something. Maybe this could be it. Don't you remember how good he was during the Blitz?'

'How many chances are you going to give him, hen? Personally, I think he's had a few too many.'

Isa plonked herself down at the dressing-table and handed over the hairbrush she'd brought with her. Standing behind her, Carrie began smoothing her hair, but her subject's attention wasn't on her coiffure. She was studying their combined reflections in the mirror.

'I'm happy for you,' she said finally. 'You'll get a bit o' bloody peace at last. Men,' she said in disgust, 'who needs them?'

Carrie snorted. 'I thought you quite liked them as a species, Mrs Cooke.'

'They're only good for one thing,' said Isa darkly, 'plus they come in handy when you need a piano shifted. Otherwise I wouldnae give them houseroom.'

Matt was still smiling as they got ready for bed that night.

'I'm happy for you,' Carrie said, unconsciously repeating the words Isa had used to her earlier in the evening. She darted a little glance at him as he took off his shirt. 'I think . . . perhaps . . . that you've needed something like this.'

He paused in his undressing. 'Carrie . . . it hasn't always been as it should have been. Maybe this could be a new start for us.'

She lifted her chin. 'Do you want it to be?'

'Yes. Oh, yes!'

He was beside her, wrapping his arms around her, kissing her eyelids, her cheeks, her lips. 'I love you,' he said, 'I really love you.'

'I know you do,' she said sadly, placing a hand on his chest and looking up at him, 'but things have got to change.'

'They will. I promise.'

Her eyes scoured his face. 'Can I believe you this time?'

'You can,' he said, and bent his head to her lips. His kiss was light, and rather formal. He had kissed her like that on their wedding day, after the minister had pronounced them man and wife. A promise given, and a promise received. A promise which had been broken so many times. 'You'll wait for me?'

'Of course I will. I'm your wife.'

'So I don't need to worry about you getting up to anything while I'm away?' he asked lightly.

She chose to take that as a joke. 'As long as I don't either. No consorting with pretty servicewomen after working hours.'

'There won't be any as pretty as you.' He put his hand to the back of her head, buried his fingers in her smooth hair. 'Kiss me again,' he said. His voice had grown husky with desire. 'Properly, this time.'

It had never occurred to Carrie that she would work anywhere else than on the railway and it came as something of a shock to find she couldn't simply walk up the stairs to the station and start. While they were sure there would be a place for her, she would have to go through the official channels and apply via the women's section of the labour exchange.

With typical tact, Isa told her she'd better smarten herself up a wee bit. Since Matt had taken most of the spare cash with him when he went off to training camp, it was a case of make do and mend. Carrie had a square-shouldered navy costume she'd bought a couple of years ago which wasn't bad, but the cheap hat she'd bought to go with it was looking a bit sorry for itself.

'It's too plain,' pronounced the fashion expert, eyeing it suspiciously. Florence triumphantly produced a box of trimmings.

'What would she be wanting wi' those old things?' said Isa in disgust. 'We're looking for something up-to-date and modern.' She picked up an ornate hat-pin and threw it back into the box with an expression of disgust.

'You hold your tongue, Isabella Cooke!' The old woman winked at Carrie. 'I know exactly what we're going to find in here.' With a cry of satisfaction, she fished out a little sprig of fabric daisies and held them against the navy felt hat.

'What d'ye think, hen? I'll stitch them on for you. It would all fit nicely together if you wore your white blouse with the scalloped collar.'

'That would be ideal,' Carrie agreed. She was perfectly capable of sewing them on by herself, but she knew Florence wanted to perform the small task for her. 'Don't you think so, Isa?'

She was trying not to laugh at the way the younger Mrs Cooke's fashion sense was warring with her accustomed reluctance to admit that her mother-in-law might be right about anything. Putting the hat on, Carrie tried the daisies in one position and then another as she studied her head and shoulders in the mirror. The little white flowers lifted the dark hat, but they weren't too fussy, and if she did her hair nicely . . . well, there would be no stopping her. Suddenly light-hearted, she whirled round, an impish smile on her face.

'You're that bonnie, Carrie,' said Florence. 'I was bonnie like you once.'

'When was that?' asked Isa with a magnificent curl of the lip. 'When the old queen was on the throne? And I'm no' talking about Mary – unless it was Mary, Queen of Scots.' She looked up at Carrie.

'She is bonnie and the hat looks good, but only because the lassie sets it off properly wi' her lovely hair. Nothing to do wi' yon daft wee trimmings o' yours.'

'So should Florence *not* sew them on then?' asked Carrie innocently.

'I suppose there's no harm in having them. It'll keep the auld yin out o' mischief for ten minutes. You know what they say – the devil makes work for idle hands.'

Carrie and Florence exchanged serene smiles.

The young woman sitting behind the small pine desk couldn't have been much older than Carrie herself, but she oozed confidence. Her suit might have been cut in approved Utility style, obeying all the wartime restrictions designed to avoid wasteful use of cloth, but you could tell by looking at it that the fabric was of a much better quality than Carrie's costume. She also had a lovely hat, which she had removed and laid in front of her. It was like a small plate, designed to be worn at a forward tilt, and adorned with two different colours of net and a large artificial lily.

'Railway work, you say.' She paused. 'And why would you think you were suitable for that, Mrs . . .' her eyes dropped to the pad of paper in front of her '. . . Campbell? It is Mrs?'

Carrie nodded. She'd felt confident when she had left the house, ready to take on the world. Florence and Isa had admired her and told her how smart she looked and both Archie and April had given her a kiss for luck. Now she was beginning to feel nervous. Why did she think she was suitable for railway work? Because she was a station-master's daughter? She swallowed. Answer the simple question first.

'Yes,' she said, 'I'm married. My husband's currently serving with the Argyll and Sutherland Highlanders. He's anticipating embarking for North Africa before the end of the year.' Maybe that piece of information would impress her interviewer. However, the girl didn't react to it, only asked if she had any children.

'Two. A boy of six and a girl of four.'

'But that would give you an exemption from war work. You do understand that, Mrs Campbell?' Her brow creased in obvious perplexity at Carrie's obtuseness.

'I understand that perfectly,' she said steadily, 'but I want to do my bit like everyone else.'

She'd changed her mind about the girl's hat. It was a ridiculous object, too fussy for words. Her own was far more chic.

The young woman looked doubtful. 'It could be very demanding on you, you know, especially if you've been merely a housewife for the past few years, and not working at all.'

Merely a housewife. Not working at all. Carrie toyed briefly with the idea of asking little Miss Snooty which window she wished to leave by. No, she'd go for the supercilious air herself. She'd been able to do it very well once upon a time.

'Perhaps in the circles in which you mix that's the case, but I can assure you that housewives in Partick work extremely hard, Miss . . .' Carrie stopped. 'I'm sorry,' she said sweetly, 'I don't know your name. You didn't introduce yourself, did you?'

Miss Snooty blinked twice. She looked like a startled haddock. Any minute now bubbles would float out of her mouth and drift slowly up to the ceiling.

'Simpson,' she said hurriedly. 'Rachel Simpson.'

'Well, Miss Simpson, I can assure you I'm no stranger to hard work and I also have a reasonably good brain. It still functions quite efficiently. Now, will you kindly tell me how I go about applying to work on the railway?'

Although she'd had a notion of working in the signal box – partially to prove to Matt that she could do it – Carrie was very happy when she was directed into the booking office. It felt like coming home. She knew quite a few of the staff members, too old for the call-up, from her father's time. One of the clerks kept calling her Miss Burgess. She liked that. It made her feel like a girl again.

A lot of the drivers remembered her, as did many of the regular business travellers. Several people from both groups shared their memories of Archie with her. She liked that too. She was part of the railway family again, in a way she never had been with Matt. He hadn't cared for her and the children visiting him at work. He'd considered it unprofessional.

It was hard work: learning the job, making sure she gave the children enough of her time, keeping the household running smoothly. She had no trouble sleeping at night, but the shift work she hadn't much fancied delivered an unexpected bonus. Every so often she found herself with the oddest of commodities: time to herself.

Normally she filled a free morning with housework, getting twice as much done without the children under her feet. Once or twice, feeling deliciously guilty, she'd given herself a home-made face mask or sat down and read a book. She'd started going to the library again. It was a long while since she'd had the time or the inclination to do that.

Carrie pondered the illogicality of the situation. Here she was, working harder than ever, effectively doing two jobs. She ought to be feeling harassed, but she was more relaxed than she'd been for ages. She wasn't too happy when the obvious deduction presented itself. Matt wasn't at home.

Apart from a brief leave in August, he'd been away now for over seven months, but she was uncomfortably aware of not missing him very much. The bed was certainly cold at night when she climbed in, but that was counteracted by other things. The most important of those was the pleasure of settling down for a comfortable evening by the fire and knowing the peace and quiet wasn't going to be shattered by one of Matt's outbursts.

He was an erratic correspondent, but he seemed to be enjoying himself. From time to time she found herself wondering if he might be enjoying himself a bit too much. His letters were full of names. Mention of male comrades was fine and she was glad he was meeting new people, but she was uneasy about the occasional passing reference to the servicewomen, nurses and female civilian staff connected with the training camp. Perhaps it was what she suspected he was leaving out. Matthew was a handsome man, and this war did seem to be having rather an adverse effect on people's morals . . .

Carrie could understand it to a certain extent. The poster beside the booking-office window might ask people if their journey was really necessary, but sometimes it seemed as if the whole world was on the move. There were so many lonely folk far from home.

There were the servicemen and women from all corners of Britain and the Empire, the Poles, the Free French, and now that the United States had entered the war, the Americans. The latter had an appeal all of their own, with their music, their stylish uniforms and their film-star accents. Overpaid, over-sexed and over here, as a well-spoken young English airman she met at the servicemen's club had put it acerbically to Carrie.

Isa had more or less dragged her along there, insisting that she needed a night out. According to her, the young man definitely had his eye on Carrie.

'He just needs a wee bit of encouragement,' she said when the two of them paid a trip to the ladies' room in the middle of the evening. 'Put your hand on his knee or something.'

'I'll do no such thing,' she said indignantly. 'I'm a married woman.'

Isa gave her a look. 'And do you think your dear husband is remembering that he's a married man? I hae ma doots.'

Carrie had her doubts too, especially when Matthew wrote to say he was going to spend a seventy-two-hour leave visiting London with a group of the chaps, rather than coming home. Rumour had it that their departure for the Med was going to be postponed until the beginning of 1943, and Glasgow was a long way to come for such a short time. She knew what the delays were like on the railway these days, what with the blackout, air-raid alerts and all the rest! He knew she'd understand.

* * *

Matt wasn't the only man who found it hard to believe that women were physically capable of operating signals. Despite all the evidence to the contrary, there was interminable discussion about it. While the signalwomen themselves insisted there was no problem, they had other complaints about their working conditions. A major one was the absence of toilet facilities in or near the box. If you were covering a shift on your own, walking back to the station to use the ladies' room meant leaving your post unstaffed for a potentially dangerous length of time.

'What did the men do?' asked one new recruit, as the female staff sat in the booking office mulling over the problem.

'Use your loaf,' said Carrie drily. She turned to Anne-Marie, the girl who'd raised the issue. She was Pascal Sharkey's fiancée. 'What about installing a chemical toilet at the box itself?'

Anne-Marie nodded her head enthusiastically. 'Aye. But this is a problem all along the line, Carrie. And there's a few other things we're concerned about. Like getting to and from work late at night or early in the morning. We're wondering if it might be possible to give more consideration to pairing women up when the rosters are prepared. Say you were on a late shift and I was too. We'd both be happier about walking home if we had company.'

'Yes,' she replied, thinking about it. 'That's a good idea.' She'd had a few nervous moments going home in the blackout, especially at this time of year. They were into November, with its attendant fogs. 'Why not put it all in a letter to Mr Gibson? You know how everything has to go through official channels. That gives him something to send to Queen Street – or Edinburgh. You could get up a petition, too. Collect as many signatures as you can to go along with it.'

'I can do that bit, but would you compose the letter, Carrie? I'm a rotten speller and you're good at that sort of thing. You'll know how to put it.'

'Gladly,' she said. 'Leave it with me.'

'Well,' said George Gibson jovially, 'you ladies have started something, and no mistake.'

Carrie looked up from her ledger. It was two weeks later, and her boss had come into the booking office with a piece of paper in his hand.

'We have?'

He nodded. 'They've decided to do a survey of all female employees. Make sure working conditions are . . .' he read out from the letter he held '. . . "comfortable, suitable and appropriate to their needs". Someone's coming through from Edinburgh to interview you all.'

'Oh, good. Are they sending a man or a woman?'

He checked the letter again. 'They don't give a name, but he or she will arrive next Monday afternoon and base themselves with us for two or three weeks, travelling up and down the line to do inspections and interviews. They wonder if it would be possible to collate and type up the information here.' He looked around 'We'd better clear that table in the corner. Can you get on to that sometime before Monday, Mrs Campbell?'

'Nae bother,' said Carrie, and went back to her columns, pleased that the petition and her letter had produced such a positive result.

She was doing a sort of half back shift, working from one o'clock till six. It meant a late tea for the children, but Florence always gave them something to tide them over. In the winter she insisted Archie needed something hot as soon as he came in from school. Glancing at the clock, Carrie knew that he and April would be sitting down right now to a plate of Florence's home-made soup. Her Scotch broth was legendary, so thick with vegetables and pearl barley you could almost stick the spoon up in it. It was a feat both Archie and April had been known to attempt. She smiled. It was good to know they were being so well looked after.

When she got home that evening, she saw that the door to the flat on the other side of the landing was open a crack. Isa emerged from it, pulling the door shut behind her. 'Your hoose. Now.' She hustled a bemused Carrie into her own kitchen.

'Fine,' she said, 'but why all the cloak and dagger stuff?'

'Because we cannae discuss this in front o' the children,' said Isa. 'Sit doon.' She pulled a chair out from the table. Carrie remained standing.

'Isa,' she said in exasperation, 'what are you on about?'

'This railway official who's coming through from Edinburgh next week.'

'What about him? Or her?' she added. 'We don't know yet whether we're getting a man or a woman. How do you know about it?' she asked curiously. 'I only found out a couple of hours ago.'

'Oh, it's a man you're getting, all right,' said Isa grimly.

Carrie sat down. She no longer needed an answer to the question she'd posed. Not now she knew who the inspector was.

Chapter 25

'Ewen's still with the railway, then?' She'd wondered about that. 'Do you ever see him?'

Isa took her cigarettes out of the pocket of her apron. 'Now and again. He gave us a great day out in Edinburgh last summer, showed us all the sights and treated us to a slap-up meal. He was celebrating his engagement. To a lovely lassie called Moira. We met her too.'

'Oh,' Carrie said. 'That's nice.' She stood up, undid her coat and walked across to hang it up on the back of the door. She turned. Isa was lighting up. 'Is he staying with you and Florence while he's on his tour of inspection here?'

'That's what I need to speak to you about. Your man's no' due home on leave soon, is he?'

The quick stab of anxiety was like a fist clenching inside Carrie's stomach. 'You think the sparks might fly if he and Ewen were ever to meet up again?'

Isa picked a piece of tobacco off her tongue. 'I think it would be like Guy Fawkes night. Or probably mair like the Blitz. The ARP would have to evacuate the surrounding area to prevent innocent bystanders getting caught in the crossfire. Or cut by the flying glass. Is he coming home soon?'

'Not as far as I know. He's got some leave, but he's going to spend it in London.'

'All right for some, eh?'

'What does that mean?'

'Oh, nothing,' said Isa airily, 'maybe I'm thinking that what's sauce for the gander ought to be sauce for the goose.'

'I'm a married woman, Isa,' said Carrie levelly.

'Aye,' came the reply. 'So you are, pet.'

Ewen was ushered into the booking office by the stationmaster at half-past three on the following Monday afternoon.

'And here we have –'

'No need for introductions. Mrs Campbell and I are old friends.'

The voice was deeper than she remembered, but then he was a lot older now. She'd done the sums over the weekend. If she was twenty-four, he had to be twenty-six.

Old friends? Maybe. She had known the boy. It was the man who was standing there smiling at her. She was having some difficulty in recognising him. Oh, he had the same physical characteristics as Ewen Livingstone, although the neatly cut fair hair was attractively windswept rather than tousled, but he had an air of sophistication about him which the rough and ready lad she had known could never have aspired to.

He came forward, and she took in the well-cut dark suit and casually unbuttoned overcoat. Beneath his waistcoat he wore a white shirt and a discreetly striped tie. He looked more than smart: the overall impression was stylish. She wondered if he'd effected the transformation himself or if his fiancée was responsible for it.

He switched the briefcase he carried to his left hand and held out the right one. 'How are you?' he asked.

'Ewen,' she said, and felt strong fingers wrap themselves firmly around her own. Out of the corner of her eye, she saw that her boss was a little taken aback by her familiarity with this representative of head office. 'You're looking well.'

'I'm all the better for seeing you,' he told her warmly. There was still something very youthful there, a sense of boundless vigour and energy. No doubt she looked to him exactly what she was, a tired mother-of-two.

'Well,' said Mr Gibson. 'Mrs Campbell has prepared this table for you to work at. And you'll render every assistance to Mr Livingstone, won't you, Mrs Campbell?' He seemed determined to keep things on a formal footing.

Ewen coughed, put a hand to his mouth and turned his head to one side. Carrie knew immediately he was covering up a laugh.

'Well,' she said, when the other man had finally left the office, 'where would you like to start, *Mr Livingstone*?'

His eyes gleamed and he gestured with his thumb in the direction of the door. 'Doesn't remember me, does he? I've been with him for the past half hour and it's been Mr Livingstone this and Mr Livingstone that. I must say, *Mrs Campbell*, I'm mightily amused by all this deference.'

His accent had undergone quite a shift. He still had a warm west of Scotland burr, but there were touches of Edinburgh in there – polite Edinburgh at that.

'That's why you were laughing,' she said, suddenly realising. 'I'd forgotten you and he had coincided for a few months.'

'I obviously made such an impact he doesn't recall he was once my boss,' said Ewen wryly, laying his briefcase on the table he'd been allocated. 'He hasn't even made the connection as to how you and I know each other.' He shrugged off his coat.

Carrie took it from him and hung it up on the coat-stand to the right of the coal fire which was burning sluggishly in the back wall. The action seemed to take him by surprise, although he murmured his thanks as she smoothed down the soft dark blue woollen folds and returned to her stool in front of the ticket window.

'It has been seven years,' she pointed out. 'You've changed a lot.'

He perched himself on the edge of the table, one leg straight, one crooked over the corner of it. 'Have I?'

'I would say so.' She waved her hand in a gesture designed to encompass his appearance, his position in the company and the respect which the stationmaster had just shown him. 'And you're obviously an important person these days.'

'I don't know about that,' he said, looking faintly embarrassed.

'But you're in a special department?' she persisted. 'Doing some kind of war work?'

'Sort of. I suppose you'd call it strategic planning.'

'How did that come about?'

'Well,' he said, 'it occurred to me a couple of years before the war broke out that the railways were going to be crucially important – in lots of ways – but especially if Hitler attempted an invasion. We had to get ourselves ready for that, I thought, have contingency plans, and not only for the obvious places like the big cities and ports.' He adjusted his position, relaxing into his subject.

'I thought German parachutists were more likely to land somewhere quiet and remote – like the Highlands, for instance. Somewhere they would stand a better chance of landing undetected.'

Carrie nodded, taking his point. 'But they would plan to be close to a railway station?' she suggested. 'Or several railway stations? The smaller ones?'

He waited while she thought it out.

'Either to use the train to get to where they needed to go,' she said slowly, 'in small groups less likely to cause suspicion.' She thought about it some more. Ewen remained silent. He'd have made a good teacher. 'Or perhaps . . . to take over a station as a base . . . maybe even a whole line. Control supplies and information – people too – coming into and going out of that particular area.'

'All of those and more,' he said approvingly. Now he even looked like a teacher, pleased but unsurprised that a bright pupil had come up with the right answer. 'I started looking into it in my own time – working out what might happen, how we ought to react to it, how we could train people to be prepared for every eventuality. Hopefully.' The face-splitting smile was exactly the same, at any rate. 'I wrote up a report, made a set of recommendations. That's when I decided to learn how to type.'

'You thought it would look more impressive?'

'Aye. I was a bit embarrassed to ask any of the lassies at Waverley to do it for me, but I got one of them to teach me the rudiments of typewriting. We had a good laugh over it,' he said. 'Me and my big hands.' He stretched them out in front of him, still smiling broadly. 'Anyway,' he went on, 'I typed it up and submitted it to the general manager.'

'He was impressed, I take it.'

He made a face, self-deprecating. 'Well, I think a lot of other people were coming to the same conclusions as me, but it all kind of came together. And the general manager's always taken an interest in me.' He glanced round at their surroundings. 'Ever since that day in here, when you coached me to make that wee speech about the waterproof clothing. This is where it all started. If I've made anything of my life, it's all thanks to you, Carrie.'

'It's nice of you to say so, but you're giving me far too much credit.' She stood up. 'Right then, I suppose you'll want to get started as soon as possible. You've a lot of ground to cover. Would you like to go straight down to our signal box now?'

'Is the bummer from Edinburgh here yet? Oh!'

The young clerkess who had just looked into the room had gone scarlet, but Ewen was laughing. 'Please introduce me to your colleague, Mrs Campbell.'

'I'm the parcels clerkess,' said the girl, letting go of the heavy booking-office door and holding out her hand. 'And foot-in-mouth specialist. Maybe you'd like to interview me first?'

'It would be a pleasure,' he said expansively. 'Take a seat.' He indicated the table. 'Oh, damn. I've left my portable typewriter through in the stationmaster's office.'

'I'll get it,' offered the girl. Carrie laid a hand on her shoulder, preventing her from rising from the table. 'No. Let me.'

Twenty minutes later Mr Gibson popped his head round the door.

'Got everything you need, Mr Livingstone?'

Ewen looked up. 'Aye, I'm fine. We've just completed the first interview of the project.' He smiled at the foot-in-mouth specialist. 'I think I'll go and see the local signalwomen now.'

'Will one of these ladies go along to show you the way? Mrs Campbell,' the stationmaster said, 'you might appreciate the fresh air, you're looking a wee touch pale today. I'll cover for you.'

'No need for that,' said Ewen smoothly. He rose to his feet, put some plain sheets of paper in a buff folder, lifted a pen and slipped it into the inside pocket of his jacket. 'I'm sure I can manage.'

'Do you have a good torch?' Carrie asked. 'It'll be dark soon. Certainly by the time you're coming back.'

The railway and all other modes of transport were as subject to the blackout regulations as everywhere else – much to the disgust of the men and women trying to operate them. However, there had been a spate of accidents during the first two winters of the war, mainly trains going into the back of other trains because the drivers simply couldn't see each other. Some railway workers moving about stations and marshalling yards had also been hurt. The government had been forced to make some concessions about lighting.

Carrie pointed to four small but sturdy paraffin lamps sitting in a neat row to one side of the booking-office window. 'Borrow one of those if you like. Your clothes are dark. A lamp will make you a lot more visible.'

'It's nice to know she cares,' said the parcels clerkess teasingly. 'Isn't it, Mr Livingstone?'

'It certainly is,' he said. He turned to Carrie. 'Will you still be here when I get back?'

'I go off duty at six.'

'Good. I'll be back well before then.'

The office seemed very empty after he had gone, although there were people coming in and out all the time: staff members on various errands and passengers at the ticket window. She thought of him out in the cold December afternoon on his way to the signal box. He must have done that walk hundreds of times. At least he was warmly clad this time, and he was wielding a fountain pen, not a pick-axe. Funny how much his life had changed. Funny how much her own had.

Her eyes lit on the fire in the back wall. It wasn't exactly a cheerful blaze. She'd better do something about that. Anyone coming in from the outside world would appreciate the warmth. Slipping off her stool, she walked across the room and lifted the poker from its hook. She gave the coals in the nest a vigorous rake, pulled out the ash pan, opened up the air vent and replenished the fire from the brass scuttle which stood beside it. Samuel the lad porter came in at that moment and she asked him to empty the ashes for her and refill the coal scuttle.

'Nae bother,' he said cheerily. 'It's a right cold day, eh, Mrs Campbell?'

'Aye,' she agreed, 'and it always gets chillier when the daylight goes.'

The late afternoon was usually something of a nightmare for Carrie. People keen to get home after their day's work were inclined to thrust their tickets at her from all directions, occasionally prompting her to issue a gentle reminder: 'I'm not an octopus, you know.' The special trains bringing the workers home from the Singer sewing machine factory at Clydebank, now given over to munitions, were the worst. A sea of impatient humanity piled off them.

At twenty to six, when the peak of the passenger traffic had passed, she took time off to warm her hands by the booking-office fire. You couldn't wear gloves when you were collecting tickets. She glanced up at the clock. Ewen was taking an awfully long time.

He came in ten minutes later, bubbling with vitality, filling the room with his presence. 'I met Martin Sharkey on the way back,' he announced. 'We were talking for a while.'

'He'd have been delighted to see you,' she said, touched by his obvious pleasure in meeting his old foreman.

'Aye,' he agreed, placing the now extinguished lamp back with its fellows. 'He greeted me like a long-lost son.' Ewen's voice had grown husky. 'Seemed quite proud of me, in fact.'

'Did he take you into the bothy?'

'Och, no.' He laughed. 'Although we stood outside it for nearly half an hour.'

Carrie tutted. 'In this cold? You must be frozen. Come here and get a warm.'

He laid his folder on the table, took off his coat and threw it over a chair before joining her by the fire. He turned and looked at her, mischief sparking in his eyes. 'Aye, Mammy,' he said, his accent pure Partick.

'Well,' she said mildly, 'I am a mammy.'

'And your bairns are a credit to you.' He stretched his hands out to the flames. She straightened up and watched the pale skin of his face reflect their flickering pink glow.

'When did you meet my children?'

'Earlier on today,' he said easily, concentrating on warming his hands. 'I dropped my bags off at Isa's before I came here. We all had our dinner together. After Isa had scolded me for something or other and Florence had made me try on the jumper she's knitted for me, of course. You know what they're like. It makes me think of the Gestapo in the war pictures.' He put on a German accent. 'Resistance is useless. Your daughter's a wee chatterbox, eh? And Archie's a fine lad, Carrie. That was nice that you named him for your father. We had a long conversation about how cruel his mother is to him.'

'Cruel?' She was busy assimilating what he'd just said. Her daughter, normally shy with strangers, had apparently taken to this one. Archie had also seemed to like him and Ewen had referred to both of them as though he knew them well.

Of course, someone might well have kept him informed of their progress. She was going to kill Isabella Cooke. Then she wondered what other information might have been given, not about the children, but about Matt and her.

'Cruel?' Carrie repeated, moving away from the fire. She couldn't bear it if he knew about the violence. She thought of it as something shameful, and that shame belonged as much to her as to Matthew. Somehow she ought to have been able to prevent it from happening.

'You won't let him have a white mouse,' Ewen teased.

'Oh, that,' she said vaguely.

He turned away from the fire and looked at her. 'Are you all right, Carrie?'

'I'm fine.' She looked pointedly at the clock. 'My relief will be here any minute. Are you going along the road now too?'

He moved over to the table and started tidying up his papers. 'Aye, if that's all right with you. It's been a long day. There was a big forward planning meeting at Waverley this morning and . . .' He broke off and looked directly at her. 'And I've had quite an emotional afternoon, what with one thing and another.'

'Emotional?' The word surprised her, jolting her out of her self-absorption.

'I didn't find coming back here too easy, to tell you the truth,' he confessed. 'I can't forget how I started off in life, and I'm sure there's a lot of folk out there who'd be only too glad to remind me,' he said grimly.

'Perhaps,' she conceded, thinking about it, 'but there are lots of others who'll admire you for how far you've got. Like Martin Sharkey. And Isa and Florence. Me too,' she added, 'if that's any consolation. And I'd appreciate your company on the way home. It's nice to have someone with you in the blackout.'

'That was one of the points you raised in your letter, wasn't it?'

'You saw my letter?'

'Why else do you think I'm here?'

'But they had to twist your arm to get you to come back to Partick?'

'No,' he said sweetly. 'I was a volunteer.' He tilted his head towards the door. 'Ah, those sound like purposeful footsteps outside. Must be whoever's taking over from you.'

Coming indoors after the darkness of the blacked-out streets always made Carrie blink until her eyes grew accustomed to the light, but she was blinking for another reason at the moment: disbelief, tinged with an edge of anxiety she hadn't felt since Matt had left. April came running forward, gave her mother a cursory greeting and turned immediately to the young man by her side. Archie was shyer, hanging back a little, but like his sister, his face was glowing as he looked up at Ewen.

When he crouched down to talk to them, April immediately put her arm around his neck and Archie came forward, thrusting out his hand. It had a large marble in it.

'This is my best one, Uncle Ewen,' he said. 'You said at dinner time you'd like to see it, so Auntie Florence let me into our house when I came home from school and I got it to show you.'

'That's a corker,' said Ewen admiringly, taking it and examining it from every possible angle. 'Thank you for letting me see it, Archie.'

'You can keep it for a while if you like,' said the little boy gravely.

'Thank you. I will.' Closing his fingers over the glass sphere, he slid it into the pocket of his jacket. 'Shall I give it back to you at the weekend?'

Carrie found her voice. 'Uncle Ewen?' she croaked.

He smiled up at her. 'You don't mind, do you? We got on to first-name terms at dinner time, and there've been too many people calling me Mr Livingstone today.'

'Och,' said Isa in disgust, 'the weans couldnae call him that, could they?'

'I suppose not,' said Carrie faintly. It didn't seem to have occurred to anyone but herself how Matt would react if he came home and found his children chattering about their Uncle Ewen. Her stomach churned at the very thought.

Chapter 26

'Hello there,' said Ewen brightly as Carrie came into the booking office the following afternoon to start her shift. He was standing at the table in the corner sifting through some sheets of paper.

She returned his greeting and walked across the room, undoing the buttons of her coat as she went. 'You look as though you've been busy this morning,' she said, indicating the papers which lay in front of him. 'More interviews?'

'Aye. Most of the female staff here.' He glanced down at them. 'How do you spell Egypt?'

She told him, and saw him run his index finger underneath one typewritten word. He looked up again, giving her a relieved smile. 'I'd got it right. The husband of one of your colleagues is serving there, but I couldn't find it in my trusty dictionary.' He tapped his fingers on a small book lying on the table.

'Is that the one I gave you?' Carrie couldn't resist picking it up. 'It's been in the wars,' she observed.

'Oh, it's been well-used,' he said, still smiling at her.

She replaced the book on the table, moved away from him and began taking off her coat.

'Can I help you with that?' he asked politely.

'I'm fine, thanks. When would you like to interview me?'

'When it's convenient.'

'Maybe not this week. We're a bit short-staffed.' She hung up her coat, took her place at the ticket window and removed the cardboard placard which communicated that fact to the travelling public. 'More short-staffed than usual, that is,' she said ruefully. 'People down with the flu. I'm starting two weeks on full back shift this Saturday though, so I'll have a bit more time next week. I won't be trying to cram everything into five hours.'

'I'll start the other stations this afternoon, then,' he said. 'I'll just make some phone calls, let them know I'm on my way.'

'That's me off,' he announced some ten minutes later, half in and half out of the door. 'Will I maybe see you tonight?'

'Probably,' she said, glancing over at him. 'We see quite a bit of Isa and Florence as it is and you seem to be an added attraction as far as Archie and April are concerned.'

'I like them too,' he said. 'They're nice children. See you later, then.'

He gave her a wave as he passed the ticket window on his way through the booking hall. He had to bend down to do it. That was funny. She didn't remember him as having been that tall. Then she recalled the defensiveness which had once cloaked him from head to toe, born of sensitivity about his mother, his illegitimacy and his lack of education. That seemed to have evaporated completely. Coupled with the aura of quiet confidence, maybe that was what gave the impression of a few extra inches of height. Or perhaps he simply stood up straighter these days.

Carrie sat for a moment or two staring into space. Then she turned and looked at the table where he'd been working. The little dictionary wasn't there. He must have taken it with him. She'd chosen it to be handy to carry, after all.

She could remember buying it. She had selected it with great care, as she had the paper and ribbon with which she had wrapped it. She had wanted it to be special: a treat for someone who didn't get many treats. He'd been so appreciative too, despite the fact that she had unwittingly upset him that day, making him think about his mother's death. She could see still the way he had bowed his head . . .

'Miss?'

With a professional smile, she turned and dealt with the customer who had just tapped impatiently on the window.

She did see Ewen that night – and Wednesday and Thursday nights too. As she'd predicted, the children were keener than usual to spend time at their aunties'. That didn't surprise Carrie. Both of them had been missing the presence of a man in their lives. Ewen played with them as Matt did – robustly and energetically – communicating with them in an entirely different way from herself.

Watching the horseplay which developed over the next few evenings she could see there was more of the boy in Ewen than she had first thought. He could almost have been their big brother. He had a way of getting on to their level which wasn't in the least patronising, and seemed to be enjoying himself as much as they were. Perhaps he was making up for lost time. She couldn't imagine that his own childhood had included much of the carefree rough and tumble he indulged in with Archie and April.

She could see that Florence was relishing it all. It was obvious she adored Ewen as much as she doted on Carrie's children, and was taking enormous pleasure in having all three of them together under her roof. Even Isa, who normally regarded the world cynically through a plume of cigarette smoke, looked on with an indulgent eye.

Everyone was having a wonderful time – except for Carrie herself. All too uncomfortably aware that she was the main reason why Isa and Florence had seen so little of Ewen over the past few years, she tried to suppress her growing feeling of unease. She would just have to hope that by the time Matt got his next leave, the memory of Ewen Livingstone and his visit would be long gone.

Coming home from the steamie midway through Friday morning, she was lugging a basket of clean clothes up the stairs when she met Ewen coming down.

'You should have called me,' he reproached her. 'I'd have helped you with that. Don't tell me,' he said, reading the expression on her face. 'You've managed fine without me up till now.'

She took pity on him, allowing him to take the laundry from her. 'Something like that. I thought you'd be at work anyway.'

He ran nimbly back up the stairs and placed the basket on the mat outside her front door. 'Lunch and a meeting at Queen Street today. With some of the high heid yins.' He grimaced. 'I seem to spend half my life going to meetings. I've got a big one at Waverley next Sunday.'

'Sunday?'

'That's the only day we can get everybody together,' he said gloomily, rejoining her on the half-landing. Today's meeting explained the extra attention to his appearance. He looked particularly smart, and she said as much.

He grimaced. 'I think I'd look a lot smarter in a uniform.'

'You're in a reserved occupation,' she pointed out, 'and you're doing an important job.'

'Maybe.' He sounded unconvinced.

'Well,' she said again, 'you do look very smart.'

'And you look very beautiful.'

She turned, and smiled at him. He had turned too, and stood now looking up at her. She was wearing her headscarf, knotted at the front as usual. She could feel a few tendrils of hair, still damp from the steamie, against her face.

Her clothes consisted of a pair of Matt's trousers she'd altered to fit herself, an ancient creamy-coloured lacy jumper and a jacket which had done sterling service as a blanket before being pressed into the war effort. It saved the good checked woollen coat she wore to work or on the rare occasions when she went out for the evening.

She'd dyed the old blanket dark green, cut a big square collar for it and put a fringe round that made out of a spare ball of Aran wool Florence had given her. Isa called the whole ensemble her Rosie the Riveter outfit.

'I don't look at all beautiful,' she said, 'but it's kind of you to say so.'

'There's nothing kind about it.'

Carrie shrugged, a little embarrassed. He was being gallant, no doubt. She moved away from him and put her foot on the first step of the stairs. 'We'll see you on Monday, then?'

'Monday?' He looked up at her in apparent perplexity.

'Aren't you going back through to Edinburgh for the weekend?'

'No. I'm staying here. In fact, I was wondering if you'd let me take the children to the pantomime tomorrow. I'm going to see if I can get seats today. It only started last week, so they might not be fully booked up for the Saturday matinées yet.'

The unease clawed at her again. The pantomime. Archie and April would talk about that for months . . .

'Isa and Florence are coming,' he said, obviously thinking she needed some persuading. 'It's a pity you're on duty or you could have come too.'

It seemed churlish to refuse. Especially as he appeared to be giving up a weekend with his girlfriend in favour of her children. And she knew the two of them would love it. 'I'll give you the money for their tickets, then. If you manage to get them.'

'No you will not,' he said. 'It's my treat.'

He did get tickets and Carrie spent Saturday morning coping with two children high as kites with the excitement of it. She felt a little forlorn at work that afternoon and evening, knowing everyone else was out enjoying themselves. She loved the pantomime, and apart from that one visit to the foreign servicemen's club with Isa and an occasional trip to the pictures with the children, it was an awful long time since she'd had a night out.

The children were full of it the following morning, chattering away as she took them to Sunday school. She heard all about it: the man dressed up as a woman, the woman dressed up as a man, the evil sorcerer. According to April, he'd been really scary. Archie pooh-poohed that idea. *He* hadn't been feart at all.

He was more interested in telling his mother how Uncle Ewen had bought them sweeties and then taken them for high tea afterwards. They had even, the little boy confided breathlessly to his mother, come home in a taxi!

Carrie handed them over to their Sunday school teacher at the entrance to the church and debated whether she was going in to hear the service herself. She decided against it. She wasn't exactly feeling full of the milk of human kindness this morning. When she got back home Florence was waiting for her on the landing.

'Come in for a wee minute, Carrie,' she said, 'we want to tell you all about our trip yesterday!'

Ewen was sitting in front of a roaring fire, relaxed in his shirt sleeves, laughing at something Isa was saying to him. He stood up when Carrie came into the room. She was perversely irritated by that. Where had he acquired those kind of manners?

'Good morning,' he said cheerfully.

'What's good about it?' she muttered. 'It's freezing out there.' Out of the corner of her eye, she saw Isa raise her eyebrows at him.

Florence had gone to fetch the theatre programme. She came back through with it, her face bright and animated. She told Carrie exactly what the children had, apparently as excited as they had been by the show, the sweeties, the meal out and the taxi. All paid for by Mr Ewen Livingstone. All guaranteed to give Archie and April an afternoon out they would remember for a very long time.

Unless Carrie made liars out of her children – as impossible as it was unthinkable – Matt was inevitably going to hear all about this from their innocent lips. It would be she herself who would bear the brunt of his reaction. Her unease ballooned suddenly into full-scale anxiety, tinged with a sharp edge of resentment.

She supposed she couldn't blame Ewen – although he must remember how jealous Matthew had always been of him – but Isa and Florence were a different matter. Isa had been concerned enough to check with her before Ewen had arrived that Matt wasn't due home at the same time. She seemed to have forgotten all about that now. Carrie hadn't realised how fragile her control was until it broke.

'For goodness' sake, Florence,' she snapped, 'you're as bad as Archie and April! It can't have been that exciting.'

She had never seen anybody's face fall in quite the same way as Florence's did at that moment.

Carrie looked up with a start when the booking-office door was pushed open at nine o'clock that evening. George Gibson, as regular on his evening rounds as her father had been, wasn't due for another half hour, and by this time on a Sunday evening things were usually pretty quiet. She was taken aback when she saw who her unexpected visitor was. Surprise – and embarrassment stemming from the circumstances of their meeting earlier in the day – lent an edge to her voice.

'What are you doing here?'

'I was out for a walk,' Ewen said, 'and found myself in Crow Road, so I thought I'd come and see you home.'

'I've still got an hour to go,' she pointed out, indicating the clock on the wall.

'I'll go through some of my interviews. Start analysing the information.' Despite his words, he made no move to take off his coat, just stood there looking at her, arms folded across his broad chest. She knew she wasn't imagining the reproach. It was evident in every line of his stance.

She shrugged. 'Please yourself, but I don't need anyone to see me home.'

'I thought that was one of the points I'm supposed to be investigating.' His tone of voice was deceptively mild. 'That it's not very pleasant for a woman to have to walk home alone on a dark winter's night.' He backed up towards his table, stood leaning against it.

'I'm used to it,' she said shortly. 'I can manage. There's really no need for you to hang on.'

'Oh, you can manage everything, can't you?' His eyes had darkened, gone the wintry blue colour she remembered as a sign that he was angry about something.

'What's that supposed to mean?' she demanded, her own temper ready to flare up. All it needed was the tiniest spark.

'You know exactly what it means,' he said grimly. 'Don't you think you owe Florence an apology for the way you spoke to her this morning?'

Carrie didn't think it. She knew it. She got up and went to stand in front of the fire, turning her back on him. His condemnation couldn't make her feel any worse than she already did. She'd been miserable all afternoon and evening, hating herself for taking it out on the woman who cared for her and her children so much, who even now was looking after them so that she was free to go to work.

'I don't want to believe this,' came the harsh voice from behind her, 'but are you put out because we were enjoying ourselves while you were stuck here?'

Did he think her so shallow she was capable of being jealous of her own children, then? She ached to defend herself, but how could she possibly tell him the truth? He would look at her with pity in his eyes . . . and she knew she couldn't bear that. She took a deep breath.

'Maybe that's it,' she agreed, allowing her head to fall forward as she put a hand out to the narrow mantelpiece to steady herself.

His tone of voice was no longer mild. It was contemptuous. 'Then I think you should grow up, Carrie. Don't you?'

Her fingers gripped hard on the warm cast iron. 'You think I should grow up?' she repeated. She sounded remarkably calm, but when she turned to look at him her eyes were glowing as brightly as the coals in the fire behind her. Looking suddenly alert, Ewen straightened up and opened his mouth to say something.

She didn't give him the chance, her apparent calmness disappearing into a series of angry questions and statements. 'How dare you say that to me, Ewen Livingstone? I've *had* to bloody well grow up! What do you think it was like for me, losing my parents within a year of each other? Archie was born the day my mother died. The very day. That was all she held on for. What d'you think it felt like to nurse my baby with my mother lying dead in a room across the hall? I was only eighteen years old, for God's sake!' Her voice quavered.

'Carrie,' he began, rising to his feet. 'I'm sorry. I didn't know that –'

She got control of herself, swallowed hard. 'I've had to do a hell of a lot of growing up since we last knew each other,' she said bitterly. 'Dealing with all that, living with my horrible in-laws, bringing up my children, holding down a job, coping with a husband who . . .'

She stopped dead. Ewen came towards her and peered into her face. 'A husband who what?' he asked.

She narrowed her eyes at him. 'What has Isa told you?'

'Not a thing,' he said, his voice grim. 'But you just have.'

Her chin flew up. 'I've told you nothing,' she said. 'Absolutely nothing.'

'Carrie . . .' He put his hand on her arm, but she side-stepped him and walked back to the ticket window. When she got there she lifted a pencil and bent her head over the bundles of tickets she'd been checking when he came in.

'I've got to get on with my work. I think you should go now.'

'I came to walk you home,' came the quiet voice from behind her. 'And that's what I'm going to do.'

She stopped pretending to check the tickets. 'Please go away. Please.'

'Is that what you really want?'

'Yes,' she said. Her voice was flat and lifeless. 'That's what I really want.'

Carrie had never felt quite so lonely as she did on her walk home that night.

'You look tired, lass,' said Florence, looking up as she walked into the kitchen. 'Shall I make you a wee cup of tea?'

'Oh, Florence, I'm so sorry! Please forgive me!' She went forward, down on to her knees beside the older woman's chair.

'Least said, soonest mended, pet,' Florence said calmly. 'Lay your head down in my lap and have a wee greet. You look like that's what you're needing.'

Carrie did as she was bid.

Chapter 27

Carrie sat down opposite Ewen on the following Wednesday afternoon and watched him feed a sheet of foolscap paper into the portable typewriter. She was on duty with another girl today and they had chosen the mid-afternoon lull for the interview so they could conduct it without any interruptions. She could hear her colleague behind her at the ticket window, dealing with a passenger who had a complicated travel enquiry.

'I'll type your answers directly on to my proformas,' Ewen said, somewhat unnecessarily. She could see what he was doing.

'Now then . . .' He was muttering to himself. 'Name, address, date of birth, maiden name . . . I know all of those. Your grade and how long you've worked here I don't.'

She told him and he typed it in without looking up. 'Your opinion of your working conditions,' he said.

'I'm very satisfied with them. Only I agree with the idea of trying to pair women up when they're working late. Like I put in the letter.'

He typed that in too. His fingers were surprisingly nimble on the keyboard. The girl at Waverley with whom he'd had such a good laugh must have taught him well.

'Your domestic circumstances. I need to ask you about them.'

'You know them too,' she said, doing her best to shrug nonchalantly. 'Married with two children, both cared for by friends when my hours don't fit in with school and crèche times.'

'I have to ask you about your husband,' he said carefully.

A train pulled in, and the other clerkess went out to collect the tickets. Behind Ewen, there was a crackle from the open fire. They both turned and looked at it. A little mound of coals had collapsed in on itself.

'I should put more on,' she said, half-rising from her chair, bracing herself with one hand on the table.

Ewen swung back round to face her. 'It'll keep for five minutes.'

She subsided. 'My husband's serving with the army,' she said. 'The Argyll and Sutherland Highlanders. What more do you need to know?'

He lifted one of his hands from the typewriter and laid it over hers. Her fingers contracted beneath his, but his grip was firm. He looked her straight in the eye. 'I need to know how best I can help you.'

'Take your hand away,' she said.

He remembered. She could see it in his eyes. He had said exactly the same thing to her once before. She bit her lip, summoned up her last reserves of strength. 'Take your hand away, please.' She looked at him, a silent plea in her green eyes.

He took his hand away.

Carrie tilted the horseshoe purse so that its entire contents slid forward and were visible, staring at the silver and copper coins as though she could conjure up the ten shillings she was sure she'd neatly folded and put in there before she'd left the house this Saturday morning. It didn't work. The note simply wasn't there.

She tugged off one glove – it was nearly as cold inside the shop on this wintry day as it was outside – and flicked her index finger over the money she did have, adding it up in her head. She was three and tenpence short for the messages which sat in front of her. She deposited the entire contents of her purse beside them and said as much. The face on the other side of the dark wood counter looked less than sympathetic.

'I'm s-sorry,' she said, stuttering in embarrassment. 'I've miscalculated somewhere. I'll need to put something back.'

'Well, what then?' snapped the shop assistant. She wasn't known for her friendly nature.

A dark-coated arm came over Carrie's shoulder. The hand which belonged to it set two florins down next to the small pile of groceries. 'She's not putting anything back. And we'll have two o' those penny caramels as well.' He lifted the paper-wrapped toffees out of a cardboard box which sat on the counter. 'Here's the sweetie coupons.'

Archie and April were looking up at Ewen with broad smiles. He handed them a sweet each. 'The dentist will love me,' he told them brightly. He gestured towards the groceries lying on the counter. 'Shouldn't you pack them away?'

When the four of them were back out on the pavement he reached for the message bag. 'I'll take that.'

Carrie swung it out of his reach. 'Haven't you some shopping of your own to do? Did Florence send you for something?'

'I can get it later,' he said easily. 'I was really out for a walk. Revisiting my old haunts. Like Keith Street and the Quaker graveyard.'

'I know where that is,' piped up Archie. 'It's a spooky place.'

His Uncle Ewen took his eyes off Carrie's face long enough to smilingly contradict him. 'Oh, no it's not. It's a special place. A magical place.'

He looked so relaxed, his woollen coat slung casually over the intricately patterned Aran sweater Florence had knitted for him. Flecks of snow swirling down from a heavy sky were beginning to settle on his shoulders. He hadn't shaved today. There was a faint shadowing of bristles on his jaw.

Carrie was in her Rosie the Riveter outfit. Now that she thought about it, she realised the wool Florence had given her to make the jacket's fringe must have come from the leftovers of that same Aran sweater, the raw material painstakingly unpicked from two smaller jumble sale finds.

'What are you doing here anyway?' she demanded. 'Don't you have a meeting in Edinburgh tomorrow?'

'Yes, but it doesn't start till late morning. I'll go through first thing.'

'Won't your fiancée be missing you?'

He looked nonplussed. 'Moira? I shouldn't think so. She joined the WAAF six months ago. Decided she wanted to see a bit of the world before she settled down.'

'She broke off your engagement?'

'No,' he said. 'I did.'

Archie was growing impatient with this grown-up conversation. 'Can we eat the sweeties now, Mammy?' he asked, already unwrapping his penny caramel.

'No,' she replied, unusually short with him. 'You know you're not allowed to eat in the street.' She turned to Ewen. 'Thank you for lending me the money,' she said stiffly. 'If you come back with me to the house, I'll reimburse you straightaway.'

'Don't be daft, Carrie. I'm not going to miss four bob.'

'I'm not short of money,' she snapped. 'My pay packet's lying unopened on the kitchen table. I forgot to put the money in my purse, that's all.'

'Take the money as a gift.' He looked down at April, tugging on her mother's blanket jacket and pleading to be allowed to eat her caramel. 'What's wrong with the bairns eating the sweeties now?'

April was still tugging. 'Stop it!' cried Carrie. Leaning down, she administered a smack to her daughter's bottom. Neither April nor Archie was accustomed to being physically chastised. It wasn't the way their mother normally went about things. A small shocked face looked up at her. Then the tears came.

'I'm sorry,' she said desperately. 'I'm sorry, pet.' But before she could get down to take her daughter into her arms, Ewen had swept the little girl up into his.

'Now, what's all this nonsense?' he said, tickling her under the chin. He had her smiling again in seconds, especially when he lifted her up to ride on his shoulders.

'Can you manage your mammy's messages, Archie son? Right then, let's get back to the house.'

Carrie gritted her teeth. 'There's absolutely no need for you to see us home.'

Ewen gave her a bland smile. 'Yes, there is. You owe me three and tenpence.'

When they got back home he set April down and took the shopping bag from Archie. Then he unlocked the door to Isa and Florence's and shooed the children in, one large hand gently but firmly on each small back.

'Tell your aunties your mother and I will be along in a wee minute.' He closed the door on any protest. 'Open up, Carrie,' he said grimly.

She started to argue with him. He fixed her with a determined look, and she thought better of it. Her hand was shaking as she took the key out of the pocket of her jacket. She couldn't seem to get it lined up with the lock. Ewen's fingers closed over hers. 'I'll do it.'

When they got in she headed for the kitchen, knowing he was right behind her. She pulled off her jacket and threw it over a chair, not noticing when it slid to the floor. The damned pay packet, as she'd remembered too late, was lying in the middle of the table. Picking it up, she ripped it open and tipped out the contents.

'Four shillings,' she said, snapping the coins down on the hard wood of the table. She slid them towards him.

'That's tuppence too much,' Ewen said evenly. 'The sweets are a present from me to the bairns. A wee treat.'

'They don't need treats.'

'Everyone needs treats, Carrie,' he said evenly. 'Children especially.'

'I don't have any change. Take the money.'

'No, I don't want it. Any of it.' He put her shopping bag on the table and laid the door key beside it. He stooped, lifted her jacket and placed it carefully over the back of a chair. Then he stood and looked at her, and the grim expression on his face relaxed.

'You look dead cute in that rig-out, you know. Especially the breeks. I hate that stupid-looking headscarf, though. It hides your lovely hair.'

'Take-the-bloody-money!'

'There's no need to swear,' he said mildly. 'It's not necessary if one has an adequate vocabulary.'

She ignored the implicit invitation to share that particular memory. 'There's every need to swear!'

'And was there every need to smack the wee lassie when what you really wanted to do was hit me? It's me you're angry with, isn't it? Because I've found out something you'd rather I didn't know.'

She moved quickly to stand in front of the range, putting the table between them. Then she turned, folding her arms across her chest. 'So you're a student of psychology among all your other talents, are you? Psychologist, child-care expert, strategic planning expert, esteemed servant of the railway company, dispenser of sweeties to the children of Partick?'

He raised one eyebrow. She hadn't known he could do that. 'My, my, Mrs Campbell, shall I fetch you a saucer of milk? That sounded a wee touch catty.'

Her precarious control shattered. 'Well, what do you expect?' she demanded, waving one arm wildly in the air. 'You come breezing back into my life, you charm my children, you charm my friends, you charm everybody. And you're all clever and debonair and attractive . . .'

He was coming round the table, heading straight for her. She hastily resumed her defensive posture.

'Clever?' he repeated, a quizzical expression on his face. '*Debonair?*' He paused, and pretended to consider. 'I think that's my favourite, Carrie. Shall we make it the word of the week? Although I like *attractive* too. In fact,' he said, sauntering forward to stand right in front of her, 'I like all of them. Especially when they fall from your lips.' His eyes dropped to the lips in question, and she took a step back – and almost burned herself on the range.

'Careful.' He coiled his fingers around her wrist and pulled her away from the heat. Into a different kind of warmth.

[illegible]

[illegible]

[illegible]

[illegible]

[illegible]

[illegible]

[illegible]

[illegible]

Chapter 28

She was a girl again, standing in the Quaker graveyard with the October sun warm on her back, the stubble on his chin pleasantly rough on the smooth skin of her face.

'Tell me you didn't want me to do that,' Ewen murmured against her mouth. He sounded calm, but his breathing was fast and shallow.

'I didn't want you to do that,' said Carrie, and heard for herself how dazed she sounded. 'Do it again,' she whispered.

His arms came about her waist, tightening around her body, pressing the lacy patterns of her jumper into her skin. Hadn't she been wearing it that day too, the last time he had kissed her? She lifted her hands and placed them flat against his chest. Through the softness of the Aran sweater she felt the rhythm of his heart: a rapid but solid thump.

Then it came to her what they were doing. This wasn't a boy kissing a girl in a corner of an old graveyard. The heat she could feel on her back wasn't the autumn sunshine of seven years ago, it was the glow of her own hearth. That hearth which belonged to Matt too.

What sort of a wife was she to be acting like this with his children mere yards away? What sort of a mother? She began to struggle, pushed Ewen violently away. For a few seconds they simply stared at each other. Then he spoke.

'Tell me one thing, Carrie. Tell me you still love your husband.' He took a quick little breath. 'Tell me that and I'll go away and leave you in peace.'

Her eyes found the willow pattern platter on the high mantelpiece above the range. It had been a similar gesture on her part which had betrayed it as the location of Ewen's letter that fateful day four years ago.

Afterwards, even while she'd been enduring what its discovery had provoked, she'd been aware that the base of the platter had been pulled out of place by Matt's furious and searching hand, forward of the thin strip of wood which kept it secure and upright. She'd been terrified that her grandmother's treasure might slide off the mantelpiece and be smashed to pieces on the range or the hard floor. But it had survived, and so had she. After a fashion. She turned her head again, met Ewen's intense gaze.

'I'm his wife,' she said.

'That doesn't answer my question.'

Carrie knew it didn't, but she didn't know what else to say. She didn't know how she felt about Matt any more. All that came to her when she considered the question was a numbness, an inability to feel very much at all. But he was her husband. And the father of her children.

'I made a commitment to him. Took vows in the church.'

Ewen's expression grew cynical. 'And do you think he takes that commitment as seriously as you obviously do?'

She took a breath, squared her shoulders. 'You can't know that he doesn't.'

'Yes, I can,' he said. 'Some sons take after their fathers. And he does hit you, doesn't he?'

'What do you want from me, Ewen?' she asked desperately.

'Och, Carrie,' he said, his face softening. 'Only to help. In whatever way I can.'

'That's why you kissed me just now then, is it?'

'No,' he said slowly. 'There was another reason for that.'

Matthew Campbell was in a state of some indecision. The pretty ATS officer had just asked him which destination she should make his rail warrant out for. He had planned to go up to London again. He loved the city, and the opportunities it afforded: especially to a handsome Scotsman in kilted battle dress. But, he thought, peering through the window behind the young woman's head at a sky filled with ominous blue-grey clouds, he was missing his family.

He thought of Archie and April's innocent smiles and how pleased they would be to see him. He thought of Carrie. She had an innocence about her too, unlike most of the girls he'd had while he'd been down here. He felt vaguely guilty about that, but what she didn't know wouldn't hurt her, would it?

'Make up your mind, soldier,' said the girl pertly.

He couldn't help sizing her up. Was she one of those who would or one of those who wouldn't? Making that judgement about every good-looking woman he met had become second nature – and there were quite a lot who would . . .

Lately, in low moments, he'd begun thinking it was all a bit sordid. During his last encounter he hadn't even bothered finding out the girl's name. She hadn't asked for his either. He'd found himself longing for Carrie: her honesty and freshness, that passion which had only ever been given to him.

He glanced once more at the outside world. The journey north was going to be hellish. The forecast was for heavy snow all over the

British Isles. Was it worth going so far for such a short stay? He thought about it.

Carrie was in his mind's eye, lying underneath him in the box bed, her vibrant hair splashed over the pillow. Dammit, he was going home.

'Glasgow,' he said firmly. 'Make it out for Glasgow.'

Carrie had to stop him saying the words. It seemed important. So she asked a question, and succeeded only in landing them both in more trouble.

'Why did you break off your engagement with Moira? Isa said she was a lovely girl.'

'She was,' agreed Ewen. 'We had some great times together. She was pretty and funny. Passionate too,' he added, a gleam of mischief lurking in the corner of his eye.

Carrie stiffened. 'So what exactly was wrong with this paragon?'

The mischievous look vanished. 'She wasn't you,' he said simply.

Despite the weather – the scenery whizzing past outside looked like something off a Christmas card – the train was making good enough progress. Crewe. Preston. Lancaster. Then the light faded and they drew the blackout curtains across the windows – not that there was a great deal of light inside the carriage anyway. The low level of illumination permitted by the wartime restrictions was barely enough to read by or to play cards, although the other men in Matthew's compartment were attempting the latter.

He'd declined an invitation to join in, preferring to think about his reunion with his family. He peered at his watch. Six o'clock. Would they make Glasgow by ten? No, that was over-optimistic. They had two notorious summits to negotiate: Shap and Beattock. They'd be hard going in conditions like these. Midnight would be more like it. The children would be sound asleep by then. He wouldn't disturb them, but he could surprise their mother, creep in beside her . . .

Train heating was subject to wartime restrictions too. Although they'd been promised it would come on again in an hour's time, it was bloody freezing at the moment. Matt had been one of the most vociferous complainants about that earlier on, but he wasn't noticing the cold at the moment. There was a warm glow creeping up his body. He adjusted his position, closed his eyes and enjoyed it. It was nothing compared to the pleasure he'd be feeling after midnight . . .

Then, brakes screeching like chalk being drawn across a blackboard, the train ground to a halt. The card-players cursed as the upended suitcase which formed their impromptu table jerked and fell over, throwing the completed hands to the dusty floor.

Matt curled his slim fingers round the curtain which covered the window, pulled it back a crack and looked out. Through the driving snow, he could just make out station buildings. There were no signs to identify the place, of course, a measure designed to confuse German spies. It also confused a lot of weary travellers.

'Where are we?' asked one of the card-players.

'How the hell should I know?' he responded irritably.

'Well,' said the man reasonably, 'you did tell us you were a railwayman in civvy street.'

'I think it might be Penrith,' he said grudgingly. And, he thought glumly, there's probably too much snow on Shap Fell and we're going to sit here for hours. He should have gone to London, after all. By this time he could have been sitting opposite a pretty girl in a nice warm bar having a drink, anticipating further delights to come – especially if she had a room of her own not too far away.

'Cover that light up!' bellowed a voice from the platform.

'One of Hitler's long-lost brothers, d'ye think?'

Matt dropped the curtain and forced a smile. He was going to be stuck with these men for several hours. He was annoyed with himself for having made the wrong decision. Nothing he could do about that now. Carrie had better be grateful for what he'd gone through for the sake of what was now rapidly diminishing into little more than a few hours with her. That was all. She'd better be extremely grateful indeed.

She had told him not to, but Carrie wasn't surprised when Ewen came into the booking office at ten o'clock that night, observing as he did so that there was quite a bit of the white stuff falling this evening.

'So I see,' she said. 'You look like you've just returned from the Russian front.'

He squinted down at his coat. The dark material was covered in lacy cobwebs of snow. 'I should have given myself a shake before I came in. Like Bobby the dog does after a swim.' He looked back up at her with a grin.

You're all sparkly, she thought, with your flashing smile and the snowflakes glistening on your coat. Even your eyes look silvery-blue tonight. You're like Jack Frost. Only he stretches out a bony finger and freezes everything solid, whereas your fingers have begun to melt something in me. But I can't allow that to happen . . .

Ewen did the one eyebrow-raising trick. 'What are you thinking about?'

'Oh . . . nothing really. I'll get my coat.' She lifted it down from the stand in the corner, buttoned it up and then reached for her scarf. It was a home-made effort, in multi-coloured stripes. She'd knitted three altogether, for herself and the children, out of leftover bits of wool. She pulled on matching mittens and crocheted tammy, looked up and caught an amused look.

'What's so funny?'

'Well, as you would say . . . nothing really. You look like Nanook of the North, that's all. Should we no' cross the scarf over your front and fasten it round the back with a couple of safety pins?'

'Ha, ha. At least I'm dressed for the weather. You haven't even got a hat or gloves on.'

'Gloves are for cissies,' he said grandly. 'No' manly types like myself.'

The snow was beginning to lie. You could see it. Despite the blackout, the deserted pavements were glowing like dull ribbons. Even Dumbarton Road, normally kept clear by the continual toing and froing of trams and other traffic, was beginning to acquire a ghostly white coating. Everything seemed eerily quiet.

'How did you spend your day?' The snow wasn't falling too heavily at the moment. There was no need to make a mad dash for home.

'I took Archie and April to the pictures. You don't mind, do you?'

'Why should I mind?'

'After last weekend,' he enquired wryly, 'when I thought I was going to get my head in my hands to play with for taking them to the panto?'

'There was a reason for that.'

She heard him take a deep breath. 'Yes,' he said. 'I'm sorry. I didn't think. None o' us did.'

'Aye, well,' she said wryly. 'I suppose the damage is done now. What did you see tonight?'

'*The Wizard of Oz*.'

'They'd have enjoyed that.'

'They did. It didn't seem to bother them that they'd seen it before.'

'It never does. April had great fun being terrified of the Wicked Witch of the West last time.'

'This time too,' he said. 'She hid her face in my coat whenever the witch cackled. I think Archie was a bit frightened too, but he was very brave about it. They were both real excited. Could hardly keep their eyes open after we got back from the cinema. More or less fell asleep into their supper. Their aunties got them undressed and into their night clothes and I carried them across to their beds. Florence is sitting with them till you get home.'

A little flurry of snow blew into Carrie's face, and she bent her head to let her hat take the brunt of it. That made her wonder why he had come out without any headgear. She asked him. It had seemed a simple enough question, but he took his time about answering it.

'I wanted to feel the snow on me,' he said at last. 'To help me relive a memory.' He stopped dead beside her. They were almost home.

'Would you come somewhere with me? It's not much further.'

'It was the day of your wedding,' said the deep voice in the soft darkness. They were in the Quaker graveyard, the snow-covered grass beneath their feet springy as a newly stitched quilt. 'I went out and got myself drunk. I thought it might deaden the pain.' He paused briefly. 'It didnae.'

She was listening carefully. Since he had been back in Partick he'd begun to re-acquire aspects of his original accent.

'At some point during the evening – I've no idea exactly when, I was well away with it by that time – Martin Sharkey noticed what I was up to and told me I'd had enough. He got this other surfaceman to help him get me to the door. I think they'd have taken me right home, only Janice was waiting outside, and she volunteered.'

'Janice Muirhead?'

'Aye.' Eyes grown accustomed to the dark, she saw him raise his head. 'Where is she, by the way? I haven't seen her around since I've been back.'

'Nobody knows. She went off somewhere. Not long after the war broke out.'

Carrie didn't think she'd intended to sound disapproving, but Ewen must have heard something in her voice. 'You shouldn't blame her for what happened the night of your hen party. That was my fault. I behaved very badly.'

'I had hurt you very badly.' Carrie hesitated. 'Did you and Janice ever . . .' She stopped short of completing the question, but he answered it anyway.

'No. Well . . . nothing to speak of.'

She wondered what that meant. Exactly.

'We might have that night,' he went on, 'but we didn't. I'd like to think it was because I came to my senses but it was probably because I was too blootered,' he said with brutal honesty. 'I was sick into the gutter, Carrie. Out there on Keith Street.' The self-disgust was evident in his voice. 'Then I came here. It was snowing then too, but it was a bit sheltered in that corner over behind where you're standing now. That's where I curled up.'

'You spent the night here?'

'Aye,' came the calm voice. 'Martin discovered me at six o'clock the next morning. He'd been worried about me. When he didn't find me at home, something made him look in here.'

She remembered very well that it had been snowing that night. While she'd been taking her ease with Matt in a warm and luxurious hotel, Ewen had been alone in the freezing darkness. Huddled in a corner like an animal which had skulked off somewhere to lick its wounds.

'You'd fallen asleep?' She was trying to emulate his own level tones, but she was aware of a turbulent mixture of emotions within her breast: guilt for the part she had played in his unhappiness at the time; pity for the boy he had been; admiration for the man he had become. No, it was a lot more than admiration . . .

'I fell asleep eventually. I spent some time thinking first.'

She whispered a question into the blue blackness. 'What did you think about?'

His answer came back at her like an arrow hitting its target. 'I thought about you. I thought about Matthew Campbell making love to you.' She heard him take a deep breath. 'And it made me so angry that I smashed my fist into the wall. Three times.'

She moved forward. 'Oh, Ewen,' she breathed. 'That must have hurt so much.'

'I wanted it to hurt.' A faint colouring of humour crept into his voice. 'My wish was granted. It was sore for weeks.'

She took another step towards him and slipped her gloved fingers into his. 'Was it this hand?'

'Aye. My right hand. My working hand.'

'It's cold,' she said, automatically beginning to rub the frozen digits to restore circulation to them.

'Always the little mother,' he said lightly.

'Don't be so bloody cheeky,' Carrie murmured, 'and don't tell me not to swear either. Does this not feel nice?'

'It would feel a whole lot nicer if you took your wee mitten off. Your skin against my skin.'

Her fingers stopped moving. Her whole body stiffened. He didn't speak for a second or two, but when he did his voice was slow and gentle. 'I know. You're not ready for that yet.'

Her next words came out on a great rush of breath: a plume of white in the darkness between them. 'Ewen, I'm not ready for any of this!'

'I know that too,' he said gently. 'But there's something I have to tell you all the same.' He paused briefly. 'Something I need to tell you.'

She waited, knowing she couldn't stop it this time. Not knowing if she wanted to . . .

'I love you,' he said. 'I've never stopped loving you.'

'Ewen . . .'

'Wheesht. It's all right. You don't have to say anything. I understand.'

Florence was sitting by the fire knitting, but stopped as soon as they came into the kitchen. Thrusting her needles into the ball of wool, she rose to her feet and started gathering together her bits and pieces. 'I looked in on the weans a wee minute ago, Carrie. They're both sound asleep.'

'Thanks, Florence,' she said softly, divesting herself of her scarf and tammy before removing her coat and draping it over the back of a chair. 'Would you be wanting a cup of tea before you go?'

'No, I'm fine, pet.' She glanced at Ewen. He hadn't taken his coat off but had gone to stand against the wall beside the range, hands behind his back. 'Will I leave the two of you to say goodnight?' she asked doubtfully.

The young eyes and the old ones met. 'Leave the door on the latch, Florence,' said Ewen in his deep voice. 'I'll not be long.'

'Aye.' Her lined face softened as she looked at him. 'You're a good lad,' she said.

Carrie saw her out, did a quick check of her own on Archie and April and walked back through to the kitchen. Ewen was still standing with his back to the wall.

'At least Florence approves of me. Though at this precise moment I can't say I'm finding that much of a comfort.'

The realisation of what he meant threw Carrie into stammering confusion. 'You mean you want to – You would have wanted to –'

'Of course,' he said calmly, pushing himself off the wall. 'If the lassie was ready and willing. But she's not, is she? And I've always made that a golden rule.'

'Oh,' she said faintly. 'Did you and Moira –'

She stopped, horrified that she'd been about to ask him such an intimate question – and for the second time that evening – but Ewen's face was alive with mischief as he walked towards her.

'A wee bit of curiosity? That's a good sign. Not only with Moira,' he murmured, 'although a gentleman should never discuss such things, of course. Suffice it to say that I'm no longer the innocent lad you once knew. Haven't been for quite some time, in fact.'

'Oh,' Carrie said again, and he laughed softly.

'Any chance of a goodnight kiss as a consolation prize?'

'Ewen . . . I can't. You know I can't.'

He lifted his hand, touched her cheek with his fingertips. 'I know that you let me kiss you in this very room this morning. I know that you kissed me back. I know that you asked me to kiss you again. That's what I know, Caroline Burgess.'

'I'm not Caroline Burgess any more,' she said sadly. 'That's the whole problem, isn't it?'

He dropped his hand. 'It doesn't have to be,' he said quietly. 'Not in this day and age.'

She could only shake her head at that.

'It's too late to talk about this now,' he said briskly. 'We'll leave it till tomorrow night when I get back from Edinburgh. And shall I come and have breakfast with you and the bairns in the morning before I go, take them to Sunday school for you on my way to the station?'

She shook her head again. 'I can't fight you any more. I haven't the strength left.'

'You don't need to fight me. We're on the same side, you and me. We always have been. Since we were a boy and girl together that day in Oban. Remember?'

'That was a hundred years ago,' Carrie said sadly. 'We're different people now.'

'No,' he insisted. He made a fist of his hand, tapped it lightly against his chest. 'Not in here. Not in the part which makes us what we really are.' He smiled at her, his eyes full of tenderness. 'I think it's called the heart.'

Another bloody delay. Matt lowered the window and poked his head cautiously out of it. The snow which blew in provoked a profane but sleepy protest from one of the card-players. The rest of them were out for the count, slumped in their seats snoring and wheezing. He called to an older man in railway uniform standing further up the platform. 'Where are we?'

'Carstairs Junction,' came the reply, the words almost whipped away by the snell breeze whistling along the side of the train.

'Any idea how long we're going to be held up here?'

'Your guess is as good as mine, pal. We're waiting for the snow plough to clear the track ahead o' ye.'

Matt slammed the window shut and sat down. He supposed it could be worse. Carstairs wasn't that far from Glasgow. He glanced at his watch. Half-past five. Maybe he'd make it home in time for breakfast.

'People don't come for breakfast!' cried April, gleeful that she had caught the grown-ups out. Ewen had knocked but then, using Isa and Florence's key let himself in to Carrie's house. 'People come for their tea, or dinner on a Sunday.'

'Well, I've come for breakfast,' Ewen told her, 'and what's more I've also come bearing gifts. One of your Auntie Florence's home-made loaves and this.' He laid the loaf on the table, put a hand to the inside pocket of his coat and, with the air of a conjurer producing a rabbit out of a top hat, set down a jar of jam. His hosts regarded it with some awe.

'Rita Sharkey,' he said as Carrie took his coat from him and hung it up on the back of the door. 'She gave it to me last week.'

'Where on earth did she get the sugar?' Carrie asked, making the tea and bringing it to the table.

Ewen tapped his nose significantly as he sat down opposite her. 'I thought it best not to enquire. Let us simply enjoy it. Come closer, you two. You're about to smell the summer.'

Obediently, Archie and April leaned forward. Ewen twisted open the lid of the jar.

Archie took a deep breath. 'Raspberries,' he said. 'My favourite!'

'My favourite too!' cried April.

Wide mouth curving in a slow smile, Ewen looked across the table at Carrie. 'Shall I pour out their milk?'

It was all so natural and relaxed. Afterwards, he insisted on doing the fire for her, giving it a thorough raking and taking the ashes down to the midden before adding fresh coal. 'To save you having to go out in the snow till you fetch this pair,' he said. 'Will I help you with the dishes before we go?'

She declined, although she was amused by the offer of help. 'No, I think you'd better watch your time. You don't want to be late for your meeting.'

She saw them out, reminding the children to be quiet as they went down the stairs. There were still people asleep at this time on a Sunday morning. She stood at the open door after the three of them had gone out of sight, smiling as she listened to the stage whispers floating back up to her. Then she heard Ewen's voice, a little louder than the children.

'Hold on, bairns, I've forgotten something.'

He was taking the stairs two at a time, his unbuttoned coat flying out behind him.

'What did you forget?' she asked.

'This,' he said, and planted a kiss on her mouth before taking off again. He paused briefly on the half landing, grinning up at her. 'If you won't give them to me, I'll just have to steal them.'

'*Ewen Livingstone!*' she hissed, but she couldn't help smiling at him.

'The word you are looking for,' he pronounced, 'is *incorrigible*.' He waved his hand and disappeared down the stairs.

Carrie went back into the kitchen and looked without enthusiasm at the breakfast dishes. Nothing could come of it, of course. He must know that as well as she did. Only he didn't seem to. She glanced over at the fire. It was burning merrily. She'd do the dishes in a minute. She'd have a wee sit down first.

Half an hour later she heard the scrape of a key in the lock.

'All right,' she called, 'what did you forget this time?' Despite herself, she sat up eagerly, looking towards the door with a smile on her face.

A soldier in battledress and Glengarry bonnet walked into the room. 'What did who forget, Carrie?' he asked. His gaze went to the table: four plates, the two chunky tumblers she used for the children's milk, her own tea cup, the extra one opposite. He lifted the tea cosy, felt the pot with his hand. 'Still warm,' he said. Quietly, as though he were talking to himself. Then he looked at her. 'Odd time of day to be entertaining,' he observed.

As he walked towards her Carrie saw the shutters come down on his beautiful dark eyes.

Chapter 29

She had to stop shaking. There were things she had to do: important things. Before she could do any of them she had to get up off the floor, and before she could attempt that feat she had to stop shaking.

He had started on her while she was still in the chair, using both hands to administer stinging little slaps to her face. First the right cheek, then the left. She lost count of how many times. Then he threaded one hand through her hair and hauled her to her feet, his long fingers digging painfully into her scalp. 'Who is he?' he hissed into her face. 'I want his name.'

'Matt,' she sobbed. 'Please let me go. You've got it all wrong. Please, Matt!'

He pushed her towards the wall, banged her head against it. 'I want his name!' he repeated. 'Tell me, you little whore! Tell me!' He spat the words out. It was like a machine gun firing, each word punctuated by him banging her head once more against the wall. 'I-want-his-name!' Every impact sent a jagged ache and waves of nausea searing through her.

Tears streaming down her face, reeling with pain and dizziness, Carrie begged him to stop, kept telling him nothing had happened, but he showed no sign of hearing her pleas. Yet, despite the blank look in his eyes, he wasn't shouting and although he was hurting her, he was controlling it too – enough to cause pain, not enough to knock her out. He had a question to which he wanted an answer.

She mustn't tell him. She wouldn't tell him. But her refusal to supply that answer told him what he needed to know. The punishing hand slipped out of her hair, and she was dimly aware of him taking a step back from her, leaving her slumped against the wall.

'It's Ewen Livingstone,' he said. 'He's come back, hasn't he?'

She had waited for him to start hitting her again, but this time he had attacked her with words. Horrible words. Terrifying words.

She had to stop shaking. She started with her hands, convulsively clutching at the material of her skirt. With all her might, she willed them to become still.

'In the name o' God, lassie! What's happened to you?'

Florence, in tartan dressing-gown and slippers and with her grey hair done up in a fat plait down the side of her neck, pulled Carrie into the flat.

'For pity's sake,' came a querulous voice from the kitchen, 'would youse both put a sock in it? It's bad enough folk coming in here shaving themselves at the crack of dawn. Has everybody forgotten that today's Sunday?'

Florence hustled Carrie out of the lobby and into the kitchen, carefully shutting the door behind them. 'It's you that's making all the row, Isabella Cooke,' she hissed. 'Now, get out o' your bed and give me a hand wi' Carrie.' Her voice softened. 'Come on now, pet. You sit doon here by the fire and we'll see what's what.'

Isa, a vision of loveliness in nightie and hairnet, swung her legs over the side of the bed. 'What's wrang wi' her?'

By the time she made it to Carrie's side, it was clear that irritation had been replaced by other emotions. First there was concern and curiosity. Then, as realisation dawned, came anger. Without taking her eyes off the red mark on the side of Carrie's face, she stretched out a hand to the mantelpiece for her cigarettes.

'I take it your man's home,' she said drily. 'Would I be correct in thinking that he dropped in unexpectedly?' She opened the packet she held in her hand, then looked up abruptly. 'My God, hen, he and Ewen didnae meet up, did they?'

'Ewen took the children off to Sunday school about half an hour before Matt arrived.' She could still speak. That was something. Then a thought struck her. How long would it have taken Ewen to walk the children to church and deposit them with their Sunday school teacher? Ten minutes? Quarter of an hour? Then he would have needed another five to ten minutes to get to the station, perhaps slightly longer on pavements still covered in snow.

'They must have just missed each other,' she whispered. She closed her eyes, visualising it: Matt's train coming in on the westbound platform as Ewen climbed up the stairs to the eastbound one. There could only have been a minute or two in it. She bent forward, burying her face in her hands. 'Thank God. *Thank God!*'

There was a silence punctuated only by the noise of Isa taking a few hasty puffs. 'Where's your ever-loving husband now, then?'

'I don't know,' Carrie said helplessly, her voice muffled by her hands. 'I don't know.'

Florence put an arm about her shoulders. 'Sit up, pet,' she coaxed.

She tried not to wince as delicate fingers went to her hair, smoothing it back to assess the damage. 'A cold compress,' pronounced Florence. 'That's what we're needing here.' She swung round to the sink to prepare the remedy.

'Will that stop it from coming up in a bruise? I don't want to look a sight at work this afternoon.'

Isa sat on the arm of the chair opposite Carrie and drew some more nicotine into her lungs. 'You're planning on going in the day, are ye?'

The message was clear. If that *was* her intention, she'd have to climb over Isa's dead body to accomplish it.

'I have to,' she said. 'I can't let Ewen come back here tonight. I can phone Waverley from work, pretend I need to speak to him on railway business. He's going to some big meeting. I might not get him the first time I call, I'll probably have to try a few times. That'll be much easier if I can do it from the booking office. Then, when I get him, I can tell him he's got to stay through there for a couple of days. At least until Matt's leave is over.'

That earned her a pitying look. 'And you really think he will? When he finds out what that bloody bugger's done to ye?'

'He's not going to find out. I'll think of some reason why he shouldn't come back tonight.'

'Ye might have your work cut out on that one, hen.'

'Do you think I don't know that?' Carrie's voice faltered, and a solitary tear slid slowly down her cheek. Approaching with a pad of lint, Florence blotted it with her finger and applied the compress to the side of Carrie's head.

Isa grunted. Florence swung round to her. 'Could you no' be making us all a cup o' tea, instead o' standing there puffing on yon horrible thing?'

'I'm thinking,' said Isa, with dignity. 'If Ewen had gone by the time he got there, how did Mr Campbell know it was him you were having breakfast with?' She narrowed her eyes accusingly. 'Ye werenae stupid enough to tell him, were ye?'

'Of course she didnae tell him,' snapped Florence. 'He guessed. Any fool would have known that with Carrie it could only have been Ewen. Not that the two o' them did anything last night. I heard him coming in, five minutes after me. The lassie's no' a trollop, jumping from one man to the next like a demented rabbit.' She lifted the damp lint and examined the skin underneath. 'Unlike some folk I could mention.'

Isa straightened up. 'Don't you talk to me like that, you old bitch!'

'Truth hurts, does it, Isabella Cooke?'

'Oh, stop it!'

Carrie pushed Florence and the cold compress away and half-rose out of the chair. 'Stop it!' she said again. 'I don't want the two of you fighting because of me. And according to Matt, I *am* a trollop! And a lot worse than that besides!'

She subsided again. The shaking had come back. She looked up at both of them through a shimmering curtain of tears. 'He said awful things to me. Called me dreadful names. He wouldn't believe Ewen and I hadn't spent last night together, said no one else would believe it either. He said he could divorce me for something like that and the judge would say I was . . . I was . . . a loose woman. Sleeping with another man while my husband was away serving his country.' Her voice rose on a note of anguish. 'They'd call me an unfit mother and take the children away from me! He said he'd make sure I never saw Archie and April again!'

She was finding it hard to catch her breath. She put a hand to her chest and broke into a storm of weeping. Florence's arms came round her immediately and Isa stepped forward to kneel at her feet, reaching for her other hand.

'Listen to me,' said Isa urgently. 'Your weans have got the best mother in the world.' She squeezed Carrie's hand. 'And you know the both o' us would stand up in court and say that.'

'Aye,' said Florence stoutly, 'and lots o' other folk in Partick besides.'

'That's right,' said Isa, glancing up at her mother-in-law. The two of them began listing names, batting them backwards and forwards like tennis balls over a net.

'But Matt could bring out all his well-connected relatives!' Carrie said when they finally stopped.

'They wouldnae all be on his side,' said Florence. 'There's that nice Mr Cunningham, for a start.'

'Aye,' said Isa, nodding approvingly. 'The weans' Uncle Roddy. He'd speak up for you, hen. Defin-ately. Come on now. Dry your tears. You've not got your troubles to seek, but you've got friends to help you.' She squeezed Carrie's hand again. 'And you've got Ewen. D'you know what it means to have a man who loves you like that? There's lots o' folk would envy you, you know.'

Carrie lifted her head and looked into wistful eyes. 'Isa?' she said uncertainly.

Her friend gave her the most rueful of smiles, dropped her hand and rose to her feet. 'I suppose I'd better make us all some tea.' She transferred her gaze to Florence. 'Will that shut you up, ye old bisom?'

'Less of the old, ye wee flibbertigibbet,' said Florence. 'There's a lot of years left in me yet. I'll maybe even see you out.'

'Huh!' said Isa.

'Mr Livingstone, please.'

It was four o'clock that afternoon and this was the fourth time Carrie had phoned. She kept getting the same telephonist, and being put through to the same secretary. It was a Sunday, of course, there would only be a skeleton staff working. The two voices were beginning to sound familiar. The secretary was beginning to sound irritable.

'Is this Partick station again?'

'Yes. It's really quite important that we get hold of Mr Livingstone.' Carrie gripped the heavy black receiver hard.

'Well, as I told you half an hour ago, he's still in the meeting. These are not the sort of people you interrupt lightly. It's a very high-level affair, you know.'

'I understand that,' said Carrie, gritting her teeth at the patronising tone of voice, 'but as I told *you* half an hour ago, my business with him is rather urgent.'

'But you won't tell me what it concerns so that I could pass a note in to him?'

'No, I'm afraid that's not possible.'

The voice at the other end of the line grew suspicious. 'Is this a personal matter?'

Carrie denied that and reluctantly ended the conversation. She could get Ewen into trouble if she kept phoning. She could get him into trouble if she didn't.

She walked across to the window to pull down the blinds. The weather was atrocious. While no further snow had fallen that morning, it had started again as she was on her way to work. Isa had insisted on accompanying her, fearful that Matthew might be waiting for her at the station.

Carrie would have preferred her to stay with Florence and the children, but both Mrs Cookes had insisted she needed an escort. There were enough able-bodied men within earshot on a Sunday afternoon if Matt decided he was going to come home and cause trouble. And despite the act she was putting on, Florence had said sternly, they could both see fine that Carrie was still feeling gey wobbly.

They were right about that. Her head ached – inside and out – and she was ready to jump at her own shadow. Anxious that Isa should get back home quickly, Carrie had confidently assured her that there were always plenty of people around at the station. She peered out of the window at the platform. That was normally the case, but on a snowy Sunday afternoon in the depths of winter there weren't many passengers, and like Waverley, Partick too was operating with the bare minimum of staff today. Everyone in the goods yard had gone home early. There was little point in trying to shunt wagons in conditions like these.

Samuel the young porter was still working. Carrie kept putting her head round the door of the porters' room across the hall, making excuses to chat to him for a few minutes. He probably thought she was checking up on him, but she simply wanted the reassurance and comfort of knowing there was someone else around and not too far away.

The stationmaster had gone home early for his tea. He'd be back on his rounds about half-past nine, he'd told Carrie. She'd been unable to think of any reason to detain him.

The snow had brought a chilly wind with it. Meeting Donald Nicholson and Bobby on their walk along Dumbarton Road, he had opined that it must be blowing in from Siberia, it was so cold.

The train driver she'd spoken to twenty minutes ago had been complaining bitterly about lack of visibility. With the blackout restrictions, it was poor enough on a December afternoon, but the snow was turning his job into a nightmare. 'It'll soon be blizzard conditions, Mrs Campbell! You mark my words. And yet folks still expect the trains to run on time! Whatever the weather.'

She lowered the blinds on the hostile white darkness. If this did escalate into a blizzard, trains would surely have to be cancelled. Oh, please God, let the trains from Edinburgh to Glasgow be cancelled!

He came off the 8.22 to Helensburgh, the only passenger to alight from the train. Expecting there to be nobody at all – the night had grown even wilder – Carrie was waiting outside the booking-office door just in case there were any tickets to be collected.

'You're not going to believe this but I left Waverley on the five o'clock. It's taken me hours to get back here!'

Ewen followed her as she backed into the booking office. As the door swung shut behind them his voice became low and intimate. 'Oh, I've been thinking about you all day!'

She went to him then, laid her head on his shoulder. The pressure on her sore face hurt, but she didn't care. She was glad she hadn't been able to reach him on the phone. She was glad the trains from Edinburgh to Glasgow hadn't been cancelled. She was glad he was here.

She could feel his surprise at her action, but instead of the joking comment she expected, two surprisingly hesitant arms settled gently about her. For a minute or two they stood together in silence. Then he pulled back, lifted his hands to her head.

'I've always loved your hair,' he said dreamily, letting the red-gold strands trail through his fingers. 'Such a bonnie colour, and as smooth as silk. You're wearing it loose tonight. Is that for me?' The caressing hands stopped abruptly. 'What's this mark on the side of your face?'

He touched it, and she started back, drawing her breath in on a hiss of pain. He frowned. 'Carrie, what's happened? Did you fall in the snow or something? You should have phoned me. I'd have come back earlier.'

'I've been trying to phone you all day,' she said sorrowfully. 'To tell you to stay in Edinburgh.'

'Stay in Edinburgh?' he repeated. 'But why?' His frown deepened.

Then she saw the same emotions chase themselves across his face as she had seen on Isa's that morning: slowly dawning realisation, followed by quick and furious anger. But his fingers were exquisitely gentle as he raised them once more to her wounded face. 'How did he do this to you?'

She told him, her voice breaking as she described the assault.

'I'll kill him,' Ewen said softly. Behind him, someone pushed open the door.

'Not if I kill you first.'

Tall and handsome in his uniform, Matt walked into the room. Ewen turned to face him, pushing Carrie behind him. The protective gesture wasn't lost on her husband.

'It's you I'm interested in at the moment, Livingstone. I've been waiting for you to arrive. I'll deal with my whore of a wife later.'

'I thought you'd already dealt with her.' Ewen sounded calm, but Carrie knew he was fizzing with anger. 'Like hitting women, do you?'

'She's my wife,' Matt said calmly. 'I'm entitled.' His gaze flickered briefly to her. 'Even with that nasty bruise she still looks lovely, don't you think? I'll have to do something about that. Prevent any more like you fancying a quick dip between her thighs.'

'She hasn't been unfaithful to you, you know.'

'You expect me to believe that?'

'No,' Ewen said evenly, 'I suppose it's too much to expect that you'd be capable of believing that.'

The irony seemed to be lost on Matthew. 'I always thought she was different, but it turns out she's just like the rest of them. Comes of being friendly with that slut Isabella Cooke, I daresay. Definitely not the kind of person children should be exposed to. Don't you think so, Livingstone?'

Matt folded his arms and tilted his head to one side, as though this were a dinner party conversation Ewen and he were having. 'You would have different views on that of course. I suppose you naturally gravitate to strumpets and tarts – being the bastard son of a whore yourself.'

Every word was deliberate. Designed to wound. Calculated to provoke.

Carrie gripped Ewen's arms above the elbows, pressing as hard as she could through the heavy material of his coat. 'Ewen, please don't. Think of your job.'

Matt snorted. 'He's not even in uniform, Carrie. What sort of a man does that make him?'

She lifted her chin and looked him in the eye. 'A better man than you,' she said steadily.

Matt's face darkened. 'His mother was a whore, Carrie. Can you not understand that? Christ knows who his father was. Any one of a hundred drunken sailors with a few pounds in their pockets.' His voice dripped contempt. 'More likely a few coins. That's all it took to buy Annie Livingstone for half an hour.'

She waited for Ewen to stride forward and smash his fist into Matt's face, but he didn't move. Instead, he struck back with words. Stunning, heart-stopping words.

'I know exactly who my father is,' he said quietly. 'I also know very well who my brother is. Half-brother, at any rate.'

And the last piece of the jigsaw fell into place.

Chapter 30

'My brother? A guttersnipe like you? Don't make me laugh.' Matt tossed his dark head. 'Bred in the sewer,' he sneered. 'And however high you climb, you'll always slide back down there. Where you belong. Where your whore of a mother belonged.'

Carrie waited for Ewen to explode into violence, but instead he turned and looked at her.

'Do you know how my mother ended up on the streets, Carrie? I don't think I ever told you that part of the story, did I?'

'No,' she said. 'You didn't.' He sounded calm enough. Maybe, just maybe, if she kept him talking, things could stay that way.

'She came to Glasgow to go into service.' He raised an arm. Ramrod-stiff, it pointed accusingly at Matt. 'Up the hill in his grandfather's house. She was seventeen years old, fresh from the Highlands. She didn't stand a chance against a man like your father-in-law.'

'He took advantage of her?' Carrie whispered.

Matt snorted, but Ewen ignored him. 'Yes. Told her he loved her, of course, promised he'd look after her. But he wasn't there when they flung her out into the snow. Pregnant and friendless and with nowhere to go.'

It fitted all too well with what she knew of Charles Campbell's character. And she recalled the acerbic comment Ewen had made yesterday morning. *Some sons take after their fathers*. Now she understood the ambiguity of the way the observation had been worded. He'd been exempting himself from that character assessment.

'How very affecting,' said Matt. 'Did she get that from some music-hall melodrama? A nice fairy story which meant she didn't have to tell you the truth. A slut like your mother wouldn't have the faintest idea who had fathered her bastard. How could she when she spent her life opening her legs for one man after the other?'

Ewen took a step forward, his hands bunching into fists. Carrie followed him, slipped her own hands over those fists. She felt him react to her touch, but knew also that every word was eating away like acid at his self-esteem and his self-control.

She recognised the strategy. That was exactly what Matt wanted.

She listened, horrified, as he continued to deploy it. There had to be some way she could stop this.

'I know what women like that are like.' He laughed suddenly. 'I should do, I've had plenty of them over the years. Professional and amateur. More of the latter than the former recently.'

Carrie's eyes opened wide. Her fingers fell off Ewen's hands. He turned to look at her pale and shocked face, then swung back round to her husband.

'No, she didn't know that,' Matthew said casually. 'I've always been a gentleman, spared her the knowledge. I won't need to from now on, will I? I'll be able to do as I damn' well please.' His voice slithered like silk. 'Considering I now hold all the cards.'

'What the hell do you mean by that?'

Matt folded his arms across his chest, apparently relaxed. 'It appears you have a brain. Try using it. Think how this will look. While I'm off serving King and Country, you're screwing my wife. Who then flaunts you in front of our innocent children.' He unfolded his arms, put one hand to his chest. 'Then, when I – the broken-hearted husband – come home and confront my faithless wife and her lover, you lay me out cold while she stands by and watches. Think any court in the country would let her keep her children after they've listened to that story? Think you'd keep your position in the company? You'd be back swinging a hammer before you knew what had hit you.'

It was a variation on what he'd said to Carrie that morning, but Ewen was hearing it for the first time. He went white. 'You evil bastard,' he breathed.

Matt raised his eyebrows. 'Strange insult for you to use.'

'Ewen! No!' Carrie grabbed the arm he'd started to raise. His eyes were glittering like gunmetal.

'Let me at him, Carrie. We cannae let him get away wi' saying all those things about you – and ma mother. I'm goin' tae fuckin' kill him!' In the midst of her distress, she registered that he had reverted completely to his original accent. Matt's strategy had worked well, searing away the layers which made Ewen what he was today, unerringly finding the lost boy beneath.

'No, Ewen, no! He's right. Can't you see that? Think of your job,' she begged again. 'Think of how far you've come! Don't throw it all away now!'

She held on to him. It was hard work, but because he didn't want to hurt her, he was allowing her to do it – while Matt looked on and watched them both.

'Come outside with me,' she urged Ewen. 'For a minute. Till we all calm down. Then we can discuss this like rational adults.'

She forced herself to meet Matt's dark eyes. 'There's nothing to discuss, Carrie,' he said calmly. 'You and the children stay with me. End of story. Unless you want to lose them – and ruin your little friend's career. Not to mention his life. I'll hold the door open for you, shall I?' His voice hardened. 'You've got ten minutes. After that I'm coming out there to get you.'

They went on to the platform, sheltering from the snow under the canopy. When they got there, Ewen turned abruptly and made as if to go back in. Carrie raised her hands to his shoulders, trying to shove him against the wall of the building.

'No! That's what he wants you to do.'

His breathing was ragged, his voice raw. 'What about what I want to do, Carrie?' But he let her push him back.

She stood beside him, staring out at the blizzard. 'What do you want to do?'

The reply was immediate. 'I want to do to him what he did to you. I want to smash his face into a pulp. I want to break all his fingers because he used them to hurt you.'

'Ewen,' she said, chilled by his words, 'he's your brother.'

'He doesn't believe that,' he said bitterly. 'Why should you?'

'Because I know your mother didn't bring you up to tell lies. She was a good woman. An honest woman.'

He found her hand. 'We'll fight him for the bairns,' he said. 'Through the courts. What he told us about himself . . .' He threaded his fingers through hers. 'We can use that against him.'

'He'll deny it. We've got no proof. And,' she said sadly, 'he does love Archie and April. They are his children.' She gave an odd little laugh. 'You really are their Uncle Ewen.'

'Aye. I am.' He squeezed her hand, but even as he was doing it she was extracting her fingers from his grasp. Something else had struck her. Something which didn't make her laugh. 'I'm your brother's wife.' She took a step back. 'You would never have told me. Would you?'

There was a train coming. Carrie turned mechanically as it pulled in to the platform and just as mechanically returned the smile and wave of a small girl sitting at the window of a third-class compartment. She and her mother were in the second last carriage and looked to be the only passengers on board. Nobody got off and the driver started up again.

The train swayed along the platform. 'They're not showing any rear lights,' said Ewen dully. 'You'd better get on the blower to Hyndland so the guard can do something about that before he leaves there.'

Carrie had also noticed the lack of illumination. The strong wind must have blown the lamps out. She swung open the booking-hall door and Ewen followed her in.

Matt was a railwayman too. He understood the urgency of the situation. When the clerkess at Hyndland phoned them back five minutes later with the news that the train still wasn't with them, he took the instrument out of Carrie's hand and tried to raise the signal box at Partick. They had all made the same deduction: that the train had halted at a red light somewhere on the brief stretch of track between the two stations.

'I'm not getting through to the box. The line's dead.'

'Maybe the wind's brought down the telephone cable,' suggested Ewen. 'The spur that goes to the box.' The three of them looked at each other. A few hundred yards along the line they had a standing train. In a blizzard. With no lights showing. Ewen asked the obvious question.

'When's the next westbound service due?'

'Nine-twelve to Dalmuir Park,' said Carrie. She took a deep breath to calm herself down.

'Then we've got less than twenty minutes,' said Matt, glancing at the clock. 'Any of the porters on?'

'Young Samuel.'

'Get him to run round for the stationmaster. You wait here and alert the driver of the nine-twelve, and the two of us will go down to the signal box. All right?' That final question, accompanied by a questioning lift of the head, was directed at Ewen. He got a cool look back, then a quick nod of agreement.

'All right,' Ewen replied. 'Let's get the hand lamps lit. Two each.'

Carrie picked up the phone. 'I'll inform Queen Street. Then they can get word through to everyone else.'

There was a rumble, the slowly building vibration which indicated the approach of another train.

'Eastbound, one trusts,' muttered Matt.

'No,' cried Carrie. 'It's not!' She thrust the telephone down and ran out on to the platform, but she was too late. The train had already rattled past. The two men were right behind her.

'If the next train's the nine-twelve, what the hell was that?' yelled Ewen, fighting against the noise made by the fast disappearing carriages and the wind.

'It looked like empty coaches, but the first Home James isn't due for another hour yet. Oh, God,' she wailed. 'Oh, God!'

They heard it thirty seconds later, the sound of the impact rising above the blizzard. An almighty bang, like the report of the biggest gun imaginable. Then a dreadful splintering sound and the screech of metal against metal. A long drawn-out banshee wail which seemed to go on for hours. Then there was silence.

The sleet was driving into their faces, so at first it was hard to make out what lay in front of them. It was Ewen who deciphered it first, memories of his days working the line helping him discern the lie of the land by the inadequate light of the hand lamps. Carrie and Samuel had followed him and Matt down, bringing four more with them. They had left the stationmaster phoning for help.

A group of men were sitting on the ground. Carrie went quickly to them and established that they were the drivers and firemen of both trains and the guard of the first one. They all had cuts and bruises but appeared otherwise to be largely uninjured.

'Ah didnae see it, hen!' said the driver of the second train. 'Ah just didnae see it! It loomed up out o' nowhere!'

'It had no rear lights,' she soothed him. 'You hadn't a hope of seeing it. Not on a night like this.' And, she thought, there was a curve in the line here. He wouldn't have seen the red signal either – especially with several carriages of a stationary train in front of it.

She did what she could to comfort him, relieved beyond words that he and his fireman and the guard of the first train were physically unhurt. They'd been at the centre of the impact. Hopefully that boded well for the mother and child she'd seen. The guard on their train, also unhurt and apparently with nerves of steel, was standing in a huddle with Matt and Ewen, all of them discussing what to do next. He had confirmed that the two had been his only passengers on arrival at Partick.

There were swaying lights approaching: staff from Hyndland also carrying hand lamps. Carrie left the shocked train crews in their care and walked over to where the three men stood. 'What about the woman and the little girl?'

'We're going to try and get them out,' Ewen told her, 'but there's a wee bit of a problem. The collision's made the standing train jackknife – the carriage they're in and the carriage in front of them. Can you see?'

She could barely make it out through the swirling snow. The two carriages, both half on and half off the tracks, now formed two sides of a triangle. Whilst the empty coach lay at a crazy angle, leaning away from them, the other coach had rolled completely. Its side was now its roof. The bogeys which held the wheels had broken off at either end and there was a large gap between them and the carriage.

It was going to be a bit of a scramble to get up there, with nothing solid remaining on the undercarriage which could be used as a stepping stone, but otherwise she couldn't see what the problem was. Braving the other coach would be hazardous – it was still tilting – but this one appeared to have fallen as far as it could go.

Surely all that was needed was for one or more of them to climb up on to the side, walk along it and get the woman and child out. Maybe someone could go for a ladder so they could give them a fireman's lift back down on to solid ground. Even if they weren't injured – and please God let that be the case – they'd be badly shocked and frightened. She couldn't hear any cries, but it was hard to hear anything in this wind. She expressed her thoughts aloud.

'If only it was that simple,' said Ewen. He lifted an arm to indicate. 'There's a sort of embankment over there, Carrie. Remember that subsidence there was a few years back? The engineers had to do a bit of earth-moving over there. They allowed the hole which had formed to exist and shored up the railway line above it. The ground slopes away steeply from the track.'

Everyone was listening carefully to him. 'The ends of both carriages are suspended over the drop. From about their middle points.' Samuel shifted nervously from one foot to the other. 'Exactly where you said the woman and wee lassie are.'

The implications were crystal clear. Any undue pressure and the coach could seesaw and fall. Not a slide down an embankment which might just protect the people inside, but a drop through fresh air with a heavy impact at the end of it.

Sombre faces were cast into relief by the paraffin lamps at their feet. If they did nothing, waited for further help to arrive, the tilting coach might fall further, taking itself and the other one with it. With the same outcome.

All at once Matt laughed. 'So it's a case of damned if we do and damned if we don't.' He squared his shoulders. 'Which one of us is the lightest?'

Carrie saw the Adam's apple in Samuel's throat bob. 'I am,' he offered gamely.

'Get away,' said Matthew. 'Your mammy would never forgive us if anything happened to you. And don't bother volunteering either, Carrie. I doubt you'd have the strength in your arms to pull them out.'

He glanced across the flickering lamplight at Ewen. 'I'm taller than you. I can inch along on my belly that bit further without tipping the balance. Hopefully,' he added, smiling wryly.

Ewen's brows knitted. 'You're sure? I'll easy do it.'

'I'm sure. I'll need someone strong enough to grab them and swing them away from the gap when I lower them down. You'll be right on the edge of it, mind. Give us a kiss for luck, Carrie,' he added casually.

He walked over to her and kissed her hard on the mouth, his arm coming briefly about her waist. 'I love you,' he said. Then he released her and headed for the tumbled carriage.

'Good luck,' called Ewen.

Matthew turned and looked at him. 'Aye,' he said. 'You too.'

* * *

'He'll have been trained how to do that, Mrs Campbell. In the army, like.'

'I suppose so, Samuel.'

The boy was chattering, giving a running commentary she didn't want or need on Matt's agonisingly slow progress along the carriage, but she wasn't going to tell him to keep quiet. Nerves took different people different ways.

In her own case, it was an inability to look away, however much she wanted to. He'd mounted the carriage fairly far back, where it still lay on solid ground. She was willing him on – and praying hard. Should she offer God a bargain in exchange for his safety? It came to her what that bargain would be, and she hesitated. There was a loud creak, and she ran forward to where Ewen and the guard stood, Samuel in hot pursuit.

'The other coach,' said Ewen. 'It's shifted a bit.' He laid a comforting hand on her shoulder. 'Don't worry. He seems to know what he's doing, and he's taking it real slow.'

She followed his gaze to where Matt was crawling along the upended side of the wooden carriage. The movement did look like something he'd learned in the army. She'd seen soldiers in newsreels doing something very similar.

'That one,' she called up through the snow. 'You've reached it.'

He stretched forward, curled his fingers around the door handle and tugged. 'It's stuck fast. I'll have to break the window.'

'It's not broken already?' asked the guard.

'Nope. Anybody got a hammer about their person, by any chance?' Matt sounded quite cheerful.

'I brought one!' shouted Samuel. 'I thought about that!' He gave it to Ewen who stretched up to hand it over, holding it by the head and extending the shaft to Matt, straining to get it as close to his reaching fingers as possible.

'Thanks.' He edged a little further forward before using it. As the glass shattered, they heard screaming from inside the compartment. A child's voice. Carrie clutched Samuel in relief. Ewen was standing on the very edge of the embankment, getting ready to receive the girl and her mother as they were handed down. She didn't want to disturb his concentration.

Matthew was reaching down, hauling someone up by the armpits. It was the mother. Her body looked limp, but she was muttering. Carrie wondered if she was concussed. She might well have been, but she was no sooner surrendered to Ewen's waiting arms than she was fighting him, trying to get back into the wreckage.

'The girl's trapped,' Matthew called. 'Her foot's caught under something.'

Hysterical the mother might be, but she had heard that comment.

She started howling, pounding her fists against Ewen's chest. Carrie moved quickly forward, pulling her away from him before her struggles could send them both over the edge. With a strength she didn't know she had, she dragged her back and shook her hard.

'Listen!' she said. 'They're doing their best to get your lassie out! Do you think you shouting and screaming is helping them any? For God's sake – for your daughter's sake – for my husband's sake – SHUT YOUR BLOODY MOUTH!'

Stunned, the woman stared into her face. Then she burst into tears. Carrie put her arms about her and held her tight. 'That's better,' she said. 'Have a wee greet. Only a wee one, mind. Your girl will need you looking cheerful when they bring her out.'

Ten minutes later they heard a shout of triumph. It was Matt's voice, carrying above the blizzard. 'Got her!'

Carrie was powerless to stop the woman from running back to the wreckage, but this time she stood and waited as her daughter was passed carefully down to Ewen. The little bundle is his arms said one word: 'Mammy.' One word was enough. He handed her over to her mother with tears sliding down his face.

'Getting a wee bit emotional here,' he said a little shamefacedly.

Carrie touched his arm. 'That's all right,' she said. 'Now Matt's got to get himself off there.'

'Out of there,' Ewen corrected. 'He had to go inside the compartment to free the girl.'

As he said the words, a head appeared through the shattered window.

'D'you want to wait till we get a rope?' called the guard.

'I'm thinking there might not be time for that,' muttered Ewen, but Matthew had already got up on to the side of the carriage, and was shaking his head. 'Maybe I should jump.'

'Don't be so bloody stupid,' said Ewen sharply, 'you'll break your legs. Come back the way you got there.'

'Matthew,' Carrie called. 'Don't take any risks.'

Snowflakes dancing around him, he smiled down at her. 'Life's a risk, Carrie. Didn't you know?'

There was an ominous creak. She called out, and her hand went to her mouth. He put his hands on his hips and shook his head at her in mocking reproach. 'That was the other coach,' he said. 'For all we know this one's as solid as the Rock of Gibraltar.'

He was standing in the elegant pose she knew so well, one leg extended a little to the side. He looked as though he was about to do some Highland dancing. The only thing missing was the crossed swords at his feet. He tapped one foot on the wood on which he stood. Once. Twice. 'See? Nothing to worry about.'

'For Christ's sake,' said Ewen. 'Get on to your front and come back down here.'

There was another creak. Then the sound of wood splintering.

'That wasn't the other coach,' Ewen said grimly. 'You're going to have to bloody jump. Do it now!'

Matt was still smiling. Then, beneath his feet, the coach fell away. He went with it.

There was help now. Plenty of it. Nurses and ambulance men and people with ropes. A squad of them were down in the gully, searching for Matthew.

'Maybe we should have waited till we had ropes,' Ewen was saying. 'Then we'd have been able to hang on to him.'

'We couldn't have waited,' said the guard. 'We'd have lost the passengers.'

Someone had slung a blanket around Carrie's shoulders and pressed an enamel mug of hot sweet tea into her frozen hands. They'd done the same for Ewen and Samuel and the guard too. Her teeth were chattering. So were Samuel's.

'Drink your tea,' she told him automatically. She was beginning to get that distant feeling, the sense of watching it all happen, like being at the pictures. Only when you were at the cinema you could get all caught up in the story, but you knew you weren't really involved in it. Here, in the corner of her brain which was refusing to allow her to drift away from what was unfolding in front of her, she knew all too well that this was cold and bloody reality.

It got colder and bloodier still. They were pulling a stretcher up the embankment. The long body on it was wrapped in a dark blanket. Including the face.

Chapter 31

Matt's funeral was every bit the ordeal Carrie had expected it to be, with Archie and April confused and bewildered and asking all sorts of questions she found it hard to answer. How could the daddy they hadn't seen for months be lying in that box at the front of the church? And how could he be in there anyway when Auntie Florence had said he was in heaven now?

Florence had told them that the day before, comforting them in the best way she knew how. Mercifully, neither of them had appeared to register Isa's muttered: 'More likely the other place.'

Carrie sat in the front pew of the church, between the children. Her father-in-law had his arm around the shoulders of a somewhat bemused Archie. His wife wasn't with him.

'Shona felt she wouldn't be able to face it,' he'd told Carrie, tenderly embracing his daughter-in-law before she had a chance to resist.

Poor Matt, she thought sadly. Your mother put herself before you until the last.

The enquiry into the accident was postponed until the beginning of February 1943. The convenor began by expressing the deepest condolences of all those present to Mrs Campbell. He was most solicitous when Carrie gave her account of events, ensuring she was entirely comfortable and had a glass of water to hand.

She caught Ewen's eye, and he gave her a little smile of encouragement. At her request, he'd gone back to Edinburgh the day before Matt's funeral. She hadn't seen him since, although she knew he'd written to Isa several times. He gave his own evidence clearly and concisely. He didn't think they could have waited for help to arrive. It had been a matter of life or death and they had done as they thought appropriate in the circumstances.

'A course of action which unfortunately led to the death of Mr Matthew Campbell. Is it your opinion that Mr Campbell was foolhardy to attempt a rescue of the two passengers on board the derailed train?'

'No,' said Ewen vehemently. 'It is my opinion that Mr Campbell acted very bravely. He saved two lives. At the expense of his own.'

Beside Carrie, Charles Campbell bent his head and shaded his eyes. She hated herself for it, but she couldn't help noticing how elegantly the gesture was performed.

The conclusions drawn at the end of the day were what everyone has expected them to be. Whilst criticisms might be made against the guard of the first train for failing to ensure that the blizzard hadn't extinguished his rear lamps, he had been checking them frequently that night. He had, in fact, intended to do so again at Hyndland. A recommendation was made that in future such a check should be made at every stop.

Otherwise, it was decided that the accident had been just that, a tragic sequence of events sparked off by the atrocious weather conditions that night. It was because of the storm and train cancellations elsewhere that the empty carriages had gone through at an unexpected time. No blame attached itself to their driver. Nobody was to be blamed. It was an act of God. Sympathy was once again extended to Mrs Campbell and her children in their sad loss.

As the enquiry broke up, she stood up and made her way to the exit. Ewen had beaten her to it. He was in his dark coat and suit, hat held politely in his hand. 'Mrs Campbell, can you spare me half an hour of your time? Perhaps you would allow me to take you to tea.'

Her father-in-law was right behind her. 'Mr Livingstone, isn't it?' he said affably. He held out his hand, but Ewen didn't take it. Charles narrowed his eyes. 'Have we met before, young man?'

Ewen took his intense grey gaze off Carrie's face. 'I believe you may have known my mother,' he said levelly.

Charles lowered his hand and pondered. He was obviously doing a mental rundown of his female acquaintanceship, the sort who might have a son like Ewen. 'No,' he said, with a charmingly apologetic smile, 'I can't think I've ever had the pleasure of knowing a Mrs Livingstone.'

A girl with a notebook and pencil materialised at Carrie's elbow. 'Both you and your late husband worked on the railways, Mrs Campbell?'

She was joined by a colleague – a gentleman of the press this time. 'Do your children know their daddy died a hero, Mrs Campbell?' he asked. 'Would you give us the wee ones' names?'

'For God's sake,' said Ewen irritably, 'can you not leave her alone?'

'It's all right,' Carrie said, 'they're only doing their job.' Josephine Shaw had told her all about human interest stories. They made good copy. She would answer their questions and they would go away happy.

'And this gentleman?' the girl asked after she'd got the information she wanted out of Carrie. 'Are you a relative of Mrs Campbell's, sir?'

'I'm the dear girl's father-in-law,' replied Charles. 'Matthew was my son.' There was a catch in his voice.

'And . . .' the reporter asked hesitantly '. . . would you mind answering a few questions about him? You wouldn't find it too painful?'

Charles smiled bravely. 'Perhaps we could go somewhere more congenial?'

They were in George Square. Carrie had declined to go for tea with Ewen, but had agreed to walk for a while. It wasn't cold – one of those bright and sunny February days which seem to carry the promise of spring not too far around the corner. They stopped in front of the cenotaph, by one of the two stone lions flanking the memorial.

'Do you think he'll work out who you are?'

'I don't know.' Ewen shrugged his broad shoulders. 'He probably hardly even knew my mother's surname. She would have been "Annie" to him. Just another parlour maid. To tell you the truth, I don't much care. I used to, but I've got other things on my mind at the moment.'

Carrie looked away. 'Ewen, please don't say what I think you're going to say.'

'Why not?'

She was studying the lion's huge paws. 'Can't you see how Matt's death has changed everything?'

'Yes, I can. It makes it much easier for us.'

She whirled round, gazed at him in horror. 'That's a brutal thing to say!'

'Carrie,' he said urgently. 'I'm sorry for the way he died. I suppose I'm sorry he *is* dead. I wouldn't wish that on anybody. Not even him. But if you're expecting me to act like a hypocrite, you're looking at the wrong man.'

'Ewen . . .'

'Just listen to me for a minute. Please? Will you hear me out?'

'All right,' she said reluctantly. 'Say what you have to say.'

'Come for tea?'

'No. Tell me here.'

He sighed. 'You're a hard woman.' He raised his eyes for a moment to the City Chambers, standing solidly behind the cenotaph. Then, as though he had marshalled his thoughts, he turned back to her and began. 'Here goes, then. They're planning on forming this railway regiment. More like a company really. Probably going to come under the Royal Engineers.'

'A railway regiment?' She was struggling with surprise. This wasn't at all what she'd expected him to say.

He nodded. 'The tide's beginning to turn, Carrie. We'll soon have Hitler on the run. Then we'll go after him, hit him where it really hurts.'

'The invasion of Europe?'

People were beginning to talk about it. For so long, Britain had been on the defensive, straining every sinew to keep the invader out. Now, with that battle at last won, it was time to start turning the tables.

Ewen nodded again. 'And wherever we go in – France or Italy or somewhere else where they least expect it – communications and lines of supply for men and materials are going to be crucial.'

'Roads, railways and bridges.'

'Aye,' he said grimly. 'We know it and they know it. They'll try to destroy it all as they retreat. So we'll need people who can throw it back down again as quickly as possible. And people who can study the maps before we go, work out where the crucial points are. So advance troops can maybe go on ahead to try to stop them from mining the bridges and railway lines.'

Carrie had been studying his face as he spoke. 'People like you,' she said. 'You've got the practical experience and the strategic planning experience.'

'Yes,' he agreed. 'People like me.'

'You want to go, don't you?'

'Aye,' he said slowly. 'I want to go. I think I probably need to go. But there's a large part of me wants to stay here too.'

He slid a hand inside his coat, brought out an official-looking buff envelope. He surprised her again, sent the conversation spinning off in another direction.

'I went to see a solicitor in Edinburgh a couple of weeks ago. Asked him about the brother's wife's business. Not that it would really matter, of course. You and I aren't related in any way, and we're also the only people who know that he and I were half-brothers. Apart from Isa, and she's not going to tell anybody.' He smiled nervously at her. 'But I thought it might be something that would worry you, so I asked the lawyer what the position is. Apparently it used to be the case that a man couldn't marry his brother's widow, but the law was changed several years ago.' He extended the envelope to her. 'It's all in here, if you want to read it.'

She looked at the letter, but made no move to take it from him.

'Carrie, did you hear what I said?'

She raised her eyes to his face. 'You really think it's that simple?'

'No. I know it's not.' He swallowed. 'First I have to ask you to marry me and hope you'll say yes. Then I have to ask you to wait for me, and hope you'll say yes to that too.'

There was a couple walking past them – a young man in a sailor's uniform carrying a kitbag and a girl clinging on to his arm. She was clutching a handkerchief and she'd obviously been crying. Carrie followed their progress across the square. They weren't going to Queen Street. They had headed off in the direction of Central Station. Probably he was going to join his ship at Gourock. Would the girl travel down with him, or would they say their farewells at the station?

'I know I'm asking you at a bad time,' Ewen said. 'Especially with this being the day of the enquiry. I'm sorry about that – but I don't have much time, Carrie. I'll probably be away within the month. I don't want to wait, but I'll understand if you think getting married before I go would be a bit too quick.'

The couple had disappeared from view, out of sight somewhere on St Vincent Place, heading for Buchanan Street and then Gordon Street.

'Say something, Carrie,' he said. 'So I'll know I haven't been talking to myself for the last five minutes.' He was wearing that nervous smile again.

'I can't say yes.'

'I've rushed you, haven't I? I should have given you a day or two to get over the enquiry.'

'Ewen, I can't ever say yes. Not now. Can't you see that? Don't look at me like that!'

For he had gone deathly pale and very still. 'I don't understand,' he said. 'I thought you loved me. Like I love you. And however it happened, you're free now.'

'Free?' She gave a harsh little laugh. 'I'll never be free. Every time I close my eyes, I go over his last moments, see it all happening again.'

'That's natural.' His voice softened. 'I've been doing that too, wondering if he might still be alive if we'd done something differently. It'll pass, I think.'

She shook her head. 'Not for me. I keep remembering that whole day, how he must have felt when he came home and found out about you . . .'

Ewen's voice was hard as tempered steel. 'When he came home and banged your head off the wall, you mean.'

'Ewen,' she said, 'you told Matt I hadn't been unfaithful to him – but I had. Don't you see that? Not physically maybe, but in my heart and in my head. I think he knew that. And I think it hurt him just as much.'

His eyes opened wide in disbelief. 'You're making excuses for him? How many times had he broken *his* wedding vows? He treated you like a dog, Carrie. Isa told me what happened after I sent you that first letter.' He slammed his fist violently into his other hand, startling her. '*Christ!* I'm so angry about that. And he didn't stop there, did he? She's told me the whole story.'

'No,' Carrie said passionately. 'Isa's told you her version of the story. There was more to Matt than that. A lot more. He loved Archie and April. He loved me.'

Ewen's hands shot out, gripped her by the upper arms. 'Carrie, for God's sake! Don't you remember the way he behaved that night? The things he said to you? How he told you about the other women he'd had? He threatened to take Archie and April away from you. Was any of that love?'

'He told me he loved me,' she insisted. 'Before he went up on the carriage. You were there. You must have heard him.'

'Oh, I heard him all right,' Ewen said grimly. 'He did it for my benefit. To remind me he was your husband and that I had no claim on you. He was so sure he was going to win.' He stopped, breathing heavily, and his hands fell from her arms. 'He has won, hasn't he?'

'He's dead,' she said harshly. 'You're still alive.' She was silent, remembering how she had thought of bargaining with God in return for Matthew's safety. She remembered too how she had pulled back from that sacrifice. It was being demanded of her all the same. If she was to have the faintest hope of being able to live with herself. She dropped her eyes and bent her head, waited for him to go.

There was a pause. Then she heard him give a bitter little laugh. 'You never actually told me you loved me, did you? Maybe I got it all wrong anyway.'

She didn't raise her head.

'Goodbye, then Carrie,' he said at last. 'I'll always love you, you know.'

She waited till she could no longer hear his footsteps. When she looked up he was almost at the station. She watched him cross the road and disappear into it. This time she knew he was walking out of her life forever.

PART IV
1946

Chapter 32

There was something different about Isa, but Carrie was having difficulty in pinpointing exactly what it was. She'd been talking to her for a good ten minutes before she worked it out. Not one cigarette had been smoked. She commented on this amazing development.

'Donald doesn't approve of smoking. I'm trying to give them up.'

'Donald?' Carrie wrinkled her brow in puzzlement. Of all Isa's gentlemen friends, past and present, she couldn't bring a Donald to mind. Pierre the Free Frenchman had lasted quite some time. Then there had been Eugene, a charming American. He had endeared himself greatly to Carrie by presenting her with an unaccustomed luxury: her very first nylon stockings – two pairs of them.

He'd gone off to help liberate Europe in June 1944 and had now returned to his home in New Jersey. Isa had received a Christmas card from him and his wife at the end of 1945. Although she refused to admit it, Carrie suspected that was the first she had known of the existence of the lady.

Eugene had been superseded by Harry. He'd been a Royal Navy man from Portsmouth but doing a shore job in Glasgow connected with the huge amount of activity the war had brought to the Clyde. He'd stayed on for six months after the end of the war in Europe, then he too had returned home.

'Donald,' she repeated thoughtfully. Then her mouth dropped open. 'You surely don't mean Donald Nicholson?'

'What other Donald would I be talking about?'

Carrie couldn't quite hide a smile. 'Well, you'd have to admit there have been quite a few men to choose from over the years.'

Isa gave her a hard stare, and reached into her pinny pocket. It was difficult not to laugh when the searching hand came back out empty.

'If Donald wants you to give up the fags,' Carrie said wickedly, 'you're not going to be able to sit there and blow smoke rings at me any more. You'll have to find another prop. Maybe you should take up knitting. Then you could jab a needle in my direction when you want to make a point.'

'Ha-bloody-ha,' snarled Isa.

Carrie responded with an impish look. 'So it's serious, is it?' she asked. 'With you and Donald?' She had always liked Bobby the dog's quiet master but the combination of him and Isa seemed an unlikely one. Now she came to think about it, he had always hovered around her a bit, but while Isa liked going out and enjoying herself, Donald's idea of a riotous time was taking his dog for a long walk or visiting the library.

'He's a good man, Carrie. Intelligent too. He's very well-read, you know. We have some great talks – about all sorts o' things.' That was another mind-boggling concept. Donald seemed to operate a kind of self-censorship, speaking only when it was strictly necessary. Nobody needed to tell him that careless talk cost lives or that loose lips sank ships.

Nonetheless, Carrie was touched by the note of tenderness in the smoke-roughened voice and by the way Isa's face had changed when she had spoken of him. She looked younger . . . softer somehow.

'You two have been getting to know each other, then?' she asked gently.

'He's asked me to marry him.' Now the expression on Isa's face was different again. She looked nervous, wanting reassurance. 'I've said yes, hen. Am I aff my heid?'

'Do you love each other?'

'Aye. I'm afraid so.' She put the back of her hand to her mouth. This was another first. The redoubtable Isabella Cooke succumbing to tears? 'He knows all about me, Carrie,' she said in a tremulous voice. 'That I've been a wee bit . . . well, what ye might call flighty . . . and he doesn't care. He says that's all in the past. It's our future together that matters to him.'

Touched, Carrie jumped to her feet and threw her arms around Isa's neck. 'If Donald said a lovely thing like that you're most definitely not aff yer heid. Congratulations. I hope you'll both be very happy. Can I interest you in a bridesmaid and pageboy for the wedding ceremony?'

So she attended Isa's wedding, and witnessed with maternal pride Archie and April's part in the proceedings. Her son, now a strapping lad a couple of months short of his tenth birthday, wore a kilt gifted by a friend whose own boy had grown out of it. The war might be over, but it was still a case of make do and mend. However, the kilt was in excellent condition and Archie looked fine and handsome in it. He had his father's dark hair and eyes, although Carrie could see a good bit of her own father in him too.

Between them, she and Florence had done their best to fulfil April's requirements. Not long turned eight, she was a mischievous red-haired tomboy, but had surprised her mother by requesting a 'fairy princess' dress for her role as bridesmaid. This was not, as she carefully explained, because she herself cared for that sort of thing, but because she knew her Auntie Isa would like it.

Rita Sharkey had come up with the material, supplying a dark green taffeta party dress which had been worn by all of her daughters in turn and was now too small for any of them. A little worn in places, its pre-war style and full skirt had allowed for some nifty cutting to fashion a new creation for April.

Florence's collection of bits and bobs had supplied the trimmings: crocheted lace at the collar and cuffs, broad tartan ribbon to tie as a sash round the waist, stiff net underneath to make a sticky-out petticoat. The colours complemented each other beautifully and the contrast between the overall green and April's red-gold hair was very striking.

'I shouldnae say it, hen,' said Florence, 'but we made a good job o' yon frock, did we no'? April looks a treat in it.'

'She does,' Carrie agreed, her eyes on her daughter. She was dancing with Donald, giggling as he twirled her round the dance floor, April standing on his feet. It looked funny, her dainty little shoes on top of his heavy ones. Bobby, an honoured guest at the festivities, currently sitting on the floor next to Carrie, was watching them with great interest.

'Aye. She's a bonnie girl. Takes after her mother.'

Carrie smiled. 'What would I do without you, Florence?'

She put her hand to the small plate in front of her and picked at the crumbs of wedding cake – a masterpiece of creative shopping and cooking over the rationing which was still in force – found a decent-sized morsel and lowered her hand to give it to the dog. 'You'll be pleased that Donald's moving in. It'll be nice for you to have a man about the house.'

'Aye.' Florence nodded happily. 'He appreciates good cooking when he tastes it, and he's already done quite a few o' the wee jobs that lazy lump Isabella Cooke never manages to get round to.'

Carrie bent solicitously over Bobby, the better to hide her amusement. She'd been worried at first that the newly-weds might set up home together elsewhere, leaving Florence to cope on her own after all these years. Then, with relief and a few covert chuckles, she had watched Isa's reluctance to admit that she didn't actually want to leave her former mother-in-law. All the excuses were trotted out.

Donald's single-end was too small for both of them, especially with the dog being there too. A bigger flat would certainly be nice, but bomb damage and proposed slum clearance were leading to a post-war housing shortage rapidly approaching crisis point. The waiting lists were as long as your arm and as a couple without children, Isa and Donald weren't going to be given priority.

It would surely make more sense for them to take over the front room – spacious enough and Isa's domain anyway – and save their pennies for something else. Donald, she had told Carrie excitedly, was talking about maybe getting a caravan on the coast. He had quite a lot of money put by already. It wouldn't be anything fancy, of course, but something cosy and comfortable, with a view of the sea. They could all use it for weekends and holidays. Carrie and the weans too, naturally. Wouldn't that be great?

All of this might very well be true, but as Carrie had worked out a long time ago, Isa and Florence were also extremely fond of each other, although brutal and prolonged torture wouldn't have dragged that admission out of either of them.

'Archie and April think it'll be great to have Bobby across the landing.' She patted him on the head. 'You'll have plenty of folk wanting to take you out for walks, son. Although you're getting on a bit now, aren't you? You must be about fourteen. What's that in doggie years – ninety-eight? My, my.' She gave him another pat. 'You're remarkably fit for your age, sir.'

Carrie straightened up and found Florence doing the folded arms and pursed lips act. 'What?' she asked.

'Would you not like a man about your own house, pet?'

A waitress carrying an outsize teapot was approaching. Carrie looked up with relief, but it was short-lived. As soon as the woman had filled their cups and moved on, Florence returned to the topic. She'd brought it up several times over the past year: since the war had ended and the men had begun to come home. Some of the men, that was. There were those who were never going to return. Others seemed to be choosing not to do so.

Pascal Sharkey and Anne-Marie waltzed past their table, and Carrie gave them a wave. Pascal was one of those who had come home safe, and three months ago she had danced at his and Anne-Marie's wedding. She was glad for them, as she was glad for all those who'd been reunited with their loved ones after the years of upheaval.

All the same, she'd been guiltily aware of a little pang of envy both at that celebration and at this one. The uncomfortable sensation had been swiftly followed by a resolution to count her blessings, as she did now.

'I'm quite happy as I am. I have my children, I have my friends and I have my work.' She hid a grimace. There was a wee bit of a problem brewing on that front. She hadn't mentioned it to Isa because she had been all caught up in the preparations for the wedding, and she hadn't told Florence because she didn't want her worrying.

With a bit of luck – and Pascal Sharkey's help – Carrie was sure she could get the problem solved. Back working on the railways after his demobilisation, he was now her official union representative.

A bony hand reached across the table. 'You don't need me to tell you what else you need. Who else you need.'

Carrie didn't reply, and Florence's thin fingers tightened around her wrist. 'Are you going to punish yourself forever for what happened to your man? It was an accident, you know.'

'I do know that, Florence,' Carrie said quietly. The waltz finished and the dancers began to leave the floor. 'For a long time I didn't, but I've sorted it out in my head now. What the enquiry found was right. It was a terrible accident. Nobody's fault.'

'I'm real glad to hear you say that, lass.' The worried look on her interrogator's face relaxed a little, but the questioning wasn't quite over. 'Do you not think you should let a certain person know that's how you feel now?'

'No,' she said firmly. 'We don't know where he is anyway. Do we?' Carrie was playing with the crumbs on her plate again. She raised her eyes. 'I suppose we would have heard if there had been bad news.'

There was a question in her voice. Florence answered it robustly. 'Of course we would. He put Isa and me down as his next-of-kin, after all.' She gave Carrie's hand a little shake. 'Of course we'd have heard.'

'But he hasn't written to either of you since he joined up, has he?'

'No,' came the reluctant reply. 'But that doesnae necessarily mean anything. At first he'd have been too busy. Then he'd have been on the continent . . .'

'Florence, the war's been over for more than a year. I've got to face facts. If he'd wanted to get in touch, he'd have done it by now. I'm sorry for your sake. And Isa's.'

The older woman dismissed that. 'You could try and find out where he is now. The army must have records of him. Or the railway. He's more than likely come back to work for the LNER.'

Carrie shook her head. 'I sent him away, Florence. I've got absolutely no right to expect him to come back and try again. Even if I wanted him to,' she added. She turned away, unwilling to continue meeting that surprisingly penetrating gaze. 'Can we talk about something else now? Please?'

She heard Florence sigh. Then her voice changed. 'Here's Pascal coming to ask you to dance, anyway.'

Carrie stood up with him with alacrity. 'So,' she asked as he steered her round the dance floor, 'what do you think of the detailed proposals for the railways?'

He gave her an enthusiastic and comprehensive response. Sweeping to power on a tidal wave of popular support the year before, the Labour Party had announced its intention of giving the returning servicemen and women who had voted for it exactly what they wanted. Evoking the spirit of Dunkirk and of the Blitz, they had declared that this time the land fit for heroes would be delivered.

There was to be a guarantee that the hardship endured during the Hungry Thirties would never be allowed to happen again. Declaring itself to be socialist and proud of it, the new government had a clear vision of how that could be achieved. Control of all aspects of life – industry, the press, the banks, the coal mines – had to pass from those they referred to as the 'hard-faced men' to the ordinary people of the country. Nationalisation of the railways, the backbone of Britain, was a major plank of this policy.

Like Pascal, Carrie was all in favour of the idea. 'As long as safety and efficiency are our watchwords,' she said as soon as she could get a word in edgeways. 'And we'll need massive investment. Everything's worn out after the war – the track, the rolling stock, the buildings. The staff, too,' she added with a rueful smile.

'Aye,' her partner agreed, doing some nifty footwork to pilot them round two of their fellow dancers who'd had one drink too many. 'We're also seriously undermanned.'

Carrie looked thoughtfully at him. She hadn't been going to bring it up when they were both guests at Isa and Donald's wedding. It didn't exactly seem the appropriate occasion, but seeing as how he had mentioned it . . .

By the time she had finished recounting her tale of woe they were seated at his table, Anne-Marie listening attentively.

'So,' she said when Carrie had finished, 'they're happy to keep you on, but only if you agree to go full-time and do all the different shifts? Is that the position?'

'Yes. They're not asking all the women to leave like the last time. They need a lot of us. As Pascal says, we're seriously under*manned*.'

Thinking of the thousands of women whose labour had helped keep the railways running over the war years, she couldn't resist giving a teasing emphasis to the second half of the word he had used. Anne-Marie got it immediately, and rolled her eyes in sympathy. Carrie grinned at her, and went on.

'But they are making it very difficult for any women with children to stay on. I've made it clear that I'll do my best to be as adaptable as possible. I'm perfectly willing to do a longer shift occasionally and cover for holidays and sickness. And I'm quite happy to start in time for the morning rush hour.'

'Mrs Cooke keeps the children till it's time for school?' asked Anne-Marie.

'Yes. And she's ready to help out if I am covering for somebody else. All I'm asking is that, as a general rule, I can work a six-hour day shift Mondays to Fridays so I've got time to do my shopping and a bit of housework and be home for my children coming out of school in the afternoon. It doesn't seem such an unreasonable request.'

'It's not unreasonable at all,' said Anne-Marie with some passion. She turned to her new husband. 'Pascal, surely you can do something to help?'

Carrie understood immediately the conflicting emotions evident in his expression.

'Anne-Marie,' he said awkwardly, 'we really can't make special arrangements for women which could be seen as giving them an advantage over men.'

'What, like paying the same rate for the same job, you mean?' asked his wife pertly. 'Perish the thought!'

He made a face at her, and Carrie leaped in. 'Pascal, during the war we all worked whatever hours were asked of us, and were glad to do it. We were flexible then. Can the railway not be flexible now?'

'Carrie, no one's denying that the women did a great job under very difficult circumstances –'

'But now we're all supposed to be content to stay at home and stir the porridge?' queried Anne-Marie.

'You wanted to give up work!' he said accusingly.

'Aye, I did. I was fed up pulling great heavy levers and being stuck in a signal box for hours on end.' She laid a conciliatory hand on her husband's arm and fluttered her eyelashes at him. 'And I wanted the chance to minister to your every need, darling boy.'

'That'll be right,' he said ruefully.

'Poor lamb,' she said, and gave him a quick kiss. 'In my case, there was also a man coming back from the army who needed his job back – the particular one I happened to be doing. But Carrie's in a different position.'

Carrie leaned forward over the table. 'That's right. I'm not taking a man's job, Pascal. You know that. We're extremely short-staffed on the clerical side. And I'm not trying to make some sort of a point either. Part of me would love to go home and be a full-time housewife again, but I'd be broke if I tried to live on my widow's pension, and Archie and April would suffer. And,' she finished up, 'I like my job. And I'm good at it. You know that too.'

'Aye,' he said uncomfortably. 'I do.'

Anne-Marie was looking hopefully at him, clearly expecting him to come up with an instant solution, but Carrie knew Pascal was in a difficult position. As an NUR representative, he was duty-bound to protect his members, most of whom were male. He had to make sure they all got back the jobs they had left when they joined up and safeguard their interests during the transition to a nationalised railway network. Part of that was ensuring that male wages and salaries weren't threatened by the employment of too many women working – through no fault of their own – for a lower rate of pay.

'I'll ask for a meeting,' he said at last. 'You can put your case directly to management.'

'You'll go with her, Pascal,' said Anne-Marie, frowning a little. 'She is one of your members.'

'What? Oh, aye. Of course.' Reminded of his responsibilities, he put a hand inside his jacket and came out with a diary. 'When would suit you Carrie? Did I hear you say you were taking the weans away over the summer holidays?'

'We're going up to see Mary and Douglas,' she said, and suggested a date in the week after the schools went back.

'Will you tell Mary and Douglas I was asking for them, Carrie?' said Anne-Marie.

'I'll be glad to.'

Trying not to be too disappointed by Pascal's obvious reluctance to help her, Carrie smiled broadly at Anne-Marie. Pity she wasn't the NUR rep. She seemed more prepared to help than her husband did.

Neither of the children wanted to get undressed and ready for bed when they got home that evening. Anxious to admire themselves in their wedding finery, they began fighting over the space in front of the long mirror in the lobby. Exasperated, Carrie threatened to cover it with a blanket if they didn't agree to take turns.

'She's had much longer than me already, Ma. I should get the first shot.'

'People said I was pretty,' contested April. 'I need to look at myself to see if they were right.'

'They said I was handsome,' retorted Archie.

'Handsome is as handsome does,' responded his sister loftily.

Carrie's exasperation gave way to amusement. That was one of Florence's sayings. Both children had picked up quite a few of her and Isa's turns of phrase over the years. They weren't always entirely sure what they meant. In some cases – particularly when it came to Isa's utterances – that was probably just as well.

Her merriment had another source. Archie was a typical boy, forever coming home with the seat out of his trousers or a rip in his shirt caused by falling out of a tree or catching it on the wall he happened to be climbing over at the time. April wasn't much better. Seeing them take such an interest in their clothes and how they looked in them was a novel experience.

'My father wore a kilt, didn't he, Ma?' asked Archie. 'When he was in the Argyll and Sutherland Highlanders?'

'He did,' she said, standing behind him and placing her hands on his shoulders. In a year or two she would have to stand up on tiptoe to be able to do that. She met his eyes in the mirror. They were shining . . . and so like Matt's.

'Can I be a soldier when I grow up, Ma?'

'If you want to,' she said lightly, 'but I'd like to think there wouldn't be any wars left to fight in by the time you grow up.' She squeezed his shoulders. 'Haven't we had enough of all that?'

April piped up, using a word she'd just learned at school. 'But our Daddy *was* a gallant soldier, wasn't he, Mammy?'

Carrie smoothed the hair whose colour was the image of her own. 'Aye,' she said slowly. 'He never got the chance to do any real fighting, but he died saving two people. A mother and daughter like you and me, April. He was a brave man.'

And a complex and complicated one, she thought as she lay in bed before she went to sleep that night. She'd spent a lot of time trying to puzzle out why Matt had turned out as he had. She didn't think the way his parents had brought him up had helped, but she'd also gone over and over the mistakes she herself might have made. Could she have handled him better?

In the end, after a great deal of soul-searching, she'd decided the answer to that was no. She hadn't deserved what he'd done to her, hadn't – in that terrible phrase people used so unthinkingly – asked for it. He had loved her, but it had been a supremely possessive love. He had thought he owned her, wanted to control her. There had been some kind of a demon in Matt, which had pulled him towards the dark side of his nature. Carrie supposed that was what all the other women had been about. They hadn't seemed to bring him much joy.

Odd how different he had been from Ewen, although with hindsight she could see some tiny physical similarities. Apart from the wavy hair, they were more in the occasional gesture. There was something about the way both of them had laughed . . .

It was sad that such antipathy had existed between two brothers. If circumstances had been different, might they ever have been friends? No, that was to live in cloud cuckoo land. Charles Campbell would never have acknowledged the relationship, let alone the existence of his second son.

She took the children to visit their grandparents occasionally, but they never stayed for long. As far as Carrie was concerned it was a duty visit, nothing more. That was sad too.

Her father-in-law was still a charmer – to those who didn't know him very well. Matthew had charmed her, she supposed. No, it was more than that. He had aroused her, and she had mistaken passion for deep and lasting love. Then circumstances had conspired to push her into marriage with him: her father's death, her mother's longing to see her settled before her own time ran out, Esther's opposition to Ewen.

'You were wrong about him, Ma,' she whispered into the darkness. 'You were wrong about both of them.' Yet how could she regret marrying Matt? He had given her Archie and April.

She lay on her back, staring up into the darkness. They had been funny tonight, admiring themselves in the mirror, although thinking about how Archie's eyes had shone when he talked about Matt didn't make her smile. It didn't help to realise that she herself was largely to blame for her children's evident hero-worship of their dead father.

She was all too conscious of the gap in their young lives. The awareness had grown keener during this past year when other children's fathers had begun coming home. So she had determined that Archie and April would at least have positive memories of their own. They would hear no criticism of Matthew from her lips.

And whatever his motives, in the end their father had given his life for others. That was surely something of which his children ought to be allowed to be proud.

There were times, however, when she feared she had gone too far in the other direction. She was anxious too in case either of the children had inherited Matt's temper. So far there was no sign of it, but that didn't stop her worrying, particularly about Archie. He resembled Matt so much physically. What if he had some of his personality traits too?

Yet there had been strengths in Matt's character too: the way he had comforted her and helped her cope at the time of her parents' deaths, his cheerful encouragement of everybody in the time they had spent in the shelters during the Clydebank Blitz. He had been such an odd mixture.

She had experienced a maelstrom of emotions after his death. There had been anger, both against herself and him, so strong that the grief which followed it had taken her by surprise. She had thought it must be guilt, then realised what she was really grieving for: the promise their marriage had at first seemed to offer, the person he might have been if the flaws in his personality hadn't outweighed the strengths.

There had been guilt in plenty, of course. Carrie did know that the accident which had resulted in Matthew's death had been just that, but there had been months, perhaps even years, when she had tormented herself over her part in the events of that day.

She had turned them over so many times in her mind, agonised over every word she had said to Matt. Had she influenced his behaviour in any way, made him act in a foolhardy manner because he had thought himself betrayed?

It had been a long process, but she had come now to the conviction that the way he had acted during his last moments had been entirely in character. There had certainly been some cockiness in it – recklessness too – but that was the way he was. He had thought himself invincible. Nevertheless, he had acted with real bravery, rising to the occasion as he had at other times. It was the way she tried to remember him.

The guilt might have gone now, but it had done its job well. Florence had hit the nail on the head tonight, as she often did. That was what had made Carrie send Ewen away. She had told Florence she had no right to expect him to come back and try again. That was perfectly true. What she hadn't told her was how much she had hoped that he would . . .

Carrie let out a long breath. Real life wasn't like the pictures, of course. You couldn't always expect a fairytale ending. You could probably very seldom expect a fairytale ending.

'Oh, very philosophical,' she muttered crossly. Then she turned on to her side and told herself sternly to go to sleep.

Chapter 22

[illegible]

Chapter 33

Laughingly declining to play yet another game of rounders, Carrie left the children on the green sward at the bottom of Douglas and Mary's large garden and walked slowly up through the neat rows of vegetables to join her hosts. They were sitting on the verandah Douglas had built on to the back of the railway cottage, Mary cradling the youngest member of the family in her arms. Her husband had a protective arm about her shoulders and was looking tenderly at his three-month-old daughter, sister to the two boys and one girl currently playing with Archie and April.

Carrie slipped off her shoes, enjoying the feel of the grass paths beneath her bare feet. She took in a deep breath of clean Highland air and looked around her admiringly. The setting of the line-side cottage was quite stunning, with wooded and heather-clad hills rising all around. The springy vegetation was beginning to acquire its purple hue, poised to decorate the autumn mountainsides with glorious bursts of colour.

She raised her eyes to the hill on the other side of the house, over the railway line. She and the children of both families had clambered up it yesterday, stopping when they reached the head of the narrow waterfall which trickled down it to wave to Mary and the baby, watching them from far below.

The Campbell family had only one complaint to make about their holiday so far. On the train journey up, Carrie had promised the children a grandstand view of the highest mountain in the British Isles. She remembered it well from her previous visit, when April had been a babe-in-arms and Archie also had been too young to take in the spectacle, clearly visible from Douglas and Mary's back garden.

However, they'd been here for a week now and Ben Nevis had remained resolutely invisible throughout that whole period, shut away behind billowing white clouds. 'It's there,' she kept telling the children. 'It really is there.'

In contrast to the wild and natural grandeur surrounding it, the vegetable garden was a masterpiece of order and method. There was a large potato patch, lines of peas supported on sticks, rows of lettuce, carrot and beetroot. Carrie had forgotten how wonderful the fresh variety of the latter tasted, especially when you had pulled it out of the ground yourself before preparing it.

She'd been doing her best to help out during their stay, taking on as many tasks in the kitchen as Mary would allow and also lending a hand in the garden. Her hostess had made a token protest that she was here for a holiday, not to work, but Carrie had assured her that she was having a wonderful time. For one thing, she was revelling in getting her hands dirty again. It was an awful long time since she'd had the chance to do any gardening.

She was nearly at the house. She looked up again as she approached. Douglas and Mary and the baby were still in the same position, all cuddled together on a wooden bench padded with soft cushions. Carrie thought a little wistfully that she missed that sometimes: a strong shoulder to lean on. But she didn't grudge them their happiness, not one bit of it.

'The three of you look like one of those religious paintings in the Art Galleries,' she called.

Douglas looked up with a laugh. 'The holy family? No' us, I don't think.' He looked beyond her to the children at the foot of the garden. 'Have that lot worn you out? I'll go down for twenty minutes. Then they can help me get the supper.' He rose to his feet and came to meet her, extending a hand to pull Carrie up the open wooden steps of the verandah before clattering down them himself.

'You sit here and talk to Mary for a while. Although,' he added, throwing a very male look over his shoulder, 'I should have thought the two of you might have run out of conversation by now.'

'Never,' said Mary cheerfully. She patted the space next to her which Douglas had vacated. 'Come and sit by me, Carrie. Do you want a shot of the baby?'

Laughing at how the question had been phrased, Carrie turned and held out her arms, then carefully eased herself back against the cushions and put her feet up on the horizontal bars of the verandah.

'Och, you're a lovely wee bundle,' she told Mary's daughter, bending to gently nuzzle the tiny nose with her own. A pair of very clear blue eyes stared straight back up at her, and she laughed again and raised her head. 'We have talked quite a lot, haven't we? And late into the night. Is Douglas worried that I've been keeping you from your beauty sleep?'

Mary looked fondly at her youngest offspring. 'Sleep? What's that?'

'Aye, you've got your work cut out, Mary. Where do they get their energy from?' she asked, indicating the older children, now gleefully welcoming Douglas' arrival. 'April looks like a jumping bean.'

Mary gave her a slow smile. 'They take it from us, of course. Although I must say you strike me as being fighting fit yourself, Mrs

Campbell. You've been running about there like a jumping bean yourself for the past hour.'

'Reliving my lost youth,' Carrie said cheerfully. 'This holiday's been a real tonic, Mary,' she said. 'We're grateful to you and Douglas for having us all. Especially with you just having had the baby.'

'It's no bother at all,' Mary said firmly, 'And it's been a break for me too. Douglas and I are just glad if we've been able to help you have a bit of a rest. You work hard, Carrie, holding down a job and bringing up the children single-handed. You make me feel quite lazy sometimes.'

Carrie looked at her in amazement. 'Lazy? With four children and this garden to look after? That's a job in itself.' Her gaze ranged over it. 'It's one I wouldn't object to having, mind you.'

Mary raised her arms above her head, stretched long and languorously. 'What's happening with your father's garden now? It was all turned over to vegetables during the war, wasn't it?'

'Yes, the railway horticultural society worked it more or less as an allotment for the duration, although it's looking a bit dilapidated now. It'll be a challenge for someone to turn it back into a real garden again, although it won't be the Gibsons.'

'Is he retiring?'

'Yes, but not till the end of next year. He's going to take us up to nationalisation, he says, then hand over the reins to someone else. I'll be sorry to see him go. He's been a good boss.'

'They've decided on the first of January 1948, haven't they? As the official date when we all become British Railways?'

'I believe so.' Carrie readjusted her hold on the baby, still reflecting on the current state of the garden at Partick. Like Mary, she continued to think of it, however much she tried not to, as her father's domain. She knew he would have been one of the first to volunteer to dig for victory, but witnessing the alterations which had been necessary to turn it into a high-yielding vegetable plot had given her a few pangs of regret all the same.

Most of his carefully thought out and laboriously built landscaping had been removed. The drying green had been cultivated, of course, the small square of grass near the back door having to satisfy Mrs Gibson for drying her clothes now. And since you couldn't eat flowers, most of them had been dug up too, although they had kept the roses round in the front garden and the red hot pokers and marguerites at the edge of the grass round the back. Carrie had been glad about that.

Mary's mind was obviously running on the same train of thought as her own. 'And the rhododendrons are still there?' she asked anxiously. 'I don't think I could imagine the garden of the station house without them.'

'Me neither,' Carrie said warmly. 'Some wee man from one of those government committees did suggest they were taking up valuable growing space, but fortunately nobody listened to him.'

'You wouldn't mind taking on the task yourself Carrie,' her friend observed. 'The garden, I mean.'

'I'd love to, but since they're highly unlikely to appoint me as the new stationmaster I don't think I'll get the opportunity,' she said wryly. 'I'm beginning to think I'll be doing well if I manage to hold on to the job I've got.'

'You'll manage. You're a fighter, Carrie. Look what you've come through already.' Mary coughed delicately. 'What with Matthew and everything.'

Carrie looked her in the eye. 'You never liked him, did you?' She paused. 'Even before you knew what I've told you this week?'

Mary swallowed, clearly torn between an unwillingness to speak ill of the dead and a desire to answer Carrie's question honestly. 'There was something about him which always made me uneasy. Do you remember the night of your hen party? When he more or less ordered you home? I was really unhappy about that.'

'Maybe if I'd stood up to him then – right from the beginning – things might have been different,' Carrie said reflectively.

'That's you blaming yourself again,' said Mary sternly. 'I thought we'd agreed you weren't going to do that.'

'Easier said than done,' said Carrie, smiling at her. 'But you're right. We did agree on that.'

'And I really don't think you need to worry about the children,' Mary said, referring back to a conversation they'd had a couple of nights ago. 'April has the same kind of nature as you. She has a temper, but it's like yours. Quick to rise and quick to subside again. She doesn't bear grudges and she forgives easily.'

'Thank you for that character assessment of my daughter and myself,' said Carrie with a smile. 'And Archie?'

'He strikes me as being very even-tempered, and he reminds me an awful lot of your father. He's got that same dry sense of humour I remember Mr Burgess as having. And while we're at it, I don't think you need to worry about them hero-worshipping their father. I think that's natural – particularly at the ages they're at now. You can always decide to tell them more later. When they're old enough to understand.'

'I'm not sure I'm old enough to understand it,' said Carrie wryly. 'I still get confused trying to puzzle it all out. The way Matt was, I mean.'

'Maybe you should stop trying, then. Just accept it as something unfathomable and get on with your life.'

Carrie dropped a kiss on the baby's head. 'What a wise woman your mother is,' she said. 'It's been really great being with you, Mary. You'll let us return the compliment at Christmas?'

'We'd love to. Are you sure you can fit us all in?'

'Nae bother. You and Douglas can have my bed. This wee one can be in with you and the children and I can sleep in the front room. We can always spill over across the landing if it turns out to be too tight a squeeze.'

'How's that working out? They haven't all murdered each other yet?'

Carrie laughed. 'No. Fortunately Donald and Florence get on like a house on fire. The two of them sometimes gang up on Isa, as a matter of fact – but only in fun. Donald's got a really wicked sense of humour once you get to know him. And he and Isa have got their caravan now, so the lovebirds can get away occasionally if they need a bit of privacy.'

'Ah, love,' Mary said archly. 'They say it makes the world go round, you know.'

'Really?' Carrie was giving her no encouragement on this one. Unfortunately she didn't need any. Shamelessly using her newborn as a prop, Mary's eyes dropped ostentatiously to the bundle in Carrie's arms. 'It suits you, you know.'

'Mary,' she responded, 'I'm not sure if I should tell you this. It could come as a bit of a shock. I know you've had four children, but you may not have realised that it wasn't the stork who brought them.'

Mary grinned, and Carrie gave the baby a little pat. 'Before you get one of these,' she said, 'you need one of those.' Her hands being full of baby, she gestured with her chin to where Douglas was running around with the children. 'And I rather think that one – a particularly fine example of the species, by the way – is spoken for.'

Mary grinned again and threw a glance down the garden towards her husband. 'Aye, he's no' a bad lad.' Her gaze came back to Carrie's face. 'But there are other fish in the sea, Carrie.'

'And that's the best place for them,' she said smartly, 'unless they're wrapped up in newspaper and covered in salt and vinegar.'

She pulled a funny face, but Mary had stopped smiling. 'You're still young, Carrie, and you won't have the children forever, you know.'

'Don't you start,' she said gloomily, turning her head away and gazing out over the garden. 'I get this all the time from Florence.'

'I can't believe you haven't had any offers. You're an attractive woman.'

Carrie's head swung back round. 'I never said I hadn't had any offers!' she said indignantly.

'Only they haven't come from the one person you'd be interested in?' suggested Mary shrewdly.

* * *

For a house containing three adults, five children and one baby, everything seemed very quiet when Carrie awoke the next morning. Although it had to be extremely early, it was already broad daylight, the sun streaming in through the open curtains of the room she was sharing with April and Mary's elder daughter.

She tiptoed through to the scullery to get herself a drink of water, glanced out of the window, and stood for a moment stock still, arrested by the sight which met her eyes. The Ben had finally decided to show itself.

She opened the back door as quietly as she could and sped out on to the grass. It was wet with dew, soaking her bare feet and the hem of her long nightie. She scarcely noticed, entranced by the view of the mountain. Ben Nevis looked almost like a piece of beautifully painted stage scenery. She felt as if she could stretch her hand up and slide her fingers down the back of it.

Even at this time of year the long plateau of its massive summit was decorated with patches of white: corries where last winter's snow had been preserved. Carrie stood lost in admiration. It looked so powerful: solid and strong, awe-inspiring in its scale and grandeur.

She felt as if she'd been given a gift, one she had better pass on to Archie and April before the day got much older. The sky was blue and cloudless now, but you didn't have to spend much time in the West Highlands before you learned how quickly the weather could change. Nevertheless, she stood a moment or two longer, savouring the moment and experiencing a strange feeling of content.

What had she thought yesterday – that she missed having a shoulder to lean on? But when had she ever had that? Certainly not since her parents had died. In a strange sort of way it had been the other way round with her and Matt.

She would have to be her own strength and support. She'd had enough practice at it, after all. And she would do as Mary had advised yesterday: stop trying to analyse it all. Perhaps you simply had to accept that to some questions there were no answers. You just had to get on with your life. And leave the past with all its broken hopes and promises where it was.

It was the future which mattered now – for herself and the children. If she was to provide adequately for them she needed to keep her job. She was going back home to fight for it.

She wasn't sure if the set-up was designed to be intimidating, but it would, she considered, be very easy to feel daunted by it. She was in the LNER's regional head office in Glasgow, in a huge and high-ceilinged room on the first floor. It could have accommodated a good-sized wedding.

It was elegantly furnished, if a little austere, all dark wood and polished floorboards. Her shoes had squeaked as she had walked across them, shown to an upright chair positioned in the centre of the room.

It faced a long table which ran almost the whole length of one wall. Like the boards under her feet, the dark and luxuriant wood of which it was made was polished to a high sheen. Behind it, backs to one of the three long and elegant windows which lit the space, sat four officers of the railway company. Pascal Sharkey had accompanied her to the interview, but they had seated him over by the door, out of her line of sight. To all intents and purposes Carrie was on her own.

'So tell us, Mrs Campbell,' began the chairman, 'why should we accede to your request in this matter?'

It was all very mannerly, but she could tell from his demeanour that he was expecting to deny that request. They were going through the motions, that was all. She had also just remembered who the person sitting on his right was.

It was the man who had turned her down for a job after her father had died, who had thought it so unreasonable that a woman should even put herself forward for a clerical job on the railway. He was unlikely to be a supporter of continuing female labour now that the crisis was over. She remembered how patronising he'd been, and thought she could see that same attitude on his face now.

She glanced at the two other members of the panel. Four of them to deal with one humble clerkess. A sledgehammer to crack a nut? Carrie straightened her shoulders. That's what they thought. She took a brown envelope out of her handbag, laid it on her lap and began to speak.

She talked for several minutes, putting her case cogently and succinctly. She had prepared it all in advance, written it out and then learned it off by heart. Donald Nicholson had listened to her, made some helpful suggestions. Then she had practised it in front of him and Isa and Florence a couple of times, made sure it sounded fluent but natural.

She reminded them of the long hours she had put in during the war, of how she had never failed to turn up for work even under the most difficult of circumstances. Neither rain, snow nor gale-force winds had stopped her from being at her post at the required time. She told them the evidence suggested that women workers, particularly those who were a little older, were extremely reliable in this regard. The man to the right of the chairman raised a sceptical eyebrow.

The gesture infuriated Carrie. It also strengthened her resolve. And she would deal with him in a minute.

'I'm not speaking only for myself,' she said. 'I know of at least eight other women in the same position. We're all widows.'

Interesting. That last comment had aroused a little flicker of unease. She opened her brown envelope and took out a letter. She had composed it and all nine of the women had signed it. She read it out. It argued that while the small concession they were seeking would cause very little disruption to the company and its operations, the resulting benefits would make an enormous difference to the lives of the loyal female employees affected.

'*. . . allowing us to raise our children without becoming a burden to the state or the community*,' Carrie finished. She'd been rather proud of that phrase. It ended by repeating what she'd said to Pascal when she had first asked him for help. '*We were flexible during the war. Can't the railway be flexible now?*'

She finished and looked up expectantly, suddenly nervous. There was a brief silence. Then the man to the right of the chairman spoke. She'd seldom seen such an insincere smile.

'Mrs Campbell, the company is deeply cognisant of the sacrifices you good ladies made during the war, but those were emergency conditions. Surely we all want to get back to normal now?'

'There are those of us who made greater sacrifices than others, of course,' she said evenly, looking him straight in the eye. 'Some of which make it rather difficult to get back to normal.'

She hadn't being going to bring Matt's death up, intending to present her case in an unemotional way, but it intrigued her that the unease she'd sensed before was now obvious discomfort. Her questioner coughed nervously and looked away. The man on the other side of the chairman shifted in his chair. They would have been briefed on who she was, of course. No doubt the accident enquiry report had been dug out of the files.

Perhaps they'd been expecting her to try and shame them into keeping her on. They weren't to know that wasn't her way.

Extracting several sheets of paper from the envelope, she stood up, walked over to the desk and laid them in front of the panel members. 'Copies of attendance records for myself and my colleagues for the past five years,' she said. 'There's also a reference for each woman relating to the standard of our work during that period. It's been provided by our respective stationmasters, who were all more than happy to do that for us. I'll let you peruse the information for a few moments, gentlemen. I believe it speaks for itself.'

Brisk and businesslike. That was the only way to be – the only way she might stand a chance of success. She resumed her seat, glancing at Pascal before she turned and sat down. He gave her a swift wink. That was all very nice, but she'd been hoping for a bit more than that . . .

The chairman was the first to finish reading. 'These are certainly very impressive,' he said. He lifted his head and his voice, projecting it to the back of the room. 'Mr Sharkey, do you have anything to add to what Mrs Campbell has told us?'

'I most certainly do,' came an enthusiastic voice from behind her. Carrie swung round in surprise. Pascal was coming across the dark floor, taking something out of his inside pocket. He had a brown envelope too, a bit fatter than hers. He came to stand beside her, resting his free hand lightly on the back of her chair.

'Firstly I'd like to back up everything Mrs Campbell has said. I've been doing some research of my own into the contribution made by our female employees both during the war and after it and I have to say that I'm very impressed.' He walked forward to stand in front of the long table. 'I'd also like you to consider this.' He leaned forward and laid his envelope in front of the panel. Somewhat bemused, Carrie watched as the chairman pulled out what looked like an awful lot of sheets of paper.

'It's a petition,' Pascal was explaining, 'in support of the argument you've just heard and with specific reference to the lady sitting in front of you.' He swung round briefly, threw Carrie a smile. 'It's signed by staff members of all grades, train crews and passengers. Mrs Campbell is a very popular employee, both with her colleagues and the travelling public. I've seen her in action, and I know that not only is she a most conscientious worker, but also that her genuine interest in the passengers and their concerns brings enormous benefits to ourselves. There's a sort of mutual respect and goodwill.' His smile grew a little grim. 'We're going to need as much of that as we can get as we make the transition to nationalisation. As we're going to need staff members like Mrs Campbell and her colleagues.'

It was a good job, Carrie thought, that none of them was looking in her direction at that precise moment. Brisk and businesslike? Fortunately she had managed to swallow the lump in her throat by the time they had finished reading and examining the petition. The chairman was smiling: a real, genuine smile.

When they were back outside she couldn't resist throwing her arms around Pascal's neck and giving him a kiss on the cheek. 'Thank you! I never guessed you were cooking up something like that.'

'Well, I think it was your arguments and the way you put them that won the day, Carrie, but I hope I helped a bit. Once I started looking into it I realised what an asset women workers are. I'm sorry if I seemed reluctant to begin with.'

'That's all right,' she said, beaming at him as they walked into the station concourse. 'You've made up for it today. And I'm really grateful.'

Pascal gave her a very rueful look. 'It's not me you should be thanking, Carrie.'

'Ah,' she said. 'I get it. Certain people used their powers of persuasion on you?'

'How did you guess?' he asked wryly. 'I didn't have a hope in hell of standing up to the blandishments of my wife and that smooth-talking father of mine.'

Carrie grinned, her eyes shining with the joy of success. 'Was the petition Anne-Marie's idea? She organised one before, of course.'

Pascal nodded. 'Aye. She told me that, said it had brought positive results. She insisted we had to try everything to help you. My father and I went round with the petition while you were on holiday.'

'Well then,' Carrie said happily, 'let's get on a train and go back and tell them both the good news.' She glanced up at the station clock. 'If we're lucky we might manage to catch your dad as he comes off his shift.'

Martin Sharkey's working day had been over for half an hour by the time they got back to Partick, but he had stayed behind, waiting for them under the canopy of the station buildings.

'Sure, you're not needing to tell me anything,' he said as Carrie stepped off the train, closely followed by his eldest son. 'It's written all over your face! I'm real pleased for you, m'dear.'

Carrie kissed him on the cheek too. He laughed uproariously, clearly delighted by the gesture. After she had thanked him several times and been told several times that she was entirely welcome, Martin informed her that he had a wee surprise for her. 'Something that might come in handy. Especially as you're going to be staying on here at the station. Would you be remembering a conversation you and me had about a month ago when you mentioned a notion you had to start up the station garden again?'

'Yes . . .' Carrie said cautiously.

'Well, look round the corner of this canopy here and see what the little people have left you.'

His benign smile broadened when he saw her delighted reaction to what she found. 'Two of my father's half whisky barrels! I thought they'd all been used for firewood!'

'I saved these two. Hid them at the back of the bothy. I've cleaned them up for you, but I'll not get the lads to put the earth in until you tell me where you want them put.'

'Whatever made you think to keep them?' asked Carrie, already working out where the tubs were going to stand.

He laid a paternal hand on her shoulder. 'I knew we'd be wanting to grow flowers again some day, lass!'

Chapter 34

Carrie was finding it harder than usual to bite her tongue today. She and the children were paying an afternoon visit to her parents-in-law, who now lived outside Largs in a pleasant sandstone villa overlooking the Firth of Clyde. It wasn't too far along the coast from Donald and Isa's caravan. In fact, they had travelled to Largs from there, having just spent a cramped but highly enjoyable few days of the Easter holidays with Mr and Mrs Nicholson, beachcombing by day and stargazing by night.

She'd rather have done it the other way round – got the duty visit out of the way first – but this last Saturday of the school holidays and her own Easter break had been the only day which had suited Shona and Charles Campbell. Allegedly.

Given that their lives still consisted of what seemed to Carrie to be an empty round of social engagements, she couldn't quite understand why they hadn't been able to see her and the children sometime during the previous three or four days. That would have allowed Archie and April and herself to get home to Glasgow earlier tonight. They could have had a relaxing evening by their own fireside before inevitably having to spend most of Sunday getting organised for going back to school and work respectively.

It was always like that, though. They had to fit in with Shona and Charles. It never seemed to be the other way round. Since the visits were few and far between Carrie had decided to put up with that, reluctant to do anything which might lead to a severing of the children's connection with their grandparents. Archie and April had very few living relatives, after all.

One whom they met now and again was Roderick Cunningham. He'd had his own share of problems over the years, chiefly occasioned by his relationship with Josephine, but Carrie thought – or hoped at least – that things were working out now. Whatever his worries, Roddy always visited at Christmas bearing presents and unfailingly remembered the children's birthdays. It was always a pleasure to see him.

Visiting his sister's house could never be called a pleasure. Carrie did her best to be polite, even chatty, but it could be hard going. Knowing what she did now, she also found it difficult to stomach

Charles Campbell's bonhomie. Sometimes it was all she could do to be in the same room as him.

He must have known that he had fathered a child. Yet he had allowed the mother of that child to be cast out without a penny, condemning her to a terrible life and a tragic death. During Carrie's first few conversations with him after Matthew's death and the enquiry into the accident she had been on tenterhooks lest he bring up the subject of his chance meeting with Ewen, but Charles seemed to have forgotten all about it.

She put that down to the selfishness and self-centredness which characterised her father-in-law's personality. His own account of the enquiry, a story he repeated interminably, revolved around the young female reporter who had interviewed him, and the article which had subsequently appeared in her newspaper.

He'd been particularly pleased with the photograph taken to accompany it. There was a framed copy of it on the small antique table which stood in the bay window of the villa's sitting room. Next to it, in a similarly ornate silver frame, stood a picture of Matt, handsome in his uniform. As far as Carrie could see, Shona seldom gave it a second glance, paying as little attention to her son in death as she had in life. Carrie herself was staring fixedly at his face at the moment, trying not to get angry at what her mother-in-law was saying.

Shona was riding one of her favourite hobbyhorses today. Since the Labour Party's election victory nearly two years ago it was always a variation on the same theme. The country was going to the dogs. Today she was expressing herself volubly on how lazy everyone had become since the war had ended.

It was all the fault of this socialist government. They were giving people ideas above their station, as well as far too many holidays. Why, they were even talking about introducing shorter hours in shops and factories! That was quite ridiculous.

Coming from someone who had never done a day's work in her life, Carrie considered it was also a quite breathtaking piece of cheek.

'Not that you get any real service in the shops these days anyway,' Shona went on. 'Service seems to be a dirty word all round. Have you any idea how difficult it is to get help in the house these days?'

Well, no, Mother-in-law, I don't actually. Seeing as how I do my own housework and always have done. And go out to work six hours a day. There was no point in saying the words out loud. Shona had little idea of what Carrie's life was like. No interest in the subject either.

'The trouble is that women of that class have far too many alternatives these days. Going into service isn't good enough for them any more. They'd rather work in a shop or an office.' Shona's cool eyes flickered over her daughter-in-law. 'I'm surprised you've continued to go out to work, Caroline. I was reading an article in the *Daily Telegraph* only last week which predicted a massive rise in juvenile delinquency due to children running riot while their mothers are at work. Young women today are so selfish, of course. And they set their children no acceptable standards of behaviour.'

Oh, it was hard not to rise to it! Carrie occasionally had daydreams in which she imagined telling Shona exactly what she thought of her, but in real life she knew it simply wasn't worth it. If she started, she probably wouldn't be able to stop, and that would certainly mean an end to the visits to Largs.

She glanced across at the children. They were sitting together on a small sofa in front of the empty grate. Charles had managed half an hour with them today before getting bored. He'd muttered something about having some business to attend to and had then disappeared. April was engrossed in one of the comics Carrie had bought on the way to the house, but Archie was looking solemnly at her and his grandmother. Carrie wondered if he'd been listening in. He looked a little worried, so she smiled brightly at him and let her mother-in-law's monologue wash over her.

It was a relief to be out of the house and into the clean salty air, happily marching the mile or so along to the town, duty done for another few months. Having left a little earlier than they actually needed to, they got to the station with time to spare, only to find that the next train to Glasgow had been cancelled. There was a wait of more than an hour till the next one.

'What will we do?' asked April as the three of them walked back out into the street.

'We're going to get home even later than we thought,' said Archie.

'Well,' Carrie said slowly, 'that is a bit of a nuisance, right enough.' She paused, deliberately spinning it out. 'We could always have our tea here, of course. Give us something to do while we're waiting.'

Two pairs of eyes lit up. 'Chips?' asked April hopefully.

'Out of the paper?' ventured her brother.

That was breaking one of her own rules, the one about eating in the street, but it had been a boring afternoon for the two of them. They deserved a treat. Carrie gave in.

'Letting my standards slip,' she said mock-mournfully as they walked along the front enjoying their tea. 'I'll just have to hope that me letting you eat chips out of newspaper doesn't turn you both into juvenile delinquents.'

The comment went over April's head, but Archie gave her a sharp look.

* * *

'How long till the train now?'

'Five minutes less than the last time you asked,' she responded with a smile, lifting a hand to smooth the lock of dark hair which had fallen forward over her son's pale brow. The three of them were sitting together on a bench in the railway station, Carrie in the middle. On one side of her, knees drawn up and wrapped in her mother's protective arm, April was asleep. On the other, Archie was all too wide awake.

'Why do we visit here?'

'Because they're your grandparents,' she replied, but the days when he was satisfied with a simple and straightforward answer were over.

'And blood is thicker than water?'

'Is that something Florence says?' she asked, amused.

Archie nodded, then wrinkled his nose in perplexity. 'What does it mean?'

'Well,' Carrie said, 'I suppose it means that what connects you to your relatives is more than what connects you to your friends.'

He digested that. She could see the wheels turning, and his next question didn't surprise her. 'Are Auntie Florence and Auntie Isa and Uncle Donald our relatives?'

'Nope. They're our friends. Very good friends.'

'Auntie Mary and Uncle Douglas aren't really our aunt and uncle either, are they?'

'No. They're very good friends too.'

Archie nodded in agreement. 'So in our case water's thicker than blood?'

Carrie laughed. 'I suppose it is.'

Tired of the subject, or perhaps simply satisfied to have worked out something which had been troubling him, he slid forward on to the edge of the bench and looked around. 'I like stations,' he said. 'And trains.'

'Do you?' enquired his mother fondly. 'So do I.'

'Then it's a good thing that you work for the railway,' he said solemnly.

'I would say so,' she replied, trying to match his seriousness. There was something else coming. She could tell.

'It's good for us too,' he said brightly. 'April and me, I mean. That's why we get free passes and privilege tickets, isn't it? We get to travel by train a lot, and we like that.'

'I'm very glad to hear it,' Carrie said.

'And you like your work, don't you?'

'Yes. Very much.'

'And when you're at the station we're either at school or Auntie Florence or Auntie Isa are looking after us. I mean,' he said earnestly, 'it's not as if we're *running riot* when you're not there.'

It was the exact term his grandmother had used. Touched, Carrie realised that he was offering her his support. What had she done to deserve this wonderful child?

'Slide back in the seat,' she said. 'Have a wee rest. Are you too big a boy to want a cuddle?'

'Well,' Archie said confidingly, 'nobody knows me here, do they?'

She slid her spare arm about his slim shoulders. 'But we'll keep coming to see your grandparents,' she suggested, 'to be polite.'

'And so as not to hurt their feelings,' he replied. 'You should always try not to hurt other people's feelings.'

'Does your Auntie Florence say that?'

'No,' he said comfortably, cuddling in to her, 'I just know it.'

Carrie smiled. 'You know something else, Archie Campbell? You're a very nice person. And your mammy loves you.'

'I love you too, Ma. How long till the train now?'

'*Russell* lupins?' queried Carrie. The name wasn't familiar to her.

'Yes,' said the passenger with whom she was discussing the subject. He ran a business in Partick, travelling in by train from his home in Dumbarton. 'They're a new strain, came on to the market the year before the war broke out. Although apparently the chap who developed them had been working on them for years. Did it all on an allotment in York, I believe. His life's work – and a remarkable achievement. I think you'd like them, Mrs Campbell. There's a splendid selection of colours, and they're very sturdy.'

'They sound lovely,' she said. 'If you're sure you can spare some?'

'With the greatest of pleasure, my dear,' he said warmly, regarding her from under pepper-and-salt eyebrows of luxuriant growth. 'Now,' he said, 'I know you don't like your flowers too regimented, but I was thinking that if you had a clump of them in the centre of each of your flowerbeds – at the back against the fence – it would add a pleasant unity to your overall design.'

'Mmm,' she said consideringly, surveying the bed they were currently standing in front of. 'You could be right.'

'Think about it anyway,' he said. He gave her a little pat on the shoulder. 'And keep up the good work. You've made a real difference here. Brightened up the gloom.'

Carrie smiled fondly after him as he strode off towards the Crow Road exit. He'd been one of the first to comment on her gardening attempts. She'd begun in a small way with the tubs Sharkey had given her the previous autumn, carefully nurturing the bulbs she'd planted in them over the cold and wintry months which had heralded the start of 1947.

Admiring the welcome splash of colour, the businessman gardener had promised to bring her some more bulbs towards the end of the year. When she'd acquired some other tubs and – with a bit of help from two of the porters – reinstated the platform flowerbeds, he'd brought her some cuttings out of his own garden to start off her summer flowers.

It had all kind of snowballed from there. An older lady who travelled regularly from her home in Westerton to do her shopping in Partick handed in a box of bedding plants. The marigolds in particular had done very well, growing bright and vigorously as a border round the central flower bed. Carrie loved their cheerful colour. They were so long-lasting too.

Other passengers had started taking an interest. She'd been given more cuttings from a very friendly couple who had an allotment. A previously rather shy middle-aged bachelor had begun discussing the plants and flowers with her, offering lots of helpful advice. She'd introduced him to the nice couple, had happily heard them trading invitations to look at each other's gardens.

A younger couple brought her some geraniums. Another man asked her if she'd like him to bring her the odd bag of manure. Carrie smiled, remembering how embarrassed he'd been, although anxious to convince her of the benefits of that particular fertiliser.

She needed no convincing now, she thought. Her beds and tubs were full of healthy soil which in turn had allowed the growth of tumbling plants and vibrant flowers. Morning rush hour over, she took five minutes to walk up the platform to review the situation. Although they were well into the autumn she was pleased to see that there was still plenty of colour in evidence.

The trailing blue and white lobelia in the whisky barrel furthest up the platform, to the side of the gate, was beginning to look a wee touch straggly. She'd give it a couple of weeks more, then plant some spring bulbs in there.

Horticultural tour of inspection finished, she walked smartly back to the booking office, deep in happy thought. If she managed an even better show next year perhaps they could think about going in for the best station garden competition, give Hyndland a run for its money. The next station along the line had a beautiful display this year, and the friendly rivalry between the competing stations which had existed before the war looked all set to start up again.

She'd need to do something on the other platform too. She glanced over at it as she came in under the canopy. So far she only had one tub of flowers there. She could do with some window boxes and plants around the station buildings too. She had some on her own windowsills at home from which she could take cuttings and was planning also on trying to raise a tray or two of seedlings next year, as much as she could find space for.

She passed through the booking hall. Its large windows would make it an excellent greenhouse. She would bring her geraniums in here before the first frosts. She was smiling as she went back into the booking office. If she mentioned to the people who now cheerfully referred to themselves as the travelling gardening club that she was hoping to go in for the competition, she'd probably be inundated with plants. The rivalry between stations extended to the passengers too.

'You look as if you're plotting something, Mrs Campbell,' observed the stationmaster.

'I am,' she said, and told him what it was.

'Well,' said George Gibson, 'you've certainly made a big difference to the station, and I can only wish you the best of luck if you do decide to compete for the title next year. I'll not be here to see it, of course.'

She knew he was looking forward to his retirement – he and his wife were moving to Stirling to be closer to their married daughter and her family – but she could hear the wistfulness in his voice.

'It'll be a wrench for you,' she said gently, 'leaving the railway.'

'Aye,' he agreed, 'but it's time to give someone else a chance. I've done my bit, I think.'

'Much more than that,' Carrie assured him. 'Through some very difficult years too. There's a lot to your job even when you're not coping with the effects of a world war.'

'You'll know that better than most, lass.'

Registering that *lass*, she realised that he must be feeling a bit emotional. He was usually so formal. 'Do you think we'll get an LNER man to take your place?' she asked brightly, pleased when she saw his face light up.

'Maybe. I know they have advertised it internally throughout the company, but I suppose it won't necessarily be the case. Not in this brave new world.'

He looked sad and she realised that however welcome the change was to many people, there would be others who would deeply regret the passing of the old railway companies and the swallowing up of the Big Four.

Coming in to see her three weeks later, however, Mr Gibson was in jovial mood, brandishing a sheet of paper. 'They've sent me a list of candidates for the job,' he announced.

Carrie looked up from her work. 'Anybody we know?'

'Yes,' he said brightly, and presented the letter to her. 'An old friend of ours. Look!' he said, and pointed out the sixth name on the alphabetically ordered list.

Chapter 35

She couldn't assume anything. [illegible] that [illegible] George Square [illegible] now. She could have [illegible] [illegible] that [illegible] [illegible] was inevitable that he [illegible] had to [illegible]

All the same, she [illegible] [illegible] [illegible]

[illegible]

[illegible]

Mother Carrie [illegible] was [illegible]

She did. [illegible] forward to seeing them [illegible]

[illegible] [illegible] anything?'

'No, it [illegible],' he said [illegible]

'You think [illegible] all [illegible]'

Chapter 35

She couldn't assume anything. It was four years since that bitter parting in George Square. Ewen could be married to someone else by now. He could have a child. And life did things to people. She knew that better than anybody. Circumstance and experience altered your perspective, made you look at the world in a different way. It was inevitable that he would have changed. He had also been to war. That had to affect a man too.

All the same, she had never forgotten his final words to her. *I'll always love you.* She remembered them . . . and she hoped.

She knew she couldn't expect a letter herself, but was surprised when one took so long to arrive for Isa and Florence. It contained a further surprise when it did. Ewen would be staying in a hotel when he came to Glasgow for his interview. Florence was upset about that, but Carrie did her best to reassure her.

'He probably feels bad because he hasn't written to you for so long. Doesn't want you to think that he's taking advantage of you.'

Florence spluttered. 'And how could he ever do that? The laddie's mair or less family, for goodness' sake!'

Another case where water was thicker than blood.

Ewen's visit would also be brief. He was arriving on a Thursday, keeping his appointment at the railway company offices on Friday, and probably travelling back south late on the following Monday afternoon.

'South?' Carrie asked when Isa read this information out to her. 'Has he been working in London, then?'

'He's no' giving very much away here. Read it for yourself.'

She did. The letter was cheerful in tone, apologetic for not having been in touch for so long. He was, he wrote, very much looking forward to seeing them again. *It'll be a short visit, but I'd like to see everybody. You and Florence and Donald – not forgetting Bobby! Archie and April, of course. Their mother too.*

'*Their mother too*,' Carrie repeated wryly. 'That makes me sound like a bit of an afterthought.'

'No, it doesn't,' Isa said reassuringly, 'but you'll have to expect him to be a wee bit cautious, hen.'

'You think that's all it is?'

She'd had no chance of trying to hide her hopes from those sharp eyes. Isa gave her a swift hug. 'I know so. Once you tell him how you feel . . .' She winked conspiratorially. 'D'ye see what else he says? He wants us to go up to Glasgow to have high tea with him on the Thursday and be his guests at a supper dance in the Burgh Hall on the Friday night.' She paused for thought. 'If he's been working in London, how on earth did he know there's a dance on at Partick Burgh Hall next Friday night?'

One week later, Carrie stood in the foyer of a Glasgow hotel watching the man who had always been able to find things out walking towards her. Beside her, April was jumping up and down with excitement. Unable to contain herself any longer, the little girl ran up to him. Ewen's arms opened as wide as his eyes. 'My, how you've grown!' he cried.

Archie walked forward too, and then it was hugs and greetings for everybody. Ewen left her till last, extending a polite hand. 'Carrie,' he said pleasantly. 'How are you?'

There was a greater maturity about his face. No doubt his experiences in war-torn Europe had something to do with that. He would have tales to tell.

As though she were sleepwalking, she allowed her hand to slip into that well-remembered firm grasp of his. He looked as energetic as ever. He was saying something. Carrie had to struggle to concentrate.

'. . . introduce my bride-to-be to you.'

She turned and looked at the woman – a well made-up blonde, giving her a cool smile which made no pretence of reaching her eyes. Her hair hadn't always been that colour. Carrie remembered her as a brunette.

The prospective Mrs Ewen Livingstone was smartly, if a little flashily dressed. She was, however, wearing a smock under her coat. Ewen might not have a child yet, but by the looks of it he only had a few months to wait. Janice Muirhead was expecting his baby.

Chapter 36

'I'm not going to the supper dance tomorrow night, and that's final! You two can take the children if you like, but you can count me out. So stop going on at me, Isa!'

The children were in bed, and she was at her own kitchen table, Florence hovering solicitously at her side and Isa sitting opposite her.

'He's going to marry Janice Muirhead,' Carrie said flatly. 'That's all there is to it.'

'He hasn't married her yet,' Isa retorted. 'You could fight her for him. If you come to the Burgh Hall the morn's night.'

'Och, Isa,' Carrie said despairingly, 'she's carrying his child. And they've obviously been living together in London. You heard all those wee hints Janice managed to drop into the conversation as well as I did.'

'What the hell difference does that make?' said Isa impatiently. She made an exclamation of disgust. 'I could fair do wi' a fag.' She looked around as though she expected one to materialise out of thin air. 'Mind you, you would think the stupid bugger could have been a wee bit more careful. He's no' a boy any more.'

'Isabella Nicholson,' said Florence. 'Mind your language!' But the rebuke had been automatic. She sat down at the table and looked puzzled. 'There's something here that doesnae quite meet the eye. How has he no' married her already? That's what ye would expect a man like Ewen to do.'

Isa looked at her as though she was soft in the head. She gestured across the table at Carrie. 'Because he wanted to see this lassie one last time before he made up his mind,' she said. 'To see if she had changed *her* mind. Why else?'

'If that's the case,' asked Carrie, 'why is he going out of his way to make sure he and I never end up on our own together while he's here? It was all of us this afternoon. It's all of us tomorrow night.'

'There's always the weekend, pet,' said Florence, frowning anxiously.

'When he's asked if he can take Archie and April out on Saturday and agreed they'll come to you for their dinner on Sunday.' Carrie threaded her fingers through her coppery hair. 'In any case, we all know Ewen's the last man in the world to desert a woman who's having a baby by him.'

Florence opened her mouth to say something, then closed it again. That argument was irrefutable.

'You're still coming to the dance,' Isa said. 'You're going to put on your glad rags and look your best. I'll do your hair.'

It was easier to give in. What did it matter really?

Half an hour into Friday evening, it seemed to matter quite a lot. Carrie had expected Janice to be all over Ewen like a rash, wasting no opportunity of showing off her ownership of him, but it wasn't like that at all. It was much worse.

There seemed to be genuine friendship and affection between them, and a good few private jokes. And although Janice was wearing an engagement ring, she certainly wasn't flashing it about.

She was friendly and relaxed with the children too. They had taken to her, as they appeared ready to resume their relationship with Ewen where they had left it off. They had known him for only a few short weeks several years ago, but they had never forgotten him. He had made an impact on them.

He asked Carrie up to dance fairly early on in the proceedings. Getting it over with, she supposed. The touch of his fingers, restrained though his clasp was, brought back far too many memories. She could barely speak, and was glad when he was apparently not very interested in making conversation either. Just as she was wondering how much longer she could stand to be in this polite embrace, he mentioned that he had been for his interview earlier that day.

'How did it go?'

'Not bad. They seemed quite impressed anyway.'

'Oh,' she said. 'That's good.'

They finished the dance in silence and when the music stopped he escorted her courteously back to her seat. Then he asked Janice up on to the floor. Donald led Isa out and a laughing Florence agreed to stand up with Archie. That left only Carrie and April at the table. She slid her arms around her daughter's waist, and the little girl leaned back against her in response.

Carrie's eyes kept finding Ewen, wherever he was on the dance floor. He looked a hundred times more relaxed with Janice than he had been with her. She pressed her lips gently against April's hair. This was awful. She shouldn't have come. The music stopped again, everyone returned to the table, and the band leader announced the imminent arrival of supper.

'But first,' he said, 'we all need to work up an appetite. Ladies and gentlemen, take your partners please for the Dashing White Sergeant!'

Ewen was still holding Janice's hand from the last dance. He looked across the table at Carrie. 'How about it?' he asked. 'For old times' sake?'

'No,' she said hurriedly. 'Take April.'

Janice sank down into her chair. 'It's too energetic for me, Ewen.' She laughed up at him. 'Especially in my condition.'

'You and April then,' he said, looking once more at Carrie.

'No,' she repeated, although she knew it was the height of rudeness to refuse his invitation a second time. 'Take Archie. Put April in the middle.'

Donald asked Florence and Isa to make a set with him. That left Carrie and Janice alone at the table. To Carrie's immense relief, the other girl excused herself and went off to the ladies' room. Almost everyone else was up on the floor, throwing themselves into the dance and concentrating on the intricacies of the steps.

Ewen was throwing himself into it too, laughing with Archie and April whenever any of the three of them made a wrong move. Carrie watched him hungrily, saw his energy and vitality, his strength and grace. He had all of those characteristics in abundance, both physically and mentally. He had laid them at her feet so many times.

Now, when she would gladly have thrown herself at his, he no longer wanted her. Her children were revelling in being with him, responding to his interest in them. She thought of how different things might have been. For all of them. And found she couldn't bear to look at the three of them together for one second longer. She turned away, glanced across the table and jumped. 'How long have you been back in your seat?'

'Long enough,' Janice said. She gave Carrie a bland smile.

'Will we all fit in round the table?'

'If we pull out both leaves,' said Donald in his slow voice, and set about performing the task.

'We'll need your chairs, Carrie,' said Isa as she went to help him.

Florence was busy at the range, looking for all the world like a benign witch presiding over a collection of cauldrons. 'And your good cutlery, pet,' she threw over her shoulder. 'We havenae got enough respectable stuff to go round.'

'We'll go and get it all now. Come on, you two,' Carrie said with a brightness she was very far from feeling. There didn't seem to be any way she could get out of being present at this meal. What excuse could she possibly offer?

After all, she had gone to the dance on Friday and allowed Ewen to take the children to the pictures yesterday. Naturally, Janice had gone too. Carrie had waved the four of them off and smiled cheerfully when they came home. She had even invited them in for a cup of tea. That had been politely declined, but she'd spent the rest of the evening listening to her children chattering excitedly about their afternoon out with their Uncle Ewen and – she supposed that one was inevitable – their Auntie Janice.

Archie and April took a chair apiece. Carrie took one as far as the landing, placed it against the wall between the two houses and turned to go back into her own to fetch the cutlery.

'Exactly what I need in my condition,' came Janice's voice. 'How thoughtful of you, Carrie!'

She put a smile on her face and turned to greet them. Janice was pulling herself up the last few stairs, Ewen behind her, jokingly pushing her towards the landing. She sank into the chair. Then Archie came out.

'Hello, wee man,' she said cheerfully, ruffling his hair. 'Are you needing my seat?'

'Go on in,' Carrie said. 'I've another one to fetch.'

'And the cutlery, Ma,' Archie reminded her.

Janice put a hand out to him. 'Be a gentleman, pet. Help me up.' She smiled at her fiancé. 'Why don't you give Carrie a hand, Ewen?' She put on a posh accent. 'Archibald will escort me into luncheon. Won't you, kind sir?'

Archie giggled. Janice let him pull her up, pretending to need a lot more assistance than she actually did.

'May I take your arm?' she queried once she was on her feet. 'Because,' she confided to him, reverting to her own voice, 'I'm growing as big as the side of a house, Archie. I need all the help I can get to move about.'

He giggled again, and obliged.

In contrast to the hustle and bustle and frantic culinary activity taking place across the landing, Carrie's own home seemed unusually quiet. She was very aware of Ewen's silent presence behind her as she walked into the kitchen. Memories were flooding back of two other occasions when she had been alone in this room with him.

'There's the chair,' she said unnecessarily. It was the only one left at the table. Feeling the need to fill the silence, she said the first thing that came into her head. 'She's quite a character. Janice, I mean.'

Ewen smiled. It made his eyes crinkle, emphasising fine lines at their corners which hadn't been there four years ago. 'Oh, she's that all right,' he said warmly. He walked forward, putting his hands out to lift the chair. Then he stopped.

'What's that?' he asked, his attention obviously caught by a small picture hanging on the wall between the range and the box bed.

'Oh,' Carrie said, wishing he hadn't noticed it, 'just a big postcard, really, but I got Donald to frame it for me. Archie and April bought it for me this summer. They thought I might like it.'

He was walking across the room to have a better look. 'Why, it's Oban, isn't? The view out over the bay?'

'Yes.' She crouched down to open the cupboard where she kept the canteen which held her good cutlery. 'We had a day trip down there in the summer, while we were staying with Douglas and Mary at Fort William. You remember Douglas, don't you?' She extracted the wooden box, then stood up and closed the cupboard door with her foot. Ewen was still standing with his back to her, gazing at the little picture.

'Oh, aye,' he said absently. 'Oban Bay,' he murmured. 'With Kerrera in the foreground and Mull of the Mountains in the background. Lovely photography,' he observed.

'Yes.' She wished he would pick up the chair. Then they could go.

'It's very tasteful,' he said. He turned at last, and smiled at her. 'Guaranteed not to provoke an attack of the screaming abdabs in the middle of Oban High Street.'

She rested the canteen of cutlery on the table. She was sure it hadn't been so heavy the last time she had lifted it. Ewen was still smiling at her.

'I can remember that day we had there so well.' His face lit up further. 'And the train journey back. "*Faster than fairies, faster than witches, Bridges and houses, hedges and ditches*",' he quoted softly. 'Do you remember the boy at Tyndrum who was clambering and scrambling?'

'It was a long time ago,' she managed.

'Twelve years,' he said.

'A long time ago,' she repeated. She hoisted up the box of cutlery, made sure she had a secure hold of it.

'Aye,' he said slowly. 'We were both very young then.' He walked across to the table, lowered his eyes to the chair.

A dismissal then. A relegation to the days of their youth. He looked up at her. 'Are you happy, Carrie?' he asked softly. 'Is life good?'

'Yes,' she said. 'I'm happy. My life is very full.' That last was true, at least. Only she had a feeling that from now on there was going to be a yawning chasm at the very heart of it.

'I'm glad,' Ewen said. 'I'm really glad to hear that.'

'They'll be wondering where we are.'

'Aye,' he said, and began carrying the chair towards the door. He paused to let her go in front of him. 'After you,' he said politely.

Carrie pushed the crocus and daffodil bulbs into the earth, rose to her feet and cleaned the dirt from her hands and her trowel. It was a sunny day, but there was an edge to the wind this Monday morning, a foretaste of the cold and dark months ahead. The snell breeze blew a strand of hair across her face, making her eyes water.

She made her way back down the platform. Funny how something as small and fragile as a bulb could survive through the cold and dark of the winter. Carrie was trying very hard not to think about how she was going to do the same. She was trying very hard not to think about a lot of things.

Something her father had once said came back to her, floating down out of the ether. Over the years, she had often been aware of his presence in this place where he had spent so much of his working life. *Dangerous occupation, thinking. Probably why lots o' folk try to avoid it altogether.*

'You were dead right there, Daddy,' she said sadly. Quietly, but out loud. Just in case he was listening.

There was a sharp tap on the ticket window. Putting her coat on before going home at the end of her shift, Carrie turned to see who it was. If she hadn't been so obviously getting ready to leave she would have come up with some excuse. As it was, good manners forced her out into the booking hall.

'I thought you and Ewen were going back to London today,' she said.

'I'm meeting him at the train. I wanted to have a word with you before I left.'

'Janice . . .'

'Please, Carrie,' the girl said quietly, with none of her usual brashness. 'Just walk up the platform with me for a wee minute.'

When Janice stopped outside the back garden of the station house, it crossed Carrie's mind that she had come to gloat. If Ewen got the stationmaster's job, his bride would be mistress of this little kingdom – but somehow that didn't fit in with the girl Carrie had got to know again over the past couple of days. And when Janice spoke she could hear nothing of that sentiment in her voice.

'The garden needs a lot o' work, eh? To get it back to how it was before the war. Ewen would enjoy getting stuck into that,' she observed. She turned and smiled, a wry twist of the lips. 'Whereas I personally would hate it. You used to help your daddy in the garden, didn't you?' She glanced down at the half whisky barrel at her feet. 'Have you been planting something?'

'Bulbs for next spring. That's when they'll sprout.'

'A bit like myself.' Janice patted her stomach and laughed. 'It's great when the baby starts moving, isn't it? You know you've got a real wee person in there.'

Carrie couldn't take much more of this. 'Janice, please say what you've got to say and let me go home. My children will be waiting for me.'

That wasn't strictly true. At the moment Archie and April were both still in school. They were going straight to their aunties' house afterwards, Florence having declared she would cook the tea for everybody tonight.

'To give you a wee rest, hen,' she had said, not bothering to hide her concern at her young neighbour's pale face and listless demeanour.

Janice moved towards a bench placed against the fence, under the rhododendron bushes. She waited till Carrie, all unwilling, had joined her.

'You know Ewen and I have been living together for the past couple of months,' she began.

'So I gathered.' Carrie knew she sounded stiff and disapproving. She didn't much care.

Janice gave her an odd little glance, knowing and sophisticated. 'Nobody gives a damn about that sort of thing in London, you know. Certainly not in the area where Ewen's been living. He has this little service flat near the station: one room and a tiny kitchen. There's one bed,' she said precisely.

She *had* come to crow. Carrie slid forward on the wooden seat, poised for flight. 'I'm not interested in your domestic arrangements!'

'You should be,' came the calm reply. 'How else would I know that he talks in his sleep?'

Carrie felt the breeze on her cheek, sensed the distant vibration of the next train about to pull into the platform. Very slowly, she turned her head and looked into the face of the woman sitting next to her. What she saw there was mischief rather than malice.

'He murmurs your name. Sometimes *Carrie*, sometimes out in full: *Caroline Burgess*. I've been getting a bit fed up of hearing it, to tell you the truth,' Janice added lightly.

The train was approaching round the curve of the track, crossing the bridge over Dumbarton Road. The engine stopped opposite where they sat, and the driver lifted his hand in greeting. Janice waited until he had started up again and pulled away.

'They've offered him the job. Someone came in person to the hotel this morning. King's Cross have said they would release him immediately, but I think he's going to turn it down. Because you're too good an actress.'

Carrie took her eyes off the retreating train, and turned once more to Janice.

'I saw the way you looked at him on Friday night,' the girl said softly. 'When you thought nobody was watching you.'

'I don't understand,' Carrie said, 'you're engaged to him, you're expecting his baby. Why are you telling me all this?'

Janice spoke very clearly. 'The baby's not his. There are several possible candidates. Well,' she admitted, her expression growing rueful, 'quite a few actually. Unfortunately Ewen's not one of them.'

'What?' Carrie's heart had begun to thump violently. 'Does he know that?'

'Oh, aye,' said Janice blithely. 'He rescued us, you see. Walked into this club in London where I was working. For some not very nice people. They didn't want anything to interfere with my earning potential,' she said carefully, her hand going protectively to her stomach. 'But I'd already decided I was keeping this one. Ewen helped me get away from them.'

Carrie pondered that for a moment. 'He couldn't save his mother, but he managed to save you?' she suggested.

'That's about it,' Janice said cheerfully.

Carrie was studying her face. No malice. No distress either. 'Don't you love him?' she asked. 'Doesn't he love you?'

'We're fond of each other,' Janice said equably, 'but that's as far as it goes. We gave each other comfort at a time in our lives when we both needed it. That's all.'

'So why has he asked you to marry him?'

'Because he's a gentleman.' She grimaced. 'Although he knows very well that he hasnae exactly ruined my reputation single-handed. And,' she added carefully, 'because even someone as strong and as determined as he is gets tired of pushing the same rock up the same hill.'

Carrie raised her face to the sky. 'I'm scared, Janice,' she said at last. 'How can I be sure that he still wants me? He hasn't told you in so many words, has he?'

'You don't think that he might be scared too, Carrie?'

She lowered her head again. Janice was smiling at her. 'You'll have to stick your head above the parapet this time,' she said. 'How often did he do it for you? Go on,' she commanded, giving the sleeve of Carrie's coat a little tug. 'If you're quick you'll catch him. He's along the road. Where you would expect him to be.'

Carrie stood up. 'You'll not get mixed up with those people again?'

Janice was still smiling at her. 'No. London's a big place, but I'm planning a move to the coast anyway. Somewhere nice and healthy for the baby to grow up. Somewhere I might stand a chance of finding a decent man, a nice chivalrous one who'll feel sorry for the young widow and her baby. Wasn't it sad that my husband survived the war, only to be run over by a bus in Kensington High Street a couple of years afterwards? And a week before I gave birth too.'

Carrie laughed, liking her. 'You're a survivor, Janice.'

'Oh, aye, I'm that, all right.' The mocking eyes grew shrewd. 'I used to envy you so much, you know.' She gestured with her head to the garden behind them. 'Living in there with your father and mother who loved you. But you've paid your dues since then, I think.'

'You could say that.'

Janice reached out, curled her fingers around Carrie's wrist and gave her hand a shake. 'Well then,' she said, 'go and grab yourself some happiness. Before it's too late.'

'Did you climb over the wall, or did you come in the grown-up way?'

He whirled round. He'd been standing with his back to the gate, looking up at the sky. 'What are you doing here?' His attitude was anything but welcoming.

'Janice sent me.'

'Oh?' He was wearing a raincoat, long and unbuttoned. He thrust his hands into the pockets of his trousers, pushing back the light-coloured folds.

'She and I have been having a very interesting discussion.'

One fair eyebrow went up, but Ewen contented himself with another one word answer. 'Really?'

'She said they'd offered you the job, but that you might be going to turn it down.'

'Aye. I might.'

Carrie glanced around her, at the old graveyard in which they stood. 'You came here to think it over?'

His chin went up. 'What's it to you?'

She reminded herself she had no right to expect this to be easy. 'I think you should take it. You'd relish the challenge.'

'Maybe I'm fed up facing challenges.' His eyes were a cool grey. 'Maybe even someone as stupid as me eventually realises when he's pursuing a lost cause.'

'Don't call yourself stupid,' she said sharply. 'You were never that. Not even when you were a wee raggedy boy out there on Keith Street. And,' Carrie enquired, 'are you absolutely certain that the cause is lost?'

He took his hands out of his pockets and two hesitant steps towards her. Then he stopped. 'There's times when I still am that wee boy,' he said. 'Lots of them.'

'I know,' she said softly. 'I know.'

Something flashed across his face then, but he recovered himself quickly. He stood where he was, making no further move towards her. He'd been hurt too many times, and he was wary. So it was up to her. Time to stick her head above that parapet. She took a deep breath.

'I'm going to tell you something, and then I'm going to ask you a question. You can say yes, or you can say no.' She took another breath. 'I love you, Ewen Livingstone. Will you marry me?'

He stared at her. She was too late. She'd left it too long, thrown his love for her back in his face so often it had evaporated. Cast to the four winds, it had vanished as though it had ever existed at all.

Ewen took a step forward. 'Are ye no' supposed to wait till it's a leap year?'

'Is that one of your pieces of useless information?' she asked. She wanted to laugh. She wanted to cry.

He took another step. Then one more.

'I think we've waited long enough,' she said breathlessly, looking up into his face. 'Don't you?'

'Way too long,' he growled, and bent his head to kiss her.

Chapter 37

'You didn't need to come and see me off,' Janice said.

Ewen contradicted her. 'Of course we did. Here, I got you some magazines and fruit for the journey. Now,' he said briskly, 'you'll remember to eat properly? Get all the vitamins and minerals you need?'

'I will. Thanks for these.' She took the magazines and fruit from him and stuffed them into the small bag at her feet. He'd already put her case on to the train. 'I'll send your things,' she promised.

'There's not that much,' he said. 'My books and a few other bits and pieces, but tell the people at King's Cross to contact me and I'll arrange to pay the carriage at this end. The room's paid for the next six weeks. Will that do you, or do you want me to send them another month's rent?'

Janice shook her head. 'No, that's more than enough. Oh!' she said suddenly. 'I'd better give you this back.' She began tugging at the engagement ring.

Ewen's hand closed over hers. 'No, no,' he said. 'It's yours, lassie. Sell it if you like.'

'Only if I need to,' she said. 'Otherwise I'm going to keep it to remember you by.' She reached up and kissed him on the cheek. 'Thank you for everything you did for me.' She looked across at Carrie. 'Is it all right if I give him a hug as well?'

'Be my guest,' she said gently. She'd been hanging back to allow the two of them to make their farewells.

Over Janice's shoulder, Ewen's eyes were far too bright. 'Good luck,' he said huskily. 'Especially when the baby comes.'

Janice gave him one last squeeze, then let him go. 'She'll give you one of your own,' she said. She held out her hand, and Carrie came forward.

'Will you write and let us know how you get on?'

'Probably not.'

Carrie looked into her eyes, and sighed. 'I suppose you're right, but we'll always remember you, you know.'

'I should bloody hope so. Cupid's little helper, that's me. You'll look after him?' Janice asked. 'And let him look after you?' She gave Ewen a smile. 'He likes to do that.'

'Oh, Janice!' Carrie threw her arms around her neck and embraced her. Janice hugged her back. When they separated, both of them had tears in their eyes.

'Would you look at the state of us! Him, too.' She gestured with her thumb towards Ewen, once more looking decidedly moist-eyed. 'Well, I'd better get aboard.'

The door was slammed behind her, and Janice leaned out of the window to say a last goodbye. Her final words were for Carrie. 'You'll enjoy giving him a wean. He's all right in that department. A lot more than all right. Know what I mean? Take it from one who knows.'

Ewen Livingstone – stationmaster designate – blushed to the roots of his hair. The final whistle blew, and Janice threw them both a wicked grin. 'Have fun, my children.'

'In the name o' God,' said Isa in exasperation. 'Where on earth can your mother have got to? She's more than two hours late.'

'Aye,' said Florence, 'the meal's going to spoil if she's no here soon. Away down to the street and see if you can see her coming, children.'

Ten minutes later, April came pelting through the half-open door of her aunties' house, giggling furiously. Archie was hot on her heels, clutching his neck and making exaggerated faces as though he were about to be sick.

'Heavens above,' said Florence, grabbing April as she ran helter-skelter into the kitchen. 'What's going on?'

'Come and see! Come and see!'

Isa went storming out on to the landing, preceded by the children and closely followed by Florence, Donald and Bobby. 'Where the hell have you been, Carrie?' she began. Then she saw what was happening down on the half landing and her face broke into a wide, broad smile.

Ewen was braced against the narrow stone sill of the long windows which lit the stairwell. He sat with his legs apart, and one of them was providing a seat for Carrie. He was grasping her waist firmly with one hand. The other rested on her knee. She had her arms coiled about his neck.

'They won't stop kissing!' said April in delight.

'It's disgusting!' exclaimed her brother in accents of horror.

Ewen took his mouth off Carrie's and grinned at him. 'It's allowed, Archie,' he said cheerfully. 'We're going to be married.'

The landing above them was a sea of smiling faces. Even Bobby, front paws up on the banister, was wagging his tail. With a supreme effort of will, Isa managed to replace a grin with a ferocious scowl.

'Is that right? And where, might we be so bold as to ask, does Mr

Ewen Livingstone think he's staying until the ceremony takes place?'

'In there?' he said hopefully, pointing towards Carrie's front door.

Isa responded to that with a snort of derision. She turned to Florence. 'You're going on your holidays,' she announced. 'To Carrie's house. You,' she announced, jabbing a finger at Ewen, 'are lodging wi' Donald and me for the duration.' She sniffed magnificently. 'This is a respectable close. We're having no shameless and unseemly behaviour in here!'

Epilogue

His hand on the bolt of the [illegible] gate, [illegible] announced, 'I suppose I'd better go.'

'I suppose you'd better [illegible] I'd very [illegible] better than [illegible] do. No one out there's going to [illegible] a [illegible] of [illegible].'

'Aye, it took me a long time to work out. [illegible] Soft as butter really, wasn't he?'

Connie's own smile [illegible] pockets roll on him, you [illegible].'

His eyes softened. [illegible]

[illegible]

[illegible] worry. [illegible]

[illegible]

'[illegible]'

'[illegible]'

[illegible]

'What's cooking?' he [illegible] Connie gave him a shove. [illegible] you can have all the [illegible] you want when you come off duty. [illegible] remember?'

He looked fondly at her. [illegible] 'And you?'

'Now I'm the matron [illegible].'

'So you are,' he said. 'So you are.' [illegible]

[illegible] words in the [illegible] language [illegible]. Swinging her round in his arms he laid a large hand [illegible] her stomach, splaying his fingers [illegible] feet up this afternoon.'

'Certainly not,' she said, [illegible] being [illegible] by the [illegible]

Epilogue

His hand on the bolt of the platform gate, Ewen paused and turned. 'I suppose I'd better go.'

'I suppose you'd better wipe that smile off your face before you do. No one out there's going to respect your authority otherwise.'

'Aye, it took me a long time to work out that was your father's trick. Soft as butter really, wasn't he?'

Carrie's own smile grew sad. 'Ewen,' she said hesitantly, 'this job took its toll on him, you know.'

His eyes softened. 'I'm a different personality to him.' He reflected. 'A bit harder, maybe. If anyone gives me a mouthful, they know I'm quite capable of giving them one back.' He slid his arm about her, gave her shoulders a reassuring squeeze. 'I'm sure he's looking down on us from somewhere, you know. Giving me a helping hand now and again, chuckling when I make a mistake.' His generous mouth quirked wryly. 'I'm not so sure I'd like your ma to be watching over us, mind.'

'She'd have come round to you.'

'You think so?'

'I'm sure she would have. Come on now. Duty calls.'

'One more kiss?'

'You've had lots already,' Carrie said sternly.

'Who's counting?' he asked, and added a few more to the tally. Carrie gave him a shove. 'Go,' she said. 'You can have all the kisses you want when you come off duty. The trains have to run on time, remember?'

He looked fondly at her. 'Always the stationmaster's daughter, aren't you?'

'Now I'm the stationmaster's wife.'

'So you are,' he said. 'So you are.' He dropped a kiss on her nose. '*The stationmaster's wife*,' he said consideringly. 'Possibly my favourite words in the entire language. Apart from *Caroline Livingstone*, that is.' Swinging her round in his arms, he laid a large but light hand on her stomach, splaying his fingers out over the bump. 'Going to put your feet up this afternoon?'

'Certainly not,' she said, although her intended briskness was being sabotaged by the soft little kisses he was dropping on the side of her neck. 'There's gardening to be done.'

He lifted his head and heaved a theatrical sigh. 'I suppose it's just as well. If you're out in the garden, I won't have a hundred passengers asking me where you are or if you're keeping well. Giving me presents and wee bits of flowers and plants to pass on to you. Hoping that you're putting the station in for the best garden competition again. You might as well still be on the payroll.'

'I know,' she said happily.

'Don't do any of the heavy stuff then,' he said. 'I'll get Archie and April to help me with that this evening.'

'Donald can help too,' she reminded him. 'They're all coming round tonight.'

'So they are. I'd forgotten. Are Florence's knitting needles still in danger of catching fire?'

Carrie laughed. 'You mean the several dozen matinée jackets she's making for the baby?' She lifted a lazy arm, found his jaw and traced the line of it with her fingertips. 'You've got to go back to work, Mr Livingstone.'

He sighed, and allowed her to turn around. 'Carrie . . . Archie and April are happy about the baby, aren't they?'

'Are you kidding? They're over the moon. Apart from arguing constantly about whether we're going to have a boy or a girl, of course. No prizes for guessing who wants what.'

Ewen smiled. 'Maybe we should let them choose the name,' he suggested. 'Would that be a good idea?'

'We're there ahead of you,' she said. 'And they actually agree on one point.'

'Which is?'

'Both their names begin with the first letter of the alphabet, so they think it would be nice if the baby's did too.'

'Fine by me.' He thought about it some more. 'In fact, that's a really nice idea. Have they anything in mind?'

'So far Archie's come up with *Andrew* or maybe *Alan*. *Alexander* is also in the running. What do you think?'

'All good names,' he said. 'And if we have a girl?'

'Oh,' she said, 'April and I have already decided. We thought we'd go for *Anne*. After your mother,' she added unnecessarily, for his reaction was there in his face for her to read.

'Hard, are you?' she enquired a few moments later.

He lifted his head from her neck and gave her a sheepish look. 'I don't know what I did to deserve you.'

'Och, Ewen,' she said tenderly. 'You do.' She patted his broad chest. 'Be off with you. Go out there and give 'em hell.'

He couldn't resist one last kiss, leaning over the fence and cupping her face between his hands.

'You're happy, then?' she asked.

His eyes were like a Hebridean sea: deep, full of quiet power, as constant and enduring as the mountains and rocks.

'Happy?' he repeated, and the sun came out and turned the grey waves a warm blue. 'Lassie,' he said, 'I'm delirious with joy!'

Look for the Silver Lining

Look for the Silver Lining

JUNE FRANCIS

First published in Great Britain in 2006 by
Allison & Busby Limited
13 Charlotte Mews
London W1T 4EJ
www.allisonandbusby.com

A catalogue record for this book is available from the British Library.

10 9 8 7 6 5 4 3 2 1

ISBN 0 7490 8222 4
978-0-7490-8222-2

Printed and bound in Wales by
Creative Print and Design, Ebbw Vale

JUNE FRANCIS was born in Blackpool and moved to Liverpool at an early age. She started writing in her forties, producing articles for *My Weekly*, and has since gone on to have twenty novels published. Married with three grown-up sons, she enjoys fell-walking, local history and swimming.

Find out more about June Francis by visiting her website at *www.junefrancis.co.uk*.

Also available from Allison & Busby

The Pawnbroker's Niece
Step by Step
A Place to Call Home
A Dream to Share

Also by June Francis

The Bride Price
Beloved Abductor
My Lady Deceiver
Fateful Encounter
A Sparrow Doesn't Fall
Love's Intrigue
Flowers on the Mersey
Friends & Lovers
Lily's War
Going Home to Liverpool
Kitty and her Boys
Somebody's Girl
For the Sake of the Children
Another Man's Child
Someone to Trust
Rowan's Revenge

Part One

1941 to 1942

Prologue

'Up, children! On your feet!' Out of the corner of her eye, 21-year-old Nellie Lachlan could see the giant crack in the wall widening. 'We're going to march out of the classroom, along the corridor, then outside. Dennis, you can lead the way.'

'But it's raining, miss,' Dennis moaned.

'A bit of rain won't hurt us.'

'Is this a game, miss?' asked one of the four-year-olds.

'Sort of.' She began to sing 'The Grand old Duke of York' and hustled the children, whose attention had obviously been elsewhere when she had ordered them up, outside to where their classmates were already lining up. 'Come on, Dennis,' she urged, 'or someone else can be leader.'

'No. You said I could be leader but do we have to go outside?' he asked.

'Just get going!' ordered Nellie, glancing at the wall. Bits of masonry were starting to fall. She knew that she mustn't panic the little ones but they had to move fast. Who would have believed the bomb that had exploded in the next street last night could have had such an effect on the old school? She remembered Teddy, her husband, saying the effects of a bomb blast should never be underestimated. He had wanted her to get away from the bombing but so far she had stuck it out, not wishing to leave the job she adored and also hoping to heal the rift between herself and her family.

'When they were up they were up,' she sang, gently pushing children through the doorway and counting heads at the same time.

Was it her imagination or was the floor really quivering? Is this what it felt like to be involved in an earthquake? She shoved five-year-old Johnny out of the door, thinking, 'Thank God, the last one!' when she remembered there was a new girl, Audrey.

She turned back and her gaze swept the room. Where was she? Could she have sneaked out to the lavatory? No! She spotted a foot sticking out from behind the sand tray. The child must be hiding, thinking the marching was just a game, and one she didn't want to join in.

Nellie wasted no time and raced over to the sand tray with the sound of shifting masonry and the singing of the marching children in her ears. She dragged the startled girl to her feet and ran with her towards the doorway. They were almost there when Nellie heard a rumbling and the floor shook violently. Audrey screamed. The urge to look behind them was overwhelming but Nellie resisted and swung the girl in an arc and then let her go. Momentum took her out into the corridor and Nellie flung herself after her as the wall caved in.

Chapter One

Nellie sat at the end of a row of children with a three-year-old boy on her knee. She could feel his skinny body shake as he giggled at the antics of a child puppet performing a jerky dance as it tried to escape a mother puppet attempting to get a miniature gasmask on its head. A smile lit her blue-green eyes as she watched another tiny puppet blundering about with its arms held out in front of it because its gasmask was on backwards. The performance went on for a few minutes longer and then ended with the message: *Don't forget your gasmask!* It was greeted by a storm of clapping and a shouted request for 'More, more!'

Nellie echoed their sentiments, thinking the poor loves had been through so much that it was good for them to forget the horrors of the bombing for a short while. Gradually the noise died down as the puppet booth was cleared away and the area set up for a game of musical chairs.

Miss Jackson, the headmistress of the Central School on the outskirts of Liverpool, crooked a finger at Nellie. With a feeling of trepidation, she eased the boy off her knee and stood up. She was aware of being the focus of numerous pairs of eyes and prayed that she did not look as nervous as she felt. This would be the first time she had played since her arm had been broken when the wall had collapsed. The librarian smiled encouragingly. He had initiated the Saturday morning hour and also arranged for lessons for those children who had not been evacuated to take place in the library after the primary school had been closed due to bomb damage.

Nellie settled herself on the piano stool and her fingers felt for the black and white keys. She tried out a few scales. It was her Great-great-aunt Adelaide who had allowed her to 'mess about making a bloody din' as her seafaring father, Bernard, called her playing on the upright piano in the parlour of Adelaide's large Victorian house, a short distance from the

LeedsLiverpool canal. Sadly, the old woman had died last year shortly after Nellie's sailor brother Joseph had been killed. It had been just six months before Nellie had eloped with her brother's best friend, the Protestant Teddy Lachlan.

She began to play 'The Teddy Bears' Picnic' and relaxed a bit when she heard the children singing as they skipped around the chairs, slowing down as they came to the end of a row, ready to scramble for a seat if the music should suddenly stop. She thought how her husband would have found pleasure in watching the tots enjoying themselves. They both wanted a family but it was too early to tell whether she was pregnant from their too-short honeymoon. He had been so tender and thoughtful on their wedding night that all her trepidation had vanished. She sighed, wishing that she could relive those few days in Southport, but she did not know when she would see him again now that he had disembarked for Libya.

She stopped playing and there was a mad scramble for the chairs. Nellie watched, her ready sympathy roused by the plight of the two littlest ones who did not reach the chairs in time. One cheerfully went and sat on her mother's knee but the other stamped away to lean against his grandfather's leg and glower at the other children.

Another two chairs were removed and Nellie began to play again. Her gaze wandered to the rows of books displayed in the children's department. It was Adelaide whom she had to thank for her love of stories. Nellie's mother, Carmel, had never told them fictional tales for fun; she made her children focus on stories of the saints' lives and daily readings from the Catholic missal first thing in the morning and last thing at night. The rest of the time, Carmel spent keeping house for Grandfather Callaghan, visiting her sister in Bootle or attending church while her seafaring husband was away for months on end. It was Nellie's paternal grandfather who had inherited Adelaide's house and the rest of the family, except her brother Francis who served as a curate in an inner city parish in Liverpool, still lived there.

Nellie lifted her hands from the piano and watched, again, that mad scramble of children trying not to be left out. Suddenly it occurred to her that the little girl with plaits and a quivering lip, who had been pushed off a chair by a larger boy, reminded her in a peculiar way of herself. Since her marriage, she had been cut off from her family. For once, her parents had presented a united front when Teddy had asked for her hand in marriage. Her father, who was home on shore leave, voiced his disapproval in no uncertain terms and refused to grant his permission.

Her parents' antagonism had shocked the young couple. Nellie had never imagined her mother would be so against her choice of husband. Teddy, despite being a Protestant, had been made welcome in their house since boyhood and she had often heard her mother and Aunt Josie saying what a nice, charming young man he was. He'd had a steady job working in a shipping office until being called up. It was just before he'd left for an army training camp in Scotland that he asked Nellie to write to him. She had done so and, over the months, their affection for each other had grown. On his first leave, the friendship forged by their correspondence had blossomed into a real love affair.

Nellie took her hands from the keyboard and eased back a strand of chestnut hair from her eyes, watching again the children's rush to secure a seat. She decided musical chairs was not a nice game but at least it served the purpose of teaching children at an early age that life was not a doddle and one had to put in effort to get what one wanted. She and Teddy had wanted each other desperately but, even so, it had taken some doing going against her family's wishes and running away to get married on his embarkation leave.

Nellie launched into 'Run, Rabbit, Run' and felt that ache inside her as she thought of her younger sisters, Lottie and Babs. She loved her sisters dearly but, although she had written to them several times since her wedding, she had not received one answer and it hurt.

'Miss Callaghan, can you spare half an hour after we've finished with the children? We're having a meeting and want you to be there,' said Miss Jackson.

Nellie nodded. She had kept secret her marital state, knowing that normally a married woman would not retain her job once she left spinsterhood behind. 'Can you tell me what it's about?' she asked.

'You'll be told at the meeting, dear, which will take place at the far end of the Adults' section of the library.' Miss Jackson hurried away.

Nellie hoped the meeting wouldn't go on too long. She had shopping to do and her rented room to clean.

Fortunately for Nellie, her part in the proceedings was dealt with first. 'Miss Callaghan, we wondered if you would be willing to accompany a group of mothers and their pre-school children to Cumberland?' she was asked.

Nellie blinked at the man. 'You mean they're being evacuated?'

'Voluntary evacuation.' He peered at her over his spectacles. 'It is not the same as the government's scheme for school children just before the outbreak of war; it is being offered to mothers wanting to escape the recent bombing. The Luftwaffe might have left us alone for a short time but, no doubt, they will be back. Their intention is to destroy the docks if they can and the morale of the people.'

Nellie remembered that day when she had almost been flattened because of a German bomb and knew what her answer would be. 'So would I be going to teach the children?'

He tapped the tips of his fingers together. 'These are pre-school children so your task will be to prepare them for school.'

'How many children will there be?'

'A dozen in your charge but there will also be younger siblings who will be in the care of their mothers. You will be staying in a large detached house called High View, which has been loaned to us by a colonel who has come out of retirement and is now at the war office in London. The house is situated a couple of miles from Ambleside.' A slight smile relaxed his rather thin lips. 'Beautiful country, and I'm sure it will do your good self and the mothers and children nothing but good. Of course, you will have some help. A Miss Finch from Kendal, who is a qualified nurse, will be responsible for the children's health, and the Colonel's housekeeper, with the help of the mothers, will see to everything else to do with their welfare.'

'Will there be other such groups going elsewhere?' asked Nellie, her face showing interest.

'Yes, but that is not your concern.' He waved a hand dismissively. 'Will you accept this job? I know the care of pre-schoolers was not what you were trained for but it is becoming increasingly obvious the care and education of this age group will take on more importance on the home front in the future.'

Nellie felt a rising excitement and was flattered that they should ask some one as young and inexperienced as herself to take it on. She would have a roof over her head and be fed and paid a wage, which meant she could save money for the day when she and Teddy would have a home of their own.

'Yes, I would like the job,' she said firmly.

The committee looked pleased and she was told they would be in touch with more details soon. Nellie thought the departure could not come quickly enough for her.

Within days, Nellie gave her landlady notice and thought about what she would need in the way of equipment. She was fortunate in that her list met with the education suppliers' approval. She was looking forward to the challenge but she knew that she could not leave without trying to heal the rift with her family, so she decided to visit them.

As she reached the front gate, she was stopped by a next door neighbour, Mrs Wainwright, who liked to have her nose in everyone's business. Silver-haired with baby-blue eyes, she looked the picture of a cuddly granny.

'What are you doing here, Nellie? If you were hoping to see your sisters, they're out.'

Nellie felt a deep disappointment. 'What about Mam and Grandfather?'

'He's at a retired seamen's meeting, I believe.' She gave Nellie a sharp look. 'So what made you leave home? You haven't joined the Forces.'

Nellie's pretty mouth tightened. 'Mam didn't tell you?'

The woman looked frustrated. 'No, but I did wonder if you'd got yourself into trouble.'

'Well, you were wrong. I did something much worse: I married Teddy Lachlan, a Protestant.'

Defiantly, Nellie walked away, forcing open the gate to her grandfather's house and heading up the path. Her heart was beating fast at the thought of confronting her mother. If Aunt Josie was with her then the meeting would be more than a little fraught. She went round to the back of the house and let herself in by the washroom door and into the kitchen.

Her mother glanced up from the book she was reading and Nellie saw that it was *The Life of St Francis*. Carmel's auburn hair was greying and her face was lined. Her lips tightened when she saw her daughter. 'You've got a nerve coming here when I told you to never set foot in this house again.'

Nellie felt tears prick the back of her eyes. 'I'm going away, Mam. I just wanted to try and make up our quarrel. Teddy and I are married now, so it seems pointless carrying it on.'

'You're not married to him in the eyes of the one true Church, Nellie, so you're living in sin. A daughter of mine behaving in such a way! I'm ashamed of you,' she said scathingly.

Nellie felt the colour rise in her cheeks but she tilted her chin. 'Then you're wrong to feel like that. You know Teddy's a good man but he has his own faith and he's entitled to it.'

'Rubbish!' cried Carmel. 'There is only one true faith and he needs to turn or he'll go to Hell.'

The mention of Hell angered Nellie. 'Well, rubbish to that,' she said. 'If there's a hell I believe it's on this earth. Think of all those soldiers who were killed in the Great War.'

'He's turning you his way,' gasped Carmel, putting a hand to her bosom. 'Now get out of this house before I throw you out.'

'I'm going. I'm sorry you feel the way you do, Mam. I'm off to Cumberland in the morning. I'm going with some children and their mothers, so if you ever did worry about me and the bombs you can stop worrying. Give Babs and Lottie my love, and Grandfather, too.'

Her mother pointed at the door. Angry tears almost blinded Nellie as she turned and walked out of the house. She would have to be asked back before she returned to this house again.

The next day Nellie left Bootle. It had been decided to ferry the party to Cumberland by charabanc because the journey by train would have entailed several changes and a bus trip at the end, which might prove too difficult for mothers with little ones.

The children were excited as they climbed into the vehicle.

'Dad said I'll see cows in fields, miss,' said one little boy, his brown eyes shining as he looked up at her. 'Is that right?'

'I'm sure we will,' said Nellie, seating him next to the window before helping his mother and baby sister into the place beside him.

'I'm gonna miss my fella,' said the woman, settling the baby on her knee, 'but the kids have got to come first.'

'Works at the docks, doesn't he?' asked Nellie, giving another mother a helping hand.

'That's right,' said the first woman, lowering her voice and adding, 'I'll worry meself sick about him, knowing there'll be more air raids, but he said if we were on a sinking ship it would be women and children first.'

Nellie took his point and determined not to worry about her family. Besides, her grandfather's house was at least a mile and a half from the docks and not in an industrial area.

Within less than an hour they had left bomb-damaged Merseyside behind and were roaring along the main road heading north into the Lancashire countryside. One of the mothers began to sing, 'We're off, we're off, we're off in a motor car, sixty coppers are after us and we don't know where we are.'

The simple refrain was taken up by most of the women and several of the older children. Nellie smiled, wondering where the song had started. Perhaps it reflected the mothers' visits to the picture house when they were girls, watching silent films in which the Keystone Cops featured. When all were sick of singing that ditty, Nellie started them off with 'Ten Green Bottles Standing on a Wall'. It was another simple song but it would help teach the children how to count down from ten to one. When that ended someone suggested 'Run, Rabbit, Run'.

Nellie loved singing and proceeded to lead them into such popular songs as, 'Look for the Silver Lining', 'Life is Just a Bowl of Cherries' and the odd children's Sunday school chorus, which she had learnt when, unknown to her mother, she had visited the Methodist chapel on Linacre Road with a Protestant friend. The building was almost opposite to where Babs worked in the office of the Diamond Match-works. 'This Little Light of Mine' kept them going for five minutes and the mothers remembered other choruses.

So the miles sped by. There had been no snow in the city but here, in the countryside, lay odd patches in the fields and on the summits of the distant mountains. She remembered once when there had been a fall of snow in the city and Teddy had told her that if you were to put some snowflakes under a microscope they looked just like stars. He had gone on to liken the stars to those in her eyes and she could still feel the thrill his words had given her. She had teased him, saying that he was a real romantic.

'I'm all in favour of a bit of a romance,' he'd responded, kissing her and then twirling her round in an impromptu dance and singing against her ear, 'Wait till the Sun Shines, Nellie'. It was a song about being happy and sighing and going down Lovers' Lane. He had reminded her of an evening in her great-great-aunt's house, when she had picked out the tune on the piano and the old lady had told them that the music was written by Harry von Tilzer in the early years of that century before the Great War.

A tiny sigh escaped her, thinking of all those young men who had lost their lives in that so-called 'war to end all wars'. She feared for her husband, missing him terribly, but knew, like many another wife and sweetheart, she just had to bear it. At least she would have his letters, and her ex-landlady had promised to send on any that might come for her after she left. Nellie had already written to Teddy with her new address and reminded him to write Miss Callaghan on the envelope.

They had several stops on the way when mothers and children scurried behind a handy hedge to relieve themselves. It was far too cold to have a picnic, so they ate meat paste and jam butties on the charabanc. As they drew closer to their destination, Nellie noticed the sweep of Morecambe Bay.

A mother cried excitedly, 'The sea, the sea!'

Then it was gone, but ahead loomed the mountains of Cumberland. By then, some of the children had fallen asleep, while others had got fed up of having sheep and cows pointed out to them and were getting fractious. Nellie drew several of them to the back of the charabanc and played 'Pat-a-Cake' with them and told them the story of 'The Three Bears', putting on a gruff voice for Father Bear and a lighter one for Mother and Baby. She wished that she had thought to keep some crayons and paper from the boxes she had packed, but they were in the luggage compartment of the vehicle. By the time Lake Windermere came into view, she was beginning to sag, but the dipping sun reflecting off the surface of the water, turning it to apricot and gold silk, raised her spirits.

'Not long to go now,' called the driver over his shoulder.

Mothers perked up and so did the children. Several of the older ones began to ask, 'Are we there yet, miss? Are we there?'

Nellie had no more idea than they did but said, in what she hoped was a reassuring voice, 'Nearly.'

To her relief they were soon making their way through Ambleside. Nellie gazed at the grey slate houses and the tiny shop windows but the light was beginning to fail, so she could see little detail. Soon they left the village behind to wend their way along a winding road, fringed by trees. Eventually they stopped near a gatepost that bore the name High View. 'All out here,' said the driver. 'I won't get up there.'

They got down from the vehicle, stretching and groaning, wanting to see exactly where 'up there' was. On the other side of the gatepost, a drive led up a hillside only to disappear round a bend but, between the bare branches of the trees, a large grey house could be seen.

It took some doing getting everyone with baggage and boxes up to the house. Some of the mothers complained about the steepness of the hill before they'd even started the climb. The noise brought forth a man, a boy and two women. The man and boy instantly started to carry in the baggage. One woman, in a nurse's uniform and with greying hair, introduced herself as Miss Finch. The other one was plump and said that she was Mrs James, the housekeeper. Nellie put both women's age in the late forties.

'Hopefully the worst of the weather is behind us now we're into March,' said Mrs James in a northern burr. Her gaze swept over the group of women and children in front of her before returning to rest on Nellie.

'January was so cold that Rydal Water froze over and we had skating on the lake.'

'What a pity we missed it,' said Nellie brightly. 'It would have been a sight worth seeing for the children.'

'It's much too far for the little ones to walk but you can take the footpath over the fells. The weather can change dramatically. You must never go out alone or without telling someone where you're going.'

'I'll bear that in mind,' said Nellie, having no intention of traipsing up mountains and getting lost. She was a city girl and if she decided that this Rydal Lake was worth having a look at, then she felt sure there would be a bus that would take them there.

'Right! Let's get them all in, Mrs James,' said Miss Finch briskly. 'You lead the way and I'll bring up the rear. I'm sure the mothers would like the children to have their suppers and to get them to bed as soon as possible.'

Supper and bed are just what I need, thought Nellie, picking up her holdall and gasmask and following mothers and children indoors. While Mrs James saw to them, Miss Finch dealt with Nellie.

'I'll show you to your bedroom first so you can leave your bag and gasmask there. Then I'll take you down to the room we've allocated as a playroom for the children. I'm sure you'll want to see what we've done as soon as possible.'

Nellie agreed and followed her up several flights of stairs to an attic bedroom. She was reminded of the ones in her grandfather's house. They were slightly smaller than this one and were full of junk. She had once suggested when her father had been on shore leave, that it would be good if the rooms were cleared out so Babs and Lottie would not have to share. He had pointed to the damp in one corner and the peeling wallpaper and the assorted leftovers from several generations. 'You going to sort this out, girl? I doubt it. And I'm not going to bloody waste my leave doing it either.' He had hurried downstairs and out to the Red Lion.

'I hope this will do you?' said Miss Finch. 'We've given the bigger rooms to the mothers and children.'

Nellie nodded. She had a room to herself and, although there was not much in the way of furniture and the bed was narrow, she saw no point in complaining. The blackout curtains were drawn, so there was no use in looking out of the window at the view. Tomorrow would do. She felt a momentary homesickness, wanting the comforting sight of familiar houses and shops and the sound of a foghorn on the River Mersey. Well, she was going to have to forgo those things for a while. She wondered what Teddy would make of the place. Most likely he would love it, having spent months in the Scottish countryside and having written of his liking for lonely, wild places.

'If you leave your things and follow me down,' said Miss Finch, standing in the doorway, tapping the wall with her fingers.

Nellie dropped them hastily on the narrow bed and hurried after the nurse as she vanished from view.

Nellie had no complaints, though, when Miss Finch showed her to the room designated the playroom. It had a large bay window with a padded window seat and, except for a grand piano, space had been cleared of what she presumed was most likely dark, heavy furniture, similar to the pieces she had noticed in the hall and on the landings. In their place stood several small tables and chairs and surprise, surprise a sandbox, which rested on a huge sheet of tarpaulin. Next to it was a cardboard box containing buckets and spades. 'Golly,' said Nellie, smiling. 'I never expected that.'

'It was the gardener's idea. He thought with the children coming from the coast they'd like it.'

'I must tell him how much I appreciate it,' said Nellie, wandering over to the boxes that had come from Liverpool. Her fingers itched to unpack them and see if she really had been supplied with what she'd requested.

'You'd best leave them until after supper,' said Miss Finch, as if reading her mind.

Nellie nodded and followed her out of the room. Yet when supper was finished, tiredness overcame her and instead of heading for the playroom, she went upstairs. After unpacking, she pulled on her fleecy pyjamas and got into bed. The sheets were cold but did not feel damp. She forced herself to lay still and prayed for Teddy, her family, the children and mothers, and, lastly, herself. Her thoughts drifted over the happenings of the day, before she fell into a deep sleep.

The next morning Nellie woke feeling a bit groggy and, when she climbed out of bed, nausea overcame her. With a handkerchief held to her mouth, she had to rush downstairs to vomit in the toilet next to the bathroom. She put her sickness down to the macaroni cheese they'd had for supper.

When she went down to breakfast, she did without porridge and ate just toast smeared with butter and a cup of tea. Then she gathered her children together and took them to the playroom. There were a couple who wanted their mothers to stay with them but Nellie decided that she had to be firm from the start and insisted they left. She knew from her brief experience of primary school that most children stopped crying after a short while.

She told the children that they would say a prayer first and then practise putting on their gasmasks. After that the older children could help her unpack the boxes that had come from Liverpool while the younger ones could play in the sand tray.

She saw that a couple of the four-year-olds were torn between curiosity of what was in the boxes and making sand-pies, but when she told them they could play in the sand tray later, they appeared satisfied with her decision.

Once the boxes were unpacked, Nellie soon discovered most of what she had asked for was second-hand. Even some of the paper had been written on the back. It was annoying but she reminded herself that there was a war on and so there were bound to be shortages. She handed out individual blackboards and chalks to the oldest children, thinking that if by the time they were five they knew their alphabet, could write their names, count to ten and distinguish red from yellow and blue from green, they'd cope with school better. Not that she expected all of them to develop at the same rate.

She thought of her younger sisters; Lottie was almost eighteen and Babs was a year younger. Lottie, plump, short, with mousy hair, had always been slow but thorough. As for Babs, she was like quicksilver, wanting something finished almost as soon as she started. Even their father made some time for his youngest daughter when he was home. She had flaming red hair, dancing green eyes, dimples and a smile that made you want to smile yourself. It was as if the good fairy had waved a wand over the youngest in the family and dished out most of the charm and good looks. Folk might say that inner beauty was more important, but from Nellie's experience of life, good looks were what made that first positive impression on people. Perhaps for that reason, she'd always had a soft spot for those children not so fortunate as Babs. She had her eye on one already who would need drawing out. She also felt music was a good place to start and, that afternoon, planned to involve all the children in being part of a band.

The morning sped by and Nellie enjoyed her lunch of cottage pie and sponge pudding and custard. While the children spent time afterwards having a break, she unpacked the box containing not only proper musical instruments: triangles, drums, cymbals and tambourines, but also blocks of wood, spoons and a small washboard. She smiled, thinking that the music they would make would definitely not be to everyone's taste but at least they would enjoy themselves.

She gathered the children together as soon as they began to drift back into the playroom. She handed a drum and sticks to Ronald, a dark-haired, thin-faced boy, who showed signs of scurvy. 'This for me?' he asked, looking amazed.

'Yes. And I want you to bang it nice and loud.'

'But Mam says I've to be quiet and behave meself,' he said.

'Not during music time,' said Nellie, giving him a brief hug.

She gave out the rest of the instruments and told the children to make as much noise as they wanted and to march once she started singing. This time she did not mind being the focus of at least ten pairs of wide eyes as she seated herself at the piano and began to play and sing 'We're Soldiers of the King, Melads'.

Slowly but gradually the noise level increased as the children banged, shook, chimed and got into step. Several bumped into each other but no harm was done and soon they were marching in some semblance of order. She thought that in the weeks to come she would teach them a few simple songs, as well as so many other things. They could draw and paint, do jigsaws. She would read them stories and take them on nature walks as the weather warmed up, just short ones around the garden at first. For the first time in weeks she felt content.

What Nellie called 'real spring' arrived in the Lake District sometime towards the end of April. By then she had something else on her mind besides her small charges. She had missed a couple of periods and had suffered from morning sickness since her arrival. While delighted to be having Teddy's baby, she was determined to keep her condition a secret as long as possible for fear that, once it was out, she would be sacked. The thought of what she'd do if that happened worried her enormously.

She had written to her sisters and brother telling them where she was living, but had not heard back from them. She had refrained from pouring out her hurt to Teddy, thinking that he had enough on his plate with having to face the Italians and Germans in Libya, but she wrote to him about the baby, knowing that he would be just as thrilled as she was. In the meantime, she would carry on working and saving as much money as possible. She sighed, wishing she could talk to someone about her situation. As it was, despite making good use of her time in the countryside getting to know the mothers, she still felt something of an outsider being 'miss' to them.

The women spent their time helping with the housework and cooking, knitting for the men in the Forces whilst listening to the wireless, as well as looking after the babies and tiny tots amongst them. Some made the effort to go into Ambleside and brought back sweets and newspapers. Others 'oohed' and 'aahed' over the films and dances taking place in Kendal or Morecambe advertised in the local *Gazette*. Nellie would have enjoyed seeing Ivor Novello's *The Dancing Years* at the Winter

Gardens in Morecambe but had to forgo that pleasure because of the distance and cost.

It had taken Nellie some time getting used to the country sounds at night: the screech of an owl, the baa of a sheep, the wind in the trees when a storm blew up. Despite the beauty of the countryside, the war could not be forgotten: occasionally the noise of aeroplanes could be heard and Mrs James spoke of the shipyards at Barrow being their target. Nellie would pray for the people there, as well as her loved ones. Posters went up in the village promoting Ambleside and Windermere's joint fundraising effort for War Weapons Week, and there was news of a war casualty – the pilot grandson of a Mr Lupton of Ambleside.

Then, on a beautiful morning towards the end of the second week in May, Nellie received a letter. She had been hoping for one from Teddy in response to her news about the baby but this was addressed in her brother's sprawling hand. The sight of it caused her a mixture of delight and apprehension and she was about to slit it open with a finger when someone called her and she remembered that the children were assembled in the hall for a nature walk.

She pocketed the letter and ushered them outside. The smell of wood smoke was in the air, mingling with the scent of hawthorn blossom and gorse. Birds twittered and warbled and she pointed out birds on the wing, carrying scraps of tawny dried grass or grubs in their beaks, explaining to the children that this meant they were building nests to lay their eggs. She thought how different these surroundings were from the city streets and felt a pang of homesickness. She asked the children what they missed most about home.

'I miss my dad,' said Ronald.

'The shops and the river,' put in another boy.

'What do you like about the countryside?' she asked.

'No bombs to blow us up,' said a rosy faced girl called Ruth, jigging about.

Nellie agreed. 'That's why we're here, isn't it?'

They nodded solemnly and a couple said, 'Yes, miss.'

Nellie suggested they look for wild flowers and see if they could spot any bees, butterflies or other insects. They ran off happily and she settled down on a fallen tree trunk and took out Francis' letter.

Dear Nellie,
There is no easy way of telling you this, so I might as well get straight to the point. Mam and Aunt Josie are dead.

She stilled, conscious of the thud, thud, thud of her heartbeat, and reread those last six words. *Mam and Aunt Josie are dead.*

'I don't believe it,' she murmured, and read them again before continuing.

I don't know if you're aware but Liverpool has suffered a week of devastating air raids. Mam and Lottie were visiting Aunt Josie when a raid started. You know how stubborn Aunt Josie was. Anyway, she refused to go to the shelter and a high explosive went off right in front of the house. They were both killed but thank God Lottie survived, even though she was buried for several hours. She is in Southport hospital now, her hip is broken and so is her left leg. She's been asking for you and so I told her that I would write.

Lottie apart, you're going to have to come home to look after Grandfather and Babs. She's of an age when she needs an eye keeping on her and the old man can't do it. She'd have him running round in circles trying to keep up with her and that won't do. Also, the match-works received a direct hit so she's going to have to find another job.

I can guess how you must feel about the loss of Mam but from what Babs told me, you mustn't reproach yourself. It seems Mam had kept the letters you sent to the girls and hid them away before they could see them. Both have been waiting to hear from you, certain you'd have kept in touch, and were hurt when you didn't write. Anyway, Babs found your letters in Mam's insurance policy box and that upset us all.

I'm hoping I can depend on you, Nell, to do what I ask. Your marrying outside the church without coming and talking to me beforehand caused me pain. Mother wanted you excommunicated but I couldn't do that to you. Besides, I've been stretched to the limit dealing with the sorrow caused by the bombing in my own parish and that is why I put off writing to you.

Yours,

Francis.

Tears welled up in Nellie's eyes and she returned the letter to its envelope. There was no doubt in her mind that she would have to do what her brother asked. She did not want to leave the children in her care, but family came first. She would have to serve her notice and go. Calling the children, she spent a few minutes inspecting and commenting on the wild flowers and odd beetle they had found, before hurrying them back to the house.

Chapter Two

It was June before Nellie was able to get away but she wrote to Francis and Babs telling them when she would be home. Tears were shed when it came to her taking leave of the children, but she said that she hoped to see them when they returned to Liverpool.

'Some of us mightn't be long following you,' said a mother. 'My fella said there hasn't been any raids worth mentioning since the May blitz.'

'See you around, then,' said Nellie, smiling as she climbed into the pony and trap taking her into Ambleside, from where she would catch a bus to Windermere railway station. She had quite a journey before her and planned to go into Southport, where Lottie was convalescing, before going home. She intended on writing a letter to Teddy on the train, bringing him up to date about her movements. She was worried about her husband because she had not received an answer to the letter she had sent telling him about the baby. Of course, letters did go missing during wartime. The German U-boats were still wreaking havoc with British shipping. She could only pray that was the problem, terrible as the thought of ships being blown up was, and Teddy was OK.

Once settled on the train at Windermere, Nellie took out her fountain pen and pad and began to write:

Dearest Teddy,

I am sitting on the train, watching the beautiful countryside go past, on my way back to Liverpool. I've become used to the hills and the fresh country air, so it's going to feel strange being back home again. As I haven't heard from you for several weeks, I don't know if you received my letter telling you about the baby or the one I wrote after Francis got in touch. If not, the good news is that I'm having a baby, which is due in October. I am thrilled to bits and now the morning sickness is over, I'm in the pink. As soon as I get home, I'll have to register with a midwife and find out what help I can get from the government when it comes to nourishing food, large clothes to cover my bump and the baby's layette. With the need for clothing coupons starting this month, I'm hoping there'll be extra for this expectant mum. I only wish you were here to share in the excitement with me because we've talked about having a baby, haven't we?

I have to confess to having had some worries about where to live once the time came for me to leave High View. As you know, Mam had told me not to darken the doors again. Hopefully, Grandfather will be pleased to see me but I'm getting ahead of myself.

Mam and Aunt Josie were killed in the blitz and Francis says I'm needed at home. I was so shocked I couldn't believe it at first. Well, I just hope the pair of them get into Heaven. I won't say anymore on that score.

Poor Lottie was injured but I will soon be seeing for myself just how bad she is. Babs says she can't walk but hopefully that isn't a permanent state. Babs has found herself another job as an invoice clerk because the match-works was blitzed, but I don't know how long she'll last there as she said there's only old women in the office and they boss her around. By 'old' she probably means twenty-five or thirty.

How are things with you, sweetheart? I hope you're not suffering from the heat too much having spent so many months up in Scotland. I do so miss you and even the memory of that lovely honeymoon in Southport can't make up for not having you with me, my handsome, wonderful husband.

At least I feel my time in Cumberland has not been wasted. All that I've learnt about small children will stand me in good stead when I have ours. Boy or girl, it does not matter to me as long as he or she is healthy and all there. If it's a boy I can just imagine you taking him to Goodison and cheering the Blues on, and if it's a girl I know you'll want her dressed in pretty frocks and for her to have the best things in life.

I love you lots and wish we could be together. Kisses and hugs and keep your head down,

Your very own,
Nellie.
XXXXX

There were tears in her eyes as she folded the letter and placed it in an envelope, which she kissed after sealing it. Hopefully, there wouldn't be too many delays on her journey and she would reach Southport in time to post it.

Nellie was in luck, arriving at a handy time in the resort where the sun was shining. She followed her brother's instructions to a T and found the convalescent home, which was a requisitioned hotel adapted for helping the wounded recover for the duration of the war. She expected the meeting with Lottie to be an emotional one and was not mistaken. As soon as Nellie walked into the small ward and saw her sister sitting in bed, looking, if Nellie was honest, rather like a stranded whale, her eyes filled with tears.

'Oh, love,' she said unsteadily. 'What a thing to happen!'

'Nellie!' Lottie's plump cheeks trembled and her chins wobbled as she held out her arms to her. 'I thought you'd never come.'

Not wanting to hurt her, Nellie hugged her sister as best she could. Lottie wept on her shoulder and it was some minutes before she gained control of herself. 'I couldn't even get to the funeral,' she said, sniffing and wiping her damp face with the back of her hand, 'but Francis said all was done as it should be. They've been buried at Ford cemetery. I'd have liked a marble angel for their grave but he said that Grandfather wouldn't fork out for it and Dad definitely won't.' Anger twisted her face. 'May the Holy Mother and our Saviour forgive me but I don't think either of them has a heart.' Her grey eyes filled with tears again.

Nellie fumbled in her pocket and produced a crumpled handkerchief. 'Here, use this, and stop getting worked up about them. You should have realised by now that the only member of the family Dad cares about is Babs. Francis said he's yet to have a reply to the letter he sent telling Dad about Mam and Aunt Josie's deaths.'

'That doesn't surprise me,' muttered Lottie, mopping her face with the handkerchief. 'I don't know how he and Mam ever came to get married. They certainly didn't have time for each other when he was home.'

Nellie nodded. 'It's a mystery to me, too. But maybe they loved each other once.'

Lottie handed the handkerchief back to Nellie and pushed back her lank mousy hair from her forehead. 'You must love Teddy Lachlan a lot to go against Mam and Grandfather the way you did and marry outside the faith.'

Nellie's blue-green eyes lit up as she pocketed the handkerchief. 'I love him to bits. He's a good man. Remember how he bought us girls ice-creams from the Italian ice-cream cart at the Pierhead years ago? It must have broke him but he was a generous soul even then.'

Lottie sighed. 'It's just a pity he's not a Catholic soul.'

Nellie frowned. 'Don't start on religion, Lottie. Teddy has his way of worshipping God just like we do. The main difference, as you know, with Proddies is that they have no time for the Pope...or priests for that matter...although, Teddy and Francis used to get on OK years ago.'

Lottie's eyes widened. 'It's not just that, Nellie, some of them don't have any respect for the host.'

Nellie groaned. 'Forget it, Lot. You're never going to convince Teddy that bread and wine becomes the flesh and blood of our Lord. Now stop this or I'll walk out of here right now and I won't give you the chocolate I bought you. Although, perhaps I shouldn't have done so but there's no bananas or oranges to be had.' As she produced the bar of Fry's Chocolate Cream, Lottie almost snatched it out of her hand.

'My favourite. You are generous, Nellie, especially as you'd have had to use some of your sweet ration for this.'

'You're my sister and I was willing to make the sacrifice because I don't want to put on too much weight myself.' Nellie placed a hand against the material covering the soft swell of her belly.

Lottie stared at her. 'There's hardly anything of you.'

'There'll be a lot more of me soon.'

'Why?'

Nellie rolled her eyes. 'Never mind. I'll tell you another time. So do you want to talk about what happened or don't you want to think about it?'

Lottie was only too ready to discuss the experience of being buried alive. The awfulness of feeling as if she had the weight of most of the house pressing down on her. She said with a shiver, 'I was terrified when I could smell leaking gas and then there was the drip, drip of water and shifting of rubble...not knowing if I would ever get out alive was awful. As for Mam and Aunt Josie...I don't want to think about them being blown up.' She swallowed and offered a piece of chocolate to Nellie.

She shook her head. 'You enjoy it.'

Lottie sighed. 'I wonder if you can get Fry's Chocolate Cream in Heaven.'

'God only knows,' murmured Nellie, amused.

'I suppose not,' said Lottie, looking doleful. 'Gluttony's one of the seven deadly sins, so it'll probably be forbidden. I did pray, Nellie, to Our Lady, Saint Joseph and every other saint I could remember to get me out, and they did.'

'I hope you thanked your rescuers.'

'Of course, between screams. The pain, I'd never felt anything like it. I thought I'd die when they moved me.'

'Well, you're here to tell the tale,' said Nellie, and continued to listen to her sister filling her in on her operation and what had happened after that. Nellie, although wanting to hear her sister's tale, was exhausted and only just about managed to prevent herself from nodding off by getting up off the chair. 'I don't want to leave you, Lot, but I'm going to have to. I've been travelling for hours and I'm whacked. I've got to get home yet.'

Lottie's face fell. 'I wish I could come with you but they say it'll be a few weeks yet.'

'Me too,' said Nellie, bending to kiss her. 'But as soon as you're on your feet I'll be back for you.'

'Thanks, Nell. But you will come to see me again before then?'

'You bet,' she said.

On reaching the door, Nellie turned and waved to her sister.

Lottie waved back.

Nellie left and headed for the railway station.

An hour later she got off the train at Seaforth and crossed the road, passing the auctioneers of Litherland and Outwaite, the Railway Arms and the Litherland Boys Club as she made for the Lift Bridge over the LeedsLiverpool canal. It was situated right by her father's favourite drinking house when he was home, the Red Lion.

As Nellie crossed to the other side of the canal, she remembered her great-great-aunt telling her that in the old days before the lift bridge and a proper road was built to Ford cemetery, the coffin would be carried across a wooden bridge. The mourners would trail after it and what with the weight of them all the bridge would creak and groan as if in sympathy. No wonder some called it the Bridge of Sighs. She chided herself for thinking of coffins and burials and making herself miserable.

Of course, it was natural she would be thinking of such things, knowing her mother and aunt were buried at Ford. She would need to visit their grave and pay her respects and leave flowers. Perhaps Babs would go with her. She strode past the shops situated opposite the newly built town hall, which housed the council offices, remembering when farm cottages had stood where the shops were now. The need for more homes, promised to those who'd fought in the so-called 'war to end all wars', had resulted in the cottages' destruction. It was an attempt to turn

Britain into a land fit for heroes. In the Thirties new housing had sprung up on farmland and the young couples who had moved in had needed shops: a bakery, a fishmonger's and greengrocer's, a Co-op, a hairdresser's, a chandler's, a chemist and a cobbler's-cum-shoe shop. A park had even been laid out with bowling greens, a paddling pool and swings for the children.

Her grandfather's house was a short distance away in a crescent known as Litherland Park. There was a chestnut tree either side of the front gate and, predictably, the house was called The Chestnuts. Having been away for several months, Nellie viewed it with new eyes and thought it could do with a coat of paint. Not much chance of that, though, with there being a war on, she thought.

The front gate was warped and not easy to open. She placed her holdall and gasmask box on the ground and was struggling with the gate when a familiar voice said, 'So, you're back, about time too!'

Nellie spun round, saw Mrs Wainwright and groaned inwardly. She recalled that the old woman had been widowed during the Boer War and knew she should be more tolerant of her.

The old woman scurried towards Nellie with hands tucked mandarin-fashion in the sleeves of a pink cardigan. Freeing one of them, she pointed at Nellie. 'Francis did say you were coming but it seems ages ago. Your grandfather won't let you in, you know!'

'They had to find a replacement for me,' said Nellie. 'So tell me why won't Grandfather open the door?'

Mrs Wainwright's lips tightened. 'He's become very suspicious of people.' She raised thinly pencilled eyebrows. 'His language is atrocious, to put it mildly. He seldom goes out, has the groceries delivered by the messenger boy from the Co-op. Surprisingly, he's also employed the boy to work in the garden digging for victory. Although, no doubt he'll soon be going off to fight.'

'What about Babs? Surely Grandfather opens the door to her?'

Mrs Wainwright snorted, blowing down her nostrils just like a horse. 'She has to go round the back. Sometimes the door's locked and it's bang-bang-bang-bang. Occasionally it's been after ten o'clock in the evening and the noise is enough to wake the dead. Sorry about your mother and aunt, by the way, you'll know Lottie's in a convalescent home.'

'Of course. I visited her on the way here. Now if you'll excuse me it's been a long day and I'm tired.' Nellie pushed the gate with some force with her hip and that did the trick. She bid Mrs Wainwright a good evening and picking up her baggage, made to go up the path, pausing when she heard her name being called. She turned and watched Babs running towards her and blinked back tears, determined not to cry. She'd had enough emotion for one day. Her younger sister, who bore a striking resemblance to the singing star Deanna Durban, was looking attractive in a green jacket and matching skirt. Babs not only possessed a figure that would have looked good in a sack but also had great hair beneath the yellow and green patterned headscarf; she could have posed for the artist Titian with that red hair of hers.

Nellie dropped her baggage and held out her arms. Babs flung herself at her, squeezing Nellie so tightly that she could scarcely breathe.

'Watch it,' gasped Nellie, remembering the baby. 'You'd think you hadn't seen me for a year.'

'It does seem ages,' said Babs, freeing her and stepping back. Sparkling green eyes scrutinised Nellie from head to toe. 'You look well. You've put weight on. It must be all that country air and good farm food.'

Nellie smiled. 'Don't make me laugh. Some of the mothers couldn't cook for toffee. I look fatter because I'm having a baby.'

Babs' jaw dropped and, for several seconds, she did not speak.

Then she took a deep breath. 'I wonder what Mam and Aunt Josie would have made of that news.'

Nellie's expression sobered. 'It's something I haven't dwelt on. I'd like to believe that it would have softened their hearts, but I never could tell which way they would take things I was made up about, so I gave up trying to please them. Remember how they were both completely against my training to be a kindergarten teacher?'

'That was because Great-great-aunt Adelaide was in favour of it. You know she and Mam hated each other.'

Nellie was shocked by her sister's use of the word 'hate'. 'I know they didn't get on. I put that down to them being so different.'

Babs picked up Nellie's holdall. 'You're too nice, Nell. I would have thought working with children would have made you realise that most human beings fight tooth and claw to be top dog and get what they want. Mam was jealous as hell of our great-great-aunt for owning this house. She was mad when the old woman left it to Grandfather and thought Dad should have got it. She'd have been in a different position then but, instead, he ruled the roost and she continued to fill the role of housekeeper.'

'How do you know all this?' asked Nellie, grabbing her gasmask box and following Babs up the path.

'I didn't have my nose in a book half the time I was home, or playing the piano the other half.' Babs chuckled. 'No offence meant, Nell. But I watch people and keep my ears open.' The light in her eyes died suddenly. 'Pity I wasn't home when the postman called when your letters were delivered: I never thought Mam could be so sneaky.'

Nellie sighed. 'We can't know all there is to know about people.'

Babs nodded.

'So how has Francis taken Mam's death? Although he's written to me, he hasn't said anything about his feelings,' said Nellie.

'He didn't seem to take it in at first but I think that was down to his already being exhausted and shocked by the sights he'd seen in his parish after the Luftwaffe tried to beat Liverpool into the ground. In a way, I think he was glad to be on what he called "the frontline" for once. I think he feels it not being in the Forces.'

Nellie's heart sank. 'You don't think he'll go and volunteer?'

Babs shrugged. 'I've no idea. He's always been one for playing his cards close to his chest. Anyway, let's not think about it now. You've got Grandfather to face.' She stopped in front of the house.

Nellie knocked on the door. The sound echoed through the house and she listened for her grandfather's footsteps, but all was still. She banged with her fist on the wood again, louder this time, but still there was no response. 'Mrs Wainwright said he's been refusing to open the door to people,' she said, turning to Babs.

Her sister giggled. 'He wouldn't open up to her…thinks she's got her eye on him since Mam went…but he has been acting peculiar…the old biddy's right about that. He locked me out last night, so I ended up staying at a friend's.' Babs went over to one of the bay windows and, standing on tiptoe, she peered inside before signalling to Nellie. 'Come and have a look in here.'

Nellie followed her over and stretched up to look through the window. Her eyes widened as she saw newspapers spread over the sideboard, on the sofa, easy chairs and the piano. 'What on earth is he playing at?'

'God only knows. When I ask he says it saves money.'

Nellie moved away from the window. 'Is he in, d'you think?'

'Probably. I think he's going deaf as well as daft.'

'Shall we go round the back?'

Babs nodded. 'I generally do. Although, he might have the door locked.' Her pretty face darkened. 'One of these days I'll give him a fright by smashing a window pane and unbolting the door and breaking in.'

They walked round the side of the house and the setting sun dazzled Nellie as she came out of the shade onto the back of the house. Shielding her eyes with a hand, she gazed over the garden. The lawn had been dug up and rows of sprouting plants showed above the soil. At the bottom of the garden there were several fruit trees. But there was no sign of her grandfather.

'He must be inside,' said Nellie, absently stroking the ginger tom that sat cleaning itself on top of the bin.

'You go and look,' said Babs, placing the holdall on the ground. 'He might want a few words with you on your own. I'll have a ciggie out here. He goes mad if he sees me smoking.'

'I should think so, too,' said Nellie, becoming the big sister. 'When did you take that up?'

Babs grimaced as she reached into a pocket and produced a packet of five Woodbines and matches. 'It hasn't been much fun here on my own with him, you know? He chunters on to himself and I don't know what he's saying then. Sometimes it's been a bit scary. I'm really glad you're back.'

Nellie squeezed Babs' shoulder lightly and, picking up her holdall, walked past the outside toilet and outhouse towards the washroom door. She did not bother knocking but turned the knob. To her relief the door opened and she stepped inside. All was quiet. She hurried across the red quarry-tiled floor to the door that led to the kitchen, opened it and went through.

The kitchen was large and bright and Nellie had loved it since she was a little girl. Her great-great-aunt might not have done much in the way of housekeeping and cooking the main meals but, on occasions, she had encouraged Nellie to help her make gingerbread men and lemon cheese and jam tarts, and in autumn the sweet fragrance of stewing apples and plums had filled the kitchen. They would bottle the fruit or make pie. Suddenly she felt like crying because those times would never come again.

There were signs of occupation. A coal fire glowed in the black-leaded range and on the draining board was a dirty saucepan filled with water. The sink was piled high with crockery and cutlery. Nellie frowned, remembering Babs had been locked out last night. Like most men, Grandfather had never lifted a finger on the domestic front.

She sniffed. Something smelt rotten.

Following her nose she went over to the walk-in larder and there on a shelf were several plates. She peered closer at one; what was that moving? She gagged. Maggots! Her stomach heaved and she backed out of the larder in a hurry.

Something pressed between her shoulder blades. 'I'm armed. Make any sudden move and you're dead,' rasped a voice.

Nellie's heart was already beating fit to beat the band and now she thought it would burst from her chest. 'Grandfather, is that you?' she gasped.

Whatever was digging into her back was removed and, turning, she saw her grandfather holding a walking stick. 'Helen, what are you doing poking about in my larder?'

She did not answer immediately but gazed at his unkempt figure. His white hair was shaggy and he badly needed a shave; his navy-blue trousers were shiny with age and baggy at the knees, his soiled blue shirt was minus several buttons and revealed a grubby buttoned-up vest underneath. She swallowed a sigh, thinking he was a lot untidier than last time she had seen him. Since his Aunt Adelaide's death he had started to let himself go. 'I was looking for you.'

'In the larder?' he said, leaning on the walking stick.

'Something smelt horrible.' She shook her head at him. 'There's maggots in there. Whatever they're eating should have been got rid of.'

'Frightened of a few maggots, are you, girl?' He chortled. 'I'll just put a match to them and that'll get rid of them. The meat will be OK.'

Nellie gazed at him in horror. 'You've no intention of eating it? You'll poison yourself.'

The amusement ebbed from his weather-beaten features. 'If you'd had to eat what I've had to eat to survive, my girl, then you wouldn't be so fussy. Sixty years I served under sail and steam and often we went without sight of land for weeks, existing on worm ridden biscuits and dried up salted meat. When we did fetch up at an island, we had to hunt and kill our food, that's if we weren't hunted ourselves by the natives and eaten.'

Nellie had never heard her grandfather speak of such things before, but then, just like her father, he had spent most of his time at sea. 'You're saying you nearly ended up in a cooking pot?' Then immediately she shook her head. 'No! You're having me on.'

Grandfather looked injured. 'Saying I'm a liar, Helen, isn't the way to worm yourself into my good books.'

She was unrepentant. 'You must have a stomach like a goat if you can eat that meat and survive.'

He grinned, showing a set of dentures that needed a good soak. 'I'm as tough as old boots but never mind that now. How about making me a cup of tea?'

Nellie was not averse to making tea. She was desperate for a cup herself but she made sure she washed the crockery thoroughly first. She was putting milk into cups, when Babs appeared in the doorway. 'So here you are, Grandfather. Didn't you hear us banging on the front door?' She placed the gasmask holders on the table, pulled out a chair and sat down.

He scowled at her. 'Get to your feet, girl! You don't sit in my company until I tell you,' he rasped. 'The trouble with you young ones today is that you've no respect for your elders.'

'I've plenty of respect, Grandfather, but I'm tired and my sitting down isn't doing you any harm.' Babs smiled up at him. 'Anyway, aren't you pleased that Nellie's back?'

He glared at her from beneath bristling eyebrows. 'I bet you are. You don't do a tap in this house...think you can twist me round your little finger. I'm not our Bernard, you know? He spoilt you.'

Babs folded her arms and said challengingly, 'You know that's not true. I might be his favourite but he's never spent enough time in this house to spoil me. A prezzie once or twice a year if I was lucky and he made landfall in Liverpool.'

'All right, you've made your point,' he mumbled, moving over to the table and sitting opposite her. He waved a gnarled, blue-veined hand in Nellie's direction. 'Give us that tea, girl, and sit yourself down.'

Nellie placed cups and saucers in front of him and Babs before fetching her own. Avoiding the chair with a wobbly leg, she sat to the right of Babs and took a mouthful of tea before saying, 'So, Grandfather, is it OK with you if I come back and live here?'

'I think you'd better. I'll soon be dead if I'm left to the mercies of this one.' He indicated Babs with a jerk of his head. 'Carmel would have done for me if she could. She was trying to poison me, you know? That sister of hers was a bit of a witch, mixed potions.'

Nellie blinked at him. 'Don't be daft, Grandfather! Mam wouldn't have poisoned you.'

'He's said this before,' said Babs with a shrug. 'I've told him Aunt Josie made herbal medicines...remedies she knew from Ireland.'

Grandfather fixed her with a stare. 'That's what she wanted you to believe, girl.' He was silent for several moments and, when he spoke again, his words stunned his granddaughters. 'Carmel wasn't the wife I wanted for Bernard. She tricked him into marriage but he was too besotted with her to see that at the time. Probably that old witch gave him a love potion.'

'What d'you mean tricked?' blurted out Babs.

'Use your nous, girl,' he growled. 'She led him astray and he had no choice but to wed her.'

'You mean she was having a baby?' asked Nellie.

'It's the only reason he would have married her. She was a handsome woman but she wasn't the right one for him. I could tell you things...' His voice trailed off.

Nellie was annoyed that the blame for her mother's

pregnancy should be laid only at Carmel's door. 'It takes two to tango, Grandfather.'

'Yes, but she shouldn't have led him onto the dance floor. Of course, I never let Joseph know he'd been conceived out of wedlock.' His voice cracked. 'I loved that boy. It broke my heart when he was killed.'

'We all loved Joe,' said Nellie, glancing at her sister. Babs rolled her eyes and got up and left the kitchen.

Grandfather wiped a hand across his eyes and then cleared his throat. 'So you're needing a berth. You thought of your old grandfather and are hoping he'll take pity on you.'

Nellie was not having that. 'I married Joe's best mate if you remember? Francis said *you* needed me and that's why I'm here. I had a nice berth up in Cumberland.'

The old man looked uncertain. 'So that's where you went. Where is he now?'

'Libya.'

'Not a navy man?'

'No. I'd best tell you that I'm having a baby,' said Nellie firmly. 'It's due in October. So if you feel that you can't cope with a baby in the house, then you'd better say so now and I'll find somewhere else to live.' She crossed her fingers.

He was silent, staring at her. 'According to Aunt Adelaide, you were a good baby, Helen. Joseph was a rascal, into everything. Perhaps you'll have a boy. You can call him Joseph.'

Nellie thought that if Teddy was in agreement and the baby was a boy, she wouldn't mind one of his names being Joseph. Edward Joseph; she liked that. 'It is a nice name,' she said diplomatically.

'A saint's name. Which reminds me...your sister...the ugly one, is in hospital somewhere.'

Nellie almost snapped his nose off. 'Lottie is not ugly! And she's in a convalescent home. I've already seen her and you could have visited her, too, had you a mind to!'

He nodded his shaggy head. 'Don't shout. You'll keep the

place tidy, Helen, do the washing and cook the meals. There's the garden…although, I have a lad, Billy, who comes in. I'll want every penny accounted for. At least you being married and having a baby means you won't have to go out and work for the war effort.'

Nellie agreed, thinking that he definitely was not as daft as Babs said. She'd be working her guts out, doing an unpaid job that she wouldn't have chosen in a million years. Hopefully, she would feel differently about housework when Teddy came home and they had a place of their own. She went off into a dream, picturing him and her and the baby living happily together after the war.

Her grandfather's voice interrupted her imaginings. 'Teddy will be sending you money, so you can chip in with some. You have your ration book?'

'Yes, I have my ration book,' said Nellie, thinking he had a nerve expecting money from her as well as work. She drained her cup. 'I'll take my things upstairs and then I'll go to the chippie. I'm starving and the last thing I want to eat is a plateful of maggots.' She left the table before he could stop her and, picking up her things, hurried out of the room.

Nellie climbed the stairs to the first landing, which was long and wide with six doors opening on to it. Once the wooden floor had been varnished and highly polished, but now it was dull and scratched and the carpet runner needed a good beating. She deposited her things on the landing, then went into the lavatory and had to hold her nose as she put down the seat. The pan was stained and she knew her first job would be to clean it. Her feelings towards Babs were not warm at that moment. How could her sister put up with such filth! There was a toilet brush in the corner but Vim was needed. After pulling the chain, she went into the bathroom where there were double cupboards from floor to ceiling. She opened the bottom one and found a half-empty container of Vim and a couple of cloths. She scrubbed and wiped the lavatory bowl and seat and then went into the bathroom and cleaned the sink and washed her hands again. When she emerged Babs was calling her name.

Nellie found her sister in one of the back bedrooms, which was crammed with a double bed that had been passed down from their parents and shared by the three sisters until Adelaide had died, when Nellie had taken over her room. There was also a tallboy and a chest of drawers, on top of which stood a Madonna and Child, mantled in a layer of dust. Nellie did not mince her words. 'You lazy so-and-so! I can't understand you. I'm not interested in housework but I couldn't put up with the state of that toilet.'

Babs' face reddened. 'I know it's terrible. I kept meaning to do it but he made such a mess every morning and was in there for a heck of a long time that, in the end, I got into the habit of using the outside one. Sorry, Nell. I told myself Mam would have had a fit if she'd seen it but that only made me feel worse in a way. I was so upset when she and Aunt Josie were killed I did go a bit to pieces. Now you're here, I will try and pull my weight.'

Nellie's anger dissolved. 'Sorry for shouting but I don't like cleaning toilets either. I know someone has to do it but it was always Mam in the past. Maybe we took her for granted too much.'

'But she never asked us to do any housework, did she?' said Babs. 'Dad used to say that she had a martyr complex.'

Nellie nodded. 'I remember her complaining that she was the only one who ever did anything round here. I offered to do the polishing.'

'She said that in front of me. I remember the old woman told her that she should be thankful that she had a roof over her head and that she and Grandfather were prepared to feed us all and help buy our clothes.'

Nellie frowned. 'Dad must have kept her short. I suppose we shouldn't be talking about Mam in such a way. She worked hard all her life. None of us are perfect and she did do a lot for the family.'

Babs nodded. 'I wouldn't talk about her to anyone outside the family. Which reminds me, what did you think of what Grandfather said about Mam and Dad having to get married? You could have knocked me down with a feather.'

'I was stunned. She was always so religious. Poor Mam.' She glanced about the room. 'Are you OK sleeping on your own? Or would you like me to share with you for a while?'

Babs smiled. 'I'm glad you offered. I'll be happy to share the bed with you. I never thought I'd miss our Lottie's company but I've had nightmares since Mam was killed. We can rethink when Lottie comes home.'

'Lottie's more likely to need a bed to herself because of her injuries, and she's put on more weight,' said Nellie. 'She can have my room because there's a three-foot single bed in there.'

'That's generous of you,' said Babs.

Neither suggested using the bedroom that had been their parents', while their father was at sea, both certain he would not like them doing so.

After collecting Nellie's few possessions, they discussed their sister's condition, wondering when she would be home.

Nellie took bedding from the drawer at the bottom of the tallboy. The sheets were old and darned in several places. One had been turned outsides in and sewn up the middle. Make do and mend, she thought, remembering seeing her mother sew them. Sadness swept over her and she wished that they could have been closer, but Carmel had always kept her daughters at a distance; it was the younger of her sons she had chosen to be her favourite.

'Does Francis visit much since Mam was killed?' asked Nellie.

'Not really. He's kept busy in the parish. I should think we'll be seeing him soon now you're back. He'll have things he'll want to say to you.'

Nellie hoped he would not go on at her about having married a Protestant. Once the bed was remade with clean sheets, she told Babs that she was going to the chippie and went downstairs. She could hear the wireless, so popped her head into the parlour and saw that Grandfather had removed several sheets of newspaper so he could sit down and listen to *In Town Tonight*.

When she asked if he wanted any chips, his response was, 'Who's paying?'

'Me,' she replied.

'I'll have some, then,' he said with a grin.

She had thought as much, and, leaving the house, headed for the fish and chip shop in School Lane, where the Catholic parish church of English Martyrs was situated. It was months since she had been to church and thought it was unlikely she would set foot in this one for a time. No doubt her mother had confessed to the priest that Nellie had married outside the church. Perhaps *he* had excommunicated her? How would she know if he had? If she went to another church and did not confess what her mother would have called the error of her ways to a priest, how were they to know she'd married a Proddy? She smiled at the prospect. If she felt like going to church at some time, then she would go and not worry about being excommunicated.

Of course, when she told Francis about the baby, he would certainly have something to say about the need for it to be baptised in the Catholic faith. If her mother and grandfather had played their cards right, then Teddy probably would have agreed if Nellie had wished it. As it was, her mother had put his back up by calling him a heretic. She then got to wondering if Francis might turn up tomorrow. If he did, then she'd best be prepared and have her answers ready.

Chapter Three

Nellie woke to the sound of birdsong and, for a few seconds, thought she was back in Ambleside. Then the memories of yesterday trickled in and she turned her head to see if Babs was awake, but the space beside her was empty.

Nellie rose and went over to the window. Moving aside the blackout curtain she gazed down at the back garden. Most of it was in shadow but the sun was shining on the fruit trees. How peaceful it looked. Thank God that the Luftwaffe had gone away. If only Teddy were here instead of in Africa. He had loved this time of year, when a day out meant not having to come back until eleven because of the long summer evenings. She prayed that he would survive the war and her dream of having a happy home with him and the baby would come true. She felt a sudden rippling sensation in her belly and, convinced it was the baby moving, a thrill raced through her. She had been aware of similar tiny sensations but this one was stronger, which meant she must visit the doctor soon so she could be referred a reliable midwife.

She dressed, washed her hands and face and went downstairs. She found Babs in the kitchen, drinking a glass of water as she gazed through the window. The ginger tom came over to Nellie and stropped her legs.

'I think it wants some milk but there isn't any left,' said Babs, without looking round.

'I should have thought to get some last night when I went out to the chippie,' said Nellie, checking the bread bin and finding only a crust. 'Same with bread.' She smiled wryly.

'I ate the last for breakfast.' Babs paused. 'Remember Mam and Aunt Josie taking us on the ferry across the Mersey just for a change from Seaforth Sands?'

Nellie experienced a flood of nostalgia. 'Of course, I do. I was twelve last time we went. They liked New Brighton because of the fair and it had nice sand. We always had to be careful at Seaforth because of the sinking sands. I remember at New

Brighton they'd watch us paddle in the seawater pool with our skirts tucked in our knickers. I'd have to hold yours and Lottie's hands because they worried about you two going out of your depth. I'd want to have a swim but wasn't allowed to. The pair of them would gossip away, handing out jam butties when we said we were hungry and giving us drinks of Aunt Josie's homemade dandelion and burdock.'

'It was always just us girls.'

'Joe and Francis were too old for making sandcastles by then,' murmured Nellie, a catch in her throat, 'and even when Dad was home, he never came with us. Remember getting sand inside the leg of your knickers? It didn't half chaff!'

'Happy days,' said Babs softly. 'When I was a bit older, Dad used to take me places. He took me to see his ship once, and to the park to listen to a brass band. I remember him bringing me a frock home. I think it was from China. It was pink and white and I loved it but Mam told him he needed glasses because the pink clashed with my hair. I'll never forget the look on his face. I hated her for that but because he wanted me to wear it, I did. I loved the feel of the material, it was all silky soft. I wondered if she was jealous because I don't remember him bringing her anything.' Babs turned to face Nellie and a solitary tear rolled down her cheek. 'I hope if I ever marry that me and my fella don't fall out of love.'

'Perhaps they never were in love,' murmured Nellie, going and putting an arm round her sister. 'He probably got carried away and she couldn't stop him. They married because they had no choice. Sad.'

Babs nodded and wiped away the tear with a finger. She glanced at the kitchen clock. 'I should be on my way now.'

'I'll walk with you as far as the shops,' said Nellie.

'Has Grandfather given you any money?'

Nellie shook her head. 'I've still some of my own.'

'I'll get my things,' said Babs.

While she did so, Nellie checked the larder and was relieved to see that the maggoty food had gone. She went in search of shopping bags and found a couple hanging on a hook next to her grandfather's mackintosh and cap in the washroom. Babs was ready by then and the pair of them left the house.

'So, d'you think you'll stick with this new job?' asked Nellie.

'No.' Babs turned her attractive little face towards her as they walked along the pavement. 'I decided I wanted to move half an hour ago. When the weather's like this I hate being indoors. I quite enjoy working in the garden.'

A startled Nellie said, 'You never have before.'

'I do now.'

'You're too young for the Women's Land Army.'

'It's something to think about, though, when I'm eighteen. In the meantime I'll try something else. I'm going to hand in my notice today. I wouldn't mind working in a shop or a restaurant, or at the pictures,' said Babs enthusiastically. 'There's a dry-cleaner's in Waterloo advertising for a counter assistant. Apparently, now clothes rationing has come in, they reckon they'll be doing more business because people won't be able to buy much in the way of new clothes. Dry cleaning means people will have to give their old ones the kiss of life,' she added with a smile.

Nellie found it hard to imagine Babs finding fulfilment in a dry-cleaner's, but kept her mouth shut about that and instead said, 'This youth Grandfather's taken on...'

'Billy.' Babs' eyes danced. 'What are you getting at?'

'I just wondered what he's like,' she said casually.

'You couldn't call him handsome but he's a worker. He reminds me of someone but I can't think who.' Babs' heels click-clacked on the pavement and her hips swayed seductively in the tight-fitting black skirt two inches above her knees. She clutched the straps of the bag and gasmask container that hung from her shoulder and glanced at the two men on the opposite side of the road.

'Much too old for you,' murmured Nellie.

Babs' lips twitched. 'I wasn't even thinking about that but you must admit, Nell, there's not much talent around these days with most of the young men in the Forces.'

'There's boys of your own age. Although, perhaps I shouldn't be encouraging you to think about going out with boys. Grandfather wouldn't be in favour and Dad would have a fit.'

'Dad would only get to know if someone told him.' Her green eyes fixed on Nellie's face. 'I can't see you telling him.'

'No, I seldom write to him because he's a lousy letter writer. Even so, I hope you don't start messing about with boys yet. Mam kept a real tight rein on me at your age.'

'Poor Nellie,' said Babs, sounding sympathetic. 'But don't think you have to take her place. You're far too young. I'm really glad you're back, though. Anyway, this is where we part.' They had come to the shops and Babs fluttered her fingers at her eldest sister and headed for the bus stop. Nellie watched her for a moment and then went into the bakery.

Babs climbed aboard the bus and went upstairs, intent on sitting in a front seat. She might not be a kid anymore but still loved gazing down on the traffic and people. If she was lucky, a youth called Ritchie would be keeping her a seat. They'd first noticed each other about a month ago but it had taken him a week to pluck up the courage to say 'Morning!' to her. Another couple of days had passed before he'd commented on the weather. Several more had gone by before he had introduced himself and asked her name. She found his shyness rather endearing, but then Billy had been slow in coming forward when he had first come to work in the garden. She put a bet on with herself that if Ritchie was there today then he would ask for a date.

Her eyes gleamed as she recognised his neatly cut hairstyle and imagined him saying to the barber, 'Short back and sides, please?' His neatness was one of the things she liked about him. He turned before she reached him and smiled. His smile was another thing that she found attractive. As he removed the haversack from the window seat next to him, she said, 'Morning, Ritchie.'

'Morning, Babs.' His brown eyes wore an expression similar to a dog that had spotted a juicy bone. She brushed past him and sat down, causing him to shift a little to give her more space. He took out a packet of cigarettes and offered it to her. 'Cigarette?'

'Thanks.' She watched him flick the wheel on the lighter before placing the end of the cigarette between her lips and lowering her head to the tiny flame. His generosity was another thing that made him acceptable to her. She thanked him again and said, 'So how are you this sunny morning?'

'All the better for seeing you,' he replied.

She flashed him a dimpling smile. 'You say the nicest things.'

He flushed. 'That's because you're nice to talk to and nice to look at.'

There was a pause as they both inhaled and then slowly allowed the smoke to trickle from their nostrils. She stretched out her legs and crossed shapely ankles. 'So are you doing anything exciting this weekend?'

'That depends on you.'

Her ears caught the slightest quiver in his voice and she warmed even more to him. 'In what way?'

'I wondered if you'd come to the pictures with me tomorrow?' The words came out in a rush.

'Maybe. What film were you planning on seeing?'

'*The Thief of Baghdad.* Sabu's playing the genie. It's on at the Trocadero in town.' He faced her. 'It'll be fun.'

'Sounds good to me,' said Babs, responding to his enthusiasm. 'There might even be a flying carpet. The heroine will be wearing Eastern costume with silky pants and a nice little top and a yashmak...and there'll be a real nasty baddie with a beard.'

Ritchie grinned. 'So you'll come?'

'Try and stop me,' said Babs with a chuckle, flicking ash from her cigarette. 'When and where shall we meet?'

He suggested seven o'clock at the bus stop where she normally got on this bus. Babs agreed without hesitation, even though it did mean she would be getting in after eleven. She would tell Nellie that she was going out with a friend and there would be no getting locked out tomorrow night because, knowing Nellie, she would wait up until she was safely in.

Nellie fought the temptation to break off another piece of the crusty fresh loaf as she walked round to the back of the house, but failed. She felt very tired this morning and reasoned with herself that not only had she had no breakfast but was feeding two. She ticked off in her mind the food she had bought, thinking she was bound to have forgotten something: porridge oats, sugar, bread, milk, onions, two pounds of potatoes because she was not sure what was in the garden, sausages, a tin of peas, two eggs and tiny portions of bacon, butter and cheese. She had also bought a morning paper for her grandfather.

Hanging up her jacket in the washroom, all seemed quiet in the house. She pushed open the kitchen door with her hip and struggled in with the loaded shopping bags, only to stop at the sight of her brother, who was bent over the fireplace, putting a match to the fire Babs had set last night. He must have heard her gasp because his head turned and he got up from his haunches.

Neither spoke. Not for the first time, Nellie was thinking the priesthood's gain was womanhood's loss. It wasn't that Francis was conventionally handsome, but there was a rugged attractiveness about him that surely caused a flutter in the breasts of many a woman in his congregation. He wore his clerical garb but was bare-headed and she noticed his hat on the windowsill. He had thick hair, which was the same shade of reddish-brown as her own.

'So you came,' he said, coming towards her and relieving her of her burdens.

'I said I would.' She flexed fingers, stiff from carrying the shopping bags. 'Where's Grandfather?'

'I presume he's still in bed. Babs gone to work?' Francis placed the shopping on the table.

'Yes. She said she's going to hand in her notice today and go after another job.'

'Surely it would be more sensible for her to get the other job first.'

Nellie smiled. 'You know our sister. Mam did her best to keep her in order and succeeded most of the time.'

'So now she's rebelling, you think?'

'We'll see.' Nellie pulled out a chair and sat down. She felt awkward in her brother's company in a way she had never done so before. Was it because she felt guilty?

He sat opposite her. 'So what's it feel like being back home?'

'Well, Grandfather didn't kill a fatted calf or put a ring on my finger.' She smiled wryly. 'His intention is the same as yours, I'm to take Mam's place – just the kind of life I was looking for.'

Francis' mouth tightened. 'Thousands aren't living the life they'd like to, Nellie.'

'I know that! My husband's in the desert fighting the Jerries and the Eyeties!' She paused, thinking what to say next. She could hear the crackling of the wood in the grate and suddenly was desperate for a cup of tea. 'I'm grateful, anyway, that you broke the silence by writing.'

'I would have written sooner but I couldn't understand why the pair of you couldn't come and see me so we could have discussed your situation. I just never thought you believed me such an ogre that you felt you had to run away and marry in that hole-in-the-corner fashion,' he said, riffling his fingers through his hair.

Nellie said stiffly, 'We didn't have time for discussions. He was on embarkation leave. I love Teddy. He's a good man and we wanted to spend his last few days here together.'

'I don't dispute his goodness, Nell, and I do understand your wanting to marry him. It's just that mixed marriages always cause trouble.' His expression was sombre.

'There wouldn't have been any trouble if Mam hadn't thought she was in the right,' said Nellie hotly. 'It's not as if

Teddy isn't a Christian, but she called him a bloody heretic as if he was the greatest sinner in the world. I found out yesterday that she was no angel, so what right had she to judge Teddy?'

'What do you mean, she was no angel?' Francis' voice was dangerously low. 'You shouldn't speak ill of the dead, especially after the way she died.'

Nellie wished she had kept her mouth shut and fiddled with the knife on the table. 'I'm sorry. I shouldn't have said that. None of us is perfect.'

'I want to know what you meant by it!' Francis hit the table with his fist causing her to draw away from him.

'That's enough,' growled their grandfather's voice from the doorway, taking them both by surprise. 'A man of the cloth should be able to control his temper.'

Francis stared at him aghast and his hands clenched on the folds of his cassock. 'Forgive me, Grandfather. I've been under a great deal of strain the last few months.'

'I know, I know,' said Grandfather. 'You had to identify your mother's and aunt's bodies and you saw sights in your own parish that were enough to turn a man's stomach.'

'A head! I found the head of a child once,' muttered Francis.

'Forgive me.' Nellie was horrified and reached out a hand across the table and placed it on his arm. She stroked his sleeve.

'Of course, he must forgive you,' said Grandfather. 'It's what Joseph would do. He taught me what can be gained by forgiveness.'

She heard the hiss of Francis' breath and as their eyes met she guessed what he was thinking: Joe had found it easy to forgive people because he was the kind of sinner who confessed regularly and then blithely went out to sin again. She winked and the muscles in Francis' face relaxed.

'Of course, I forgive you.' He squared his shoulders. 'Now, Nellie, what have you got in these bags? I hadn't got as far as seeing if there was any milk for the tea. I'm hungry, too. You wouldn't have a loaf in there, would you?'

She gave him a knowing look. 'As if you couldn't smell it.'

Grandfather leaned across the table and sniffed. 'I can smell it.' He reached for one of the bags. 'Butter. Did you get butter, Helen? The stuff Billy brought has all gone. Crusty bread with butter makes my mouth water.'

She tapped the back of his hand. 'Butter is on the ration, which means there's not a lot.' Getting to her feet, she began to unpack the shopping.

Francis took the bread knife and the loaf she passed him. The expression in his eyes was quizzical as he said, 'I think the mice have been at this.'

'Very funny. I am eating for two.'

He froze a moment before beginning to slice the loaf. 'You didn't mention that in your letters.'

'We didn't jump the gun. It's due October…and before you start talking about its baptism, I'll tell you now I'll make no decisions about that until it's born and I've discussed it with Teddy.'

He nodded. 'OK. Is there any jam? I seem to remember Mam making some last autumn.'

'It didn't set properly, so it's runny.'

'I'm not fussy,' said Francis, as he disappeared into the larder.

Nellie saw that the fire was still not ready to boil water, so made do with half a cup of milk and more bread. She was relieved that she had managed to get away without explaining to Francis why their mother was no angel.

As the three of them sat at the table eating, Nellie told Francis about having seen Lottie. 'I thought she might have been out of bed by now.'

'She has to rest, Nellie, but they do get her up and I've wheeled her out in a wheelchair. Naturally she's still broken-hearted about Mam and Aunt Josie, but thanking Our Lady and Saviour for her survival. Time will heal but it'll take a while. So many are grieving for the loss of their loved ones.'

'Were there many lives lost in your parish?' asked Nellie.

He gave a sharp nod. 'There's an Italian couple I've been visiting weekly since the May blitz. They lost a son in the bombing.'

'A child?' asked Nellie.

He shook his head. 'No, but Michelangelo helped out at the boys' club and was the apple of their eye. At the beginning of the war he was put in a POW camp on the outskirts of Liverpool, despite having lived here most of his life but then he was moved. His crime was that he hadn't registered for British nationality.' There was a note of bitterness in Francis' voice.

Nellie's heart went out to the parents. 'How unfair, and how sad that he should die. But how did it happen if he was in a POW camp away from Liverpool?'

'He was freed after a year and he joined the merchant navy. His ship was damaged by a torpedo, so he was on leave. It would have been better if he'd stayed on the Isle of Man.' Francis' expression was bleak.

'I'm sorry. I shouldn't have mentioned the blitz.' Nellie covered his large hand with hers.

Grandfather mumbled, 'No use talking about long ago sad things.'

Nellie and Francis glanced at him, both wondering what he was referring to. They knew scarcely anything about his early life and guessed that now was not the time to ask.

An hour later Francis left, saying he would call again in a week or two. As soon as he had gone, Nellie made a start on the housework. While she polished and scrubbed, she thought about visiting the doctor and the need to buy maternity clothes. She waited until the afternoon before going into the parlour where her grandfather was listening to the wireless and reading the newspaper she had bought. She began to gather the old ones from surfaces.

'What d'you think you're doing?' he asked, lowering the *Daily Post*, and pushing himself up out of his chair and fumbling for his walking stick.

'This is a lovely room and you've got some lovely things. It's a shame to cover them all up,' she said, folding the sheets of newsprint.

His face worked and spittle appeared at the corners of his mouth. 'It saves money having them covered, saves on polish and dusters! I won't have you interfering with my decisions, Helen.'

'Come off it, Grandfather. I won't polish every day. I like to see the things you've brought back from your travels.' She picked up a sandalwood box and sniffed it. 'Doesn't the smell take you back to the Far East?' She put that down and picked up a conch shell. 'What about this?' She stroked the blush pink inside of the shell and then held it to her ear. 'I remember being told that if I did this, I'd hear the sea.'

'Load of rubbish,' he muttered. 'You can't hear the sea in a shell but I do remember where I picked that up. It was in Jamaica.'

Nellie's eyes sparkled. 'You've had such an exciting life. Hiding your things away is like saying you want to forget that life.'

'I'm not going to do that, girl. It's inside here.' He tapped his skull.

'Dad used to always point at this if I was ever in here with him.' Nellie picked up a brass ornament of the three wise monkeys. 'He'd say, "See no evil, hear no evil, speak no evil", and then he'd squeeze my shoulder really hard and talk about the man being the boss of the house and women needing to heed what they said. He'd talk about the dangers of sinning and Hell until I could almost feel the flames.'

'Aye, well, Helen, he had more experience of sin than you did. Foreign ports can be right dens of iniquity, not that I'm saying our Bernard would do more than get roaring drunk,' he added hastily. 'Anyway, if you're going to disturb my peace by messing about with my things, make sure you polish those monkeys... and you can give some money towards the polish.'

She was indignant. 'I've already paid for the shopping I bought this morning. I do need some money for myself, Grandfather. I'll need maternity clothes and a layette for the baby. I'll need a cot and a pram, although, it probably won't be easy getting the latter.'

He scowled. 'You should have thought of all this before you went and ran off with Teddy Lachlan and got yourself in the family way, girl.'

Nellie rolled her eyes. 'I wouldn't have had to run away if you had stuck up for me.' She thought of the last time she had seen her mother; a lump rose in her throat and she was unable to say another word. Instead, she left the parlour with her arms full of newspapers, thinking that tomorrow she would visit the doctor's surgery up the road.

The next day Nellie's pregnancy was confirmed and the doctor congratulated her, recommended a midwife and told her that she was entitled to an extra pint of milk a day. She would also be allowed sixty extra clothing coupons for maternity wear and to buy the baby a layette. That news came as a relief.

When Babs arrived home at two o'clock the following afternoon, Nellie asked her if she would like to go shopping for maternity clothes with her.

'I can't, Nell,' said Babs. 'I got that job, by the way. The boss said that he thought I'd be good for business. It doesn't sound exciting but at least I'll be meeting different people. Anyway, I'm going to the pictures tonight with a friend and I've also told Billy I'll help him in the garden later this afternoon. I'll need the time to get myself ready to go out that I'd be giving up if I went with you. We can go next Saturday afternoon.'

Nellie was disappointed but decided that next week would do just as well. 'OK. So when will Billy get here?'

'As soon as he finishes his deliveries for the Co-op,' said Babs, and went upstairs to change.

* * *

Nellie stood at the top of the garden, listening to Billy talking to Babs. Since setting eyes on the seventeen-year-old, she knew what her sister meant about him reminding her of someone but, just like her sister, she had no idea to whom. He was a well set-up young man with floppy mousy hair and straight eyebrows.

'You want to try and persuade Mr Callaghan it would be a good idea to have some pullets here. He really should have bought them weeks ago but there's some still to be had,' he was saying.

'But how would we look after them? Where would they live and what would we feed them on?' asked Babs, who was kneeling on an old cushion, weeding between the rows of peas and runner beans.

'It tells you in the *Crosby Herald.* I did woodwork at school, so I wouldn't mind having a go at building them a house. They'll need an enclosed run as well because we wouldn't want them digging up the vegetables.'

Babs wrinkled her nose. 'I doubt I'll be able to persuade him. They'll cost money and he doesn't like spending money.'

'Eggs are getting as rare as gold dust. He'd have a ready supply and a nice chicken at Christmas, too,' said Billy.

'It sounds good, but…'

Nellie interrupted her sister. 'I'll talk to Grandfather. Most likely if I offer to go half with the cost and appeal to his greedy nature by painting pictures of yummy yolky eggs with soldiers, he'll agree.'

Billy looked her way and she saw that his eyes were blue-grey. 'I'm Babs' sister,' said Nellie, smiling. 'I'm sure she's mentioned me.'

'Yes, Mrs Lachlan. It's nice to meet you. Just let me know when Mr Callaghan gives you the go ahead,' he said.

'I'll go and ask him now.' Nellie left Babs and Billy alone, convinced by the way they looked and spoke to each other that there was nothing of a romantic nature between them, but then at that age maybe they were hiding their feelings.

She found her grandfather gazing down at the letter that had come that morning. She had recognised her father's handwriting on picking up the envelope from the mat. She wondered what he had to say but knew the old man would tell her soon enough if there was anything he thought she should know. Bernard had written to his wife regularly once a month. Carmel would read them and then rip them up and put them on the fire. Nellie presumed they had been duty letters. It saddened her to think that her parents might have realised very early on in their marriage that it had been a mistake but were trapped because the church did not accept divorce. At least she and Teddy had married for love. She felt a niggle of anxiety, wondering when she would hear from him. It seemed ages since his last letter but maybe with his being in the desert, it wasn't easy to get letters to a ship.

'What is it you want, Helen?' asked Grandfather, without looking up.

'Billy thinks we should buy some pullets. We'd have our own eggs and a chicken at Christmas.'

'Can he get them cheap?'

'I don't know what cheap is. I'll give something towards the cost,' said Nellie.

'Do it then.'

Nellie could not conceal her surprise. 'Are you feeling well?'

He glanced up at her from beneath bristling eyebrows. 'What's that supposed to mean, girl?'

'I expected to have to persuade you.'

He grunted. 'Impudent miss! By the way, Bernard's hoping to make it home soon. This letter is dated two months ago. If you ask me, he writes a few lines and then puts it aside and then does another couple when he's got nothing better to do.'

'Does he mention me?'

'Of course he does. He'll give you a right earful when he comes home. Wouldn't be surprised if he thinks he can have the marriage annulled.'

Nellie's stomach flipped over but she said defiantly, 'I was over twenty-one when I got married, so he couldn't have stopped me.'

Her grandfather cackled, 'That's what makes him mad. But you weren't married in our church, were you, girl? So you're not married in the eyes of God.'

'We were married by special licence in St Andrew's on Linacre Road, so it's legal and that's good enough for me.'

He muttered, 'Bernard won't agree. His being captain of a ship makes him think he can order things the way he wants. He forgets when he's home that we've all managed to live our lives without him.'

'And we'll carry on doing so, too,' said Nellie, tilting her chin. 'What does he have to say about Mam and Aunt Josie?'

He folded the letter and did not answer her.

Nellie walked out of the parlour, guessing that whatever her father had written concerning the death of his wife was best not being repeated to his children. Could he have referred to what their grandfather had told them the day she had returned from Ambleside? Could be that he was glad to have his freedom. The thought grieved her, but she put it from her mind as she went into the garden and told Billy to go ahead with buying the pullets and building them a home. He looked delighted and promised to get onto it as soon as possible. She was glad that at least she had made him happy.

That evening Nellie wrote a letter to Teddy telling him that she was now at her grandfather's house and that she had seen a doctor and would most likely have a talk with the midwife during the coming week. She told him about Babs changing her job, of her visit to Lottie and of Billy's plan to get them some pullets, adding that he seemed to know only slightly more about gardening than herself but he was strong and a great help when it came to digging and weeding. Both of them had asked questions of Grandfather, but his years at sea meant he knew little more than them, so she'd have to become an avid reader of the advice given weekly for amateur 'Diggers for Victory' in the local *Crosby Herald.*

She made no mention of the conversation she'd had with Grandfather concerning her father's homecoming, deciding it was best not to annoy him with that news.

Having finished her letter, she went and had a bath before joining her grandfather in the parlour and listening to a murder mystery on the radio, thinking she probably would have enjoyed a trip to the pictures with Babs, herself.

'You're a perfect gentleman, Ritchie, but I think it would be best if you didn't see me home,' said Babs, as they stood in front of the town hall that evening.

'But it's dark, Babs. I hate the thought of someone jumping out and hurting you,' he said earnestly.

'You're a sweetie,' she said, planting a kiss on his cheek, 'but I think I'll be safe enough. It's not pitch black at this time of year and we have a real nosy neighbour, who never seems to sleep. If Grandfather knew I was seeing a fella, then I wouldn't be able to go out with you again.' She squeezed his hand before releasing it. 'Now go.'

'But when will I see you again?' asked Ritchie.

She thought about that. 'Thursday. I won't go home but stay in Waterloo. I'll meet you outside the Plaza.'

He hesitated but then nodded. 'OK!'

Babs had not missed that pause. 'We can go Dutch. Or even just have a walk. We'll see what the weather's like.' She kissed him lightly on the lips and left him standing there, knowing he was staring after her. She hoped he would not take it into his head to follow her. She did not want him knowing where she lived because, sooner or later, she knew that she'd have to break it off with him. She liked him a lot but had no intention of things getting too serious between them. She wanted to have some fun while she was young and no doubt he'd be joining the Forces within the year.

Chapter Four

As Babs walked along the pavement the following Thursday evening, she became aware that despite the lateness of the hour, Mrs Wainwright had her in her sights. She was leaning on her gate and Babs knew there would be no getting past her without some comment being made.

'I wouldn't like to be in your shoes,' said Mrs Wainwright. 'I'd get a walloping if I'd dared stay out until this hour when I was a girl.'

'When was that? The Stone Age?' said Babs with an innocent air.

The old woman's hands tightened on the gate. 'Don't you give me your cheek, girl. Your father's just gone into the house and I'll speak to him about you when I see him. The whole family's been far too soft with you. Short skirts, smoking and staying out late! It's asking for trouble.'

'It's none of your business what I do, Mrs Wainwright. Good night,' said Babs airily.

She walked away, humming a tune from the film she had just seen as if she didn't have a care in the world. The truth was that she was going to have to put on an act. When her dad was around, she always felt she had to please him and pretend to be the person he believed her to be. It wasn't that she was exactly scared about how he'd react if she let him down...no, that wasn't true, she was a teeny bit scared. She just wished his expectations of her weren't so unrealistic. Of course, she was looking forward to seeing him because he was her dad but, in the past, his arrivals had always created an atmosphere in the house that was uncomfortable; perhaps she was worrying too much. With Mam no longer around, he might be completely different. Then Babs remembered Nellie and her heart sank. There was no doubt in her mind that their father wouldn't pull his punches when he faced his eldest daughter.

Babs burst into the washroom to the accompaniment of mild

chirping and clucking from the pullets in the wooden crate, waiting to be housed in the home Billy was constructing for them. She hoped Nellie had thought about keeping an eye on the cat where the birds were concerned. There was a dozen of them, eleven hens and one cockerel. They were ugly things, in-between that fluffy and cuddly stage and full-grown strutting birds.

She hung up her jacket, her ears alert for the sound of raised voices but, to her surprise, all was quiet. She opened the kitchen door, only to pause in the doorway, as the first person her gaze fell on was Nellie.

She was standing against the table, her hands gripping the wood. Her face was pale and strained but when she spotted Babs her expression changed to one of relief. 'So there you are! I told Dad there was nothing to worry about and probably you'd missed a bus.'

'I did,' lied Babs. She and Ritchie had walked back from the picture house in Waterloo, taking a shortcut using the lane that ran along the allotments and across the canal via the footpath that came out on Field Lane by the park. They had stood gazing down at a coal barge for a few minutes, and his arm had slipped round her waist as he pulled her to him for a stolen kiss.

'You should have allowed extra time in case you missed a bus,' said Bernard.

She sensed his disapproval but pretended not to have heard him. 'Did I hear you right, Nellie? Did you say Dad's home?' She did not wait for her sister to answer but hurried forward to where she could see Bernard standing by the fireplace. He was a fine figure of man with broad shoulders and a strong frame. He was clad in a navy blue jacket and trousers and had loosened his tie so that his white shirt gaped at the throat, revealing the neck of his vest. He had a Clark Gable moustache and Brylcreem-slicked-back reddish brown hair, flecked with silver at his temples. He was not exactly handsome but he had attractive, if stern, features. 'It's lovely to have you back, Dad!' She stood on tiptoe and kissed his chin.

He hugged her to him and then held her at arm's length. 'You get prettier each time I come home.'

Babs sought for the right word. 'And you get more distinguished looking,' she said.

He looked pleased. 'We're a good-looking pair. That's why I was worried about you being out late. There's blokes around who'll take advantage of a lovely girl like you.'

'I don't let them get close enough, Dad. Mam warned me to keep my distance.'

'As long as you remember what she said, even though she's gone. Nellie didn't heed her and look what happened to her.'

Bernard frowned in his eldest daughter's direction. It infuriated him that she had dared to go against her Catholic upbringing and that, as a married woman, he had no control over her. She had moved away from the table to put on the kettle. He could see the slight swell of her belly and was reminded of his dead wife. Carmel had looked just the same when she had first broken the news that she was pregnant. He had been mad for her then and had willingly married her, but he had soon realised his mistake after Joseph was born. No wonder he felt that women couldn't be trusted. It was the same with Lottie. He had always wondered if she was his child. She had supposedly come early but was so different physically to his other two daughters that he couldn't help doubting his wife's fidelity. Still, he'd been blessed with Babs and had done his duty by her and the church all these years. He hugged her against him.

'I'll never forget Mam,' said Babs, a catch in her voice. 'Or Aunt Josie. Will you be visiting the grave, Dad?' She looked up at him from lovely green eyes, the same colour as his own.

He hesitated, unsure what to say. His mother had died when he was only young and he hated cemeteries. Besides, he was glad to be rid of Carmel and her carping sister and felt it was hypocritical to go and visit their last resting place. 'Not just yet, Babs. I'm still coming to terms with their deaths.'

'I haven't been yet,' said Nellie, wishing she and her father could be closer. 'Perhaps the three of us could go together?'

'Didn't you hear what I said, Nellie? I don't want to go just yet.' Her suggestion exasperated him.

'I thought that visiting the grave would help you to come to terms with Mam's death,' she said. 'But if you don't want to go that's up to you.' She turned away from him and fetched a packet of cocoa from a shelf.

'I didn't say I *didn't* want to go,' he snapped. 'Don't mention this subject again.'

Nellie nodded, convinced he had no intention of paying his respects to her mother. She turned to her grandfather. 'Cup of cocoa, Grandfather?'

His rheumy blue eyes fixed on her face. 'I don't see why not. But remember, Helen, what I said.'

She stared at him. 'About what?'

His brow puckered and his mouth worked and then his face brightened. 'Angels. That was it.'

'Angels!' exclaimed Bernard. 'What the hell are you talking about, Father?'

There was a crafty expression on the old man's face and he tapped the side of his nose. 'Careless talk cost lives. I'll say no more.'

Bernard shook his head in disbelief. 'Please yourself.' He turned to Nellie. 'Have you anything for me to eat?'

She said, 'How about jam on bread? With not knowing when you'd arrive, I haven't much in the larder.'

He looked annoyed and, noticing his expression, Babs said, 'I'll make some jam butties.'

'Isn't there anything else?' demanded Bernard.

'There's a bit of bacon but that's for Grandfather's Sunday breakfast treat,' said Nellie.

'Can't take that away from him, I suppose,' muttered Bernard, glancing at his father.

'No, you can't,' said the old man, hunching a shoulder.

'That's mine. I bet you eat better at sea these days than I ever did.'

'Depends on the cook and the weather,' said Bernard, digging his hands in his pockets. 'I suppose it's too late for the chippie.'

Nellie nodded and Babs went and fetched the jam from the larder.

Supper passed off without anything contentious being said and then everyone went to bed. As she and her sister undressed, Babs said, 'What did Dad say before I came in?'

'What d'you think he said?' murmured Nellie, leaving the bottom two buttons on her pyjama jacket undone and stroking her belly, wishing it was Teddy who was home and not her father. She'd love to relive that short honeymoon in Southport.

'That you're a bad example to me?' Babs sat cross-legged on the bed. 'I wish he'd stop thinking I'm so blinking marvellous.'

Nellie laughed. 'You're not? Anyway, that was the least of what he said. Not only am I a disgrace and a disappointment but also that, most likely, I've been excommunicated and won't be able to go to Mass. I'm wayward, disobedient...and I'm too much like mother. What do you think of that last one?'

'He's crazy thinking you're like her. You're easygoing. Mam never was.' She changed the subject. 'What did you think of Grandfather going on about angels and careless talk costing lives?'

'Maybe he was thinking about Mam. Remember him saying that she was no angel? She could have been a bit of a girl in her day and only got religion when life stopped being fun. If she did have to get married, it could explain why she was so strict with us,' said Nellie.

Babs yawned. 'Poor Mam. She must have felt the shame of it. I suppose I'll have to go to Mass with Dad tomorrow?'

'What about visiting Mam's and Aunt Josie's grave with me?'

'OK. Dad hasn't said how long he's going to be home, has he?'

'No.' Nellie prayed that it would not be too long.

Her prayer was to be answered.

Within the week Bernard was back at sea but he had made his presence felt during the days he was home, especially after he'd had a few drinks at the Red Lion. The old man had grumbled his disapproval of his son's drinking and what a thorough waste of money it was as he'd stood watching Nellie mop up Bernard's vomit. She and Babs had also had to help their father to bed one night. Nellie had received a clout on the ear from his flailing arm for her pains. She wondered how he related his religious beliefs to his excessive drinking and his reluctance to visit his wife's grave. She and Babs had wept real tears when they'd gone to pay their respects and Nellie knew she would have to go through it all again when Lottie came home.

A few days after Bernard had departed, Babs let slip the news that she would be working Saturday afternoon and would be going straight out afterwards with a friend.

'I was hoping you'd come shopping with me,' said Nellie, wondering about this nameless friend.

'Sorry, Nell. It's this new job. I have to work Saturday afternoon.'

Nellie was disappointed but understood. Smiling, she said, 'At least that means you won't be spending money on clothes.'

Babs grimaced. 'I don't have money to spend once I've handed over for my keep to Grandfather.'

'You have my sympathy but we all have to pay our way. Wouldn't it be great if women got equal pay with men...but even teachers don't get that.'

'Perhaps one day after the war,' drawled Babs, and left for work.

The following morning, to Nellie's delight, several letters from Teddy arrived. Some had been redirected from High View and she wasted no time in putting them in some semblance of order and opening them one by one. They all started with the same words,

My darling Nellie,
I hope you are well. I am OK, so you're not to worry about me. I am missing you more than words can say and wish I was with you.

The letters consisted of only one page but were written on both sides in her husband's neat hand. The most important letter was his reply to the news that she was expecting their baby.

I was so overjoyed to get the news of the baby that I danced around the tent, yipping and yowling like a madman. You couldn't have sent me better news. It's pretty rough out here. Sand gets into everything and it's so hot that...well, I won't go into how unpleasant it makes things. I have dreams of Britain's cool green fields and woods and strolling arm in arm with you. Now I can imagine three of us enjoying the countryside. Dreams are what I live on, Nellie. When this war's over, we'll find a little place that's just our own. It would be nice if it had a garden but the main thing is the three of us being together as a family. I know that's what you want too.

I can't really say much about things here...careless talk costs lives...but you must take care of yourself and keep the letters coming. They mean so much to me. I have enclosed a photo that one of the blokes took. Lots of love, kisses, hugs,

Yours for ever, Teddy.

With eyes that shone with tears, Nellie gazed down at the photo of her husband. He was wearing shorts and a shirt. His hair was already showing signs of being bleached by the sun and his skin looked tanned. She kissed the picture and propped it up against the statue of the Madonna and child. Then, after reading the letters, she put them in a cardboard box and placed it inside the tallboy. After doing that she sat quietly on the bed, smiling as she imagined Teddy dancing about. She could only echo his wish that he was here with her.

She went downstairs and found the parlour unusually

deserted, so she sat at the piano. Memories of days gone by when her great-great-aunt had been alive were evoked as she played 'Come into the Garden, Maud'. 'Wait till the sun shines, Nellie' reminded her of the music hall and Teddy. 'Run, Rabbit, Run' recalled the children she had left up in Cumberland. She wondered how they were getting on and how old they would be when they came home. As the music echoed round the parlour, her anguish at being parted from Teddy eased a little, and after a while, she closed the piano and, collecting her purse and shopping bag, she left the house.

The next day Nellie received a surprise visit from the midwife. It appeared that the doctor had got in touch with the woman and given Nellie's details to her. The midwife examined her and seemed satisfied with Nellie's condition. She talked about what Nellie could expect as her pregnancy advanced and about the birth. The woman was so down-to-earth that Nellie felt reassured she was in good hands.

With that hurdle over, Nellie went out into the garden and found her grandfather keeping an eye on Billy as he put the final touches to the henhouse. He had already enclosed an area of the garden for a run where they scratched about in the soil. First thing that morning, she had made them a mash consisting of a mixture of porridge oats, corn and greens, which they appeared to have enjoyed.

'I'm looking forward to my first egg,' said the old man, rubbing his gnarled hands together.

'Aren't we all,' said Nellie, noticing that he looked a lot cleaner and tidier since her return, although his hair could do with a trim. 'We'll need to give Billy some.'

Grandfather's overgrown eyebrows twitched together like hairy caterpillars. 'Don't be making promises in front of the lad, Helen. We don't know how many eggs there are going to be. After all they're my birds.'

'Our birds,' said Nellie, winking at Billy. 'I paid half the cost.

Billy got them for us and is making them a home so he's entitled to a share. Fair's fair, Grandfather.'

The old man seemed about to argue with her but she gave him a stern look and, grumbling beneath his breath, he stomped away into the house. She had been about to mention her trip into town that afternoon but on second thoughts decided it was best to keep quiet. He'd only moan and tell her not to waste the fare and to shop local. She could see the sense in that but today she felt a need to get away. Besides, if she went into town, she could always call in on Francis and tell him of their father's visit. If he wasn't in, then she could slip a note through the presbytery door saying she had called and ask whether he had any news of Lottie, as she hadn't had a chance to visit her again yet.

Nellie got ready and caught the bus into town. She did not have much in the way of money to spend and she had yet to apply for her extra coupons, so she limited herself to buying one maternity smock and skirt, a brassiere and a couple of pairs of big knickers. There was little in the way of cots and prams to be seen, even if she'd had the money to buy new. It occurred to her that it might be worth checking up in the attic rooms before advertising for second-hand items or buying any baby clothes.

She walked from C&A Modes to her brother's parish near Scotland Road. Unfortunately, he was out, but she left a note with the housekeeper and caught the bus home. That evening Nellie showed her purchases to Babs.

Her sister shook her head dolefully. 'Blinking heck, Nell. I'm never going to get pregnant if I have to wear clothes like that.'

Nellie agreed that they weren't flattering. 'But they're not meant to be and as soon as the baby's born, hopefully, I'll be like Mam and get my figure back dead quick.'

Babs looked thoughtful. 'It'll be strange having a baby in the house. I've never known there to be one.'

Nellie smiled. 'That's because the last baby was you.'

'Was I a good and beautiful baby?'

'There's no need to fish for compliments,' said Nellie. 'You've seen the photograph. All those curls! When Dad eventually saw you he said that your hair should never be cut.'

Babs said ruefully. 'I hated it when I was twelve. Mam thought it was lovely that I could sit on it but it was a real nuisance getting it dry, remember?'

'I remember you hacking at it with a pair of blunt scissors,' said Nellie.

Babs' eyes danced. 'I got you into trouble, didn't I? Mam caught you trying to tidy it up and hit the roof.'

Nellie rolled her eyes. 'I was seventeen but she still whacked me with a hairbrush across the head! I saw stars.'

'I did confess I'd done it myself.'

Nellie nodded. 'You might have been a pest at times but you always did try and make things right.' She folded the maternity clothes and placed them in a drawer. 'I'm going to bed.'

'Me too. Did you remember to get the hens into their little house?'

Nellie gasped. 'No, I didn't.' She headed for the bedroom door.

'Stop, stop, stop!' cried Babs. 'I did it. I was just seeing if you'd remember. Billy made a good job of the henhouse.'

'You can say that again.'

Babs nodded and found herself comparing Billy with Ritchie. She liked them both but neither was her Mr Right. She got into bed, watching her eldest sister put on a spotless white nightdress. 'What's happened to your pyjamas?'

'This is looser and more comfortable. I wore it on my wedding night and I thought I might as well make use of it, rather than keep it until Teddy comes home.'

Babs said, 'It's pretty. You putting the light out?'

Nellie did so. Babs wished life was more exciting. Should she let Ritchie kiss her more passionately next time? She was still thinking about that when she fell asleep.

* * *

Babs duplicated the woman's name and address on the bottom half of the slip, tore that off and handed it to her. The other half of the slip she pinned to the jacket and said 'Good morning!' as the customer left the shop, closing the door behind her and setting the bell at the top of the door frame jangling.

Babs went into the back of the shop and hung the garment on a hanger on a rail. She had worked at the dry-cleaner's six weeks now and was fed up. Outside the sun was shining and she longed to be in the fresh air. Her mind was busily working on several thoughts at once. A fortnight ago, she had read in the *Crosby Herald* that due to the government wanting to encourage people not to go away for their holidays and thereby save fuel and pressure on transport, various groups had got together to arrange family fun days and open air dancing in parks. She had celebrated her seventeenth birthday whilst Nellie had been in Cumberland but had never had a proper dancing lesson in her life, although Nellie had taught her a few steps. Babs did not feel very proficient but was keen enough to give it a go, so she had got Ritchie to agree to go dancing that evening in the grounds of Potter's Barn in Waterloo. The name was a local one for a building that was supposed to be an exact replica of the farmhouse that the British troops had used during the battle of Waterloo. History was a subject Babs was not particularly interested in so she could not remember its real name, which was French anyway. She decided it should be fun and could not wait for the evening to start.

The other thing on Babs' mind was changing her job. Without having said a word to Nellie, she had made enquiries about joining the Women's Land Army after remembering hearing stories of youths lying about their age to go and fight in the Great War. Poor lads, thought Babs, so many had died so young. Still, that wasn't going to happen to her and she saw no reason why, at seventeen, she shouldn't be doing her bit for the war effort. She wanted to work on the land. There was something so satisfying about planting seeds and seeing vegetables and fruit grow and picking the fruits of your labour. She had discovered that it was a Lady Denman who was in charge of the scheme. She had devised a minimum wage of twenty-eight shillings a week for her army of women. Of course, male farm labourers earned ten shillings more, but Babs was not going to get herself worked up about that; it would be the same no matter what job she went for.

Out of the twenty-eight shillings, Babs would have to pay for her board and lodgings, but as she didn't earn much in her present job, and she handed most of it over to Grandfather for her keep, that was something she was philosophical about. She would be provided with a uniform and wearing a uniform appealed to Babs, although she had no desire to go into the Forces and be sent far away from home. The farmlands of Lancashire were almost on her doorstep, so she was convinced she would be able to come home every week and see Nellie. She felt slightly guilty about leaving her sister alone with Grandfather, but no doubt that wouldn't be for long. Lottie would be out of hospital soon and, in October, Nellie would have her baby to look after and so wouldn't have time to miss her youngest sister.

Babs decided to join straight away. She had a perfect excuse for not being able to produce her birth certificate if those in charge wanted to see it because it had been in her mother's capacious handbag, along with other important papers and their ration books, that evening in May when she had stayed at her Aunt Josie's house and the bombers had struck. Hopefully the Land Army would take her on and, if they suggested she get a replacement and send it on later, she would conveniently forget to do so. She couldn't imagine them considering her so important that they would chase the matter up.

That evening as Ritchie taught Babs to foxtrot to the music of the band from the local dance hall, he held her much too close for her liking. The air was tangy with the salty smell of the river and the scent of roses. She could see the faint outline of the moon in the sky and really, she thought, if Ritchie had been her Mr Right her heart would have been beating ten to the dozen with excitement but, as it was, she could only feel his hammering away. She glanced around in an attempt to distract herself from the thought of her breasts being squashed against his chest, certain that her mother would not have approved. But then she would have been shocked at so many couples dancing out in the open air.

'Babs, I'm crazy about you,' whispered Ritchie against her ear. 'I wish we could get married.'

'Married!' squeaked Babs, treading on his foot.

Ritchie winced. 'I shouldn't have blurted it out like that but you look so-so lovely, I couldn't help myself.'

She gazed up into his pleasant face and saw the yearning in his eyes. A sigh escaped her as she decided that it was definitely best for him if she went away. 'It's nice of you to say these things, Ritchie, but I'm only just seventeen.'

'People do get married at seventeen. I'd like us to get married before I get called up.'

'I don't think my father would agree,' she said.

'But he's at sea, isn't he? Does he have to know?' Ritchie had come to a stop.

Babs patted his collarbone and gently drew away from him. 'Let me think about it. Do you have the time? I daren't be late tonight.'

Ritchie checked his watch. 'It's only half nine.'

She pretended dismay. 'It'll be ten by the time I get home. I'm going to have to go. The dance will soon be coming to an end anyway because it's getting dark.'

'I'll come with you.'

Babs knew she had to allow him to walk her most of the way home. On the way, she gave him no chance to bring up the subject of marriage again. It was ridiculous. She was far too young and, besides, she didn't love him. She chattered away about her job and the garden, telling him about the henhouse that Billy had made. Ritchie asked who Billy was and how old he was. 'Ancient,' she said. 'He's Grandfather's old gardener.'

He accepted that because so many young men's jobs were being taken by men coming out of retirement. He stopped her on the footbridge and drew her into his arms. She allowed him to kiss her but when his hand brushed her breast she pulled away. 'None of that, Ritchie. I'm a respectable Catholic girl. Now I must get home.'

She hurried ahead but he soon caught her up. 'Sorry,' he said. She smiled and said that she forgave him. He reached for her hand and she allowed him to hold it. When they came to the town hall, she bid him goodnight.

'But when will I see you again?'

She looked up into his earnest young face and said that she'd see him on Sunday afternoon and arranged a meeting place, but she had no intention of keeping the date. As she walked the rest of the way home, she knew that she should have told him to his face that she did not want to see him again but it was easier to lie rather than see his hurt expression. She thought of Nellie and knew that her sister would try to stop her leaving if she could, so she decided the best thing would be just to go without saying goodbye. She would just walk out of the front door one morning carrying her holdall and use the excuse that she was having some things dry-cleaned. She would leave a note in her underwear drawer in the hope that when Nellie found it, she would understand why she had done things the way she had.

It was a week later, a few hours after Babs had left for work taking some dry-cleaning with her, that Nellie decided to go and pay Lottie a visit. She had received an answer to the note she had left for Francis, telling her that he was going to be staying in Ireland for a fortnight. The first week would be taken up with a series of religious seminars but during the second week he planned on visiting their mother's childless aunt and uncle, who farmed a few acres in County Wicklow. He would visit Lottie before he went but would appreciate it if she could find time to go and see their sister. He was concerned about Lottie's slow recovery and wondered how much longer she would be allowed to convalesce in Southport. Nellie had been wondering about that herself, so as soon as she could, she told her grandfather where she was going and left.

It was a beautiful July day when Nellie set out and she was wearing the maternity smock and skirt that she had bought at C&A Modes. Beneath the blue and red floral smock, she wore a pink crepe-de-chine blouse that she had bought for her wedding. It was a bit tight round the bust and she had been unable to fasten the bottom buttons. The baby was getting more active and often she found herself marvelling at the miracle of life that was growing inside her womb. Because of the heat, she had pinned up her chestnut hair on top of her head, leaving her slender neck feeling much cooler. She took the train to Southport and enjoyed gazing out on the gardens of big houses, the fields and woods, sand dunes and golf course. She thought that on such a day, there was nothing so lovely as the countryside.

When Nellie arrived in the resort, she bought her sister a copy of *Peg's Paper*, which was light reading, and headed for the convalescent home. She was directed to the garden and found Lottie sitting in a wheelchair, toying with her rosary beads. A Catholic missal was balanced on a belly that was as large as her own. She was dismayed, concerned that her sister was putting on so much weight. It couldn't be good for her damaged hip and legs, or her heart for that matter.

'Hello, Lot.' Nellie bent and kissed her sister's cheek.

Lottie looked up at her and there was a fiery light in the grey eyes beneath the straight slashes of her eyebrows. 'I prayed you'd come and here you are.'

'Yes, here I am,' said Nellie, sitting on the wooden bench a couple of feet away. Taking the magazine from her bag, she placed it on the bench.

'Isn't prayer wonderful?' said Lottie. 'I pray to the Holy

Mother and the saints for healing and one day I think I will be healed. Perhaps right now, though, I'm still sitting here because I've indulged in wicked thoughts.'

'Wicked thoughts! You?' Nellie laughed. 'I don't believe it. Hitler's Luftwaffe dropped a bomb, that's why you're here. It would be better if you'd get out of that wheelchair and try walking some more.'

Lottie pushed back a hank of lank mousy hair and screwed up her eyes against the sun. 'But it kills me to walk.'

'I'm sure it does, but you *can* walk.'

Lottie hesitated. 'If I said it hurts, I must be able to walk, mustn't I? I get puffed, though.'

Nellie refrained from saying that was because she was overweight and instead said, 'I get puffed sometimes.' But that was when she forgot she was pregnant and ran upstairs or climbed on a chair to clean windows and the like.

Lottie shielded her eyes from the sun and scrutinised Nellie. 'You've put weight on. You're getting as fat as me.'

'That's because I'm pregnant.'

'Pregnant!'

Nellie nodded. 'I wish you could come home, Lot. I'm sure it would be better and easier for both of us if you were home.'

Lottie was distracted and looked uncertain. 'We don't have a wheelchair there,' she said, as if that was the deciding factor. 'Why haven't you mentioned before that you're pregnant?' she added.

'I thought I'd tell you face to face. Anyway, now you know. It's due in October and hopefully you'll be home by then.'

'I hope to God I will be.' She frowned.

Nellie wondered if Lottie was about to mention her not having married in the Catholic church and the baby being illegitimate, so she swiftly changed the subject. She talked about Babs and Grandfather, the hens and how the cockerel was starting to wake them in the morning.

Lottie had little to say and eventually Nellie rose to go. Her sister stopped her with the words, 'Couldn't you take me out in the wheelchair? We could go along the prom.'

Nellie hesitated and glanced towards the gate at the bottom of the garden. Could she manage the drop to ease the chair down off the step? Perhaps she should ask for help.

She did so and, after a word of warning to come back immediately if she found things difficult, a nurse helped her out of the garden into a back lane. It was hard work pushing Lottie in the wheelchair so Nellie did not rush but took her time. There was quite a crowd along the prom and the sound of a brass band playing dance music floated on the air. Nellie headed in that direction. When she saw people dancing, she wished that Teddy was there so they could dance, too. There was a bench nearby so she sat down, glad to have a rest. The band was playing 'Look for the Silver Lining' and she thought that everyone must be looking for a silver lining to lighten the dark clouds of war.

They stayed for a while, listening to the music until at last the band packed up its instruments and left. Nellie got up and pushed Lottie back to the convalescent home, said her goodbyes and departed.

The train was crowded with day trippers heading back to Liverpool and she was so weary when she got off at Seaforth that she decided to buy fish and chips to save her cooking. She entered the kitchen, wanting nothing more than to kick off her shoes and put her feet up, but her grandfather was not alone. Billy and a strange young man sat at the table.

'Who's this?' asked Nellie, putting down the wrapped newspaper parcel on the dresser.

Billy stood up and offered her his seat. 'Please sit down, Mrs Lachlan.'

'His name is Ritchie,' growled Grandfather, 'and apparently he's been seeing Babs and wants to marry her.'

Nellie sat down on the vacated chair. 'He's been what?'

'We haven't done anything wrong,' said Ritchie, his hands clasped tightly together.

Nellie stared at his unhappy young face and then glanced at

her grandfather. 'Where is Babs? Surely she should be home by now?'

Ritchie answered. 'She's gone off. I called in at the dry-cleaner's and they said she'd quit. Not a word did she say to me about that.'

'Us neither,' whispered Nellie, stunned by her sister's duplicity.

'I didn't even know where she lived. She would never let me see her home.'

'So how did you find this house?' asked Nellie.

'The woman at the dry-cleaner's gave him the address,' rumbled Grandfather.

Nellie did not speak for several moments and then she stood up and left the kitchen. She went upstairs and into their bedroom. Going over to the chest of drawers, she opened the ones used by her sister. It was in the bottom one she saw the envelope and took it out with shaking fingers.

Tearing open the envelope, she spread the sheet of paper flat on the top of the chest of drawers and read,

Dear Nellie,
I know you would have tried to persuade me not to go and that's why I've done what I want this way. After all, you set me an example by running off with Teddy. I've joined the Women's Land Army. It was easy enough to get in because they're desperate for workers. I'm not going far. Up Lancashire that's all. As soon as I'm settled I'll write again. In the meantime don't be too angry with me and take care of yourself and the baby.
Lots of love,
Babs.

Nellie sank onto the bed. Daft! That's what Babs was. As if she would have stopped her if she really wanted to do something towards the war effort. If she had run off with that Ritchie in the kitchen, that would have been a mistake. Thank God, she'd had the sense not to do that. The cheek of her, saying that Nellie had set her an example. She smiled and shook her head.

Her stomach rumbled and she remembered the fish and chips that she had bought. She got up and went downstairs and handed the note to her grandfather. The two young men stared at him as he read it.

When Grandfather had finished, he raised his eyes to Nellie's face. 'Stupid child! Believes because she's done a bit of gardening with Billy that she knows all there is to know about growing things. Probably thinks it'll be lovely working in the countryside at this time of year, but wait until winter comes,' he chortled, 'that'll be another story.' He dropped the note on the table and reached for the fish and chips. 'You lads can beat it. Supper time's for us.'

Billy and Ritchie got up and Nellie followed them out. She felt sorry for the latter. It was obvious he was smitten with Babs and Nellie doubted her sister had been intentionally cruel. Hopefully, he would soon get over his feelings for her. As for herself, she would miss her youngest sister, but at least she had not gone far away. Even so, Nellie bet a pound to a penny that when their father heard about his darling daughter's behaviour, he would find some way of laying the blame not on Babs, but on her.

Chapter Five

'Here, lass, wash that cow down.' The farmer, Mr Rowland, indicated the beast he had just finished milking with a nod of his head and passed Babs a bucket of soapy water and a cloth before moving on to milk the next animal.

She gazed at the cow in dismay, thinking this was not what she joined the Women's Land Army for. The beast was huge and she had no idea where to start her task. Its horns looked really sharp and the sound of its hooves, as it shifted in the cowshed, scared her to death. She could just imagine how it would feel if her Wellington-clad foot got trodden on. She shuddered and knew she had to stay alert. Trouble was that she had been roused at four o'clock that morning and still felt half-asleep. Perhaps she should start at the top and work her way down. It seemed the most sensible thing to do.

Babs soaked the cloth in the water and told herself to show no fear but stare the cow in its surprisingly beautifully fringed eyes and start with its head. She reached up and slopped water over the cowlick between its horns. The cow reacted by blinking water out of its eyes and jerking its head.

'Sorry,' she said, attempting with trembling hands to mop the water away.

'Wha' the hell d'yer think yer doin'?' demanded the farmer.

She stared down at him. 'I'm washing the cow.'

'Yer don't bloody wash all the beast, lass, just its udders.'

Babs could not help but giggle. 'Sorry.'

He looked at her as if she was an idiot. 'Gerron with it.'

Laughter was still bubbling away inside her as she bent down with the dripping cloth clasped in her hand. She stared at the dangling skin bag with its set of teats and stopped laughing. Taking a deep breath, she rested a hesitant hand on the animal's flank and prayed it would not kick out at her as she gingerly began to wipe the teats. To her relief the cow just stood there and the tension seeped out of Babs.

She had arrived at the farm yesterday evening, having been picked up by the farmer in a horse and cart at Ormskirk railway station. Mr Rowland looked to be a man in his late thirties, with a weather-beaten face and a front tooth missing. Beyond telling her to get 'oop' into the cart, he had not spoken to her on the journey to the farm. On arrival she had been shown to a cottage that had looked quite pretty with honeysuckle and a rambling rose climbing round the door and up the wall of the house.

Inside was a different story. The front door opened straight on to a room that was small and dark, and there was no electricity. The only furniture was a saggy-looking sofa and a gate-legged table and two chairs. On the stone-flagged floor there was a rag rug in front of a black-leaded grate, to the side of which was a coal scuttle. A blackened kettle stood on the hob but the fire was unlit. Lighting was provided by a couple of oil lamps. Babs' heart had plummeted as she had put down her holdall and gasmask container.

Mr Rowland had showed her the scullery with its deep white sink and shelves with two of everything in the way of crockery and cutlery, as well as a couple of saucepans and a frying pan. He then pointed to another door in the corner of the living room, which led to a flight of stairs. 'Flo will be back in the morning,' he'd said in a Lancashire accent. 'Come over to the house in half an hour and Sister will have some supper ready for you.'

She nodded, relieved that at least she was being fed that evening because she was starving. Upstairs there was one large bedroom with two narrow beds, a large wardrobe and a chest of drawers. One of the beds showed signs of being in use. On the other was folded bedding and this one was next to the window, which was open at the bottom. She had thrust her head out and gazed at the view. A variety of smells had assailed her dainty nose: honeysuckle, manure and what she took to be the smell of the fields, which stretched towards the distant hills and encompassed several small woods. There was only the odd building and, realising she had really come to the back of beyond, she felt homesick for Liverpool. The other room upstairs was only big enough for a cot and chest of drawers. There was no bathroom. When need had driven her to go in search of a lavatory, she had discovered a primitive privy at the bottom of the garden.

Babs sighed as she plunged the cloth into the bucket of soapy water again and wiped the udder of another cow. This was her third and she thanked God that Mr Rowland went in for mixed farming so didn't have a huge herd but just a round dozen. By the time she had washed the last cow, her knees were shaking, her back ached and her hands were red from being in and out of water.

As soon as she had finished, Mr Rowland told her to skedaddle to the kitchen and get herself some breakfast. 'Tomorrow, you'll cook for yerself, lass.'

Babs wiped her hands on her brown dungarees, wondering whether he would take her into Ormskirk to buy food. Then she remembered the other land girl, Flo, and hoped she would bring some groceries back with her.

Once outside, Babs felt a bit better. Dawn had arrived but she was still glad of the brown jacket that covered her working dungarees; there was a definite chill in the air. As she trudged across the cobbled yard, she thought about her 'walking out' uniform hung in the wardrobe upstairs. She could only hope she would get a chance to wear it.

She eased off her wellies at the back door of the farmhouse and entered in her stockinged feet. The farmer's sister looked up as she entered the kitchen. There was a lovely smell of freshly baked bread and the room was warm. The woman said something incomprehensible in a thick Lancashire accent. It amazed Babs that she was only about twenty miles from home and this woman might as well be speaking a foreign language. Thankfully Babs could understand what her brother said much better. Miss Rowland repeated her words and waved a hand towards the sink beneath the window. Babs presumed that she was telling her to wash her hands.

She did so reluctantly, wishing there was a jar of glycerine and almond oil handy to moisturise her skin. She washed her poor mitts and then dabbed them dry on a towel. She noticed Miss Rowland had placed bowls of porridge on the table. Porridge was not Babs' favourite food and she would have liked to refuse it but guessed she might not get anything else to eat if she did. There was a stone jar of honey on the table and Babs reached out with a greedy hand for it. She had just got the lid off when a wooden spoon descended and caught her a stinging blow on the back of the hand. The woman said something but Babs did not need words to get the message. The honey was not for the likes of her.

Miss Rowland pointed to a small dish of salt and one of sugar. At least she had a choice, thought Babs, and while the woman's back was turned, used the sugar liberally. There was also a jug of cream on the table and she made swift use of it, so the lumpy porridge did not taste too bad. As she ate her breakfast, Babs thought of Nellie. Tears pricked the back of her eyes and she wanted to go home. She wondered what her sister had thought when she found her note and what she would say if Babs suddenly turned up on the doorstep as unexpectedly as she had left the house. 'Come in, love,' she'd probably say and would refrain from adding that she had known her sister would find the job harder than she imagined. Grandfather would be a different matter.

The farmer sat down at the table and said something about potatoes to Babs. As his sister placed mugs of tea in front of them both, he carried on talking and Babs stared at him with dawning comprehension. It seemed he expected her to begin digging up potatoes that morning. She remembered the potato plot at home and how Billy had done most of the digging. She reached for the mug of tea and knew she was in for a long, hard day.

To her relief, Babs was not to work alone with the farmer in the potato field, which seemed to stretch to the horizon. The other land girl, Flo, was back and he left them to it and went off to do something else.

'Howdo,' said Flo, who was small and lean but soon proved to be much stronger that she looked. 'I'll do the diggin',' said Flo, wielding a spade. 'Yous can pick up the spuds and place them in them baskets over there. Don't be lookin' so worried. We'll get more help. Mams and kids generally turn up with it being the school holidays. Them's glad to make a few bob.'

Looking at the size of the field, Babs thanked God for that.

Potato picking on such a large scale was back-breaking work but, as the day progressed, Flo was proved right and they were soon joined by an army of women and children. Miss Rowland also appeared and a trestle table was set up. Babs reckoned she had the easy job of weighing out the potatoes and totting up the earnings at the end of the day.

That night Babs fell into her lumpy bed, muscles aching and fingers bleeding. She went out like a light. It was the same every single night of that first week. Too exhausted to indulge in chitchat with Flo, she ate what the other girl put in front of her morning, noon and evening.

The second week Flo began to lay down some ground rules. 'I know what you're sufferin',' she said. 'I've been there, but you'll soon toughen up and in the meantime, you've got to do your share of the cookin' and cleanin' and everythin' else.'

Babs did not argue but smiled and thanked her for being so patient with her. 'I never thought it would be like this.'

'Naw! Neither did I. I worked at mill and thought what a lovely life it would be away from Bolton in the country.' She gave a wry smile. 'He does a bit of everythin' here, as you'll have noticed. Cows, pigs, poultry, spuds and...wheat...you're just in time for harvest, Babs.' She threw back her dark head and laughed. 'It might look luv'ly on the pictures but it's bloody hard work. What we really need is a tractor here and mebbe by the end of the war this bloody tight-fisted farmer will have one, but I've no intention of hangin' around here till then.'

As they lay in their beds that night Flo told Babs about what she'd found out while she'd been away for a couple of days. Mobile gangs of Land Girls were being organised to work in different parts of the country as the need arose. Great swathes of Lancashire countryside that were once farmed but had been left to go wild since the Great War were being dug up to use for crops. 'Bigger fields where they can use machinery will be more productive. The German U-boats are still sendin' merchant ships bringin' food to Britain to the bottom of the Atlantic. The country has to be fed and it's the job of the farmers and the Women's Land Army to make sure nobody starves. The billets will be much better, Babs. I've heard some are in country houses and there's wardens who'll look after our every need.'

That really appealed to Babs. Instead of having the energy to go out to the nearest town to the pictures or dancing, here she had to work until she dropped. Thinking about the pictures and dancing reminded her of Ritchie. He'd have had her letter by now and would know it was over between them. Then she thought of her sister and remembered guiltily that she had not written to her yet. She must do so as soon as she had the time and the energy to put pen to paper.

'Helen! Where is that girl? Helen!'

'Coming!' called Nellie, drying hands that were chapped and sore from washing clothes, before hurrying into the parlour.

The wireless was on and her grandfather was sitting in an armchair with the light from the window falling over his bowed shoulders onto a letter on his lap. He removed his Woolworth's spectacles and stared at her.

'What is it?' She stared back at him, trying to conceal her impatience. Seeing the open sheet of paper reminded her of Babs, who had not yet written. She felt cross with her. Then there was Teddy, who faithfully wrote to her still. The poor love! In his last letter he had mentioned having a heat rash that itched unbearably. He had called her his lovely wife. She thought ruefully that it was a good job that he could not see her right now with her chestnut hair falling in damp wisps about her sweaty face and her body clad in a wraparound dingy pinny that could not conceal her advancing pregnancy.

'Who's the letter from?' she asked.

'Two things,' said Grandfather. 'The Hun has invaded Russia.'

She nodded, thinking poor Russians, although, they should have had more sense than to align themselves with someone as untrustworthy as Hitler. 'And the letter?'

'Your sister, Lottie, who was the least favoured amongst you girls when the looks were doled out.'

'That's not kind,' said Nellie. 'What about her?'

'They want her out. They need the bed.'

Nellie's feelings were mixed. She wanted her sister home but how would she cope? 'When is she coming?'

He tossed the letter to Nellie. 'She's got to be fetched. There's nothing more they can do for her. She's got to leave Friday at the latest.'

'But that's the day after tomorrow,' cried Nellie. Her eyes scanned the page. 'It says here that she won't be able to climb stairs just yet. I'll have to get Billy to bring down the single bed from Adelaide's old room. If you agree, it can go in the dining room as we never use it.'

He nodded. 'I hope you'll be able to manage looking after the house and the pair of us. If her being here means I get neglected, then other arrangements will have to be made.'

Nellie ignored him, thinking, not for the first time, that he was a selfish old man. She left him to his newspaper, wondering how she was going to get Lottie home. There would be the walk from the hospital to Southport railway station and then the walk up from the one at Seaforth and she would need to get the room ready. It was at times like this that she needed Babs, but she was going to have to get help from another quarter. So, that evening, Nellie spoke to Billy when he arrived to help in the garden.

Instantly, he said, 'No problem, Mrs Lachlan.'

Relieved, she almost hugged him.

Between them they managed to move the table and chairs out of the dining room, dismantle the single bed and bring it downstairs. As he reassembled the bed frame in the dining room, they talked about the beans and peas that were ready for picking.

After Billy had carried the dining chairs out of the way upstairs to the attic, Nellie gave him thruppence and thanked him. He pocketed the money with thanks. She had wrapped vegetables and a couple of eggs in newspaper and now handed them to him.

'There's something else I want to ask you, Billy.'

'Fire away,' he said.

She told him about Lottie having to be brought home from the hospital. He had already heard about her being buried in the blitz and spending months in hospital. He looked thoughtful. 'I could probably give her a ride on my delivery bike up from the station.'

Nellie visualised Lottie, who must be all of twelve stone, sitting in the wicker basket fastened to the front of Billy's bike and smiled. 'It would be a disaster,' she said frankly. 'She'd have the pair of you over.'

He sighed. 'If that's what you think, Mrs Lachlan, we'll have to come up with something else. I could ask my dad. This used to be part of his beat years ago, but now he's a desk sergeant at the police station.'

'I didn't realise your dad was a policeman,' said Nellie.

Billy flicked back a lock of hair from his forehead. 'He wanted me to join the force but I'm going in the army. I might get to see a bit of the world.'

'As long as you keep your head down,' said Nellie, and brought the conversation back to Lottie. 'So will you help me bring my sister home?'

He said that he would speak to his father and let her know tomorrow.

The following morning, Nellie had just finished feeding the chickens and was washing her hands when there was a knock at the door. She went to answer it and found a policeman on the doorstep. He was well over six foot, with a sturdy build and had a cherubic rosy face with grey eyes and thick eyebrows.

'Sergeant McElroy, at your service, Mrs Lachlan,' he introduced himself with a smile. 'My lad Billy told me you have a problem.' He removed his cap to reveal receding salt and pepper hair. 'Your sister, love. What you need is a wheelchair and I can get you one, just for tomorrow, mind,' he said in a low voice. 'I'll leave it at Seaforth Station. Billy can return it after your sister's safely delivered here.'

Nellie thanked him. 'It'll make things so much easier for me.'

'All in a day's work,' he said cheerfully. 'The wife and I really appreciate you having Billy here and the eggs and veggies he brings home.'

She smiled. 'He deserves them. He's a hard worker.'

'Glad to know you appreciate him.' He touched his helmet and strode off down the path.

The journey to Southport was achieved with the minimum of fuss. Sgt McElroy had oiled the wheels for Nellie and she and the wheelchair travelled in the guard's van. She found it hard work pushing her sister through the bustling streets of the seaside resort and it was a relief when Lottie and the wheelchair were deposited on the Liverpool-bound train.

It was only as they neared Seaforth that Lottie began to babble on about how nervous she felt seeing Grandfather again. 'He never liked me, Nellie.' Lottie's lips quivered and her double chin wobbled. 'Is-is he as m-much a whingeing, m-miserable, tight-fisted, old so-and-so as he used to be when Mam was alive?'

Nellie nodded. 'Although, it can't be much fun getting old,' she murmured, gazing out of the window towards the Beach Road allotments as the train approached the station. 'Quick-tempered, unreasonable, autocratic – he's them, too. Just comfort yourself with the thought that he spends most of the time in the parlour listening to the wireless and reading the paper.' She stood up. 'Here we are.' Helping her sister to her feet, she added, 'Chin up, shoulders back, best foot forward...and, whatever you do, Lottie, don't let him see that you're scared.'

Lottie promised to do her best. Yet half an hour later as her exhausted sister pushed her up the path, Lottie was thinking that it was easy for Nellie to say she shouldn't show any fear of their grandfather. He had been something of a bogeyman to Lottie as a child. Aunt Josie had often threatened that if she didn't behave herself then they'd tell him what a naughty girl she had been. 'He'll put you in a dark cupboard and throw away the key,' she'd warned in her squeaky voice. Holy Mother of God, she had almost wet her knickers when her aunt had said that. She'd had nightmares about being locked away in the dark for years.

'Rouse yourself, Lottie. We're here,' panted Nellie, placing a hand on her shoulder. 'Can you get out now?'

'If you can take my belongings and hold the chair, I think I can manage.' Lottie leaned on the arms of the wheelchair and pushed herself up. Her feet searched for the ground and Nellie took her arm and helped her to stand. Lottie took a cautious step forward and then another. She was walking but there was no way she could scud along the ground as she had once been able to. Before the operation, she had looked forward to being out of pain. Yet here she was almost four months later and still in agony.

'So here she is,' grunted a voice.

Lottie lifted her head and stared from wide, frightened eyes at the old man with his white hair and straggly moustache. She attempted to speak but could not get the words past the constriction in her throat. Her father had once said that she was no oil painting and, although the words had puzzled her, she had guessed they weren't complimentary. She was suddenly

conscious of just how tight the brown frock was and she felt the blood rush to her face with embarrassment. Why couldn't she be like her sisters?

'Cat got your tongue, girl?' he said.

'Grandfather, can you help me here?' Nellie thrust Lottie's bag at him. 'It hasn't been an easy journey and we both need a rest.'

'A rest,' he barked. 'Hasn't she been resting for the last few months?'

Nellie sighed. 'Can't you see she's in pain? Please, get out of the way so we can both get inside. The quicker you do that, the quicker I'll get dinner on and you'll have less to complain about.'

'Don't you be pert with me, Helen. I'm the boss here. You're here because I allow it,' he muttered, ambling up the lobby and dumping the bag outside the dining room before going into the parlour and closing the door.

Lottie glanced at Nellie and accompanied her sister to where her bag had been dumped. Nellie opened the door of the dining room and ushered her sister inside. 'You're to sleep here,' she said. 'Hopefully you'll manage the outside lav without too much trouble.'

Lottie gazed about the sunlit room and whispered, 'It's so much bigger than the bedroom upstairs and I'll be sleeping here on my own. It's going to feel strange without Babs here, too.'

'You'll soon get used to the space, and you can have the cat for company. You can see the back garden from here. I've brought in an armchair so you can watch the garden birds and the hens, as well as Billy when he comes to give a hand.'

Lottie did not ask about Billy because her sister had talked about him before. She limped over to the easy chair near the window and lowered herself onto it carefully. 'Thanks, Nell, for getting me here.'

'No trouble.' Nellie picked up Lottie's bag and carried it over to the bed. 'What have you got in this? Do you want me to unpack it for you?'

'A new ration book and identity card, the missal that Francis gave me.' She ticked the rest of the items off on her fingers. 'A couple of changes of clothes, nighties...oh, and a medallion from Lourdes that a woman who visited gave me.' Her grey eyes searched Nellie's face. 'Mam didn't believe in accepting charity but giving is good for people's souls, don't you think?'

Nellie smiled. 'I'm sure you're right. After I've done this, I'll make us a cup of tea. Perhaps you can come with me to the kitchen.'

'I'd love a cuppa. Will Grandfather be joining us?'

'Probably not.' Nellie placed her sister's clothes in one of the sideboard cupboards but when she straightened up dizziness overcame her and she had to sit on the bed.

'I don't think he likes me,' said Lottie, heaving a gusty sigh.

Nellie murmured, 'Don't let it bother you. I don't think he likes anybody much. You know Joe's death knocked him for six.'

'I liked Joe. Aunt Josie used to say he was a naughty boy. To be honest, Nellie, I didn't know him as well as Francis. I love Francis. Do you think he'll visit me? You and him used to get on really well before you...' She hesitated.

'Married Teddy,' supplied Nellie. 'Things aren't that bad between us. He's busy, though, so he mightn't be able to get here as regularly as he'd like to.' The dizziness was passing and she changed the subject. 'D'you think you'll manage to do some jobs for me? It'll mean Grandfather won't have as much to moan about.'

'I want to be useful,' she said eagerly. 'I can sew. I can peel potatoes.'

'You can knit, too, can't you? I need things for the baby.'

'Oh, Nell! I've been thinking about your baby. You'll have to get married in the Catholic church now. Otherwise, it'll be a little...'

'Don't you dare say that word!' warned Nellie. 'Besides it's not true. Our marriage is legal. I'll go and put the kettle on. You can follow me when you're ready.' She walked out of the room.

'Oh, Mary, mother of God,' whispered Lottie, feeling for her rosary beads. 'I've gone and upset her now but she has to be told. Help me, Mother, to make her see the error of her ways.' She sat for a few minutes in the silence, aware of the ticking of a clock and the muted clucking of hens. Then she pushed herself up out of the chair and limped across the room.

Nellie looked up as Lottie entered the kitchen and forced a smile. 'You OK?'

Lottie's face was tight with pain but she nodded and made for a chair at the table.

'Don't sit on that one. It's the one with the wobbly leg.'

'A bit like me,' joked Lottie. She lowered herself onto a different chair. Once seated she looked up at her sister. 'I'm praying to St Giles for a miracle.'

'Good for you,' murmured Nellie, remembering he was the patron saint of cripples and beggars. As she placed a cup of tea in front of Lottie, she prayed her sister's devoted religious zeal would not get on her nerves.

As they drank their tea, Nellie filled her sister in on the everyday routine of the household, as well as any other of Grandfather's foibles of which she might be unaware, such as his still covering furniture with newspaper despite her telling him that it should be reused for the war effort.

'What about Mass?' asked Lottie.

'Grandfather doesn't go regularly and the priest doesn't visit.'

'And you?'

Nellie gave a twisted smile. 'Not yet. Now finish your tea and don't say another word about religion.'

'One more thing?' squeaked Lottie. 'Mam's grave?'

Nellie's fingers tightened on her cup. 'What about it?'

'I'd like to visit and put flowers on it.'

Nellie felt a stab of guilt. She had not visited her mother's and aunt's graves since her father had been home. 'Maybe we'll go there in a few weeks' time. At the moment the walk'll be too much for you.'

'What about the wheelchair?'

'I told you Billy's coming for it.' Nellie rose from the table and began the preparations for the evening meal.

Later when Billy arrived, she introduced him to Lottie, realising they were much of an age. 'It must have been scary being buried alive,' he said.

Lottie nodded. She had never had much to do with boys. Aunt Josie had warned her never to be alone with one and if she found herself in a boy's company by accident, she must certainly not allow him intimacies. Lottie had had no idea what her aunt was talking about.

Billy persisted. 'My dad's mate was killed in Bootle during the blitz. He was a hero and was awarded a posthumous medal.'

Lottie managed to mumble something about there being lots of heroes around then. Billy was about to say something else when Grandfather appeared and barked an order at him. Relieved, Lottie limped back into the house and managed to reach her bedroom, where she sat and watched through the window what was going on outside. She felt much more comfortable being an onlooker.

The following day Nellie received a postcard from Teddy. It had a photo of palm trees and pyramids. She told herself that she must not worry about him because that way madness lay. She longed for him and it was only the thought of them being together as a family in the future that helped her keep going when she felt so unbearably tired.

The days fell into a pattern. Nellie would help Lottie to get out of bed and leave her to dress herself. Then her sister would join her in the kitchen and they'd have porridge, toast and tea with their grandfather before Nellie went shopping and did some of the household chores. Lottie was given the task of doing all the darning and mending, as well as preparing vegetables. Nellie went to the library and brought books for them to read.

Lottie spent more time reading her missal, promising herself every day that she would make the effort to get to church on Sunday but so far she had not managed to do so. She was shy of being asked questions about what had happened to her and having to talk about their mother's death. Francis had not been to visit and there had been no letters from Babs.

Every evening when Billy arrived, Lottie would settle herself in the chair in front of the window with the wool and knitting needles Nellie had bought and knit for the baby, watching him work among the rows of vegetables. She found it restful, spending that hour or two in such a way, and gradually the nightmares of being buried alive and the awfulness of losing her mother and aunt began to lessen.

Chapter Six

'There's a letter here for you here, Helen.'

Nellie glanced down as Grandfather dropped it in her lap. Instantly she recognised the handwriting and eagerly slit the envelope with a finger. It was little more than a note but it was from Babs who, it appeared, was not far from Ormskirk. Immediately Nellie was reminded of the article in the *Crosby Herald* about hundreds of acres of land in Lancashire, which had lain neglected since the last war, being ploughed up by the Women's Land Army. It did not appear that Babs was one of them because her note said that she was working on a small mixed farm. She said it was back-breaking hard work and she missed her home comforts and hoped Nellie was well and that she would be able to visit home before the baby's birth.

Unfortunately Babs had forgotten to write her address on the top, which was annoying, but Nellie was relieved that her baby sister had written at last and that she was doing exactly what she wanted. She looked forward to seeing her.

But they were to have a surprise visitor the following week. Nellie had set up a deckchair in the garden, so Lottie could have fresh air while sewing a vest for the baby and she helped Billy pick vegetables. The three of them were gainfully occupied when a loud voice hailed them. Nellie turned and saw a man dressed in a tweed jacket and tan trousers coming towards them. He was bareheaded and smoking a pipe and she did not immediately recognise him.

'It's my dad,' said Billy in a low voice. 'What's he doing here?'

Nellie wondered the same herself. 'Good evening, Sgt McElroy,' she said.

'Mrs Lachlan.' He gazed at her pregnant shape from slightly protuberant eyes before giving his attention to Lottie. 'This your sister?'

'Yes. Lottie, this is Billy's father,' said Nellie.

'How d'you do?' said Lottie, slanting him a look before resuming her task.

'Billy mentioned you were managing to get up and about a bit, so I thought I'd come and say hello. How are you coping after your terrible experience?'

'Fine.' Lottie did not look up.

'Billy was quite concerned about you,' said the sergeant.

'Billy's very caring for someone of his age,' said Nellie with a smile.

'Well, we did our best with him. It wasn't easy.' He was silent a moment and then said, 'If everything's all right then I'll be getting back to the missus. She's an invalid, you know. Good evening, Mrs Lachlan.'

'Good evening.' Nellie watched him until he was out of sight before turning to Billy. 'You didn't say your mam was an invalid,' she said.

'No,' he said tersely.

'Was the wheelchair hers?' asked Nellie.

Billy shook his head. 'She's not sick that way.' He turned his head away and resumed picking beans.

His behaviour roused Nellie's curiosity but, as it was obvious he did not want to talk about his mother, she let the subject drop.

The Sunday in August when the clocks went back, Nellie arrived home from the shops to find Francis in the kitchen, talking to Lottie and Grandfather. She wondered why it was that priests and vicars wore their clerical collars when they were not working. She said, 'Hello,' and proceeded to unpack the shopping and put it away.

He followed her into the larder. 'Grandfather says you're fine. Is that true, Nellie? You look tired to me. He and Lottie aren't expecting too much from you?'

She was touched by his concern. 'I'm managing.'

'And Lottie? He's not bullying her?'

'He ignores her most of the time.'

Francis looked relieved. 'Better that than have her cowering in corners in fear of him.'

Nellie agreed.

'Pity Babs decided to go off and be a land girl. You could have done with her here.'

Nellie nodded. 'She's young and I think part of her leaving was due to wanting to get away from an overzealous boyfriend.'

'Boyfriend!'

She smiled. 'Grandfather not mention him?'

'No.'

'Probably forgotten. He is getting old.'

He nodded and sighed. 'It's a shame Lottie's still in pain.'

'She's a good help to me, though. She's knitting for the baby.'

He tapped his fingers against the shelf holding packets of oats, sugar and tea. 'She is worried about you both...' He let the sentence hang.

'Ahhh!' murmured Nellie, her body tensing. 'I presume you're not referring to my physical health?'

'You know the church's teachings, Nell,' he said gravely.

She stared into his sober, rugged face. 'I thought we agreed not to mention the baby's need for baptism until after it's born. I know you feel it's your duty to broach the subject but we'll end up at loggerheads if you persist.'

'Have you mentioned it to Teddy yet?'

She shook her head. 'Truthfully, I've so many other things to think about and, besides, the poor love has enough to deal with out in the desert without me giving him that to worry about.'

'He's still safe, then.'

'I hope so,' murmured Nellie, her heart flipping over. 'Africa's such a long way away and it takes time for news to filter through.'

'I'll hold him in my prayers,' said Francis.

She thanked him and asked whether he'd heard from their father.

Francis shook his head. 'Like Mam, he might have been pleased to have a priest in the family but I think he's always resented our closeness.'

'That doesn't surprise me. He's a possessive, jealous man.' She flushed, 'I know I shouldn't have said that but I can't pretend that he's the perfect father.' She cocked an eyebrow. 'Shall we join Grandfather and Lottie and have a cup of tea?'

He nodded and she went to put the kettle on.

A few weeks later, on a Sunday afternoon, Nellie was out in the garden, thinking about Teddy as she washed down a cot she had found, dismantled, up in the attic. She still did not have a pram but it was six weeks until her confinement and she had decided to wait until the baby was born before putting an advertisement in the Wanted column of the *Crosby Herald* for a second-hand one. Billy was up a tree picking apples. Lottie was at the foot of the trunk, taking them from him and placing them in a bucket. Nellie's eyes were dreamy as she thought of the baby, convinced it was going to be a boy. She hoped that when her grandfather set eyes on him her son would take the place in his heart that Joe had once filled.

'Helen, come here, girl!' Her grandfather's brusque voice took her by surprise.

'What is it?' she said, wringing out the cloth into a bowl of water and glancing up at him, where he stood in the doorway of the washroom.

He did not speak but held out a light orange envelope to her. She did not move, staring at it in disbelief. The cloth slipped from her fingers and a pulse began to hammer in her head. The old man's mouth trembled and he moved towards her.

Wordlessly, Nellie took the envelope from him and with shaking hands removed the telegram. The message abruptly informed her that Corporal Lachlan had been killed in action. She felt as if she had been stabbed in the heart, swayed, and had to grip the cot to prevent herself from falling. For what felt an eternity she rested against it as waves of icy desolation swept over. Her vision blurred as she stared down the garden at Lottie and Billy, working together beneath the apple tree. She could not believe that Teddy was dead. She crushed the telegram in her hand as if somehow that would obliterate the news, but the words hammered inside her head: Dead! Teddy was dead.

He was not going to be one of the survivors who would come marching home. Never again would she see his face or feel his lips on hers. Never again would he take her in his arms and make love to her or call her sweetheart. They'd spent so few days of married life together. The dreams they'd had for their future would never come true; they had died in the desert with him.

She felt a hand on her shoulder and looked up at her grandfather. To her amazement she saw that his eyes were moist. 'Come inside, Helen, and sit down. You look as if you're going to faint.'

Me, faint? thought Nellie. She felt dizzy and sick, so perhaps she would just slip to the ground and lose consciousness, at least then she wouldn't have to think or feel. She felt hot and cold, and then blackness descended on her and she knew no more.

'Are you OK, Nell?'

Nellie blinked and stared up at Lottie and Billy. What had happened? Why did they look so worried?

'Of course she's not all right. She fainted,' snapped Grandfather.

The ground was hard and Nellie's back ached. She looked at the cot and saw what looked like a sheet of yellow paper stuck to one of the bars

'Is it the baby?' asked Billy.

'The baby!' Lottie's fat jowls wobbled. She had no idea what to do if it was the baby that had caused her sister to pass out.

Nellie said nothing but continued to stare at the yellow paper.

'Let's get her inside,' said Grandfather. 'Billy, you help her up.'

Billy placed his arms round Nellie and she clutched at his pullover with trembling hands. She was cold and felt strange. Something terrible had happened but she did not want to think about it. Her baby needed her. Billy carried her into the house and she flopped against him as if the strength had drained out of her. He took her into the parlour and placed her on the sofa on a sheet of newspaper. She did not care about that but was thankful to lie down.

Her grandfather and Lottie had followed them in and Lottie carefully lowered herself onto the edge of the sofa. Her grandfather had told her about Teddy's death and she did not know what to say to Nellie or what to do, but could only pray for guidance. She reached out and took one of her sister's hands and chaffed it. 'You're cold, Nellie.'

'That's shock,' said Grandfather. 'A hot water bottle and a cup of tea are what she needs.'

Lottie looked up at Billy. 'I'll put the kettle on,' he said, and left the parlour.

'You go and help him, girl,' said Grandfather. 'I'll sit with Helen.'

Lottie hesitated and then dragged herself up. She limped into the kitchen and saw that Billy was pouring milk into a cup.

'Best put in several spoons of sugar,' he murmured, glancing at Lottie. 'Mam says that's good for shock.'

'OK,' said Lottie, going in search of the sugar bag. 'I hope she's going to be all right. Her husband's been killed. She ran away and married him, you know? He was lovely even if he was a Proddy. She really loved him.'

'It's a blinking shame,' said Billy, shaking his head. 'Why is it that terrible things happen to good people?'

'It's not God's fault,' said Lottie, spooning sugar into the milk. 'It's the devil, who tempts people like Hitler into wanting power. They think they're somebody great and all they are is evil.'

Billy mooched around the kitchen with his hands in his

pockets. 'D'you think Mr Callaghan and Mrs Lachlan will want me to carry on picking apples?'

Lottie was not used to making decisions. 'What do you think?'

'She wanted them all picked by tomorrow.'

'Then why ask me? Go and do it.'

He nodded and made for the washroom, only to pause in the doorway. 'I hope she'll be OK,' he said, before vanishing outside.

So do I, thought Lottie, carrying the cup of tea into the parlour.

Nellie sipped the hot tea, scared silly, fearing she had damaged the baby when she had fainted. The ache in her back was spreading and she wanted to be up and doing something, anything to get rid of the dark thought hovering on the edge of her consciousness. She wanted to scream at it but knew if she did that she would only frighten Lottie and Grandfather.

Lottie brought in a hot water bottle and placed it next to Nellie and then sat at her feet. 'Billy's carrying on picking the apples,' she said.

'That's good,' said Nellie, feeling as if the words were coming from a distance. 'What about supper? Will you be able to make it?'

Lottie said, 'I'll have a go.'

Nellie ate her supper off a tray. She was feeling like a cat on hot bricks and could not relax. Grandfather sat with her, listening to the wireless. The drone of men's voices caused her to grit her teeth. That scream inside her still lurked and she got up, unable to bear doing nothing any longer.

Her grandfather lifted his head and stared at her. 'You all right now, Helen?'

She nodded and carried the tray outside. Her body felt in the grip of one of those monsters of steel she had seen in a sci-fi film with Teddy. A chill seized her heart and she felt a sense of panic. 'Teddy, Teddy, I want you,' she babbled silently as she walked into the kitchen.

Lottie was washing dishes and looked pleased to see her. 'You're on your feet, Nellie. Are you OK?'

Nellie thought, if anyone asks me that again, I'll scream. She made up her mind to go to bed and lumbered out of the kitchen and climbed the stairs, knowing she would be left alone up there. She went to the lavatory and then undressed and got into bed with a sigh of relief. Teddy, she thought, hugging her pillow against her cheek. A tear slid down her face and then another and another, dampening the pillowcase. No, she mustn't cry. What was there to cry about? He wasn't dead! He couldn't be dead! She and the baby needed him.

She tried to shut out the thoughts but the same ones kept coming. Teddy was dead. She would never see him again. Never, never! Stop it, stop it, cried her brain. You'll make yourself ill. Think of the baby. The baby. Generally, as soon as she lay down to sleep, the baby started moving and she imagined her son practising football in her womb. Tonight she could feel nothing, just that ache and cold fear. She told herself that the baby had probably had as big a shock as she had and was resting. 'Look on the bright side. Things are going to be fine,' she murmured, determined to sleep.

But Nellie could not sleep. Every nerve in her body was alert for any movement from the baby. Minutes and then hours ticked by and still nothing. She got up and went to the lavatory and was shocked to see a smear of blood when she wiped herself. Her heart began to thud. What was happening? Oh God! Something was wrong. Outside it was dark and she did not know what to do. She needed the midwife. Lottie would have to fetch her.

Nellie went downstairs and banged on her sister's door. Normally it took Lottie some time to get up and open it but to her surprise it opened instantly and she stood there in a voluminous nightgown with her hair in disarray about her flushed face. She looked wide awake. 'What is it, Nellie?'

'Get dressed. You must fetch the midwife,' said Nellie without preamble.

'But-but where does she live?' stammered Lottie, who had been no further than the garden gate since she had arrived home.

Nellie told her. 'You must hurry,' she cried.

Then she sat on the stairs in her night attire, white-faced with misery.

Lottie wasted no time wishing that Babs was here to run for the midwife, but got dressed and limped out of the house. Fortunately the woman was home and came immediately. She was middle-aged with a hatchet face and a brisk manner. Lottie suggested she and Nellie might like to use her bedroom to save her sister climbing the stairs. Then Lottie went into the kitchen to see if the fire was still burning so she could boil a kettle for tea.

Soon Nellie was lying on Lottie's bed. 'Let's have a listen and a look at you,' said the woman, easing up Nellie's nightie. Her face was grave when she finished her inspection. 'Hospital for you, my girl, and straight away.'

'No,' she whispered. 'No.'

'My dear,' said the woman gently. 'You must be brave.'

'But...'

The midwife shook her head and went in search of Lottie. 'Stay with her while I arrange things.'

Nellie wanted to scream that this could not be happening to her. Within the hour an ambulance had whisked her to the hospital. Various unpleasant things were done to her and then the pain started. It went on and on. A doctor came to visit and spoke to her kindly and after that everything was a blur. Hours later, still gowned and masked, the doctor told her that her baby boy had been delivered stillborn. Despite her utter desolation, she asked to see him, only to be told that was not a good idea. Besides, he had been taken away and disposed of.

Chapter Seven

Babs hummed 'Life is just a Bowl of Cherries' as she brushed her hair in front of the cracked mirror she had bought from the white elephant stall at the local church's fundraising sale in aid of the Red Cross. Flo had shown her the nearest village that lay hidden out of sight beyond a wood and could be reached in twenty minutes by a footpath.

Flo, who had been ready for the last ten minutes, said, 'There won't be any talent there, yer know.'

Babs' red hair whirled about her shoulders as she looked at her. 'How do you know? It could be different from when you went last year.'

'Tradition,' said Flo, inspecting her fingernails. 'There'll be Lancashire hotpot wiv mebbe a choice of red cabbage, beetroot and brown sauce, as well as bread and butter. For pudding there'll probably be apple pie and custard...and there's the barn dance. Yer knows what that's like.'

'No, I don't,' said Babs.

'Stamping feet and couples charging up and down centre of the hall. There'll be lots of clapping and dosey-doein'. If you get a man to partner yer, and you probably will because yer a looker, he'll do his best to swing yer off your feet.'

'It sounds fun,' said Babs, her green eyes bright with excitement.

'Aye! It was fun last year. Yer can have a laugh if you don't worry about not knowin' what yer doin'. If you can forget yourself and let yerself go.'

'I've been working that blinking hard I'm determined to have a good time,' said Babs, easing back aching shoulders from cutting cabbages and milking. 'Mr Rowland certainly likes his pound of flesh.' She puckered her brow. 'I wish I'd brought a decent frock, but I didn't have any room in my holdall.'

'We're best wearin' breeches and brogues, anyway, as we'll be usin' footpath.'

'I suppose you're right. Besides, I'm getting used to not having a skirt flapping about my legs,' said Babs, glancing down at herself in the WLA uniform of green V-necked ribbed jumper worn over a fawn aertex shirt with brown corduroy breeches and knee length fawn socks. 'Even so…' She didn't finish what she was saying, wondering instead what Nellie and Grandfather would say when they saw her dressed like this. She was disappointed that Nellie had not replied to her note but perhaps she had believed Babs would be visiting in days so hadn't bothered. Unfortunately, Mr Rowland had refused to allow her the time off, saying they were too busy, despite a group of land girls turning up to help gather in the harvest. She and Flo had picked their brains about the new scheme and planned to get in touch with the organiser. But her mind had strayed away from Nellie. She must write to her tomorrow as she was sure the baby was due any day now. Would she have a niece or a nephew? She felt a thrill at the thought of being an aunt.

'Yous ready then?' asked Flo.

Babs reached for her waterproof brown overcoat and felt porkpie hat and put them on before slipping her gasmask holder and bag containing her torch, purse, comb and ticket over her shoulder. 'Now I'm ready,' she said, smiling. 'I hope you know the way in the dark.'

'It's spooky but I'll get us there,' said Flo. 'Mam always said eat plenty of carrots and you'll see in the dark.'

'It's a pity Mr Rowland didn't offer to take us in the pony and trap,' said Babs, leading the way downstairs.

'If we were local he might have but we're only the hired hands and *furriners* to boot,' said Flo.

'Who did you go with last time?' asked Babs.

'Oh, there was a bloke workin' here but he joined up with his mate from village. Both are in army now. I write to Pete now and then.'

Fortunately there was a harvest moon and lots of stars overhead, so there was no need to switch on their torches. Babs was glad to be warmly clad. There was a definite nip in the air and she had noticed that morning it was getting lighter much later and the leaves were beginning to change colour. She thought of Nellie and the time she had spent in Cumberland and wondered if she ever missed the countryside or her job with the children. It had probably been more interesting than being at home looking after Grandfather. She wondered if Lottie was back home and how Francis and her father were, and thought that she must get round to writing to them, too, but right now she wanted to have some fun.

The village hall was already filling up when the two girls arrived. They hung their coats and hats in the cloakroom and entered the main hall. It was brightly lit and the walls were festooned with berry-encrusted greenery. Vases of Michaelmas daises were placed on trestle tables set with white cloths and crockery and cutlery. At the far end of the hall, a female pianist, a grey-haired male violinist and a youth with a penny whistle were in a huddle with a stocky man wearing corduroy trousers, a checked shirt and a red 'kerchief knotted at his throat.

Babs noticed that most of the women and girls were wearing full skirts or frocks and envied them. 'Do we dance or eat first?' she murmured.

'Eat. So they can clear everythin' away for dancing. Man wearing red scarf is master of ceremonies. He tells us what to do when it comes to dancin',' said Flo.

'Will people feel like dancing after eating?'

'Folk don't get up straight away and some have to be dragged onto floor 'cos they worry about makin' fools of themselves. 'Sides, yer not goin' to get that much to eat yer can't move.'

Which was a pity, thought Babs, who had only eaten a jam butty because of the hotpot supper.

They found themselves a place and sat down. Babs glanced at the other people at their table and was pleased to see a couple of young men in uniform. She guessed they were on leave and eyed them up, wondering if either was married, not wanting to go poaching another woman's man. One of them, fair-haired and with a lively expression, had noticed her looking at him and stared boldly back.

'Evening,' he said.

'Hello,' said Babs, thinking he had a cheeky grin.

'Yous must be redhead working on Rowland's farm. Heard about you,' he called across to her above the din in the hall.

'What have you heard?' she asked, thinking that the village gossips must be as busy as Mrs Wainwright back home.

'Don't want to make yous think too much of yerself but they said yous were trouble.'

Babs was indignant and her cheeks flamed. 'I don't know what they mean by that but if you're going to take any notice of them, why bother speaking to me?'

''Cos I fancy a dance with you. Shame, it's wild west kind of dancing but they'll probably throw in a waltz towards the end. Yous fancy getting up with me?'

'I don't mind, although, I tell you now I've never done this kind of dancing before.'

'No problem. Half the fun is having a go. Don't you go letting any other idjit persuade you to get up.'

Before she could say that she'd please herself, a man in a clerical collar rose and called for hush. He had to repeat himself several times before the noise subsided. The proceedings were opened with a thanksgiving prayer for the harvest and then a blessing on the food they were about to eat. No sooner was that over than the hotpot was served by a team of middle-aged women.

Babs did not waste any time eating hers and would have enjoyed a second helping but, as none was offered, she had a couple of slices of bread and left room for pudding. This turned out to be what Flo had prophesied, apple pie and custard. She laid down her spoon with a satisfied sigh and placed a hand on her stomach. 'That was lovely.'

'No argument,' said Flo, reaching for her cup of tea. 'So yer've found yerself a partner already. Well, just don't go acceptin' any invitations to go outside and look at the moon. Eric has busy hands.'

Babs got the message but was determined to enjoy the dancing, anyhow. She wasn't looking for trouble.

Half an hour later the tables had been cleared away and the musicians were tuning up. The master of ceremonies was urging people onto the floor and Babs expected Eric with the busy hands to appear at her shoulder but that did not happen, so Babs sat watching the first dance with lively interest. There were several sets of four couples who whirled and skipped backwards and forwards; men twirled their partners and did what the master-of-ceremonies called dosey-doe-ing. She thought it looked really complicated but the music set her feet tapping and she decided that if Eric didn't make an appearance soon, she would accept any offers to dance that came her way.

She did not have long to wait before a distinguished looking elderly gentleman wearing a navy blazer and flannels approached her. 'May I have the pleasure, my dear?' he asked.

He was not the partner she wanted but was aware that several pairs of eyes were watching her and among them were those of Mr Rowland and his sister. She smiled and stood up. 'I'll probably tread on your toes. I've never done this before.'

'Just listen to what I tell you and not that fool in the red handkerchief and we'll do fine.' He held out a hand.

Babs placed her hand in his and was led onto the floor. As the music started, he bowed. She curtseyed and within moments joined hands with the other women and was skipping forward and back, forward and back. Her partner caught her hands and said, 'Swing around.' He continued to give her orders throughout the dance but she still got muddled up and ended up giggling madly.

Yet when the music stopped, he told her she had done wonderfully well and led her back to her seat, where a smiling soldier sat. He stood up and waved her to it. 'So d'yer think yer've got the hang of it now, Babs?'

She thanked the elderly gentleman before saying, 'You have to be joking, Eric,' with more than a hint of breathlessness.

'Prepared to have another go?'

'Once I've my breath back,' said Babs, whose legs were aching too. And talking of breath, she thought, catching the smell of beer on his.

His blue eyes widened. 'Come on, lass. Yer not one of these oldies.'

She laughed. 'No! But I work bloody hard all day, mate.'

'Then yer won't have any strength to resist when I take yer in my arms.'

'You've got a nerve,' said Babs mildly. 'But I'd better warn you my brothers taught me self-defence.'

'Yer've brothers?'

'Only one now,' she said, looking up at Eric, who wasn't half bad looking. 'Joe was killed in the Battle of the Atlantic.'

Eric's smile faltered. 'Sorry about that.'

'It wasn't your fault but thanks. My dad's still out there.'

'Bloody war,' said Eric.

'Yeah.' She decided not to mention her mother and aunt; their deaths were still too raw. 'So are you good at this barn dancing?'

His smile reappeared. 'I'll not make a hash of it.'

'Glad to hear it,' she said.

He proved himself right and, although he laughed when she made mistakes, Babs sensed his laughter was not unkind. Even so, when he asked to see her back to the farm at the end of the evening, she refused and that wasn't only because she'd sensed the farmer's eye on her while she danced. 'I'm with Flo.'

'She could go back with the Rowlands,' said Eric, still holding Babs' hand after the last dance.

She shook her head.

His blue eyes gazed into hers. 'Oh come on, lass. Have pity on a poor soldier! This is my embarkation leave.'

'Sorry.'

'What about the pictures on Monday evening?'

She hesitated. 'I work long hours and I'm whacked at the end of the day.'

He persisted. 'I'll borrow Dad's motorbike and take yer into Wigan. Yer'll hardly have to walk a step and if yer fall asleep during the film, yer can rest yer head on my shoulder.'

The offer was tempting and knowing he would be leaving soon lowered her resistance. 'OK. But you'll have to cut the engine, so Mr Rowland doesn't hear it. I'll meet you at the end of the path leading to the farm.'

His eyes lit up. 'Yer won't regret it. I'll give yer a good time.'

Babs said, 'Does that mean I get a box of chocolates?'

He smiled. 'Mebbe. See yer Monday.'

She watched him walk away and was glad there was no time to get fond of him. He could get killed and she did not want the pain of grieving again.

'You ready to go?' said Flo, appearing at her side with their coats and hats. 'Mr Rowland said we're to go back with him.'

Babs nodded. 'I thought he might.'

On the short journey back to the cottage in the pony and trap, she thought of Nellie and reminded herself that she must write to her in the next few days.

'It's good to have you home, Nell,' said Lottie, her grey eyes concerned as she looked into her sister's strained face. 'I'm really sorry about Teddy and the baby.'

Nellie's eyes filled with tears and, wordlessly, she squeezed her sister's hand and walked slowly over to the fireplace. She felt so down that she just wanted to sleep and not wake up. She rested her head on the mantelshelf and gazed down into the fire. If only she had seen her baby and held him in her arms. Had he been fair like Teddy or chestnut like herself? Had his eyes been blue-green, brown or grey? Would he have grown to be tall or of medium height? She would never know these things and her grief weighed heavily.

'There you are, Helen,' said her grandfather gruffly, entering the kitchen. 'How are you, girl?'

She lifted her head. 'How do you think I feel?'

'Bad. As if there's nothing to live for,' he surprised her by saying. 'But moping about won't solve anything. I remember when I lost your grandmother I felt terrible. But what could I do? I was on the high seas when she died. I was expecting her to be there when I docked but she'd been dead months and I didn't know about it. I could have been killed and she wouldn't have known, either. I've lived on memories ever since.'

Nellie was deeply touched by his words. 'You've never spoken of her before.'

He looked embarrassed and pulled on his moustache with a trembling hand. 'You never knew her, so what was the point? She was a stranger to you.'

'But if you'd spoken about her, I would have got to know her. It's-it's like reading a book. The more you read about people the more they become real.'

'Like reading about the saints,' interposed Lottie.

Grandfather ignored her. 'It was a long time ago. Time goes some way to healing but you have to get on with your life or go under.' He gave Nellie a ferocious stare. 'Work, girl, that will help you. Work.'

Work, she thought. A job. I could do with getting away from this house, but not yet. In her present mood and state of health she wasn't fit.

'Something to eat, Nellie?' asked Lottie, rousing her from her reverie. 'I've managed a bit of shopping and cooking while you were in hospital.'

'That's good.' She managed to sound enthusiastic, thinking that if her sister was able to do more in the house then she, herself, could seriously consider going out to work.

The next day Nellie received a letter from Babs and this time there was an address in the right hand corner. She wondered why her sister had not come home as she had said and, with a lift of the heart, hoped this was to tell her when she would visit. She began to read,

Dear Nellie,
I hope you are well. I thought I might have had an answer to my last letter but perhaps you thought you'd see me before you had a chance to write. I'm sorry I didn't get to see you but we're up to our eyes here and Mr Rowland, the farmer, refused to allow me time off. God only knows when I'll get home. I had some fun, though, at the village Harvest Supper and Barn Dance. You would have laughed to see me, Nellie. I made a right muck of it. This soldier, Eric, was on embarkation leave and tried his best to teach me, as did some other elderly gentleman, but I think I'd have to take lessons to get the hang of it. The village is one good thing about this place, I don't feel so cut off and Flo says there's an Autumn Beetle Drive to look forward to, whatever that is, and a Christmas Bazaar with a bottle stall and all kinds of things to make money for the church and the Red Cross.

But enough about me. What about the baby? My niece or nephew should have arrived by now. Whatever it is I'll love it. I can't wait to see it and hope you are OK.

A sob burst from Nellie and, crushing the letter in her hand, she ran out into the garden and down to the trees at the bottom. She placed her head against a tree trunk and cried and cried. It felt as if her heart was breaking, not only for her child but Teddy as well. She did not know how she was going to go on despite what her grandfather had said. What was there to live for, if she could not have Teddy or her son to love and care for?

'Are you all right, Mrs Lachlan?'

Slowly Nellie lifted her head and turned round to see Billy's father standing a few feet away. She swallowed and managed to say, 'Where did you come from?'

'I came to see if Billy was here. He spent more time helping out while you were in hospital.' He tugged at his full lower lip. 'Do you think he and Lottie get on well?'

Nellie wiped her wet face with the back of her hand. 'Yes. I'm glad about that. She's never had many friends. Mam and Aunt Josie always kept such a watch on her.'

His eyes seemed to bulge and for a moment she thought he looked haunted. She was surprised when he said, 'I remember your mother. She was unhappy because she was treated like a skivvy in this house.'

'She never complained. We'd have helped if she'd have asked but often she just seemed to want us out of the way.'

'I'm not talking about you girls but the old woman and your grandfather.' He paused, tapping the fingers of his right hand against his left wrist. 'Anyway, it's all water under the bridge now. Both women are dead and...' He paused again as if remembering something. 'I'm sorry to hear about your husband and the baby. You've had a bad time.'

'Yes.' She resisted screaming at him that she was still having a bad time. Wanting to get rid of him, she added, 'Would you like some apples? Billy's already taken some but maybe your wife would like more. Fruit's good for invalids.'

He thanked her and they walked up the garden together. She put some apples in a paper bag and handed it to him and said she'd see him to the gate.

'There's no need, Mrs Lachlan. I know the way out.'

She ignored his words and began to walk to the front of the house. He followed her and, at the gate, thanked her again, adding, 'If you ever feel Billy's here too often, just send him away.'

Nellie shook her head. 'You don't have to worry about him. I'm always pleased to see him. He's no trouble at all.' She turned and went back into the house.

Making herself a cup of tea, Nellie opened Babs' crumpled letter and finished reading it.

I hope Lottie's home now and is being a help to you. Give her and Grandfather my love. I'll be writing to Dad and Francis. Do, do write, Nellie.

Lots of love to yourself and the baby.

Your affectionate sister, Babs. XXXXXX

Nellie did not immediately reply to Babs' letter. She made several starts but her tears just soaked the page. Eventually, though, she managed to write down the terrible news and posted the letter to Babs.

Somehow Nellie got through the following days. She had a reply from Babs almost by return post. It was brief.

Dear, dear Nellie,

I am so, so sorry. I wish I could be with you but Mr Rowland is a selfish swine. He's got Flo and me ploughing with the horse now and won't give me the time off. He has no sympathy at all but says there's lots of people in the same boat. I wish he'd drop dead. By hook or by crook I'm determined to see you soon.

Love Babs.

Nellie realised she was glad Babs could not get away, knowing she would have trouble coping with her sister's sympathy.

Francis had already visited her in the hospital briefly but now he wanted to do something more positive for her. She cut him short when he said that the church was there to help her at such times. 'Not now, Francis,' she said, placing a steaming mug in front of him. 'At the moment I'm angry with God and don't want anything to do with him.'

'I can understand your feelings, Nell,' he said earnestly, pausing to take a large gulp of the Camp coffee that she knew he liked, 'but don't separate yourself from the best help you can have at such times.'

Her eyes were sad. 'It's too soon. I'm hurting too much. I know you can say that it wasn't God that caused the war but

Hitler but that still doesn't help me. I need to come to terms with this in my own way…and don't even think of mentioning that perhaps I'm being punished for marrying outside the faith. If you did then I would never speak to you again.'

Tears shone in Francis' eyes and he clasped her hand, which rested on the table. 'What kind of priest do you think I am?'

'Sorry,' she said, tears trickling down her cheeks as she gazed at their joined hands. 'But I need a brother more than I need a priest right now.'

He nodded and, holding her hand tightly, said no more.

A few days later, it came as a shock to turn on the wireless and discover that the Japanese had bombed the American naval base of Pearl Harbour. Within no time at all, America and Britain were at war with the Japanese and, shortly after, America's declaration of war with Germany and Italy followed. Soon it would be Christmas and Nellie wondered where was that peace and goodwill to all men that so many longed for?

She was in no mood to celebrate Christmas but Lottie was so desperate to try and get to Midnight Mass that, in the end, Nellie gave in and said she would go with her. Grandfather surprised them by accompanying them. Somehow Nellie managed to remain dry-eyed throughout the service but there were those who cried.

It was one o'clock in the morning by the time they arrived home but they were worried when they entered the house by the front door and saw a light in the kitchen. Grasping his walking stick tightly, Grandfather crept towards it, followed by Nellie. Lottie collapsed on the chest in the hall, exhausted by the effort she had made in getting to church after a long day preparing for the Christmas festivities.

Then Babs appeared in the doorway. 'Surprise, surprise!'

Nellie burst into tears.

Babs hurried forward and put her arms round her. 'Is my face that ugly? Please don't cry, Nell.'

'You've got a nerve, girl,' growled Grandfather, stumping past her into the kitchen. 'You should have visited ages ago.'

'I didn't have the money and besides, I wasn't allowed leave. I knew that after twenty weeks I was entitled to a free journey home but that swine of a farmer still kicked up a fuss. I couldn't stand it any longer and so I've walked out.'

Nellie rubbed her damp cheeks and cleared her throat. 'I'm glad you've made it at last. Heck, I'm desperate for a cup of tea.'

Babs smiled. 'I've something better. Homemade wine. I bought it at the bottle stall at the Christmas Bazaar. I thought it might help.'

Lottie called from her place in the hall, 'I don't hold with strong drink.'

'I do,' said Nellie, thinking a strong drink would be very acceptable right now.

Lottie placed her arm through Nellie's and Babs', and the three sisters walked across the kitchen. Nellie could see more clearly now that Babs was wearing a green V-necked, ribbed jumper and baggy brown corduroy breeches with knee-length socks.

'You look a right cut,' she said.

Babs laughed. 'I know. Would you believe I went to a dance in this outfit and was asked out to the pictures. They're lovely and comfortable and warm. Even so, I'm longing to get into a frock.' She opened a cupboard door and took out some glasses. 'Bloody hard work, it is, working on the land. I must have been crazy applying but in summer the countryside looked so lovely and after doing my bit for the vegetable patch, I thought it would be a piece of cake.'

'Serves you right,' said Grandfather, casting a disapproving eye over the bottle of wine. 'You girls shouldn't be drinking.'

Babs ignored him and, having found a tin opener with a corkscrew attachment she drew the cork, sniffed the bottle and filled three glasses. She handed the first to Nellie, the second to Grandfather and kept the last for herself. 'It's peapod.' Raising her glass, she added, 'Here's to better times.'

'Cheers,' said Nellie, and took a large gulp. It was sweeter than she expected and went down a treat. She drained her glass and held it out for a refill.

Grandfather made a disapproving noise in his throat but Nellie noticed that he'd emptied his glass, too. He did not ask for a refill but left the three sisters on their own and went upstairs.

Clasping her drink, Nellie moved over to the fireplace and sat down. 'So how long can you stay?'

'A couple of days.' Babs followed her over and sank onto the rug in front of the fireplace. 'I'd best go back. If I'm in luck, he'll tell the powers-that-be he wants rid of me and I'll get somewhere better than the cottage. You'd probably think "how picturesque", like I did when I first got there but in winter it's cold and damp. And as for the lav! That consists of a wooden board with a hole over a bucket, which we had to empty into a trench we dug ourselves...and there's no hot running water. This time of year it's a nightmare.'

'But you managed to go dancing.' Nellie sipped more wine.

'So it hasn't stopped your gallop,' said Lottie.

Babs stuck her tongue out at her. 'We manage the occasional night out but I must admit, if I have any choice in where I go next, I'll make sure it's near somewhere there's more life.'

Nellie was beginning to feel light-headed and could not hold back a giggle. 'How are they going to keep you down on the farm?' she sang.

Babs chuckled. 'You said it, Nell. But I reckon I'm stuck in the Land Army for the duration and God only knows how long that will be.'

A silence followed her words. Nellie wished she had a crystal ball. The war seemed to have been going on for ages. She yawned suddenly. 'Time for bed. Still want to share the double one?'

'Sure. It'll be almost like the old days,' said Babs.

Nellie knew those days were long gone. They were different

people. They had suffered great losses and life would never be the same again.

Having Babs in the house over Christmas and Boxing Day had a beneficial effect on Nellie. Maybe it was because she did not want to upset her eldest sister that Babs avoided the subject of the baby and her husband. Instead she talked some more about her life and mentioned Eric.

'I hope you kept him in order, Babs,' said Nellie. 'He'd have been looking for comfort.'

'I'm not daft, Nell. I know what's what,' she said with a twinkle.

Nellie found herself remembering hers and Teddy's honeymoon and felt a fierce gladness inside that she had defied her mother and married him. Hadn't someone once said that it was better having loved and lost than not to have loved at all?

Chapter Eight

'So, Nellie, what are you going to do with yourself now?' asked Mrs Wainwright. 'You've had tragedy in your life but you're only a young woman and doing something for the war effort will be good for you.'

'You think so, do you?' Nellie clenched her teeth as she dragged the front gate towards her until it jammed shut. 'For once, Mrs Wainwright, I think you're right. Good morning!'

She crossed the road and carefully walked along the pavement on the other side. It was February 1942 and there had been a frost the previous night. The last few months had been the worst of her life but now it was time to move on. Teddy would want what was best for her and that meant not wallowing in misery. He would want her to go out and do some good. She considered how attitudes had changed since before the war. The government was now positively encouraging married women to go out to work. But what was she to do? Could she go back to her job as a kindergarten teacher? She would find it tiring working full-time with children in a proper school. She had enjoyed working with the pre-school children up in Ambleside. Perhaps she should think of repeating that experience here on Merseyside. Not so long ago, she had seen an article in the *Crosby Herald* about the need for a wartime nursery that would enable mothers of babies and small children to work in factories. She had not read anything more about it but maybe it was worth looking into. Perhaps someone at the council offices would know something about it.

So that's where Nellie went and was directed to the Department of Education. There she spoke to a woman who informed her that plans were afoot for a nursery to be built in the Litherland area by next spring.

'That's no good to me. I was looking for a job now.'

'There is a woman, a Mrs Perkins, who has just opened a

private nursery in Linacre Road. She was hoping for a government grant but the building she is using doesn't meet with our criteria.' The woman tapped the base of her pen on the blotter on the desk. 'She is a trained nursery nurse and is filling a need, so we haven't closed her down. Could be that she'll appreciate your help.'

Nellie thanked her and asked for the address. She crossed the canal and made her way past the library and sausage factory and along Linacre Road until she came to a bicycle and repair shop. Inside, an elderly man was mending a puncture. She asked him where she would find Mrs Perkins.

'Upstairs, love. But I heard say that she was full up. Lots of young mothers are keen to earn money and can't get the kiddies' names down quick enough.' He fixed her with unblinking eyes. 'Of course, you can always put your child's name down on her waiting list.'

Nellie experienced the familiar pang of loss but managed to say, 'I have no children. I want to work with them.'

His face brightened. 'In that case. You've come at the right time. One of the school leavers she had helping her walked out yesterday. Got herself a job in a factory earning more money. I'll show you where to go. Can't be having the little 'uns coming through here, so you need to go through the side door.' He took a bunch of keys from under the counter and led her outside and opened the door for her.

Nellie thanked him and headed up a flight of uncarpeted stairs to a landing at the top. Several doors faced her but she crossed to the one where the din seemed to be coming from and knocked. There was no response so she knocked louder and tried turning the knob. The door did not yield, so she banged on it. She heard a bolt being drawn and the door opened to reveal a woman in her late twenties. She looked harassed and had a struggling toddler wedged between her knees. 'Quick, say what you want,' she said. 'If you want to enrol your child we're full up.'

'I'm a kindergarten teacher interested in pre-school children. I heard you might be in need of help.'

The woman looked hopeful. 'I can't pay you what you could get in a proper place but perhaps money isn't as important to you as looking after children, otherwise you'd be after a job in a school.'

Nellie smiled. 'You're partly right. I love children but I do need some kind of wage.'

'I'm Polly Perkins.' The woman smiled. 'Hopefully we can come to some kind of agreement because it sounds like you're an answer to a prayer.'

Nellie stepped inside and bolted the door behind her. Almost immediately, a little girl came over and slipped a hand into hers. While Mrs Perkins dealt with the toddler between her knees, Nellie allowed herself to be led over to a corner where two children were building with bricks. They were so absorbed in what they were doing that they did not seem to notice her, that is, until the girl dragged her hand free and tumbled the boy's tower of bricks.

The boy turned on the girl with lightening speed and walloped her one. She screamed so piercingly that the sound seemed to go right through Nellie's head. 'Stop that noise. You shouldn't have knocked over the boy's bricks. That was asking for trouble.'

She did not wait to see the effect of her words but turned to the boy. 'Boys should not hit girls.'

He looked up at her from angry brown eyes. 'Why?'

'Because boys are generally bigger and stronger and it's not kind to pick on someone smaller than yourself,' said Nellie.

'But she was naughty.'

'She was but if she does it again then she won't be allowed to play with the bricks again today.' Nellie knelt on the parquet floor beside him. 'Now let's see who can build the highest tower. I'd like one of blue, one of yellow and one of red.' She smiled at the three children. 'I'll do a green one. Who can tell me which bricks are red?'

The girl had stopped screaming and now scrambled over to the pile of bricks and picked up a red one. The boy sniffed. 'I don't want red ones. Blue for boys.'

Nellie told him to take all the blue ones and asked the other little girl to take the yellow ones. She hesitated and Nellie nudged a yellow brick towards her hand. Immediately the girl picked it up and soon the three children were absorbed in carefully piling brick upon brick. Nellie felt a hand on her shoulder and looked up at Mrs Perkins.

'Thanks for that. The one doing all the screaming is my daughter Daisy. She thinks she can do what she wants because I run the group. I'm sure you can imagine that doesn't make things easy for me.'

Nellie nodded and got to her feet. 'Is she one of your helpers?' she asked, spotting an adolescent girl across the room.

'Yes, she's fifteen years old.' Polly grimaced. 'I'm not sure how long she'll stay. She says she loves children but I don't imagine she thought it would be like this.'

Nellie glanced about the rest of the room. There were two babies in a playpen – one had managed to pull herself up and was rattling the bars – and about twelve other children were involved in a variety of activities. It was not exactly pandemonium but there were several running around, exercising their lungs to their full capacity. 'You have your hands full.'

Polly nodded. 'I was a children's nurse until I married. After I was widowed I decided to do this for the war effort but I've discovered that a group of lively toddlers isn't the same as nursing sick children.'

'I'm Helen Lachlan. Most people call me Nellie.' She held out her hand. 'I'm a widow, too. I can only do part-time because I live with my grandfather and younger sister. She was injured during the bombing and can't get around as well as she used to. So I'm needed at home.'

Polly's pleasant features lit up. 'Part-time will be great. I can only offer you twenty-five shillings a week. Nowhere near what you're probably worth but it's the best I can do.'

If Nellie had to pay all the overheads involved in running a house then the money would not have been enough, but situated as she was, living with her grandfather, the money would do for now. 'I accept.'

Polly looked delighted and, reaching out a hand, squeezed Nellie's. 'Thanks. I'm sure we'll get on fine.'

Nellie said, 'I'm sure it won't be from want of trying if we don't.' She noticed a piano against a far wall. 'Do you have a music time with the children?'

Polly shook her head. 'It belongs to the dancing class that rents the room in the evening. Why, do you play?'

'Self-taught. I've found musical games use up lots of energy, much more than kids running around, going mad. I hope you don't mind my saying that?' she added hastily.

'No! I'm happy with any suggestions you make.' Polly frowned. 'Such as what to do with that little horror over there? He's a real nuisance at the moment.'

'Which one?' asked Nellie.

'The one on the rocking horse.'

Nellie gazed in the direction she indicated. The young helper was attempting to drag a boy from the horse but he was clinging to its mane and yelling. As she watched, she saw the girl prising his fingers away from the horsehair. The boy spat at her and she smacked his bare leg. 'You little monster! I don't put up with that from no one.'

Polly sighed. 'She shouldn't smack him. Trouble is that's what she does to her younger brothers at home. There's your second challenge. Separate Jimmy from Dobbin the horse, but in a way that doesn't mean he kicks every child in sight once he's down. He's been through a bad time, poor lad, but we can't encourage such behaviour. Fortunately, he'll be off to school in September but that's some way off yet.'

Nellie nodded and strolled across the room with Poll, avoiding children and passing a table where five older children chalked patterns on blue sugar paper. As she approached the child on the horse, she asked, 'What's the bad time he's been going through?'

'His father was killed at the docks during the May blitz. Jimmy's a twin and shortly after losing his father, his brother was hit by a coal cart when the horse panicked and bolted.'

'No!' cried Nellie, distressed. 'The poor child...and his poor mother.'

'Yes. It was terrible for them both. There's a baby girl in the family, Irene. She's the younger one in the playpen; she's no trouble. In fact, I wonder sometimes if she's too well behaved. Of course, she never did know her daddy or her other brother but I think babies pick up on the way we adults feel, don't you?'

Nellie nodded. Of course children could sense how their parents were feeling without understanding why they were angry or violent. She thought of her own double bereavement and wondered how the mother coped. Perhaps she had found caring for the baby difficult, so ignored her as much as she could and Irene had given up trying to get her attention.

Nellie placed a hand on the horse's mane and smiled. 'Hello, Jimmy. I see you like Dobbin.'

'Yus,' he said sullenly.

'I can see why. He's got a lovely mane, hasn't he?' she said, stroking it.

He pushed her hand away. 'He's my Dobbin and does what I tell him or he gets a smack.' He hit the horse's neck with the flat of his hand. 'Smack, smack, smack!'

Nellie covered his hand with hers. 'I bet he'd rather have something to eat or a hug than a smack.'

'He's naughty, so he has to be smacked,' said Jimmy, attempting to drag his hand free.

Nellie released him. 'Why is he naughty?'

''Cos!'

Nellie was tempted to ask ''Cos what?' but was certain Jimmy would have difficulty putting into words the grief and angry bewilderment he was feeling. It was difficult enough for an adult to cope with loss, as well she knew, so how much harder was it for a child?

She made a decision and climbed up behind Jimmy and put her arms round him. 'Do you know this song?' she said, and began to sing:

'Ride a cock horse to Banbury Cross,
To see a fine lady upon a white horse,
With rings on her fingers and bells on her toes,
She shall have music wherever she goes.'

Jimmy threw back his head and stared up at Nellie. 'I'm not a lady and Dobbin's not white.'

So Nellie changed the words to Jimmy sitting upon a piebald horse. The boy appeared to like the rewrite and smiled, asking her to sing it again. She did so and then said that she wanted him to help her.

'Help you do what?' he asked.

'I'll show you,' said Nellie, climbing from the horse. She lifted Jimmy down and held his hand as she led him away. 'How would you like to do some marching, Jimmy?'

'Like a soldier?' he asked, turning his thin face up to her. 'My uncle Marty's a soldier.'

'Where is he?'

'Somewhere hot.' He sighed gustily. 'Mam's cross 'cos he's gone away.'

Nellie sympathised with her. Aloud, she suggested to Polly that she organise the children into a line while she played the piano. 'That's if you think the dancing group won't mind?'

Polly smiled. 'Why should they mind? It's not going to do the piano any harm. It's locked but I know where the key is.' She went over to a jar on the windowsill and seconds later brandished the key.

Nellie asked Jimmy if he would like to be the leader.

He put a finger in his mouth and looked worried. 'What's a leader do?'

She told him he was to stand at the front and all the children were to follow him. He seemed to like that idea, so she left him in Polly's charge and unlocked the lid of the piano. She ran her fingers over the keys and after a few seconds, launched into 'The Grand Old Duke of York'.

'The Grand old Duke of York, he had ten thousand men.

'He marched them up to the top of the hill and then marched them down again.

'When they were up they were up, and when they were down, they were down.

'And when they were only half way up, they were neither up nor down.'

By the time the children had marched round the room three times, Nellie could hear some of them having a go at the words. She smiled, thinking it did not matter to them that they did not know who the Duke was or how many ten thousand men were or that the rhyme was about an event in British history they were learning without realising it. For the first time in months Nellie knew she was doing something she really wanted to do and, whether her grandfather liked it or not, she was going to carry on doing it.

Later over a cup of tea, Polly told Nellie about the need for more toys for the children. 'Trouble is, just like everything else, they're in short supply. I did advertise for second-hand stuff but had no luck.'

Nellie recalled Billy helping her to take the cot up to the attic and, if her memory wasn't playing tricks on her, there was all kinds of discarded stuff there, including a dolls' house. Perhaps it had once belonged to her great-great-aunt. There might even be some other toys in the tea-chests. It wouldn't do any harm to have a look. She decided not to mention it to Polly until she had had a chance to see what there was. Instead, she asked her the hours she was expected to work.

'What if we say ten o'clock to three and I'll throw in lunch?'

'Saturdays?'

'Nine till twelve?'

Nellie agreed, thinking Lottie was coping with walking so much better now that she might be able to manage more shopping and to prepare lunch for Grandfather and herself.

'I'll start tomorrow,' she said.

Polly beamed at her. 'I just know you're going to be the best thing that's happened to this group,' she said. 'I'll see you out.'

Warmed by Polly's words, Nellie hoped she was right. As she passed the window of the bicycle shop, she noticed the old man looking out and waved to him before going on her way. Her heart felt lighter as she walked along Linacre Road, thinking about Polly and the likelihood of her being a war widow. If that was so, then she was certainly working hard at overcoming her loss and supporting her child.

Nellie crossed the canal and did some shopping in the Co-op, buying what she thought they would need for today and tomorrow. Life would be easier once the days were longer and the weather was warmer. Although, that would mean more work in the vegetable garden. Hopefully Billy would still be willing to help there but she could not expect to have him much longer. She would miss him when he was called up and Lottie probably would too.

Nellie had no sooner entered the house than her grandfather appeared in the kitchen doorway. 'Where've you been, Helen? I was starting to believe you'd had an accident and I was stuck here with your sister,' he said in a grouchy voice.

'After a job,' she said, knowing there was no point in putting off what she had to say.

'A job! What kind of job?' he demanded.

'Essential war work. I'll tell you as soon as I've put the shopping away and sat down.' Despite her words, she had to squeeze past him into the kitchen because he stood in her path.

She dumped the shopping on the table and smiled at Lottie who was sitting by the fire, darning the heel of one of her grandfather's thick woolly socks.

'I heard what you said, Nellie. What job?' asked Lottie anxiously. 'Will it be full-time?'

Nellie removed her gloves, noticing there was a tiny hole at the base of the thumb. She dropped it in the mending basket next to Lottie's chair. 'Will you mend that for me, please?' Taking a deep breath she said, 'I can't stay at home when I'm fit and healthy. There's a war on and we all have to do our bit in whatever way we can. The government needs more women, mothers included, working in factories making munitions and armaments and other essential things. Someone has to look after their pre-school children when there's no family to do it, so I'm doing that part-time. It doesn't pay much but...'

'How much?' growled her grandfather.

She did not answer but said, 'I'll still put money in the kitty, Grandfather, but I do need to save some for a rainy day.'

Lottie burst out, 'Is it wise you working with little children, Nellie? Won't it upset you after losing the baby?'

Nellie turned to her. 'Of course I feel it,' she said unevenly. 'But most people aren't having it easy. Why should I be any different? I love children and...'

'What about the housework and the shopping?' grunted her grandfather.

'The house won't get very untidy if we all make an effort to clear up after ourselves every day,' said Nellie pointedly. 'On Sundays I'll try and catch up on the big jobs, such as the washing. Although, I'll only be working from ten until three...nine till twelve Saturdays.'

'You shouldn't work on the Sabbath, Nellie,' chided Lottie.

Nellie frowned. 'I won't be the only person in the country working on the Sabbath, Lottie. The enemy doesn't take the day off then, I bet.'

'It's not right,' muttered Grandfather, glaring at her from

beneath his bushy eyebrows. 'You'll wear yourself out, girl.'

'Not if we all help out in the house as I said,' insisted Nellie.

There was silence and she took that for agreement and got lunch ready.

After the meal, Nellie went upstairs into the attic rooms. Her brothers had slept in the larger one before they had left home. It was in a right mess. A dismantled bed stood against a wall and other stuff had been dumped in there. Damp was coming through the ceiling in one corner, causing the wallpaper to peel off. She couldn't remember when the paintwork had last been done anywhere in the house. As for the net curtains, they were filthy. She decided that, when the weather got warmer, she would take them down and wash them.

She gazed through the window and saw Mrs Wainwright standing in the middle of the road, gossiping with one of the neighbours. She wondered whom she was talking about now. Probably not this household because there wasn't much happening. Although, no doubt she'd pass the word around once the news got out that Nellie had a job.

Nellie turned away and saw the dolls' house on the floor in the part of the room where the ceiling slanted down and ended a few feet from the floor. She knelt and discovered that she could remove the front of the house. Five rooms were revealed: two on the ground floor, one larger one on the first floor and two on the top floor. Only a couple of the rooms had fireplaces and there was no furniture or dolls to be seen at all. Her brow puckered. She could not remember ever playing with the dolls' house. Was it because there was no furniture or dolls? But what use was a dolls' house without furniture or dolls? They must be somewhere in one of the attic rooms.

She went over to one of the tea-chests filled with junk and began to rummage through its contents. She dragged out strings and strings of red, white and blue bunting and dropped it on the floor. There were several old-fashioned dresses and she held one against her. There was lots of material in the skirt which reached almost to the floor; the neckline was high with a mandarin collar. The dresses followed the bunting. Pity the frocks weren't smaller. The children could have had great fun with a dressing-up box. If she and Lottie had more time they could have altered them, but in the circumstances...

She delved further, looking for anything that might contain small furniture or dolls. She found a couple of other boxes that might prove useful. Inside one was what she realised, when she put it to her eye, was a kaleidoscope; the other had 'Shadow Pictures Punch and Judy Show' printed on the box. Inside were black figures with rods attached and tiny screens. Nellie smiled, thinking that perhaps once she'd had a bit of practice with them, then she would be able to show the older children how to use them. She put the puppets aside with the kaleidoscope and, as there didn't seem to be anything else of use to her in that tea-chest, she dumped the dresses, bunting and everything else back inside and turned to the other one.

Almost immediately she struck lucky. Besides finding boxes of furniture and dolls, there were also dominos, a tin drum and an odd shaped teddy bear with holes either side of his body and a loop of woven wool attached to his shoulders. She felt certain that the children would like him.

She gathered her spoils together and carried what she could downstairs. She was unsure how to get the dolls' house to the nursery but the rest she felt certain she could manage. But, first of all, she supposed that she had better ask Grandfather if she could borrow them.

To her surprise she found him sitting by the fire listening to the wireless in the kitchen. 'When did you bring that in here?' she asked.

He glanced up at her with her arms full of toys. 'What have you got there?' His tone was sharp.

'Toys. I found them in the attic.'

'You've no right to go rooting up there.'

'Sorry, but I thought you'd want to help with the war effort,' she said, determined to get him to agree to her borrowing them. 'Toys might not appear to be as important as making battleships or guns but children do need to play.' Nellie held out the teddy bear to him. 'He's a funny one.'

'It's a children's muff.'

Nellie's blue-green eyes sparkled. 'The children will love it. Can I borrow these and the dolls' house upstairs for them, please?'

He pulled on his moustache. 'They'll damage them,' he grumbled. 'Can't be letting kids pull them apart...been up there for years.'

'Doing nothing!' cried Nellie, wanting so much for the children to have them. 'Giving nobody pleasure, forgotten, gathering dust. I don't ever remember seeing them before. Have a heart, Grandfather!'

'Why should I?' he grumbled, gazing into the fire. 'I don't know these kids.'

'You could get to know them,' she suggested rashly. 'I bet most of them haven't a granddad and would like one. I could bring some of them to visit. I'm sure they'd love seeing the hens and...'

'That's enough!' He looked horrified. 'Take the bloody things. They won't be of any use to me once I'm dead.'

Nellie was so delighted that she did something she had seldom done before and bent to kiss his wrinkled cheek. 'Thanks. You'll get your reward in Heaven.'

'As long as there's no bloody kids up there,' he said, touching his face where her lips had pressed against his skin.

She left the kitchen singing, thinking all she needed now was for someone to take the dolls' house to the nursery. A consultation with Polly would hopefully sort out that problem.

Polly was delighted when Nellie produced the toys the next morning. 'I said you were going to be the best thing that happened to this place.'

Nellie was warmed by her praise and broached the subject of getting the dolls' house to the nursery.

'If it's not too big you could balance it on a pram.' Her eyes met Nellie's. 'Maisie Miller lives near the library. Perhaps she'll let you borrow hers. I'll suggest it when she comes to pick up her two. I'll let you know what she says in the morning.'

That suited Nellie.

Later, Polly suggested that Nellie might like to heat up Irene's bottle and give it to her. It was a bittersweet moment holding the baby in her arms but at least Irene did not kick up a fuss at being handled by a stranger. She simply gazed up at Nellie from curious blue eyes. Tears clogged her throat and she pressed a fierce kiss against the girl's curly fair hair, thinking, if only...

The following day Nellie asked Polly if she had spoken to Maisie.

'Yes. She said you can borrow the pram. She suggested that you take her kids home, drop them off and take the pram home and then pick them up at eight tomorrow morning with the dolls' house. That does mean you staying here until four and I did tell her that you didn't start here until ten. She suggested that you knock off earlier the next day. I don't mind that if you don't?'

Nellie said that it was fine with her.

So several hours later, Nellie wheeled the pram along the street where Maisie Miller and the children lived. Jimmy was sitting at the foot of the pram, gripping the sides of the handle. His eyes were intent on the front doors of the terraced houses as they passed. Nellie could hear the baby sucking on her fist. Poor lamb, she's hungry, thought Nellie, hoping her mother would have a bottle ready for her. Growing children were allowed two pints of milk a day, although young babies had to have skimmed. Her heart ached, remembering that moment when the doctor told her that her son was dead.

'There's Mam!' cried Jimmy.

Hastily Nellie wiped her eyes with the back of her hand and looked up to see a woman standing on the doorstep.

'So yer here,' said Maisie, eyeing her up and down. 'You don't look a bit like I thought you'd look. Teachers aren't generally young and attractive.'

Nellie laughed. 'I'm not attractive and I feel ancient some days.'

'Well, you don't look it. That's not having children of your own.'

The laughter died in Nellie's face and she lifted Jimmy down from the pram. 'I lost a baby. Stillborn.'

Maisie looked mortified. 'I am sorry, luv. I heard you were a widow. This war's a bugger. My brother's been sent abroad. I think he's in the Middle East somewhere.' Maisie reached beneath the hood and unfastened Irene's harness. 'I'd ask you in for a cup of tea, so we could have a chat, only the woman I lodge with has a man friend in.' She lifted her daughter into her arms. 'Sorry.'

'Doesn't matter. I'll see you tomorrow morning.'

'Sure. You take care,' said Maisie.

'And you three.' Nellie glanced down at Jimmy. 'Bye. See you tomorrow, too.'

He half-lifted an arm and then let it drop and ran into the house.

As Nellie pushed the empty pram past the sausage factory, she noticed an indicator for War Week on the wall; the local target was to raise seventy thousand pounds to buy a motor torpedo boat. She thought what an enormous sum that was and wished that instead of it being for weapons it could have been spent on houses and hospitals and schools. She did not notice the policeman until he was a couple of feet away and only just managed to avoid him.

'Mrs Lachlan, isn't it?' he said, peering down at her from beneath the rim of his cap.

'Sgt McElroy! You startled me.'

'What's this we have here?' He bent his large burly frame and peered inside the pram before straightening again and looking down at Nellie. 'No baby. For a moment I thought...'

'Thought what?' asked Nellie, staring at him.

He flushed brick red.

She realised what he was thinking and was shocked. 'You thought that I'd stolen a baby.'

'Losing a baby can do queer things to a woman. So what's with the pram? No black market goods or bottles of booze hidden inside?' he said with heavy humour.

'Very funny,' said Nellie, pulling a face. 'I've borrowed the pram to carry a dolls' house. You can search it if you like.'

'I'm sure there's no need for that.' He rocked back and forth on his heels. 'It's my job to uphold the law. There's too many people around ready to break it. They think because there's a war on that it's an excuse for all kinds of things.'

'I'm sure you're right...but I haven't broken the law. So if you don't mind, I'll be on my way.'

He nodded. 'You mind how you go.'

Nellie pushed the pram in the direction of the Red Lion but stopped at one point and looked back in time to see the bobby turn into the street where Maisie lodged. Remembering Billy lived near the library, she guessed that the Millers and McElroys were neighbours. She crossed the canal, wondering if he really had believed she was desperate enough to steal a baby. What had he meant 'losing a baby can do queer things to a woman'? No. She could imagine only too easily the child's mother's grief. She had to accept that she would never have her own child because no man could ever take Teddy's place. She would spend the rest of her life looking after other people's children.

Chapter Nine

Nellie picked up the letters from the coconut mat and turned them over. She was pleased when she saw they were from Babs and Francis, but wondered what her brother was writing to her about. She decided to open his letter first and read it over breakfast. Lottie and her grandfather were still in bed, so she would have the kitchen to herself.

She sat at the table and took a gulp of tea before slitting open the envelope.

Dear Nellie,
I thought I'd best write and let you know that I'll be bringing a solicitor to visit Grandfather on Friday afternoon. Last time I visited, you were at the nursery and I don't know if he's mentioned what we discussed that day. He is getting forgetful. He must have been feeling his age because he wants to make a will. You don't have to be there but I thought you should be aware that he's taking this step. It seems he appreciates what you do for him and wishes to provide you with some security for the future now you are widowed. I had mentioned to him that one of my parishioners, widowed when her husband was killed at Dunkirk, had said her war pension was not enough to live on. I hope you are feeling much better and not working too hard. May our Saviour bless you.

With love,

Francis

Nellie was astounded and read the letter again. She had presumed that when her grandfather died everything he possessed would automatically go to her father. It seemed that she was wrong. She remembered his uncharacteristic behaviour when she had not only lost Teddy but the baby too, and found herself wondering how her grandmother had died. She imagined him as a young sailor away at sea for months on end and thought how awful it must have been to arrive home to be greeted with the news that his wife had been dead for months. She remembered the tears in his eyes. Perhaps he had never married again because he couldn't bear to put another woman in her place. She recalled her father's reaction to her mother's death and her eyes darkened. Why couldn't he have pretended to feel some affection towards her memory and regret for her untimely death? It would have cost him little to have shown some respect by visiting her grave. Her feelings towards him hardened, and, not wanting to think about him anymore, her thoughts returned to Francis' letter.

Should she mention it to her grandfather? Should she try to get home early from the nursery? Or should she just carry on as usual as if she didn't know anything about the will or the solicitor? She decided on the latter and naturally wondered how much money her grandfather would leave her. A hundred pounds would make a nice little nest egg. She vowed she would be more patient with him, feeling warmer towards him. Who knows, maybe he might even leave some money to Lottie and Babs.

Thinking of her sisters reminded Nellie of Babs' letter. She glanced at the postmark and saw that it said Warrington. So Babs had left the first farm. Was she finding her new billet any more exciting than her last one?

Nellie stretched out a hand for her cup and drained it to the dregs before beginning to read,

Dear Nellie,
Sorry I'm late in answering the letter you sent me at the end of February telling me all your news. Would you believe that I'm living in a mansion? It makes the cottage on the farm seem like a dog kennel. I'm sharing it with nineteen other land girls and you want to hear the noise when we all sit down for supper in the huge dining room! It has oil paintings on the walls of hunting dogs and horses. Flo moved with me but we're making other friends, so are not as close as we were at the cottage. Some of the older girls can

already drive tractors and this is something I want to learn. Today work's been back-breaking and it makes planting seed potatoes in the garden look like a doddle. We've planted thousands on some of the land that had lain fallow and was ploughed up last year. But you don't want to hear about work. Guess what the big news is here right now? The Yanks are here, Nellie! I mean they're here at Burtonwood, the airbase. So far we've only seen a dozen or so of them strolling about town but rumour has it that there's going to be thousands of them coming over. I've never met a Yank before and I'm expecting them to speak like they do in the pictures. I'll keep you posted to when I actually speak to one.

Anyway, enough of them. How are you, Nell? How are you getting on with the kiddiewinks? I bet it's hard work. How's Grandfather and Lottie? Is he still as much of a grouch as ever, and is Lottie any better? It must be tough being in pain the way she is. Has she lost any weight since she's had to help in the house and garden? How's Billy? He can't have much longer to go before he gets called up. Do write and bring me up to date, Nell.

Lots of love,
Babs. XXXXX

Nellie smiled as she folded the letter and replaced it in its envelope. She loved the way Babs wrote, could almost hear her voice in her head as she read her words. She pondered on whether she should tell her youngest sister about Francis' letter but decided not to count her chickens before they were hatched. Who was to say Grandfather might not get a cob on with her and change his mind? She thought about what Babs had said about the Yanks. Would she keep her head or lose it to a handsome American airman? A timely bit of sisterly advice might be in order. She could also tell her about Lottie and Billy and how they seemed to get on well. Most likely he would be calling round this evening, now the days were starting to draw out.

Nellie placed the letters in her handbag and, putting on her jacket, left for work. She looked forward to seeing the children and having a chat with Polly. She supposed that she would also have to give thought to who could replace Billy when he was eventually called up.

Lottie looked out of the window and saw Billy come out of the outhouse with a spade. A bag of seed potatoes had been delivered that morning and she had been waiting for him to come all day to dig the trenches, planning on helping him plant them out. It might give her hip gyp but she was prepared to put up with the pain to spend time in his company.

As Lottie limped through the kitchen, Grandfather glanced up from his newspaper. 'Where are you going?'

'To help Billy.'

'Billy? Who's Billy? Can't have strangers here.'

Lottie sighed. She had noticed that her grandfather was getting forgetful. 'Billy's not a stranger. He's been coming here for the past year. Not that he'll be coming much longer. He'll be eighteen soon and is going to be a soldier.'

Grandfather scowled at her. 'Nobody's told me that. A soldier, you say? Handy having the armed forces around the place. There's a war on, you know, and there could be spies around.'

'Spies! There's no spies here,' she said, wondering if he was going doolally as well as forgetful.

'That's what you think,' he said, rustling the newspaper. 'They're crafty, them spies.'

Lottie decided to humour him. 'If you say so. I'm going out in the garden.'

She left him to his newspaper and went outside. Billy looked up as she approached and smiled. 'Hi, Lottie. You coming to give me a hand?'

She smiled shyly. 'If I can be of use.'

'Of course, you can. There's nobody I'd rather have in the garden helping me.'

She blushed. 'You mean that?'

'I wouldn't say it if I didn't. Shall we get cracking?'

She nodded, glad that he never seemed to stare at her as if he found her fat and unattractive. He was kind and helpful and she would never forget how quickly he had reacted when Nellie had fainted and how, later, he had asked her for her opinion about what to do about the apples.

Billy began to dig. Lottie watched him, wondering if he could ever fancy her. Of course, she was older than him and probably looked it too, she thought sadly, limping over to the potato bag and taking out some sprouting potatoes and going over to where he was digging the trench. He indicated exactly where he wanted her to put the potatoes and the distance between them. As they worked together as a team, she said, 'It's a miracle, isn't it?'

'You mean a whole load of potatoes growing from each little one you plant?'

'Yeah.' That was another thing she liked about Billy. He seemed to know exactly what she meant without asking her to explain herself. 'How is it you're so good at this, when you only have a back yard at home?'

He smiled down at her. 'It's like anything. You learn about it by having a go. No other way of going about any job in my opinion.'

'You think I could learn about things the same way?'

Billy rested on his spade. 'Practise makes perfect. Although, I reckon if your heart's in it, then you're more likely to make a good job of things.'

Lottie nodded. That made sense. 'What would you like to do when the war's over, for a living, I mean?'

He resumed his digging. 'I don't think that far ahead. Your grandfather was telling me about your brother Joseph. I wonder what plans he had for after the war, if any?'

She realised what he meant. If you were a young man and had to go and fight, what was the use of making plans when you might be killed? She shivered at the thought of Billy being killed. She liked him a lot and didn't want anything bad to happen to him. She decided not to think about the future either. 'D'you like potatoes?' she asked, getting on with the job in hand.

He nodded. 'Chips. I love Mam's chips. She makes them the gear.'

'I thought your mam was an invalid,' said Lottie, and was surprised to see hot colour stain his cheeks. 'Have I said something I shouldn't have? I'm sorry if I have.'

He said roughly, 'You've got nothing to be sorry about. Mam is sick and what makes her sick does mean she's laid out flat sometimes, but she can get about.'

'You mean her illness comes and goes like the pain in my hip and leg?'

'Exactly like that,' he said, smiling, and leaning forward, he brushed her lips with his. Lottie's lips tingled. She could scarcely believe he had just kissed her and wanted him to do it again because it had felt so nice. She held up her face, closed her eyes and puckered her lips. 'I shouldn't,' he murmured, but he did.

This time it was a proper kiss and lasted until a voice startled them apart with the words, 'What's going on here?'

Lottie almost fell over the bag of seed potatoes but was steadied by Billy's hand on her arm. He helped her to straighten up and they both stared at his father. Sgt McElroy did not look pleased and Lottie was scared.

'What are you doing here, Dad? It's like you were checking up on me,' said Billy, an angry note in his voice.

'Don't be impertinent, boy! I'm-I'm here on police business,' he stated.

'What kind of police business? This isn't your beat,' said Billy.

His father said sternly, 'More cheek. You get on with your work and keep your distance from Miss Callaghan or I'll be having words with her grandfather. I can't see him approving of you taking advantage of this young lady here.'

'He hasn't done anything wrong! I-I'm not a little girl. I-I liked him kissing me,' said Lottie boldly.

Billy hid a grin and got on with the digging.

Sgt McElroy stared at Lottie and she stared back defiantly. He spoke quietly as if to a child, 'I'm only thinking of what your grandfather and Mrs Lachlan might say if they knew you'd been canoodling with the hired hand. They might tell him not to come here anymore. You don't want him sacked, do you?'

Lottie certainly didn't want that to happen and shook her head.

'I knew you were a sensible young woman,' said Sgt McElroy, smiling. 'And how is your grandfather and Mrs Lachlan keeping? I saw her a short while ago pushing a pram.'

'She'd borrowed the pram to take the dolls' house to Mrs Perkins' private nursery. She's helping with the children.'

'Now that's good.' He nodded his head several times. 'She's showing sense by doing something useful to take her mind off her loss. My wife lost a baby and ended up with a form of paralysis.'

'That's sad,' said Lottie.

'You can say that again,' he said, a grim smile playing about his mouth. 'You tell your grandfather to be on his guard. There's been a few break-ins round and about. I'll be going now but don't you forget what I said, Miss Callaghan, if you don't want Billy to stop coming here.'

She nodded, thinking that perhaps kissing wasn't the good thing she had thought it.

Later when Nellie came home, Lottie told her that they'd had a visit from Sgt McElroy.

'What did he want?'

Lottie pursed her lips. 'He said it was on police business and there'd been some break-ins.'

'Where?'

'Round and about. I was to put Grandfather on his guard.'

Nellie's brow furrowed. 'How did he react?'

'He talked about guns. He doesn't have a gun, does he, Nellie?'

'I shouldn't think so. He talks about spies but we haven't seen any, have we?'

Lottie chuckled. 'No. It would be funny if Billy's father came round again and Grandfather thought him a spy.'

'That man does have a habit of popping up when one least expects it. What else did he have to say?'

'He asked how you and Grandfather were keeping. He mentioned having seen you. He also said that his wife lost a baby and ended up with some kind of paralysis. Billy told me, though, that she can get about a bit.'

Nellie nodded, thinking perhaps she might make a point of seeing Maisie Miller and asking her about Mrs McElroy. With them living in the same street Maisie might know something about her.

She did that two days later after telling Lottie and her grandfather that she would be late home that afternoon. She had completely forgotten that it was Friday and the solicitor and Francis were coming to call.

To save Maisie Miller picking up her two children, Nellie had said that she would drop them off at the house. She was invited in for a cup of tea and as they sat in the kitchen, Nellie brought up the subject of Mrs McElroy.

'My sister's been told that she lost a baby and it resulted in some kind of paralysis. I feel really sorry for the woman.'

Maisie said, 'Save your energy. She drinks.'

Nellie's eyes widened. 'What!'

'She's a boozer.' Maisie looked disgusted. 'Don't ask me how she can afford the amount she gets down. Poor Terence! He's had to put up with it for years. So she lost a baby but she had Billy and we all have to get on with life as best we can. We both know that as well as anyone.'

Nellie nodded. 'They must be embarrassed by her drinking and that's why we were told she's an invalid.'

Maisie agreed. 'Trouble is she depends on Billy a lot, so she'll miss him when he's called up. Still, we all have our crosses to bear and have to cope as best we can.'

Nellie agreed and left soon after.

When she arrived home it was to find Francis sitting in the kitchen drinking Camp coffee. It was only then that Nellie remembered about the solicitor. 'Where's Grandfather?' she asked. 'Did the solicitor come? Did everything go according to plan?'

Francis nodded. 'Once I'd assured Grandfather he could be trusted everything was agreed. Once it's drawn up all he has to do is sign it. The solicitor had another appointment and had to leave. I thought I'd stay and see you.' He rubbed his jaw with his hand and yawned.

'You tired?'

'I'm always tired. I don't sleep very well.'

She knew the feeling. 'Memories?'

He grimaced. 'Too many bad ones. The sights I saw in the blitz...having to identify Mam and Aunt Josie. It'll be a year soon.'

'I bet you never thought your faith would be tested in such a way when you went into the priesthood,' she said softly. 'Have you ever doubted or had regrets about the life you've chosen?'

'By regrets I presume you mean never having a wife and children? Is that what you're trying to say, Nellie?'

'I suppose I am.'

'I'll let you know that at the end of my life.' His large hand grasped her small one and squeezed it. 'Remember when we were young?'

'Young? We're not old, Francis.'

'I feel old. When I do sleep I have terrible nightmares. I question how I would cope on a battlefield. I wonder sometimes whether it's another testing ground where God wants me.'

'No!' cried Nellie, her fingers tightening on his. 'I've lost too many. I don't want to lose you as well.' Her voice sank to a whisper. 'Surely it says in the Bible that God does not test us beyond that which we are able to bear?' He stared at her. The moment was fraught with emotion. 'Don't volunteer! You're needed here,' she insisted.

He took a deep shuddering breath. 'Perhaps. I'll stay for a few more months at least, and will see how things go after that.'

Nellie knew that she had to be satisfied with those words for now. Neither of them moved straight away but stayed grasping the other's hand as if it were a lifeline.

Lottie came through the door and they drew away and looked at their younger sister. Nellie said, 'Have you heard anything from Dad, Francis?'

'No. I thought you might have. I did write and tell him about Teddy and the baby.'

'I haven't heard a word. I'm sure if anything had happened to him one of us would have heard.'

Francis nodded and stood up. 'I'd best be going. But first would you like me to give you a blessing, Nellie?'

She nodded, thinking that perhaps he needed to do this more than she did. He placed his hands on her head and asked God to comfort her in her grief, heal her pain, guide her for the future and bless her that night with peaceful sleep.

She thanked him. He kissed the cheeks of both his sisters and then picked up his hat from the dresser. 'I'll see myself out.'

There was a silence after he had gone.

Nellie made herself a cup of tea and sat at the table. She sensed her sister was dying to ask what they had been talking about and wondered if Lottie knew about their grandfather having a will drawn up. She realised that she didn't want to talk about it but there was something that needed saying. She repeated what Francis had said about it almost being a year since their mother and aunt had been killed.

Lottie cried in horror, 'How could I have forgotten?'

'So much to do,' said Nellie. 'If you think you can manage, we'll visit the grave on the anniversary of their death.'

Lottie said, 'We can pick the bluebells under the fruit trees and cut some hawthorn blossom and put them in water in a jam jar.'

So they visited Ford cemetery together. Afterwards Nellie wished that Lottie had stayed at home. She had watered the grave with her tears. The next day Nellie felt duty-bound to visit Bootle cemetery where Teddy's parents were buried. They had died some years before. She was not the only one there because so many had died that week in May just over a year ago.

Nellie began to have strange nightmares about Sgt McElroy arresting her for having stolen a baby. Perhaps it was because she had bumped into him coming round the side of the house. He'd told her that he was just keeping an eye on the place because of the reported break-ins.

'I haven't heard of any,' Nellie had said.

'That's because we don't want to worry people,' he'd replied.

She'd thought his answer was too glib, not to mention peculiar in the light of his having told Lottie to warn their grandfather about them. She'd been so irritated that she asked how his wife's paralysis was with a knowing look. He had turned a funny colour and hurried away. Afterwards she felt ashamed of herself, and the nightmares had begun. In one he arrested her for being drunk and disorderly!

This state of affairs might have persisted if it were not for a visit from Babs. Nellie was sitting in a deckchair, relaxing for once while Lottie and Billy worked in the garden, when a familiar voice whispered in her ear, 'What's this? You skiving off?'

Nellie started and opened her eyes and smiled up at her youngest sister. 'Why didn't you say you were coming?'

'I wasn't sure if I'd make it. As it was I got a lift.' Babs' heart-shaped face was alight with excitement. 'I wish you could have seen him, Nell. He was the spitting image of Cary Grant. I think I'm in love,' she said dreamily.

'Who was?' asked Nellie, amused.

'The Yank who gave me a lift to Warrington station in his jeep.'

'Oh!' Nellie stared at her lovely sister, thinking about her flirtatious ways and remembering what had happened with their mother. 'Don't you get carried away and do what you oughtn't,' she warned.

Babs' expression changed. 'You're a right one to talk about getting carried away. What about the way you rushed into marriage?'

Nellie was not to be diverted. 'At least I'd known Teddy for years before we took the plunge.'

Babs pouted. 'Don't be a such a fuddy-duddy, Nell. You're sounding like my mother. I suppose you don't believe in love at first sight?'

'I've never given it much thought.'

'Think about it now. This love I feel could be the real thing. It could last for ever,' she said, striking a dramatic pose.

Nellie said, 'It depends on what you mean by real love. I suppose people can be instantly attracted to each other but it didn't happen that way for me and Teddy. It grew on us. I suppose if he hadn't been on disembarkation leave, we mightn't have realised how much we cared about each other and got married in a rush the way we did.'

'So you weren't desperate to go to bed with him?'

Nellie fixed her younger sister with a stare. 'You shouldn't be talking about such things.'

'Why not?' Babs flushed. 'That's nearly all some of us talk about after being out on a date. So did you enjoy sleeping with him?'

Nellie smiled and then realised Lottie was present and straightened her face. 'You're not married, so get such thoughts out of your head.'

Babs giggled. 'Your expression said it all, Nell. A bit of all right, was it?'

Nellie said severely, 'Sex outside marriage is a mortal sin for a respectable Catholic girl like you!'

'I don't know why you have to sound so scandalised and talk about mortal sin to me. You eloped and were excommunicated.'

'Was I? I've yet to receive a written notice saying so. Anyway, I don't want you ending up in trouble just because an airman has Cary Grant looks.'

'Yes, Nell,' said Babs, her voice subdued and her eyes downcast.

Nellie wished her mother was there to reinforce the pitfalls of sex outside marriage. Although, on the other hand, perhaps it was just as well that she wasn't. 'Now you're here, how about the three of us going the flicks together? It's ages since we've done that.'

Babs hesitated and, for a split second, Nellie wondered if her sister had made a date with the Yank until she said, 'Why not?'

Nellie then thought that perhaps they should ask Grandfather, but he shook his head and said, 'Someone has to stay here on guard. There might be spies.'

Babs rolled her eyes and said as they went upstairs, 'Why's he talking about spies?'

Nellie told her about Billy's father warning them that there had been some break-ins. 'For some reason Grandfather has it fixed in his head that they're spies.'

Babs looked thoughtfully. 'I suppose it makes some kind of sense with there being a war on.'

They went to see Gracie Fields in a re-showing of *Shipyard Sally*. The newspapers had panned the star for divorcing her comedian husband and marrying an Italian-born director, Monte Banks. She had further displeased them by exchanging England for Canada, according to the press, so he wouldn't be interned. However, her fans had remained loyal, especially as, recently, she had returned home to perform live in front of factory workers and troops.

When they got back, it was to find that Grandfather had locked all the doors. It was only by persistently knocking and calling to him that he eventually allowed them into the house. 'You shouldn't have gone out,' he complained querulously, 'leaving me all on my own for the spies to torture me.'

Nellie hugged him and kissed his cheek. 'Sorry, Grandfather, but you're perfectly safe. There are no spies here. I'll go and make you a nice cup of cocoa.'

He appeared soothed by her attentions and Nellie determined not to leave him alone in future. Perhaps she should think of having the local bobby to keep an eye on the place if she and Lottie were to go out at any time and let Grandfather know help was at hand.

The warmer weather arrived and Polly insisted on their young charges spending more time outdoors. Polly and her helper took the smaller ones to the park, while Nellie went with the older ones along the canal where they could watch the barges bringing coal from Wigan to the gasworks in Bootle and Liverpool. Nellie enjoyed these outings. The weather was beautiful and being outside made her feel more hopeful about life. She knew Polly so much better now and discovered that her husband had been in the RAF, and had been shot down over the Channel. Nellie asked how she had coped with his death.

Polly answered simply. 'What else could I do?'

Nellie told her about the baby. They discussed whether it would have been easier for Nellie to cope if she had been able to hold her child in her arms. Polly said that to hold him and then have to let him go would have been unbearable.

Then she went on to say, 'We'll be losing some of the children in September to big school.'

'I know. Jimmy for one. Will you advertise for more?'

'We've got a waiting list. Although, I'd give it all up if I got the chance of working in a council nursery. I wouldn't have to worry about the mothers forgetting to hand over their money some days. We must keep a look out for any news of a nursery being built in the area.'

Nellie remembered what she had been told a few months back when she had called at the council offices but decided not to say anything until she had more information. In the meantime, she had plenty of other things on her mind; not only would they be losing Billy soon but Babs had not written since her last visit when she'd had a lift from an American. Could it be that it was time Nellie took a trip to Warrington one Saturday, while Billy was still around to keep an eye on Grandfather and Lottie; see if she was getting up to anything with that airman. She would write a letter to Babs and post it that evening.

Chapter Ten

Babs pocketed the letter from Nellie, thinking she would read it later when she had time. No doubt her sister was wanting to know why she hadn't heard from her recently. Well, that was OK because she had good reason for not having written. She was worked off her feet but this evening she had a date with Luke, the Cary Grant lookalike, and was late already. She was meeting him in the village and no doubt he would give her chocolates and suggest they went for a walk. He approved of the countryside around Culcheth and it seemed to have slipped his mind that, as a land girl, she saw enough of fields, trees and farm animals.

She outlined her lips with an orange-red Max Factor lipstick she had bought from one of the other girls, and then smiled at her reflection in the mirror. She thought she looked pretty good. Reaching for her shoulder bag, she remembered how she had believed herself in love with Luke when they'd first met because he looked the stuff a girl's dreams were made of: tall, dark, handsome. He was also kind and had good manners. Trouble was, last week he had told her that he didn't approve of make-up and had asked her to wipe off her lipstick. It seemed he was a Baptist and didn't approve of tobacco, alcohol or any of the other activities she considered fun. She had told him that she was Catholic and he had immediately begun to talk about the Bible. Discussing religion was the last thing Babs wanted from Luke but she had agreed to another date and made up her mind if he was not prepared to do a few things to please her, such as going into Warrington to a dance or to see a film or a variety show at the theatre, then she would call it a day.

Babs knew she was more than three quarters of an hour late as she approached their meeting place under a chestnut tree, near the parish church. There was a jeep parked at the kerb and she expected the waiting Luke to be a little cross with her. It was not until the airman in the olive green uniform turned round that she realised he was not her date. He removed his cap and she saw not only was his hair fair but that he wasn't handsome either. His nose was crooked and his mouth too wide and he looked to be a few years older than Luke.

'Miss Callaghan? Miss Barbara Callaghan?' he drawled.

'That's right. Who are you? Where's Luke?' Her voice sounded snappy.

'Name's Jake. Sergeant Jake O'Donnell. Luke couldn't make it.' He held out a hand.

She took it, noticing that his eyes were blue and fringed with dark-gold lashes. 'So he sent you.'

Jake's tawny eyebrows rose. 'You'd rather he'd just stood you up? I was beginning to think that's what you'd done but he did say you were often late, so I decided to wait exactly an hour.' He glanced at his watch. 'You just made it.'

Babs' cheeks pinked. 'I'm sorry. It's been a long day for me out in the fields.'

'Understood.' Jake squeezed her fingers gently before releasing them and replacing his cap. 'So where would you like to go?'

'Pardon?'

'Granted.'

'I meant...what do you mean by asking me where I'd like to go?'

A lazy smile started in his eyes and dimpled his lean cheeks. 'I thought the question was a simple one,' he drawled. 'I'm Luke's replacement. If you'd rather not go out with me, then perhaps I'll just walk you home.'

Startled by the change that smile made to his face, Babs said, 'For goodness sake, it's Saturday night, the last thing I want to do is stay in.'

'So what would you like to do?'

'Make me an offer,' she challenged.

He looked her up and down, taking in the curves beneath the floral printed summer dress with its accompanying bolero, and the neat ankles and dainty feet in the low heeled court shoes, and gave in to temptation. 'Do you like swing?'

'Swing?'

'Jazz. Bopping?'

'I've heard of jazz and jive but not bopping?' It was as if he was speaking a different language.

'Do you dance?'

Immediately Babs smiled. 'Now you're talking, Sergeant O'Donnell. I'm not a brilliant dancer but I'm a quick learner. Although, I'll warn you now that I've heard there are dance halls that don't allow jive.'

'I wouldn't know that as I haven't been over here long...no time to case the joints. One thing's for sure, they're gonna have to get used to it or we'll be holding our own dances back at the base,' he said, opening the passenger door of the jeep. 'Climb aboard.'

She did not need asking twice and, in no time at all, she was being whisked along the road in the direction of Warrington, having dismissed Luke from her thoughts.

The dance hall that Jake chose to patronise turned out to be strictly ballroom. 'Are you sure you're OK with this?' he asked, having found them a small table. She nodded and he went off to get them a drink. She watched the dancers circling the floor, wondering if he had volunteered for the job of taking her out or had had it thrust on him.

Jake returned after the next dance and placed a long glass in front of her before pulling up a chair. The band struck up another tune and she began to hum, 'Goodnight, Irene'.

'Now that number is from back home,' said Jake.

Babs nodded, sipped her drink and realised it was lemonade, refreshing but without a kick. 'There's no alcohol in this. I am over eighteen and allowed to drink in this country.'

'Sorry, Miss Callaghan, but I don't have it in mind to get you drunk and have my wicked way with you.' He took a long drink of his beer.

His words startled her. 'Why not? Don't you find me attractive?'

A muscle in his jaw twitched but he did not answer her straight away and asked did she mind if he smoked. She shook her head and watched him take out a packet of Camel cigarettes. 'Can I try one of them?'

'Nope. Smoking is a bad habit and I don't want to lead you astray. To be honest, you remind me of my sister back home. She's always trying to push back the boundaries. Luke treated you right but I can see how a guy like him would eventually drive a girl like you nuts.'

Babs was annoyed. 'You don't know anything about me, so how can you say that?'

'You haven't mentioned his name since you climbed into my jeep.'

'If I remember rightly you haven't either. In fact we didn't speak at all on the way here.'

'I was waiting to see if you'd ask why he couldn't come.'

She flushed. 'You could have told me. Now *you* have mentioned him, perhaps I can say that Luke isn't the person I thought him, so I was going to end it tonight.'

'He'd come to the same conclusion about you, realised you didn't have much in common.'

Babs was hurt. 'He could have had the guts to say so to my face.'

'He was going to but had an accident this morning...dropped a wrench on his foot. He gave me a note for you.' Jake reached into his pocket and held out an envelope.

The colour in Babs' cheeks deepened. 'Don't bother. You've said it all.'

He reached for her hand and placed the envelope in it. She stared at him and then ripped it up. 'My, you've got a temper, must go with the red hair,' said Jake mildly, shaking his head.

'None of us is perfect.'

He drawled, 'No. But you have got looks, so I can see why Luke fancied you.'

Babs was about to say that there was more to her than just a pretty face, when she remembered that it was Luke's handsome face that had attracted her. 'You obviously don't fancy me,' she said.

'I wouldn't say that but I'm older and wiser, so I don't believe in rushing my fences. Have some of your drink and if you're still in the mood to dance then I'll take you round the floor.'

Babs recovered her nerve. 'It's the only reason I came here with you,' she said, reaching for her glass, 'and I hope you don't tread on my toes.'

She was to wish those words back after he led her onto the floor because she was so nervous of making a fool of herself, she stumbled over his feet and found herself lifted into the air. He danced her round the floor in that position and she felt so embarrassed she wanted to hit him but that was impossible; clamped to his chest and with his shaven cheek against her smooth one she couldn't. Instead she gazed up at the twirling, glistening ball hanging from the ceiling, so that she didn't have to meet anyone else's eyes and experienced a sense of floating.

When that dance ended and he took her back to their table, she drank her lemonade down in almost one draft and then stared at him. 'Is that how you usually dance with women?'

'Nope! I usually dance with mature women who can dance. Another drink?'

If she hadn't drunk all her lemonade, Babs just might have flung what was left in his face but as it was she had to make do with saying, 'D'you mean to insult me?'

'I was just speaking the facts as they are, Barbara. Drink?'

She nodded.

When he returned to the table and placed another lemonade in front of her, she made no comment but acted like he was not there, continuing to watch the activity on the dance floor. When the dance finished, she expected him to say something but he didn't. So she remained silent and reached for her glass, taking tiny sips of the lemonade. The next half hour was one of the most frustrating since she had moved from the farm near Ormskirk. He sat there as silently as she did and she could not help thinking that he was making her suffer because she had ripped up Luke's note. It had been a childish thing to do. She wondered if Jake was a close friend of Luke's and whether he came from middle America. With a name like O'Donnell there must be some Irish in him, so most likely he was Catholic, but that didn't say she and he would have anything else much in common. He was too old for her, anyway, and besides, she didn't feel the least bit attracted to him. It would be a relief when they said their goodbyes.

When the interval arrived and he asked her if she would like to go, she said yes and strangely felt near to tears. Despite her telling him to drop her at the entrance to the drive, he drove her to the front door of the house. As she was about to let herself out of the jeep, he left the driving seat and helped her down. 'Thanks,' she said. 'Although, you didn't have to.'

'Sure, I didn't.' Abruptly he seized her shoulders and brought her against him and kissed her long and hard.

When he released her she stared up at him from blazing eyes. 'I beg your pardon!'

'Again. Think before you say yes in future, Barbara.' He saluted her and climbed back into the jeep. 'Goodnight. Sleep tight.'

She watched him drive off, wishing she had thought to slap his face. Then she skipped into the house, thinking she was free of Luke and could now do damn well anything she wanted to do. It was not until she was in bed that she remembered Nellie's letter, but decided she was too sleepy to read it. Tomorrow would do and she'd reply to it the same day.

* * *

Nellie pounced on the letter and hurried with it into the kitchen. She slit it open and spread the single sheet of paper on the table.

Dear Nellie,
This is just a quick scribble as I'm up to my eyes. It would be lovely to see you but it's just not worth your while coming here at the moment. We get sent off places where we're needed and sometimes we stay there, so I can't guarantee I'd be here even if I gave you a date. You mustn't worry about me. I'm fine. I've finished with the Cary Grant lookalike and at the moment I'm fancy free and have no intention of getting serious with anyone. I hope you and Lottie are fine, and Grandfather, too. Seen anything of Francis? I had a letter from Dad but he didn't ask after you, which surprised me because I'd told him about Teddy and the baby. Having said that, a lot of the letter was blacked out. At least we know when he sent it he was still alive and kicking.
Lots of love,
Babs.

Nellie was disappointed about not seeing her sister but accepted that, because of the war, things weren't easy for anyone. She was hurt by her father's failure even to send his condolences via Babs. Still, nothing he did that was hurtful should surprise her but it did depress her. She realised that she really was in need of a break.

There was a sound at the kitchen door and Nellie looked up and saw Lottie in her pyjamas. 'You not gone to work yet?' she said.

'In a minute,' said Nellie, smiling. 'There's some tea in the pot. I've a letter from Babs. I had thought of going to see her but she says not to bother because she can't guarantee when she'll be there.'

Lottie poured herself a cup of tea and said sadly, 'Billy'll be off soon. He's had his call up papers.'

'We're going to miss him, aren't we?'

Lottie nodded and then rested her chin in her hands, causing her lank hair to flop about her face. 'There's only one good thing about him going and that's we'll see less of his father.'

Nellie nodded. 'Although, he might still come round because of the break-ins.'

Lottie muttered, 'I don't know one person around here who's been broken into. I think he only comes to keep an eye on me and Billy. At least Grandfather won't be sacking him now.'

Nellie stared at her. 'What d'you mean "keep an eye on you and Billy"? And why should Grandfather sack him?'

Lottie hesitated. 'Nell, is it wrong to kiss someone you like?'

'Why, have you been kissing Billy?'

'Only once,' said Lottie, flushing. 'He kissed me first and it was only a little kiss but when his dad caught us he said Grandfather would sack Billy if he knew about it. So I made sure it didn't happen again.'

Nellie said tactfully. 'It could be that Sgt McElroy thinks Billy's too young for you and, with him going away, doesn't want either of you getting hurt.'

Lottie's face brightened. 'It could be that. It was a really nice being kissed. I never thought any boy would want to kiss me.'

Nellie was glad that she had a happy memory. Eying Lottie from head to toe, she realised that she had lost weight. She had good legs and shapely ankles and, although she could never be classed as pretty, she was growing into a handsome woman. She had an air of innocence about her that some men might find attractive.

'Well, you know different now, Lottie, so let it boost your confidence and don't let anyone pull you down,' said Nellie.

Lottie blushed. 'Thanks, Nell.'

'My pleasure. Anyway, I've work to go to. You relax and stop worrying about Grandfather and Sergeant McElroy. You're probably right about there not being any break-ins.'

'Does that mean we can have a night out? There's a film on in Liverpool I'd like to see.'

'You think you can manage a trip into Liverpool on the bus?' asked Nellie.

Her sister nodded. 'It's on at the Paramount and is called *Moonlight in Havana*. It stars Allan Jones, the American tenor. You know the one. He sings 'Donkey Serenade'.

'He's the one with blond wavy hair and a lovely voice, isn't he? OK! As long as you don't end up complaining because of the walking and Grandfather doesn't mind.'

'I won't complain,' said Lottie cheerily, 'and we could ask him if he'd like to come with us.'

But when they approached their grandfather, he first asked what the film was about and when they said it was a musical, he shook his head. 'Not my kind of thing. Anyway, someone's got to stay home and keep guard.'

'I don't think there's anything to fear, Grandfather. Neither of us has heard of anyone being broken into, so you won't lock us out, will you?' she teased.

He scowled. 'I'm not a fool, girl. You give the password and I'll let you in.'

'What is the password?' she asked.

'V for Victory,' he said.

She nodded and left him sitting in front of the fire with the *Liverpool Echo* on his knee, listening to the wireless.

The film was as enjoyable as the sisters expected and, for a couple of hours, they were transported to Cuba and taken out of themselves. Nellie told herself that it was as good as going to Warrington. But by the time they arrived home, Lottie's limp had worsened and her mouth was tight with pain.

'In future we'll stick to the Regal,' said Nellie firmly.

They went round the back of the house but the washroom door was locked. She banged on it loudly but there was no response so she banged again and shouted, 'V for Victory!' Still no answer.

'Perhaps he's fallen asleep on the parlour sofa,' said Lottie. 'You go round the front and he might hear you better. I'll sit on the step and wait here.'

Nellie nodded and retraced her steps. She not only banged on the front door but called, 'V for Victory!' through the letterbox. She also knocked on the parlour window but without any effect.

'Hello, hello, hello! What's going on here?' called a voice out of the darkness.

Nellie jumped and turned round; she could just about make out a dark shape looming behind the torch. 'Is that you, Sergeant McElroy?' she asked.

'Yes.' He shone the torch in her face.

'Lower that!' said Nellie, half-blinded. 'What are you doing here? You didn't half give me a fright.'

'Sorry about that. What's up?'

'We can't get in. Grandfather must have locked all the doors and fallen asleep.'

'Where's your sister?'

'Waiting round the back.'

Immediately he set off round the side of the house. Nellie hurried after him, arriving seconds later. The first thing he did was ask Lottie if she was OK.

'I'm tired and in pain and I want to go to bed,' she said fretfully.

'All right, love, we'll soon get you inside.' He tried the handle but it didn't open. He shone his torch up at the first-floor windows. 'There's a window open up there.'

'You'd never get up there,' said Nellie. 'You're too large. And I'm not shinning up the drainpipe in my best stockings.'

He returned to the washroom door and tapped a small window pane with his truncheon. The glass broke and, carefully, he slipped his hand through the gap and turned the key.

Nellie was surprised that the door was not bolted. She hurried inside, followed by Sgt McElroy. A limping Lottie brought up the rear. Nellie could feel her heart beating heavily, not knowing what she would find inside. She clicked on the electric light and led the way into the kitchen. She stopped abruptly as she saw her grandfather lying on the floor with his stick beside him.

'Oh God,' she whispered, hurrying over to him. She looked into his ashen face and knelt down to search for a pulse; his skin was still warm.

'Oh dear, oh dear, oh dear!' said Lottie.

Nellie looked up at Sgt McElroy. 'I can't find a pulse. I think he's dead. Could you fetch a doctor? I'd rather stay with him.'

'Let me try.' The sergeant knelt down and fumbled for the old man's wrist and then felt the vein in his neck. Slowly he shook his head before getting to his feet. 'You're right. He's dead. You wouldn't like me to look around before I go for the doctor? Make sure there's no one here? That window upstairs…'

'Please, the doctor. If anyone got in, they've probably got out by now.'

He nodded and left the house.

Nellie told Lottie to sit with Grandfather. 'Where are you going?' she asked, looking scared.

'I'm just going to check that nobody is here.' She picked up the poker.

'Why didn't you let Sgt McElroy search? If Grandfather's dead, there's nothing a doctor can do about it,' said Lottie.

'I was surprised to find him hanging around here when Billy's not working,' said Nellie.

Lottie's brow puckered. 'Could be that there really have been break-ins. Don't go up, Nell! Stay here.'

Nellie hesitated but then shook her head and left the kitchen, switching on lights as she went, checking Lottie's room and the parlour, thinking she'd need to go through the latter again before she could be sure nothing had been stolen. She went upstairs and into the bathroom and closed and locked the window. Then she crossed the landing to her grandfather's room and opened the door. It swung silently open and she switched on the light.

To her relief the room was empty but in the middle of the

floor was a black tin box with the lid flung open and envelopes beside it. She looked inside, expecting to find it empty, but there were a heap of half-crowns and several sepia photographs. She gathered the coins together and pocketed them. Then she picked up the papers and placed them with the photographs in the tin box and shut it. She took a blanket from her grandfather's bed and checked the other bedrooms but found no sign of them being turned over. She returned to the ground floor and covered her grandfather with the blanket, swallowing a tightness in her throat. Then she sat beside her sister to wait for the doctor.

'We shouldn't have gone out,' said Lottie, gazing down at the covered body. 'I suppose I'll miss him despite his being a moaner.'

'He's left me something in his will,' murmured Nellie.

Her sister gave her a sidelong glance. 'How d'you know?'

'Francis told me. I suppose he died of a heart attack.'

She got up and felt the kettle. It was hot enough to make tea. She was trying to analyse how she felt about her grandfather's death. Although she had known that he would die one day, somehow she had expected him to last longer. Was she upset? Yes, but the way she felt could not compare to her grief over the loss of Teddy or her baby.

She made tea and handed her sister a cup. 'Did he have much money, d'you think?' asked Lottie.

'I've no idea. I did find a bag of half-crowns upstairs. We can use them for anything we have to buy until the insurance money comes through,' said Nellie, wondering what had happened to disturb her grandfather while rooting in his box. Perhaps he had heard a noise and come downstairs. Maybe it had been fear of attack, alone in the house, that had killed him. Just like Lottie, she felt guilty for having left him but there was nothing she could do about that now.

A few minutes later the doctor arrived with Sgt McElroy and pronounced her grandfather officially dead. In answer to

Nellie's question about it being a heart attack, he said, 'Yes. Not surprising in a man of his age and with all the stresses of wartime. My sympathies, Mrs Lachlan and Miss Callaghan.' He scribbled on a slip of paper all that was necessary and handed it to Nellie. 'Perhaps the sergeant and I can help move your grandfather out of the kitchen.'

A relieved Nellie thanked him.

'Perhaps to his bedroom, said the sergeant, teetering on his heels, his arms behind his back. 'I'd like to look around upstairs with that window being open.'

'There's no one up there, I've looked. You can put Grandfather on Lottie's bed in the old dining room, that would be the simplest thing,' said Nellie.

'Makes sense,' said the doctor, slapping the policeman's back, adding, 'Come on, man! Let's do it so we can leave the young ladies to sort themselves out.'

As soon as the two men left, Nellie wiped the urine off the kitchen floor and then, looking at Lottie, knew she needed to be in bed. 'Can you manage the stairs?' she asked.

Lottie nodded. 'Can we sleep together, Nellie? I feel cold and a bit shaky.'

'Of course,' said Nellie, putting an arm round her. 'I'll take the shelf out of the oven and wrap it in newspaper and pop it in the double bed. Then I'll help you upstairs.'

'You'll have to get the priest to say absolution and what about Francis? You'll need to get in touch with him to arrange the funeral.'

'That can wait until the morning,' said Nellie.

Once Lottie was in bed, Nellie went back downstairs. There was something she felt she must do. She fetched clean clothes for her grandfather, as well as soap, hot water and a towel. She went into the parlour and, taking a deep breath, she did for him what she hadn't been able to do for her mother. She stripped, washed and changed him before his limbs stiffened. Only when she had performed that act did she go upstairs and run a bath.

She lay in the water, tears in her eyes, thinking about the old man. What would her father's reaction be to his own father's death? This house would be his now and no doubt he would expect her to look after it. She must speak to Francis. Tomorrow she would tell Polly that she needed a few days off to arrange things.

Polly was understanding. 'Of course you can have time off. I don't know how I'll manage without you,' she said seriously, 'but I'll have to cope.'

Nellie apologised and wasted no time in heading for her brother's parish. Francis was not at the presbytery but the housekeeper told Nellie that she would most likely find him at the boys' club in the church hall. So Nellie went in search of her brother. She had once expressed her disgust to him and Joe about what some men called the art of boxing. Both had told her that boxing was popular in the deprived parishes of Liverpool because lads knew that there was a chance of escaping the streets by making money in the ring. She thought she knew what to expect when she walked into the boys' club but no one was using the ring, there were only a couple of youths hitting punch bags and another was skipping with a rope. She saw her brother's black-clad figure at the other end of the hall speaking to a man. She waved and Francis spotted her.

Immediately, he excused himself and made his way towards her, a concerned expression on his rugged face. 'What is it, Nellie? For you to be here at this time of day it must be something serious.'

She told him what had happened and he placed an arm about her shoulders. 'It sounds like you've done as much as you can. I presume you've spoken to your parish priest?'

'Not yet. I thought I'd speak to you first.'

'Perhaps that's just as well. I know Grandfather's wishes. He wanted to be buried at sea.'

'Why didn't I think of that?' murmured Nellie, surprised. 'How do we go about arranging it?'

'There's no need for you to worry, Nell. I spoke to Father Waring at Atlantic House after Grandfather made his will. He agreed to arrange everything when the time came.'

'That's a relief!'

'Did you think to bring the papers that were in Grandfather's black box?'

'Yes. I haven't opened anything.' She handed several long, narrow brown envelopes to him.

'I can tell you what's in his will right now, Nellie. He left the house and its contents to you. Any money that's left after funeral expenses is to go to the church.'

Nellie rocked on her heels. She must have misheard him. 'Say that again?'

'Grandfather left the house and its contents to you,' repeated Francis with a faint smile.

'What about Dad?'

'Dad was a fool. That's what the old man thought and not only a fool but a selfish, opinionated one, who drank too much and took things for granted.'

'Goodness!' exclaimed Nellie. 'I never thought he felt that strongly about him.'

Francis nodded. 'He appreciated you returning to the house and taking responsibility for the family. Of course, if Joe had been alive, he would have got everything.' He grimaced. 'As it was you were second in line favourite after your husband was killed.'

Nellie shook her head. She felt positively odd, remembering her mother banning her from the house which now seemed to belong to her. 'I can't believe it. Dad'll have a fit. He'll say I wormed my way into Grandfather's good graces,' she babbled. 'I'll have to make the house over to him. It's only right. He was his son.'

Francis said sternly, 'Pull yourself together, Nellie. Don't rush into doing anything of the sort. You need a cool head to make any big decisions. Carry on just as you are.'

Nellie gulped and a shudder went through her. 'You're right. Dad's not here, so there's no rush.'

'Exactly. You need to think hard before considering going against Grandfather's wishes.'

'I told Lottie he had left me some money, I never imagined this. Do I tell Babs?'

'I suggest you keep mum for now. A will does reside with Grandfather's solicitor. He'll not be getting in touch with Dad because he's not a beneficiary. I'll write to Dad about Grandfather's death but, for the moment, I won't mention his will. If you decide to keep the house and Dad cuts up rough when he comes home, if I'm not around then the solicitor will help you.'

A ripple of fear raced along her nerves. 'Why shouldn't you be around? Don't you go enlisting in the Forces as a padre, Francis. I've told you before, I don't want anyone else I love dying on me.'

He hesitated and said gently, 'If I feel it's God's will and not just my own guilt, then I'll have to go. In the meantime, our next move is to comply with Grandfather's wishes. In the meantime his body will have to be taken to the undertaker's.'

After Nellie had written to Babs telling her about their Grandfather's death, Nellie thought a lot about her grandfather's wishes. Several times she considered making an appointment with his solicitor after the burial at sea was over. Then she would wander through the rooms of *her* house and down the garden, feeling a strong sense of possession. An idea started to grow in her mind about how she could put the house to good use for the war effort but she didn't tell anyone about her plan because it needed a lot more thinking out.

Ten days after his death, Grandfather's body was carried aboard a pilot boat that would take it to the Mersey estuary. There, Nellie, Lottie and Francis would say their farewell to the old man. Babs could not get away so it would just be the three of them. Although only a short voyage, it was not without its fraught moments. There was the danger of floating mines, and buoys marked the numerous wrecks where ships had sunk during the blitz. Just like the shifting sandbanks, they needed the navigation skills of an experienced pilot.

At last they reached the spot deemed the right one to launch Grandfather's body into the deep. Francis said the words of committal and the old man's earthly remains slipped into the sea. Nellie and Lottie dropped a wreath of lilies and roses on the surface of the water. It was a moving moment. The old man had not always been easy to live with but both sisters would always be grateful to him for providing them with a home when they needed one.

Part Two

1943 to 1944

Chapter Eleven

January 1943

Dear Nellie,

Sorry I couldn't make Christmas but I'm about to go off to a New Year's Eve party. You wouldn't believe the changes the Yanks have brought to the area. Lively is not the word for the place these days. The airbase at Burtonwood is growing. It's going to be huge with shops and cinemas and dance halls...oh, and they do have runways, hangars and warehouses, too. It'll be like a little town in itself. They call it Little Detroit or Little America. The natives are already calling it

Babs paused and chewed on the end of her pen. She had been about to write *Sodom and Gomorrah* but decided that might bring her eldest sister running to see for herself if the rumours about the American servicemen being over-sexed were true. Instead she wrote, *other names.*

I doubt they have anything to complain about. The Yanks are spending money around here like there's no tomorrow. I'd really love for you to visit but now is not the right time. It's real bleak out here at this time of year because the winds blow icy across the flat fields from the Mersey. Wait until the spring and then we'll have a good time. In the meantime don't worry about me. I have got a head on my shoulders and no man in uniform is going to sweet talk me into doing something daft. By the way, I had a letter from Dad. Has he written to you? Seems his ship was hit but managed to limp into Greenock in Scotland and he's up there now. Maybe you'll get a visit. It's been ages since he wrote but he seems to think that Grandfather's death was a blessing. Hope to see you when the weather gets better,

Love and kisses,

Babs.

She blotted the letter and slipped it into an envelope and addressed and stamped it. Then she placed it, with the one she had written to her father, in her shoulder bag. She looked up as a couple of young women entered the lounge. One was Flo and the other, a tall blonde, was Heather, who had initiated Babs into the workings of a tractor's innards. She was wearing a kilt and a frilly cream blouse beneath a tartan waistcoat, because although she had not been born in Scotland she was of Scottish descent.

'You ready yet?' asked Heather, without a trace of a Scottish accent.

Babs nodded. 'I needed to get a couple of letters written. I'll post them in the morning. Nobody else going from here?'

'No,' said Heather. 'Some have still got hangovers from last night's celebrations in the village.'

Babs had missed out on last night but was raring to go out that evening. Captain Stuart McGregor, a Yank and officer of Canadian and Scottish descent, had invited her to the dance, which was to take place in the hall where he was billeted. He had told her to bring a couple of friends. She was hoping to see him in a kilt. She put on her hat and waterproof coat over her frock and followed the other two outside.

It was pitch black and raining but, fortunately, Heather was driving the farm truck and knew the area well. Soon they were heading towards the hall a few miles from Burtonwood. Babs marvelled at how quickly the Americans had extended the base in the last nine months or so. It had been Stuart who had told her of its attractions and she hoped one day to have the opportunity of being set loose in the shop. She knew that pleasure would have to be deferred but tonight she was intent on having fun.

Heather parked the truck in the driveway alongside several jeeps and cars, and the girls hurried through the rain into the hall. Lights blazed inside and they were directed to a room where they could leave their outdoor clothes. They did not need to ask directions to the ballroom because the sound of a big band led them to it. The noise reverberated round walls festooned with streamers and there were already couples on the dance floor.

Stuart must have been looking out for Babs because no sooner had the three girls entered the room than he came over to them with two other airmen, one of whom Babs recognised with mixed feelings.

Stuart seized her hand and pulled her towards him. 'It's great you made it, honey. I was just starting to think the weather had put a kibosh on things.'

'No, a bit of rain wasn't going to keep me away.' She smiled up into his pleasant, fresh-skinned face and then eyed him up and down. Yes! He was wearing a kilt and looked OK in it. They had met a fortnight ago in a pub in Warrington. He had been with another airman and she'd been with Flo. The men had bought them a drink and they'd got chatting.

'You've met Chuck,' he said. 'Let me introduce you to Jake.'

'We've met,' she said, thinking that if Jake had been invited for Heather she was going to top him by at least four inches.

'Barbara.' Jake inclined his fair head.

She turned to her friend. 'Heather, this is Jake O'Donnell. You'll have gathered the other two are Stuart and Chuck.'

Chuck nodded in her direction and then whispered in Flo's ear. She said something in a low voice and the next moment the two of them were heading for the dance floor.

Heather stared after them before turning back to the other three and giving Jake the once over. 'I suppose it's me and you then, if Stuart's Babs' date.'

Jake drawled, 'I really appreciate that gracious invitation to dance.'

Babs suppressed a giggle but Heather said, 'Are you trying to be funny?'

He raised his eyebrows. 'Perish the thought. Shall we give it a go?'

'That's what I've come for.' She seized him by the shoulder and almost yanked him onto the floor.

'Why is it I think they're not going to get on?' said Stuart.

'No comment,' said Babs, watching the other couple and wondering why she was glad Jake and Heather weren't hitting it off.

'You ready to dance?' asked Stuart.

Feeling confident of making a good impression on the dance floor this evening because she had been practising, she turned to him and smiled. 'When you are.'

He took her hand and led her onto the floor but they'd hardly got into the rhythm of the dance when the music stopped. Stuart grimaced. 'Bad timing. Drink?'

She nodded and watched him hurry away, kilt swinging as he dodged between people. 'Left you already, hey?' whispered a voice against her ear.

She did not need to look round to know who had spoken, but did anyway.

'He stood on my foot,' complained Heather.

Babs gave Jake a severe look. 'Is this true?'

'I'm saying nuthin'!' he said, straight-faced.

Heather glared at him. 'If you're saying it was my fault then that's not true. If you'd been paying attention, you'd have realised the music was coming to an end and stopped dancing.' She slipped off her shoe and made a painful show of wriggling her toes.

'OK! I admit that my mind was on other things,' said Jake.

'Now there's a confession. I'm going to have to sit out the next few dances if I'm to be fit for the Gay Gordons,' said Heather.

'Perhaps you'd like me to find us a table,' said Jake.

Heather smiled. 'Now you're talking.'

The two girls watched him disappear into the throng before exchanging glances. 'Do you think he'll come back?' asked Heather.

'Why shouldn't he?'

Heather wiggled her toes, replaced her shoe and walked a few paces without any sign of a limp.

'That got better quick,' said Babs.

Heather said, 'I need a taller guy. See you later.' She went in the opposite direction from Jake.

Babs stood waiting for Stuart and Jake to reappear, knowing there was nothing for it but to tell Jake the truth. She doubted he would care about being ditched if his earlier comments were anything to go by.

He was the first to arrive at Babs' side and smiled when he saw her standing alone. 'I reckon I've been ditched,' he said. 'As for you...'

'I could lie and say she's gone to rest her foot but...'

'Let's stick to the truth. Tall women are not my cup of tea.' His blue eyes took in Babs' appearance in one sweeping glance as the band launched into a boogie and she began to tap her foot. 'Do you want to dance?'

She was tempted to accept his offer, so she could show him how good she'd got since their last meeting, but said, 'I'm waiting for Stuart.'

'If he's gone to the bar he could be some time. Come on,' he said. 'Admit you're dying to dance with me.'

'After the last time when you made a show of me! Don't make me laugh.'

'Could be fun.'

She glanced at the dance floor and wanted to be on there amongst the boogying couples. 'OK!'

He wasted no time leading Babs onto the dance floor and whirling her around before launching into an energetic jitterbug. His enthusiasm was infectious and she had no trouble matching his every step and coming up with a few of her own when he held her by the waist and lifted her up in the air before swinging her down between his legs. She managed to retain her footing and do a bit of a step dance before he turned to face her.

She laughed. He grinned as he grabbed her by the waist and pulled her close. They still danced fast but now they were cheek to cheek. When the music ended she was out of breath and had to cling to him while she recovered. She could feel the heat of his body against her hand and thought how useful he would be in bed as a hot water bottle. She giggled, thinking it wasn't a romantic thought.

'What's so funny?' he asked, gazing down at her.

She noticed the smile in his eyes and the sweat glistening on his face. 'You don't want to know.'

'Yes. I do. A dollar for your thoughts.'

She shook her head. 'Not this one.'

'What about when we get to know each other better?'

She did not answer because out of the corner of her eye she noticed Stuart standing on the edge of the dance floor, staring at them. 'Time to go. Thanks for the dance.' She freed herself and made her way over to her date.

Close up she could see that Stuart was not pleased. 'What happened to your friend, Heather?' he asked.

'Jake stood on her foot.' She reached for one of the glasses he held. 'This one mine?'

'Sure. So how come you're dancing with him?'

'He said you'd be some time and could see I wanted to dance.'

'You said you wanted a drink.'

'You asked if I wanted a drink. I just didn't expect you to be away so long.' Babs was thirsty and thought this exchange might go on for some time. She lifted the glass to her mouth and gulped down half the shandy.

'How well d'you know Jake? He hasn't mentioned going out with you.' There was suspicion in his voice.

'I know him hardly at all.'

'It didn't look like that to me.'

'It's true. This is only the second time I've met him.' She was getting annoyed by his possessive attitude and knew she wouldn't be accepting any more invitations from Stuart. 'Can we change the subject now? You asked me to come. I'm here. So let's not waste time arguing. Let's down our drinks and dance.'

Grudgingly, he agreed.

They danced on and off for the rest of the evening but exchanged little in the way of conversation. Several times Babs gazed about her for Jake but he was nowhere to be seen. She had to admit that the fizz had gone out of the evening without him around.

As she climbed into bed that night, she wondered whether she would see Jake again. Trouble was she could hardly go asking for him at the base, so it seemed she was going to have to wait until he came looking for her. She thought of Nellie, wondering what she would make of Jake, and remembered that she must post those letters tomorrow.

Nellie seethed as she re-read that part of Bab's letter referring to their father. She could understand a son calling his father's death a blessing if he had been gaga or in terrible pain and bedridden from some horrible disease, but that couldn't be said about Grandfather. The truth was that the two men had never got on and whether that was because they'd spent so much time apart she just didn't know. She guessed now that her father's only interest in Grandfather's death was what he would get out of it. She could only pray that he would stay in Scotland and not come south. She glanced at the clock and realised she should be on her way to work. Pocketing the letter, she left the house.

As Nellie walked, she thought about the number of women on Merseyside who had husbands, sons or brothers in the navy. The Battle of the Atlantic was still being waged and the deaths of so many sailors must surely be having its effect on the morale of their women. Yet like herself, they had to come to terms with their loss because life went on, but the end of this terrible war couldn't come quickly enough for all of them.

At least up here on the north-west coast of England they

were not suffering like those in London, which was being bombed again. Still, there were a lot of less worrying things to think about. The government had warned that there would be coal shortages and the British Gas Company was urging people *To save Gas, to smash the Axis Powers.* The local press said shortages of fish and green vegetables were likely during the rest of winter. The nation was being urged to tighten its belt to give, give, give, save, save, save. There was hardly an iron railing to be seen anywhere. Regular collections of waste paper were made and the *Crosby Herald* was urging people not to hoard their Christmas cards and old calendars but to take them to the post office.

Even the libraries were at it now; thousands of books had been destroyed in the blitz and they wanted people to give books purchased at Christmas to their local branch. She was in favour of that because she borrowed books to read to the children. While all this was going on, the Anglican bishop of Liverpool was concerned that women and girls were turning to alcohol to calm their nerves. Nellie, for one, did not blame them. She thought of Mrs McElroy and wondered whether she had lost a father or brother in the Great War as well as a child. Perhaps if she'd had more children, she would never have turned to drink.

Nellie was thinking about her own son when she spotted a notice on the waste plot of land close to the lift bridge. Her curiosity was roused and she went and read it. As she did, her spirits lifted and, singing a Cole Porter number under her breath, she hurried across the bridge and along Linacre Road. She came to the bicycle shop and climbed the stairs and burst into the room above.

'Polly, guess what?' she blurted out.

Her friend looked up from the register. 'What?'

'The council nursery is being built on the waste land the other side of the canal, near the lift bridge. It'll be a single-storey prefabricated building and should be opening the first week in April.'

Polly's eyes shone. 'So they've finally got down to it.'

'You know why, don't you? Now the Allies have almost won the war in Africa, the next stop will be Europe. It'll be more men in the Forces, more bombs, bullets, guns, tanks, uniforms.'

'Poor sods,' said Polly softly.

Both were silent, remembering their own husbands.

A mother and child stopped in front of the table. Polly took the woman's money and ticked off the child's name. As soon as she had gone and the toddler had settled with chalk and a board with a handful of other children, Polly asked Nellie what else she knew about the nursery.

'Nothing,' said Nellie. 'But I'll go into the council offices and find out on the way home.'

'Great,' said Polly. 'Now Margaret's started school, I'll apply for a job there as a nursery nurse. I'd best do it straight away because there could be any number of children's nurses applying.'

Nellie glanced about her. 'What about our children?'

Polly frowned. 'Depending on the cost and what the nursery is offering, we could lose most of them.'

'There'll be more wanting to fill their places,' said Nellie with conviction. 'The other day I passed a woman with two little ones. I remembered them from Ambleside. She told me that she wasn't the only one who's back. They all reckon it's safe to come home now and are keen to earn money. She told me that she'd apply for a job in an Ordinance factory, filling shells and things if she could get someone to look after her kids.' Nellie added ruefully, 'Would you believe, Polly, that the government are promising not only good money to get them into the factories but a canteen, stockings and make-up at special prices? It's shift work, mind, and that includes working part of Sunday. I think we're in the wrong job.'

Polly shook her head. 'It'll only last while the war's on. Us widows need jobs that'll pay us a regular wage for life.'

Nellie knew she was right and, on the way home, dropped in

at the council offices to discover that the only jobs available were for trained nursery nurses. She found that disappointing but it made her plan all the more appealing. She wrote down the details for the nursery nurses' jobs for Polly and hurried home.

When Nellie woke the next morning, she could hear the wind whistling in the eaves and rattling the windows. She wanted to snuggle down in bed but had to drag herself up. In such weather her plan seemed all the more attractive. She went downstairs, shivering as she lit the fire, and then went out to see to the hens and collect the few eggs they produced at this time of year. Soon there would be work to be done in the vegetable patch and she would have to ask around or advertise for a replacement for Billy.

Polly was excited when Nellie gave her the information about the nursery. 'This is great. Sister Mary Moore's to be matron. She worked at the First Aid Post in Litherland during the blitz, so she's well known in the area. You're a true friend, Nellie.'

Nellie shrugged. 'It's the least I can do. Unfortunately they only want trained nursery nurses and I have no medical background.'

Polly sighed. 'It's a shame. You're so good with the kids. If I do get the job, then perhaps you'd like to take over here.'

Nellie hesitated, knowing it would take capital to get her own nursery up and running. 'I'll think about it,' she said.

'Do. There's no rush. I mightn't get one of the posts.'

'The hours'll be longer. It's going to be open from seven in the morning to seven at night six days a week.'

'Probably be shift work. What do you think of their charges?' asked Polly.

'Incredible. A shilling a day and the children will get three meals for that and medical care. They plan to take fifty children from six months to five years. With staff and meals to pay for, the government must be subsidising it.'

'We'd have trouble competing,' said Polly.

Nellie agreed, wondering if her plan was sensible after all, but she still believed there would be a demand for more pre-school childcare in the area. Fifty nursery places wasn't that many considering the number of families in Litherland. She really had to give it serious thought.

It was in her mind to mention the possibility of taking over Polly's nursery to Lottie as soon as she arrived home but, when she walked into the kitchen, it was to find her brother sitting alone in front of the fire.

'Hello, Francis,' said Nellie, pleased to see him. 'Where's Lottie?'

'She's forgotten something for supper and gone out to see if she can get it.' He rose to his feet. 'You look tired. Lottie thinks you're working too hard.'

'I'm no different from most of the country. What are you doing here?'

'I had a phone call from Dad.'

Nellie's smile faded. 'He's not coming here, is he?'

'No.'

'Thank God for that.' She sat down at the table and eased off her shoes.

'But he did ask me to come and check the house, see if anything needed doing and get it done. How he expects me to make that happen when there's a shortage of materials and manpower beggars belief.'

'He's presuming a lot like we thought. He didn't say how this work was going to be paid for, did he?' asked Nellie.

Francis tapped his thumbs together. 'He suggests you sell some of Grandfather's stuff...but that's not all he said. He thinks you and Lottie should be paying him rent.'

Nellie gasped. 'You are joking! Who does he think is paying the rates?' She poked her breast bone. 'Soft pot here! Ooh, I can't wait to see his face when I tell him the house is mine. You didn't tell him, did you?'

Francis shook his head. 'He just might have had an apoplexy and we don't want that, do we, Nellie?'

'Oh I don't know,' she said, tongue in cheek.

'Nellie!' Francis shook his head at her but with the faintest of smiles in his eyes. 'He is our dad.'

She nodded. 'A pity he doesn't remember it and do the nice things dads are supposed to do for their children. Our lives would have been much easier if he hadn't spent so much time in the pub when he was home. I bet Mam never saw much of the money he got when he cashed his advance note before a trip. So what's he up to?'

'He's signed on another ship. Says he's going to the Americas to pick up supplies but once they're loaded his destination is hush-hush.'

'Doesn't trust his son enough to tell him?'

'I honestly think he doesn't know,' said Francis.

'OK. So it's unlikely he'll turn up on the doorstep in the next few months, so I'm free to do what I want,' said Nellie casually.

Her brother stared at her hard. 'What have you in mind?'

'Hot drink?' She did not wait for his answer but put the kettle on.

'Nellie, come on. Tell me! You've got that look on your face.'

'What look? Like I'm plotting something?' She chuckled as she spooned Camp coffee into cups. 'I should really put my idea to Lottie at the same time as you but that will mean my telling her that the house is mine.'

'Come on, Nellie, get to the point,' said Francis.

She sat and stared at him because she wanted to see his expression when she unfolded her plan. 'Polly, who runs the nursery group, is applying for a job as a nursery nurse at the new council nursery being built. If she gets the job she's asked if I would like to take over her group.'

Francis frowned. 'You mean work there full-time? You'll be exhausted, Nell. I mean, it takes time getting there and back everyday and then there's the house and garden. Lottie might be a lot better now but she couldn't possibly cope with the work involved on her own. She'll be lonely, too, here all day on her own.'

Nellie smiled. 'Exactly, that's why my own plan is better than Polly's.' She paused.

He looked at her warily. 'Go on.'

'I want to open a nursery school here in the house.'

Francis' jaw dropped.

'No need to look like that. It's for the war effort. Now the desert war's won, there'll be a big push to get into Europe. That's why the government is desperate to get more women into the factories. You can imagine the guns and ammunition that are going to be needed.'

'And men,' murmured Francis, with a tortured expression.

Nellie nodded and could not continue for the lump in her throat, thinking of the suffering so many would experience in the coming months and possibly years, but what could they do? Britain and America were committed to defeating Hitler and Mussolini and winning this war.

The kettle started steaming, so she made coffee and took Francis a cup. Then she picked up her own and sat across the fireplace from him. 'The mothers will be paid good wages. I've spoken to at least one who would jump at the chance of nursery care. Some of these poorer women have hardly two pennies to rub together. You must know what it's like in your parish. Holes in the kids' shoes and trips to the pawnshop.'

'All right!' Francis eased back his broad shoulders. 'You don't have to lay it on with a trowel. But what happens when their husbands return from the war?'

Nellie said softly, 'I believe most mothers want to be with their children but they'll make sacrifices for what's best for them. Anyway, some of the mothers won't have husbands coming home and will need to work to support themselves and their children. Not everyone has family to help them out and, even though I now own this house, I have to work to support myself and Lottie. It isn't easy. I can't save anything and every farthing is accounted for.'

'But surely you'll need money to have a nursery school here?'

said Francis, glancing round. 'You'll need equipment and toys. Where will you get them from and how will you pay for them?'

'What Dad said about selling some of Grandfather's stuff has given me an idea. If Polly does get the job at the council nursery, I'll have a sale and raise cash that way. I can't rely on Polly's nursery closing down and my buying stuff from her. I can take the toys that are mine back but I'll need money, not only for equipment, but to pay myself a wage. I mightn't get in enough money from the mothers at first.'

A reluctant smile lit up Francis' face. 'You've got some guts, Nellie. Dad will probably go through the roof like a rocket when he eventually gets home.'

Nellie did not doubt it. 'I'll worry about that when he arrives.'

During the next few weeks, Nellie made enquires at the council offices as to whether she needed planning permission and whether she would be entitled to a grant if she opened a nursery school in her house. Her proposal was welcomed, which proved to her just how advanced the government's plans to get a foothold in Europe must be. No grant was promised but she was ready when Polly next asked her whether she was prepared to take over the nursery group above the bicycle shop.

'I need an answer from you, Nellie,' said Polly, as they cleared equipment and toys away so the room was ready for the dancing class that evening. 'I've been waiting until now to talk to you, so we wouldn't be disturbed. I've got the job in the council nursery.'

'That's great,' said Nellie, smiling with delight. 'So when do you start?'

'April. Towards the end of Wings for Victory Week.'

'They're really pushing up the target this year, aren't they? Eighty thousand pounds to fund two Lancashire bombers,' said Nellie, thoughtfully.

'Don't change the subject,' said Polly. 'If you don't want to carry on here then say so. It's just that I need to tell the mothers to make other arrangements for their kids.'

Nellie popped the piano key in its jar on the window sill. 'No. I won't be staying on here. I have a plan of my own.'

'What plan?' asked Polly, looking taken aback.

'I've decided to use the house for my own private nursery school. I never told you but Grandfather left it to me.'

Polly's eyes almost popped out of her head. 'You jammy thing. But that's marvellous.'

Nellie smiled. 'I couldn't believe it. Nobody else knows. I haven't even told my sisters...or my dad. He thinks the house is his and I know there'll be trouble when he eventually gets home and finds it isn't. He's been known to be violent when he loses his temper.'

'Bloody hell, Nellie! I just hope you've got someone big and strong in the house when he does.'

'Don't worry,' she said, 'I'll make sure my brother's there.'

Polly nodded. 'Makes sense. Anyway, back to your plan. How much room have you got? What about lavs? Equipment? Toys?'

'I've got more space at home than here. I've also got outdoor space for the children to play and a washroom to hang their outdoor things. There's an outside toilet and one upstairs. I've a lovely big kitchen, too. As for equipment and toys...I'm going to have a sale to raise the money. Grandfather might have left me the house and its contents but cash...no! I'm going to have to advertise for children's toys.'

Polly grimaced. 'You'll be lucky if you can get more toys. The council nursery's having a problem. They've made an appeal but there hasn't been much of a response. People could do with searching their attics...or it would be great if some of the old ladies could knit some small dolls, teddies or golliwogs.'

Nellie agreed but she was of the mind that most old ladies thought that knitting socks, balaclavas and gloves for the troops was of far more importance than toys. She felt certain, though, that she could persuade Lottie to knit some for her children.

'I'm sure some of the mothers here will be interested, others might consider your house too far away. You're going to need an assistant,' said Polly.

'I'll think about that when my nursery school is up and running,' said Nellie. 'In the meantime my sister can help out.'

'Naturally you'll take back the dolls' house and everything else you brought...but if there's anything from here you want...except for the rocking horse, which I've promised to the nursery...take it.'

Nellie said, 'I'd like to buy your small tables and chairs.'

'No, take them. You've well earned what they cost me second-hand,' said Polly.

'Thanks.' Nellie was truly grateful. 'There's a piano at home so that won't be going in the sale. I need to get rid of some of the larger furniture: a Victorian sideboard, as well as one of the dining tables.'

'They'll be snapped up. The old stuff is better than this utility furniture that's in the shops now.'

'There's loads of ornaments, china and porcelain that belonged to my great-great aunt, as well as mementos Grandfather brought back from his travels. They'll make nice presents with there being so little in the shops these days. I'll be selling clothes, too.'

Polly looked surprised. 'Surely you'll want to keep some of them...and what about your family, won't they want something to remember your grandfather by?'

'I'll ask Lottie what she wants and I'd best write to Babs and tell her what I'm up to. It's time she visited. I was hoping to visit her but I just haven't had time.'

'How many children will you start with?'

'A round dozen? I'd rather they were made up of three- and four-year-olds...although I'm prepared to make exceptions in special circumstances.' Nellie brushed back a strand of chestnut hair, thinking of Irene Miller, who wasn't yet two.

As they made their way out of the building, Polly said, 'We will keep in touch, won't we, Nellie?'

'Of course. You can always bring Margaret to tea one Sunday.'

Polly smiled. 'And I'll definitely be at the sale.'

Nellie arrived home an hour later, having done some shopping on the way. She had yet to tell Lottie of her decision about the nursery and knew that the time had come to tell her about the house, too. When she broke the news to her sister, Lottie stared at her from rounded eyes and then slowly smiled. 'It'll be one in the eye for Dad but I think you're doing the right thing.'

Nellie wished her sister had not mentioned their father but at least she genuinely seemed pleased about her idea. 'I'm planning on making you my assistant, Lottie, and your first job will be to knit some toys for the children.'

Lottie flushed with pleasure. 'Your assistant. Will it count as essential war work?'

'Of course,' said Nellie. 'It's much more labour-saving for just two people to look after twelve children instead of having, say, eight mothers.'

Lottie said eagerly, 'You get patterns and wool and I'll get cracking. When will we be opening?'

'I'm not sure yet. I thought we could have the sale on the Sunday at the end of Wings for Victory Week. I'm sure we'll get more people coming then and we can say we'll give a donation from what we raise to the appeal. As for wool for toys, you can use a couple of Grandfather's old woollies. We can unravel them and I'm sure we'll be able to find a pattern book in the library.'

Lottie wriggled in her chair. 'It's exciting! I've felt so out of things being home all the time and it's been worse since Billy left. I like kids. I'll be made up helping in any way I can.'

While she made a pot of tea Nellie told her sister what she expected of her.

Lottie added a few thoughts of her own. 'If I just had a couple of the older ones at a time, I could show them how to make jam tarts and things.'

'Of course, you could.' Nellie put an arm around her shoulders and hugged her.

Lottie frowned. 'What about the vegetable patch, Nell? We'll be needing to plant soon and buy seed potatoes.'

'I'll see what I can do,' promised Nellie, whose mind was buzzing with ideas. 'Perhaps one of the mothers might know someone willing to barter their time for vegetables and fruit and a couple of fresh eggs a week.'

But help with the garden was to come from an unexpected quarter the next day. 'I believe you're looking for some help in the garden, Nellie,' said Mrs Wainwright, catching her as she walked home after visiting the library. 'Labour in exchange for vegetables, fruit and eggs?'

'Who told you that?' Nellie had been on her feet all day and couldn't wait to kick off her shoes and put her feet up. She just couldn't see their busybody neighbour being of help to her.

'One hears these things.' The old woman waved a be-ringed hand dismissively. 'I have a nephew, my widowed sister's only son. He's not got much upstairs,' she tapped her head significantly, 'but he is harmless and strong. I'm sure he'd suit you.'

'That's kind of you to offer his help.' Nellie would have sympathised with any nephew of Mrs Wainwright, but one who was backward she felt even more sorry for. 'Send him along.'

'Certainly, my dear.' Mrs Wainwright seized Nellie's sleeve as she made to walk away. 'And while we're talking, I really do admire you for the way you seem to be coping with everything. I suppose there's no news of Bernard coming home yet?'

Nellie shook her head. 'Last time he docked was in Scotland and then he was off to the Americas and then an unknown destination.'

'Well, let's hope he's safe. Perhaps he'll give up the sea once the war's over now your grandfather's dead. It's good to have a man around the place. I was really worried when those break-ins were going on.'

Nellie stilled. 'You weren't broken into, were you?'

'No, thank God. Terence McElroy probably frightened them away.'

'I believe this used to be his beat,' said Nellie.

'Yes. I remember having a reason to call upon him when your brother Joseph kicked a ball through my window.'

'I see. Thank you, Mrs Wainwright.' Nellie was about to walk away but then had second thoughts and turned back. 'I wonder if you could help me.'

'Help you!' The woman's pencilled eyebrows arched and she tittered. 'My goodness, fancy you asking me for help!'

'I thought you should be the first to know that I'm starting a nursery school in the house.' Nellie saw her expression change and added hastily, 'You'll find they won't make any more noise than the music teacher a few doors away. If you could spread the word that I'm having a sale to raise money for the children and that I'm giving a donation to Wings for Victory Week from the proceeds, then I'd be grateful.'

'Well! I don't know what to say,' said Mrs Wainwright, looking flabbergasted. 'What kind of sale?'

Nellie told her and her neighbour's eyes gleamed and she rubbed her pale hands together. 'I'd be happy to help you price things. Adelaide had some very nice porcelain. You won't know the true value of it and I wouldn't like you to be robbed.'

Nellie could see the sense of having the help of someone who knew what was valuable and what was junk. Besides, if she was to help her, then she could hardly complain about the nursery. 'Thanks.'

'Just tell me when you're ready to do the pricing and I'll be there. And have you thought of making a charge and serving refreshments?'

Nellie had not done so but now welcomed the suggestion. Smiling, she thanked Mrs Wainwright again. 'I'll see if I can rope in some mothers to help.'

'Good. What date are you planning for your sale?'

'The Sunday at the end of Wings for Victory Week. It's my only free day.'

Mrs Wainwright patted her shoulder and hurried off in the opposite direction. Nellie hummed 'Sing as We Go' as she carried on into the house, thinking back over their conversation and what her neighbour had said about Sgt McElroy. So he'd been around here when Joe was a boy. Why didn't she remember him? Perhaps she had been too young. Francis might remember him, though. She dismissed him from her thoughts, remembering that she still had a letter to write to Babs about the sale.

Chapter Twelve

Babs watched intently as the farmer tied the pieces of string firmly into two separate knots round the umbilical cord before cutting the cord between the knots. The afterbirth was disposed of and within a short space of time, the calf was standing rather shakily on her spindly legs, a black and white replica of her mother.

'Do you ever get used to seeing calves being born?' Babs asked when she and the farmer left the byre.

'Never,' said the ruddy-faced woman easing her back. 'I'm just grateful when everything goes as well as it did today and I don't have to call in the vet. You can be off now. I hope you've learnt something here.'

'You can say that again,' said Babs on a laugh. 'I'm made up my first was a female calf. She won't become veal, will she?'

'You can't be sentimental in farming, girl.' The woman's expression was severe. 'But you're right. When the time comes, if I'm lucky, she'll be as good a milker as her mother.'

'Great,' said Babs, beaming.

'I suppose I'll see you on Sunday with your gang. You'll be bringing a tractor?'

Babs shook her head. 'Not me. I've managed to get a whole day off to go and see my sisters. My grandfather died and my eldest sister wrote to me about a sale she's having of some of his things and those of my great-great-aunt. Dad gave her the idea apparently. Anyhow, she wants me to go and choose something as a memento. Grandfather was a sailor and he brought home some interesting stuff. I'm bound to see you again, though. Bye.'

She raised a hand in farewell and walked towards the footpath that would take her across the fields to her billet. The sun was setting and she had forgotten her torch so she wanted to be back before it got dark. She was desperate for a bath and to get out of her working clothes which stank to high heaven.

Birds swooped and dived. Were they swallows catching insects on the wing? she wondered. Spring had arrived and the air smelt different. The countryside was full of cheerful sights and sounds. She had discovered a clump of primroses in a sheltered spot near a hedge the other day and they had smelt so sweet, unlike the pretty white flowers of wild garlic. The countryside was a revelation to a city girl like herself and she was beginning to love it, even when it seemed empty of human habitation, like now.

Ten minutes later she realised that she did not have it to herself. A man was coming along the footpath towards her and, for a moment, she was nervous because he was in shadow and she could not make out who it was. Then he raised his arm in way of greeting and she realised it was Jake O'Donnell. Her heart seemed to flip over as he came to a halt a few paces away. He was scowling.

'What do you think you're doing walking alone in the country at this time of evening?' he demanded.

Her hackles rose. 'Hello, Barbara! How nice to see you, long time no see.' She mimicked his American accent.

The muscles of his face relaxed. 'I do believe you've missed me,' he said.

'Like I'd miss a nest of red ants,' she said, brushing past him and carrying on along the path, wishing he hadn't come along right now and caught her looking such a mess. God only knew what he thought of how she smelt.

He turned and followed her. 'I came looking for you.'

'How did you know I was here?'

'I hung around the entrance and asked anyone I saw if they could give you a message until I struck lucky. I have to admit to being as surprised as hell when I was told you'd gone to watch a calf birthing. If I had a dollar for every calf I saw born when I was a kid I'd be rich.'

She stared at him. 'Were you a cowboy like in the Westerns?'

'Glad you had the right schooling,' he drawled. 'I'm from

Montana. My father has a herd there. I left when I was fourteen after we had a bit of a disagreement.'

'So how did you keep yourself?'

'Worked at anything I could to survive but it was machines I really liked, especially aeroplanes. Eventually I ended up in the air force as a mechanic. What work did you do before becoming a land girl?' he countered.

'Nothing exciting. I was an invoice clerk and then I worked behind the counter in a dry-cleaners'. This war has plenty of downsides but at least I've had my horizons widened.'

'By seeing a calf born? Smelly business, calving.'

She flushed. 'I know I stink but it's an experience I'll never forget. New life after so many deaths.'

'You've lost folk?'

She nodded. 'My brother, my mother, my aunt. More recently my grandfather died, although, he was old. My sister's husband was killed in the Desert War and her baby was stillborn.'

Jake swore under his breath. 'You poor kid.'

'I'm not a kid!' She glared at him. 'I've had to grow up fast. Now why did you want to see me?'

'To ask you out but you must be whacked.'

She felt a tingle of pleasure, but this evening was just no good because she was worn out and wouldn't be good company. 'What about another time?'

'I've the whole day off on Sunday.'

A sigh escaped her. 'Sunday I'm visiting my sisters who live on the outskirts of Liverpool. I can't get out of it. Nellie's getting rid of some of my grandfather's stuff and she wants me to pick something to remember him by. I'll be out most of the day and can't say when I'll be back for sure.'

Jake looked thoughtful. 'I could tag along. Unless you don't want me to meet your sisters?'

She hadn't even considered him meeting Nellie and Lottie. How would they react after what Nellie had had to say about American servicemen?

'Your face says it all. You don't like the idea.' He sounded hurt, which surprised her because she saw him as a tough guy.

She looked up at him. 'My elder sisters have preconceived ideas about Yanks. I don't want Nellie thinking that...'

'I'll be on my best behaviour,' he said softly, taking her hand and toying with her fingers.

'Stop that!' She attempted to free her hand.

He drew her hand through his arm and continued walking. 'I can guess the kinda ideas they have.'

'You can?'

'Sure.'

'Good. I don't want them worrying that I might get hurt or end up in trouble. I don't want to get serious about a bloke. After seeing how Nellie suffered after her husband was killed, I can do without that kind of pain.'

Jake gazed down at her and kissed the tip of Babs' nose. 'I get the message but we can still have fun going places together. The movies, a meal, a dance. I'm sure your sisters won't begrudge us that and, if they cast an eye over me, that's surely better than imagining I'm some good looking fly-by-night guy.'

Babs wasn't so sure about that. He mightn't look like a movie star but there was definitely something about him that attracted her. 'OK! But best behaviour, mind.'

He raised a hand in a kind of salute. 'Scout's honour. And afterwards we'll take in a movie in Liverpool.'

Babs agreed, hoping she could trust him to keep his word.

Nellie was in the parlour, arranging a few things and considering going up to the attic to see what was in the back room, when she heard a knock on the door. She stopped what she was doing and hurried to open it. On the door step was a strapping young man she had never seen before. 'Yes?'

'Aunt Ethel told me to come,' he said, breathing noisily through his mouth, which seemed full of overlarge teeth. 'My name's David and she said you wanted me to dig.' To her astonishment he burst into song, 'Dig, dig, dig, dig, dig, dig, you dig the whole day through.' He stopped abruptly and beamed at her. 'Dwarfs! They were funny. You seen them?'

'I can't say I have.' She was amused by his partial rendering of the song from the Disney film, *Snow White*.

'They dug for diamonds. I don't suppose you've got any of them?' he said, with a twinkle in his eye.

'I wish I had but you'll have to make do with seed potatoes. Come round the back and I'll show you where everything is.'

She introduced him to her sister, who was polishing brasses in the kitchen. 'Lottie, this is Mrs Wainwright's nephew David. He's come to help in the garden. I thought we could give him a trial period. Do you want to show him everything?'

Lottie eyed David up and down and was impressed by his physique. 'I don't mind if I do. It'll be a nice change from doing these brasses.' She dropped her duster and told him to follow her out.

Nellie left her sister to it and went back to what she was doing.

Lottie led David into the back garden. 'So have you done much vegetable growing?' she asked.

'A bit for Mum but she's getting on and gets angry when I do things wrong.'

Lottie looked at him. 'What kind of things?'

He shook his head. 'Don't want to talk about it.' He stared at her unwaveringly from hazel eyes. 'You limp. Something wrong with your leg?'

'My hip. I was buried during the blitz. These things, they're nothing to do with growing vegetables?'

She realised he had stopped listening to her and was looking about him. She saw his face light up as he spotted the hens scratching in the dirt. 'Chickens, you've got chickens! I wanted us to have some of them but Mum said, no, too noisy, too messy.'

'They're both that but what does it matter as long as they're not in the house because they lay eggs and one makes a nice roast dinner at Christmas. Come here now.' She took his arm and led him over to the outhouse where the gardening tools were kept. 'We need a trench digging for potatoes. You wouldn't want to make a start now, would you?'

'Don't mind.' He picked up a spade and grinned at her.

Lottie was astounded by his smile. *All those teeth!* she marvelled. And then asked herself what had his teeth to do with anything. They needed a strong man and he certainly looked that. She showed him where she wanted him to dig and then stood back and watched him. After seeing how fast he could shift soil, ten minutes later she decided he would do and went indoors to speak to Nellie about him.

She looked in the parlour for Nellie but she wasn't there or anywhere else downstairs. She shouted for her but, on getting no answer, climbed the stairs. She found Nellie in the back attic room, staring about her with a vacant expression. 'What are you doing, Nellie, standing like a statue? There's loads of work to do.'

Nellie started. She had been thinking about Teddy and children, but now her gaze focused on her sister. 'What is it? You should have shouted for me to save you climbing all the way up here.'

'I did but you mustn't have heard me. I think David will do. He's very strong.'

Nellie smiled. 'Good. Perhaps he can come up here and help me down with a few things.'

'You want me to ask him now?'

Nellie nodded. 'I'll come down with you.'

David was perfectly willing to do what Nellie asked and left his digging and went upstairs with her. He gazed about him with obvious interest and went over to the window and stared out. 'There's Aunt Ethel's garden. Mum says she's bossy and nosey and that's why she won't have her living with us.' He turned and looked at Nellie. 'She likes to know what Mum's up to and asks me but I won't tell her.'

'Good on you,' said Nellie, trying not to smile. 'Now these tea-chests. I want you to help me carry them down.'

He eyed them up, looked inside, placed his strong arms as far as they could reach around one of the tea-chests, heaved, lifted it a few inches. There was a rattling sound and he shook his head and replaced the tea-chest on the floor. He started to remove the newspaper wrapped parcels before she could stop him but then she realised what he was about and so she began to do the same with the other tea-chest.

Half an hour later the chests had been emptied and everything was in the parlour. She thanked him and sent him out to carry on with the digging whilst she set about unwrapping the parcels. The first was a china plate with a pattern of dark red roses and had a stamp on the back saying Royal Albert. She unwrapped another piece and so on and so on, placing crockery, cutlery, glassware and ornaments that consisted of china figurines, brass bells and trays from India. She had also found rolls of wallpaper. A fortnight ago she had found a single roll of a different design of wallpaper in one of the chests in the front attic and had used the back of it to make notices advertising her sale.

With Lottie's help she set to washing and polishing their spoils, reflecting on the positive reactions she had received about her nursery school scheme and the sale. The old man who owned the bicycle and repair shop had offered to display one of her notices in his window, and so had the librarian, the lady in the sweet shop and the man in the post office. Even so, she could not help worrying that either enough people wouldn't come or that so many would turn up that she wouldn't have enough things to satisfy everyone. A banging on the door curtailed her reverie and she went to answer it, wondering who it could be this time.

On the doorstep stood Mrs Wainwright. 'Just come to see how David's doing,' she said, her head held to one side like a perky bird.

'He's only been here a short time but I'm sure he'll do fine,' said Nellie, guessing her nephew was not the real reason behind the old woman being there. 'Do you want to come in and I'll show you what I've gathered together so far?'

Mrs Wainwright's eyes gleamed. 'I was just waiting to be asked.'

She bustled inside after Nellie. So far nothing had been priced and Mrs Wainwright stood inside the parlour, assessing what was there.

'Just as I thought,' she said at last. 'Some really nice stuff amongst the bric-a-brac your grandfather brought home. Although, no doubt, that will go, too. If you like I could start pricing things now? Best not to leave it until tomorrow.'

'Thank you,' said Nellie sincerely, 'and please, Mrs Wainwright, tomorrow, after Babs has had her pick, I want you to choose something in appreciation of your help.'

The woman was obviously touched. 'You're very trusting, Nellie. How do you know I won't take something expensive?'

'I would expect you to take something decent.'

'Yes, but what will Bernard say?'

'It was Dad who gave me the idea for the sale,' said Nellie smoothly, 'so I wouldn't worry.'

Mrs Wainwright's face lit up with pleasure. 'Well, if you say so, dear.'

Nellie went and found paper and pen and gave them to her neighbour and left her to the pricing, while she returned to the kitchen. Lottie had vanished but Nellie found her in the garden, helping David plant the seed potatoes. Smiling, Nellie left them to it and went to put the kettle on.

As she made tea, she thought of the mothers from Polly's group, who had enrolled their children. Among them had been Maisie Miller, who had lent her the pram to carry the dolls' house back home, anxious to ask if she would bend her rules for Irene. Nellie had become fond of the little girl with her blonde curly hair and big blue eyes, thinking, with a catch at her heart, that her own child would have been of a similar age if he had lived. Tears pricked the back of her eyes but she told herself that now was not the time to get upset. She had to be focused on raising money for her new venture.

On the morning of the sale, Nellie was up at six. She had been lying awake for ages, a dozen things running through her head. She prayed the rain would stay away so Maisie and another of the mothers who had volunteered to help with the refreshments could serve them in the front garden, so making the house less crowded if her sale turned out to be a success. But uppermost in her mind was what time Babs would arrive. In case she was late, Nellie had set aside a couple of pieces of porcelain that Mrs Wainwright had said were the genuine article, but even so Nellie would have preferred for her sister to make her own choice.

'So this is your home,' mused Jake, gazing at the people in the front garden, some sitting on child-size chairs at child-size tables, while others stood chattering and drinking tea. Children played with toys on the grass and the buzz of conversation was loud enough to compete with several swarms of bees.

'It doesn't normally look like this,' said Babs, wondering what on earth Nellie was thinking of having all these people in the garden. She imagined their father would have a fit if he saw them crowding on the front lawn. 'She must be having a proper sale. I just thought she'd be taking things to the second-hand shop.' She tugged on his arm. 'Come on, let's find Nellie, so I can introduce you and find out what's going on.'

As they walked up the garden path, Babs would have had to be blind and deaf not to be aware of the attention Jake was attracting, but she told herself that she did not care what these people thought because she didn't know most of them from Adam.

She found Nellie in the parlour with a ferrety-faced man and Mrs Wainwright arguing over the price of the heavy, dark oak sideboard that had been there as long as Babs could remember.

She was astounded, wondering what the hell her sister was playing at. So the sideboard was a monstrosity and she, herself, much preferred modern stuff, but it wasn't Nellie's to sell. It struck her that the room was almost empty of most of the furniture and ornaments that had been there for years. Then she saw that Nellie had spotted her and Jake. To say her sister looked surprised was an understatement. She whispered something to Mrs Wainwright and hurried over to them.

'So you made it at last,' said Nellie, smiling brightly. 'Any later and there might have been nothing left.'

'What are you up to, Nell?' demanded Babs. 'I presumed when you said you were getting rid of a few things, you didn't intend emptying the whole house.'

Nellie flushed and shoved a dangling lock of hair behind an ear. 'Don't be daft! We need the beds and furniture in all the bedrooms for when the war's over and you and Dad come home, but there is too much stuff in this house and I needed to raise money for my nursery school.'

'Your nursery school! What are you talking about?' asked Babs.

'The one I'm opening here, but never mind that now,' Nellie paused and looked at Jake and smiled. 'Introduce me to your friend.'

'You've gone off your trolley,' said Babs, her green eyes sparkling. 'You can't have a nursery school here.'

Nellie shifted her attention from the American, whom she considered no oil painting, back to her sister. 'I'm having one and nothing you say will alter that. It's my contribution towards the war effort.' She turned back to the airman and held out a hand. 'I'm Nellie Lachlan. Who are you?'

He shook her hand and said gravely, 'Jake O'Donnell. I don't know if Barbara will have my hide if I say it's a pleasure to meet you.'

Babs glared at him and then walked out of the room.

Nellie said ruefully, 'Oh heck! I should have said more in my letter but I wanted to explain to her face. Having said that, she hasn't mentioned you to me.'

'Shocks all around,' he said, with the faintest smile.

She nodded. 'You'd best go after her. I'll find you in a few minutes after I find out if Mrs Wainwright's got me a fair price for that sideboard.'

Jake said, 'See you later,' and left the parlour.

Nellie put him out of her mind and looked over to where Mrs Wainwright and the dealer seemed to have come to an agreement. He was in the act of removing a wad of banknotes from an inside pocket and was peeling several off. He counted them onto the old woman's outstretched hand and Nellie realised he had paid forty pounds for the sideboard. Hallelujah! She decided to talk to Mrs Wainwright later and sort things out with Babs.

She slipped out of the parlour and into the kitchen, where she found her sister whispering vehemently to Jake. She started guiltily when Nellie said, 'I do have a right to hold a sale of Grandfather's things and use this house for a nursery school, but you're not going to like it. If I tell you why you must swear on the Bible that you won't tell Dad.'

A rosy-cheeked Babs said, 'What right?'

'I want your promise first,' said Nellie.

Babs' curiosity was such that she cried, 'OK! I promise.'

Nellie took a deep breath before blurting out, 'Grandfather left the house and its contents to me. I want you to know, though, this will always be your home as long as you wish. There's also a couple of pieces of Royal Doulton upstairs in our bedroom that Mrs Wainwright says are worth something. They're yours if you want them.'

Babs gulped and then she swore, uttering words that Nellie had never heard her say before. She looked at Jake, who held up both hands and said, 'Don't look at me, Mrs Lachlan! She hasn't heard them from me. You have to admit, though, you've given her a helluva surprise.'

'No more than the surprise I got when she turned up with you. Anyway, the truth's out now and you heard her promise not to tell Dad,' said Nellie.

Babs turned on her with a furious expression on her lovely face. 'I'm taking my promise back. How could you steal Dad's inheritance?'

Nellie counted to ten, tapping her fingernails on the table. 'I am shocked that you could believe I'd set out to do such a thing. If you doubt me, speak to Francis. Grandfather asked him to arrange for a solicitor to call here. I was out at work. Francis had told me that Grandfather wanted to leave me something so I'd be secure. I thought he meant something like fifty pounds. He cut Dad out of his will because he...' She stopped abruptly, remembering Jake's presence. 'Enough said. This is family business.'

'And I'm not family,' he drawled. 'It sure is interesting, though, why you get it all and Babs gets nothing.'

'Lottie doesn't get anything either,' said Nellie. 'I think Grandfather believed I'd never marry again and that nobody would want to marry Lottie. As for Babs,' she glanced at her youngest sister and her face softened. 'Look at her. She won't have any trouble finding a husband.'

'What about Dad?' asked Babs, feeling calmer.

Nellie's face hardened and she folded her arms across her chest, thinking with half a mind that they were fortunate not to have been disturbed by anyone in the last five minutes. 'You know that Dad's first love is the sea. You might have been his blue-eye but you can't have forgotten the way he treated Mam or the time he spent in the pub. He's only ever used this house as somewhere to sleep when he docked. Well, Lottie and I will be here keeping the home fires burning and we'll try our hardest to welcome him.'

'Are you going to tell him you own the house?' asked Babs.

Nellie's mouth twisted in a smile. 'Only when I've a big strong man in the room to protect me.'

There was silence in the kitchen and faintly they could hear the sound of people talking, the cries of children and the clucking of hens. Then Babs stirred and went over to Nellie and put her arms round her. As they hugged each other there were tears in their eyes.

'I won't spill the beans,' whispered Babs. 'Now where's my inheritance, did you say?'

Nellie felt too emotional to speak and it was Jake who said, 'In *our* bedroom, I heard her say.'

Inexplicably his answering caused them both to laugh. 'That's right,' said Nellie. 'You go and get it while I collect my money from Mrs Wainwright.' She left Babs and Jake alone, thinking that he knew a family secret that even their busybody neighbour hadn't latched on to yet.

Babs stared at Jake. 'Well, what do you think of my sister? If you were looking for a woman of property, she's the one to go for.'

Jake gave a crooked smile and placed a hand on the side of her face and caressed her cheek and chin. 'You're a nice person, Barbara Callaghan. You go and collect your inheritance. I'll be waiting here for you.'

His touch had its usual effect on her and for a moment she closed her eyes and kissed one of his fingers. 'Thanks. I won't keep you waiting long.'

She hurried out of the kitchen before her emotions completely got the better of her. She found the figurines where Nellie had said they'd be and, feeling they were a bit old-fashioned for her taste, she decided to ask Mrs Wainwright to sell them for her. After all, thought Babs, she didn't need something to remind her of her grandfather. He had been part of her life since her birth and she wasn't going to forget him. Money would be much more useful.

When Babs arrived downstairs, she found Jake still waiting in the kitchen for her and that was a comfort despite his not being alone. Lottie was handing him a cup of tea while Nellie was talking to a woman whom she introduced to Babs as Polly Perkins, her former boss from Linacre Road. Babs asked a few questions about Nellie's proposed nursery and when she listened to the answers, wondered if her sister had given any thought to what would happen if their father arrived home unexpectedly. She kept her thoughts to herself, though. Soon after, she and Jake said they'd have to go if they were to catch the first house at the pictures.

'You'll come again soon, Babs?' asked Nellie, following the pair out to the front gate.

'If I can. We're getting really busy now but you mustn't worry about me, I'll be fine.' Babs kissed her sister's cheek.

The sisters drew apart and Nellie looked at Jake with a smile. 'It was nice meeting you.'

'Same here, Nellie.' He tipped his hat at her, and drawing Babs' hand through his arm, walked away.

Nellie watched them go with mixed emotions. Part of her envied Babs for having a man in her life but another part of her felt it was disloyal to Teddy's memory to think in such a way.

She returned to the house to see how things were going but it was obvious the sale was a success. The weather had been a great help and so had people's curiosity. Neighbours, acquaintances and those mothers who had not helped with the refreshments had come to support the venture even if they had not bought anything. They had paid their entrance fee and had a tour of the house and gardens and every penny was appreciated by Nellie.

By the end of the day Nellie knew she had made more than a hundred and fifty pounds. It was a small fortune to her and she was over the moon because it was enough to get the nursery off the ground and keep her and Lottie for months, even after making a donation to Wings for Victory.

Mrs Wainwright was obviously pleased with herself. She had looked down her nose a few times at the accents of some of the mothers from the other side of the canal but, fortunately, she had refrained from making comment.

'A very satisfactory sum, Nellie, considering your sale came at the end of Wings for Victory Week and on a Sunday. Fortunately lots of people accept that while there's a war on there's no rest on the Sabbath.'

'Have you chosen something for yourself, Mrs Wainwright?' asked Nellie.

'I have.' The old woman took the brass ornament of the three wise monkeys from her bag.

Nellie stared at it in astonishment. 'I would have thought you'd have chosen a piece of porcelain.'

'No. My father served with the army in India and I remember him bringing one like this home...but my sister was given first choice after he died and chose the monkeys because she knew I wanted them.' Her fingers caressed the shiny backs of the monkeys. 'It will help bring back happy memories.' She returned the ornament to her bag. 'Babs has asked me to sell her porcelain for her. I'll collect the pieces tomorrow. Thank you, dear. I've enjoyed myself. Bye.'

Nellie thanked her again and saw her out, thinking about what she had said about Babs wanting her to sell the porcelain for her. She hoped her sister wasn't short of money because if she was, then sometime in the future maybe, she was going to have to do some rethinking.

The following day, the dealer arrived with a horse and cart. David was in the garden, so Nellie roped him in to help the men to carry out the sideboard. The parlour was now empty apart from the piano, sofa and the small tables and chairs. The sofa would be ideal for either her or Lottie to sit on to read to the children on cold, wet days. She would bring down the old nursery guard from the attic and have a fire in here. Her aim was to follow the routine she had kept as a kindergarten teacher as much as possible. She wanted *her* children to have the start in life that was seldom given to those of working-class parents. If most could begin school knowing their alphabet, numbers up to twelve and write their names, they were in with a chance.

Due to the paper shortage, she had decided to supplement her stationery supplies by giving the children cut-up sheets of wallpaper to practice their writing. There were items she would not be able to get due to the war but she did not doubt that she would be able to keep the children occupied. She had her round dozen and was looking forward to the time when the nursery was up and running and, like her sale, could be deemed a success.

Chapter Thirteen

Babs lay on the bed, gazing up at the ceiling with her father's letter held against her chest. It was short and to the point.

Dear Babs,
Hope you're keeping well. I haven't heard from you for some time and Francis and Nellie haven't been in touch either. I thought you, at least, would have dropped me a line but maybe you're too busy to think of your old dad thousands of miles away out on the briny. Anyhow, I'm still alive and I want you to do something for me. If you haven't visited Nellie recently I want you to make time now. I want to know if what I asked to be done has been done. Let me know.
Yours,
Dad

Her first reaction had been annoyance and then guilt for having given him little thought in the last few months but then he hadn't written to her either. He must be referring to the sale but she had no idea what his plans were for the money raised. She groaned and eased herself over onto her side. Every muscle in her body seemed to be aching after being out in the fields all day. She would have to get in touch with Nellie and ask what she wanted her to say to Dad. It was months since the sale, so perhaps it was time she paid her sister a visit to find out for herself how the nursery school was doing. Nellie seemed happy with the way things were going, saying so in the letter, which had enclosed a postal order for the sale of the Royal Doulton. The amount had surprised Babs but she wasn't going to look a gift horse in the mouth. She wouldn't bother trying to get a day off as most likely it would be refused. The light summer evenings meant they were working most of the hours God sent but an evening visit was not out of the question. If she could persuade Jake to get the use of a jeep and take her there, she could be back in time for work the next day.

Jake! She sighed, wondering if she was doing the right thing by allowing herself to get so fond of him. It would have been wiser to carry on playing the field but, even if she had the time, she wasn't interested in finding someone else. He was generous, a great dancer and, inexplicably, considering he was no Adonis, she was attracted to him like a nail to a magnet. She would have to drop him a line and arrange a date.

The door opened and Heather entered, still in her working dungarees. 'Babs, Jake's at the gate.'

Babs sat up, wincing and smiling at the same time. 'Great! But talk of the devil, I was just thinking of him.'

Heather winked. 'Like that, is it?'

'Never you mind what it's like,' said Babs, her feet searching for her shoes.

'You've done it then?' Heather giggled. 'Was it worth the risk? Some say it's a real disappointment and the men just want to satisfy themselves.'

'I wouldn't know,' said Babs, easing her feet into highly polished brogues and reaching for her shoulder bag. 'When I do it, I aim to have a wedding ring on my finger.'

'Good for you,' said Heather, flushing. 'I hope you get your wish but you know what they say about Yanks.'

'No, tell me,' said Babs in a mocking voice, taking out the compact and the Max Factor lipstick that Jake had purchased from the shop at the Burtonwood base. He would have given them to her but she had insisted on handing over the cost from her inheritance. 'You sure are one stubborn dame,' he'd said.

'You know exactly what they say and most of it's true,' muttered Heather.

Babs made no comment because she was applying lipstick. Her green eyes smiled at her reflection in the small mirror, and she found herself humming 'Look for the Silver Lining', thinking Jake had not pushed his luck in trying to get into her knickers and that couldn't be because he didn't fancy her. He could undo her bra single-handed and for a moment she dwelt on the hungry kisses he had lavished on her and felt hot all over. She dusted the freckles on her nose with the powder puff and said, 'Did he have a jeep with him?'

'Aye. He must be hoping to take you somewhere,' said Heather.

Babs replaced her lipstick and compact in her handbag and took her hat from a wardrobe shelf. 'See you later,' she said. 'But if I'm not back, don't worry, I'm hoping to persuade Jake to take me to see my sisters and that will take some time. Bye.'

She hurried out of the hall and down the drive to the gates where she found Jake, sitting in the jeep, smoking a cigarette. Immediately he saw her, his face lit up and he stubbed out the cigarette and opened the passenger door for her. 'Hi, honey. I was praying you could make it. I've news.'

Her heart flipped over as she seated herself. 'News! What kind of news? You're not going away?'

Jake grimaced. 'Me and my big mouth. I shouldn't have broken it to you so soon. I should have waited until later.'

Babs' throat felt tight and she had to swallow before she could speak. 'You're not going on a bombing raid over Germany, are you?'

He smiled. 'Do you listen to anything I say? I'm an aeroplane mechanic. I don't fly the darn things.'

She touched his arm, caressing his sleeve. 'I do listen. I just wasn't thinking straight. So what's your news?'

'Shall we get away from here first?'

'Yes. Go somewhere quiet where we can talk.'

'Sure.' He drove off along a country lane.

A warm wind tugged at her hat and automatically she put up a hand to hold it in place as her gaze fastened on his craggy profile. 'So you're going away?'

He nodded. 'You know the Allies have taken Sicily and Mussolini's quit.'

'No, I didn't. I don't read newspapers or listen to the news. Grandfather was forever wanting to know what was happening with the war. Not me. I do know the Battle of the Atlantic's being won because one of the girls mentioned it.' She smiled. 'I've told those who follow what's going on just to tell me the good news.'

He thought of those in her family who had been killed and said, 'Understandable. But getting back to what's going on now. The next stop for the Allies will be the Italian mainland and more experienced aeroplane mechanics are going to be needed in the south of England.'

Babs was torn between relief that he was not going abroad and a sense of loss because he would be hundreds of miles away from her. 'I don't know what to say,' she murmured.

He placed a hand over hers without taking his eyes off the road. 'You could say you're going to miss me.'

'Of course I'm going to miss you,' she said vehemently. 'I mightn't have wanted to get serious but you caught me while my guard was down.'

His cheek creased into a smile. 'I'm kinda fond of you, too. What say we get wed?'

Babs felt a rush of warmth and happiness. 'I never thought you'd ask.' She flung an arm around his neck and the jeep swerved.

'Hey, hey, woman, control yourself or you'll have us in the ditch.'

'Sorry.' She kissed his cheek and resumed her former position.

'Do I take that for a yes?' he drawled.

'No, a no.' She chuckled. 'Jake, you'll be able to get me some parachute silk, so I can have a wedding dress made from it, won't you?'

'I was hoping to dispense with the fancy stuff,' he said wryly. 'I want to marry you before I go away, take you with me, even. We'd have to do it within the week.'

The excitement in Babs' face died. 'You mean no white wedding in church? I've dreamt of a white wedding in church.' She saw the expression on his face. 'OK!' she said hastily. 'There's a war on and we can't all have what we want. I'll do without the white wedding but you're forgetting, I'm under age. I need Dad's permission to marry.'

The expression on Jake's face this time would have been comical if the subject under discussion had not been so serious. 'Hell! Your dad's at sea. How long will it take to get in touch with him? How long before he writes back?' He stopped the jeep and stared gloomily through the windscreen and then his face lit up. 'We could send him a wire.'

Babs' concept of how a radio telegraph worked was nonexistent but perhaps it was possible to find her father's ship in such a way. Then she thought this was her father they were talking about and she knew that even if he received the wire, he wouldn't say yes. She groaned and dropped her head on Jake's shoulder. 'It won't work. I'm his favourite daughter. Even if you weren't a Yank, he'd want to look you over before giving his permission.'

Jake put his arm round her. 'OK. I suppose any father worth his salt wants what's best for his daughter, but there's a war on and some things just have to go by the wayside. I reckon we'll just have to elope. What's that place up north in Scotland?'

'Gretna Green! You must be joking.' Babs thought it might sound romantic to elope but she didn't fancy tying the knot over an anvil. She wouldn't feel properly married if it wasn't in church. It occurred to her that to suggest such a thing Jake mightn't be Catholic. 'You are Catholic, aren't you?' she asked.

He shook his head. 'Grandpa was but he married a Protestant and Dad was brought up in the Episcopal church. He met Ma at a church social. I didn't suppose it mattered to you what I am.'

A dismayed Babs nodded glumly. 'I'm sorry. It does.'

He rubbed the back of his hand over his jaw. 'I never realised you felt so strongly. You don't talk religion. I'll convert. I'll get married in your church.'

'You will?' Her spirits yo-yoed again. 'But that still means I'll need Dad's permission.'

Jake swore long and hard.

Babs said, 'What's the point of swearing? What are we going to do?'

He stared at her from hopeful blue eyes. 'We could always jump the gun and hope you get pregnant. Then your father would have to give his permission.'

'No way!' Despite understanding the way his mind was working, all the talk about her father reminded her of what Grandfather had said about her parents having to get married and she did not want a marriage like theirs. She drew away from Jake. 'If you want me, then you're going to have to wait for me. It's not as if you're going off to fight.' Her pretty mouth set firm.

'Sure, but we are going to be parted. After this evening, we probably won't see each other for months.' His voice had deepened and he reached out for her.

She knew he wanted her but she placed a hand against his chest. 'You were listening to me, weren't you, Jake? No going too far. I've got strong doing the job I do now and I wouldn't want to hurt you if you really tried it on.'

He frowned and then the muscles of his face relaxed. 'I'm really scared, honey, but I sure get the message.' He took her hand and drew her closer. 'Isn't there any way we could get married this year?'

'I'll have to think about it,' said Babs, remembering Nellie running off to marry Teddy, but that was a no-no. Even so, thinking about her sister reminded her that she had been going to ask Jake to take her to see Nellie but now was not the right time. If he was to leave within the week, she wanted to spend that time alone with him, so decided her sister would have to make do with a letter.

* * *

'Nellie, you don't ever wonder if the nursery wasn't a good idea, do you?' asked Lottie anxiously, eyeing the boy that had just snatched a sheet of paper from Irene, who had been happily scribbling until that moment.

Nellie did not answer because she was reading Babs' letter, which had just arrived. The news that her father had asked Babs to find out whether Nellie had done what he'd asked annoyed her but she was more worried about what her sister had to say about wanting to marry Jake. For a moment she felt a pang of envy that Babs was in that wonderful state of being in love, which probably accounted for the letter being so garbled and Babs forgetting to say whether she had received the postal order. Nellie hoped it hadn't gone missing because she had added a few pounds to the amount Mrs Wainwright had handed to her from the sale of the china. As she read the last paragraph, Nellie frowned. Babs seemed to want her to write to Dad and persuade him to give his permission so Babs could marry Jake.

'She must be mad,' murmured Nellie, 'thinking he'd listen to me.'

'What did you say?' asked Lottie.

Nellie looked at her sister. 'Babs. She wants to marry Jake and expects me to get Dad to agree to it.'

'You'd be better getting in touch with Francis and see what he thinks,' said Lottie. 'But what *I* want to know now is are you going to deal with Tommy? He's just ripped up Irene's paper.'

'OK!' said Nellie, pocketing the letter and squeezing her way between two tables to where the young miscreant was scattering the paper like confetti. She still marvelled that even the most cherubic looking child could be an imp in disguise. She supposed that as children even Hitler and Mussolini hadn't looked like the monsters they turned out to be. Thinking of the Italian dictator reminded her that a short while ago twenty-two thousand Italian POWs had been landed at a north west port. Probably Liverpool but the press had to be discreet. Recently the Ministry of Information had let it be known that Italy had now surrendered unconditionally. Their declaration of war on Germany had followed soon after. She wished the Italians had realised earlier who was the real enemy. Perhaps if they had, Teddy might have still been alive.

Nellie took Tommy by the shoulders and turned him round to face her. 'That wasn't kind, Tommy.'

'It was rubbish she was doing,' he sneered, trying to wriggle free.

'Not to Irene. You can go in the garden and help David dig up potatoes. I want you to try and count as many as you can and write down the number for me when you've done that.'

His sullen expression lifted and he would have run out of the parlour if she had not darted after him and told him to slow down. 'We don't want any accidents, do we?' she said, smiling down at him.

He nodded and she let him go before returning to where Irene had already taken another square of wallpaper and was scribbling on the back of it. She rested a hand on the girl's fair curls, feeling a strong affection for her. Another child might have attempted to snatch the paper back but not this one. Nellie thought of Maisie, who was worried sick about her brother fighting with the Allies in Europe. The feeling in the country was that there were still tough days ahead but the tide of war had turned. Africa was in the hands of the Allies, and thanks to Captain Johnny Walker, who had led his U-boat destroyers out of Gladstone Dock in Seaforth to a band playing, 'A-Hunting We Will Go', more Allied ships were reaching their destinations.

She left Irene and returned to the table where she had originally been showing the four-year-olds how to write the letter s. Having the children in her home was a real joy. They had brought the old house alive and she hoped that if her grandfather could see her now, he would approve of the way she was using her inheritance. She wasn't making much money but at least she was doing something worthwhile and, although not completely happy, she was content.

The only fly in the ointment was Mrs Wainwright who, when it came to music time or the children playing in the front garden, complained of the noise they made. Nellie was disappointed in her, having believed after the sale that the old woman was on her side. Still, there was no use worrying about her as she had enough on her plate.

Later over a cup of tea, Lottie said, 'I forgot to mention that I saw Billy's father when I went looking for our cat last night.'

'Did you ask him about Billy?'

'He's up in Scotland and enjoying being a soldier. Sgt McElroy was really friendly, asked how we were and whether the nursery was doing well.'

Nellie smiled. 'And what did you tell him?'

'I said it was great and that I was learning a lot about children.'

'You're doing really well.'

'David likes the children, too. They accept him for what he is,' said Lottie. 'Grown ups can be too judgemental.'

'I noticed Tommy was happy to go and help him.'

There was a pause before Lottie said, 'So what about Babs' letter? Will you be going to see Francis this evening?'

'This evening!' Nellie screwed up her face, thinking about that.

'No time like the present. David will keep me company. He's whittling something from wood for the children. He's really good with his hands,' said Lottie eagerly. 'You don't mind him staying on a few hours, do you?'

Nellie shook her head, and decided if David was staying then she could safely leave Lottie in the house. He was so big and strong that a burglar would think twice before breaking in.

Nellie almost changed her mind when the time came to catch the bus to Francis' parish. The wind had got up and it was threatening rain.

'If you put it off, the weather could be the same tomorrow and the day after that,' said Lottie, who was settled by the fire with the cat. David was sitting opposite her, whittling a piece of wood, whistling while he worked.

'OK! I'll go but don't be worrying about me if I'm late,' said Nellie, putting on her outdoor things. 'See you later.'

By the time she was making her way to the presbytery near Byrom Street, it was dark and pouring with rain and Nellie was wishing she had ignored what Lottie had said and stayed at home. With her coat collar turned up and the brim of her hat pulled down as far as possible, she focused her torch on the ground a few feet in front of her, worried in case she fell into a hole. As she passed the looming bulk of the darkened church, she heard what she thought was a groan. She paused and spun her torch round but could not see anything unusual so continued walking, only to hear the sound again.

She retraced her steps and shone her torch into the porch. The beam fell upon the shivering, huddled shape of a man, who had one leg thrust out. His breathing was laboured and his clothing looked soaking wet. She reached out a tentative hand and touched him. He jerked back causing her to almost jump out of her skin. With a heavily beating heart, she waited for any more sudden movements, but when he remained still, she touched his shoulder. 'Are you hurt?'

He did not answer.

She shone her torch on him and saw a large rip in his trouser leg, exposing bloodied flesh beneath. 'Nasty,' she said. 'Are you hurt anywhere else?'

He did not speak and she shone the beam of the torch on him and saw that, despite the heavy boot he was wearing, his left ankle was swollen. She was going to need help.

'I'll go and fetch the priest,' she said.

Without further delay she hurried to the presbytery, praying that her brother was not at the boys' club or out visiting a parishioner. As it was, she did have to knock several times before she heard the sound of hurrying footsteps and her brother's voice informing her that he was coming.

Nellie's shoulders sagged with relief as the door was flung open. His dark bulk was a reassuring presence. 'There's a man in the church porch, Francis. He needs help.'

'Nellie! Is that you?' He peered out.

'Yes! Hurry! He's injured and he's soaking wet.'

'OK! I'll come. You must be soaked yourself. Come inside. I'll just get my coat and a torch.'

Nellie stepped inside and closed the door on the filthy evening. 'Perhaps you'd prefer to wait here while I go and take a look at him,' said Francis.

'No. You'll need my help to get him up.'

'I'm not an eight-stone weakling,' he said, sounding amused.

'I know that! But you'll need someone to hold the torch because you'll have your hands full.'

'You're right! Father would have helped but he's away at a conference and I've given Mrs Riley a couple of days off to go and see her sister. So why are you here, Nellie? What can I do for you?' asked Francis, putting on his coat and reaching into the drawer of an ornate umbrella stand. He took out a torch.

'Babs and Dad. *She* wants to marry a Yank. *He* wants to know if I've done what he's asked.'

'Dad's written to you?'

'You're joking! He's wrote to Babs.' Nellie almost blurted out, 'Bloody cheek!'

He opened the door. 'So what do you want me to do?'

'Speak to Babs, see her fella, write to Dad,' she said, following him out. 'You've got your key?'

He felt in a pocket, sighed and went back into the house, reappearing a few minutes later and closing the door.

Nellie held onto her hat as she walked alongside him, taking two paces to his one. 'So will you do it?' she asked.

'Do what?'

'Speak to Babs, see Jake, write to Dad. Although, she didn't ask me to speak to you. She wanted my opinion because he's not Catholic but says he'll convert,' panted Nellie, trying to keep up with him as they turned a corner and felt the full force of the wind.

'Good. But instruction will take time. She'll have to wait.'

She was indignant. 'You can tell you've never been in love.'

'Good thing, too, from what I've seen of what it does to people.'

Nellie opened her mouth to say something good about love but they were now nearing the porch. Francis flashed the beam of his torch onto the man. He had moved and Nellie could now see his face clearly. One side of it showed heavy bruising and there were scratches on his cheeks and nose. His eyes were closed and, although his eyelids flickered, they remained closed. If he'd had a hat then the wind must have whipped it away because his dark hair shone wetly.

'He's completely out for the count,' said Francis.

'I'm sure he was conscious before. One of his legs is bloody and he's hurt his ankle.'

The stranger opened his eyes and muttered indistinctly.

'Did you hear what he said?' asked Nellie of her brother.

Francis did not answer but handed his torch to her. She kept its beam on the man as Francis lifted him upright. 'Be careful of his ankle,' she warned.

The man groaned as Francis heaved him upright and hoisted him over a burly shoulder. 'You light the way, Nellie.'

She did as told, flashing the torch on the ground in front of them, aware every now and then of the painful hiss of the man's breath. She wondered who he was and where he had come from.

Francis told her to take the key from his pocket and open the door. She did so and held the door open while he carried the man inside. Once the door was closed, she switched on the light. Now she could see the man's damaged face more clearly. At some time he had been in the sun because his skin was tanned, his cheeks were thin and his nose was swollen, his dark eyebrows were thick, sooty slashes. She placed his age at twenty-six or seven.

'I'll take him into the study, there's a fire there,' said Francis. 'Could you put the kettle on and make some tea? The matches are on the shelf near the cooker.'

Nellie headed for the kitchen, knowing what to expect. Unlike the one at home, the room was freezing with no friendly fire in a black-leaded range. She had no trouble finding the matches and lighting a gas ring. She filled the kettle and put it on before removing her wet hat and coat and hanging them on the back of the door. She was hungry but considered it good manners to ask her brother before making herself something to eat. Besides, the injured man might be in need of food.

She made the tea and carried it into the study. Francis was not there but the stranger was sitting in an armchair in front of the fire. All she could see of him was the top of his dark head and steam rising from his clothing. She placed the tray on the desk, poured the tea and carried a cup over to him.

His injured foot was resting on a stool and the trouser leg had been cut away, exposing a nasty gash on his shin. He stared up at her from eyes that were almost black and she had trouble reading his expression. Her heart fluttered beneath her ribs and she felt breathless. She thrust the cup and saucer at him, wanting to get away. As he took it, his fingers brushed hers and her skin tingled. She hurried back over to the desk and picked up her cup of tea and gulped down a mouthful.

To her relief, Francis entered the room, carrying a bundle of clothes, a blanket and towel. As if in answer to an unspoken question, he said, 'The church jumble. Not given by the local poor, I might add, but from a richer parish in South Liverpool. Comes in handy at times like this.'

She burst out, 'Do you recognise him?'

'I don't know everyone in this parish.' Francis placed the clothes on a chair and reached for his cup of tea. 'I want you to look at his leg; best sort that out before he puts on a clean pair of trousers.'

'Me!'

'You look after children so you must know something about cuts and bruises,' said Francis.

'OK,' she said reluctantly, 'but I'm no Florence Nightingale. He looks like he's had a good clout to the head. He could be suffering from concussion. He should see a doctor.' The man's head turned and she saw the apprehension in his eyes. 'He understands English OK,' she murmured.

'Were you thinking he mightn't?' asked Francis.

She hesitated. 'He's got real dark eyes and hair, and his skin...'

'That doesn't mean a thing, Nellie. There's plenty of men in this parish with those same dark eyes and hair.'

'Maybe. But why isn't he knocking on his family's door?'

'He could be from Holy Cross parish; been away and not realised the church there was bombed and that's why he's turned up here.' Francis drained his cup and placed it on the tray. 'Anyway, I'm not about to start questioning him. He came to the church for help. No doubt he's hungry.'

'I'm hungry, too. I thought of making myself a jam butty.'

Francis smiled. 'I can do better than that...there's the remains of a pie, a gift from a grateful parishioner in the larder. It's tasty, although I'm not sure what's in it.'

She left the study, thinking of that grateful parishioner, guessing that half the women in his congregation were in love with him. She found the pie and cut it into wedges and put it on plates.

Back inside the study, she found the man had changed into a flannelette shirt and Fair Isle pullover and he had a blanket draped over his shoulders. Francis had pulled up a chair next to him and was talking to him in a low voice.

'Has he told you anything yet?' asked Nellie.

Her brother shook his head.

The man's dark eyes washed over Nellie's weary face. Then he noticed the plates in her hands and she saw that he was hungry. 'I wonder when he last ate,' she said, going over to him.

'Never mind that. Give him his pie,' said Francis.

Nellie did so and then handed another plate to her brother before sitting in a shiny leather armchair to eat her pie. It had an unfamiliar flavour but was as tasty as her brother had said. She only hoped it wasn't somebody's moggy; these days, people were eating meat they wouldn't normally touch.

Francis polished off his slice in no time. 'I'll just nip upstairs for the first aid box. If you could get some hot water and there's clean rags in one of the kitchen drawers.'

Nellie nodded but did not rush to do what he said. She was tired and, besides, the man was still eating. She watched him surreptitiously, wondering how he'd got his injuries. He looked as worn out as she did; how far had he travelled before finishing up in the church porch? She swallowed the last bit of pie, rose from the chair and went into the kitchen.

She ran hot water into a bowl and took the clean rags from a drawer. When she entered the study, her brother still hadn't returned. She placed the bowl of hot water on the hearth and knelt on the rug. Blood had crusted over the wound on his shin at some time but something had happened to cause the injury to open up again. She picked up a clean rag and dipped it in the hot water and gripped the man's calf. She felt him tense and then relax, only for his calf muscle to tense again when she began to clean the wound.

She was unaware that Francis had entered the room until he said, 'There's no Dettol or iodine.'

'Have you any whiskey?'

'Whiskey?'

'Remember the parable of the Good Samaritan?'

Francis looked pained. 'You're not suggesting using good Irish whiskey as an antiseptic?'

As her brother moved into her line of vision, she was aware that the man was watching her. 'I only want an eggcup full,' she said.

'That's approximately a dram. That whiskey came to me at great cost.'

'Illegally, I bet,' she said dryly.

'I'm a priest, Nellie. How can you accuse me of breaking the law?' His expression was one of mock horror.

'Come on, Francis, you don't want this poor man ending up with septicaemia, do you?'

With a sigh he fetched the bottle from the sideboard cupboard, found three small glasses and poured out the whiskey.

'Is one of them for him to drink?' she asked.

'You're the nurse. Would it do him good?'

Nellie looked at the man. 'What do you say?' she asked.

He gave her a ghost of a smile. Goodness! He'd be quite nice looking if it weren't for the bruising and the swollen nose, thought Nellie. 'Give him some,' she said, 'and while you're at it, I wouldn't mind a dram.'

'You drink whiskey, Nellie, what would Dad say?' He handed her a glass and gave one to the stranger. Francis raised his. 'Good health and may God bless us all.'

'Ditto,' said Nellie, taking a cautious sip.

The stranger gave a sharp nod and downed his drink in one go.

'Do you think he's used to whiskey? Perhaps he's an Irishman, who's been in the sun,' said Nellie.

Francis smiled and took the man's glass from him and half-filled it. 'Here's your antiseptic, Nell. Don't let it evaporate.'

Nellie tossed off her whiskey and felt it burning a path down her throat. She gave a small cough before reaching for a piece of cotton wool and dipping it in the whiskey. She hummed beneath her breath as she swabbed the wound. It was deep and she felt the man tense again and considered suggesting Francis give him another shot to drink. His warm breath stirred her hair and, for a second, her fingers faltered but then she told herself not to be so bloody silly and finish the job.

She got to her feet and turned to her brother. 'I think that cut needs a few stitches.'

'I'm sure it'll be fine. That whiskey's powerful stuff. What about his ankle?'

'Cold water compress?'

'I'll get fresh water,' said Francis, lifting the bowl and carrying it out.

Nellie eased aching shoulders and glanced at the clock on the wall. It was a shock to see that it was ten o'clock.

When Francis re-entered the room, she said, 'I should be going.'

'It's still throwing it down outside. Stay. You can have Mrs Riley's bedroom.'

She shook her head. 'Lottie will be worrying about me. Besides, the kids will be coming in the morning.'

'It's Sunday tomorrow.'

'Is it?' Nellie put a hand to her head. 'I'd forgotten what day it is.'

'Lottie's not stupid. She'll realise you've stayed here because of the rain.'

Nellie eased tired shoulders. 'You're probably right. I just hope she's not frightened in the house on her own.'

'She's not a child, Nellie.'

'I feel like she is at times.' She glanced at the stranger. 'What about him? I take it you'll be putting him up here?'

'I can hardly throw an injured man out in the rain.'

She relaxed. 'OK, I'll stay but I want a hot water bottle in my bed.'

Francis shook his head and said in a droll voice, 'I can see you're going to be a troublesome guest. You'll find the hotties in the kitchen. Fill three.'

'So you're going to be Florence Nightingale now while I fill hotties?' She glanced down at the wounded man and he smiled back at her from drowsy eyes. She felt a similar thrill to when a troublesome child surprised her by behaving well, and hurried out of the study.

She boiled water and filled the stone hot water bottles,

forcing her thoughts away from the two men in the study and thinking, instead, about Babs and Jake. He had seemed OK to her but whether he was the right man for Babs Nellie did not know. Perhaps Francis was right in thinking that there was no rush to sort out Babs' problem and that her having to wait until she came of age to marry him could be the wisest course to take.

She returned to the study with two of the hotties. The man had his foot in the bowl of water and a glass in his hand; his eyes were closed. She realised that his leg between his ankle and just above his knees was dark in comparison to part of his thigh. 'He's been wearing shorts and has been in the sun,' she said.

'What did you say, Nell?' asked Francis, who also had a glass in his hand and was sitting in the leather armchair.

'I think he's been abroad.' She thrust the hotties at him. 'You'll have to take these up. I don't know where they go.'

'I'll show you Mrs Riley's room,' said Francis, getting up. 'Have you done the other one?'

Nellie nodded. 'I'll fetch it. I'll go to bed now if you don't mind. I'm whacked.'

She went over to the door but paused to glance back at the man. His eyes were open and he was staring at her. He looked anxious and who could blame him? He must be in trouble to have sought out the help of the church. She watched as he turned his head away and gazed into the fire. Then she went to bed and wasted little time worrying about him, or anything else for that matter, but fell asleep, clutching the hot water bottle wrapped in her vest.

'So did you find out anything about him after I went to bed?' asked Nellie the following morning. She placed toast on a plate and handed it to her brother.

'I can't answer you,' said Francis, crunching into his toast with strong teeth.

'Can't?'

He nodded.

She thought about that and murmured, 'I see.' Her mind buzzing with possibilities, she reached for the teapot. 'Nothing more I can do to help?'

'No. You've been a good Samaritan and can leave things to me now. He needs to rest, so I won't wake him yet. You can go home and check Lottie's OK.'

'Thanks.' Nellie knew it was pointless being annoyed with him but after the part she'd played in the drama last night, she felt that she was owed an explanation. Yet she knew her brother well enough to know it was not going to be forthcoming, so she let it go and finished her breakfast.

When she was ready to leave, she said, 'Will you let me know how he gets on?'

He nodded. 'I'll come and see you and Lottie soon.' He opened the front door.

She had the impression he couldn't wait to get rid of her, which surprised her as she had thought he might have tried to persuade her to attend Mass at his church. Obviously the man's needs were more important. But before she was prepared to say her goodbye, she had something else to ask him. 'Dad and Babs, anything further to say?'

'Let me think about it. As I said, I'll come and see you soon.'

Nellie had to be content with that and so she said her goodbye and left.

The rain had dried up and the sun was peeping through clouds which scattered before a stiff breeze. She decided not to worry her head about the man. It could be that he was a soldier who had gone AWOL, but he was not her problem. So what if she had felt something towards him? She was a woman, after all, and was not immune to the opposite sex.

When Nellie arrived home, she was surprised to find Lottie in the kitchen peeling potatoes, talking to David. 'You're here early for a Sunday morning,' she said.

'I didn't hear you come in, Nellie,' said Lottie, looking flustered and dropping a potato.

'Obviously, you weren't worried enough to look out for me.'

'I was a bit worried about you,' said Lottie, darting a glance at David, who had picked up the potato. 'But-but when I saw the weather, I guessed you w-were staying with Francis.'

'Good. I'm glad you weren't frightened on your own.'

'No. I was fine,' said Lottie, her face scarlet. 'So what did Francis have to say?' She took the potato from David who stood awkwardly, his head turned away from Nellie.

'He wants time to think about it. We had a bit of excitement, so we didn't talk about it much,' said Nellie, sitting at the table.

'What excitement?'

'I found an injured man in the church porch and Francis has taken him in.'

'What was wrong with him?'

Nellie told her. 'Anyway, Francis didn't need me anymore, so I came straight home.' She smiled. 'If you don't mind getting on with the dinner, I'll go and have a bath.' She turned to David. 'I suppose you've seen to the hens?'

He nodded jerkily.

'Thanks. You can go home now if you like.'

David glanced at Lottie. 'Will I go?'

She hesitated. 'It's up to you.'

He stood there indecisively. Nellie sighed and left them to it.

As she lay in the bath with her eyes closed, she could see the man's face against her eyelids. 'Man of mystery,' she murmured, wondering what his name was and where he had come from.

During the days that followed, he haunted her dreams and on wakening, she felt guilty for his doing so. She gazed at Teddy's photograph and felt a mixture of sadness and guilt but realised that she was no longer heartbroken. She replaced the photograph, wondering whether love really could last a lifetime.

A week later Francis called with the news that his unexpected visitor had left.

'Where's he gone?' asked Nellie, her heart quickening.

'To find his family.'

'Oh! So we won't see him ever again?'

Francis shook his head. 'I doubt it, Nellie. Best to forget that you ever met him and concentrate on Babs' problem.'

Nellie felt depressed and knew that she did not want to be bothered with Babs' love life. Yet she knew she had no choice. Jake was not the first fella in Babs' life and it could be that he wouldn't be the last. She was still young and perhaps their not rushing into marriage would test whether he was the right one for her or not. In the meantime, she listened to what her brother had to say and made up her mind to visit her sister.

Chapter Fourteen

The decision to speak to Babs face to face having been made, Nellie wasted no time in getting in touch. She wrote that she didn't believe their father would take any notice of what she had to say but that she'd spoken to Francis and he was going to write to him. In the meantime, perhaps it would be a good idea if she visited Babs.

Nellie received Babs' answer by return post, consisting of a few lines telling her which bus to catch and promising to meet Nellie on her arrival. She began to look forward to the outing, relieved to have the anniversary of Teddy's death and the loss of her baby behind her.

When the day came for her visit, Nellie put on her best frock and twisted her hair into a knot on top of her head. Unfortunately she was delayed by a traffic jam in getting to the city centre and had to run for the bus. She was greeted with a resounding cheer as she jumped aboard.

'Yer just made it,' said a blonde, touching Nellie's arm as she swayed up the aisle.

'Not that yer'd have had long to wait,' said another girl, giving a wriggle of excitement. 'They've laid on extra buses for the big dance tonight. They've a real swing band over from the States.'

'What!' exclaimed Nellie, startled.

The girl patted the seat next to her. 'Sit here.'

Nellie thanked her in a breathless voice. She'd have to be blind not to notice that nearly every place on the bus was taken by her own sex. 'You-you don't mean this bus is going to Burtonwood base?'

'That's right. Where did you think it was going?'

'Warrington.'

'Wrong bus.' The girl looked at her sympathetically. 'What are you going to do?'

Nellie fiddled with the strap of her handbag, imagining what

Francis would say if he knew she was on a bus heading for the airbase. Perhaps she should get off but Babs had told her to catch this bus and would be waiting for her at the other end. She must have meant for her to go to Burtonwood, perhaps to show her that there was nothing for her to worry about. She glanced about her at the young, excited faces and couldn't blame them for wanting some fun, to dance with one of those glamorous GIs when there was such a shortage of home-grown young men around. As long as they kept their heads, she thought, relieved that Jake was a couple of hundred miles away, which surely meant Babs would stay out of trouble.

'Well, have you made your mind up?' asked the girl, smiling.

Nellie nodded. 'I'm staying put. My sister's meeting me at the other end and she'd only wonder what had happened to me.' She sighed, wondering what she was letting herself in for.

'Great! I'm sure you'll have a smashing time even if you can't dance.'

'I can dance OK,' said Nellie affronted.

'Then you're in for a treat,' said the girl.

Nellie smiled and kept quiet, feeling certain Teddy would not begrudge her enjoying herself. In fact she was beginning to look forward to the prospect of being asked onto the dance floor.

Babs kissed Jake's letter and placed it under her pillow. She wondered why she had doubted him, just because he had not been in touch as soon as he had arrived at the base in Essex. Well, she need not have worried. The poor love had been up to his eyes in work since he got there and she had to remember that winning the war was uppermost in most servicemen's minds. She wished they could be together. Perhaps she should have eloped with him as he'd suggested. After all, she had the money that Nellie had sent her in her post office saving account. A sigh escaped her and then she mentally shook herself and, reaching for her bag, walked slowly out of the room. She must not forget the trouble Nellie marrying Teddy had caused in the family. She wondered what her sister would do when she realised that she was heading for Burtonwood. Maybe she'd get off the bus and go back home, but hopefully not. Nellie could do with a bit of brightness in her life and, with her love of dancing and music, what could be better than dancing to a swing band?

A bus had just pulled up and passengers were disembarking when Babs arrived at Burtonwood. Almost immediately she spotted Nellie and was relieved to see that her eldest sister was wearing a brightly coloured frock of red and blue. Her cheeks were rosy and her chestnut hair shone as if it had been polished with a silk handkerchief. Babs hurried forward with a skip in her step to greet her.

'Hi, Nell, long time, no see,' she said, flinging her arms around her.

'Not since April,' said Nellie, returning her hug.

Babs' jaw dropped. 'That long! Where does the time go?'

'Being busy helps,' said Nellie, holding her sister at arms' length. 'You've lost weight.'

'Hard work, and I haven't eaten much the last week or so.'

'Why is that?'

'No letter from Jake, but I got one today.' Babs' green eyes sparkled. 'He's not the best of letter writers but then neither am I. Still, he said all that needed to be said.'

'So marriage is still on the cards,' said Nellie, releasing her sister. 'Because if so, what are we doing here?' She glanced about her at the crowds and the buildings, which her sister had once referred to as 'Little America'.

'I thought you could do with having some fun,' said Babs, linking her arm through her sister's. 'You haven't sworn off men completely, have you?'

'No, but that doesn't mean I'm looking to hop into bed with one.'

Babs gaped at her. 'I should think not. Who gave you such an idea?'

'Listening to some of the talk on the bus. Not for them a walk down the aisle first,' said Nellie dryly.

Babs grimaced. 'Hopefully you'll trust me to use my nous.'

Nellie nodded. 'You seem serious enough about Jake, so I can't see you chancing ruining what the pair of you have. Although, Dad will probably refuse his permission for you to marry until he sets eyes on him. Could be you might have to wait until the war's over.'

Babs nodded. 'You could be right. Although, I'll be twenty-one in forty-five, so I'll be able to do what I want then. It seems ages away.'

'It'll probably go over quicker than you think,' said Nellie, smiling. 'Now where's the dance hall? I can't wait to hear the swing band.'

Babs' face brightened up and she hugged her sister's arm. 'All we have to do is follow the crowd.'

So that's what they did. Nellie had never seen such a large ballroom or so many men in uniform, except in a war film. Couples were already on the dance floor and she felt excitement and pleasure as she recognised 'Lullaby of Broadway'. Memories of dancing with Teddy caused her a moment's sadness but then her feet began to tap to the rhythm of the music and she hoped someone would ask her to dance.

Babs insisted on their finding a table first but, no sooner had they sat down than two men appeared. 'I didn't think I'd see you here, Babs, with Jake gone.' The younger airman's sarcasm was evident.

Babs stiffened. 'I'm surprised to see you here without Heather, Stuart.'

He flushed. 'She didn't tell you it's over between us? I caught her with another bloke. I wasn't putting up with that. I can't see Jake putting up with it from you, either.'

'Jake and I trust each other,' said Babs, her eyes flashing green fire. 'But if you want to go telling tales, don't forget to mention I was chaperoned. This is my sister, Nellie. Nell, Stuart McGregor.'

Before Nellie could even offer her hand to shake, he turned on his heel and stalked off. 'What's wrong with him?' she asked.

'Sorry about that, ladies,' said the remaining airman. 'Stu can be a bit touchy. I'm Ray Jones, by the way.' He held out a hand.

Babs barely touched his fingers but Nellie shook his hand firmly because she liked the look of him. He had a pleasant face and his uniform was spotless. 'Nice to meet you.'

'Likewise.' He smiled. 'Are chaperones allowed to dance?'

Nellie glanced at Babs. 'Will you be OK?'

'Of course!' Babs rolled her eyes. 'I brought you here to dance. You deserve some fun after spending most of your time looking after kids.'

Ray looked startled. 'You're married?'

'Widow,' she said hesitantly, hating the word. 'And they're not my kids. I'm a nursery school teacher.'

'Now that's what I call heroic,' smiled Ray. 'I've a couple of boys back home and my wife says two's enough of a handful for her.'

'I've none of my own.' Nellie wondered if he would have been honest with her if Babs hadn't mentioned children. Still, he hadn't had to tell her he was married. 'Shall we dance?'

'Sure.' He led her onto the dance floor to the strains of 'Don't Sit Under The Apple Tree'.

Babs watched them dancing a speeded-up quickstep and thought if Jake had been here they'd have been jitterbugging. Of course, she had no intention of dancing but, even so, she couldn't prevent her foot tapping.

A clean-shaven, gum-chewing airman stopped in front of her. He was tall, dark and had surprisingly vivid blue eyes in a square-jawed face. 'I spotted you from across the floor and thought you looked kinda lonely. So I thought I'd mosey on over and see whether you'd like to cut a rug with me,' he said.

'I'm not dancing,' she replied.

He stopped chewing. 'Why? It can't be that you don't fancy

dancing with me, so you must have broken your foot or something.'

Her lips twitched. 'No. But my boyfriend isn't here, so I'm just watching.'

'Why did you come?'

'I brought my sister. She deserves a good time.'

'She the one dancing with Ray?' He took out a packet of gum and offered it to Babs.

'Yes. Thanks.' She tore off the wrapper and popped it into her mouth. It was cinnamon flavour and one of her favourites.

They chewed companionably for a few moments before he said, 'Name's Pete Rand. You want a drink?'

'Thanks. Lemonade.'

He nodded and left her. Babs looked for Nellie and Ray and spotted them still on the dance floor, talking animatedly. The two had certainly clicked but she doubted that would lead to a date. She bet they were talking about kids. She thought of Jake and wondered how many kids he'd like. She considered two boys and two girls were the perfect family. She wondered what he was doing right now. Would he be off duty? If he was then maybe he had gone out with some of the other guys. Perhaps even now he was dancing with a girl somewhere. She frowned.

'So where's your chaperone?'

Babs groaned and looked at Stuart. 'None of your business,' she said.

His face hardened. 'I saw you talking to Pete.'

'Is it against the law to talk to someone now?' said Babs.

'No, but Jake might not like it.'

Babs felt her temper rising. 'Go and find yourself another girl to annoy.'

'Annoying you, am I? Good.' His expression was ugly. 'I'm going to carry on doing it. Because you sure as hell annoyed me the way you threw me over for him.'

'Something wrong?' said Nellie.

Babs had not noticed her sister approaching the table and flashed her a grateful look. 'Nice dance?'

'Great. Our steps matched perfectly.' She smiled up at Ray. 'Thanks. Perhaps we can dance again later. Right now I'm going to sit this one out.'

'Sure.' He glanced at Stuart and was about to speak when Pete arrived with his and Babs' drinks. Stuart glared at him and then deliberately brushed against him, almost knocking one of the glasses out of his hand as he walked away.

'What's up with him now?' demanded Pete.

'Ignore him,' said Babs. 'Give me that glass. I'm really thirsty.'

He handed the lemonade to her and glanced at Nellie. 'You're the sister. I'm Pete.'

'Nellie.'

'D'you want a drink, Nellie?' asked Ray.

'Thanks. I'll have a shandy.'

He went off to the bar as the band launched into 'My Heart Belongs to Daddy'. A female singer sank huskily into a microphone. Pete put down his drink and looked at Babs.

Nellie said with a smile, 'Why don't the pair of you dance. I'll keep my eye on you both from here and if there's any shenanigans, I'll be on that floor separating the pair of you before you can say Jack Flash.'

'Thanks, Nell,' said Babs, who was longing to dance.

Pete grabbed her hand and led her onto the dance floor.

Nellie sang along with the singer as she watched them. She had so much enjoyed her dance with Ray and him being married meant she didn't have to worry about him making a pass at her.

'So she's dancing after all. I knew she wouldn't be able to resist flirting with another guy,' said Stuart.

Nellie stared at him. 'Not you again. You really are a pain in the neck.'

'Don't you care that your sister's a flirt?' he said, sitting on Babs' chair.

'Go away!' said Nellie. 'She's not engaged to Jake, so if she chooses to dance with someone else that's none of your business. You've no right to pester my sister the way you do.'

'God, you're as bad as her. Ray's married you know?'

'I do know. Now get lost.'

'Are you here again, Stu?' said Ray, appearing at his shoulder. 'There's plenty of other girls around, so go find someone else.'

Stuart got up and walked away silently.

Nellie took her shandy and thanked him. 'He must have really had it bad for Babs.' She looked for her sister and Pete. The music had changed and they were both giving their all to 'Jeepers Creepers'. She was pleased to see Babs enjoying herself.

'She's a lovely girl but it really got his goat that she preferred Jake. They'd only been on a couple of dates. He needs to move on.'

Nellie agreed. They dropped the subject and talked about music until they got up and danced again.

For the next few hours Nellie and Babs enjoyed themselves, dancing with a variety of partners but Babs happened to be dancing with Pete again to 'The More I See You' when Stuart made another appearance. He forced himself between Babs and Pete and managed to fasten his mouth onto Babs'. She thumped him on the back but the next moment Pete had him by the back of his collar and dragged him off her. Stuart struggled but Ray seized one of his arms and he and Pete marched him away between them.

Couples nearby had stopped dancing to watch what was going on.

'He's made a complete show of me,' seethed Babs. 'Let's get out of here, Nell.'

'Yes, I agree! Show's over,' cried Nellie, waving the curious away. 'I'd best be getting home anyway.' She took her sister's arm as they walked off the dance floor. 'You OK?'

'Yuk! He put his tongue in my mouth. It was just like I

imagined a slug would taste. I felt as if I was choking,' said Babs. 'I won't be coming here again.'

The sisters left the dance hall, arm in arm, and walked to the gates. Nellie thought that the air smelt lovely and took deep breaths of it. There was a bus waiting outside with Liverpool on its destination board and she could see quite a number of women and girls already inside. It seemed they weren't the only ones who'd had enough. Nellie felt a spurt of anger every time she thought of Stuart and was worried for her sister.

'You working in the morning?' asked Nellie.

Babs said wryly, 'When don't I work mornings? Why, what had you in mind?'

'You're coming home with me. I think you've had a shock and need a bit of spoiling.'

'That sounds lovely,' said Babs wistfully. 'Although, normally I can handle Stuart, you know? He just took me by surprise.'

Nellie was not convinced. 'You could do with a break. Come home. I'll give you breakfast in bed and then you can catch an early bus.'

Babs hesitated and then smiled. 'What the hell! I'll probably get into trouble for not starting work at the crack of dawn but it'll be great to get away and be spoilt just for a few hours.'

'Then let's get aboard before someone comes looking for us,' said Nellie.

'You mean Pete and Ray,' said Babs.

Nellie nodded as they settled themselves on a seat. 'You seemed to be enjoying yourself with Pete.'

'He's a great dancer but I told him straight off that I had a boyfriend,' said Babs. 'What about you and Ray?'

'Nice guy but that's it.' Nellie yawned. 'My feet are tingling. I haven't danced so much for ages.'

'You enjoyed yourself, though?' said Babs.

Nellie nodded and closed her eyes.

They were almost asleep on their feet by the time they

reached home and it was past the witching hour. They crept into the house via the washroom, and Nellie pushed open the kitchen door only to freeze when she saw her father sitting in front of the fire.

'What time d'you think this is to be coming home?' he rasped.

'Is that Dad's voice?' asked Babs, wriggling past Nellie.

Bernard's expression changed and a smile creased his face. 'Is that my dearest, darling daughter, Babs?'

Babs blinked. 'Are you being funny, Dad?'

Bernard's smile wavered. 'Why should you think that?'

'You don't generally call me your dearest, darling daughter even when you've been drinking.'

'So I've been drinking,' growled Bernard, holding out his arms. 'Come and give your ol' dad a kiss.'

Babs glanced at Lottie. Her face was fixed and her lips were pressed together in a thin line as she sat at the table, knitting. She wondered what he had said to put that expression on her face. With a sigh, Babs went forward and succumbed to her father's embrace. He smelt of beer, tobacco and sweat and she did not like it when he smacked her bottom before releasing her. She stood, looking down at him, considering how best to approach the matter of getting him to agree to her marrying Jake. It seemed providential that she should have come home with Nellie and found him here. 'So what are you doing here, Dad? It's not so long since I got a letter from you and you made no mention of coming home.'

'Didn't know I'd be home, did I? And I'm only on turnaround, girl. Just in dock while some minor repairs are done. Be off again tomorrow.'

'So where will you be sailing next? Or shouldn't I ask?'

'Good God, girl, if I can't trust my own daughter, who can I trust?' He laughed. 'The Americas for supplies and then the Italian coast. The Eyeties might have signed the Armistice but the Allies have still got to get the Jerries out of Italy. I've heard there's some nasty things going on there. The Jerries aren't pleased with their former allies. I won't upset you by mentioning some of the things they're rumoured to have done.'

For a moment there was silence and Nellie paused in spooning tealeaves into the teapot to glance at their father. Her imagination ran riot, thinking of bombings, rape and the shooting of innocent people.

'So-oo,' said Bernard, scraping his unshaven chin with a fingernail. 'It doesn't look to me like you've done anything in the way of decoration, Nellie. Instead, I hear you've got rid of stuff and now run a bloody children's nursery school in the house. You've got no right, girl. You should have asked me first. Not that I'd have given permission.'

Nellie could feel her heart beating. Was it confession time? She could imagine what Babs was thinking. Here was the perfect opportunity to tell their father about Jake and ask his permission to marry him. Could she, herself, risk putting her father into a filthy temper and so spoil any chance of his saying yes to her sister? She decided to keep her secret a little longer. 'I had to do something for the war effort, Dad, as well as earn money to pay the household bills. As for getting work done in the house, no chance of that with the shortage of materials and manpower.'

He looked put out but didn't persist and instead said, 'The kids bring in money, do they?'

Nellie's fingers curled into her palms. 'How else could Lottie and I keep ourselves?'

'You don't expect me to send you money, do you?' he muttered. 'You're living rent free as it is.'

'I pay the rates,' she said, hanging on to her temper.

'I should think so, too!' His eyes narrowed. 'Wouldn't surprise me if I'm stuck with you and that slob of a sister of yours for life now your husband's dead!'

Nellie felt like hitting him. 'Thanks for the sympathy. I was really glad to receive your letter of condolence when I lost Teddy and the baby.'

He flushed but only said, 'By the time I got the news what was the use of writing. Anyway, it was a marriage that should never have taken place.'

Babs took a second look at Nellie's face and said, 'You really have a gift for saying the right thing, don't you, Dad? Our Nellie's suffered.'

He turned on her. 'Keep your mouth shut, girl. It's God's punishment on her that she lost that baby for marrying outside the faith.'

His daughters gasped.

Nellie's eyes glinted and the truth hovered on her lips but she held back for Babs' sake. 'I'd watch what you say, Dad, or you might find you're the one on the sharp end of God's punishment.'

He got to his feet and raised his hand as if to hit her. Nellie reached for the poker. 'Just you dare!'

Babs cried, 'Back off, Dad. Use your head. I can't be here looking after this place while you're away. Our Nellie's the only one fit to do that. Isn't that right, Nell?' she said, not looking at her sister. 'I might be getting married. There's an American airman who's popped the question.'

Bernard swore. 'You've been seeing a bloody Yank without a word to me?'

'Probably knew what you'd say,' muttered Lottie. 'You want to be the only man in her life.'

'Shut up, bitch. I don't want to even look at you,' he said.

'I've noticed,' said Lottie. 'It's as if you think the gypsies brought me.'

'Don't you give me lip, girl,' he yelled, 'or you'll be out on your ear. I'm going out. Don't wait up for me.' He stalked out of the kitchen.

Babs glanced at her sisters and then hurried after Bernard, catching him up at the front door. 'Jake. Can I marry him? He's a good bloke.'

'Sez you! I'll not have a Yank in this house. Forget him, girl.' He opened the front door and slammed it after him.

For a moment Babs stood there, staring at it, and then she returned to the kitchen. Nellie handed her a cup of tea. 'I take it the answer was no?'

Babs nodded. 'He's selfish and unreasonable.'

'I know what I'd do,' said Lottie. 'Tell him to go to hell.'

Babs stared at her. 'What's got into you? I've never known you so lippy.'

Lottie smiled. 'I'm not scared of him anymore. I know the ten commandments and that I should honour my father but I can't. Anyway, all I can say is that I'm glad he's only on turnaround: our gain is Italy's loss. The sooner he goes back to his ship, the better I'll like it.'

Nellie nodded. 'Let's forget him. I'm whacked and want my bed.'

She did not wait for them to answer but went upstairs. She did not expect to sleep straight away because she was feeling so angry but having cleaned her teeth and undressed, she fell asleep within minutes and did not even remember Babs getting into bed with her.

Bernard did not return to the house until the following morning and by then Babs had left. She said that she didn't see the point of hanging around waiting for him to make an appearance. Nellie agreed. When he did arrive, he had an almighty hangover. She almost wished it wasn't Sunday, so the children would have been there making a din. He asked after Babs.

'She left early,' said Nellie. 'Had to get back to the land.'

He swore and went upstairs to shave and put on a clean shirt. That done, he said to Nellie on his way out: 'Things had better be different here when I get home again, or I'll be making changes myself.'

'Yes, Dad,' she said calmly. 'Say hello to Italy for us.'

'Those kids will have to go for a start,' he warned, giving her a dirty look before striding down the path without a backward glance.

'We'll see about that,' said Nellie, and closed the door, knowing she mustn't pray that a torpedo would sink his ship.

Chapter Fifteen

'Polly!' Nellie's eyes lit up as she spotted her former employer outside the Co-op. 'Long time no see. How are things with you?'

'Fine! I was thinking of coming to visit you to see how you were getting on but what with Christmas and the dark nights…' Her voice trailed away.

'I know what you mean. Anyway, we're OK. Although, we lost half of our intake to school in September. We've taken on four three-year-olds but I'm still not making enough money to pay me and Lottie a decent wage.'

Polly looked concerned. 'How's your sister doing?'

'Not bad actually. She's good with the kids and there's David, he helps out, too.' Nellie told her a little about him.

Polly listened before saying, 'Do you think they could cope without you? Because if they can, you might be interested to know that the nursery's expanding in April and they're looking to employ a nursery teacher for the older ones. If you like, I could put your name forward and they'll probably get in touch with you bearing in mind your experience. What d'you say?'

Nellie felt a buzz of excitement. It seemed ages since her outing to Burtonwood and Babs had not written for a while, so it would be good to get away from the house, and as for getting a proper wage, that really appealed. 'I don't mind giving it a go.'

'I'll do that, then.'

After Nellie finished the shopping, she went home with her head in a whirl but she decided not to mention having met Polly and the job in the nursery until she knew more.

A week later Nellie received a letter, asking her to write to the matron at the nursery detailing her experience and qualifications. It was then that she told Lottie about the job and asked if she thought she could cope with running their little nursery school herself.

Lottie looked anxiously at David, who was eating an apple, and said in a trembling voice, 'I honestly think, Nellie, that only a few of the mothers really care whether their kids know their alphabet and can write their names before they go to school. As long as they're getting looked after while they're at work that's all they care about. I'd still carry on with the older ones doing what you want me to if you think I'm capable.'

'Of course you're capable,' insisted Nellie, putting an arm around her sister's waist. She realised Lottie had gained a few inches during the winter months. 'I wouldn't even be thinking of applying for the job, if I didn't believe you were.'

'I can carry on helping Lottie,' said David eagerly, rocking backwards and forwards on his heels.

Nellie's forehead creased. 'I'm sure you'd be a great help with the music and games but once spring comes, you'll be working in the garden more. We could do with roping in a volunteer as well. I'll speak to the mams and see if they can suggest anyone.'

She took the opportunity of doing that the next day and was delighted when Elsie, one of the mothers, said that her fella had been home and she was expecting again. 'I'm going to have to give up me job but I'd hate to be home all the time. I wouldn't mind helping out a couple of afternoons, if I don't have to pay for our Mo.'

Nellie accepted the offer and applied for the job at the nursery. Within a month she had an interview and a week later was informed she had the job.

In the intervening weeks before she started at the council nursery, she made sure that Lottie and the mother worked out a schedule of activities for the children. David's input was logged, as were the times he would be spending in the garden. Nellie suggested that the children might enjoy having a little patch of land of their own to plant seeds and watch them grow. 'You'll have to make sure they don't dig them up to see what's happening to them, David,' she said.

He nodded vigorously. 'You bet I will.'

Having done as much as she could to help them, Nellie had to trust that they would cope without her when she started her new job in April.

It was difficult at first getting up at the crack of dawn to be in work before seven in the morning. Most of the mothers would already be there, waiting for the doors to open. Nellie was glad that she had not started in the depths of winter and decided not to think what it would be like getting up next November. Most of her class were eager to learn but there were always those who just wanted to muck about. Generally it was boys who didn't want to keep still. She stuck to the plan she had adopted when teaching the children in the Lake District: prayers, learning their letters, writing, numbers and colours. Then it was story time, music, and she even started a nature table, taking the children for walks in the park or along the bank of the LeedsLiverpool canal. It was almost the same as dealing with the children in *her* nursery school but with the added pleasure of nipping into the nursery and seeing the babies in their cots.

The hours were longer and, of course, she had to take orders from Matron and give account of herself, the children and the progress they were making. She would have preferred not having to obey orders and explain such things but at least she had more money and that was a relief. She did not see as much of Polly as she had thought she would, though. Her friend looked after the smaller children while they played, making sure they had an afternoon nap on the foldaway, washable canvas beds provided and that they drank their milk, orange juice and cod liver oil daily.

Absorbed in her new job, Nellie had little time to worry about Babs, from whom she had received only a scribbled note saying that Jake was not happy about their father's reaction. He wanted her to try and visit him in the south, but that was impossible at the moment as she could not get the time off. She just wished the war would end but that appeared some way off still.

At the beginning of June, Nellie woke up to the news that the invasion of France had begun. She felt for the thousands waiting anxiously to hear the outcome, fearing that their menfolk would be amongst the fallen or seriously wounded. During the weeks that followed she took an avid interest in the progress of the Allies across Europe, especially as a couple of the mothers had husbands with the army. She soon realised that it was going to take months rather than weeks before the Germans were defeated.

Nellie's every hour was filled with activity or sleep so that the weeks flew by. She noticed that Lottie had put on more weight but perhaps that was because she was contented and was eating more now she wasn't there to watch her. She stopped worrying about how Lottie and David were coping with the nursery because nobody complained to her. Then one sunny morning in August, Nellie was roused by screams from a dream about a dark-haired stranger reaching out to her through mist and rain. She fell out of bed and for several moments just lay on the floor, winded, wondering what the hell was making that noise. For a second she thought it might be the cat, only to hear Lottie screeching her name.

Nellie pushed herself up and not bothering to throw on a dressing gown, ran downstairs. Before she reached the ground floor she caught sight of her sister writhing on the floor in the lobby. She was panting and both her legs were drawn up onto her fat belly beneath the cotton nightdress. Nellie could see Lottie's private parts and watched in astonishment as her sister groaned, gasped and panted. When she realised what was happening, she was so astounded that she could not move but felt glued three steps from the bottom. Then she saw the crown of the baby's head appear and flew upstairs and into the bathroom.

'Oh my God,' she muttered. 'Oh, my God!' She flung open the cupboard and grabbed a couple of towels and thundered downstairs. Just in time to put a towel between Lottie's legs as the baby slid out covered in mucus.

Nellie stared blankly at the little girl. Having been out for the count when her own dead baby had been delivered, she did not know what to do and had to rack her brains. She had to make the baby take its first breath. Wrapping the towel round her, she carefully turned the child upside down and hit her gently on the back. She was rewarded with a choking noise.

'What's going on, Nellie? What's happening to me?' asked Lottie weakly.

Before she could answer, there was a banging at the front door. Nellie could only hope it was someone who had come in answer to her prayer.

'Don't move!' she croaked, placing the baby on Lottie's belly.

She opened the door and to her horror saw that it was Mrs Wainwright. 'What's going on, Nellie? What's all that screaming? I mean it's bad enough hearing those children during the week when they're playing outside but today's Sunday and I was just on my way to church when...'

Nellie made to close the door in her neighbour's face but Lottie groaned and the old woman thrust it wide open and forced her way past Nellie. If the sight of Lottie giving birth had been a shock to Nellie it came as an even bigger shock to Mrs Wainwright to see the afterbirth arrive.

'I don't want to believe this,' she said weakly.

'You're going to have to,' said Nellie, deciding to make use of her neighbour. 'You go and fetch the midwife.'

Mrs Wainwright said in a trembling voice, 'Your sister is unmarried. It would be kinder to let the baby die.'

Nellie was furious. 'Don't ever say that!'

'What's going on?' interrupted a second voice.

Nellie whirled round in surprise to face her youngest sister. 'Babs, you're not going to believe this!'

'I'd like not to,' said an amazed Babs, taking in the scene, 'but it can't have been an immaculate conception.'

'I don't suppose you can help?' asked Nellie.

Babs hesitated and then knelt down besides Lottie. 'Scissors and some string, Nell.'

Nellie asked no questions but rushed into the kitchen. As she searched for the required items, she counted back nine months. When she returned to the scene in the lobby it was to the sound of the baby's cry. In delight and amazement she watched Babs deal efficiently with the umbilical cord. Once that was done the baby was wrapped in another towel and handed to Lottie.

'You're marvellous!' cried Nellie.

Babs stood up, easing her back. 'You'd better get some rags to bind her.'

'I know that much,' said Nellie, wanting to hug her youngest sister. 'How did you know what to do? I'm sure you saved their lives.'

Babs shrugged and smiled. 'I've helped deliver calves. I never thought it would come in handy here, though.' She looked down at Lottie, who was gazing into the baby's tiny face in disbelief. 'We're aunts,' said Babs. 'Who'd have ever believed our Lottie would have a baby before me?'

'It's a disgrace,' said Mrs Wainwright, tight-lipped. 'She's just like her mother.'

The sisters had forgotten the old woman but now stared at her. She was standing in the doorway, dressed in her Sunday best suit, clutching her missal.

'Yes, I can see how you'd think that,' said Nellie, her eyes sparkling. 'But I'd think twice before you go spreading the word. There's only one person who can be the father, in my opinion, and that's David.'

Mrs Wainwright's face reddened. 'Prove it!'

Babs and Nellie looked at each other and then both got down on their knees beside their sister. 'Think back nine months, Lottie,' said Babs.

'Did you do something you'd never done before with a fella?' asked Nellie. 'Something that involved removing your knickers and getting very close to David?'

Mrs Wainwright spluttered, 'You're putting words into her mouth.'

The sisters ignored her.

Lottie lifted her eyes from her perusal of the baby's face and, if there were to be a competition for whose face was the reddest between her and the old woman, it might have been a draw. 'It was when you stayed overnight at Francis'. I was scared being in the house on my own, so David stayed with me. I didn't know what I was doing,' said Lottie hastily. 'At least I didn't know it would make a baby. It was just so comforting being together and loved.'

Babs and Nellie exchanged satisfied smiles and looked up at Mrs Wainwright. She did not speak but retreated in a hurry.

'Wedding on the cards or not?' asked Babs, grimacing.

'Not if she has anything to do with it,' said Nellie, getting to her feet. 'But at the moment, she's the least of my worries.'

Babs nodded. 'Let's make Lottie and the baby comfortable. The rags, Nellie, and we'd best try and get her to bed and call in a midwife to check that she and the baby are OK.'

With a concerted effort, Nellie and Babs managed to get Lottie into bed. While Nellie dressed and then fetched the midwife, Babs saw to her sister's basic needs. Lottie was grateful. 'You do surprise me, Babs. I never thought you'd be so kind and not say how terrible I am for committing a mortal sin.'

'What's the use of that. It'll be punishment enough you're having to put up with the consequences of being an unmarried mother if David doesn't marry you. Now shut up and put this lovely little baby to the breast.'

Lottie's cheeks were rosy as she unbuttoned the top of the nightgown. 'Mam and Aunt Josie would have killed me. They'd have sent me away for bringing disgrace on the family. They'd have said I was a sinner and I'd go to Hell.'

'I'd stop worrying about that,' said Babs. 'They're not here, are they? Dad will have a fit, though, so let's hope David will marry you. That's if you want to marry him?'

Lottie did not answer because she had managed to get a nipple into her baby's mouth and when her daughter began to suckle, she felt such a feeling of warmth and love that she could think of nothing else. Babs shrugged and moved away, deciding that it was pointless worrying about what was going to happen to Lottie and the baby right now.

When the midwife arrived, her manner was brisk and non-judgemental and she complimented Babs on her actions and told Nellie that she would look in again on Lottie and the baby tomorrow. Then she left.

After she had gone, Nellie made tea and toast and, after taking some in to Lottie, she sat down at the kitchen table with Babs. 'So what brings you home? Any news from Jake?'

Babs brushed back a strand of red hair and sighed. 'Would you believe he's been sent abroad. I don't know where. Something to do with keeping the planes flying. I tell you, Nell, I'm really fed up. I'm wondering if we'll ever get together again. I should have eloped with him when he suggested it. At least I could have had his baby by now and be done with working on the land.' She scrubbed her face with her fingernails. 'I almost envy our Lottie.'

'Me too,' murmured Nellie, reaching for the milk jug. 'A perfect healthy little girl. Anyway, I'll need to have words with David when he arrives.'

'You think they'll get married?'

'The baby needs a name and the pair of them get on well. He might be a farthing short of a shilling but he's a hard worker and is genuinely fond of her. I'll put it to them both. They can live here.'

'Dad will be made up with that.'

Nellie shrugged. 'He'll just have to lump it if he wants to carry on using this house as a base when he gets shore leave.'

Babs toyed with her fingers and said, 'Do you want me around when you tell him?'

'I'd appreciate some moral support but don't worry about it. I'll make sure Francis is here.' She paused, thinking suddenly of the mystery man she had met at the presbytery and wondering where he was now.

Babs interrupted her thoughts. 'I haven't told you about Stuart.'

Nellie reluctantly dismissed the mystery man from her mind. 'He hasn't been pestering you, has he?'

'Nothing that I can't handle.' She paused. 'Our Lottie's not the only one who surprised me recently. My friend Heather had a baby. Don't ask me how she managed to keep it a secret so long but she did. She said it's Stuart's but he's denying it. I told him he was a right heel. I just thank God I finished with him and got together with Jake, even though we've spent more time apart than together.'

Nellie topped up their tea. 'You're in the same boat as thousands of others. It's hard but you just have to bear it.'

'I know, I know.' Babs sighed. 'So getting back to our sister. The baby's going to need clothes.'

Nellie nodded and said softly, 'At least I can help there.' She drained her cup and went up to the attic. She had stored the shop-bought layette and knitted garments Lottie had made in an old chest of drawers. As she removed them she experienced that pain of loss and tears tingled the back of her eyes, but she thought of the baby downstairs and wasted no time on regrets.

Lottie was sleeping and Babs had placed the baby, still cocooned in a couple of towels, in a sideboard drawer. As she took the items from her, she said, 'You might marry again, Nell, and have babies.'

For once Nellie did not shrug off the idea. 'Who knows? I'd have never have believed our Lottie would end up in trouble, so there's no use trying to foretell the future.' She glanced at the clock. 'David's generally here by now; I wonder what's keeping him?'

But David did not turn up that day and he had not arrived the next day when Nellie had to leave for work. Babs said that she would stay and have a word with him when he turned up and speak to the mothers.

'Do I tell them Lottie's had a baby, Nellie? I don't see how we can keep it quiet with them bringing the kids here,' she said.

Nellie agreed. 'One of the mothers stays and helps on a Monday; she's having another baby. You can tell her what's happened and leave it to her to spread the news.'

Babs nodded and Nellie left her to it. Later she explained to Polly what had happened. Her friend tried not to look shocked and offered the services of her cousin. 'She's having her third child and I'm sure she'll help Lottie out for a few days as a favour to me...until Lottie's on her feet.'

'Thanks. I can't pay her but I'll give her some vegetables and she can help herself to apples from the tree.'

With that settled, Nellie got on with her work but she could not concentrate, uneasy about David not having turned up yesterday. She determined if he didn't arrive that day then she would call on Mrs Wainwright that evening.

When Nellie arrived home it was to find Lottie alone with the baby. 'Babs had to leave. David hasn't arrived, Nell. What am I going to do?' she asked, tears rolling down her cheeks.

'Right!' said Nellie, storming out of the house and up Mrs Wainwright's drive. She banged on the front door but got no answer, so went round the back. The curtains were drawn and the door was locked.

A voice the other side of the fence, said, 'She's gone on holiday. She went yesterday. I was told she'd be away a fortnight.'

Nellie's heart sank. 'Did you see David with her?'

'I only saw him briefly. She had him in and out of the house in no time. She mustn't have gone to church after all.'

Nellie realised she had no choice but to concede defeat for the moment. She returned to the house. 'He's been whisked away by that old witch,' she said to Lottie in a seething voice.

'What do we do, Nellie?' asked Lottie, sniffing back her tears.

'Wait,' she replied. 'There's nothing else we can do. We'll register the baby's birth as Callaghan. Have you thought of a name for her, Lottie?'

She nodded and murmured, 'Lucia Helen Barbara.' She looked up at her sister. 'You and Babs are the best sisters in the world.'

Nellie was so touched she could not speak for a moment, and then she squeezed her sister's shoulder and said huskily, 'Word's bound to get around and, if you ask me, Mrs Wainwright hasn't done herself any favours by going off the way she did. The neighbours know David's always round here. They'll put two and two together and guess he's the father. If she and David's mother insist on keeping the two of you apart, I think it'll rouse people's sympathy.'

'I hope you're right, Nell,' said Lottie.

Nellie hoped she was, too. One thing was for sure, there would be no placing this child in an orphanage. She was a little love with dark curls and the sweetest little mouth.

By the time the fortnight was up and Mrs Wainwright was a visible presence in the neighbourhood once again, Lottie had convinced herself that David did not want her; she was too ugly, too fat and, besides, neither of them had any money to look after a child. Even so, she hoped that he would visit just so he could see how lovely his daughter was. But he did not come and it was only when Nellie went round to visit Mrs Wainwright that the truth came out.

'His mother needs him,' said the old woman defiantly. 'It's all right for you, Nellie, you're young and strong and can cope without a man about the place. My sister can't. She's got a weak heart and so the pair of them have gone to live in the country with our cousin.'

Nellie was angry. 'Does David know about the baby?'

Mrs Wainwright flushed. 'Don't be silly. You think we'd have told him? Best he doesn't know in case he gets any stupid ideas about marriage. They'd have more children and how would they cope without help? You tell me that, Nellie. You mightn't like the idea but my sister and I have done the sensible thing and you'll realise that sooner or later.'

'You should have given him a choice. You and your sister will rue the day you made your decision. Lucia is a lovely baby. Your sister could have found a lot of pleasure in being a granny but that's her loss. Good day, Mrs Wainwright.' She walked away, wishing that she knew the whereabouts of the cousin.

Lottie greeted the news bravely and said little. She accepted that David's mother needed him but she wanted to scream that she and the baby needed him too. Not knowing where he was meant there was nothing she could do about it. David wasn't strong-willed and bossy like some men, so she could understand why his mother and Mrs Wainwright could have such a hold on him that he would fall in with their wishes. So she accepted life as it was and got on with it. Somehow she managed without complaint to cope with the baby and run the nursery school with the help of the volunteer mother.

Several weeks passed before Nellie decided Francis should know about the baby. Telling him was something she was not looking forward to but she couldn't put it off indefinitely. Lottie wanted the baby baptised but was too ashamed to go to the parish priest.

Francis looked rightfully stunned when Nellie told him the news. 'I can't believe it. Lottie of all people. Now if you'd said Babs had got herself into trouble...' He shook his head in bewilderment. 'I can imagine what Mother would have said.'

Nellie leaned back in the leather chair and stared at him from beneath drooping eyelids. 'So can I, but she was in no position to judge having been pregnant herself when she got married.'

He looked shocked and several moments passed before he said, 'So that's what you meant about her being no angel. Dad'll have Lottie out.'

'Over my dead body,' said Nellie fiercely.

'Let's hope it doesn't come to that,' said Francis, riffling his fingers through his hair. 'He wrote to me about Babs and Jake. You didn't let me know he'd been home and knew about them.'

'Sorry, but my life's so busy.'

'You're too busy. You need to be careful you don't crack up, Nellie.' He twiddled his thumbs. 'You must keep me up to date with what's happening with you girls.'

'Women, Francis, not girls,' she said firmly, getting to her feet. 'Anyway, you know everything I know now, so what do I say to Lottie? She wants the baby baptised.'

'She hasn't visited her parish priest?'

Nellie shook her head. 'Lottie hasn't been to church since Lucia's birth. She's too ashamed.'

Francis met her gaze squarely. 'Get her to go to English Martyrs' and make her confession. I'm sure the priest will baptise the child as she's an innocent in all this.'

She nodded and stood up, fiddling with her gloves. 'She'll find it difficult.'

'Tell her to look upon it as a penitence and let's pray David turns up.'

Nellie nodded. 'I hope so for Lottie and the baby's sake. It will be easier for Lucia if she has her father's name as she grows up.'

She returned home and told her sister what Francis had said. Lottie closed her eyes briefly. 'Will you come with me, Nell?'

Nellie nodded, knowing it was essential to Lottie's well being that her spiritual needs were met. She only hoped that Lottie would not go all religious on her again because she did not want to have to cope with that. She reckoned her mother being overtly religious was due to her sense of shame in having sex before marriage and, sadly, she must never have really felt forgiven. It was taking Nellie some time to get back on friendly speaking terms with God, and perhaps that wouldn't come about until the war was over.

Part Three

1945 to 1946

Chapter Sixteen

Babs climbed down from the tractor and eased her aching shoulders. A bath, a meal and bed, she thought. Her breath misted in the frosty air as she made her way across the farmyard. Then she spotted an airman leaning against the barn wall, smoking a cigarette. Only for a second did she think it might be Jake, because he had written saying he was coming home but then she recognised Stuart and swore inwardly. Could she get away with ignoring him?

He killed that idea stone dead by dropping his cigarette stub in the mud and coming towards her. 'I'd almost given up on you,' he said.

'What are you doing here?' She did not pause but carried on towards the footpath that would take her across the fields to her digs.

'I've got news of Jake.'

Her stride faltered and she glanced at him. 'What is it?'

'He's missing.'

She felt the blood drain from her face. 'I don't believe it,' she whispered.

Stuart shrugged. 'Please yourself, but the plane flying him home never arrived. Radio contact was lost and nothing has been heard since.'

She croaked, 'Where did it go down?'

He took out a packet of cigarettes and offered her one. She shook her head, not wanting to take anything from him. In a fever of impatience, she watched him light up, knowing he was deliberately keeping her waiting.

'Most likely they ditched in the sea. The same kind of thing happened to Glenn Miller on his way to Paris. His plane just vanished. I'm really, really sorry, Babs.'

'Don't be such a hypocrite. You're not sorry,' she said in a trembling voice. 'Now, if you don't mind going away, I'd like to be alone.'

His eyes narrowed. 'That's not very friendly or sensible. We don't want you doing anything silly now, do we? I'm perfectly happy to provide a shoulder for you to cry on.'

Babs looked at him in disgust and walked away. She didn't want to believe what he had said was true but surely even he wouldn't lie about such a terrible thing? Her eyes filled with tears and her throat felt as if it had a plum blocking it. She wanted to howl, but with Stuart still in earshot, didn't want to give him the satisfaction of hearing her give way. She began to run as if she could escape the terrible news she had been told.

'Hey, wait! Don't run away,' shouted Stuart.

She ignored him, running along the frost-hardened ground and remembered it was on this path that she had met Jake one beautiful spring evening. Tears trickled down her cheeks. She could hear Stuart shouting and he sounded closer. She spun round and saw him a few feet away. He stopped and smiled. 'You're being silly.'

Despite her tears she could see him clearly and without hesitation she walked towards him. Before he could realise her intention, she drew back her arm and then let fly with her fist and hit him smack on the jaw. His body seemed to crumple as he slid to the ground. She left him there and carried on back to her digs. She needed Jake still to be coming home but if she couldn't have him, then she wanted Nellie.

Nellie hummed 'Brahms' Lullaby' as she carried the sleeping baby into Lottie's bedroom and placed her in her cot. She tucked the blankets in around her niece and then kissed the top of her head before tiptoeing out of the room.

She was halfway to the kitchen when the knocker sounded and hurriedly she made for the front door, not wanting the baby to wake. She opened the door and to her surprise saw Babs standing there. Immediately, her sister's wan features told Nellie something was terribly wrong.

'What is it?' she asked.

Babs gulped. 'Jake's missing. His plane lost radio contact and vanished.'

'Oh, Babs,' breathed Nellie, seizing hold of her sister and drawing her into the house. 'You poor, poor thing,' she added, putting her arms around her. Babs burst into tears and wept on Nellie's shoulder. She felt helpless in the face of such grief and could only pat her sister's back and whisper, 'There, there now, get it all out.'

She had no idea how long she stood there, nursing her sister, before a drowsy voice asked, 'What's wrong? Where's the baby?'

'In her cot. Put the kettle on, love,' said Nellie, glancing at Lottie.

Lottie blinked. 'Is that our Babs?'

Babs sniffed and wiped her damp face with the back of her hand and drew away from Nellie. 'Yes, it's me.'

'You look terrible,' said Lottie, concerned.

'Jake's missing,' said Nellie. 'Will you put that kettle on?'

'OK, OK, I'm doing it,' said Lottie, leading the way into the kitchen. 'When did it happen?'

Babs shook her head. 'I don't know.' She stood in the middle of the kitchen, gazing about her as if she had never seen the place before.

Nellie helped her off with her coat and hat and ushered her over to a chair by the fire. Babs stared into the flames and gulped convulsively.

Lottie glanced at Nellie. 'Shall we have cocoa?'

She nodded. 'Put an extra spoonful of sugar in Babs'.'

Lottie said, 'It's a terrible shock. Us three don't half seem unlucky when it comes to men.'

Nellie made no reply but drew a footstool close to Babs' chair and reached for her sister's hand. She held it firmly but did not speak, not wanting to say anything that would upset Babs further.

Lottie made the cocoa and took the tray over to the fireplace. She handed a cup to each of her sisters before sitting down herself.

Babs stared at her and said in a vague voice, 'You've lost weight.'

Lottie was gratified and said, 'You think so? It must be chasing round after kids and looking after Lucia.'

Babs sighed. 'I suppose I'll never have kids.'

'You don't know that,' said Nellie. 'Drink your cocoa.'

They drank in silence and only when the empty cups were placed on the tray did Babs say, 'I don't know what to do.' Her lovely features were pale and drawn. 'It was Stuart who told me. He said he was sorry but he wasn't really.' Her green eyes darkened. 'A couple of the girls think he'll start pestering me to go out with him again but I told them that I'd punched him on the jaw and he'd be a fool to try.'

Nellie said, 'Good on you, but if I was you, I'd think of making a move.'

'I feel I need to get away. Go where nobody knows about me and Jake.'

Nellie stood up. 'Makes sense. What d'you say to a glass of sherry? I've some left over from Christmas. I presume you'll be staying the night?'

Babs nodded, slipped off her shoes and tucked her legs beneath her. 'Do you remember the peapod wine I brought that first Christmas I was away?'

'It went down a treat,' said Nellie, going over to the dresser.

'If you'd stayed at that first place you would never have met Jake,' said Lottie.

Babs' eyes filled with tears. 'I'm glad I met him. I'm just bloody sorry I never married him.'

'It's no use thinking like that. Get that down you,' ordered Nellie, handing her a tumbler of sherry.

Lottie gasped. 'You'll get her drunk drinking all that.'

'It'll help her sleep,' said Nellie, taking a generous mouthful of the sherry herself. 'Anyway, missing doesn't mean that he's dead, just presumed dead.'

Babs stared at her from dull eyes. 'Stuart said it went missing over the Channel.'

'How does he know that if radio contact was lost?'

'I-I presume that's where the plane was when contact was lost.'

Nellie nodded. 'Of course. I was just trying to give you some hope.'

Babs' eyes brightened. 'You think there is hope?'

'I can't say.' Her tone was sad. 'But if there is a chance he's survived, then they'll find him, won't they, and you'll get to know? I mean, even if they ditched in the sea, it has been known for sailors to have been found alive weeks after going missing. If it was me, then I'd want to believe Jake would turn up again.'

Silence.

'Nellie found a man that went missing,' said Lottie, yawning.

Babs stared at Nellie. 'What man?'

'Didn't I tell you about him?'

'I can't remember. Tell me again in case?' She downed half the sherry.

So Nellie told Babs about discovering the stranger in the porch of St Joseph's and how she had dealt with his injuries but that she had never seen him again.

'So what happened to him?'

'Francis said that he'd gone in search of his family. I never knew his name,' said Nellie.

Babs swallowed the last of her sherry. 'Was he young? Was he good looking?'

Nellie smiled. 'He was in his twenties and, yes, I think that if his face hadn't been bruised and his nose swollen then he wouldn't have been half bad.'

'So who do you think he was?'

Nellie shrugged. 'Either he was a soldier who'd gone AWOL or...' she hesitated, 'an escaped POW. He looked like he had Italian blood.'

'An Eyetie! And you helped him? You do surprise me,' said Babs, 'although, we're supposed to be mates now. There's a couple of camps not far from us that have Eyeties prisoners and they've helped on the land.'

Nellie nodded. 'It could be that he wasn't one of the enemy. There's hundreds of immigrants of Italian descent in Liverpool and some were put in POW camps at the beginning of the war and later were freed to fight. I remember Francis mentioning it ages ago.'

'If he was from Francis' parish, he should have known his name and where his family lived,' said Lottie.

'I know. Anyway, it's unlikely I'll ever see him again.'

The light in Babs' eyes died. 'Just like I'll never see Jake again,' she muttered. 'Why is it men like Stuart survive and the Jakes and Teddys of this world are lost?'

'It's useless thinking like that.' Nellie fetched the sherry bottle. 'So where are you thinking of moving? Somewhere nearer home?'

'But what if…' began Babs.

'What if what?' asked Nellie, draining the sherry bottle.

'Jake turns up and I've moved?'

'He'll come here,' said Nellie. 'So chin up and think of doing what I said.'

She nodded and no more was said on the subject.

Babs waited a little while before putting in for a transfer and by then, she had given up hope of ever seeing Jake again, convinced she would have heard from him by now if he had survived. It was a struggle to carry on but what else could she do? Nellie had survived double heartbreak losing her husband and baby, so could she do less?

Spring came to Merseyside and Nellie and Lottie planted seeds, both thinking that this time last year David had been there to help them, and before him there had been Billy.

'Remember Billy?' said Nellie.

Lottie nodded. 'I hope he's still alive.'

During the previous weeks there had been Allied victory after victory and the latest news was that Cologne had fallen. 'If one of us sees Sgt McElroy, we should make a point of asking him,' said Nellie. 'Although, Maisie Miller will probably know.'

So Lottie asked Irene's mother. 'As far as I know, he's still OK,' said Maisie.

Babs visited. Despite having a healthy colour with spending so much time outdoors, it was obvious to her sisters that she was still grieving. How Nellie wished that the war would be over, not next week or next month, but now!

In April, President Roosevelt was succeeded by President Truman. Nellie received the news with sadness, thinking it was such a shame that he should die when victory was in sight.

Within weeks American and Soviet forces met in Germany and the horrors of Hitler's death camps were discovered. Shock vibrated through Nellie, wondering how men could be so cruel to their fellow man. Yet she was avid for more news that spoke of the war coming to an end.

In Italy, the Allies captured Bologna, and the following day Mussolini was shot dead by partisans. Venice was taken and Nellie was reminded of her father and she worried about him coming home. Not only did he need to know she owned the house but also about Lottie and Lucia.

On the thirtieth of April, Hitler committed suicide. The news of his death created wild expectations of an immediate end to the European war with Germany's unconditional surrender; a two-day holiday was promised.

Nellie was weeding in the garden when Lottie called her in to say that Churchill was about to speak to the nation. It had started to rain, so she was more than happy to stop work and run inside. Lottie had been in the middle of making a cake while Lucia crawled about the place. She picked her up and settled her on her knee. Nellie turned up their grandfather's old wireless and the unmistakable tones of the Premier came over the airwaves, announcing that the war in Europe was over. The sisters cheered and danced round the kitchen. Within minutes, ships' hooters on the Mersey blared out a cacophony of sound and church bells began to ring. There was no mistaking what that noise meant; it was time to celebrate.

Nellie's throat tightened with emotion. How many others would be feeling as she did? They had survived the war but, having lost loved ones, their lives would never be the same again. There would always be a tiny core of sadness in their hearts. She wanted to sit quietly and let the thought of peace sink in but such stillness could not last long. The neighbours had decided on a party.

Lottie popped her cake in the oven, while Nellie made meat paste sandwiches. Once ready, they were carried outside to where trestle tables were erected and spread with cloths. People chattered and sang as food and drink were placed on the tables. When she looked at the amount of food displayed, Nellie wondered where it had all come from. There were meat paste and sardine sandwiches, ham and egg, cakes, jellies, custard, chocolate and lollipops. There was a barrel of beer, as well as bottles of sherry, port, ginger ale and lemonade.

Nellie noticed Mrs Wainwright was missing and asked the neighbour who lived the other side of the old woman whether she knew where she was. Nellie had not spoken to Mrs Wainwright since she had told her David and his mother had gone to live with a cousin.

'Gone to celebrate with her sister. She said that she hadn't been too good. Heart. Pity you couldn't have followed them, you might have seen David.'

What heart! thought Nellie, still angry that the two women had kept David away from Lottie and his daughter. Perhaps she should have thought of shadowing Mrs Wainwright. She smiled wryly. What would be the use? She and Lottie were coping and Lucia was a contented baby and that's what mattered. She thought about her other sister. Poor Babs! It would be great if she could make it home. No sooner had she thought that than she heard someone say, 'Here's Babs Callaghan.'

Nellie turned and saw her youngest sister coming towards them. She was dressed in her land girl uniform but still managed to look feminine and attractive. 'So you made it,' said Nellie, her face lighting up.

Babs forced a smile. 'It wasn't easy but I managed to get a lift. So when do we eat? I'm starving. And what about a drink?'

The children were seen to first and then drinks were poured for the adults and food was handed round. The three sisters sat together on the chairs that Nellie had brought from the house. 'We should toast the valiant dead,' she said.

So that's what they did and there was many a tear shed when Nellie said, with a break in her voice, 'Without their sacrifice we'd never have won this war.' She was conscious of that feeling of unreality that had held her in its grip on previous occasions and wished that the victory in Europe had not cost so many lives.

Afterwards there was dancing and singing and Nellie admired Babs for joining in because she must have given up hope now of ever seeing Jake alive again. She could only pray that her younger sister would find someone else one day.

If Nellie had believed everything would change overnight now the European war was over, she was soon proved wrong. Rationing remained and the mothers still worked long hours, but at least lighting restrictions were lifted, so they were able to take down the black-out curtains and go out in the evening without torches. But Babs continued working as a land girl and the troops did not immediately come marching home.

In July, an election was held and the Labour party won a resounding victory. Churchill was out and there were many who thought it was a slap in the face for him. It was said that it was the soldiers' vote that had won the socialist victory. Nellie could understand why they had wanted a change and it was the reason she voted for a Labour government. They were determined to improve the lot of the working classes and promised new homes, jobs and, most of all, a health service, where nobody would need to pay to see a doctor or to go into hospital. Lottie still suffered from the injuries she'd received during the blitz and Nellie hoped that, one day, something could be done to help her.

The following month the Americans dropped two atom bombs on Japan, bringing the war in the Far East to a speedy end. VJ Day followed with more parties to celebrate. The numbers said to have been killed when the two bombs were dropped astounded Nellie. She realised that such explosive power would change the way war was waged in the world for ever, but at what price?

Happily, Lucia had her first birthday towards the end of August. She was a bright-eyed, lively child and was toddling everywhere. Lottie had saved some rations and made her a cake. Nellie bought her niece a pink sun-bonnet and she looked a picture in it.

Lottie had her hands full but said to Nellie, 'I'm glad we've still got enough mothers interested in the nursery, because it means she has other children to play with.'

'Numbers could start going down, though,' warned Nellie. 'Once the men start coming home, most won't want their wives out at work but looking after them and the house and kids.' She was reminded that Bernard's homecoming was something she really must give more thought to but until she heard from him, she could not really make any arrangements to sort things out.

It was October before Nellie heard from her father. The letter informed her that he was in hospital in Italy after falling through a hatch into the hold. He had broken several bones but said that his life was not in danger, so they were not to worry as he was in good hands. She breathed a sigh of relief, glad that his homecoming was to be delayed for a while longer.

The first Christmas of the peace was to come and go before Nellie heard from her father again. She had written to him, wishing him a happy Christmas and hoping his bones were healing, but had not received an answer. Francis was the first to get up-to-date news of Bernard having been moved from hospital to a villa further down Italy's western coast to convalesce. His bones were taking longer to mend than the doctors had predicted but, hopefully, he would be home some time in January.

'I would have thought his bones would have healed ages ago but I have been praying he'll stay away longer,' said Lottie. Her knitting needles were going ten to the dozen. 'I can imagine what he's going to say about Lucia.'

Nellie tapped the letter against her teeth. 'I suppose we can expect him any day now, seeing that we're halfway through January.'

She was right. Two days later a telegram arrived saying that Bernard would be with them by the end of the week and that he was bringing a surprise with him. Immediately Nellie wrote to Babs, asking her to get some time off, so she could be there when Bernard arrived. She also wrote to Francis but she was still waiting for an answer to her letter, or for him to call, when Babs turned up the following evening. 'It's dull, dull, dull on the farm,' she said. 'I hope the surprise he's got is a good one. He never even sent me a card for my twenty-first. I hope it's something I can wear.'

'It won't cost much that's for sure,' said Lottie, not looking up from her knitting. 'He's even more tight-fisted than Grandfather was. Anyway, he's not the only one about to spring a surprise, is he?' She grinned at Nellie.

'I wish Francis was here. Dad mightn't believe Grandfather left the house to me but he'd have to believe Francis.' Nellie closed her library book and put coal on the fire. 'Of course, I could always speak to the solicitor.'

'Dad'll probably try and force you to make the house over to him,' said Lottie.

Nellie sighed. 'You mean contest the will. Francis said that if I made the house over to Dad, I would be going against

Grandfather's wishes. He trusted me to make this a place where all the family could feel at home.'

'You really believe that?' asked Babs.

Nellie said softly, 'He didn't tell us to go away when we needed somewhere to live. We had our disagreements but this house has been a refuge to all of us in times of trouble.'

Babs said, 'It's going to be tough on Dad but I'll never forgive him for not giving his permission for me to marry Jake.'

'He doesn't care about your feelings,' said Lottie. 'As for the house, he only needs somewhere to hang his cap when he's on leave.'

'Yes. This will still be his home,' said Nellie. 'For all his faults he is still our father.'

'OK! You've made your point,' said Babs, her brows knitting. 'Are we going to do something special to welcome him home? I can guess the first thing he'll say is that you haven't had the place done up.'

'He never handed over any money.' Nellie gazed at the dingy eggshell-blue painted walls and smoke-stained ceiling. 'I wouldn't have used it if he had. It's my responsibility. The whole house needs a lick of paint and hopefully I'll get some of it done this spring.'

'So we can't paint the walls but we could write a big notice saying Welcome Home, Dad,' suggested Babs.

'And where do we get a clean sheet of paper that big?' asked Lottie. 'There's been a war on, you know.'

Babs made an exasperated sound and turned to Nellie. 'Can't you get some paper from the nursery?'

'There's a paper shortage.'

Babs persisted. 'How about crepe paper? Remember making red, white and blue paper roses for the coronation and twining them through a trellis round the front door?'

'Don't start getting nostalgic. I haven't got any crepe paper, but what I have got is bunting,' said Nellie.

'Bunting?' said Babs.

'Upstairs in the attic.' Nellie got up. 'And there might be some other stuff we can use. Anyway, I'm going to take a gander through what was left over after the sale.'

'I'll come with you,' said Babs, her eyes alight. 'It's ages since I've had a nose up there.'

Immediately Lottie said that she'd like a root around as well. 'I'll just check that Lucia is sleeping OK. She's been a bit fretful lately because she's teething.'

'Won't you find it difficult climbing all those stairs?' asked Babs.

Lottie sniffed. 'Don't you worry about me. I'm tougher than you think.' She put down her knitting and followed them out of the kitchen.

Once in the attic, Nellie dragged out yards of bunting, triangles of red, white and blue flags.

Lottie entered the room a few minutes later and immediately delved into another tea-chest. She lifted out a couple of gowns, dropped one and held the other against her. 'What d'you think?'

'Holy Mary, mother of God, Charlotte Callaghan, you're not thinking of wearing that? It's touching the floor and goes up to your neck,' said Babs.

'I like it.' Lottie tilted her chin. 'Lots of lovely material in it and I love the flowery pattern in orange and brown and that it'll fasten to my throat...as for the length, I'll shorten it a bit.'

Her sisters exchanged looks but made no comment. Nellie remembered how she had thought of altering some of the frocks for dressing-up clothes for the children, but she had never had the time.

They continued to root in the tea-chests and eventually, with a triumphant shout, Babs dragged out a remnant of a roll of wallpaper. 'The back of this will do for a notice.'

Nellie looked at it in surprise. 'I thought we'd used up all the wallpaper.'

'Obviously not this bit,' said Babs, waving it in the air.

Carrying their spoils between them, the three sisters went downstairs, discussing whether to put up the bunting outside or in the kitchen. Babs was all for hanging it on the chestnut trees but Nellie said, 'It could rain or even snow at this time of year...best inside.'

Babs gave in and said she would hang it up in the morning after Nellie had gone to work. 'I'll do the welcome notice, too. It's a pity we haven't got any paint. The words won't show up much in ink or pencil.'

'Try the outhouse,' said Nellie, spooning cocoa into a jug. 'You just might be lucky and find some dregs in a tin.' It seemed strange to her that in a day or two her father would be home and she would have to face his wrath, not only over the house but also for allowing the unmarried Lottie to get pregnant and bring up her daughter here without a word to him. If only it had been Teddy coming home instead of her father, but there was no chance of that and so she had to make the best of what she had.

Chapter Seventeen

Less than twenty-four hours later Nellie came out of the nursery to the sight of falling snow. To her surprise, standing at the gate was Irene Miller. 'What are you doing here?' asked Nellie, thinking that Maisie should have collected her daughter from The Chestnuts an hour or so ago.

'Mam didn't come for me, so I decided to walk home on my own,' said the little girl who would be five that year. 'Your sisters were arguing, so I sneaked out. Then I saw you and wanted to say hello.' She smiled up at Nellie.

'I don't think you should be going home on your own in this weather and in the dark,' she murmured.

'But the snow's lovely,' said Irene, looking skywards.

Nellie's face softened, remembering as a child she had found the snow magical. Sadly, what with the war and all that had entailed, life had lost much of its magic. Suddenly she had a deep longing to feel carefree, to sing and be happy and to have that childish sense of wonder about life. She felt the cold kiss of a snowflake on her flushed cheeks and another one stung her chapped lips.

A small hand slipped into hers. 'Do you like it, too?'

'I love it!' said Nellie. 'I'll see you home.' If Bernard had arrived then their talk was going to have to wait.

As they trudged towards the lift bridge, fat snowflakes continued to pirouette lazily from an overloaded sky in what seemed like a never-ending stream. The child tried to catch them in her mouth and Nellie smiled, recalling doing the same thing with her sisters.

'Mrs Lachlan, look! The snow's melting in the canal.'

Roused from her reverie, Nellie gazed at the oil-streaked surface and saw that indeed the snowflakes were being swallowed up by the mass of water. Strangely, it reminded her that she was one of millions in the world, all in the same boat, weary after a war that had taken so much from and out of them.

They crossed the lift bridge, passed the smithy and the Red Lion pub; ahead lay Litherland library and the factory where Maisie worked. On its wall hung a model of a perky pig, carrying a meaty sausage on a fork. She noticed the figure of a boy making his way towards them.

'It's Jimmy!' cried Irene, jiggling about. 'It's me big brother.'

The boy slithered to a halt a foot away and Nellie saw that the thin face of the eight-year-old was not only pinched and flushed with cold but was tight with distress too. Her heart sank. 'Oh, Mrs Lachlan, Mam's acting crazy and I don't know what to do,' he said.

Nellie's heart flipped over. 'What d'you mean crazy, Jimmy. You just calm down and explain yourself.'

'She threw the potatoes at me and smashed the teapot. Then she picked up our only saucepan and began to bang it against the fireplace, screaming at the top of her voice.'

'Has she been drinking?'

'I couldn't smell it on her breath. I think she's just gone off her nut.'

Nellie took the boy's hand and began to hurry the two children in the direction of Linacre Road. 'Couldn't the woman you share the house with help?'

'She's gone. She married a fella. She lives across the water now.'

'Have you any idea what it's about?'

Jimmy shook his head. Nellie asked no more questions.

The front door was ajar and Nellie paused only to give Maisie warning that she was there by knocking and announcing herself before walking in. She found Maisie sitting in front of a fire struggling for life in the grate. Her shoulders were bowed and she was sobbing as if her heart would break. Nellie signalled to the children to sit on the sofa and went over to her. She placed a hand on her shoulder. 'What is it, Maisie? What's wrong?'

The woman did not answer at first and Nellie waited for her to gain control of herself. After a couple of minutes she raised a tear-stained face and said in a wobbly voice, 'Our Marty's gone and got himself married without a word to me. I thought he'd come and live here...get his old job back and I could work part-time and we'd cope fine. Me and him were always there for each other when we were kids,' she said, biting back a sob. 'We never knew our dad and, as for me mam, she wanted rid of us as soon as she could. Now he's married this girl in the ATS. I just don't know how I'm going to manage with all the rent to pay on this house.'

'He's alive, Maisie! You be thankful for that. You want him to be happy, don't you?'

'I wanted him to be happy here with me...that's what we planned,' she said angrily.

'You're not the only one whose plans have been wrecked,' said Nellie. 'For the kids' sake, pull yourself together. You can get a lodger to help you with the rent.'

'I suppose I can. I didn't think of that. I had me mind set on our Marty living here.' Maisie wiped her eyes with the back of her hand.

Nellie signalled to Jimmy to put on the kettle. 'Well, you've got your children and I'm sure they're a blessing to you, Maisie. At least you have part of your husband to love.'

Maisie sniffed. 'I suppose you're right. Marty's survived the war and I should be thankful for that. I just hope this girl and I will get on.'

'I'm sure if you meet her half way, things will be fine,' said Nellie, bending to pick up a potato. She motioned to Irene to help her gather the rest together before taking off her coat and peeling the spuds. Maisie thanked her and said that she would be all right now and wasn't she wanting to get home.

'Yes. My father's coming home. He could be at the house when I get there.' Nellie hugged the children and said that she would call again soon.

'Well, yeah, thanks, luv. Jimmy, see Mrs Lachlan out.'

The boy walked with Nellie to the front door. She stepped

outside and then turned and looked into his young face and saw the anxiety there. It touched her heart. 'Don't be worrying. If your mam gets upset again then come to me. In case you've forgotten, the house is called The Chestnuts; Irene knows where it is if you ever need help.'

His face brightened up. 'Yes, Mrs Lachlan.'

'Bye, Jimmy.'

'Tarrah!' He waved his hand and then turned and went back inside the house.

Nellie put her head down and hurried towards the main road. She did not see the figure looming ahead through the whirling snowflakes until she almost walked into him.

'Watch where you're going,' said a rough voice.

Looking up and blinking snow from her eyes, she realised it was Sgt McElroy. 'Oh, it's you! I haven't seen you for ages.'

'I didn't realise it was you, Nellie. My wife died, you know?'

'Oh, I didn't know. I'm sorry.' Here was something that Maisie hadn't mentioned, but then she had not asked. 'How's Billy?'

'He's in Germany. Won't be coming home just yet.'

Nellie said, 'I'm so glad he survived the war. I'll never forget what a help he was to me when I needed it.'

'Aye. He's a good lad.' He hesitated. 'How's Lottie? I did hear she had a baby.'

Nellie flushed. 'Yes. She was a bit of an innocent was our Lottie. I must rush. My father's due home.'

'Is he now? If he stays for long that would be something new.'

'You remember my father, then,' said Nellie.

'I remember your mother more than him. I remember her saying when she had a bit of trouble that he was never there when she needed him.'

She knew he was right but only said, 'Mam wasn't alone, although, I agree that a woman needs a man about the house. I must go. Nice seeing you again. Sorry about your wife and give my love to Billy when you write.' She hurried away, thinking that her sisters would be wondering what had happened to her.

But Lottie and Babs were more worried about the telegram they'd just received than Nellie being late home.

'I don't believe it,' cried Babs, her green eyes glinting with anger as she paced the floor. 'Dad wouldn't go and do something like that...not without telling us first.' Her shapely figure, clad in a navy blue skirt and jumper with a blue cardigan on top, was stiff with outrage.

'Read the telegram for yourself.' Lottie waved the yellow slip under her sister's nose. It had come while Babs was at the shops. 'I found it hard to believe, too. But he's a man and most of them generally do what they like without consulting us women.' Her face flushed with annoyance. 'You think I'm not upset? He's always behaved like I'm a changeling. A child the gypsies placed in a basket and left on the doorstep. I'd be the first he'd have out of the house if it was what *she* wanted.'

Babs said impatiently, 'Don't be daft. Nellie won't allow it.'

Lottie groaned. 'I know you're right but I'm still worried. He-he's so aggressive. I wonder what Mam's thinking of him right now. Perhaps she's looking down from Heaven, saying he's run mad.'

'You still believe in Heaven?' Babs shook her head as if in disbelief. 'I bet this woman isn't the first he's had. You know what they say about sailors. Maybe she's the reason he's stayed away so long. She could be a nurse who's looked after him.'

Lottie clutched the towel turban that covered her curler-clad head and cried, 'But he'll expect her to live here and how can Nellie say no after her talk of this being a family home? And what about the nursery? She might hate kids.' She limped over to the oven.

'Talking of our Nellie...she's late,' said Babs, lighting a cigarette.

'It could be because of the snow.' Lottie opened the oven door. 'I just hope this woman remembers to bring her ration book. Imagine what it's going to be like when he goes back to sea, leaving *four* women in this house. I'm going to have to pass off Lucia as an orphan that we've taken in,' she said gloomily.

'Don't be daft! The neighbours know she's yours. Still, another woman in the house...' muttered Babs, sitting in the armchair and kicking off her shoes.

There was a noise at the washroom door and Nellie walked in. She eased off a sodden glove and hung it over the open oven door without taking her eyes from Babs' face. 'What's this about another woman in the house?'

'Dad's bringing a woman home and he says they'll be here this evening,' said Lottie bluntly.

Nellie dropped her other glove on the hearth. 'You're joking!'

Babs raised her eyebrows. 'Would we joke about something as serious as Dad being married?'

'Yeah! It's no joke,' said Lottie, taking a pie dish out of the oven and placing it on a cork mat on the table. 'Although Babs jokes about things, I never would.'

'I want to see the telegram. I need to see exactly what he's written,' said Nellie, white-faced. 'Some surprise! What's he playing at getting married at his age?'

'We knew you'd hit the roof,' said Babs.

Nellie stared down at her sister sprawling in the armchair, her stocking feet resting on the brass fender. 'You're taking it in your stride, are you?'

'No, but...' Babs reached for the telegram on the alcove shelf beside the chimney breast and held it out to her.

Nellie read, *Thought I had better tell you my surprise. I am bringing a new mama for you. Be with you Friday evening. Dad.* She swore and flopped onto the sofa. 'A new mama. How old does he think we are? We don't need another bloody woman in this house. In fact, I won't have it.'

'He'll hit the roof,' said Lottie, dishing out the fish pie. 'He might start smashing things, including us.'

'In front of her? I don't think so,' said Nellie, a glint in her eye.

'We'll soon know,' said Babs, glancing at the clock on the mantelpiece. 'I'm surprised they haven't arrived already.'

'I suppose with Dad being captain, he has to sort things out with the Mersey Dock and Harbour Board,' said Nellie.

'I'll have to feed them and there's barely enough fish pie left here for us three, despite Lucia refusing to eat any earlier,' sighed Lottie. 'She's gone to bed after only having bread soaked in warm milk and sugar.'

'Never mind feeding them. I'm hungry. I can always run the chippie if they want something,' said Nellie.

'I wonder what she looks like?' said Babs.

'I don't want to think about it,' muttered Nellie.

Lottie said, 'Would you believe there's an article in the *Echo*, saying Britain's so drab at the moment we women should be dressing in shades of myrtle green and the like. Apparently the servicemen returning from the near East and the Med have learnt to like the lovely soft dyes worn by the natives, so we're supposed to brighten ourselves up for the men.'

Nellie flinched. 'I don't wish to know that. It's going to be hard enough for Babs and me to cope when the men come home as it is.'

'Sorry,' muttered Lottie. 'You can't hide from it, though. The men will soon be everywhere wanting their old jobs back. You can bet a pound to a penny they won't find it easy, either, having to cope with everyday life after living on a knife-edge for so long.'

'I only hope to God that Dad doesn't decide to get a shore job,' said Nellie, pulling a chair up to the table.

Lottie gasped, 'He'd be complaining about Lucia running around the place. I'll have to get another job and find myself somewhere else to live.'

'You'll do nothing of the sort,' said Nellie. 'Just calm down.'

Lottie forked fish and potato into her mouth and mumbled,

'I suppose they'll sleep in Mam and Dad's old bedroom.'

Nellie nodded. 'I can't see them sleeping anywhere else.'

'I wonder why he got married again,' said Babs. 'I mean it's not as if he had a happy marriage. Surely it can't be for sex? He's a sailor and they know where to find it when they want it.'

'You're terrible talking of such things,' said Lottie.

Babs gave her a speaking look. 'Don't be coming the innocent with me, Lottie. I was there when you gave birth.'

Nellie looked at Lottie's face. 'Enough said, Babs,' she murmured. 'Get on with your supper. They're going to be here soon and I don't know about you but I'm going to put on my best bib and tucker to face the enemy.'

'D'you mean her or Father?' asked Lottie.

Nellie did not answer because her mouth was full. It was Babs who said, 'We could be wrong about her. She could be a nice woman, all motherly.'

'She might also be like the wicked stepmother in *Snow White*,' said Nellie. 'Whatever, we've got an ace up our sleeve.'

'*You* have, you mean,' said Babs.

'Should we light a fire in the parlour?' asked Lottie.

Nellie shook her head. 'It'll take ages to warm up. Now let's get finished and wash the dishes and get changed.'

Once the dishes were out of the way, Nellie made do with a wash down before changing into a blue and green tweed skirt and blue jumper. She found a darned pair of lisle stockings and pulled them on, folding the tops over garters, hoping they wouldn't wrinkle at the ankles. She hesitated only briefly before slipping her narrow feet into a pair of court shoes. Her breath came out as a sigh as she looked at the photo of Teddy and traced the outline of his face with a fingertip. She imagined him massaging away the stiffness in her shoulders and she rolled her head round one way and then the other, hoping and praying that her father would not decide to find a shore job. As it was, she could imagine the names he'd call her when she told him the house was hers.

Her grandfather had created a difficult situation for her because Nellie knew deep down she could not turn her father and his new wife out of the house. The housing situation was horrendous. Grannies, grandpas, aunts and children were having to share homes, sleeping in the parlour or kitchen on sofas or a couple of chairs put together. If her father was to give up the sea, then somehow they all would have to learn to rub along together.

As Nellie entered the kitchen, she saw Babs balancing on the brass fender on one foot so she could see herself in the mirror above the fireplace.

'You'd better get a move on. Although, I can imagine what Father's going to say when he sees you wearing lipstick.'

Babs' mouth formed a moue at her sister's reflection. 'I've had this lipstick for ages. Jake got it for me.' She could now say his name without getting too upset. 'It's Max Factor from the American stores.' She turned away from the mirror and said seriously, 'I don't mind giving you a bit, Nell. You could do with a dab to brighten yourself up. It might help with your chapped lips, too.'

Nellie smiled. 'OK. But I don't want you making me look like a painted doll.'

'Of course I won't. A bit of lippy is good for a woman's morale, though. You can have a dab of my face powder, too. Close your eyes.'

Nellie did as she was told and felt a feather-light touch on her nose, chin and forehead, accompanied by the delicate sweet perfume of the face powder. It was lovely. Then came the greasy feel of lipstick on her chapped lips.

'That'll do you,' said Babs briskly.

Nellie opened her eyes and glanced at her mirror image. She did look better. Lottie limped into the kitchen and her sister's lips twitched. She had removed the pipe-cleaner curlers from her mousy hair and brushed it into a frizz. She had also changed into the brown and orange floral dress that was buttoned up to the neck and floated down to her surprisingly shapely ankles. The style was completely unlike the skimpy skirts and dresses worn by most women due to shortages of material.

Lottie returned their stares. 'Don't look at me like that. At least I'm decent. That neckline plunges too much, Babs, and as for that skirt of yours, Nellie, I can see your knees, and you're wearing make-up.'

Babs said mischievously, 'Want a dab, Lottie?'

She shook her head. 'I don't know what you want to put that stuff on your face for. It doesn't do your skin any good.'

'Is that why you've got spots?' taunted Babs. 'From using the finest face powder?'

Lottie turned a dull red. 'You think yerself so funny.'

'I do try to give people a laugh.'

'You'll be laughing the other side of your face when Father sees you're wearing nylons. He'll know where they've come from.'

Babs' smile ebbed away. 'So what? I bet he'll be so full of this woman that he won't even notice unless you draw his attention to them.' She adjusted the sweetheart shaped neckline of her turquoise taffeta dress. 'You know what's wrong with you? You're jealous of me.'

The atmosphere in the room was suddenly charged with tension. Lottie's face turned ugly and she made a swipe at Babs, catching her a stinging blow on the ear.

'That hurt!' Babs lunged at Lottie and managed to seize a handful of frizzy hair.

Nellie cried, 'Stop it! We haven't time for this. I don't know what's got into the pair of you. You're not kids anymore and we've got to present a united front. If we can't get on how can we expect to get on with this woman?' She was ignored. Both her sisters panted as they struggled to get the upper hand. Suddenly there came the ring of a bell. 'That must be them,' whispered Nellie.

Her sisters froze. 'You go, Nellie,' urged Lottie, frantically smoothing her hair.

'Yes, you go,' gasped Babs, adjusting the neck of her frock.

Nellie noticed a scratch on her cheek. 'You're bleeding.'

She touched it gingerly. 'You bitch, Lottie.'

'Cover it with face powder,' suggested Nellie, and left the kitchen. She felt as if a hundred moths were re-enacting the Battle of Britain in her stomach and wished she did not have to face her father and the woman on her own. Yet, if she was to give Babs and Lottie time to tidy themselves up, there was no choice. The bell sounded again.

She clicked on the light and almost ran down the lobby, only to pause on reaching the door because she could hear Bernard muttering under his breath. She bit hard on her lower lip to stop it trembling and then flung the door open.

It was no longer snowing but the light from the lobby reflected off the fallen snow so that Nellie was able to see her father's tall figure clearly. He was wearing his seaman's cap and a heavy navy blue duffle coat and, to her surprise, he was alone. 'Where is she?' she asked.

'She'll be along,' he said. 'Has Babs managed to get here?'

'Yes.' Nellie heard the sound of footsteps to the rear of her and quickly got out of the way to allow her younger sister her first look at their father. Bernard stared at her and then Nellie caught the white flash of teeth from beneath his Clark Gable moustache. 'How's my girl? Come and give your ol' dad a spanking kiss.'

Babs hesitated, remembering his refusal to allow her to marry Jake, then she leaned forward and kissed Bernard's cheek. 'How are you, Dad? Broken bones healed?'

'What kind of welcome is that?' he growled. 'You're not sulking because I wouldn't let you marry that Yank still?'

'That Yank is dead.' Babs' voice was unemotional. 'You didn't answer my question, Dad. How are you?'

He frowned. 'Not too bad. Nothing like a nice long holiday in the sun to get a man on his feet.'

The sound of someone clearing their throat caused Bernard

to look beyond Babs to Lottie standing at her shoulder. 'You,' he said. 'Still lazing about the house?'

She stiffened. 'I don't laze. I'm in charge of the nursery and I cook, clean and look after the hens.'

'Don't back answer me. You're just like your Aunt Josie. She always had too much to say for herself.'

'I wouldn't argue with you about her. There were times when she frightened the life out of me but I don't think you should be disrespectful to the dead, Dad. Anyway, where is she? You said you were bringing us a new mama,' said Lottie.

Bernard's mouth tightened and he reached for the kitbag he had placed carefully on the ground. 'Let's get inside.'

'But where's our new mother? You said you were bringing us a new mother,' insisted Lottie.

'Inside,' hissed Bernard. 'I don't want to be discussing my business in front of the neighbours.'

'Hardly in front of the neighbours,' Lottie bridled as she limped up the lobby.

'You wouldn't have spoken to me like that before the war,' he muttered, following his daughters to the kitchen.

He placed his kitbag in a corner and his gaze roamed the bunting decorated walls with the Welcome Home, Dad notice. 'Still no improvements, I see, Nellie. You're going to have to do something about this place.' Bernard removed his cap and riffled his greying hair with stubby fingers. 'But first things first. We've hardly eaten a thing all day, so what's there to eat?'

His daughters stared at him. 'What made you do it, Dad?' asked Babs.

'And where is she?' asked Lottie.

'The bottom of the road. I thought it best if I came on ahead and put you more in the picture.' He glanced at the clock on the mantelpiece, 'She'll be here in five minutes.' But the words were no sooner out of his mouth than the doorbell rang.

Lottie clutched the cheap rosary beads about her neck and muttered, 'Mary, mother of God, help us.'

Bernard scowled at her. 'Adriana's been through a hard time, so you're to make her welcome.'

'Adriana! What kind of name is that for a stepmother?' asked Babs.

'It's a fine name for a stepmother because she sure is love and joy to me. So listen, the three of you...you'll be out on your ear if you don't do and say the right thing to her.' The bell rang again and he left the kitchen, slamming the door behind him.

'That's what he thinks,' said Lottie with a grim smile. 'When are you going to tell him this is your house, Nellie?'

'Let's just wait a while,' she said, a tiny pucker between her eyebrows. 'I want to see if he'd actually kick us out.'

Babs said, 'I never thought I'd see the day when Dad would threaten to turn me out. I'm glad Grandfather left you the house.'

Nellie wondered if the old man had ever considered his son might marry again after their mother was killed. It made sense his leaving her the house if he had. She caught the sound of a woman's muffled voice and strained to hear what was being said but was defeated by the thickness of the door. Then it opened and Bernard stood in the doorway holding a woman by the hand. Nellie drew in a breath that positively hurt, whilst Babs and Lottie just gaped at their stepmother.

Adriana was no middle-aged mama. Nellie judged her to be about her own age. She had smooth olive skin, dark eyes and shoulder length black hair on which perched a maroon beret. Her face was oval and from her expression, Nellie guessed she was a tough cookie. She wore a navy blue duffle coat and trousers tucked into Wellington boots. The sharp brown eyes reminded her for a moment of someone else as they rested on the three sisters. '*Buona sera*!' she said in a husky, accented voice. 'Good ee-vening, la-dees.'

'You're foreign,' gasped Lottie.

'Give that woman a medal for observation,' murmured Babs.

He's taken leave of his senses, thought Nellie.

Bernard placed his arm about his wife's shoulders. 'Adriana, let me introduce you to my daughters, Nellie, Babs and Lottie.'

The sisters inclined their heads stiffly but Bernard's fixed expression resulted in Nellie holding out a hand to the woman. 'How d'you do?'

Adriana looked amused and said something to Bernard in her own language before taking Nellie's hand and shaking it. His expression altered. 'How understanding you are, *cara mia.* It is a shock to them but that's no excuse for such formality.'

'What do you want me to say, Dad? Welcome, Mama, you're just what we need?' asked Nellie.

Bernard snapped, 'Don't be rude. She's what *I* need and you either like it or lump it.'

'That's no way to endear her to us. I take it *she* is Italian?' said Nellie.

'Don't refer to her as *she* in that tone. You'll either refer to her as Adriana or Mama.'

'Adriana it'll have to be then,' retorted Nellie with a distinct lack of warmth.

'So be it.' He turned to Babs and his face softened. 'Now, come on, sweetheart. Adriana's going to need all the friendly faces she can find when I go back to sea.'

Nellie experienced a flood of relief. 'So you are going back to sea and leaving her here alone with us?'

Babs said, 'Is that wise?'

'What d'you mean by that?' An angry flush darkened Bernard's face.

Nellie jumped in quickly, 'She means...how much English does she speak? How will we understand each other?'

His expression lightened. 'She speaks some English...not much, though. She'll learn soon enough.'

Lottie said, 'Has she been to Rome? Has she seen the Holy Father? I'd love to hear about it if she has.'

For once Bernard viewed her with approval. 'It's a question I never thought to ask...but I can see that you've got the right attitude for a change.'

Such praise astounded Lottie so much that she was struck dumb.

Nellie said, 'She looks cold. Perhaps she should sit by the fire. It must be terrible for her coming from a hot country to an English winter.'

Lottie found her voice and said, 'I feel sorry for her.' She held out a hand to Adriana, who hesitated only a moment before grasping it and allowing herself to be led by her limping stepdaughter to the armchair by the fire.

She sat down and stretched out her legs before glancing up at her husband. To his daughters' astonishment, he got down on one cracking knee and proceeded to remove her Wellington boots. Babs looked at Nellie and shook her head with a barely perceptible movement. Nellie raised her eyebrows, only to start when Bernard said, 'So what about rustling up some grub, Lottie, seeing as how you're the chief cook and bottle-washer here.'

She looked at Nellie in dismay. 'We decided it would be best to get you something from the chippie,' said Nellie.

'Good idea, girl. It seems ages since I've had home-grown fish and chips. I've told Adriana that Liverpool has a Little Italy and the best chippie is run by Italians.' Bernard smiled as he dug into a pocket and produced a ten shilling note. 'Two portions of fish and chips and an extra portion of chips if you three are feeling hungry as well.'

A surprised Nellie thanked him and put on her outdoor clothes and left the house, wondering if the ten shilling note meant that Adriana's influence on her father was a good one and had led to a loosening of his purse strings. But his mention of Little Italy reminded her that some of the old streets that had made up that area had been pulled down in the Thirties and corporation tenements built in their place. The neighbourhood had changed even more since the Blitz. She decided that perhaps she should telephone Francis from a telephone box as soon as she could and tell him about their brand new Italian stepmother.

As Nellie waited in the warm steaminess of the fish and chip shop, she wondered if her father could possibly have fallen in love at his age. It was the only reason she could think of for his marrying Adriana, but it also raised the question: why had the Italian woman married a foreigner so much older than herself? He wasn't exactly the sort of man that women's dreams were made of. Could he have boasted of owning a large house in England?

As she trudged back to the house through the snow with the newspaper wrapped package of fish and chips stuffed inside her coat to keep warm, she thought that if Adriana was a gold digger, then she was in for a big surprise.

She found Babs standing in the washroom doorway with the cat in her arms. 'So why do you think she married him?' Nellie asked.

'She saw Dad coming and conned him into marrying her. They say, *There's no fool like an old fool.* A young woman making out she wants him? He'd feel flattered.'

'So you think she married him for what he could have in the way of money?'

'He might have a Clark Gable moustache but he's no film star.'

Nellie smiled. 'Should we feel sorry for her? There's no doubt that Italy's one of the big losers from the war. It'll be in a heck of a mess with the Nazis and Allies having fought over its ground.'

'I wouldn't argue,' said Babs. 'But I'm going to wait and see before giving her my sympathy.'

Nellie entered the kitchen and was taken aback to find Adriana perched on Bernard's knee. She had removed her duffle coat and wore a seaman's jumper that clung to her breasts. Her dark head was bent over his and she was kissing his ear. A mixture of emotions tore through Nellie. Uppermost was the pain caused by knowing she would never again sit on Teddy's lap or hear him whisper sweet nothings in *her* ear.

Her father lifted his head, and looking slightly embarrassed, eased his wife off his knee. 'Hurry up and dish out them fish and chips, Nellie. We're starving.'

She tore open the newspaper and placed the fish and chips on two plates and the extra portion of chips on another one. Her ears caught the sound of Bernard murmuring to his wife. The next moment Adriana came over to the table and was about to pull out one of the chairs when Nellie stopped her. 'That one's got a wonky leg.' She called over her shoulder, 'Dad, explain to her what a wonky leg is. You could do with fixing it.'

He looked at her as if she had suggested that he sprout wings and fly, and walked over to his kitbag and removed a couple of bottles from its interior.

As he approached the table, Adriana patted the chair beside her. Before he could sit down, Lottie entered the kitchen, carrying a hot water bottle. She glanced at the Guinness and the wine bottle in his hand and her mouth turned down at the corners. Before Lottie could put her foot in it by voicing her disapproval, Nellie said that she would get the bottle opener.

Babs picked up the wine bottle and looked amused as she read the label. 'Aussie White's! I would have thought you'd have brought us something from sunny Italy. Is this to toast you and Adriana?'

'Indeed, it is,' he said, taking the bottle from her with a smile. 'Besides, it's not always sunny in Italy, girl. Fetch us some glasses.'

'I don't want any, thanks,' said Lottie, tightening the top of the hot water bottle. 'I'll put this in your bed.'

Nellie tried to imagine what her grandfather would have thought of his son and this woman sleeping between his sheets. She glanced at Bernard as he poured the wine and then shifted her gaze to Adriana. The Italian was stuffing chips into her mouth as if she hadn't seen food for a week, and then she caught Nellie's eye. 'The foo-od on the shee-p of your poppa...' She shrugged expressively.

'The cook's fault for almost severing his thumb,' said Bernard apologetically, placing a glass of wine next to his wife's plate.

'You don't have to explain, Adriana,' said Nellie, trying to sound friendly as she made chip butties. 'We all know what it's like to go hungry.'

'Of course you do,' said Bernard heartily. 'But now the war's over things can only get better. You girls and Adriana will soon learn to rub along. I'll have a word with Francis and see if he can find me someone to talk to her in both Italian and English.'

Nellie thought that her brother shouldn't find that too difficult but she'd like to see his face when he set eyes on Adriana. No doubt he would disapprove as much as they did. She raised her glass. 'Cheers!'

'Congratulations,' said Babs.

Adriana regarded her stepdaughters with a smile. '*Salute*!'

Babs drained her glass and licked her lips. 'I doubt I'll get halfway merry on that but it was a nice change.' She ate her chip buttie and then glanced at the clock. 'My bedtime and yours, Nellie, if you're to be up in time for work and I'm to get an early train to Ormskirk. I'll use the bathroom first if you don't mind?'

Nellie said that of course she didn't but, before she could leave the kitchen, her father said, 'D'you have a nightie you can lend Adriana, Nellie? She doesn't have much in the way of clothes.'

Nellie glanced up at the drying rack where that week's washing was being aired and smiled. If her father was imagining his wife in a sexy nightie, he had another think coming. She dragged a pair of pink winceyette pyjamas, patterned with teddy bears, from the rack and held them out to her stepmother. 'Best I can do.'

To Nellie's surprise, a smile eased the corners of the Italian woman's mouth, making her face almost beautiful and her thin fingers stroked the fleecy material. '*Orso*.' She pointed to one of the bears. 'Cute.'

Cute! thought Nellie. Not a word that sprang readily to mind, taking into consideration her father's use of the English language. 'Glad you like them.'

'*Grazie.* Thank you. I...follow...you,' said Adriana in careful English, clutching the pyjamas to her chest and hurrying out of the kitchen.

'Follow me where?' asked Nellie, hastening after her.

Her stepmother was moving at a fair lick but she halted at the bottom of the stairs and faced Nellie. 'I desire *gabinetto!* You understand?' She mimed pulling a lavatory chain.

'*Si,*' said Nellie, having heard that word for yes in an American film set down Mexico way.

The smallest room was empty and Adriana scuttled inside and closed the door in Nellie's face. Not a way to endear yourself to me, she thought, crossing the landing to switch on the light in her parents' former bedroom. She wandered inside to check everything was OK. She felt for the hot water bottle that Lottie must have placed in the bed and thought how she would have to go without that night.

She returned to the lavatory and found the door open but noticed the bathroom door was closed. From inside came the noise of running water. She knocked on the door but there was no response. Then came the sound of splashing. She was convinced her stepmother was having a bath. How dare she? Nellie remembered how she had made do with a quick wash earlier when a hot bath would have been bliss. She swore under her breath and used the lavatory before running downstairs to wash her hands at the kitchen sink.

Bernard glanced at her. 'Adriana OK?'

Nellie managed to swallow her anger. 'She's having a bath.'

Bernard smiled. 'It'll do her good. I don't think she realised how bloody cold it can get at sea. It's going to take her some time to get used to our weather.'

'So where does she come from in Italy?' asked Nellie, wanting to know as much as she could about the Italian woman.

'I'm not sure exactly where she was born and brought up but I do know she spent some of the war in Rome. I've picked up some of the language but they speak so fast, the Eyeties.'

'We wondered if she was a nurse at the place where you convalesced?'

He ignored the question. 'The Amalfi coast? Lovely place, sheer drops to the sea.' He got to his feet. 'Time I was getting to bed.' His eyes were bright and his cheeks rosy. 'Don't wake us when you get up in the morning, Nellie. We both need the rest.'

'Wouldn't dream of it, Dad,' she murmured, thinking that was surely a polite way of saying he wanted to spend time in bed with his wife. The thought of the pair of them at it made her feel slightly sick. She forced herself not to dwell on the prospect, wondering if Lottie had gone to bed. She hoped Lucia would not wake up in the night and disturb the household; at least that was less likely with her sleeping downstairs in Lottie's room. She wondered how long it would take for the news of her father's Italian wife to spread over the neighbourhood. She could guarantee as soon as Mrs Wainwright got wind of it, it would only take hours. She noticed the bathroom door was ajar and went inside. The green painted walls showed signs of condensation and on the floor was a wet towel. She hadn't stayed in the bath long, thought Nellie, picking up the towel and dropping it in the bath. Already her stepmother was making her mark. Two extra people in the house, one of them a young foreign woman and the other a father who believed he owned the place. She had no doubt that, in seamen's terms, there would be rough waters to navigate in the days ahead.

Chapter Eighteen

Nellie crept downstairs in the dark, only to pause as she heard a sound. Then she realised the noise she could hear was Lucia singing her babyish version of 'Pat-a-Cake'. Nellie smiled, thinking that it would not be long before her niece's speech improved in leaps and bounds. She frowned, thinking that could be a problem if her father and Adriana were to hear Lucia address Lottie as Mam. She saw that her sister's bedroom door was open and peeped inside, making out the humped shape of her sister in bed. She decided to leave her sleeping for the moment as Lucia wasn't there and went into the darkened kitchen. The singing was clearer here and accompanied by the growling of the cat. Nellie clicked on the light switch and child and cat blinked up at her from the hearth rug.

'What are you doing up so early?' asked Nellie quietly.

'Dinkies,' said Lucia, releasing the cat and toddling over to her aunt.

Nellie swung her up into her arms and kissed her before plonking her on the sofa and going over to the sink. She half-filled a cup with water and handed it to Lucia. Then she lit the fire, thinking of her father and the mothers and children that would be arriving in a couple of hours. She heard a noise behind her and turned to see Babs. Her red hair was in a tangle and she was still wearing pyjamas.

'Did I disturb you?' asked Nellie.

'I had to get up.' Babs curled up on the sofa next to her niece. 'So d'you think Lottie'll be able to keep secret that Lucia's hers for long?'

'No. Impossible. I'd suggest to her that she pretends to have married the father and for him to have been killed in the war, but one of the neighbours could let the cat out of the bag.'

'I don't see why. The only one I can think of is Mrs Wainwright and I can't see her talking to Dad about it. What would you do about a wedding ring for her?'

Nellie barely hesitated. 'I could lend her mine if you really believe it could work.'

'It's worth a try, and better than Dad threatening to throw her and Lucia out of the house,' said Babs. 'Not that you'd allow him to do it. How long d'you plan on keeping quiet about the house being yours?'

'I'm playing it by ear. If you're hungry, you'll have to make do with bread and jam and a cup of milk. Sorry.' Babs nodded and nothing more was said on the topic of the house.

After Nellie had told Lottie her plan and handed over her wedding ring, she and Babs left the house, the latter to make her way to Ormskirk and Nellie to the nursery. Several times throughout that day they were to think about their sister, wondering how she was coping with their father and his Italian wife in the house.

The nerves in Lottie's stomach quivered as she limped over to the pantry, carrying a half-empty jar of homemade plum jam. As she tried to open the door, the knob came away in her hand. She had mentioned it needed fixing to her father but he had ignored her. It was not the only thing that needed mending in the house but she had decided it was a waste of time pointing them out to him. It was only because he had complained about Nellie not having done any of the things he had asked her to that had got up her nose and made her mention the knob. That and the language he had used when she had asked for his and Adriana's ration books. 'Use your bloody nous,' he'd said. 'We've only just bloody set foot in England.'

She had yet to tell him about Lucia and her fictitious marriage, and prayed she wouldn't go red when she did. Lying did not come easy to her and she hoped God would forgive her. Her father hadn't even noticed the wedding ring and had made no mention of her having lost weight. Probably that was because he seldom bothered looking at her. Fortunately, when he'd glanced into the parlour, most of the children had been listening to a story so there had been no cause for him to complain to her about any noise.

A short while ago he had gone upstairs, carrying a breakfast tray of Camp coffee, toast and jam for Adriana, despite it being almost noon. As soon as he had disappeared to the bedroom, Lottie had put her assistant in charge so that she could go shopping. She could not understand why her father got so mad with her but decided not to mention ration books again. Somehow she would manage to produce a really tasty supper without his contribution. If he asked why there was so little meat, she would tell him exactly why.

She put on her outdoor clothes and slipped out of the house. She was halfway down the front path when she heard her father calling her name. For some reason that panicked her and she put on a spurt, only to slip in the snow. Her leg gave way beneath her and she fell heavily to the ground.

'Hell's bells, what d'you think you're doing, you bloody fool of a girl?' demanded Bernard from the front doorway. 'How d'you think I'm going to get you up? I'll need a crane to lift you.'

Lottie tried to get herself up but collapsed in pain. Her brother's welcome voice said, 'What have you done to yourself now, Lottie?' And slipping his strong arms beneath her armpits he heaved her into an upright position.

She clung to him, balancing on one foot, remembering the shame of his knowing about her fall from grace. He patted her shoulder and looked to where Bernard stood in the doorway. 'If you could give me a hand here, Dad, we could get her into the house and off her feet.'

'Did our Nellie get you on the blower?' rasped Bernard, walking gingerly down the path. He seized one of Lottie's arms and dragged it about his neck, causing her to gasp in pain.

'No. I had an interment at Ford cemetery and thought I'd kill three birds with one stone by visiting a former parishioner in Seaforth and dropping in on my sisters, too. Why, what's wrong if she did?' asked Francis.

'Nothing. I can make use of you now you're here. Let's get this one inside.'

Before they could make a move towards the house, there came the sound of hurrying feet and the next moment Adriana appeared in the doorway. Her dark eyes flickered in her husband's direction before passing over Lottie to Francis. For several seconds her gaze lingered on his face and then she gestured with her hand. '*Buongiorno, Padre.* Come!'

Lottie whispered to her brother. 'This is our new "mama".'

Francis almost dropped her but she managed to cling onto him and he made a quick recovery. 'What did you say?'

'Our new mama,' said Lottie. 'Her name's Adriana and she's Italian.'

Francis glanced at his father but Bernard avoided his eyes and said, 'Let's get her inside.'

'OK. You can tell me about your wife later,' said Francis in an undertone.

Adriana hurried ahead to the kitchen and opened the door wide. The two men settled Lottie in a chair close to the fire. Francis fetched a stool for her to rest her foot on and inspected the damage. 'It looks badly swollen, Lottie. I hope it's not broken.'

'Me too,' she said shakily, her face white with pain. 'I don't want to go to hospital, Francis. I've the children. I can't expect my helper to do all the work.'

'You might have no choice, love,' said her brother.

Bernard said, 'They'll have to go home. I don't like the idea of having a nursery in my house, anyway.'

Francis opened his mouth but Lottie gave a tiny shake of her head. 'I'll speak to my assistant,' she said. 'What about some cold water, Francis? I'm sure Nellie would say putting my foot in some would help bring the swelling down.'

'You're probably right.' He glanced at Adriana, who appeared to be searching the shelves. Suddenly she pounced on a bottle of Camp coffee and then looked at Francis and waggled the bottle at him with a smile.

Hurriedly, Francis switched his attention to Lottie's ankle and undid her laces and eased off her shoe before saying to his father, 'Could you ask your wife to run some cold water in a bowl and fetch it here?'

'I'll get it,' said Bernard.

As he walked over to the sink, Lottie said, 'He wants you to find someone who speaks Italian to teach Adriana English.'

Bernard glanced over his shoulder. 'It can wait until I go back to sea. I want her spending time with me and nobody else right now.'

'Please yourself,' said Francis.

'*Padre*!'

He looked up and saw Adriana holding out a steaming cup to him and realised he had no choice but to accept it from her. He thanked her in a cold, polite voice and saw the smile die in her dark eyes and experienced an unfamiliar sensation beneath his ribs. As she turned away, Francis gulped a mouthful of the coffee before rattling off several questions to Bernard.

'Has she any family, Dad? Where is she from? How did you meet her? When and where did you get married?'

'What is this? An inquisition?' demanded Bernard, slopping water onto the floor as he carried the bowl.

Francis' eyes glinted. 'I'd say they're natural questions to ask when a father turns up with an Italian wife young enough to be his daughter.'

Bernard flushed a dull red. 'OK, OK!' He placed the bowl on the stool and straightened. 'Her brothers died in the Desert War. The rest of her immediate family was slaughtered by the Nazis after the Allied landings. She doesn't want reminding of the past, so don't pester her with questions.'

'That would be a bit difficult as I don't speak Italian, just some Latin...and in my experience the past isn't so easily forgotten,' said Francis.

'Well, she wants to try and forget it,' muttered Bernard.

Lottie said, 'I agree with Francis. The past isn't easily

forgotten. I'll never forget the explosion that crippled me and killed Mam and Aunt Josie.'

Bernard turned on her. 'Don't start on about your mother! You've no idea what I had to put up with from her.'

'OK, Dad, that's enough,' rasped Francis. 'We won't mention Mam. Now if you'll step out of the light, I'll see to Lottie's foot.'

But before he could do anything, Adriana suddenly knelt down and seized the injured foot. Lottie screamed with pain and slapped Adriana's hand away. 'You're stupid!' she gasped.

Bernard was furious. 'Bloody hell, girl, don't be such a baby. She was trying to help you.'

Adriana stepped back and a furious stream of words burst from her and she stabbed the air with a finger.

'There, sweetheart, don't take it to heart,' Bernard said, placing an arm round her and ushering her from the room.

Lottie turned to Francis. 'He doesn't know the truth about Lucia or Nellie owning the house yet. He's threatened to have us out of the house if we're not nice to her. Nellie said she's waiting to see just how far he'll go before she tells him. His marrying this woman has really put a cat among the pigeons.'

'I can see how it's made things difficult.' Francis gently lifted Lottie's swollen foot and placed it in the cold water. A shiver ran through her. 'Keep it there for a while, Lottie. Regard it as a penance for hitting our stepmother. What have you told him about Lucia?'

'Nothing yet. Nellie's given me her wedding ring and has told me to tell him that Lucia's father was killed in the war.' Lottie bit her lip and stared hard at her brother to see what he thought of the suggestion.

He lowered his head and said, 'I didn't hear that, Lottie.'

She was about to repeat what she had said when she realised what he meant. Instead she said, 'I was going shopping, now I can't.'

'Write a list and I'll drop it off at the shops and explain the situation. I'm sure they'll deliver what you want. I'll also drop by at the nursery and leave a message for Nellie, telling her what's happened.' He placed his cup on the hearth and produced a pencil and a small notebook from an inside pocket and handed both to her.

As Lottie wrote she said, 'I'll need to speak to my assistant, Francis. Could you pop your head in the parlour and explain to her what's happened?'

He nodded and ten minutes later the woman came in and she and Lottie discussed what was the best thing to do. They came to the decision that until Lottie was up and about again, and her father back at sea, the assistant would run the group from her house. 'It won't be as good as from here but it means the other mothers won't have the worry of no one to look after their children.'

Lottie thanked her and then said her goodbye to Francis.

He left without seeing his father or stepmother again but could not get either out of his mind as he called in at the shops before heading for the nursery to speak to Nellie. However, he did not get that far as he saw her on the other side of the road with a child clinging to each hand and in company with more children and another woman. He hurried over to them.

Nellie spotted Francis and her face lit up. 'Have you been to the house? Have you seen her?'

'Yes!' He drew his sister aside and said in a low voice, 'Without wishing to be disrespectful to our father, he must be mad. She's far too attractive and young to be left behind when he returns to his ship. She's trouble, Nellie. I can feel it in my bones...and talking about bones, Lottie slipped in the snow and has damaged her ankle.'

Nellie's face crinkled up with dismay. 'Poor Lottie! Is it bad?'

'You can decide that for yourself. The woman who helps her is going to have the children at her home for now. Lottie was worried about the shopping, so I've arranged for it to be delivered.'

Nellie was glad about that. 'Did he tell you anything about Adriana?'

'Not much. Her brothers fought in the Desert War and were killed. The rest of her family were murdered by the Germans.'

Nellie was shocked. 'He said she'd suffered. I should feel sorry for her. I *do* feel sorry for her losing her family...but why did she have to marry Dad and complicate our lives?' she said ruefully.

Francis gave a ghost of a smile. 'Security probably. Italy's in a mess. I think you're doing the right thing at the moment not mentioning about the house being yours.'

'I'm glad you agree. I need to get to know her better before I decide what to do. If we can't get on, then I'm going to have to make some difficult decisions.' Nellie sighed. 'By the way, did he ask you to find someone to teach her English?'

'Told me to leave it until he goes back to sea. I'd best be going. See you soon,' said Francis, squeezing her arm gently.

The rest of the day could not go fast enough for Nellie. She was weary by the time she arrived home and not looking forward to having to be polite and friendly to her father and his wife. She pushed open the kitchen door expecting to find them both there, but only Lottie was present.

'Where are they?' whispered Nellie.

'They went out ages ago before the nursery finished so they don't know yet that Lucia lives here. She's asleep in her cot now. I'm going to have to tell Dad about her tomorrow.'

Nellie nodded. She knelt, feeling her sister's ankle with gentle fingers. 'It doesn't feel broken but I'm no expert. You should have it X-rayed.'

Lottie shook her head. 'No hospitals.'

Nellie did not argue with her. 'Then you'll have to rest and keep putting on cold compresses.'

'I know. It was a good job Francis arrived. I think *she* was impressed by us having a priest in the family. He was cool with her, though.'

'He says she's trouble. Mind you, he'll have more difficulty than us in accepting her in Mam's place with him having been so close to Mam.' She stood up. 'Where have they gone, by the way?'

'Dad's taken her into town for a meal and a dance at Reece's.'

Nellie's eyebrows shot up. 'A dance! What on earth did she wear?'

Lottie hesitated. 'I told her to go up to the attic and look in the tea-chest.'

Nellie giggled. 'And?'

'She looked OK.'

'I bet.'

Nellie was still smiling when she took her supper out of the oven. After she washed the dishes, they discussed the rest of their day but it was not long before their stepmother became the subject of their conversation again.

'How do you think she'll cope with you being laid up?' asked Nellie.

'She'll have to do the housework. What choice has she?' Lottie shrugged.

'What about Lucia? I can't see Dad allowing Adriana to look after her.'

Lottie agreed and her eyes looked worried. 'I doubt I'll manage her with my ankle the way it is.'

Nellie agreed. 'I could ask Matron if I could bring her to the nursery with me just until you're on your feet again.'

'Would you, Nell? I'm sorry to cause you so much trouble.'

'You're no trouble,' said Nellie, kissing the top of her head.

Any sympathy Nellie might have for her stepmother being landed with the housework over the next few days was misplaced. Bernard did not want his young wife getting her hands chapped and sore and insisted on the washing being sent to Kwok Fong's laundry. He also hired a woman to come in daily to do the housework and cooking.

Nellie remembered how hard her mother had worked and

was exasperated with his mollycoddling his young wife. She, herself, had to see to the hens before leaving for the nursery, as well as in the evening. Fortunately, Matron had agreed to Lucia attending the nursery until Lottie was on her feet again. Both sisters saw little of the newlyweds as they did not get out of bed until halfway through the morning and were out gallivanting every evening.

'It can't last,' said Nellie when she arrived home one Saturday evening in early February to find Bernard and Adriana out yet again. 'He'll run out of money.'

'She's been buying clothes,' said Lottie, holding out her arms to her daughter. Her father and stepmother were still unaware that Lucia was hers, despite the little girl's presence in the house on Sundays, as they had seen no reason to explain with them rarely seeing the child. Bernard's only comment was that he hoped that Nellie was getting extra pay for looking after the child on a Sunday. The sisters had exchanged looks and smiled.

'I didn't know she'd registered for clothing coupons,' said Nellie, easing off her shoes and putting her feet up on the fender.

Lottie leaned towards her sister and said in a whisper. 'Who says she has? Some poor Hindu draper in Everton was robbed of thousands of clothing coupons. I bet they've been sold on the black market.'

Nellie stared at her. 'You think Dad...?'

'He'd do anything for her. Anyway, she's bought a corset. A real lovely one. It's red and black and made of real whalebone with satin and cotton elastic,' said Lottie. 'She showed it to me. I'd love one like it. I'd feel safe in it.'

'Safe from what? Or from whom, should I say?' asked Nellie.

'Men. A good corset can match a suit of armour,' said Lottie with a twinkle.

Nellie laughed. 'I doubt that was her reason for buying it.'

'No. She'll look glamorous in it, unlike me.'

Nellie took a hard look at her sister. 'Don't pull yourself

down. You have nice skin and eyes and a neat pair of ankles once the swelling's gone down, you've lost weight and now curve in the right places.'

Lottie blushed. 'Thanks, Nellie. You've done me the power of good, but I can't see a bloke wanting to take me on with Lucia. There must be more women than men in this country due to the war. They'll have their pick of the best.'

Nellie said, 'You're doing it again. Who says you're not the best. Any decent bloke would accept Lucia if he loved you enough. Anyway, any news of when Dad's going back to sea?'

'Shouldn't be long now. I think I heard him mention the ship was having a complete overhaul and it's nearly ready.'

It was to be another fortnight before Bernard finally left with the promise that he would be back in a couple of months. In an aside to Nellie, he told her to get some work done on the house, as well as keep a close watch on Adriana. 'She's an attractive woman and the young men are coming home now. It's not that I don't trust her, Nellie, but some men will make a beeline for her.'

Just like you did, thought Nellie, wondering how her father could imagine she would be able to spy on his wife while she was out at work all day. Even so, with him away, she was bound to see more of Adriana and have the opportunity to get to know her better.

Chapter Nineteen

Nellie crept downstairs, intent on not waking the household. But as she neared the kitchen, she realised that the wireless was switched on to the shipping forecast. She opened the door and, to her dismay, saw Adriana sitting in front of a glowing fire, still clad in pyjamas, and Lucia on the rug, looking at a book. The girl was so absorbed in the pictures that she did not lift her head. Adriana was smoking a cigarette and, in her other hand, she held a cup. Nellie's nose caught the distinct smell of chicory. Adriana's expression was sombre and it did not change as Nellie, dressed in her working green blouse and dark skirt, took the tea caddy from a shelf and spooned tealeaves into a brown teapot.

The kettle was on the hob and steam was coming from its spout so she infused the tea, cut a couple of slices of bread and reached for the toasting fork. Lucia lifted her head and smiled. She pointed a finger at the picture of a dog. 'Dog,' she said.

'Yes, dog,' said Nellie, holding the bread to the bars of the grate. She was aware that her stepmother was watching her. Should she say something? The question she wanted to ask was what was Adriana doing up so early. Until the Saturday just gone, Nellie had left the house with Lucia without her stepmother being any the wiser about her being Lottie's daughter. Today would be different because the nursery was starting up again in the house. How would she explain to Adriana that Lucia was Bernard's granddaughter when they didn't speak each other's language? She puzzled over it and was no nearer to solving the problem by the time the bread was toasted and spread with margarine. She offered half a slice to the Italian woman.

'No... *Grazie*!' Adriana waved the toast away and flicked the cigarette butt into the fire. She stood up and left the room.

Despite being glad to have the kitchen to herself, Nellie would have welcomed the opportunity to try and make friends with Adriana. She would have enjoyed asking her about Italy and how she and Bernard had met but that was impossible.

What was her father thinking of leaving his wife here without arranging for her to have English lessons? As she ate her toast, listening with half an ear to the shipping forecast, she wondered whether she should arrange the lessons herself. According to Lottie, Francis had not visited since she had damaged her ankle, so maybe she should call on him at the weekend. Nellie went over to the window and drew back the curtain to see what the weather was doing. It was not quite light and she could make out a few faint stars in the sky, which boded well for a dry day. She decided that she had best get a move on or she was going to be late for work.

'Me come?' asked Lucia, scrambling to her feet as Nellie put on her coat.

'Not today, sweetheart.' She picked her up and carried her into Lottie's bedroom and woke her sister before leaving the house.

Lottie watched as Adriana put on the new scarlet woollen coat with the black fur collar and wondered where her stepmother was going. It was no use asking her, of course, because neither could understand what the other was saying. At least she was going to be out of the house when the mothers and children started arriving in half an hour's time. Something was going to have to be done soon about Adriana having English lessons. It would be of help to Lottie if Adriana could do the shopping and contribute to the household budget, but so far she hadn't turned over any money. Of course, lessons would cost money, too, but then perhaps her father had provided for them out of his advance money. She and Nellie had no way of knowing without Adriana telling them. She was going to have to speak to Nellie about it later.

When Nellie arrived home that evening, she was surprised to find Babs digging in the garden, despite it being almost dusk. 'Who's got you doing that?' called Nellie.

'Our Lottie!' Babs straightened up. 'It's not what I planned to do when I got here, but I'd only put my foot inside the kitchen when she begged me to make a start. She said you two had enough on your plate. As for our dear step-mama, I doubt she'd know where to begin growing food. There's talk of a wheat shortage, you know. She'll soon be wishing she'd stayed in Italy when bread goes on ration.'

'Have you seen her?'

'No. Which is just as well because I wouldn't know what to say to her.'

Nellie frowned. 'I wonder where she is?'

'God only knows. Lottie said she went out early wearing her best coat.'

Nellie wrinkled her nose. 'Who would she know? Anyway, don't do anymore digging. Come inside.'

Nellie went indoors while Babs put the spade away, thinking about Adriana and how they could pay for English lessons for her. There was no sign of Lottie or Lucia in the kitchen, so she went upstairs to get washed and changed and was on her way downstairs when the knocker sounded. She hurried to open the door, wondering if it was Adriana.

It was, but she was not alone. Nellie darted a look at the man standing beside her. He wore a cap, and due to it being almost dark, she could not see his face clearly. She looked at Adriana, expecting her at least to make some attempt at introducing her companion, but she only took a shopping bag from him with a muted '*Grazie*,' before brushing past Nellie and going inside the house.

For a moment she wondered if the man was a taxi driver and she was expected to pay him, but then he removed his cap, revealing a head of dark hair, and said, 'Good evening, Mrs Lachlan. I am happy to meet you again.' He had a slight foreign accent that was pleasant to the ear.

She was mystified, certain she had never heard his voice before. 'I'm sorry. Do I know you?'

'We met only briefly but I have never forgotten the help you gave me at the padre's house.'

The breath caught in Nellie's throat so that she couldn't speak for a moment. She clutched the door lintel for support because her knees seemed to have turned to water and her heart was racing fit to beat the band. 'You can't be...Francis said I'd never see you again.'

'I, too, believed that at the time, but the war destroyed so many lives.' He gestured with both hands. 'I returned to Liverpool. The padre knows I need work, so he asks me to teach Mrs Callaghan English. Also he says that there are things that need mending in the house and walls that need painting. I will also work in your garden and see to the chickens.'

'That would be marvellous but I'm not sure how much I'll be able to pay you.'

'I do not ask for money. The padre, he say that we can agree terms that will be of benefit to us both.'

Relief flooded her. 'What terms are they?'

'I need somewhere to stay. The padre, he suggests that I lodge here for the time the work takes.' He hesitated. 'I also have a small son and hope that he'll be able to stay here, too?'

Nellie's spirits plummeted. 'You have a son?'

'*Si*! The padre, he says that is no trouble because your sister, she has children here.'

'Of course, he'll be no trouble but-but what about your wife?'

He twisted his cap between his hands and she sensed his dismay. 'I would not be standing here on your step, Mrs Lachlan, if my wife was alive.'

Her spirits rose mercurially, causing her to feel dizzy. 'Sorry. Of course you wouldn't. I don't know what I'm doing keeping you out here on the step. Come inside!'

He shook his head. 'No, I must go now because my friends are looking after Tonio, but I will return tomorrow if you are in agreement.'

'Yes! *Si*! I mean. Please come. I really do need a man about the place.'

She caught the gleam of his eyes and thought he smiled. 'That is good. I want to be of use to you. But for now I say *buona sera*, Mrs Lachlan, until tomorrow.' He replaced his cap and walked away.

She watched him go and then remembered she did not know his name. 'Wait!' she called.

He turned and she hurried down the path. She could see his face much more clearly now by the light of the street lamp. Finely drawn lines were etched between his nose and mouth and at the corner of his eyes. The marks of suffering, she thought, hating that the war had aged them all beyond their years.

'You have not changed your mind, I hope?' he said anxiously.

'No! I want to know your name.'

His hesitation was barely noticeable. 'Michelangelo Gianelli. When I come tomorrow, I will bring my ration book and identity card.'

She smiled. 'Good.'

'*Arrivederci*!' He lifted a hand in farewell and went on his way.

Nellie hurried back into the house and found her sisters in the kitchen. She noticed a bulging shopping bag on the table. 'Where's Adriana?' she asked.

'Upstairs,' said Babs, who was washing her hands at the sink.

'Guess what she's got in this bag,' said Lottie, placing a hand on it.

Nellie was momentarily distracted from what she was about to say. 'A mutilated body?' she suggested flippantly.

Babs raised her eyebrows. 'You seem different.'

'That's because we're going to have a man about the house. A man who will not only fix things and decorate the house but also dig the garden, care for the hens and teach our stepmother English. Would you believe she went to see Francis herself about English lessons?'

'Bloody hell! Who'd have believed she'd be able to find her way there?' said Babs.

'Perhaps Dad took her to show her Little Italy and Francis' church,' said Lottie.

'Anyway, who is this superman?' asked Babs.

Nellie's eyes sparkled. 'My mystery man! But now I know his name is Michelangelo Gianelli.' The name rolled off her tongue and it sounded vaguely familiar.

'Another Italian,' said Lottie.

'He speaks good English.'

'Why didn't you bring him in?' asked Babs.

'He had somewhere to go but he'll be back tomorrow.'

Babs' face fell. 'That's no good to me. I'll be gone.'

'You'll see him again. He's going to stay here in lieu of wages. He's also bringing his son.'

'His son! You mean he's married?' said Lottie.

'A widower. Thank God Adriana's married to Dad, although if he were to set eyes on Michelangelo Gianelli, I don't think he'd be too happy about his teaching her English.'

'Good-looking, is he?' said Babs, looking amused.

'Hmmm. I just hope Adriana doesn't start fluttering her eyelashes at him.'

There was a sound behind her and Nellie turned and saw their stepmother standing in the doorway, and was relieved that she didn't speak English. Even so, there was an uncomfortable silence as she walked over to the table and picked up the shopping bag. She began to remove its contents, placing them on the table.

When the bag was empty she hung it on the back of a chair and faced the sisters, waving a hand over the newspaper wrapped packages and jars. 'Good Italian food.'

'Lottie does the best she can and she's yet to see your ration book,' said Nellie.

Adriana shrugged and muttered something in Italian. She began to unwrap a package. 'Pasta. *Fresca.*' She sniffed it and the expression on her face was one of such bliss that Nellie was reminded of the Bisto kids. She watched as Adriana took a saucepan from a shelf and half filled it with water.

Nellie's stomach rumbled, reminding her that she was hungry. 'What are *we* having for supper?' she said.

'Liver and onions,' answered Lottie, 'and it's in the oven.'

'Lovely. I'm ready for it now,' said Nellie, although she would have loved a change from liver and onions, but she knew it was an economical meal.

Lottie's face brightened. 'I'll serve up. We might as well scoff Adriana's share seeing as she doesn't want it.'

The sisters ate with half their attention on their stepmother, as she sliced and grated ingredients. 'I wonder where she got that cheese from?' muttered Lottie. 'There seems a lot of it. We only get a tiny bit on the ration...and what's that thing she's peeling? Can you smell it? It stinks.'

'It's garlic,' said Babs. 'It grows wild in some parts of Lancashire. I bet she bought it from an Italian shop in Francis' parish.'

'Same with the cheese, then,' said Nellie, pushing away her empty plate. 'I remember Italian ice-cream makers had cows in their backyards. Some probably still do.'

'D'you think Adriana knows how to make ice-cream?' whispered Lottie. 'I'd forgive her preferring her own cooking to mine if she could make Italian ice-cream like it tasted before the war. Look! She's got tinned tomatoes! Where did she get them?'

Babs stifled a giggle. 'This is crazy. We've become obsessed by food.'

Nellie smiled. 'That's not surprising given that we've just come through a war and there's still shortages.'

'If the harvest this year is as bad as it was last year here and in Canada, then she won't be getting her pasta either,' whispered Babs. 'It'll be potatoes, potatoes and potatoes – that's if we're lucky.'

They groaned in unison.

Adriana seated herself at the table and began to eat her pasta. The three of them watched her until Nellie could stand it no longer and began to collect their empty plates. She carried them over to the sink and was soon followed by her sisters.

'It makes me hungry watching her,' said Babs.

Lottie agreed. 'I wouldn't mind having a taste of what she's got. I wonder if they have pancakes in Italy?'

'Is that a reminder that Lent starts the day after next?' said Nellie.

Babs chanted, 'Pancake Tuesday's a very happy day, if you don't give us a holiday we'll all run away.'

'We'll be able to have lemon with them this year,' said Lottie. 'It says so in the *Echo*.'

Babs winked at Nellie. 'If it says it in the *Echo* then it must be true. Just a shame I won't be here to enjoy them and say what I think about Michelangelo Gianelli.'

'I can't wait to see him,' said Lottie, looking forward to tomorrow.

'Pancake Tuesday? What name ees this?' asked Adriana, lifting her eyes from darning a stocking and gazing at Lottie and Lucia. The little girl was kneeling on a chair at the table and clattering a spoon inside a small bowl.

'So you don't have pancakes in Italy,' said Lottie with a satisfied smile, pausing in beating batter and glancing in Francis' direction.

He stood over by the window, talking in a low voice to Michelangelo Gianelli. What a name for such a good-looking man, thought Lottie. Had his mother taken one look at him and thought of the Archangel Michael? His son was a nice-looking lad, as well, although he hadn't opened his mouth since his father had brought him into the parlour, where she had been reading to the children. She waited until there was a lull in the men's conversation and asked Michelangelo to explain what Pancake Tuesday was to Adriana.

He turned his dark head and spoke in Italian, causing Adriana's face to brighten as she answered him in the same language. He looked at Lottie and said, 'She will make supper this evening because you are cooking the pancakes. I tell her today is also named Shrove Tuesday and is the day before Lent begins here in England, but that you have no carnival beforehand.'

'But there is the Exposition of the Blessed Sacrament,' said Francis, glancing at the clock on the mantelpiece. 'I must go. You're quite satisfied with the arrangements, Michelangelo?'

'*Si.* I have brought all I need.'

Francis nodded. 'And you'll be strict with Mrs Callaghan, won't you? We don't want her babbling on in Italian because you understand her. No one knows better than you that to fit in she needs to be fluent in English.'

Lottie flashed both a startled look and then lowered her eyes as her brother turned to her. 'I'll see myself out, Lottie. Enjoy your pancakes,' he said with a smile.

Instantly Adriana tossed her darning aside and rose gracefully from the chair. 'You go, Padre?'

He said stiffly, 'Yes. I go.'

She gazed up at him from soulful eyes. 'You return, how you say…soon?'

'That depends.'

'Depends?'

Francis hesitated. 'Michelangelo, explain that it depends on how busy I am in the parish, which is likely to be very busy,' he said, avoiding looking at Adriana directly again and hurrying out.

Michelangelo said something in Italian to Adriana. She jerked her head in Lottie's direction and sat down in front of the fire and took up her mending. He fired a short burst in Italian at her but she ignored him and dug her needle into the fabric.

He turned to Lottie. 'I have heard that many repairs need to be done in this house, furniture and door knobs which are broken or damaged. I will need a bedroom for me and Tonio.'

Lottie said, 'Did Nellie say which bedroom you were to have? There's Grandfather's old room and Great-great-aunt Adelaide's on the first floor. Although Adelaide's is really Nellie's, but there's no bed in there at the moment, so she has the bedroom we sisters shared when we were younger.' She added hastily, 'Babs, my younger sister, is in the land army and will be coming home sooner or later. I suppose she'll have to have Grandfather's room if she wants one to herself. At the moment I sleep downstairs because of my hip...and Lucia.' She indicated her daughter with a fluttering hand. 'I-I didn't want her disturbing Dad while he was home.'

His brow knitted. 'There are no other bedrooms?'

'There's two rooms in the attic but they're in a bit of a mess.'

'Perhaps Mrs Lachlan wishes me to clear out one of the attic rooms for myself and Tonio?'

Lottie said with an air of helplessness, 'I've no idea. There is a bed up there but it's in pieces.'

'I will have a look.'

'You don't need me to show you, do you? Only my hip's a bit painful today and you should be able to find the attic rooms with no trouble.'

'I will manage,' he said, hoisting a well-worn haversack over his shoulder. 'Come, Tonio, you will watch and learn.' He held down a hand to him and father and son left the room.

Nellie entered the house over an hour later. The kitchen was deserted but something smelled good. Her nose twitched and her mouth watered. Then she heard hammering and, realising the sound was coming from overheard, she hurried upstairs and glanced in her grandfather's old room, but it was empty. She was puzzled when she realised the hammering was coming from the attic. She climbed upstairs and managed to squeeze past the paraphernalia on the landing, and saw Michelangelo doing something to an iron bedstead inside the front bedroom.

The air struck chill when she went inside. 'You've come,' she gasped, attempting to tell herself that her breathlessness was due to her rushing upstairs. 'What are you doing up here?'

'Mrs Lachlan, how pleasant to see you again.' Searching brown eyes took in her appearance. 'You did not say where we were to sleep. It is good that Tonio and I sleep up here. It means you ladies will have your privacy.' He shoved a screwdriver into the breast pocket of his shirt.

Her eyes searched the room, taking in the damp patch in the corner, and she shook her head. 'You don't have to sleep up here. In fact…'

He cocked an eyebrow. 'You would prefer we sleep on the roof?'

Her lips twitched. 'Of course not. You said "we". Where is your son?'

He turned his head and said, 'Tonio, come here, please.'

A small, dark-haired boy stepped out from behind the door. Nellie stared at him and her heart felt as if it was being squeezed. He was beautiful. Tears filled her eyes, thinking of the mother who would never have the joy of rearing such a son. 'He's the image of you,' she said huskily.

'Yes. His name is Antonio but his pet name is Tonio.' He hesitated. 'The padre, he told me about your losing your baby son. I am sorry.'

'Thank you,' she murmured, lowering herself so that her face was level with that of the boy's. 'Hello, Tonio. Welcome to my home.'

He flashed her a shy smile before burying his head against his father's trouser leg. Michelangelo protested, 'Tonio, that is not the way to thank a lady.'

'He gave me a lovely smile,' said Nellie, her expression tender as she straightened up.

'Payment in smiles, you would be happy with this?' he teased.

She laughed. 'Why not? After years of war there were times when I felt I might never smile again.'

His expression sobered. 'Much has happened to make you sad and yet this house it…' His hand painted a circle in the air, 'it is not an unhappy house.'

Nellie nodded. 'Having the children here has changed the atmosphere. Grandfather was miserable after my brother Joe was killed. Then when he died, I felt the house was too big for just Lottie and myself, and could be used for a nursery. You don't mind having to put up with the noise of children while you work?'

He shook his head. 'Of course not.'

'I'm glad.' She changed the subject. 'There is a bedroom downstairs that you and Tonio can have. I'm surprised Lottie didn't tell you.'

'She mentioned several bedrooms but I found what she had to say confusing. When she told me of these attic rooms, I decided to have a look.'

Nellie sighed. 'I understand your confusion. We lost several family members during the war.' She hesitated, 'Has Lottie told you about Lucia?'

'Only that she sleeps in her room. Mrs Callaghan had spoken of a little girl doing so and thought that perhaps she was an orphan.'

Nellie hesitated, not wanting to lie to him, but if she told the exact truth it could get back to their father. 'Lucia is Lottie's daughter but her dad was killed in the war.'

He nodded. 'So many men killed. If there is nothing else you wish me to do up here, I will come downstairs with you.'

'Right,' said Nellie, leading the way.

She took the stairs sedately, aware of the man and boy following her. Life was no longer humdrum and she did not know how she was going to handle the excitement that bubbled inside her when in the company of this man. She was unsure which bedroom would be best for them. Grandfather had slept in a single bed and there was no bed in the room that she still thought of as Adelaide's. She decided it would be more sensible to give him and Tonio the room she was using because of the double bed. She would move into Grandfather's old room, and if Babs should visit while Michelangelo and Tonio were here then the bed in the attic could be moved into Adelaide's old room.

Having worked that out, Nellie explained to him what she intended doing. Immediately, he offered to help her move her things. 'It's mainly clothes,' she said, switching on the light. 'You can carry the statue of the Madonna and Child, if you would. The furniture's pretty much of a muchness, so it's not worth changing that around.'

Clicking on the lamp beside her bed, she turned and saw him hovering in the doorway with Tonio and it took her a moment to realise he was waiting to be invited inside. 'Come in.' She pointed to the Madonna and Child and then, noticing the book next to it, suggested that the boy carry that for her.

As Michelangelo lifted the statue, the photo propped against it fluttered to the floor. He bent and picked it up and glanced at the man in the picture. 'This is your husband?'

'Yes. That's Teddy.'

'The padre said that he was killed in the Desert War.'

'Yes!' She avoided looking at him. 'It seems to me that my brother told you a lot about me.'

'That is because I asked. I wanted to know more about the woman who helped saved my life.'

'Saved your life?' She lifted her head as she pocketed the photograph. 'I'd say that's an exaggeration.'

'That is because you do not know all there is to know about me.'

Before she could ask what he meant by that, he left the bedroom, carrying the statue, with his son trotting at his heels.

Nellie gathered her clothing and shoes, bundling them in her arms, and followed them. She wanted to know more about him but didn't know how she could begin to ask him personal questions.

He held the door open for her. 'If you will give me the bedding, I will make up the bed.'

She looked at him in surprise. 'You will?'

'I have managed such things for myself for several years.'

'When you were abroad during the war? I remember how sunburnt you were when I found you.' She dumped her clothes on the bed.

'I spent some time in India.'

'India! It was 1943 when you turned up wounded; I'm surprised they brought you home instead of sending you to fight in Burma.'

He flushed. 'The tides of war had changed and a large number of us were brought to England.'

She was puzzled but before she dared question him again. Lottie called upstairs to tell them supper was ready.

'We must not let it spoil.' He lifted his son up in his arms and followed her downstairs.

Nellie was in for another surprise when she saw the concoction of pasta and mince in a delicious smelling sauce heaped on plates. She glanced at Adriana, who was wearing a Cheshire cat smile. 'You've cooked for us all?'

'I cook good. You enjoy.'

Amused, Nellie said, 'I bet we have Mr Gianelli to thank for this. They do say the way to a man's heart is through his stomach.' No sooner were the words out than Adriana stiffened. 'What do you mean by the heart and the stomach and Mr Gianelli? Are you suggesting I have my eye on him?'

Her reaction amazed Nellie. 'Your English has improved. He must be a brilliant teacher.'

'*Sciocca*!' Adriana's tone was scornful.

'Translate,' snapped Nellie.

Adriana turned to Michelangelo and said something in Italian.

'What's she saying?' asked Nellie suspiciously.

He hesitated.

'The truth,' demanded Nellie.

'*Sciocca* means idiot. She says your father is mad about her and you would be wise not to forget that.'

Nellie glared at her stepmother. 'Tell her if that is meant as a threat then she'd better think again. Things in this house are not as they seem.'

He looked puzzled. 'What is that supposed to mean?'

She hesitated. 'You don't need to know. Tell her that I want to be her friend. If she feels the same then threatening me is not the right way to go about it. Even so, I'm surprised she understood what I said, although I didn't mean it the way she took it.'

He said carefully, 'It is possible that she already understands more English than your father gave her credit for, but she has not had the confidence to use it.'

'OK. I can accept that. I don't want to make an enemy of her. This house is big enough for all of us if she remembers that we're her family now and this is our home as well.'

He nodded. 'I will tell her that.'

Turning to Adriana he spoke to her first in Italian and then in English. She nodded and wagged her finger at Nellie. 'I no enemy.'

'Good,' said Nellie.

She reached for her cutlery and glanced across the table to see what her sister thought of what had taken place, but Lottie, who had allowed Lucia to stay up late for once, appeared oblivious to what had just happened and was staring at the window with an odd expression on her face. 'What is it?' asked Nellie. 'You look like you've seen a ghost.'

Lottie slowly brought her gaze to focus on Nellie. 'What did you say?'

'It doesn't matter,' said Nellie. 'You and Lucia eat your supper before it gets cold.'

Adriana placed a plate of pasta on the table in front of Michelangelo and a smaller plate for Tonio, who was sitting on his father's knee. 'But before I eat, I will hand over my ration book and show you my identity card, Mrs Lachlan,' said the man.

'You don't have to,' said Nellie, plunging her fork into the pasta. 'If Francis has vouched for you, that's good enough for me.'

'I insist,' said Michelangelo, reaching into a pocket.

Nellie glanced at the identity card. 'Michelangelo Gianelli,' she read.

'Does it make you happy, Mrs Lachlan, to know I belong here?' His dark eyes were intent on her face.

She smiled. 'Yes, Mr Gianelli, it does.'

Nellie spoke the truth, although, it did not really matter to her anymore what his name was: it was the man himself who was making her feel things she had never thought she would experience again.

Chapter Twenty

Nellie breezed into the house, waving a newspaper. She was fit to burst with the news that the Labour government had promised free medical treatment from the beginning of 1948. That was still some way off but it did mean that there was hope of something being done for Lottie. It had never been made clear to them exactly what was causing the pain she endured some days. If they could have afforded doctors' fees, Nellie had always believed something could have been done to ease her sister's suffering.

She pushed open the kitchen door, only to stop short in the doorway. The smell of the distemper he had used on the walls was strong in her nostrils. Michelangelo was over by the sink cleaning brushes and belting out 'Come back to Sorrento' at the top of his voice.

'Have you ever been to Sorrento?' she called.

The singing stopped and he whirled round. He had flecks of distemper in his dark hair and splattered on his face. 'You like this song, Mrs Lachlan?'

She smiled. 'I play the piano and enjoy most music, but I especially like love songs.'

'Ahhh, that is good. Perhaps I will sing one evening and you can accompany me on the piano? Although, I will not sing "Sorrento" because it did not start out as a love song.' His dark eyes twinkled.

'I like the idea of a musical evening but explain what you mean about "Sorrento" not being a love song,' said Nellie, perching on the edge of a chair and gazing up at him.

Michelangelo folded his arms across his chest and leaned against the sink. 'It was written by a fresco painter and dedicated to Italy's prime minister at the beginning of this century. Parts of the city were run down and it was hoped that, having seen the deprivation for himself, he would set in motion plans for improvements. The song urged him to return to Sorrento in better days.'

'And did he?'

Michelangelo shrugged expressively. 'Alas! He died the following year.'

'That's sad.'

'It is life.'

'True.' She gazed at the newly painted walls.

'You think I do a good job?'

She smiled. 'I think you're fishing for compliments. It's great. No runs. Have you done much painting before?'

'When I was young. I am glad it pleases you.' His smiling dark eyes met hers.

She felt the colour rise in her cheeks. 'I'm sure my stepmother and sister have already admired your work,' she said lightly.

'Of course. Mrs Callaghan is in the garden. She wishes to grow the herbs oregano and sweet basil for the Italian cooking. The padre, he bring the plants but only stays long enough for coffee. This does not please her because she believes he hates her for taking his mother's place.'

Nellie protested. '"Hate" is too strong a word. He's a priest and takes his calling seriously. I wish I'd been here. I wanted to speak to him.'

'He wishes to speak to you, too. He suggested you might like to attend Mass at St Joseph's this Sunday and share a meal with him afterwards.'

Nellie's eyes lit up. 'That'll make a change. Where's Lottie and Lucia? Were they invited as well?'

'She refused. After the mothers collect their children, she went out with Lucia.'

Nellie was surprised. Lottie seldom went out in the evening. 'Did she say where she was going?'

'Not to me but perhaps she tell Mrs Callaghan.' He changed the subject. 'The *bambini,* they have been good for you today?'

She presumed by *bambini* he meant children. 'On the whole, although, some of them can be holy terrors. Where's Tonio?'

He grinned. 'I ask myself why is it that Mrs Lachlan asks where my Tonio is after mentioning *holy terrors*?'

Nellie laughed. 'He's an inquisitive little boy, so naturally he gets into mischief sometimes.'

'I am glad you say that because he is in the garden. Hopefully he is not chasing the hens and pulling out their tail feathers.'

'I'm sure he'll think twice about doing that again after getting a peck from the cockerel.' She rose to her feet and put on the kettle. 'Tea? Coffee?'

He shook his head and carried on cleaning the brushes. She gazed at his back, thinking how broad and strong it was and wondered what it would feel like to be held in his arms. The more she saw of him, the more she felt that strong tug of attraction. Occasionally she felt guilty for feeling the way she did, as if her feelings were a betrayal of the love she had felt for Teddy. She was usually sensible, so why was she allowing herself to fall for him? He was the reason why she wanted to speak to Francis. She needed to know a lot more about Michelangelo's background. It was obvious from his having a British identity card and ration book that he was a nationalised British Italian, but she was still puzzled about his being brought back from India in 1943; and what about the family he had gone in search of? Where had his wife lived and when did she die? What about his parents? She decided to chance her arm and ask him about the latter at least.

'Are your parents still alive?'

He did not answer immediately but placed the wet brushes on a sheet of newspaper before turning to face her. 'Poppa was killed in the Great War. Mama was a companion to a rich old lady, a Mrs Simpson. I was brought up in her house. Sadly they were both killed in an automobile accident in 1937.'

'That's sad. Do you have other relatives?'

'I had an aunt and uncle. They lived in Liverpool but were killed in the Blitz...but this I did not know until the padre told me.'

'So when I found you in the church porch, you'd been looking for them?'

'Yes. But the house was not there, so I search for the church, knowing the padre would help me.' He smiled, showing even teeth. 'And I was right. Now if you will excuse me, Mrs Lachlan, Tonio and I go to visit friends this evening so I must fetch him from the garden and get ready.'

She wanted to ask who his friends were but thought she had pried enough into his private life that evening. She wondered where Lottie had gone and whether she would be out long. It could be that she was visiting the mother who hadn't brought her child to the nursery the last few days, possibly because the father had been demobbed and wanted his wife at home. Nellie could see the numbers dwindling away and Lottie having to close down. Still, their nursery had served its purpose and it had done a lot to bring Lottie out of her shell and give her confidence.

Michelangelo and Tonio entered the kitchen but went straight upstairs. Adriana followed them inside and surprised Nellie by saying, 'Lottie said she and Lucia would not be back until late, so I wonder, would you like to go to the cinema with me?'

Nellie could not conceal her astonishment and, although she would rather have been asked out by Michelangelo, said, 'Thanks. I'd like that. I'll have a look at what's on at the Regal. Do you know where Lottie and Lucia have gone?' she added, reaching for the *Liverpool Echo*.

'She did not say.' Adriana spooned Camp coffee into a cup. 'I have not made supper. I thought maybe you like fish and chips?'

'Fine,' said Nellie, guessing she would be paying for the fish and chips and feeling a tiny spurt of irritation. She ran a finger down the list of cinemas on the front page. 'How about Tyrone Power and Linda Darnell in *Blood and Sand*? I've seen it before but I don't mind seeing it again.'

'It is good?' asked Adriana.

Nellie nodded. 'Rita Heyworth and Anthony Quinn are in it as well. I remember they do this marvellous dance number. I saw it with my husband. He was a good dancer.'

'You must mees him?'

'I do. Although, we spent more time apart than together,' said Nellie.

Adriana's expression was sympathetic. 'That is sad. One day you meet someone else and be happy again, *si*?'

Nellie flushed. 'Perhaps. I'll go and get the fish and chips and change into a frock when I get back.'

Adriana was to surprise her again by paying for the cinema tickets. The film was as good as Nellie remembered and if she shed a few tears at the end, then she was not the only one. They left the cinema with Adriana still dabbing her eyes with a handkerchief. 'I am glad you did not tell me that the handsome Tyrone Power dies.'

'That's Hollywood for you. He sinned by committing adultery, so he had to be seen to be punished.'

'But he had confessed and the lovely Linda Darnell forgave him,' protested Adriana, tossing back her long black hair. 'I thought we would have the happy ending but no, the bull, it keells him.'

'It's only a film,' said Nellie. 'You're English has really improved.'

'Mr Gianelli is a good teacher,' said Adriana.

'He must be. It's come on in leaps and bounds.'

Adriana looked at her with a hint of suspicion in her eyes. 'What does this "leaps and bounds" mean?'

Before Nellie could answer, from behind them came a voice, 'Did you both enjoy the film?'

The women's heads turned and they saw Michelangelo with Tonio astride his father's shoulders. Nellie felt the colour rise in her cheeks. 'I thought you said you were visiting friends.'

'It is true. I am with my friend Salvatore and his wife Teresa.' He indicated the couple at his side.

Nellie noticed Teresa was heavily pregnant and that Salvatore was holding out a hand to her. 'You're Father Francis' sister,' he said. 'Pleased to meetcha! I grew up in St Joseph's parish but my wife and I live in Seaforth now.' He was a tough looking man with a broken nose and a scar on his cheek.

'It's nice to meet you,' she said, shaking his hand.

'I used to work out at Father Francis' boys' club, and now I teach lads boxing at a couple of clubs in Seaforth. I've roped in Mick to help out.'

'That's nice,' said Nellie, hoping Michelangelo wouldn't end up with a broken nose or a cauliflower ear.

Introductions made, the five of them stood apart from the crowd while Adriana asked Teresa when her baby was expected and whether she wanted a boy or a girl. The other woman answered in Italian and Adriana's face lit up. Nellie's attention wandered as the two rattled away in that language. She noticed Tonio's head drooping and mentioned it to his father in a low voice. 'He should be in bed.'

'You are right,' replied Michelangelo.

They said their goodbyes to his friends and returned to the house, where they found Lottie sitting in front of the fire, gazing into the flames. Michelangelo did not linger but took Tonio up to bed.

'You're late in,' said Lottie, glancing up at Nellie. 'Where've you been?'

'The pictures. Where've you been?' Nellie placed a hand on her sister's shoulder.

'Out.'

Nellie smiled. 'Where's out?'

'To see a friend.' Lottie rose from the chair. 'Was it a good film?'

'*Si*! I cry at the end,' sighed Adriana. 'Then Nellie and I meet Mr Gianelli and Tonio outside the cinema and we are introduced to his friends. They both speak a little Italian and Teresa has invited me to dinner on Sunday. Lottie, if you cook that day, I cook on Monday.'

Nellie had been unaware of the invitation. 'I won't be in on Sunday either, Lottie. I'm going to see Francis.'

'I know. Mr Gianelli and Tonio are going to be out as well. He told me this morning.'

Nellie could only presume that he had arranged before that evening to have Sunday lunch with his friends. She hoped there really wasn't anything developing between him and Adriana and, worrying, went upstairs, chiding herself for already being too fond of a man she still knew little about.

Michelangelo was coming out of the bathroom as she reached the top of the stairs. 'Tonio is asleep. I think that perhaps next time I take him with me to the cinema then it will be to see a film more suitable for a four-year-old,' he said ruefully.

'Mickey Mouse or Donald Duck. You could take him to the Tatler in town,' she suggested. 'They only show cartoons and newsreels.'

'That is a good idea. Perhaps you would like to come with us?' There was such warmth in his dark eyes that she could not believe there was anything going on between him and her stepmother. 'I'd enjoy that.'

'Then we will make a date, but first, if you permit, may I call you Elena? And you could call me Michelangelo.'

She loved the way he pronounced her name, presuming it was the Italian version of Helen. 'Why not? I've been thinking for days that Mrs Lachlan and Mr Gianelli sounds so formal.'

His eyes twinkled. '*Si*! Good night, Elena. Sleep well.'

You can guarantee it, thought Nellie.

On Sunday, Nellie left the house early to reach her brother's church in time for the service. She found it intensely moving and when it ended ran out of the church. She hurried not in the direction of the presbytery but towards the main road. The first lines of the Lenten preface repeated itself in her head: *Passer invenit sibi domum, et turtur nidum, ubi reponat pullos suos:* The sparrow hath found herself a house, and the turtle a nest, where she may lay her young ones. She had seen several pregnant women with their husbands in the congregation and had found herself grieving afresh for her dead husband and child.

She wiped her eyes and gazed at a bombed site situated at the end of a row of shops. Amongst the rubble children played and already a haze of green showed where seeds had blown in the wind and taken root. She thought in a few months the purple flowers of fireweed would bring colour to bombed sites throughout the country. She wondered how long it would be before new housing was built to provide homes for the thousands of couples starting families, who were going to have to make do for now with maybe just one room in a parents' house.

'Elena, what are you doing? You are supposed to be having lunch with the padre. He is worried about you.'

Nellie started and looked up at Michelangelo, dressed in a pinstriped suit and wearing a trilby on his dark head. To say that she was surprised to see him was an understatement. 'What are *you* doing here? Where's Tonio?' she asked.

'With the padre. I saw you leave the church.' He removed a handkerchief from his breast pocket and, taking her chin between his fingers, he wiped her damp face with the linen. She was touched by the gesture and a sob broke from her. 'Shush,' he murmured. 'The time for tears is over. You have lost much but there comes a time when we all must look to the future.'

'Why didn't say you were planning on coming here?'

'Because I thought if you knew then you might not come.'

'Why should you think that?'

'Did you not want to question the padre about me?' His dark eyes smiled into hers.

She returned his smile. 'I'm not going to answer that. I know how good he is at keeping secrets. He never did tell me how you came by your injuries. I did wonder if you were a soldier who'd gone AWOL at one time.'

'Close. I was an escaped prisoner of war.'

She could not take her eyes from his face. 'I did wonder about that, too. Escaped from where?'

He hesitated. 'Many Italian immigrants were interned at the beginning of the war because the British government saw them as a threat.'

'I know that. Some went to the Isle of Man. You said you were in India.'

He nodded. 'That is true. Perhaps we talk of this another time. The padre will be waiting for his dinner.' Michelangelo put away his handkerchief and reached for her hand. 'Tell me, Elena, what caused you to train to become a kindergarten teacher? Did you not believe you would marry one day?'

'I was in no rush to marry.' She was aware of the calluses on the palm of his hand as they crossed the road that was Sunday quiet. 'My parents' marriage was not a happy one and my great-great aunt knew I loved children, so she encouraged me to train for the job. Mam was far from pleased but Francis thought it was a good idea.'

'Your mama listened to him, of course?'

Nellie nodded. 'He was her favourite.'

'So when your father married again a much younger woman, what were your feelings?'

'Shock, horror,' said Nellie. 'I still ask myself why she married him.'

'For security.'

She gave him a sidelong glance. 'Francis gave that as a reason. You sound very sure about it.'

'A young woman marries a much older man, a foreigner, who is away most of the time. A young woman living in Italy, who believes all her brothers dead and saw her own mother taken by the Germans. Naturally she needs security,' he affirmed.

Nellie felt a rush of jealousy. 'She's talked to you about her past?'

'Only yesterday. The padre thought it would be helpful for her to speak of it to someone in her own language.'

'So she's spoken to Francis as well as you?'

'Yes. He is concerned for her but does not want to get too involved. Besides, he says that the British have no idea what it is like to live in terror of someone banging on their door at night,' he said softly. 'So much fear that a person could faint away with the strength of the horror. To be dragged from one's home and taken where one does not want to go, knowing most likely one will never return but be tortured, raped or killed.'

Nellie shivered. 'It would be a living nightmare. Poor Adriana.'

'*Sì*! Poor Adriana. That is why we must be a friend to her.' His hand tightened on Nellie's. 'Forgive me. I did not mean to upset you. I am glad the Allies won the war but now let us speak of something else.' He asked her whether he should ask Adriana about doing up one of the attic bedrooms. 'Who is to say that there might not be another *bambino* in the house one day?' he said.

'You mean Adriana and Dad?' asked Nellie, not liking that thought at all.

'You have not considered it?'

She shook her head, thinking if Adriana did get pregnant then things would become even more complicated. She suggested that he just went ahead with the room and to give her the bill for the paint and anything else he needed.

He looked at her askance but dropped the subject.

Nellie was quiet at the dinner table, choosing to listen to the men's conversation as they discussed not only the youth of the country whose fathers would not be coming home, but also what the Pope had said about the need for Britain to move more swiftly in repatriating its Italian prisoners of war.

'He says this perhaps because he believes the British are using them for cheap labour,' said Francis' superior. 'He has a point. Despite thousands of our own men being demobbed there will still be a shortage of labour when it comes to rebuilding our country.'

'It could also be because there are soon to be elections in Italy,' said Michelangelo. 'There is a need for true representation from its people.'

'Surely it's possible for Italy to do what our government did last year in the lead-up to the General Election?' said Francis. 'They provided all servicemen abroad with a postal vote.'

Nellie could not resist murmuring, 'Don't forget the women. Their votes count as well. What about Bessie Braddock MP? She's done a lot for the poor in Liverpool.'

'It would be a big mistake to forget the role women played in winning the war and the new society we need to create for justice for all,' said Michelangelo gravely.

'Which reminds me,' said Francis. 'I'm glad you spoke up, Nell, because I want a few words in private with you before you go.'

She nodded and took no part in the rest of the dinner talk, thinking of what Michelangelo had said about being an escaped POW and wondering what her brother was going to discuss with her.

'Well, what did you want to say to me?' she asked once seated in the study.

Francis steepled his hands and rubbed his fingers against his chin. 'The house, Nellie. I think Adriana should know it belongs to you.'

She was astounded. 'Why? I still haven't told Dad yet.'

'She became very emotional last time she was in my company. She said that she feels as if she's a lodger, not the mistress of the house.'

Nellie sat bolt upright. 'She said that to you? She should have come to me.'

Francis reddened. 'I'm sure you can see her point.'

'Yes,' she said through gritted teeth. 'But Adriana should have spoken to me. I've tried to make her feel at home but it's not easy when I'm out working all day and it's me paying the bills. Dad must have given her some money before he left if she can afford to buy Italian food and cinema tickets. She might need security after the lousy time she had in Italy but I need to feel safe just as much as she does. I lost loved ones during the war, too.' Nellie rose to her feet. 'I'll tell her the truth when I get home.'

'No,' Francis said hastily. 'I want your permission to tell her. I can explain how it came about without getting angry and feeling guilty about it.'

'You're saying I feel guilty?' said Nellie, smoothing down her skirt. 'I don't see why I should feel any such thing these days.' She met her brother's gaze squarely. 'You tell her the truth and don't forget to add that I have more right to Grandfather's house than she has if anything should happen to Dad. Bye, Francis. Thanks for the meal. It was lovely.' She walked out of the study before he could say anything more.

'Something has vexed you. Is it something I have said?'

Nellie switched her attention from the busy pavement in Stanley Road to Michelangelo. 'Sorry. No, it isn't. It's something my brother told me.'

'About me?'

She shook her head. 'You didn't come into the conversation. We were talking about my father and stepmother. There's something they both need to know and I'll have to tell him when he comes home and I'm not looking forward to it.'

'Is it that you are thinking of leaving home?'

'No, never! But what I have to say will make him hit the roof.'

'Hit the roof?' His dark eyes were puzzled. 'What does this mean?'

'He'll explode...be furious.'

'Is it to do with my presence in the house? Mrs Callaghan

thinks I should leave before your father returns.'

'That probably would be best,' sighed Nellie. 'When you do, you won't go without saying goodbye, will you?'

'Of course not,' he said gravely. 'But I would hope that it would not be goodbye but only *Arrivederci*!'

Chapter Twenty-One

Nellie woke, blinking at the shaft of sunlight shining through a gap in the curtains. Her heart was pounding. She had been chasing Michelangelo Gianelli along a winding lane and had almost caught up with him when she was seized from behind and dragged backwards and her father's voice hissed in her ear, *'What do you think you're doing falling in love with a wop and giving him my house?'*

She glanced at the clock and shot out of bed. It was Grand National Day, the first since before the war. Not only that but her father was due home any day now. Her spirits plummeted. She wished Michelangelo and Tonio were not leaving but his work was finished here for now and Salvatore and Teresa had offered to put the two of them up for the time being.

She washed and dressed and went downstairs to find Michelangelo in the kitchen making toast. 'You're up early,' she said casually, delighted to see him.

'I wanted to catch you before you left for work.' His gaze rested on her neat figure in green and white. 'You look *chic.*'

'Thank you, kind sir,' she said, her cheeks rosy. 'You don't look so bad yourself.' He was wearing his pinstriped suit and she wondered if he was going for an interview for another job.

'It is a beautiful day,' said Michelangelo. 'As the poet said, "Oh to be in England now that April's here".'

'I must admit it's my favourite time of year and the mini heat wave we're having makes it even better.' She reached for the teapot. 'I suppose in Italy this wouldn't count as warm.'

'It is warm enough for me.' He scraped butter on a couple of slices of toast and handed one to Nellie.

'Thanks. Are you going for a job interview today?'

He nodded. 'Salvatore has recommended me to the owner of an Italian marble company. He says it will be hard work but I'm not afraid of that. I must earn money to support myself and Tonio.'

'I was reading in the *Echo* that there have been demonstrations in Italy against unemployment.'

His eyes darkened. 'I read that too. They are ex-servicemen, who demonstrate also against the high cost of living. There were clashes with the Carabinieri and many people were injured. Two old women Fascists were hanged.' His expression was grim. 'Italy is paying a high price for having allied herself with Germany.'

'Wasn't there trouble before the war between the Communists and the Fascists in Italy?'

He sighed. 'This is true and why I prefer to live in England.'

'I'm glad you're happy here and I'm sorry you're having to move out of this house. We'll all miss you both.'

'But your lives will be so much more peaceful without us,' he said with a twinkle.

'It'll be dull. You must come and see us.'

'Of course. We have yet to take Tonio to the Tatler and we have not had our musical evening.'

Nellie was pleased that he had remembered those suggestions. 'I love a good musical.'

'I too. We will arrange it next time we meet. It will be a treat to look forward to. Now I must waken Tonio and so must say *arrivederci* until the next time.'

Before she could be alerted to his intentions he bent his head and kissed her. She did not resist and the kiss lasted for perhaps half a minute before they drew apart. Neither of them spoke but stared at each other, a question in their eyes. He stroked her cheek with the back of his hand and then kissed her lightly on the lips again before leaving the kitchen.

Nellie could still feel the imprint of his mouth on hers and she felt like singing. She finished her tea and toast and reminded herself that when she returned to the house later that day, it was possible that her father would be here. She didn't know whether her brother had raised the matter of the house with Adriana but, if he had, she was keeping quiet about it. Hopefully she would carry on keeping quiet until Nellie had a chance to speak to her father.

'So who's done this?' asked Bernard, his eyes scanning the kitchen walls and ceiling.

Adriana wagged a finger at him and pouted prettily. 'Do you not read my letters, Bernardo? Francis finds a man to speak Italian. We converse and that is why my English is so much better. He also paint and mend things, so now this house is much brighter. Is it not good?'

Bernard said grudgingly, 'It's not bad and I have to admit your English has improved. We'll have to celebrate by going to a dinner dance at Reece's tonight.'

'You'll be lucky getting in. Unless you've already got a ticket from somewhere,' said Lottie, looking up from the picture book she and Lucia were perusing. 'It's Grand National Day and everywhere will be booked.'

He scowled down at her. 'You don't know that for a fact. Anyway, what's that kid doing here? I thought I told you, I wanted no kids in this house.'

'Nellie and Adriana don't mind children in the house,' said Lottie, not planning on telling her father that Lucia was her daughter right then.

'Well, I bloody do,' he growled.

Adriana said hastily, 'What is this Grand National Day?'

He explained.

'It's a pity we couldn't pick a winner,' she said with a smile.

'Too late,' said Bernard. 'But we can still go out and celebrate. We'll need to get changed.' He rubbed his hands together and his eyes ran rapidly over Adriana's figure in the tight-fitting floral frock. 'Lottie, you can go and get the *Echo*.'

'No,' she said, without looking up. 'I've had a hard day and my hip's killing me.'

'What did you say?' he said, colour flooding his face.

Lottie looked up at him. 'I've had a hard day and my hip's killing me,' she repeated.

He swore. 'You'll bloody do as you're told, girl, or you're out on your ear! You and that bloody kid.' He flicked her cheek with a finger.

It stung, angering Lottie. 'It's not your house!' she blurted.

'What was that you said?' asked Bernard, placing a hand behind his left ear.

Adriana said loudly, 'The nursery will be closing for the Easter holidays soon and while you're home it will move to another place. Is this not so, Lottie?'

She nodded.

'You must not get yourself excited, Bernardo. It is not good for the heart,' said Adriana.

'There's nothing wrong with my heart,' he said irritably. 'She has too much to say for herself. If she still wants to carry on living here, then she'd better do what I say.'

Like hell I will, thought Lottie, a cold knot of resentment settling in her chest, but she kept her mouth shut as Adriana ushered Bernard out of the room.

Nellie strolled along the pavement, enjoying the warm breeze and the sight of the spring flowers blooming in the neighbouring gardens.

'Nellie!'

She jumped and glanced around her to see where the voice had come from and spotted Mrs Wainwright waving to her. She was so astounded that she should speak to her that, instead of ignoring the old woman, she obeyed her summons.

'What can I do for you, Mrs Wainwright?'

The old woman grabbed her arm. 'David! You know where he is, don't you?'

'I beg your pardon! I haven't seen him since before Lucia was born. You saw to that.' She wrenched her arm free.

Mrs Wainwright's lips trembled. 'I don't believe you! He's

gone off, leaving my sister to fend for herself. She'll be wanting to come here and live with me and I just couldn't cope with that. She's not as sprightly as she used to be and would expect me to wait on her hand and foot.'

'Poor you,' said Nellie with mock sympathy. 'Sorry, I can't help.'

'I don't believe you! You just want to get back at me. Anyway, what's happened to your lodger? It seems fishy to me that he's beetled off just as Bernard arrives home.'

Nellie stared at her coldly. 'I don't see what business it is of yours but Michelangelo finished the work he came to do and left for another job.'

The woman's baby-blue eyes sharpened. 'On first name terms with him, I see. He's a workman! You need to be careful, Nellie, those dark-eyed Mediterranean types can't be trusted.'

'I think you've said enough,' said Nellie. 'Pity you don't imitate the three monkeys I gave you: see no evil, hear no evil, speak no evil.'

She walked away with a sinking heart, knowing that she was going to have to face her father in the next few minutes. The front door was ajar, so she went straight inside but had only just started rehearsing what to say to him when she heard her sisters talking. She pushed open the kitchen door and found them sitting at the table with a heap of coins in front of them.

'Hi, Babs! Where did you spring from? And that money, where did you get it?' asked Nellie.

'I had a couple of days due and one of the other girls suggested we go the races,' said Babs.

A smiling Lottie answered, 'She backed the winner and the horse that came second in the National.'

'Backed them both ways,' said Babs, her eyes dancing as she looked up at Nellie.

'You lucky duck! Good odds were they?'

'The winner came in at twenty-five to one and the second a

hundred to one,' said Lottie. 'She's quids in and is taking us the pictures and buying us an oyster supper.'

Nellie let out a whoop. 'I can't believe it!'

'True,' said Babs solemnly. 'I thought I might as well spend some of the money on pleasure. I want to see Deanna Durban in *Lady on a Train*. The reviewer said it was a screwball murder mystery and she's been allowed to grow up in this one. It should be good.'

Nellie agreed and then remembered her father. 'Mrs Wainwright said Dad was home.'

Babs' expression tightened. 'I'd only been in the house ten minutes when he said they were going out. I don't mind Adriana but she's all he can think about. He was in such a rush to go gallivanting with her that I'd be surprised if we exchanged more than a dozen words. Didn't have time to tell him about my winnings, so I thought *pot on him*.'

'Don't blame you,' said Nellie, sitting at the table opposite Lottie. 'What did he have to say to you?'

'Gave me orders as usual. Swore at me, flicked me in the face and told me he didn't want any kids in the house. He threatened I'd be out of the house on my ear.' A grim smile played round Lottie's mouth. 'I told him that it wasn't his house.'

Nellie gasped, 'You what?'

'Don't worry. He didn't hear me properly. I think he's going deaf in his old age. Adriana jumped in and told him I'd said something else. I wondered if she knew something.'

Nellie rested her chin in her hands. 'Francis told her about my owning the house but it looks to me like she doesn't want Dad to know yet. Was anything said about Michelangelo?'

'Not by name and nothing was said about him staying here.' Lottie's eyes gleamed. 'I wish I'd thought to mention how good-looking the painter and language teacher was. He'd be as jealous as hell, although he'd have no cause to be. It's you Michelangelo fancies, isn't it, Nell?'

'Maybe,' said Nellie casually. 'Anyway, what about the pictures? Where's this Deanna Durban film on?'

'Town,' said Babs.

'Town!' echoed Lottie in dismay. 'I don't think I'm up to getting into town this evening, my hip's really been giving me gyp and I'd have to wake up Lucia, anyway, and take her with us.'

Nellie's and Babs' faces fell.

Lottie said, 'No need to look like that. You two don't have to stay with me. You go and enjoy yourselves.'

Nellie looked at her youngest sister. 'It's your decision.'

Babs hesitated and then her face brightened. 'I'll tell you what, Lottie. I'll give you the money I would have spent on you and you can use it for whatever you like. What d'you think of that?'

Lottie's face lit up. 'Thanks! I hardly ever have money to spend on myself. You two go and get ready and don't worry about me. I'll enjoy having the house to myself for once.'

Her sisters hugged her and went to get ready.

Nellie washed and changed into a yellow, green and white patterned frock before giving her chestnut hair a good brush. She would have loved to be dressing up for Michelangelo but it was a while since she had been out with Babs and was looking forward to spending time in her company and seeing the film.

By the time they reached town it was dusk and there appeared to be people everywhere enjoying themselves. They linked arms and set off along Lime Street in the direction of the Futurist cinema, passing the American Bar. It must have been packed inside because people with drinks in their hands had spilled onto the pavement. Amongst them were several Yanks, enjoying a cigarette with their beer. A couple of them wolf-whistled but Nellie pretended not to notice. Babs raised a hand behind her head and fluttered her fingers in their direction.

'You surprise me,' said Nellie.

'Why? I have to accept that Jake's dead and I don't want to

remain a spinster all my life. Besides, they mightn't follow us,' said Babs. 'Not with full glasses in their hands.'

'Obviously you haven't seen how fast some men can down a pint of beer, but I admit they'd have to be really keen to follow us into the pictures. Thank God, there isn't a queue. We've probably got the Grand National celebrations to thank for that.' She made to go up the steps but Babs dragged her back.

'If we go in now we'll see the end of the film, and as it's a murder mystery, I don't want to do that or we'll know who-dun-it.'

Nellie sighed. 'Listen, Babs, I've been on my feet most of the day dealing with kids. I can't be doing with standing outside. Besides, if we stay here, those Yanks might just come and try to get off with us.'

Babs rolled her eyes. 'For God's sake, the way you talk you'd think they were rapists.'

'I'm sure they're not but even so...'

'Not all Americans are after one thing,' said Babs. 'Mine wasn't.'

'You don't know how the pair of you would have gone along if he hadn't gone away,' said Nellie, glancing at the men in the drab green uniform. One winked at her and she thought the other looked vaguely familiar. 'I think we should go and buy the tickets and wait in the foyer for the film to finish,' she added.

Babs scowled and with a toss of her flaming red hair, said, 'I'm never going to get married if I don't go halfway to encouraging a fella.' The words were hardly out of her mouth when the Americans made a move in their direction.

Immediately Nellie said, 'Please yourself. I'm going inside to rest my feet.'

A rebellious Babs stayed outside. One of the airmen backed off but the other taller one came towards her and, on closer inspection, she came to the conclusion they had met before. He had vivid blue eyes and the smell of his chewing gum took her back to an evening of dancing at Burtonwood.

'Hi, doll! How are you doin'?'

'I'm doing fine. How's yourself?' said Babs, fiddling with a strand of hair.

'You don't recognise me, do you?'

'I do. I've forgotten your name, though.'

He grinned. 'Wow! I thought I hadn't made any impact on you at all.'

'We jitterbugged.'

'We sure did. We were good together too.'

'Until Stuart interfered.'

'He sure was mad but he got his comeuppance eventually. Heather's menfolk caught up with him and worked him over.'

Babs experienced a spurt of pleasure. 'I'm glad to hear that.'

'My aim is to please,' he said, sweeping her a bow. 'Name's Pete by the way.'

She held out a hand. 'Babs.'

He claimed her hand and held it firmly. 'You moved away. I heard that your guy ditched in the sea. Shame.'

'Yes.' Babs knew that she would never forget Jake but she could not spend the rest of her days wishing that she had married him. If her sisters had taught her anything, it was that life went on and one had to make the best of things. 'We were just going the pictures to see Deanna Durbin,' she said.

'Good film.'

'You've seen it?'

He nodded. 'But I wouldn't mind seeing it again.'

Babs' smile deepened. 'Perhaps I'll see you inside then.'

'You can count on it. I'll just have a word with my buddy and finish my drink.' With a show of reluctance he freed her hand.

She tripped up the steps and went inside the cinema, still smiling.

Nellie had been watching Babs through a windowpane and demanded to know what the American had said to her and had she remembered him.

Babs' eyes sparkled with excitement. 'Yes. His name's Pete

and we've danced together.' She headed for the ticket kiosk.

'So what's happening?'

'He's finishing his drink and then coming to see the picture.' Babs bought two tickets and handed one to Nellie. 'I hope you don't mind sitting on your own but you'll cramp my style.'

'As long as we go home together,' said Nellie, not wanting to spoil her sister's chances. She noticed Pete approaching and smiled. 'Here he comes. Good luck and see you here afterwards.'

Babs turned to face him. 'Rear stalls?' he asked.

'Yes, but I have my ticket.'

'Golly, a girl that pays her way. I like that,' he joked.

As they walked into the auditorium, she asked how long he had before returning to the States. 'Long enough for us to get to know each other better, Babs.' As they sat down he drew her hand through his arm and began to ask her about herself.

By the time they stood for the National Anthem after the performance, their knowledge of each other had developed rapidly. They both enjoyed dancing, liked Bob Hope and Bing Crosby *Road* movies, hot sunshine, chocolate, chewing gum and growing things. She had told him she'd like a place in the country with a big garden and he told her that he lived in California. During the interval, he had asked her how she felt about kids.

'Four...two boys, two girls,' said Babs.

'Perfect,' said Pete. 'Pops has his own canning business and I'll be working for him when I get back.'

'Sounds good,' said Babs, crossing her fingers and hoping Pete was Catholic, but decided that question could wait until their next date.

As Nellie waited in the foyer, watching Babs and Pete come towards her, it was obvious from their expressions that they would be seeing each other again. She felt a little sad that her sister's future might be in America but she wanted her to be happy. Babs re-introduced them to each other and Pete suggested that they join him at Gianelli's fish and chips bar in Christian Street.

Nellie started at his mention of the name Gianelli but thought they couldn't be related to Michelangelo or he would have mentioned them. She smiled at Pete. 'Thanks, but we've left our other sister at home alone and I think we'd best skip supper here in town and be on our way.'

'Sure,' he said, obviously trying to hide his disappointment. 'Another time perhaps?'

Nellie nodded and walked on ahead so as to give them time to say goodnight. On the way home she talked about the film and it was obvious from Babs' responses that it had not held all her attention. 'When will Pete be going home?'

'He reckons six weeks.'

'You don't have much time then.'

Babs agreed. 'Don't mention him to Dad. I don't want him coming the heavy father. I know I'm over twenty-one and I can do what the hell I like but I don't want any hassle from him.'

'I won't breathe a word,' said Nellie.

When they arrived home, there was no sign of anyone in the kitchen. Nellie was making cocoa for them both when Lottie wandered in.

'So did you have a good time?' she asked.

Nellie nodded and Babs told her about Pete. 'Don't mention him to Dad, though.'

'As if I would. Anyway, the pair of them are in bed.'

'Already!' said Babs, surprised.

Lottie nodded. 'I went to bed early but I heard them come in and him staggering upstairs.'

'How d'you know he was staggering?' asked Babs.

'I recognised the sound from when I was a kid.'

Her answer silenced Babs and in that lull, they heard the sound of heavy footsteps descending the stairs. Bernard lurched into the kitchen and almost fell into a chair.

'Hello, Dad,' said Nellie, knowing that now was definitely not the time to tell him about the house.

He gazed bleary-eyed at his daughters. 'Where've you three been until this time of night?'

'Babs and I have been to the pictures,' said Nellie, eyeing him warily. 'I'm surprised you're in before midnight.'

'Everywhere decent was crowded, so we had a few drinks and then came home and went to bed early.' He yawned widely.

'So what have you come down for?' asked Babs.

He scrubbed his face with the back of his hand and stared into space. 'This Gianelli, who did the decorating an-and helped Adriana with her English, I want to get in touch with him to pay him. She said she didn't give him any money. I asked her for his whereabouts but-but I couldn't make sense of what she said.'

'Probably Adriana's brain couldn't cope with translating what she had to say into English because she'd been drinking,' said Nellie casually.

He squinted at her. 'I get what you're saying but I still want answers. This-this Gianelli bloke, what's he like?'

'A good man, a hard worker.'

'Were-were he and Adriana ever alone in the house?'

Nellie shrugged. 'I wouldn't have thought so, not with Lottie and the children here.'

He reached up and prodded a finger in her cheek. 'You've got your answers all pat. They'd be in another room.'

Nellie felt like prodding him back but made do with moving out of his reach. 'Mr Gianelli is a gentleman. He wouldn't carry on with a married woman.'

'You really believe that?'

She nodded. 'I don't think Adriana would betray her marriage vows either.'

'You think?'

'She's your wife, Dad. You should trust her.'

He stared at her and then struggled to his feet and left the room.

The sisters glanced at each other but did not speak just in case their father was listening outside. It was not until they heard the door slam upstairs that Babs said, 'It's started already. He doesn't trust his own wife.'

'He didn't when he left,' murmured Nellie. 'He asked me to spy on her.'

'As if you would,' said Babs.

'As if she could,' said Lottie, getting up. 'I'm going back to bed. Let's hope he'll be sober in the morning.'

'I probably won't see him. I'll have to be up at the crack of dawn to get back to the farm.'

When Nellie entered the kitchen the following morning, to her relief there was no sign of her father. Babs had already left and not bothered to light the fire. Nellie decided she wouldn't either and made do with a slice of bread and jam and a glass of water. She sat at the kitchen table, thinking about Lottie and David. She had forgotten to mention to her about Mrs Wainwright asking about him. On hearing a sound at the door, she turned to see a wan-faced Adriana standing there.

Without preamble, her stepmother said, 'We've got to talk.'

Nellie noticed a bruise on her cheekbone and her heart sank. 'Did Dad hit you?'

Adriana's eyes smouldered. 'He drink too much and I scold him. Then he accuses me of being unfaithful. I know why this is so because he told me that his first wife was unfaithful.'

Nellie was stunned. 'He told you that?'

Adriana nodded. 'Bernardo is a dull lover but my expectations were not high when I married him. It came as a great surprise to me that he could be so suspicious and jealous but I understand now it was because your mother betrayed him.'

Nellie sprang to her mother's defence. 'You only have his word for it. Mam was religious. She wouldn't break her marriage vows.'

'You would want to believe that but to have a husband who

spends so much time away is not easy for a woman.' She smiled wryly. 'But I do not regret marrying Bernardo. It was fate we met.'

'Fate?'

She nodded. 'I would not have met Francis and through him Michelangelo if I had not married Bernardo.'

Nellie's stomach seemed to turn over. 'What are you saying? It sounds like you believe that *you* were meant to meet Michelangelo.'

Adriana's dark eyes gleamed. 'That is the truth. I feel respect and gratitude towards him and that is why I will not tell Bernardo where he is but I have no doubt he will still try to find him.'

'He'll ask Francis.'

Adriana nodded. 'But he will not tell him. Now I have something to give you. I came down earlier and I speak to Babs but when I look in Lottie's room to see if she is OK, she and Lucia are not there.'

'What d'you mean, they're not there?'

'There is a note addressed to you.' Adriana reached into a pocket and withdrew a folded sheet of paper. 'It is as you say in England, an eye-opener.'

Nellie almost snatched the note out of Adriana's hand and unfolded it swiftly.

Dear Nellie,
I will be gone when you read this. I've been keeping something from you. My little secret. David turned up at the house several weeks ago. It was a real shock but I was glad to see him. We had a good talk and I learnt that he didn't know about Lucia being his daughter. They'd whisked him away to some relatives miles away but now he's back. He was so upset but I said that just being upset wouldn't get us far. I told him what he needed was a regular job and us to find somewhere we could be together. I know that won't be easy. We've been writing to each other and now Dad's home, I've decided we should get married. We mightn't be able to be

together as a family just yet but at least Lucia won't be illegitimate anymore. I pray that God will forgive me for being so deceitful and that you will, too.

May our Saviour bless you,

Your loving sister, Lottie

Nellie reread the letter and laughter bubbled inside her. She hadn't thought Lottie had it in her. 'You've read this?'

'As much of it as I could understand. I was worried for them both.' Adriana's brown eyes showed no shame. 'Bernardo, he does not know Lucia is his granddaughter. He thinks no man wants Lottie. I, as a woman, knew!' She hit herself on the chest. 'I tell him she run away to be married. I will like doing so. You go and work. If mothers and children come, I say Lottie gone away. *Bambini* have holiday.'

The laughter died in Nellie's face. 'What if Dad loses his temper and hits you again?'

'I will leave.'

'Leave! Is that because you know this house belongs to me? You don't have to go because of that. You're welcome to stay, we can both gang up on Dad.'

Adriana's face softened. 'You are a kind woman, Nellie, but you worry about others too much. I will leave because since coming to England, I learn something that gives me much happiness.' Her sudden smile dazzled Nellie.

'What is it?' she asked.

Adriana placed a finger to her lips. 'I tell you soon. You go to work and not worry.'

Nellie nodded. 'OK! Keep your secret. A warning, though, Adriana, keep Dad away from Mrs Wainwright.'

'Mrs Wainwright?'

'Baby-blue eyes, white hair, looks like butter wouldn't melt in her mouth. You might think she's a sweet old lady but she's a gossip and has told me she thinks it's suspicious Michelangelo left just before Dad arrived.'

'Ahhh! I know the woman you speak of.' Adriana's face hardened. 'She is polite to me but I know she is thinking I have no right to be here. When she speak to me, I pretend not to understand and when I leave her I make the sign of the cross to protect myself from her evil eye.'

Nellie was amused. 'Let's hope it works.'

Later that day, as she washed paintbrushes and pinned up the children's pictures to dry, she wondered what Michelangelo had done for Adriana to make her so happy. Was she being honest when she had said that she felt only respect and gratitude towards him? She thought of her own feelings towards him and tried not to compare them with what she had felt for Teddy: then she had been a starry-eyed romantic and she was a different person now.

When Nellie arrived home that night, it was to find Adriana sitting in an armchair with her eyes closed, smoking a cigarette. To all appearances she was at ease, but Nellie took one look at her father standing over by the fireplace and knew that it had to be an act. He was fiddling with the jar of spills used to get a light from the fire, and his hand was shaking.

'What's going on?' asked Nellie.

'I'm waiting for your stepmother to tell me where that impostor is!'

'What impostor?' asked Nellie.

'The Eyetie who supposedly taught her English,' snarled Bernard.

His wife opened her eyes and fixed him with a stare. 'You tell me you see the Gianelli brothers in their fish and chip shop. They tell you their cousin Michelangelo Gianelli killed in Blitz, so you think one who worked here is impostor. If true, what does it matter? We not pay him, so we lose nothing.' She gesticulated with her hands, causing the cigarette smoke to spiral jerkily upwards.

'I don't believe it,' said Nellie.

Bernard ignored her and thumped the mantelpiece with his

fists, causing several spills to drop onto the hearth. 'Maybe he's someone you knew back in Italy and he's followed you over here!'

Adriana's mouth tightened. 'It not true. He was a stranger to me. Francis introduce us. Speak to him if you wish to know more.'

Bernard drew in his breath with a hiss. 'Who do you think I bloody asked? He's out to cause trouble between the pair of us. He was always Carmel's favourite and is furious because I've put you in his mother's place. Every time I came home from sea he resented my being in the house and that's why he sent that Eyetie here. He doesn't approve of my having married you.'

Adriana gazed at him incredulously. 'How you think this of your own son? A priest! A holy man! I think it is you who resent him because your first wife loved him.' She jumped up from the chair and stalked out of the kitchen.

Bernard turned on Nellie. 'Tell me the truth! What the bloody hell was going on between Adriana and this impostor?'

'I don't know.'

Anger twisted Bernard's face. 'You're in it, too. You and Francis were always close. Neither of you could see what your mother was. She was a tart, plain and simple. I couldn't have been Lottie's father, the months didn't add up.'

'What?' Nellie stared at him, scarcely able to take in what he had just said. 'You can't believe Mam really had another man?'

'Of course she had another man. I only wish I bloody knew who he was,' he rasped. 'I tell you, the months didn't add up.'

Nellie began to doubt her mother herself. 'Perhaps you should have asked Mam why she needed to find affection elsewhere. You were never there, Dad, for any of us.'

He caught her a stinging blow on the ear. 'How dare you say that? I had to work, didn't I?'

She put a hand to her ear. 'Yes, but you weren't there for us even when you were home.'

He loomed over her and she thought he was going to strike her again. Stretching out a hand, she grabbed a fork from the table and held it in front of her. 'Try it!'

He glared at her and then walked out. She dropped the fork on the table and took a deep breath. There was the sound of hurrying feet on the stairs and the next moment her stepmother entered the kitchen. 'Where is he?' she asked.

'Gone.' Nellie felt her throbbing ear gingerly.

Adriana's face softened and she dragged a clean tea towel from the drying rack and dampened a corner of it. 'You are brave, Nellie.' She pressed the wet material against her ear. 'You miss your mama?'

'Yes. I only wish we could have made up our quarrel before she died.'

'I, too, miss my mama. She sacrifice her life for me. She say, "Run, run, my angel". I do not wish to leave her but she push me away. So I run and hide. I see the German soldiers capture her and it hurt me here what they do to her.' Adriana placed a hand in the vicinity of her heart and tears filled her eyes. 'I never see her alive again but when a German do bad things to me, I stick a knife between his ribs and kill him for my mama. Then I run again.'

Nellie wondered if she had misheard her. 'You killed a Jerry?'

Adriana's dark eyes glinted. 'It not easy to kill someone but is lot easier when they not expect it.'

Nellie knew that she'd find it almost impossible to kill anyone. 'What happened next?'

'The Americans come, have food and chocolate. It is good to be free of the oppressors. I learn a leetle English and then I meet your father. I think his liking me so much is good. I would like to escape the-the misery in my country, so I marry him. I not know Michelangelo before but he is a good man, believe me.'

Nellie wanted to believe her and have faith in Michelangelo. 'Dad says he's deceived us.'

Adriana hesitated. 'You need to know the truth. You-you must speak to him. I see him, tell him what happen and you meet.'

Nellie wondered why Adriana could not give her Salvatore and Teresa's address so that she could go there herself, but agreed to her stepmother's plan.

Chapter Twenty-Two

Bernard did not return to the house until after Nellie was in bed and the next day, Saturday, the house was empty when she returned from the nursery. Jimmy and Irene Miller surprised her by appearing on her doorstep, so Nellie got them to help her plant seeds. Jimmy told her that his uncle and new aunt had been to visit them last week and this afternoon Sgt McElroy had dropped in to see them. 'He told me about the boys' club at Our Lady, Star of the Sea, and said I might like to join. They do different things for different ages.'

'Sounds fun,' she said.

Later, when she saw them over the lift bridge and across the main road, she wondered if the church boys' club was one of those Michelangelo and Salvatore were involved in.

Nellie was to be proved right when she arrived back home to find Adriana in the back garden, smoking a cigarette. 'Where's Dad?' asked Nellie.

'He says he get in touch with the police,' she said in a low voice. 'I am angry with him but I could not stop him.'

'He's a fool,' said Nellie angrily. 'What good will that do?'

'He was drinking and will not listen.' She scowled.

'Did you get in touch with Michelangelo?'

Adriana nodded and dropped her cigarette stub on the soil. She glanced in the direction of the neighbouring garden. 'We go inside. Even trees might have ears and I don't want anyone else knowing about my brother.'

Nellie stared at her in amazement. 'Your brother? I thought all your brothers were killed in the Desert War.'

Adriana's dark eyes glistened with tears but she did not speak until they were inside the house. 'Not Alphonso. I have seen him. He went missing. This Mama and I knew but we not know he found by the British and made prisoner of war and shipped to India. We believed him to be dead but no, he blind for a while and very sick. By the time they discover who he is and he manage to-to write to Mama, it was too late.'

'I see…but how…what has Michelangelo to do with this? Oh, I see, or I think I do.' Nellie's head was buzzing. 'He went to India.'

Adriana nodded. 'I say only a little more and leave the rest for him to tell you. I did not know im-immediately the truth about Michelangelo. It was only when I talk to Francis about my-my grief and anger, my brothers and mother and I confess the b-ee-g sin I committed, that I discover Michelangelo was a prisoner of war in India. He asks my family name and Michelangelo recognises that of Alphonso. It seems like a miracle to me that he should do this out of lots and lots of names but then he explain. His English is so good, unlike most Italian prisoners, that he act as an interpreter.'

'Stop right there,' said Nellie, holding up a hand. 'What do you mean *unlike most Italian prisoners*?'

Adriana sighed. 'That is what he was and when Alphonso very ill, he speaks to him and the doctor and that is how he remembers him.'

'It's wonderful for you,' said Nellie, trying to take in that Michelangelo had been a different kind of Italian prisoner of war to the one she had believed him to be. 'So what happened next?'

'Italy signs the…' she paused as if searching the right word in English, 'ar-armistice and those in India are asked if they like to go to Britain and help with the war effort. Many want to do this, and so Michelangelo and Alphonso come to England but they are put in separate camps.' Adriana sighs. 'Do you know, Nellie, how many POW camps there are in Britain?'

Nellie shook her head. 'Fifty, maybe.'

'More than a hundred and fifty. But Michelangelo, he write to my brother. Alphonso being so young when captured, only eighteen, and so ill, Michelangelo had compassion for him.' Adriana gave a beauteous smile. 'I meet my brother and we are so happy to find each other.'

Nellie imagined how she would feel if Joe had not been killed but only missing and then found like the lost sheep in the Bible. 'I'm so pleased for you, Adriana,' she said sincerely. 'Have you told Dad about this?'

Adriana frowned. 'You know Bernardo's jealous heart. It will not please him that Alphonso is alive, so I stay silent. It is possible that soon Alphonso will repatriated but that means we will be separated again and we do not want that to happen.' She fell silent.

Nellie stared at her worried face and instantly guessed why she was so concerned about Bernard getting in touch with the police. 'I'd like to see Michelangelo!'

'Of course. He sent a message asking if you could meet him this evening at Our Lady, Star of the Sea. He helps with the younger boys at the church club but at seven he will be free. He will wait in the church. You know where this church is?' asked Adriana.

'Yes,' said Nellie firmly, 'and I'll be there.'

Nellie dipped a finger in the bowl of holy water and crossed herself before slipping into a rear pew and kneeling down. She prayed for Michelangelo and Tonio, Adriana and her brother, Lottie, Lucia and David, Babs and Pete, Francis and herself. She even tagged on a reluctant prayer for her father and Mrs Wainwright and her sister before rising and going over to the statue of Our Lady, Star of the Sea. She smiled up at the calm face and touched the painted blue gown before reciting the Hail Mary.

She waited, staring dreamily into space and knowing she looked her best, having enjoyed dolling herself up for this meeting. The frock she wore was primrose yellow cotton scattered with white daisies, its bodice buttoned up the front and its waist was fitted and the skirt fluttered just above her knees. White sandals, white gloves and a matching handbag completed her outfit. She wished that she'd had time to give her chestnut hair a bit of a curl but had made do with tying it back with a yellow ribbon.

She did not have long to wait before Michelangelo made an appearance. The expression in his eyes caused the colour to flood her face. '*Bella*,' he said, taking her hand and lifting it to his lips.

She guessed that was a compliment and, trying to keep her voice light, said, 'Nice of you to say so.' Her fingers quivered in his grasp. 'Now I'd like you to tell me why you deceived me.'

Immediately he looked grave and his hand slid down her arm and caught her fingers. 'It is a complicated story.'

'I'm all ears. First of all, what is your real name?'

'My baptismal name *is* Michelangelo but my family name is Riccio.'

She was glad that she would not have to begin thinking of him by another name. 'Tell me more?'

'That is my intention. But first, if you are not too tired, perhaps you would like to walk as far as Cremola's Corner for an ice-cream?'

'Sounds good to me,' she said brightly.

They began to walk in the direction of the Mersey. 'Explain how you became Michelangelo Gianelli?'

'The padre found the ration book and identity card on the offertory plate. He presumed they had been stolen because he knew that he had buried the owner. So the padre puts them away in a drawer, intending to hand them over to the authorities, but forgets.'

Nellie burst out, 'I remember now his telling me of an Italian couple who had lost their son. He had been imprisoned at the beginning of the war but then released. So Francis remembered them when you turned up and told him your story. Which was?' She fixed him with a stare.

'Some of it you already know from Adriana's lips.'

'I still want to hear it from you.'

He took a deep breath. 'Mama was English but married an Italian.'

'So you're half-English?'

'Yes. My father was killed in the Great War and she died, as I said, in an automobile accident. I joined the navy when I was seventeen. The war broke out while I was at sea. I did not want to fight the English because of my mother but I had no choice.' He sighed. 'Later my ship was torpedoed in the Mediterranean and I was rescued and taken prisoner and shipped to India. I was in company with thousands of others and was to spend almost three and a half years in the Bengal. When Italy capitulated, we were asked if we wanted to help the Allies in the final defeat of Germany. Of course, I jumped at the chance of coming to England. I had a wife and I was determined to escape. I do so but I have to cross the English countryside in winter and I fall climbing over a fence. I thought that if I could reach my aunt and uncle in Liverpool, then they might help me to get on a ship sailing for Italy. I was desperate to discover what had happened to my wife who was expecting our first child.'

Nellie gasped. 'So when you disappeared you went to Italy?'

He nodded. 'The padre, he arranged it.'

She said wryly, 'Francis really knows how to keep a secret. Wasn't it dangerous?'

He shrugged. 'It is true that I had no illusions what the Germans would do to their former allies once the Armistice was signed, but I still felt I had to find Maria. It was not easy. Eventually I discovered that she had died of a fever and my son had been placed in an orphanage.'

She squeezed his arm gently, guessing how he most have felt. 'Were the conditions bad in the orphanage?'

He nodded. 'I did not find Tonio immediately and am sick with anxiety. By then the German soldiers were wreaking a terrible revenge on Italy. The orphanage was bombed and if it had not been for the nuns, I might have lost my son. But I will not dwell on those times. I find him and he looked like what my mother used to say of an underfed child, a skinned rabbit. So I take him and feed him. I hide him inside my greatcoat and I bring him to England.'

'Did you go by the name of Michelangelo Gianelli when you were on the ship?'

'Yes. I took on his identity. The war, it is over and a small boy is not so difficult to smuggle aboard a ship and keep in a cabin. When I reach Liverpool, I go to the padre. He is willing to help me again, despite I am officially an escaped POW and my son is in England illegally.' He paused. 'My mother, she often talked of England and so, although I miss the sun and the sea, the food and wine, I want to stay in her country.' His face softened. 'Besides, I remember a woman with hair like a polished chestnut and blue-green eyes, who was kind to me and who had suffered herself. I hope maybe we can help each other forget the past.'

Nellie was moved. 'I suppose you didn't tell me the truth immediately because my husband was killed fighting the Italians?'

'This is true. But also I am still an escaped POW and wanted by the police. If I was to give myself up to the authorities, I could be sent back to Italy.'

'But surely you'd be able to return to England?' she said earnestly.

'I could apply to return here but Italian bureaucracy being what it is we could be parted for years.' His eyes darkened. 'I have strong feelings for you, Elena, and I fear if I was to leave England I might never see you again.' He drew her into his arms and, despite their being in full view of passers-by, he kissed her.

She enjoyed the kiss and when it ended she remained in his arms with her head resting on his shoulder. 'That was nice,' she murmured.

'Only nice?' he mocked.

She smiled. 'More than nice, then.'

'I enjoy kissing you very much.'

With obvious reluctance he released her and she slipped her

hand through his arm. 'So what are we going to do?'

'I have a new job. I will work hard and save money and then I will ask you to marry me,' he said. 'Perhaps, by then, I will be allowed to stay in England.'

Nellie had a better idea but did not voice it, guessing that his pride might cause him to turn it down out of hand. Besides, she had to sort out her father first, because she had no intention of waiting for years to marry Michelangelo. 'Adriana said that Dad decided to visit the police, so you're best keeping your head down until he goes back to sea.' She hesitated before adding, 'and the same goes for Alphonso if he's not gone back to his POW camp.'

'Adriana has told you about Alphonso?'

She nodded. 'But she's not telling Dad because she's already got him sussed out.'

'Sussed out?'

'She knows the way his mind works. He's a very jealous man.'

He frowned. 'I cannot understand your father. He has a young Italian wife and three lovely daughters and a son to be proud of! He should be happy for Adriana that she has found her brother. Why does he have to be like this?'

Nellie could have told him what Bernard had said about her mother as a way of an explanation, but surely there was more to her father being the way he was than that. 'I doubt Dad's ever been a happy person. It's just the way he is.'

'It is a pity.'

She agreed.

The Seaforth Naval Hospital came in sight and they turned onto the main road heading in the direction of Waterloo. 'How is Tonio? As soon as Dad leaves you must bring him to the house. Now Lottie's left, we won't have the nursery, but Jimmy and Irene Miller sometimes come and see me and he could play with them.'

'A Jimmy Miller came into the club this evening. He seems a nice boy.'

Nellie smiled. 'He's improved a lot since he was a four-year-old.'

She talked about when she first saw him and of the first months after she had lost her baby and Teddy had been killed.

'You are a strong woman, Elena. I admire you greatly,' he said.

She blushed. 'Shucks! I had to pull myself together. There was Lottie and Grandfather needing me.'

At last they arrived at Cremola's. The waitress seemed to know Michelangelo and in no time at all, dishes of ice-cream were placed in front of them. 'I sometimes bring Tonio here,' he said, dipping his spoon into the confectionary.

'I thought you might, the way that waitress smiled at you.' She spooned ice-cream into her mouth and winked at him.

'I would like to kiss you right now,' he whispered. 'Your lips would be cold and creamy, real tasty.'

Nellie giggled. She felt slightly naughty and young all over again. 'You shouldn't say such things.'

His mouth made a moue. 'OK! I will give all my attention to the ice-cream. What do you think of it?'

She spooned some into her mouth and let it trickle slowly down her throat. She remembered buying ice-cream from an old Italian who used to sell it from a cart down by the Pierhead in the Thirties. 'Lovely, but not as...'

He leaned towards her and said in a conspiratorial whisper, 'good as that which you remember eating as a young girl.'

'You're a mind reader. Tell me more about yourself and where you come from.'

'I was born in Castellammare di Stabia, a seaside town, which is situated opposite Vesuvius in the bay of Naples, about ten miles from Sorrento.'

Her eyes widened. 'So you lived opposite a live volcano. Didn't it ever worry you?'

He shrugged expressively. 'One becomes accustomed. It is thousands of years since 'Stabia was buried, along with Pompeii and Herculaneum, by the eruption of Vesuvius. It is famous for many things and many ships sail from there to America and England. Before the Great War visitors come from Britain to see the glorious scenery, its cathedral and archaeological sites. Some came to visit the spas, to drink the waters. Mama was a companion maid to a rich, widowed lady from Liverpool and she meets Poppa down by the harbour because he worked in the shipyard.'

Nellie was enchanted. 'Tell me more about your parents.'

'They did not consider marrying each other at first but the rich lady decides that the climate is to her taste and decides to stay. She rents a villa and so Mama and Poppa they get to know each other better and wish to marry, but the rich lady will not give her permission unless Poppa works for her. So he leaves the shipyard and becomes her servant, doing what is needed. The war comes and he goes off to fight and is killed. Fortunately, Mama is expecting me. She often say I am her little miracle because she did not want to live after Poppa died.'

Nellie sighed. 'It's a sad story. But it was good that the old lady took your father on and they were able to get married.'

'She saw to it so that I had a good education and I do lots of sports, javelin, discus and basketball. I win medals for the women in my life.'

'Was your wife from the same area?'

Michelangelo shook his head. 'I met her in Sorrento but she was from Caiazzo, a small town further south. We have…what you say…a whirlwind romance, get married in her church in Caiazzo and I return to my ship. She remains there with her grandmother. Like myself, her parents are dead and she has no family except for the old woman. Unfortunately, the Germans committed many atrocities in Caiazzo as they retreated before the Allied invasion and Maria's grandmother was killed.'

'So much sadness,' said Nellie softly. 'It's strange how some families seem to suffer more than others.' She glanced at the clock on the wall and realised that it was time she was going home. 'I will walk with you,' said Michelangelo, helping her to her feet.

'Only so far. I don't want you bumping into Dad,' she said. 'Now tell me about the new job?'

'I think I will like working with marble and doing tiling. It is creative and I am told that sometimes we do work on the liners. I will find that interesting.'

'You wouldn't go back to sea?'

'No. I would not like to leave Tonio or be away from you.'

It was the answer she needed.

When they reached the corner of Litherland Park, Nellie insisted that he leave her there. Michelangelo shook his head. 'I do not fear your father.'

'I'm sure you don't but I'd still rather that you didn't meet yet. I've still something to say to him that he's not going to like.'

'OK. But we will see each other soon? Perhaps we go and see a film?'

She nodded. 'How about Wednesday? I'll meet you outside the library at eight o'clock and we can decide where to go.'

He nodded and they kissed goodnight.

Chapter Twenty-Three

Nellie was singing 'Look for the Silver Lining' as she entered the house the following Wednesday evening. She had three quarters of a hour to get ready and be at the library to meet Michelangelo. She had seen nothing of her father and Adriana in the past few days and wondered what they were up to. She was going to have to face her father before he went back to sea but when would that be? She entered the kitchen and immediately the song died on her lips.

Bernard was standing in front of the fireplace, drumming his fingers on the mantelpiece. His hand stilled when he saw her and his expression darkened. 'So you know nothing, do you? Why didn't you bloody tell me that impostor was living under my roof while I was away? If that wasn't bad enough, the old bitch told me that she saw Adriana kissing him on the doorstep only two days ago.'

Nellie could only presume that Mrs Wainwright's resentment towards Lottie and herself had caused the woman to say such things. 'Where's Adriana?'

'Is that all you've bloody got to say?' he roared. 'I expected to find her here waiting for me but she's probably bloody gone off with him.'

Before Nellie could tell him how wrong he was, the washroom door opened and Adriana entered. She was smiling but then she spotted her husband and her smile faded. Nellie waited for the explosion but before Bernard could open his mouth Adriana said brightly, 'Happy news, Bernardo, you are going to be a Poppa again.'

For a moment no one spoke and then Bernard moved swiftly. 'You whore!' he yelled, and hit her.

The blow sent her flying and Nellie went to her aid, falling on her knees and putting both arms round her. But her father was not finished. He seized his daughter by the hair and attempted to separate the two women. Both screamed and Nellie tried to ward him off with one hand but he managed to get in a couple of blows to her face. 'Stop it, Dad, stop it!' she cried.

'Don't you tell me what to do. I'll beat that baby out of her,' he snarled. 'I should have seen from the start that she was just like your mother.'

'Let go of my hair,' said Nellie. Unable to prise his fingers apart, she resorted to sinking her teeth into the back of his hand.

He swore and let go of her hair, nursing his hand.

Both women managed to scramble to their feet and backed away from him. Adriana reached for the bread knife and held it in front of her and Nellie pulled open a drawer and took out the rolling pin. Bernard stood there, his chest heaving, staring at the pair of them. Then he turned and stormed out of the kitchen. They heard the front door slam and sagged with relief.

'Where d'you think he'll go?' asked Nellie.

'To get drunk,' said Adriana.

Nellie realised that if he went to the Red Lion and drank outside, as men did sometimes on a warm evening, he might see her meeting Michelangelo and realise who he was. 'I'll have to go out.'

'Where are you going?' asked Adriana, massaging her swollen cheek.

Nellie explained. 'I need Salvatore's address.'

Adriana told her and added, 'I will not stay here alone. I will go and tell Francis what has happened. He must speak to Bernardo.'

Nellie did not argue but headed for the front door with Adriana hot on her heels. Nellie told her what her father had said just before Adriana had come in. Her stepmother shook her head in disgust. 'It was Alphonso. He risk coming to see me here and I insist he must not do so again until Bernardo is back at sea.'

'It was your saying you were having a baby that did it with Dad.'

'It is his baby. I have not cheated on him.'

Nellie was glad to hear it and nothing more was said because they had reached the bus stop where they parted. She decided to take a shortcut to Salvatore's house, praying Michelangelo would not have left early for their date. She crossed the canal by the footbridge and followed a dirt path to Beach Road and past Lewis' clothing factory to another path that skirted the allotments. It was not a shortcut she would care to take on a wet and windy night because it was low-lying and given to flooding, but this evening was dry. She came to Sandy Road and ran up the street where Salvatore's house was situated. Her heart was beating with heavy thick strokes by the time she knocked on the door of the terraced house. To her relief it was opened by Michelangelo who was changed ready for their date. She saw the start of pleasurable surprise in his eyes and then shock.

'What are you doing here? What has happened to your face?' He reached out a hand and drew her towards him and ran gentle fingers over the bruising on her chin and cheek.

'It was Dad! I must talk to you,' she said urgently.

A spark of anger lit his eyes and he placed his arm around her. 'We will go into the parlour.' He ushered her into the tiny front room and sat her down on a sofa. 'Tell me everything before I go and find him and beat him into pulp.'

Right at that moment Nellie would have enjoyed seeing her father beaten into pulp but she knew that violence was not the right way to handle the situation. 'No! There are other ways of dealing with my father and it wasn't only me who suffered but Adriana too.'

'Was this to do with me?'

Nellie slipped her hand into his and held it tightly. 'Yes. Mrs Wainwright told him that you stayed at the house and that she saw you kissing Adriana. Of course, I knew it wasn't you because you wouldn't behave in such a way, but then Adriana told me it was Alphonso.'

Michelangelo swore softly in Italian. 'Once he hears that

your father has hurt his sister, then he will be determined to confront him. We must stop him.'

'Adriana has gone to see Francis. She wants him to reason with Dad. I think she's wasting her time. He's beyond reasoning and he's going to be worse once I tell him something I should have told him ages ago.'

His dark eyes were intent on her anxious face. 'What is this something that worries you so?'

She hesitated. 'It's the house. Grandfather left it to me instead of Dad. I looked after him and I suppose it was his way of saying thank you.'

Michelangelo looked stunned and then he nodded his head slowly. 'It will be a big disappointment for your father but perhaps your grandfather knew him better than you realised. Now I must ask you why did you not tell me of this wonderful news earlier? Is it that you thought I might want to marry you for your property?'

She said, 'It never occurred to me. I didn't tell you straight away because I thought your pride might get in the way of you marrying me sooner. You sounded so keen on supporting Tonio and me.'

He laughed. 'I am not that proud, Elena. One of my big concerns was where we would live. I would be a fool not to be relieved of that worry.'

'That's a relief,' she said, planting a kiss on his mouth.

He held her tightly and returned her kiss before saying, 'I cannot remain in hiding now. I will not have your father hurting you.'

She took a deep breath. 'Then you'd best come home with me. If Adriana persuades Francis to return with her this evening then, hopefully, Dad will have second thoughts before resorting to violence again.'

'I hope so. It is not good that I might have to hit the father of the woman I wish to marry.' He drew her to her feet. 'I will tell Salvatore and Teresa where I am going. It is best you wait outside, otherwise they will keep you talking and we'll be delayed.'

When Nellie and Michelangelo arrived at the house, it was to discover Lottie in the kitchen with Lucia asleep on her knee and the wireless playing dance music.

'You're back! I didn't think I'd be seeing you so soon,' said Nellie.

'I told you me and David and Lucia wouldn't be able to live as a family just yet. Francis married us by special licence and...'

'He what!'

Lottie flushed. 'I would have liked you there, Nell, but I wanted the knot tied as soon as possible.'

'So where's David now?'

'With his mother. I've been to see her and we've had a talk. I've told her she has twenty-four hours to decide whether she wants to be friends. If she does then I'm prepared to move in there and look after her, so she can enjoy Lucia's company.'

Nellie shook her head in disbelief. 'You astound me. I never thought you had it in you to make so many decisions yourself.'

Lottie smiled. 'You helped me to do that, Nell. Anyway, where's misery guts and Adriana? And what's Michelangelo doing here?'

Nellie explained while she put on the kettle.

It was Lottie's turn to look amazed. 'I wouldn't have believed so much could happen in such a short time.'

'Well, it has, and as soon as Dad returns, I'll be having words with him.' She wondered whether she should tell Lottie what their father had said about her not being his daughter, but her sister said, 'Have you eaten, Nellie? I'm starving and there doesn't seem much in the larder.'

Nellie remembered she hadn't had anything to eat. 'I am hungry.'

'What about an omelette,' said Michelangelo. 'I make good omelettes. The hens, they are laying?'

Nellie said ruefully, 'I've no idea. I haven't seen to them this evening.'

'It is getting dark so I'll go and have a look,' he said cheerfully.

He had scarcely left the kitchen when Lottie said, 'I'm really glad to see the two of you together.'

Nellie nodded. 'I never thought I'd feel this way again, but I'm glad I do.'

'It seems that things are coming right for us at last, Nell,' said Lottie.

Nellie crossed her fingers. 'I hope so.'

A silence fell and Lottie closed her eyes. Nellie decided to leave mother and daughter to rest and went outside. Immediately she heard voices and realised they were coming from over the fence.

'Here he is, Sgt McElroy, and don't listen to any excuses from him,' shrilled Mrs Wainwright. 'He's up to no good, snooping round the garden.'

'Just you hang on. You've had me out on wild goose chases before,' said the sergeant.

'Nobody's snooping in my garden,' said Nellie, realising Mrs Wainwright must have spotted Michelangelo. She looked to see where he was but he wasn't in sight.

'Where did you pop up from, Nellie? I thought you'd gone out with your stepmother and the house was empty,' called the old woman.

'Well, I'm back now, Lottie's here and everything's fine,' said Nellie.

'I definitely saw a man,' sniffed Mrs Wainwright.

'It'll have been Dad.'

'No. I saw him go out a while ago, too. He looked in a temper and who can blame him with all the carrying on in your house.'

'What goes on in this house has nothing to do with you! You made that clear when you and your sister got David out of the way. Instead, you should have stood by the pair of them and done what you could to help,' said Nellie fiercely.

'Never mind that,' said Mrs Wainwright, sounding flustered. 'I was thinking about your lodger and Bernard finding kids in the house when he arrived home.'

'Were you? You surprise me.' Nellie's sarcasm was plain.

'Now, now, Mrs Wainwright, Nellie and Lottie have done wonders for the youngsters,' said Sgt McElroy. 'My friend, Mrs Miller, has told me all about it.' The policeman rested his elbows on the fence and smiled down at Nellie. 'How is Lottie and her little girl?'

'They're fine,' said Nellie bristling, remembering what Mrs Wainwright had told her father. 'In fact, Lottie got married the other day to Lucia's father, David.'

She heard a strangled noise and guessed it was Mrs Wainwright. 'Well, well, that is good news,' said Sgt McElroy.

'What's good news?' said a voice to Nellie's rear.

She almost leapt out of her skin and whirled round to see her father standing with his hand against the wall of the house. How long had he been there?

Bernard squinted at her and then looked up at the bobby leaning on the fence. 'Here! I want a word with you about aliens,' he shouted.

Nellie prayed that wherever he was hiding, Michelangelo would not choose this moment to make an appearance. The sergeant said heavily, 'You want me to come over there, Mr Callaghan?'

'Aye, I do. Inside the house.' He staggered over to the outside lavatory and went inside.

'I'll see you in a few minutes then, Nellie,' said Sgt McElroy.

Oh God, thought Nellie, wondering where Michelangelo was. Now was hardly the time for him to face her father.

'Well, I wonder how that meeting will go. He was in love with your mother, you know,' said Mrs Wainwright's disembodied voice, taking Nellie utterly by surprise. 'And his feelings were reciprocated. They were the talk of the neighbourhood.'

Nellie's stomach did a somersault and she hoped her father had not heard that. 'Why don't you go inside before you cut yourself on your own tongue, Mrs Wainwright,' suggested Nellie.

'Not polite, Nellie. Is my nephew inside your house?'

'No. He's at his mother's. You'll be pleased to hear that Lottie and Lucia might go and live there. Goodnight, Mrs Wainwright.'

'What did you say, Nellie?' cried the old woman.

'I think you heard me,' said Nellie.

She glanced about her, still wondering where Michelangelo had gone.

The lavatory door opened and Bernard staggered outside. 'Where is he?'

'Where's who?' Nellie crossed her fingers.

'The scuffer. I'm going to tell him about that bloody impostor.'

'He's coming round the back, Dad. You go on ahead inside the house. I need to shut the hens in.'

'Naw, leave them. Come over here and lend me your arm.'

She hesitated, wondering if the drink had caused him to forget what had happened earlier that evening, and then decided she should be safe enough inside the house once Sgt McElroy arrived.

As they headed for the washroom, Nellie noticed out of the corner of her eyes that the outhouse door was open. Her heart began to thump and she forced herself not to look round as she helped her father over the threshold and steered him towards the kitchen. She pushed open the door and left it ajar, hoping Michelangelo would remember that Sgt McElroy would most likely come round to the back of the house and conceal himself somewhere. The light in the kitchen caused her to blink and she realised that Lottie must not have heard anything that had gone on outside because she and Lucia appeared to be sound asleep.

'So she and that bloody kid are back are they? Well, I won't have them in my house,' muttered Bernard.

'It's not your house,' said Nellie.

She began to withdraw her arm but he clamped it against his side. 'What do you bloody mean, it's not my house?'

She took a deep breath, hoping that Sgt McElroy would not waste time getting here. 'What I said. Grandfather left it to me. Now if you'll let go of my arm, Dad, we can talk about this later.'

Bernard made no move to release her but squeezed her arm even tighter. 'You conniving little bitch!' he roared.

Lottie started to wake up and Lucia whimpered. Nellie heard a sound behind her and Michelangelo's voice said, 'That is not the proper way to address your daughter. It would be best, Mr Callaghan, if you released Elena without any fuss.'

Nellie's heart was beating so fast now that her head felt light. Her father made no move to free her but turned and faced Michelangelo. The two men stared at each other. 'You'd better run, sonny. The police are on their way.'

The words were no sooner said than they heard the sound of boots in the washroom. Michelangelo moved towards Nellie. 'Let her go or it will be the worse for you,' he said in a dangerously low voice.

'Don't threaten me! You've been bloody carrying on with my wife. Where is she?' snarled Bernard.

'Hello, hello, hello,' said Sgt McElroy.

Nellie stared at him and saw his gaze pass slowly from her face to Bernard before it grazed over Michelangelo and came to rest on Lottie and Lucia. His face softened. 'You'd best get the little girl out of here, Lottie. I think we have here what I'd call an incident.'

Lottie stood up with her daughter in her arms. 'You haven't come to arrest Michelangelo, have you? He did nothing but good while he lived here. I prefer him to my father any day of the week.'

'But he's not your father,' said Sgt McElroy. 'I am.'

Bernard's face suffused with colour and he looked from Lottie to the policeman and then to Lottie and Lucia and back to the policeman. 'I knew it!' he said. 'You're a bloody, bastard child!' He thrust Nellie from him and lunged towards the policeman. Michelangelo caught Nellie and cradled her in his arms.

For all his size Sgt McElroy was light on his feet and sidestepped the attack. Bernard landed up against the table gasping and tried to catch his breath before turning and launching himself at the sergeant again. Once more the policeman got out of his way but this time there was no table to halt Bernard's progress across the floor and he slipped on the rug and fell heavily, his head hitting the hearth.

He lay still.

For several seconds nobody moved, and then Sgt McElroy lowered himself onto one knee beside Bernard and inspected the skull where it had made contact with the brickwork. Nellie watched him feel for a pulse, aware of her blood rushing through her veins and of the throb, throb of Michelangelo's heart against her ear. 'Is he alive?' she asked.

The policeman did not answer but stayed with his fingers against her father's neck for what seemed an age before shaking his head. He stared at her and Michelangelo. 'You saw him go for me.'

'It was an accident,' said Nellie.

Michelangelo nodded. 'You didn't touch him.'

'Is it true what you said?' asked Lottie, staring at Sgt McElroy.

He did not answer but took a tea towel from the drying rack and placed it over Bernard's face. 'There'll be an inquest.'

'Will we all have to be there?' asked Nellie.

The policeman looked at Michelangelo. 'Little Irene and Maisie told me about you and your son and said you were OK, so as far as I'm concerned I haven't seen you,' he said woodenly.

Nellie sighed with relief. 'We're getting married so he'll be legal after that.'

'Shush, Nellie. I don't exist,' murmured Michelangelo.

Sgt McElroy's mouth twitched.

'You haven't answered my question,' said Lottie.

He went over to her and put a shaking hand on her head and stroked her hair. 'We never intended things to get out of control. I loved your mother and grieved terribly when she was killed.'

Lottie believed him. She knew all about losing control and, hearing the sadness in his voice, accepted that he had truly cared for her mother. Besides she much preferred him to the man she had believed to be her father all her life. 'I understand now why you didn't want Billy and me getting close.'

'Aye. It wouldn't have been right with his being your half-brother.'

Lottie was pleased that Billy was her half-brother. 'Will you tell him?'

'If that's what you want. Right now I'd best go and call an ambulance.'

The ambulance was just pulling away from the kerb when Adriana arrived with Francis. 'What's happened?' he asked Nellie and Michelangelo, who were standing on the path.

'Come inside and we'll tell you everything,' said Nellie, and led the way.

By the time she finished talking, Adriana was already making plans. 'Alphonso will return to the camp and be repatriated and I will return to Italy.'

Francis had been silent and stern-faced until then but now he seemed to come alive. 'You don't have to do that.'

'I must, Padre.' Adriana smiled at him sadly and, lifting one of his hands, she kissed it. 'It will make things easier for all of us,' she said softly. 'Nellie and Michelangelo will want to raise their family here in her house. I marvel at her being able to keep quiet about it for so long.'

'Perhaps I learnt something from Francis about keeping secrets,' said Nellie lightly.

'It is wonderful that he can do so,' said Adriana.

'People wouldn't trust me if I couldn't, but it isn't easy,' said Francis, gazing at Adriana, knowing he was going to have to live with his longing for her locked inside him for the rest of his life.

Nellie noticed the way Francis looked at their former stepmother and bit back the suggestion that Adriana should come and visit them after she had the baby. Instead she said, 'What about money? Italy's in a mess, so how will you manage?'

Adriana turned to her. 'You must not worry about us. Bernardo took out extra life insurance when we came to England. And Alphonso has friends he made in the POW camp. We will not starve. You and I will keep in touch and, perhaps one day, you will come to Italy and see your half-brother.'

'I'd like that,' said Nellie, glancing at Michelangelo.

'I will show you my home town and you can taste the waters,' he said with a smile.

'I'd rather make do with wine,' she teased.

'Perhaps I can officiate at the wedding this time?' said Francis.

'Of course,' said Nellie, gazing at him fondly. 'You might even have to officiate at two weddings. Babs is seeing an American she met at a dance a couple of years back and it looks like it could be serious.'

'I'm glad,' said Francis. 'I'd like to see her happy, too.'

Nellie thought, so would I. She wondered how Babs would feel when she knew about their father's death. Most likely she would not grieve for him as deeply as she would have once. He had caused her a lot of unhappiness when he had failed to understand how much she cared for Jake, just as he had shown the same lack of understanding when he had refused his permission for her to marry Teddy. If only her father had been a happier and more loving man, then his homecoming would not have cast a dark cloud over them all. But his death had lifted that cloud once and for all, and she and her sisters had a shining future ahead of them.